LETTERS TO ALICE

a novel by

KING GROSSMAN

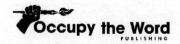

Occupy the Word
PUBLISHING

"Writing is prayer."
  —Franz Kafka, almost all of whose work got published posthumously.

⌀

Emily Dickinson penned 1,775 poems, of which a mere dozen were published during her lifetime.

⌀

Vincent van Gogh painted 909 canvases to sell one he ever received any money for.

I glanced at her and took my glasses
off—they were still singing. They buzzed
like a locust on the coffee table and then
ceased. Her voice belled forth, and the
sunlight bent. I felt the ceiling arch, and
knew that nails up there took a new grip
on whatever they touched."I am your own
way of looking at things," she said. "When
you allow me to live with you, every
glance at the world around you will be
a sort of salvation." And I took her hand.

—*When I Met My Muse*
by William Stafford

O when the world's at peace
and every man is free
then I will go down unto my love.

O and I may go down
several times before that.

—*The Mad Farmer's Love Song*
by Wendell Berry

For Clarice and Alice, my muses, indeed.

CHAPTER ONE

He was a slumbering man. Not a sleepwalker, or awake, slumbering, eyelids droopy to the world, all its corruption, its death march with violence and bad religion, the corporatocracy pulling all the strings, a non-conspiracy, conspiracy of bloated power, where things just happened, and bombs were dropped, and oceans were poisoned, and people of the land were pushed off their land, and so much more doggerel went down in the name of "human progress," which really meant flowing all the money up to the top until, what? ten rich guys in New York City, who weekend in the Hamptons and summer in Aspen, have 99 percent of it—to hell with the planet—to hell with 7,000,000,000 everybody elses. This great white whale, this Moby Dick, was so big who was going to stop it? Nobody could turn things around now. And that's why he slumbered purposefully, and with exuberant style. That, and he had a job to keep, a family to be a partner in feeding, a reputation that had never been built.

To assist him in this endeavor, he had a secret weapon. At all times the world looked sparkly, tree branches wore bangles, lights were stars, the sun furry, the moon a giant pearl, and most importantly people's faces appeared nondescript, their features flattened like people in a Georges Seurat painting. At all times, that is, unless he chose to see things clearly, but doing that was mostly too angering or depressing, often triggering a one-two punch of both monkeys-on-the-back, so he usually used his secret weapon. At first he thought all those years working as an editor for a third-rate literary agent, poring through poorly written manuscripts under bad fluorescent light, had stolen something from him. Then, as things kept getting worse, he realized it all had been a gift, and ultimately a secret weapon of protection. He sort of fell into this realization, actually.

He had been walking along the street, on his way back to the office after a quick Subway meatball sandwich for lunch, when a group of four pretty snarly-looking guys hemmed him in in the alleyway he regularly used as a shortcut. They demanded all the money he had on him, which he handed over without protest. The one with the fewest visible tattoos, to this day still striking him with a certain irony, reared back to take a swing at him. Which he returned in kind, surprising himself with his dexterity and strength. His fist swooshed through the air right in front of his assailant's retreating nose, as the blow coming at him glanced off his shoulder. He tumbled backward onto his not overly meaty butt, which pinged with pain a hell of a lot worse than his shoulder. They laughed at him, and while they did, they seemed like fuzzy caricatures of people incapable of being taken seriously. He laughed back at them nervously, and then from the belly. "F- you, man," one of the young men grumbled. He laughed harder as they turned and ran. This was a new way of seeing the world or, for that matter, not seeing it. And he liked the effect. Gone were his humiliation and anger. Not gone, but covered over with a warm, fuzzy Christmas-y feeling he hated; flashes which would always show up during the holiday season, but this was like one long flash along with a hit of Percocet to add just the right amount of I-don't-give-a-shit. Besides, it was June. Reaching over, he picked up his eyeglasses, which had come off with the fall. The right lens was cracked, the left ground into pieces on the concrete. His muggers had stomped on them. "Thanks," he muttered, stuffing the black horn-rim frame in his jacket pocket. As he stood up and brushed himself off, he devised the greatest plan ever for his life.

Okay, fine, in the month before he had become desperately nearsighted. Myopia. A rare almost sudden onset of it. His pride had kept this a secret, even from his wife Margaret and their two kids. But then they were always so busy with their lives, it hadn't been hard to pull off. The ophthalmologist had assured him the condition was hereditary, but he suspected all the editorial work in harsh lighting had done in his eyesight. Whatever. Myopic, he had just found out, was his preferred way to see. He would go back to the optometrist who had fitted him with the beefy horn rims, and choose slim reading-glass frames. That way he could look over the top of them and remain in this I-don't-give-a-shit-fuzzed-out-on-Percocet world all the time he wanted. That's how his myopia became the mainstay of slumbering. And he had gotten good at it.

Don't get this wrong, he had no illusions of grandeur, wasn't in a position to change much, never had been, never would be, but still if there were just some people, anybody really, at the top worth following, or enough underneath to follow well, then maybe it would be worthwhile not to go around like this. What were we leaving to our children and grandchildren? Yes, everything mattered so much more once Mattie and Doug came out of Margaret. That had been a trip, there in the delivery room witnessing the miracle of life. A very good trip. It had taken his breath away. But life was fast, too fast to keep up with each other. Their family had gone all *Cat's in the cradle, and the silver spoon.* So it wasn't only what was missing from afar that had worn him down; love seemed to be nothing more than a word nibbled on like a piece of stale toast until it had been totally consumed with a belch.

He thought of the word *symbiotic* when he thought of what he and Margaret had together. It remained an unspoken word between them that had grown like a malignancy. Was there love underneath it? He had all but stopped asking himself. Motions, going through the motions, that's what they had sunk to doing. Oh, there was still some pretty awesome sex, and their pillow talk afterward felt intimate enough to scare him out of bed for a cigarette and coffee at the kitchen table. They spoke the L word to each other, and when they did, it didn't feel entirely wrong. Just mostly wrong, the cancer more and more imperceptibly spreading.

When hadn't it been that way, really? Back at NYU in the creative writing program, her prose had been the surest, the strongest, and when he finally got the courage up to ask her for a beer and sushi, her conversation had held up with her prose. Back then her eyes glimmered not with wonder, but with a certain kind of togetherness. And for the upstart, untogether novelist he was, it sure felt like falling in love. As she went to work for Harpers as a copy editor, he waited tables in the evenings so he could write all day. While she zoomed up the ladder to become a senior editor and then vice president of creative nonfiction, he stopped waiting tables and penned three manuscripts in three years. All of which were still collecting dust in the bottom of his desk drawer.

Every time he had opened that drawer and took a look at them, trying to get the spark back for writing, all the words on those pages seemed to be the only ones he'd had in him. No more were left, not any worth writing down for others to potentially read anyway. Over the past four years, since the last manuscript had been finished, he had opened that drawer less and less often. In the past six months the count was zero, a big fat goose egg.

Now, as he walked into the Javits Convention Center to attend Book Expo 2010, his job was manning the booth for Flying Pens, and what kind of name was that supposed to be for a literary agency? *Go figure*, he thought on approaching the booth, which he thought about most things concerning his work. He didn't have the authority to take on new clients even if a great writer came over and bit him on the ass. That was okay, though. The role of slush pile rejectionator he had actually taken a sulky affection for. He sat down behind the poster for the outfit's one and only best-selling author, Manny Baton. On it was a blowup of the guy's newest pulp fiction book's dust jacket, which looked something like a lustfully spray-painted railcar making love to an angrily spray-painted road sign. The book's title was *Graffiti Junk*. He hadn't read it, and had no plans to. The box with the actual books in it hadn't arrived, or better yet, probably had never been ordered by Lucia, who was responsible for doing things like this in the office. So he sat there staring at all the flat faces passing him by. Maybe some of them glanced over in dismay at the pitiful state of the booth, but then he couldn't tell. He was a slumbering man with his glasses resting on the end of his nose, eyes set above the frames.

This went really well for over two hours. The main thing he'd accomplished had been not calling Lucia to get some books delivered. And then the inevitable happened. One of those out-of-focus people approached his booth. A slender, tall man or a woman with runway model potential, he could make out that much. She or he had a fuzzy shock of blond hair that resembled wheat blown sideways in a windstorm. Jeans and some sort of loose-fitting jacket glowed as if with a bluish aura surrounding them. Infiltrating Nerdsville, a probable hipster. He looked down at his boots, through his eyeglasses. This was a refinement of the secret weapon he had developed. In sharp clarity he studied the white stitching along the soles of his brown leather work boots, up the insoles to the laces, around the eyelets for his shoestrings, the right boot, the left one, then back again. It felt like riding a train to nowhere, on an endless figure eight of track. Magnificent Solitude, Cold Isolation, Ironclad Protection were the names on the sides of its railcars.

"Pfft, this is shit." It was said with a lilting high tone in broken English and a lovely French accent.

A woman then; a Frenchwoman. He kept looking at his boots. He could not deny the sound of her French-ness felt pleasing. There had been a time he dreamed of penning novels in an apartment along the banks of the Seine, but that had fizzled out altogether, hadn't it. This was not a question, but a statement of fact. With or without looking through those eyeglasses, he no longer could spot the Francophile within. Somewhere along the way of getting all the rejection letters for his manuscripts, he even stopped trying to imagine such a life. Marcel Proust, Victor Hugo, Gertrude Stein, Ernest Hemingway, F. Scott Fitzgerald, Ezra Pound, yes, Edith Piaf too, while he was at it—*be damned.*

A long silence settled between them, which would've been awkward had he not been on the train. It was painful enough for her, though.

She spoke to the poster, not him, when she finally went on. "Graffiti art must profound, or they'll simply laugh it off."

True enough... probably. But what's the use?

"What you doing here, I mean, you work this boot?"

He picked up the speed of the figure eights with his eyes. *Boot*, man, he liked how the Frenchwoman clipped the h off booth, and the clarity borne by words she left out entirely. It was like how a birth mole above the lip, a slight lisp, or a misaligned tooth in the middle of a smile made those women more sexy. Not beautiful. Desirable. Imperfections drew him in only as good stories did. The odd off-center things reminded him of himself, he supposed. And with all the time in the world to think while being a slumbering man, he'd developed the theory we were attracted to things that were more like us, bad or good. Until right now, in the past four years, since he'd laid his pen down, most any human connection that mattered at all had been made with the bad stuff. His growing lethargy, cynicism, matching up with any number of women who seemed to be swimming in them too, those were the times he'd considered lighting off into affairs. No shortage of opportunity there. Not that he was overly handsome, sort of short actually, hair thinning, and he'd developed a little paunch after abandoning exercise, also about four years ago. But several of those certain types of women had played the game with him, which proved his point about pain attracting pain, and he couldn't be sure, but it only made sense that joy attracted joy. Another thing about being a slumbering man, though, was in a reverse sort of way, it protected him against going through with an affair. He didn't care enough to have one.

"You and I from different worlds."

Correct-a-mundo. After all, he heard no I-don't-give-a-shit in her tone, only music.

"Humph."

Then, the tap of footsteps moving away on the concrete floor.

"Yeah, and what world are you from?" Why had he said this? His figure eights went to breakneck speed.

The footsteps moved closer again. "One that cares!"

Another long silence, save for the bustle of the convention—two worlds away.

"Look me."

As if in some sort of spell, he did. There was her windswept hair again, her blue aura, her sloe eyes, all safely out of focus. But he no longer felt so utterly that way.

"You not look me, really. Your eyes no dead, no alive, they…what, they suspended." She raised a hand. "I feel sorry for you."

This was freaky aware, the first person to truly see *him* who *knew it* since he became a slumbering man. The first with enough oomph to tell him, anyway. Even Margaret had remained oblivious, especially her, he thought. A spike of redness rose in him toward Margaret. She wasn't suspended, no, she was dead inside, or honestly, had she never cared enough to notice him? "I'm sort of a frustrated writer these days," he said.

"You kidding, me too!"

There seemed to be a smile that went with this, but of course he couldn't see her mouth that well.

"I am artist who use words on canvas, and more with color and black squiggles." She indicated the poster. "I make good graffiti, not this, but I want go deeper with words. I think they go deeper now."

"Why?" he said, surprising himself at meaning it. Evidently, a small part of him still did believe if he could've only gone deeper with his writing, people would've wanted to read it.

She sat on the edge of the table and leaned on a hand nearer him. "I have gotten good with my art. People like it." A lighthearted chuckle. "It's in galleries all over place. But they don't get what have to say. I want write a book."

"They probably won't get that either."

"Don't tell me that. Art gone too professional, have less, how you say, diversity of thought."

"I hate to burst your bubble, but it's the same with books." Now, he gestured at the poster. "This is what people like these days."

She shook her head. "Not all people, not people who change world."

"What if it's too far gone?"

"It doesn't matter, we do for art's sake, because we have something needs say."

Yes, that's what he had thought. Why he started writing to begin with. He wanted to go back to gazing at his boots; he wanted to lower his eyes behind his fake reading-glass lenses and bring her into focus; he did neither. "Let the universe take care of the outcome, huh."

"Something like that. Here, take card." She reached inside the bag slung over her shoulder and between her breasts, then came out with it. "I have opening at gallery tomorrow night. You maybe come."

He took the card and brought it close to his myopic eyes. *Anastasie Moreau*, he read her name written out in cursive script, underneath it the word *Artist*, a phone number and email address in the bottom corners. "Maybe," he said dully.

"You hide."

"What?"

"You read card without glasses. You no need them. You hide."

"Maybe I will come." He smiled crookedly, always keeping his eyes above the frames.

CHAPTER TWO

The Stalin Epigram

Our lives no longer feel ground under them.
At ten paces you can't hear our words.

But whenever there's a snatch of talk
it turns to the Kremlin mountaineer,

the ten thick worms his fingers,
his words like measures of weight,

the huge laughing cockroaches on his top lip,
the glitter of his boot-rims.

Ringed with a scum of chicken-necked bosses
he toys with the tributes of half-men.

One whistles, another meows, a third snivels.
He pokes out his finger and he alone goes boom.

He forges decrees in a line like horseshoes,
One for the groin, one the forehead, temple, eye.

He rolls the executions on his tongue like berries.
He wishes he could hug them like big friends from home.

This poem by Osip Mandelstam, my father's friend, slapping down Stalin's atrocities, got Mandelstam years in prison, and got my father, mother, and brother killed; nearly got Boris Pasternak, the great Russian poet and author of the most wonderful novel, *Doctor Zhivago*, killed too. I was just a young girl when given the original version of it, written in Mandelstam's own hand, to keep safe. Now I am a woman, and I cherish being put in care of such a courageous thing, and I hate the blood spilled on this one page. Deaths of people who held my whole world together at the time. We were all poets then. You had to be to not lose your mind.

With your permission, I'll tell this story. It begins in 1934.

My name was Katya Ivashov, my father's Demitri, my mother's Marfa, my dear brother's Radko. I am married now, but that is of no concern to you. Our little hovel on the outskirts of Moscow was dank and chilly, poorly insulated, but not the spirits inside, who most every night (often in the daylight hours too, to tell the straight of it) plied themselves with vodka as though there would be no tomorrow. This night was no different. We were the intellectuals, university professors, doctors, writers, students, dissidents of most any ilk, and of course, like me, their children. Our home was where countless times we gathered. Where else but our homes? The regime had closed the schools and clinics where many of the adults worked, or had been banned from if the establishments remained otherwise open. The Stalinist Bolsheviks, the Communist Party of Russia, called us "rootless cosmopolitans" and "corrupt Jewish bourgeois nationalists." That wasn't true. We were committed to sharing of wealth, honest work, the communist ideal, the bulk of Marxist thought. We just wouldn't kill you if you disagreed or had ideas for improvement. And we wanted to remain Jewish amid the schizophrenia of a brutal state that declared it was absolutely opposed to anti-Semitism and all religion. We were expected to quit what made us ourselves for the "good" of the state. I was leafing through Pasternak's unfinished manuscript of *Zhivago*, reading bits about Yuri meeting for the first time some captivating young woman named Lara—whose melancholic beauty awakened his conscience and his poetry—when the phone rang. My father answered, and in seconds his face fell ashen. Holding the phone toward Pasternak, he said, "Stalin wants to speak with you."

Pasternak nodded with the phone to his ear a couple of times, then shook his head vehemently. "He is my friend. I like his poem." Pasternak locked eyes with Mandelstam, who rocked back on the legs of his chair at the kitchen table and furrowed his brow. Pasternak winked before going on. It almost seemed he was winking at me but I knew better, for I sat next to Mandelstam. "You should read it every morning over coffee and before you fall asleep in your bed."

Then he held the phone out from his head. "The old man hung up on me again."

Pasternak walked over and sat down next to Mandelstam, and the others, several of whom I'll tell you about later, also sat down or gathered round the table. Evidently, there had been a previous call from the Goat-faced

Murderer—as we often called Stalin—to Pasternak that I hadn't been made privy of. But then, I was just a fourteen-year-old girl, merely a budding dissident poet in *the adults'* estimations. Not in mine; I felt old and wise, scarred sufficiently to believe in myself, different enough in having fallen impassioned before my time, to have taken a seat at the table. There were other kids here, of course my younger brother Radko, but from the giggles and harmless screeches coming from the bedroom, they were pillow fighting or involved in some such children's goings-on. Most around the table agreed a second call from Stalin trying to persuade Pasternak to have Mandelstam publicly renounce his poem, "The Stalin Epigram," meant things would be heating up. People at this gathering could get disappeared, sent to rot in prison, or worse. My blue eyes must've been saucers as the men and women talked.

Solomon Mikhoels: "Of course, Osip's poem must stand; it already is being read across the country. If he were to denounce, it would be denouncing the voice of all Soviet dissidents."

Emilia Teumin: "As the editor of international news releases for us, I can tell you it is being read across the world! It is doing more than standing; this poem is flying!"

(Nods of agreement all around.)

Osip Mandelstam: "Thank you all. I am lifted on your wings."

Boris Pasternak: (a hearty laugh) "Spoken like a man flowing poetry through his veins. Then it is decided. To hell with the Goat-faced Murderer's silencing of reason and love! Long live 'The Stalin Epigram!'"

(With that, the vodka flowed.)

Dimitri Ivashov: "Sadly, we cannot meet here again. They are already watching my home. Do you agree?"

(Scratched chins, some yeses.)

My mother hurried into the room, interjecting in a stressed tone hardly above a whisper, "I have been on watch at the window. Cars are outside and men are getting out. They're armed!"

Chairs skidded across the room as people stood up. Others made their way over to the back door, while some went into the bedroom to fetch their kids.

"They want this as much as they want us," Mandelstam said. He unfolded a piece of paper on the table. Before us—directly beside Pasternak's unfinished draft of *Doctor Zhivago*—lay the original of the poem in Mandelstam's own handwriting. On it were a few hen-scratched cross-outs, rewritten lines.

People stopped in their tracks. The stillness of the reformation movement gone sour settled over us. Only the stultifying sounds of children at play remained. Anyone who took the transcript would probably meet a terrible fate, and if no one kept it from the Bolsheviks, how many more good Russians, people not drunk on power, most of our countrywomen and men, would meet a similar fate because of the difference us possessing it could have made? The people in this house could make without giving in to handing this original over and publicly denouncing it? In the tinsel glimmers of these men's and women's eyes, I saw the willingness to curate this poem, and the despair, that by the sheer act of doing so, it very well wouldn't see the light of many more days. They were all too well-known as dissidents. In my mind's eye, our collective blood began hemorrhaging from that page.

That's when I spoke up for the first time at one of these meetings. "I'll take the poem."

Mandelstam raised an eyebrow at Pasternak, who, pursing his lips, nodded slowly and thoughtfully.

"There is no more time!" my mother hissed. Visibly shaking now, she moved in behind me. "She is only a child. Leave her out of this."

The sound of our front door being kicked open, and mayhem coursed through the little apartment. It all happened in seconds that felt like hours. Many of my comrades broke toward the back door, poured through the exit-way like trout in a fast-running stream. Some grabbed up little children in the bedroom or took the older ones by the hands; then they joined the current flowing away into the Moscow night. There was no alleyway or street behind our place, just a maze of apartment buildings and merchants' stores. No place for the Goat-faced Murderer's lackeys to easily be lying in wait for them. Some would get away safely, at least for tonight, although, other unlucky ones wouldn't.

I refolded the poem and slipped it down the front of my peasant dress into the bra for which I had recently received breasts; tiny little nuggets, though, with enough undulation for me to have convinced Mom into letting me start with a bra. There was plenty of room for "The Stalin Epigram" to cozy up underneath the cup with one of them. To tell the truth, I felt as proud of these first fruits of womanhood as of having the poem in my keeping. Sticking my chest out, I grabbed with both hands onto the bottom of my chair.

"Oh, come, Katya!" Mother pleaded.

Her dark expression and piercing eyes cut into my resolve to stay somewhat, and I loosened my grip on the chair a little. Would I ever see her or my father or brother again if I didn't get up and go right now? Was I, face it, a mere girl, prepared to make this highly possible sacrifice? "I love you... I love you, Father, and Radko," I cried out to her.

"You must come," she insisted.

I found myself shaking my head, and then set my eyes on Boris Pasternak, hoping this poet with wavy dark hair, chiseled features, and luscious full lips would find me as attractive as my courage and impetuousness. Secretly, I had been sweet on him for as long as memory allows. He still sat at the table, hadn't budged, except to gather up his manuscript, which I had been reading, and clutch it against his chest.

"They're here for me," Mandelstam, who also had made no attempt at leaving the table, said to Pasternak and me. "You should go. The more of us left to do our work, the better."

"You are my brother." Pasternak shook his head too. "You are Russia at her best. There is no other place for me to be."

I melted into Pasternak's words, and the fact that he didn't try to melt my resolve to stay.

"Marfa, Katya, we must go now!" my father called out, and she and I looked that way.

He stood by the back door, holding Radko's hand. I had never outright disobeyed him before, but by the God of Sarah, Abraham, Rebekah, Isaac, Leah, Rachael, and Jacob, I held on to the bottom of that chair tighter. "I'm sorry, Father," was all I could think of to say.

Then came the unmistakable blasts of Fedorov Avtomat rifles, precursors for the Kalashnikov AK-47s years later we would come face-to-face with, tonight's ordnance spitting into living room walls just outside the kitchen, death rattles all too common in Stalin's Russia. My father ran over and grasped my mother's and my arms almost gently. "Come," he whispered gravely, but as if blowing pebbles of sadness and resignation in my mind. He must've known me too well. I smelled on his breath the onion and mayonnaise sandwich he'd eaten just before the meeting. As my mother went with him, I toppled over in my chair, still gripping it, still in it. She cried out my name, "Katya! Katya! Katya!" over and over.

"I will care for her," Pasternak said, though there was no way my family heard him over her yowls.

I watched Mother, Father, and Radko disappear through the doorway into darkness. I never saw them again.

Boots clomped into the kitchen from the living room, and suddenly assault rifles were inches away from Mandelstam's and Pasternak's heads. I lay there trembling on the floor. Don't kill them! ... Don't kill them! I inwardly screamed. It wasn't so much a teenage girl needed one of them alive to care for her. We were the only three comrades left in the house. If they got killed, maybe in all of Russia there would be only one left like me.

One of Stalin's men shoved Mandelstam's arms behind his back and cinched tightly a slim black leather strap around his wrists. It brought to mind a snake choking someone around the neck. Mandelstam winced, but put up no resistance. My trembling settled some over him not dignifying them with a flailing man. I then wondered why they weren't doing the same to Pasternak. Were they just going to kill him outright?!

While they removed Mandelstam from the house, Pasternak sang: "Stand up, damned of the earth stand up / prisoners of starvation / reason thunders in its volcano…"

It was the Russian National Anthem, and I began singing with him.

"…this is the eruption of the end. / Of the past let us make a clean slate / enslaved masses, stand up, stand up / the world is about to change its foundation…"

When we heard the cars drive off, our singing stopped. Pasternak got down on one knee beside me, smiled warmly.

"They wouldn't want me; I'm a nobody," I said. "But why didn't they take you with Mandelstam?"

He chuckled. "Would you rather they had?"

"Don't toy with me."

He turned serious again. "I'm more subtle in my critiques of them than Mandelstam. Who knows, maybe I'm more cowardly than him. Whatever the case, they'll let me be for now."

I let go of the chair and, sitting up, gestured toward his manuscript. "Until that's completed and comes out in print." I winked, though tears gathered in the rims of my eyes.

He shrugged. "Don't sell yourself short. You, too, have stories to tell."

I tilted my head. "Most certainly I do. What do you mean by that?"

"You're the only other one brave or crazy enough to be here now."

"I need you," I said without thinking.

"And I you."

"Do you think my family is okay?"

He said nothing for the longest time, then, "I'll do everything I can to get you back with them."

"They're already in one of our friends' homes, right?" I hugged him, and he put a hand on my back. "Don't answer that," I went on. "We both know it's up to the fates."

As we walked out into the night together, I felt heartened he hadn't asked for Mandelstam's poem back.

In the middle distance those cursed Fedorov Avtomat blasts rained again, as if from a thunderstorm, but the giant white moon and all the stars shined brightly in the clear sky.

CHAPTER THREE

Rachel Maddow's pedantic report, tracing money from a secret super PAC funded by the Koch brothers and a bunch of other rich tea party crazies, droned out of the small TV over in the corner on their kitchen countertop. He very well knew Margaret loved this liberal marshmallow stuff, agreements met on things she had already agreed with, over and over, every day the *World Turns*. All the choices on cable networks for most any political persuasion had turned newscasts into soap operas. That's how he took journalism's descent. There had been the time he listened intently, but he was doing a better job of training his mind to tune the noise out too, in addition to all the garbage his eyes fuzzed away. It was an upgrade. Still, he had this nagging desire for Margaret to wake up and smell the coffee. Funny, as in odd, this mattered, he thought, being a slumbering man himself. Maybe it was why he cheated here and there, looking through his lenses to bring into focus her shapely figure and nice tush, while she hustled round the kitchen preparing breakfast with him.

He took four slices of toast out of the toaster, placed them on plates, lathered them with almond butter, and set them on the table. He did this partly by feel. He had gotten good at degrees of deception. She set glasses filled with orange juice beside their plates, then sat down at the table. "Mattie, Doug, get in here," she called out. "I've got a meeting and I won't be able to walk you to school if you guys do the slow-play thing this morning." A couple of "Okay, Mom" replies came through the kids' bedroom doors down the hallway. He used to get inwardly angry she never asked him to walk them to school when having to run out for work. On the occasions he had volunteered, she would hurry herself and the kids to the point of making everyone edgy before whisking them outside the apartment. Now, he just ate his toast, took a sip of coffee he'd poured for himself, stared at the glass of orange juice—which looked like glowing yellow fur inside crystallized water.

✂

Margaret wasn't really listening to the news report relegated to mere background noise. It usually worked for calming her down to a dull roar inside.

Why couldn't he help with the kids? Why did it make her feel like a failure when he did? She had that manuscript on the radical Tunisian poet to get through by noon. Her foot began tapping incessantly on the floor, clattering; *stop it*; she put a hand on her knee to steady her leg. This, what did they call it? "nervous leg syndrome" had more than once embarrassed her in the office at staff meetings. She didn't care if her husband saw it, but then if she did, it would be a bitch. He had become increasingly tuned out over the years. But she loved him then and now…admittedly in varying degrees. It couldn't be for the looks; he had never been much of a looker. Cute in a boyishly vulnerable sort of way, not purely an ass man like the football player she had dated or the hipster, or the artists and writers for that matter. But lately he had gotten, well, more on the pudgy side, and a hell of a lot less vulnerable. She didn't have a clue she wasn't giving him the very thing she needed most. "Kids, we have got to go!" she yelled again, raggedness in her tone this time. She stood up and went over to her backpack on the countertop, where she took out the file on her project. She sat back down, then read through the poem. "Are these dissidents consciously living a death wish?" she said, almost to her husband.

✂

Before he could think of a neutral reply, one that wouldn't offend or spawn additional conversation, the kids clambered in, slugged down their OJs, then grabbed their pieces of toast and started in on them, chewing like jigsaws. He and Margaret touched dry lips, their version of a toot-a-loo kiss. Good-byes were said to the kids as they walked out the doorway with their mother in tow.

   One hundred and sixty-three days in a row, he mentally noted. Other than his kids calling him Dad, and Margaret's occasional "hon," he had been referred to as "you" by her and them for that amount of time, "would you," "could you," "see you later," "get your ass in gear," "you write so well, I wish you would get back into it," "you are a good man," even "I love you"—but not by his name. Not once. "Frazier Pickett the Third." He said it out loud, as he had made a ritual of doing during first moments alone each day. No more, no less would he say his name. He thought it could be some sort of item for the Guinness Book of World Records, this string they were on. Maybe he would contact Guinness's editor. But then, it couldn't be proved. What is more, Margaret hadn't seemed to pay any mind whatsoever to him changing from regular eyeglasses to reading-glass frames; yes, she'd completely missed or purposefully overlooked, take your pick, the addition of his one major accoutrement for slumbering. Noticing she had rushed out with her file but without the piece of paper she'd commented on, though he couldn't quite remember what she'd said, something about death wishes, he picked it up off the table. Quickly, he made his way over to the door and looked along the street. She and the kids were nowhere in sight. When he went back inside, he walked over and turned the TV off, setting down the paper next to it. There on the countertop lay his iPhone, and he texted her she'd left it, that he would be willing to drop it off at her office on his way to the second day of Book Expo.

Absently, he began reading the poem on her piece of paper:

Tunisian Muscle

The people pour their muscle into the factory for
    pennies
and a dictator flexes his muscle to stop them
from going to the streets to ask for a nickel
    per day
but the muscles of the Tunisian people are stronger
raised against the muscle of brutality of a dictator's
    bicep,
to which nonviolent muscle for all is better than the
    oppressor's.

Sing along with the workers in the streets:
Tunisian muscle is helpful and the dictator kills.
Tunisian muscle is helpful and the dictator kills.

He spoke that repeated line in a low tone. If this was a death wish, it sure felt a whole lot more alive than slumbering, just saying this line. What would it be like to be this poet, this dissident poet? Some of the poems he'd written critiqued politics of the day, but they had been airplanes flown into the void, nothing more. He had gotten a couple of nature poems and a contemporary life angst poem or two published in literary journals back when, but none of his political ones. He continued reading:

Those who support the dictator muscles become flabby,
    one and all.
Emaciated!

The workers who toil will be heard in the streets with
    entire bodies
the muscles that will outlive the corrupt government.
We must not be owned by multinational corporations
whose contracts protect dictators and not people!

whose contracts protect dictators and not people!

He set the poem down and picked up his iPhone again; went to speed dial Margaret, but came up short of prompting it. Even back when he was writing and she was his first reader, her thinking had been overly precise to talk something like this through. And hadn't she had the cynic in her voice earlier this morning when she said something about this poem? Sophistication wasn't all it was cracked up to be the moment it shut down one's humanity, he thought. His humanity hadn't been shut down, just driven underground. *But what's the difference if we live lives of quiet desperation. Now there's a death wish...*

In his Dockers's front pocket, he fingered Anastasie Moreau's calling card, wishing he wasn't a writer, a deep thinker, so to narcissistically speak. Blasé over it, too, for the secret lay in how you directed your fear, he believed, and all he could come up with was slumbering.

A gnawing in his chest told him he needed to feed the only part of himself still free of slumber, consciously not shielded—his mind—that was his playground and gristmill, an open door only he walked through, though brought little out of the room, and why not have it this way? Any really good ideas that came always got slapped down in the rickety machines his family and the publishing business were, or always had been; besides, machines didn't notice much even in this age of digital artificial intelligence nanotechnology. The velocity of paying the bills for his fellow working stiffs and the poor, or hoarding wealth for the elites, all of this, the entire setup, seemed as if everyone was hooked on some neurotic polishing of brass doorknobs past their sheen down to the core of metal, until the quarry would be worn down to nothing, none of them able to stop themselves. In their small apartment, though not so cramped by downtown West Village Manhattan standards, he went into their "Discovery Arena," the only family room really, open off the front door, where he and Margaret had put together two side-by-side Apple laptops, mounted a world map to the wall that had pins in it signifying places the kids had learned about or wanted to travel to someday, and a few pins had been stuck in his and Margaret's trip destinations. Since becoming a slumbering man, he had always let Margaret stick their pins in. Thank God, they hadn't given up on parenting of a sort, he thought, as he walked over and sat down at one of the computers. He moved with a finger his eyeglasses along the bridge of his nose until he saw clearly directly through the lenses. In the Google search rectangle, he typed in the name of the poem. As the cyber mining took place and a list of selections flashed onscreen, he held down a smirk at having mentally chastised Margaret for her morning fix of MSNBC news. But that was different, they had been hardly listening, and what's more, he often suffered through Fox News and reading *The Weekly Standard* before allowing himself a dessert helping of *The New Yorker*. No, the bigger problem was he always felt like a voyeur when taking in serious news. He recalled yesterday's headlines on his favorite news source, *Democracy Now!*—of a drone strike killing innocent civilians in Pakistan, Israeli military night raids on Palestinian homes rarely targeting terrorists but everyday families instead, how with millions of foreclosures over fraudulent and loose home mortgage lending, none of the financial executives involved were going to jail, and every time he thought of courageous investigative journalists doing real jobs often in dangerous locales, he could not help but berate himself for being stuck in such a small life. Then, he mouse clicked into the first Google offering, a freelance journalist's story about Tunisians taking to the streets in protest of sweatshop working conditions and poor wages; how labor organizing fueled nonviolent civil society movements that may well spread across the Middle East, along with a Tunisian poet making waves about the confluence of these events with a poem entitled "Tunisian Muscle"—and at that his jaw dropped.

He went over and retrieved the poem from the kitchen countertop, took a quick glance at his iPhone, noticing Margaret had not texted him back. In a flash he was again at the computer, reading the poem. Then he went back to the article that explained the poem had been first read by its author, Yassine Lotfi Khaled, at a workers' rally, and then it got posted online. The poem attracted more than a few hits, mostly in the Middle East, which had ruffled the feathers of some beefy guy named Zine El Abidine Ben Ali, the president of Tunisia. Word on the street was the big bird had sent a death squad out looking for the poet, who was now underground. Even this limited spotlight on those repeated lines *"whose contracts protect dictators and not people"* was not sitting very well with old-guard Tunisians backed by the U.S. government and American oil money. *The tangled web we weave*, he thought. What had Margaret gotten involved with? Did she know the whereabouts of the poet? Had whatever she was doing on this been authorized by him?

He checked out the next article in Google's queue, which shed similar light on the situation in Tunisia, though mentioned nothing about the poet. Having seen enough for now, he got up, went over to his iPhone again, and then speed dialed Margaret.

It was answered with a "What's up?"

She was too professional to tell him details, something that had always bugged the bugeeses out of him. This would have to be good. "I've read that poem you forgot to take to the office, and am just wondering whether you want him to fulfill his death wish or not?"

Over in the Upper East Side of Manhattan, Margaret lowered her chin, leaned on her elbows at her desk in the glass-walled office. She felt exposed at her reaction to his question, but he hadn't said anything to her in months with this much interest. She wanted a breakthrough with him, at times yearned for one, though how? He used to be the dreamer, the salt and pepper, oftentimes the cyan to her tossed-salad way of thinking. He spiced her imagination, her creativity, focused it into a zone in which she had once almost started her novel. When had it all gone south? What had she done to close him down? Somewhere inside she knew her summa cum laude, Phi Beta Kappa, valedictorian-filled family constructed walls with their intellects, and she had done her share of this too. Parts of her truth wallowed in a place too shadowy and ghoulish to do more than peek at from time to time. If she admitted this fully, even to herself, she felt as if she would bounce off the ceiling and walls before shriveling on the floor like a blown-up balloon let go of at the stem. So she did what she usually did when this part of herself got tweaked, and defended herself. "I wish no one harm. I get assigned projects, and they take on a life of their own. You should know that."

⸦

Immediately, he knew what he'd said hadn't been good enough, not nearly good enough. This was just the kind of copout that had sent him into slumber, professionalism at its worst. His and Margaret's typewriters, turned keyboards along the way, were people of letters' AK-47s. If we couldn't stop shooting our own kind, called enemies, and stay in the imperious infantry, then we should lay our weapons down and go home, or to prison if need be. For this much he felt courageous; slumbering was a kind of gulag. But there was something else eating at him: those in the truest of loves would do almost anything to remain home, stay together in wartime. Even upset with him, she wouldn't call out his name—he'd gotten the proverbial "you" again. "I'm not asking you to slant anything, Margaret," he finally said. "If you can tell the truth in a way that would keep the poet alive, I trust you will do so."

"I'm not responsible for him!" she blurted, and could've kicked herself. She didn't mean that, exactly.

In part you are, he did not say. "I hope you can calm down by the time you come home. Otherwise, have a nice day." A pause. "Oh, I almost forgot, it may be a late night at Expo. We'll see each other when we see each other, I guess."

CHAPTER FOUR

Pain hanging like a black cloud relentlessly overhead had cast Russia's long shadow over my awareness of starving peasants, slum-ridden Moscow, and ever larger intellectual frozen tundra regions, as if our minds, too, were being exiled to the Ural mountains in Siberia—while also in close ground fog, devastation over not knowing what had happened to my family may just as well have been The Red Sickle slashed through my side, always oozing blood. I couldn't have cared less about the Mother Land right now, and was pouting mad Pasternak had left me with his wife, Miss Zinaida, and his son near my age, Yevgeni, to have a meeting with some man named Bukharin at Isvestia newspaper. I frequently read Isvestia, as a copy of it could always be found in our home. It was a liberal intelligentsia newspaper if there could be such a thing in Russia. How was him talking to this Bukharin going to help get the three people I loved most back?

Pasternak had been on the phone to comrades who had been at our home during that awful raid two nights ago. He would ask about who they knew had made it safely away, and who they hadn't seen or heard from. Then he spent a great many minutes explaining what he had said to Stalin on the call he'd gotten from him, and why this proved he wasn't the one setting up Mandelstam for the Bolsheviks—as many in our circles had evidently thought he may have done after whatever he'd said to Stalin on some previous call. "I was tough with the old man, not like that other time. I admit I needed to toughen up on our cause, and I did just that," he had said to them. After ending each call he looked over at me, us in his library brimming with books, me sitting across from him at his modest leather-topped writing desk, and he shook his head with the saddest eyes I had ever seen. "Sorry, Katya, not yet," he would say.

Miss Zinaida, as she had told me to call her on Pasternak bringing me home with him, sat erect, at a mahogany desk with claw feet, while going through a stack of papers. She made quick, concise notes here and there. Midmorning light coming through the windows threw a golden sheen over her statuesque frame and creamy, strong face, held taut by high cheekbones that made her seem further unapproachable. Chilly and accommodating she had been, nothing more. It felt as if she wanted Pasternak to know I wasn't approved of in encrypted code only they could decipher. Unable to take the sight of her silence any longer, I put my book down and walked over to the window. "Pasternak," I mouthed, and the pane glistened with my breath's moisture.

"Do you play the piano?" Yevgeni whispered over my shoulder, breaking my trance.

How long had I been staring out the window? I shook my head.

"Let me show you a few things on it. It could be fun."

I squinted slightly in an effort to keep my eyes set at a distance. His offer sounded delightful, indeed, but I didn't think I could do anything other than stay fixed at my station without breaking down into tears. "Not now, but thanks anyway," I managed, also in an undertone.

"Okay, but let me tell you about Stepmother. She's this way sometimes."

"Even to your father?"

"Yes."

I could understand why Pasternak had left his wife to marry her; she was strikingly beautiful. It had been the scandal of the year for Moscow poets and dissidents to gossip about. But learning her blue control got directed at all comers without exempting Pasternak, a shiver of girlish wile coursed through me. I wouldn't treat him like that. Using my reflection in the window, I ran a hand through my hair, pressed down puffiness beneath my eyes with my fingertips, and pulled my shoulders back. Okay, maybe I wasn't as comely as Miss Zinaida, but I had a slender, swanlike neckline, feline eyes, slim lips, narrow hips. I would be young while she got older and older. This was a teenage girl's fantasy love affair, I knew that. It sure worked better than the ten-kopeck romance novel I had been reading to lift me a little ways out of my hole. "If your offer's still open, I'd like to go to the piano with you," I said at last.

He smiled warmly and nodded his acceptance.

I wanted to return his smile, but couldn't quite muster one of my own.

Yevgeni was kind and gentle toward me, with quick brown eyes and easy hands that placed my fingers on the keys while I plodded into them. "Don't worry, you'll get it," he'd say, and then we'd go through the piece again. The morning turned into afternoon as if time stood still. Somewhere along the way I began playing the tune like soft, clear rain. When he informed me I was performing a Bach minuet in G major, I kissed him lightly on the cheek. This must've inspired him at least a tad, because he then flung himself into a Rachmaninoff piece. He was a virtuoso, and the song's baroque darkness caressed my sorrow like the befriending devil. In a way that could only be described as Godly, it came over me so pure and peaceful—his black playing healed.

"Where did you learn to play that way?" I said as he finished, really wanting to know.

"My father gets me lessons. It sort of is in our blood, I think. He went to music conservatory, wanted to be a pianist before becoming a writer. My grandmother was better than him, and I don't think he could take it, so he switched. My grandparents were friends with Rachmaninoff." He passed a hand above the keys. "This must be dreadful for you; it feels like I'm bragging."

"Are you kidding? You just taught me how to play Bach." For the first time since the Goat-faced Murderer's men raided our home, I allowed myself to believe that my parents and brother hadn't been shot down with those unseen Fedorov Avtomat blasts. I pictured Pasternak's sad eyes at the end of each of the phone calls to determine whether anyone had seen them, and knew he wouldn't let me down. I even allowed myself to be mildly bothered his first passion wasn't writing. I had never wanted to be anything else. I looked at Yevgeni, noticing his rosy cheeks retained a tiny vestige of baby fat. "Have you only wanted to play the piano?"

He nodded. "But neither of my folks are better than me."

"Nor mine...as writers I mean." I smiled inwardly. Maybe I should shift my romantic swoon over to Yevgeni.

It began snowing, and I turned my gaze beyond the curve of the grand piano out the bay window. Wet snow fell in big flakes, the kind sure to turn slushy. Behind this white curtain, a gray sky drew me toward it. Miss Zinaida had let me use one of her cashmere sweaters that I now brought close in front. Steps clicked too lightly on the cedar floor for them to be Pasternak's. Yevgeni and I looked that way as Miss Zinaida stopped in the doorway of the music nook.

"I'm free to help you two with your lessons now." She steepled her hands. "Shall we start?"

Since I arrived Pasternak and Miss Zinaida had held us out of school. This had been explained as a decision to let things settle down some after Mandelstam's arrest. They didn't want Yevgeni to suffer a reprisal against Pasternak, get kidnapped or something of the sort. I had been too traumatized to attend school, still was. She hadn't asked to help with my studies yesterday, probably out of respect for a shaken kid. I appreciated it. Was my earlier assessment of her unfair? There was something about this lady which made me want to please her. Maybe I wanted to know more about the woman Pasternak loved. Maybe I liked that she rarely smiled. I didn't have it in me to accept too much niceness.

She ushered us in near the fireplace, where she had started a cozy flame. Yevgeni and I sat down on the floor before pads and pencils on the coffee table, while Miss Zinaida folded onto the sofa directly behind us. The book used for algebra was, of course, Yevgeni's, and he was a grade ahead of me, so keeping up with this lesson's train of thought from the very start challenged my capabilities. Miss Zinaida's patience came as another welcome surprise. She straightforwardly would go over each problem until I understood how to do it and why it should be worked that way. The studies brought a certain momentum of spirit. Nevertheless, every opportunity I got, glances were stolen out a window at the falling snow and gray day. We were well into Russian revolutionary history when the blast of cold air from the front door opening told us Pasternak had returned.

He looked gravely at Miss Zinaida, only allowing his head and neck in the doorway. Why couldn't he at least acknowledge my existence? I suddenly felt invisible. Something bad had happened with that Bukharin man. Had he found out my family had been purged? "We need to talk," was all he said. Without a word, Miss Zinaida left us with our measly schoolwork. I began drawing the Star of David over my algebra equations.

"Are you okay?" Yevgeni said.

I kept drawing stars. "I wonder what they're saying?"

"Come with me, and we'll find out."

"What?" I said, incredulous, though setting down my pencil. "In your home the walls are too thick, and the doors too solid to have voices."

"In Russia we must know all we can." He held out his hand, and I took it. "Shhhh," he added. This Yevgeni was not like most other boys.

He led me along the hallway into his room, then inside his closet. Quietly, he rearranged some boxes on the floor until a small opening in the wall close to the baseboard came in view. Gesturing at it, he sat down with his back against the opposite wall underneath clothes on hangers. On my hands and knees, I looked through the hole and could only see the back of some dresser or chest of drawers. Putting my ear to it, I could hear them clearly.

"The state-controlled newspapers are reporting Osip was arrested from his home with no others there," Pasternak said.

"Stalin is isolating us, Boris, no," Miss Zinaida said.

"He sure as hell doesn't want anyone disappeared or killed from the other night linked easily to him."

Those words landed like blows to my chest.

"The reports include my first conversation with Stalin," he went on. "When I said Osip and I had a completely different philosophy about poetry, and Stalin told me I wasn't able to stick up for a comrade. It makes me look weak."

"Will Bukharin publish that you stood up to the Goat-faced Murderer on your second call with him? Will he report the whole truth?"

"He will not."

"So all of Russia who wasn't in the Ivashovs' home the other night will think you're a traitor to your comrades," she said, her soprano voice rising an octave.

He chuckled mirthlessly. "At least the Bolsheviks won't kill me, for now."

"They'll leave it to the dissidents."

"*No!*" I almost yelled through the peephole. I couldn't lose my family *and* Pasternak!

"It seems so. Just be glad Solomon Mikhoels, Emilia Teumin, and other leaders were at the Ivashovs'. Could be they'll get the word out I was strong with Stalin. Even so, it may not be enough."

"Bukharin will do what he can to press for Mandelstam's release, but he is watering his reporting down along with the rest." A smacking sound, as Pasternak probably slammed a hand onto a piece of furniture. "He admits he's losing his power to persuade."

She sobbed once fiercely and stopped abruptly, the stern lady catching herself? "Don't say 'it may not be enough,' Boris…" Her voice tapered off. "Don't say that."

The quietness of their embrace followed; I brought myself to hope that was happening on the other side of the wall. Whatever they were doing, it seemed this conversation had ended. I met Yevgeni's eyes, still on me, and gestured toward the way out. He nodded. As I stood up, he replaced the boxes in front of the opening. We walked briskly back into the great room and resumed positions on the floor at our schoolwork. Yevgeni started in on reading the history lesson where we had left off, while I went back to drawing stars. In my mind's eye, I constructed various versions of what would happen to us, most all of them bad. I even imagined us escaping the country and seeking asylum in America. That felt worst of all.

In about five minutes Pasternak walked in and asked me to go into his study with him. Seated once again across his writing desk from each other, I blinked back stinging wetness, a reflex. "You are a little like Zinaida," he said softly.

I would be more loving to you, I wanted to say. "Is my family dead?"

"I don't know. But the man I met with will make sure not one safe house in Russia is left unchecked."

My lips began trembling. He was wrong; I wasn't like Miss Zinaida. I didn't want to hide my fear from him. "Thank you for trying."

He nodded uncomfortably. He lowered his eyes to the blank paper on his desktop, picked up his fountain pen, and then began writing.

Is this discussion over? How insensitive! It felt so out of character for him.

He had not acted with anything other than, well, poetic aplomb toward me until he'd come back from meeting with Bukharin. I squirmed in my chair, gathering courage. "Who do you think you are treating me like this?" I said.

He looked at me oddly, as if fireflies flitted in his sadness. "A fellow writer."

I opened my mouth to say something more, but nothing came out.

"All of life is our material, Katya."

He opened a drawer, reached in, and came out with another pen. He placed a few sheets of blank paper in front of me, then laid the pen on top. "Write," he said.

"But what of?"

"Your deepest truths."

As my words turned into ink on these pages, I can't say I felt better or worse, or the power of what hung overhead dissipated like some thoughtless, wispy cloud. This was fog, thick fog, and it had set in. I couldn't make sense of it, could hardly describe it. I wondered what Pasternak was writing, but didn't dare look at his prose.

CHAPTER FIVE

The *squish...squish...squish* of Maisie Bilkman's panty hose rubbing against her abundant thighs always preceded her, which for the slumbering man offered a distinct advantage, so he closed the book of W. H. Auden poetry on his lap and set it on the floor underneath the tablecloth, out of sight. Folding his arms on the table, he set his eyes over the hazy flow of bodies at Book Expo. It had been a successful day, filled mostly with reading the elegantly subversive Auden. A few fans of Flying Pens' featured author Manny Baton had inquired about the guy's new book *Graffiti Junk*, and without any copies at the booth, it had been easy to get rid of them with an explanation the books were selling like hotcakes; he seemed to be almost always sold out. His boss's overly abundant lilac perfume flew up his nostrils, tweaking a nasty sneeze, and then in his line of blurry vision, her formidable short bulk replaced the hazy people.

"You are a piece of work, James Joyce," she said.

That's what Maisie had called him since the day she hired him a little over three years ago. Clearly, he had been too honest on that interview. He didn't bother to check whether he'd dropped some mustard off the hot dog he'd eaten for dinner on his wrinkled plaid shirt, washed but not ironed, its tail not tucked inside his jeans. He knew Maisie pretty well, and liked her. She had broken free of small-town Pennsylvania to come to New York, just as he had fled rural West Texas. She started in the mailroom at a big literary agency and worked her way up to representing its noir clientele. Five years ago she went out on her own and formed Flying Pens. She had done all this with a community college degree and her love for reading, especially cheesy, melodramatic stuff. With plusses and minuses, he admired this about her. It showed a certain kind of tenacity. Many of his friends back in Texas hadn't made their way completely through a book of any kind. He'd been called a sissy more times than he'd like to remember. Reading had been his escape from the chaos of his clan, and at the age of twelve, he had turned to writing as well. Imagining better ways on the page, back then, brought possibilities to his life. These literary escape hatches and his family's near poverty had gotten him a scholarship-grant-loan-free ride at NYU, but that was ancient history. If he hadn't fallen prey to reading the classics, really great literature, maybe he could be more like Maisie. Secretly, he also admired her for knowing how to turn a buck better than him. She was pretty much always on the move, and mostly friendly, even when ticked off. "Just helping you get rich, Jane Austen," he said.

"Uh huh." Her index finger looked something like a giant Vienna sausage curling back a few inches in front of his nose.

Performing another miraculous feat only available in slumber, he briefly crossed his eyes as it neared, and her finger turned into two Vienna sausages.

"Come with me," she said.

Following her swishy broadness, he went outside the Javits Center over toward a waiting taxi. He hoped she didn't have some writer client for him to show around Expo, or worse yet, Manny Baton, the man himself, chomping at the bit to be entertained.

She opened the door to the backseat and indicated a large cardboard box. "Aren't you the lucky one? I brought some of our author's books so you can practice your masterful selling skills."

He lifted the box and brought it out of the taxi. "You've put bricks in here."

"They sell for $27.95 each. In fact, they're so valuable, I want you to take them home with you tonight. Expo closes in ten minutes. Can't risk leaving them all by themselves at our booth, now, can we?"

"No, I suppose not." He hadn't checked the time, didn't wear a watch, for slumbering occurred in the sort of timelessness embodied in Einstein's theory of relativity. Not to worry. He would've left for the day when those fuzzy people started making their way out of the Javits Center en masse, like he had yesterday. They said their good-byes as she sat down where the box had been, and then she was all red taillights and the taxi's yellow trunk as it pulled away into Manhattan traffic. The books, no kidding, weighed his arms down. Momentarily, he considered flagging a taxi, but raising two kids and living in the West Village kept his and Margaret's finances too close for indulging in such a luxury. Instead, he tilted his head back and looked through his eyeglasses just long enough to spot the Penn Station entrance to the subway, his normal mode of maneuvering through the city, other than hoofing it. Once underground walking toward the dock for the red line downtown, he heard an amped-up guitarist riffing blues that echoed off the walls, and farther in, a street poet belted urban staccato words of the oppressed and the oppressor in all of us—which none of the pedestrians seemed to care about other than him. That particular quandary came with his kind of slumber, to a man who used to be as awake as the poet. But then, maybe some others down here liked the poet too, and were going along their merry ways, just as he was? The train he needed to get on began slowing up ahead; its brakes made that steel-against-steel sound, its wheels clacking on the tracks. He quickened his gait while others rushed by him, several breaking into jogs. Someone jammed his shoulder, and suddenly he was going down. He stuck an arm out to break his fall as the box tumbled to the floor, books spilling out. Checking for aches and pains in his body, he found none other than bruised pride. When he started to refill the box, a woman bent down on her haunches to help him.

"You trying to catch the nine train?" she said.

He nodded. "Thanks for the assist."

They worked fast but to no use; the train pulled away with five books still on the floor. Finally, he stood up with the fully loaded box in his arms again, then gave her a smile and friendly nod.

"You must leave this area now, miss, or I'll have to cuff you," a cop said, in a thick New York working-class accent, out of nowhere making this a threesome.

"For what?" the slumbering man said, nonplussed. "Helping me?"

The cop shook his head. "She's been down here protesting without a permit. Until you came along I'd almost convinced the lady to vacate. But then, that's none of your concern."

This guy waited for her to pick up my books, and then this. Unbelievable! "Cut her a break for being the Good Samaritan. What do you say?"

"I've nonviolently exercised my right of free speech," the woman said to the cop. "Your city ordinance violates the constitution of the United States."

"I'm just doing my job, lady. Now, what's it going to be?"

There it was again, thought the slumbering man. This guy was simply doing his job for Ginsberg's Moloch. Maybe he should offer him a copy of *Graffiti Junk* and be done with this. If the cop read books, it would probably be right up his literary alley.

She proudly stood more erect and placed her arms behind her back. "Cuff me if you must, officer."

To see her care about anything enough to go to jail in an act of civil disobedience felt clarifying to the slumbering man. He watched the cop, with a hand clasped over her cuffed wrists, guide her toward the subway's exit. Once more, he tilted his head enough to look through the eyeglasses. The woman had olive skin, and she wore a flowery headscarf in the style of a Muslim hijab. "What are you protesting?" he called out.

She turned her head as far as she could his direction, but the cop tightened his grip and she could only look out to her side. "Check out the hateful billboard on the wall!" she said, and then they were gone up the stairs.

The subway terminal shook as if with a tremor before a big earthquake, or more likely his sudden loss of inner equilibrium. Her words haunted him. Things were happening too fast. His slumber, which always had a hairline fracture in its bedrock, formed a fault line. Looking again over the top of his eyeglass frames, he stood in the ebbing and flowing sea of watery humanity. They were mostly fellow slumberers, though how many of them knew it? Without being able to make out their masks in all variety of facial expressions, he more clearly saw their commitment to roll along like waves upon waves, heading toward a shore no longer there. Most would defend this rite of passage to the death, believing the tides that drove the waves were powered by a distant sun and moon, or some god bent on Armageddon. Yes, there existed great differences between him and them. He had entered into a dark friendship with slumbering, and in doing so the hairline fracture appeared. Most of these people were as solid as granite in their slumber. Some aficionados would call it sleepwalking, but they were wrong about the underlying condition. In the midst of all but the hardest of freezes, there burned a pilot light that thawed. It was the part of themselves they had forgotten, the heat of the flame fallen so faint in the furnace of chaotic modernity that it no longer singularly singed. He began feeling at least a little grateful his languid, writerly, overthinking personality disorder had over the years slowed him down long enough to discern the pilot flame. It had made conscious slumber possible. Still, the billboard called to him in the voice of the Muslim woman taken to jail. Would turning toward it bring on the earthquake that would swallow him whole into the cracked earth? This was the problem with conscious slumbering; most if not all the battles you considered fighting were losing ones before started. And caring about them but not joining in the fray made him depressed. Slowly, he turned until facing the billboard. It brought to mind a night sky filled with white stars, these letters, the words she wanted him to take in. They almost glimmered and ran together, unreadable. Sweat beaded on his brow, annoyingly tickling him like his mother's and older sister's feathery touches of long ago. What a thing to have passed through his thoughts now. He set down the box of books, then with an open hand wiped away the perspiration. He couldn't bring himself to look through his eyeglasses, and he couldn't leave. The world didn't shake; instead, it stopped turning. He walked over close to the billboard, and then as if reading in Braille, the slumbering man went along the shape of the letters with his fingers:

> *The Arab street mobs are fueled*
> *by Al Qaida terrorists*
> *The poem Tunisian Muscle*
> *Is terrorism incarnate*

Death to the poet Yassine Lotfi Khaled
Death to all who hate freedom and civilization
Death to all who hate Zion
The tent-dwelling heathen Muslims
Are right about one thing
We are in Holy War!

He moved his fingers along the margins of the billboard, trying to find the fine print that would indicate who sponsored this incendiary garbage. Down in the far right corner, he traced the letters TMZ. Slipping a hand into his pants pocket, he wanted his iPhone to call Margaret, and when he came out with it, the artist Anastasie Moreau's card was stuck on the touchpad screen. He removed the card and speed dialed his wife. He explained what had happened with the Muslim woman and the billboard, and then he said, "What is TMZ, and who is behind it?"

"That's one of the things I'm trying to figure out," she said. "I agree, they are misguided."

"Mis…what?" That was just the thing about Margaret. She could be conscious, aware, awake, but her Boston brogue and her Boston liberal MIT and Harvard professor parents could make anything sound like an academic study. They hid behind their correctness. In this way she was a special kind of slumberer, and so were her folks. But there was more to her than this. She had a grittiness that reminded him of the desert plains of West Texas. Her nails were kept short and free of polish, her face honest and without much makeup. They had been card-carrying members of the ACLU in college. He renewed his membership every year, but had been reluctant to ask Margaret about her card. They hadn't been to a street protest since the transit workers strike a couple years after graduating. This young woman he had fallen in love with, but somewhere along the way she had turned and headed into comfortable retreat. "What do you feel about this, Margaret?"

"I hate it, but—"

"Doesn't it start and stop right there?" he interrupted. "If you feel that way, you can't only sit on the sidelines and dispassionately report about it, at least not with your husband."

A pregnant silence fell over their call.

✑

With an ear to her iPhone, Margaret was one-handedly preparing salmon burgers and sweet potato French fries for herself, Mattie, and Doug. The most pressing question she had for her husband was whether he would be home for supper. He had indicated he could be working late this evening, and now she gets this crazy call. But then, there was something about it that had gotten her hackles up in a good way. Not enough to call him by name. That ended when he stopped being the one to lead them into social justice causes, and she felt something die inside her. She was too afraid, too polished in her thinking to calculate success for the oppressed. And then there was her aunt Judy, grandfather Joe, and cousin Bill, who had spent stints in mental institutions over manic depression brought on by failing in causes they championed. This was not the way she wanted to raise her kids, isolated and hip in bohemian Camelot. She needed his pushes to make what she believed about solidarity and human interconnectedness real, although, until this call they had been as dormant as deciduous trees during a winter lasting for years. Once, they would have shared great sex and cigarettes, even smoking the occasional Mary Jane, after attending a rally, or a march, or storming a government building, or the university president's home with a list of demands. "I would tell you about TMZ if I knew anything," she finally said.

✍

There were rare moments Margaret opened windows for him to climb through, and most every time his reaction had been reaching for the sill and pulling himself in. But when he had, she quickly retreated into her well-organized way of coming at him, at the world. If she would just let things stay messy for a while, maybe they could find each other, take off the masks. He heard Mattie ask in the background when her meal would be ready. Their daughter was hungry. He felt hungry too, for Margaret to stay flesh and blood exposed long enough to feed his condition until strength returned, awakening happened, in himself, in their marriage. He slipped the French artist's calling card from the back of his iPhone, where he'd been pressing it against the casing with the palm of his hand. Looking through his lenses at it, he thought of Anastasie Moreau's claim that too much professionalism was bad for art.

"Are you going to be home for supper?" Margaret said.

"No," he said.

They exchanged quick good-byes and ended the call.

He sent the French artist a text message, asking the location of her gallery opening. As he waited for her reply, the thing that bothered him most—above his marital woes; above the churning in his gut that told him having an affair would be a very bad idea; above slumber he felt as addicted to as if in a $1,500-a-day cocaine habit; above having to haul around those crappy books—was the fact no one, other than himself and the Muslim woman who had been arrested, cared enough about what was written on this billboard to slow down and ponder the words. Leaning against the wall near it were two people who seemed to be stationed here as advocates, and another cop stood guard a few feet away. The sea of humanity continued flowing by in harried bliss. How could he expect them to take action while he slumbered? What if they did? *Get real*, he answered himself. And the circle that kept him slumbering completed itself, again.

Glancing at his iPhone through his lenses, he found there was nothing from the French artist. He walked over in front of the two people leaning against the wall, careful to keep several feet distance so their faces remained blurry. They were white and probably male. "Are you with TMZ?" he said.

"Yes," the taller of the two said.

"What does it mean?"

"It's some acronym," the shorter man said. "We don't know what it stands for."

Just as he suspected, this group had to be well organized and far underground. On checking his iPhone again, he read Anastasie Moreau's return text. The address indicated a gallery in the meatpacking district. "Let's see if I get this right," he said to the men. "One of you is Christian, the other Jewish."

"We are brothers in faith, who worship the same God in slightly different ways," the taller said.

"Certainly not the violent God, Allah," the slumbering man said, switching to a sardonic tone.

Their radio silence told him he'd hit the mark.

As he lifted the box of books and began walking toward the subway dock, he sang softly the old Beatles tune, "All you need is love, love. Love is all you need..."— not so softly that the two men couldn't hear.

✍

The gallery had no name on the outside that he could see, but then that wasn't saying much, now, was it? Since he'd estimated the location of her venue—by using his eyeglasses to take a look at the nearest address after exiting the subway and arriving at street level—every step he took led him unwaveringly into slumber. Along a row of warehouses, the windowed storefront poured out yellow light, casting shadows off people who milled around on the sidewalk, most in conversation with one or two others. He wanted more and less of something hot in his chest. Maybe he should turn the other way, go get with Margaret, Mattie, and Doug. He could say he contracted some serious heartburn and decided to come home early, without lying. "Her work is intense," he overheard from a cadre of talkers. "Yes, and beautiful in its pain." Feeling kind of dorky—a result of the box that tagged along with him like an old friend he'd outgrown but couldn't seem to shake—he went inside.

Standing a couple feet beyond the entrance, he panned the gallery until he spotted her wild shock of hair the color of wheat. Across the room it looked more like the morning sun. He breathed a little easier, because she was all the way over there. Cursorily, he surveyed her art: mostly big pieces, covering large portions of the walls. Some had been painted in all black strokes and squiggles, with handwriting he couldn't make out, and wasn't ready to. Others had splashes of color entangled in those unruly forests of darkness, and the few whitish or light gray canvases, she had chosen to fill almost entirely with blank space. He was a fan of postmodern art, especially Jackson Pollock, Louise Nevelson, John Chamberlain, Dan Flavin, and Donald Judd, but Anastasie Moreau's show held another dimension. What was it? Yes, something about her artworks' existential vagueness and his own settled him down. Perhaps that, and he knew a little of her thinking about professionalism. This place felt like a home he'd never entered before, a real home. One with relatives he'd never met who were weird, though not creepy or strange. They invited him in by demanding nothing, not even that he take on a recognizable shape.

"I am delight, my writer friend, you are here," Anastasie said, and all at once she stood directly on the other side of the box.

"Me too." The heat turned up again in his chest.

She leaned close to his ear and lowered her tone to a whisper. "It's okay you hide; I do too now that you show me."

Turning his head, the slumbering man's shill reading glasses on the end of his nose clicked against cat-eye frames resting on the tip of hers. Neither of them tilted their sight angle to see each other more clearly. Never mind, at this distance her eyes shined like blue sapphires, her skin smooth as silk.

She wasn't nearly as vision impaired as him. But she didn't have to tell him everything.

They chuckled at the same time.

A part of us needs to stay in hiding not to get crushed underfoot, he thought. The delicate yet tenacious part, masculine and feminine integrated and unafraid, where Orlandos created art, music, poetry and prose, great relationships if there were such things; the part that dreamed of better ways of living in cooperation with each other, the earth, and then set out to create all this, everything possible and impossible. Maybe it was too hard to be in hiding alone, and that's why he'd taken up slumbering? Did Anastasie Moreau feel this too, or was she just having a little fun with him? *Don't get so heavy so fast.* Rubbing two fingers together, he pressed against the hard gold of his wedding band. But this was already beyond good and evil, and lust. He noticed small slivers of dark moons beneath her eyes, and something about the insomnia and inner grit they revealed made him want to know more. "Will you show me your art?" he said.

"Only you look real at it."

"Yes, I look real. I'm sorry, it's just that I love the way you talk."

✍

She held his gaze for a moment, then led him over toward a big squiggly-lined canvas. Anastasie had spotted his wedding band at the Javits Center. As an attractive single woman in New York, she had learned to always check. There was something about his dormant sadness that attracted her to him, and of course, him being a writer. Most of her friends were painters and sculptors, with intense attention spans that erupted like orgasms. Writing a book would take her past the exhaustion of ecstasy long enough to slow dance with agony, heal more of it. Wouldn't it? She knew a few writers, but they were what? happier than him. When she looked at this boyishly handsome man about her age, whose name she didn't know, she saw what it took to pen the kind of words she wanted pulled out of her. No, she didn't sleep with married men and wasn't about to start now, Anastasie reminded herself. "This airbrush on canvas seventy-two inch by seventy-two inch," she said. As he looked through his lenses at her artwork, monarch butterflies, orange and black, swarmed in her stomach.

✍

Her dark forest of art snared him in its vines, and like Tarzan he untangled himself and swung from tree to tree. The people outside had been right about her intensity. His eyes were drawn to a single splash of purple underneath everything else that he had to get to. In Cy-Twombly-like offhand shaky script, the word "help" could barely be made out amidst her black squiggles. He didn't want to rescue the purple splash of color; he wanted to sit next to it on a limb forever. "Fantastique," he said, in his best Transplanted Texan-New York-French accent.

"Merci," she said. "You like put package down?"

"Better not." The box had fatigued his arms, but he needed something between him and her. "If someone stole it, I'd have to shoot myself before my boss tortured me to a slow death."

The next piece of art had a childlike sunflower with a sketchy bee pollinating it in free white space, surrounded by her squiggles with the offhand written words: *You say I love you so much I can't hear you anymore and then you are really gone.* He wondered who had inspired this painting. The other canvases, in black squiggles and words and color, took him closer to her jungle of raw vulnerability, until he began looking forward to getting to the more minimalist paintings. Maybe they would break his fall into her heart. The few other times love had entered felt as though his significant other tumbled directly into his heart. Now, he was the out-of-control gymnast performing floor exercises on her wonderful paintings. He had no idea what her heart held for him. The lyrics "She came in through the bathroom window" crossed his mind.

When they arrived in front of the wall with five light gray canvases, he stood so still he could feel his chest rise and sink with each breath. The small pencil drawings on the large canvases seemed to take him on a journey with a lone stick figure in each one trapped behind off-kilter walls of some institution that the figure tried to escape from, though never made it outside the walls.

✍

The monarch butterflies almost lifted her off the floor as she and this writer, clutching the box, stopped in front of these paintings. These were her best, most renowned efforts, had been in museums across the world for a reason. They screamed her long-muffled truth out loud. Usually, she stayed away from them at gallery showings. She didn't want to be questioned about it; the explaining without really explaining exhausted her. Why had she brought him to them? She heard no answer. The butterflies flapped too loudly.

✍

"You don't have to tell me about it if you don't want to," he said, keeping his eyes set on the paintings. He had been institutionalized three years as a kid for something called inverted chest syndrome. The surgeon had to drill holes in his malformed breastbone and place a metal rod underneath it. If the rod moved hardly at all, the chest collapsed and then it would've been lights out, his heart and lungs flattened. So during that time he was treated like one of those chickens raised in a cage that never touched ground until sent to the slaughterhouse. It made him crazy. It made him a voracious reader. It made him a writer. The institution that saved him became the slaughterhouse. And some godforsaken place had done the same to her.

✍

His words released the butterflies, as if flying from her to circle once round these paintings, then out a window. She could tell him about the incest her father inflicted since before she could remember that stole her mind and sent her to the asylum for five years. Or how her father and mother claimed in court she had made it all up. She knew in her bones he'd threatened to kill her mother if she said otherwise, just as he'd threatened her. She could also tell him about the institution having a stake in keeping her thinking she was crazy so they could keep treating her. Instead, without a word, she moved to face him, that damn box still between them, and she gently but firmly placed her hand on his chest.

✍

The fire inside him went calm, his entire body, inside and out, feeling like dewy dawn. "You will write your books," he said.

"You help me."

He couldn't tell whether it was a question…probably not. "We'll help each other."

CHAPTER SIX

We had arrived at the Pasternaks' dacha in Peredelkino outside Moscow along with the bitter cold of winter. All around—through the spring, summer, and fall—hope then heat then autumn's wait had passed, while I stayed stuck in the season that brought me here, numb so much of the time without any sign of my mother, father, and brother. It comforted and scared me that the weather turning frosty again felt like an orphaned friend entering the room. Miss Zinaida carried on better here, away from Moscow's literati and politicos. I envied as well as benefitted from her compartmentalized ways. A sort of out-of-sight-out-of-mind ease like a small brook babbled from her in this arcadia, always on the ready to gift self-isolation, if one wanted such. Worse than missing the spark lit in me by the discussions of Jewish Anti-Fascist Committee members after and between their formal meetings around those tables in Moscow, I was having a harder and harder time remembering how that fire had burned beneath my ribs. Yevgeni and I attended the local school, and he had been kind to introduce me to many of his friends. He almost constantly had someone over for me to meet, "get me out of my shell," as he called it, but I couldn't bring myself to do more than go through the motions of politeness—which his friends took as earnestness, so they kept coming over and often merrily asked me to spend the night in their homes. I accepted their invitations the bare minimum of times in an attempt to stave off being totally found out. And so far so good with them, I supposed, though not with my dear, patient Yevgeni. Thanks to his tutelage I now could play ten pieces on the piano. I was grateful over my progress, but for the life of me couldn't let the music move my soul, so I found myself on the piano stool with him less and less. It was the writing I ultimately, almost against my will, turned to, as if wrestling scarlet fever out of my body, or tuberculosis. Blame Pasternak, for he kept to his daily writing schedule like a Cossack warrior with a tulip between his teeth, no matter how good or how bad things got. I developed the impression he felt everything, every last morsel. Mostly he wrote poetry, periodically giving his novel some work. He asked me to read his additions to this manuscript, *Doctor Zhivago*, and tell him what I thought. It was flattering, especially because I hadn't heard him ask the others in the house. I could no longer connect to Yuri, Lara, and Tonya's wounds or delights over love, though the Russian struggle kept my mind spinning with thoughts and questions. Some of which I would share with Pasternak, who seemed to like my often under-formed but willing contributions. Outside of those less than frequent visits to his studio, it was different for me. He would break away from his writing long enough it seemed for pouring his heart out—about the chaos of the purges, or Stalinist pressure applied in harnessing intellectuals, or some other vital issue—to Miss Zinaida, Yevgeni, and me over dinner. These, and the occasions with a passage of *Zhivago*, were the times I thought of Moscow, of Russia, at her best. Miss Zinaida participated in the discussions as though applying the cool deftness I used in interacting with Yevgeni's friends; whereas Pasternak's son pitched in fervidly enough for me to still consider him a possible suitor, someday; but I too many times got choked up at adding something. Mostly I ate the meals and listened intently, nodding my agreements, frowning my terrible concerns. Before these evening meals and afterward, whichever or both, once my homework had been done, I would invariably open my journal and start writing. I didn't have great stories to tell like Pasternak, only the recording of my own personal hell. It throbbed onto the pages like a disease being bled out, though the agony I could not truly feel—one of the side effects being nerve damage. There wasn't healing in this, closer to destiny actually, while my pen flowed as freely as the cold snowflakes that for most of the long winter floated hither and thither, relentlessly downward, heading toward the huge white cloud of heaven already on earth.

At precisely the eighth chime of the foyer grandfather clock this particular evening, Pasternak came out of his writing studio and made his way over to the dining table, while I assisted Miss Zinaida in putting the finishing touches on bringing in from the kitchen bowls of cabbage borscht and a platter of kulebiaka salmon filet pastry pies stuffed with mushrooms and rice pilaf. He had been to Moscow for the past two days, and on entering the dacha earlier had walked briskly into his study with nothing more than a grunted hello to any of us. "Hurry, Katya," Miss Zinaida said in a low tone, as we neared the swinging door into the dining room with plates held by all four of our hands. "He has been through a rough time at the Congress of Soviet Writers."

An ever-smaller part of me flickered with hope his sour mood had nothing to do with my parents and brother being found dead, imprisoned, or exiled. No news of them each day led me closer to one of these bleak conclusions; I could take my awful pick. In crisp movements we placed the plates on the table and took our seats, me across from Yevgeni, and Miss Zinaida at the other end of the nicely set table from her husband. She rarely pandered to him this much;

whatever it was must be bad. Pasternak, as usual on sitting down at a meal, made hand motions an inch or so in front of his chest, as if genuflecting a tight little cross he wanted to keep hidden but simply could not. This never failed to confuse me, us suffering the ills of Jews in Russia without otherwise flinching from our heritage, if not our mildly practiced faith. He looked at me, then set his eyes directly on Yevgeni and said, "They are demanding a complete selling out of the arts, of Russian literature, to the propaganda machine of the Communist party. You and Katya will be reduced to windup dolls if this keeps up. Me too."

"I'm not trying to change the world, Papa." Yevgeni served himself kulebiaka.

I puffed my chest like a peacock over Pasternak thinking I would someday be a writer with readers of any kind. Picking at my food, I set my eyes between Pasternak and Yevgeni, unable to look at the boy teetering on the pedestal I'd placed him on. I would try and change the world if Pasternak thought I had a ghost's chance.

"What are you going to do, Boris?" Miss Zinaida said, too quickly, her voice hardening more like it had been back in Moscow. Her plate remained empty.

Pasternak knitted his brow for a long moment as if thinking. "I need to do something to connect more with the people." Before going on he slurped a spoonful of borscht. "The only thing keeping us out of the gulag is the following Stalin perceives me to have with everyday Russians."

"You really think it's that bad?" Miss Zinaida said.

Pasternak dabbed his lips with a napkin and looked past her, as if the words "death sentence" were written on the innocuous fleur de boheme wallpaper.

"Then you best learn to write better for them," she added.

I had never seen such transparency in her expression. Her hazel eyes were on fire with sadness, her creamy skin somehow looser over those high cheekbones. This was not a woman reacting mainly out of her own fear. It felt as though she spoke for the illiterate peasants, the hardly literate proletariat, and the voraciously reading strivers such as...well...herself? Did she come from proletariat or peasant stock? That would explain her schitzy behavior in Pasternak's writerly wonderland. She loved it, and in doing so betrayed her past. I wanted to ask Miss Zinaida about her family, but doing that right then in front of everyone would have been cruel. My parents came out from behind the Ural Mountains in Siberia's coal mining region to become a physician and nurse in Moscow, and they kept their feet straddling both worlds, which brought with it a sort of hard-earned grace, an evenness. I also wanted to share this with Miss Zinaida. But there was something else; she was right about Pasternak. Who was

I to tell him? He had surely been humoring me to encourage my comments on his *Zhivago* manuscript, allowing me to fantasize my future as a writer. The gravity of our circumstance falling through the roof like rocks that crashed onto our dinner table made this perfectly clear.

"Are your good friends Vladimir Mayakovsky and Nikoliai Aseev the ones leading the charge?" Yevgeni said, his tone dripping with sarcasm.

Pasternak nodded. "They think I am anticommunist. I am not. If communism is such a good idea, which I think it is, then tell it to the people, make it come alive in the way we live. Feed them, give them work for Christ's sake. Let the naysayers be naysayers, let the majority rule. Open elections, I say, not the rigged ones we have that we call open. We must inspire the worker with great art, great stories." He intently looked at each of us, then leaned his elbows on the table and put his face in his hands. "That's my work."

I got the feeling Pasternak meant for the safety of all of Russia, as well as his family and me.

"Stalin should like what you are saying about inspiring people," Miss Zinaida said. "But Boris, please tell me you did not speak of open elections to the committee."

He looked her directly in the eyes. "I did not. Tell me, Zinaida, how many more will die unless someone does who could make a difference." It was said in the tone of a rhetorical statement of dark fact.

"Do it with your writing, Boris, not your public comments," she said.

"Yes, I must admit you make a good point," he said. "I like to think I'm nothing if not subtle with my prose."

"And that is wise for one trying to change the world," Yevgeni said.

Pasternak shot Yevgeni a look of spite; then Pasternak's eyes fell absent, as though searching for how to make this happen. They drifted once again over at the wall.

"Your beautiful music changes the world without you even trying, Yevgeni," I said. "You are more subtle than your father, for you trick even yourself."

"Thank you...ah...I think," the boy stammered. He stabbed a fork into his kulebiaka.

I glanced at Miss Zinaida, and her lips spread almost imperceptibly into a knowing smile that as quickly faded.

Splendid, I had put Yevgeni on his heels, and his mother appreciated it. Pasternak needed time to think this through, not barbs. I felt everything good about this man, genius even, had him fenced in a corral too small. His manuscript of *Doctor Zhivago* read magnificently, magical to be fair, but his vocabulary, though earnestly toned down, was still overly high-minded for the readers he wanted to influence. He had proletarian dissident friends, wild mustangs, though Pasternak had been saddled and broken in as a thoroughbred on bourgeois pastures. This much was clear to my eye. All but unbelievable, especially to myself, I believed I could help. Straightening in my chair, I said, "Mr. P., I need to talk with you about something in your studio after dinner, if that's all right." I also posed this more as a statement.

This seemed to bring his mind back in the room with us, and he looked at me as if with a forced smile. His eyes measured my need, perhaps my intentions. He said nothing for the longest time, took a slow sip of wine, swilled it in his mouth before swallowing.

I felt like I could've used some of that wine. Slowly, I lifted my water glass and took a drink. "Can't get tipsy on this stuff, Mr. P., but it's tempting, self-medicating ourselves out of this conversation, isn't it?"

"You are the precociously bright writer, Katya," he said. "If you let this wit romp on your pages."

"I hope you think so after I talk with you." I set my water glass down, and with a wink he did the same with the wine goblet.

"Are you sure it can't be said at the table?" he probed.

Turning serious again, I nodded. "I'm sure."

He took the white cloth napkin from his lap and placed it on the table, as if waving a flag of surrender at me, while offering a dove of peace to his wife and son. "I say there's no better time than the present to have this talk, Katya." He glanced at Yevgeni before setting his eyes on Miss Zinaida. "May we be excused?"

She and Yevgeni approved. She finally began serving her own plate with the delicious kulebiaka stuffed pastry pie.

Pasternak and I stood up, slid our chairs close to the table, and then walked into his studio. Motioning at a chair off to the side of his desk, he sat down in his writing chair. I closed the door, then took my seat.

"I know your mother was a magnificent classical pianist. I want to know more about her, and your father," I said.

His brown eyes narrowed into slits of bemused curiosity. He said nothing.

"I think I can help you with your writing."

He let out an uneasy guffaw, but did his eyes relax a bit? I couldn't be sure.

Maybe my comments on *Doctor Zhivago* in the past were at least mildly impressive. Hopefully he hadn't been merely humoring a distraught young girl, and little more.

As if deciding to let someone walk into a vault containing his most valued possessions, ones worth much more than money could touch, he leaned back in his chair and folded his arms across his chest, offering some sort of tedious trust.

Or was Pasternak about to toss me out of his studio on my tailbone?

My breathing stopped. The upcoming moments I suddenly realized were much more important than Mother Russia, or my being sweet on this larger-than-life man; this was about whether Pasternak thought I had what it took to be an artist, not just a writer talking to walls but an author with readers. Without that distant hope, there would surely be no air, no oxygen supply. What else did I have to love or love me back than the story I created for myself, which someday, with hard work and improvement, could be forged into many scrumptiously piquant stories?

"Damn editors," he said straight-faced, "they always think they have all the answers." The great author winked again, and I resumed my breathing.

"My mother's name was Rosa," he went on. "She was a fabulously famous concert pianist who played for audiences all over Russia and most of Europe. I tried to be like her, even went to music conservatory, but it was no use. She was so, what? so elegantly sensitive and at the same time strong over the keys. People loved to hear her play. They loved her as a human being. She played for the Tsar's family many times before…well, prior to the revolution." His expression became distant. "I wish you could've heard her play."

Wetness had sneaked into my eyes as he spoke of her. In my mind I heard Yevgeni's magical playing of Mozart's Fantasia in C minor, my favorite. This was going to be harder than I had imagined. "I am honored to meet her through your words."

He smiled sadly. "Now you want to know about my father."

I nodded, getting the sense he hadn't been down into this tender vault in quite a while, and once opening the door, it was hard to shut. "Please, sir."

"His name was Leonid, and he was a distinguished professor at the Moscow School of Painting, Sculpture, and Architecture. He was a masterful Postimpressionist painter in his own right. That is one of his." Pasternak indicated a painting across from his desk.

The modestly wood-framed piece was of two boys sitting comfortably on a sofa with artwork on the wall behind them. It held something of the broad brushstrokes of Van Gogh, the earthiness of Gauguin, and the seriousness of Russia. "Is that one you?" I gestured at the slim-faced boy with dark, chiseled features.

"The one and only. The other boy is my brother. What do you think of it?"

"My parents taught me something about art. I recognize it as coming after the French impressionists. I like it."

"Very well, then. As you can imagine, I do too." A brief pause. "He was as good a father as he was a painter."

"I'm sure he was, sir."

Pasternak carefully placed his palms flat against his desktop, barely touching its surface. "So, story doctor. How can you knowing this help my writing?"

I straightened my spine. "A couple more questions first."

"Okay, fine enough."

"How did your family fare after the revolution?"

"We were assimilated into communist living. I won't lie to you, it was hard on us, especially my parents. We lost a lot of our possessions. But they wanted stars in the new state, so we were accepted."

"You never left the upper crust, then?"

"To the extent there was an 'upper crust,' as you call it, after the revolution, no, I suppose not. But we have always been friends of the people. Always. That is what keeps this family alive."

Yes, I thought, and your touchiness over it is the problem with your writing. "But you never lived with peasants or the proletariat."

His eyes narrowed again, this time with a flare of anger. "And you have, young lady?"

"I have family in the Urals. My parents and I spent summers there." My heart pounded against my blouse. "And your writing is too formal for those people."

"What do you mean? I've simplified and simplified it already."

"Still, it's not enough."

"I cannot have you redlining *Doctor Zhivago* or my poetry. I cannot."

Such a man, such a Russian man. "But you'd like for me to."

"You are a child."

A knife to my belly. We had been communicating not as equals, but as writers, and he well knew it! I slumped in my chair.

"No, no," he said, softening his tone. "That wasn't fair. Please accept my apology."

For probably about thirty seconds, which felt like ten minutes, we just sat there looking at each other.

Then the most wonderful idea came to mind.

"Accepted." I broke our silence. "Hold on. I'll be right back." Before he had a chance to respond, I was up out of my chair and bounding into my bedroom. I got what I came for and quickly returned to his studio.

Still at his desk, he shook his head with a smile. "You are precocious, Katya."

"Oh, tell me something we both don't already know." I set down my journal on his writing desk. "Read that."

CHAPTER SEVEN

Treetops melded into green swells on an ocean of meadows that as they receded turned bluer and bluer until giving way to purple, and the sky at the horizon was laced with orange and red and pink gently curving string taffy clouds. That's how the Berkshires outside the train's window looked to the slumbering man. Admittedly, this was the best part of his condition, the way nature presented its essence rather than its detail. This morning, as the low, rising sun warmed and lighted his face, in his mind's eye he danced over these waters better than at other times on trips to visit Margaret's family; he moved freely like an old-timey zoot-suiter or Alvin Ailey or the street kids in Central Park. Margaret and Mattie sat across from Doug and him in their private berth, and as long as he gazed out the window, Anastasie seemed right where he wanted her, in the essence of his life, not in its details. He could not deny, and didn't want to, he felt sort of eternally alive when thinking of her—which happened not so often to fall into the category of always, though often enough for him to have once, while rolling through these mountains, prayed for keeping her outside the window, like the Berkshires. This, he knew, would require some deft slumbering, maybe to some small extent because he wasn't much of a talking-with-The-Big-Guy-Upstairs kind of man. But then, the televangelists and the Catholic priests certainly weren't keeping their sexual escapades at bay. Just face it, praying had become little more than a long hangover from his Bible Belt upbringing.

The French artist and he had not been together after the night of her gallery opening. Neither of them had suggested a clandestine meeting, or anything of the sort. They had, instead, fallen into being cyber pen pals, trading texts, photos of her latest pieces, a list of ten things that were important to her: long, hot showers, novels swimming in adjectives and adverbs, leaving plenty of time for long silences in conversation, allowing messiness, celebrating a certain amount of it, etc. He had sent her a poem he'd written ages ago called "Tick Tock," about without clocks there would be no time, as only the contraption of civilization fathomed linear things. He had not been able to bring himself to attempt penning something new; the fog of his slumber was too thick for that, even with her warm, breezy, thinning ways. Partly, he felt like a fraud. She thought of him as such the writer. True, he had helped her writing sprout new buds but was his beyond fertility, like crapped-out soil from years of no crop rotation. Momentarily, he pictured the fields turned to dust outside Monahans, where he'd grown up, thought of the Kilpatricks and the Jennings, who lost their farms to mega-agribusiness concerns, and along with that he'd lost some of his best friends. They moved back to San Antonio and Del Rio to take menial jobs. He was the thief, the smart one who got away to college, a scholarship escapee. The train tracks he'd ridden on to get this far seemed a million miles long. And he felt like he hadn't gone anywhere.

Without a word, he looked at Margaret's blurry face, their heads bouncing slightly as the railcar crossed seams in the tracks. *Just bob, bob, bobbing along...* he inwardly sang. Lacing an arm across Doug's shoulders, he glanced at his boy and smiled. Mattie seemed to be reading a teen novel, though he couldn't be sure; it could be her journal or some children's magazine, God forbid not her homework. This was his life's detail, replete with their luggage stowed overhead, something that simply didn't exist between himself and Anastasie. They had not brought their baggage off the canvas of her artwork, or out of the desk drawer that contained his manuscripts. He tried to convince himself it would've been better had they never met, but that did feel like denying God. The part she had awakened in him was good and pure. That much he was certain of. But without opened baggage, dirty laundry and all, it wasn't a lie, but an incomplete truth and unfair comparison. Not that Margaret had shared herself with him fully, or she knew herself well. He noticed her eyelid twitch, which about this time on nearing Boston, it always began doing. This was such a pronounced foul-up of motor skills, appearing as if she squinted at the sun with one eye, he could spot it every time. Certainly, she wasn't winking at him, not now. She got jumpy, even more intense if that were possible, heading into these visits with her folks. Her dips into ultra self-absorption also made the kids off balance, and him. Who could blame her, though? This was part of his essence too, a big part of it. And somehow it sucked even more with Anastasie in the background. If one of the kids or Margaret would just say his name, maybe they could start there? Just when he was about to ask Margaret whether she realized how long it had been, and how she thought that made him feel, her eye twitched again. He decided against it, for now anyway.

∅

Finally, Margaret had thought when he faced her. Sometime before that she had inwardly asked herself how long he could just gaze out the window. Granted, their conversations had gotten more surface-y on these trips to her parents, but they kept her mind off the inevitable lying ahead. The infuriating part was this train ride didn't have to be that way. She had uncovered the group behind the acronym TMZ, and the hell of it was, she would tell him about them for the asking. But after that day two weeks ago when he'd worked late after the ruckus with the protester over TMZ's poster, he hadn't cared enough to inquire, and he knew she was working on Yassine Lotfi Khaled's poem referenced in that poster. He had been so interested then, and then just to drop the whole subject. But the strangest thing, ever since that night, their sex had gone wild, most nights oral pleasures performed like dueling violins, and two or three go-rounds of the whole nine yards in all sorts of creative new positions. She loved it, literally ate it up, but she knew someone needed to break the stalemate on, well, their emotional intimacy. Could doing that make their sex seem less cheap, less exciting? she asked herself, and quickly mashed the thought. Maybe she would go ahead and offer up the information on TMZ; it would be a peace offering. With that thought, her eye twitched. *Damn.* The closer she got to these gatherings with her family, the more it felt as though she was being asked to go out in the backyard and get some tall reed grass for her mother to "switch" her legs with back when a child. She would do so promptly and cried all the way, somehow wanting this negative connection. The bluster of the switches at least had passion in them, the only times she could remember reason-be-damned in her family. Or was her eye twitching over her bamboozled marriage? He looked like he was about to say something; then her eye twitched for the second time. *Damn.*

🍃

The slumbering man's eyes drifted over outside the window once more, and in little over a minute he was dancing on the water again, with thoughts of those things Anastasie loved doing. Until he spotted the train station, and the dancing stopped, Anastasie vaporized. As the train slowed to a stop, there next to the dock stood the white-haired Comrade, the name the four of them called her father behind his back, and beside the Comrade had to be her mother. Even the slumbering man could spot her dad at a distance. He looked like a six-foot-three-inch cotton-topped Q-tip ear swab.

"Why do I do this to myself?" Margaret said as they stood up.

"Enough to make you want to roll up a doobie and get right beforehand, like we used to, huh?" the slumbering man said, while getting their luggage down.

"What's a doobie?" Doug said.

"Yeah, I wanna know too. What is it?" Mattie chimed in.

"Something I'll talk to you about in a year or so," the slumbering man said. He was glad his kids were still "innocent preteens," as the smart-ass child psychologist had called them during the three sessions they tried earlier in the year that did nothing to end this nameless existence for him, though, in fairness, had helped the kids lay off the computer games some, and get their homework done on time more often. Of course, they never got around to putting Margaret's issues on the table. Come to think of it, they stopped making the sessions when it got to be her turn to say something about herself, anything really. He had hoped it would be his turn after that.

"Grow up," Margaret said to her husband.

"Grow up, *who?*" he said, on impulse.

She curled her lower lip underneath her teeth as if to start with the F in Frazier, then said, "You, you grow up. We're not kids anymore if you haven't noticed."

"Maybe we could benefit from some more good old-fashioned Freudian regression, if you know what I mean." After all, their sex had been awesome lately. He handed Mattie and Doug their backpacks, and then walked off the train carrying his bag by one hand and Margaret's by the other—while she rushed ahead.

"Grams, Grams," the kids called out, breaking into runs to greet their grandmother with hugs, who when actually presented with love usually found a way to return it. Lydia lowered at the knees to their level, putting an arm across each one's back. They kissed her cheeks, though she couldn't go so far as to give that sort of affection. The slumbering man couldn't see all this very clearly, but from back before entering this private world, he knew well enough what was happening. He exchanged hellos and shook hands with Margaret's father, Horace, who had such a wimpy grip for the grand pooh-bah in atomic physics he carried himself as, and arguably deserved the title. He had never witnessed the Comrade hugging his daughter or his grandchildren, and Horace didn't break his hot streak this time. The most you could expect was stiff pats to the kids' heads, and maybe a hand on Margaret's shoulder, but true to form, none of that went down this time around.

In the Land Rover on the way to the Mandts' brownstone, he counted three of Margaret's eye twitches; make that the equivalent thereof. She never failed to raise a hand beside her left eye like a horse blinder to disguise them. The conversation had ranged from how the kids were doing in school, to Margaret, who seemed as though she could use a weekend away from her work in New York by the look of the dark circles beneath her eyes. The Comrade and Lydia never had much to say to the slumbering man, and so far it had been little to nothing, which felt as if he was flying underneath enemy radar. *Success.* Once settled in the house, and after a quick lunch of tuna melt sandwiches with iced tea Margaret insisted on preparing, rather than having the Latina domestic helper do it (a move that impressed the slumbering man sufficiently to pitch in on the meal's preparation), Margaret and Lydia headed out to shop, while he took Mattie and Doug for a walk along Boston Bay—with the Comrade last seen fixed erect on the front porch, hands on hips, politely declining an invitation to join him and the kids. *Success*, again. But it wouldn't last through supper; he couldn't duck them at the evening meal. For some reason it was the only time everyone was expected to contribute to the conversation. Margaret had said it was just in their blood. As the three of them watched schooners, yawls, and the occasional catamaran sail in and out of harbor, to the slumbering man they seemed like fish confused over which way to school.

"Aren't the boats awesome, Dad," Doug said.

"Yes. Which one would you like to be on?"

Doug scanned the bay for a few seconds, then said, "The long, slim dark blue one with three sails, heading out to sea."

"Me too," the slumbering man said. He put a hand on Mattie's back. "How about you, Mat?"

"The same. I'll go anywhere with you and Doug."

"And Mom," the slumbering man said, more stridently than he would've liked. "She's got to come with us too."

Mattie nodded, maybe a little tentatively, and Doug's expression darkened, or was that cloud cover blocking the sun? The slumbering man looked through his lenses long enough to see his children clearly.

"I think Mom would want to stay close to land, in the bay," Doug said.

"So that's as far as any of us could sail," Mattie said, her tone turning whiney. "It's not fair."

"We'd work it out." The slumbering man didn't much believe his own words, and from the looks of the kids, neither did they. This exchange left him stinging. The only way out of West Texas had been to make the world his oyster. Maybe it depressed him to be like this now, but he knew no other path. Besides, *let your kids see you live your life well.* That's what he thought of as the best way to raise them, in the manner of great poets and authors and artists and, since he was at it, great seafarers too! Yet, all the while he felt himself falling short every day. "Let's go find a slide and a jungle gym, what do you guys say?"

✑

"Blessed are You, *HaShem*, our God, King of the Universe, who creates a variety of sustenance." The Comrade said this Jewish blessing.

All heads round the table were bowed, except for the slumbering man's. It wasn't that he didn't like the prayer, he did, and he didn't consider himself to have an anti-Semitic bone in his body; my God, he'd married into this family, hadn't he? But he and Margaret liked soft-playing their religious differences so as not to confuse the kids, kept things low-key at their home. It wasn't like they went to church or synagogue much at all, only on the three "biggies" as they called them. The only unavoidable convergence being the Christmas tree and Hanukkah menorah candles displayed side by side over holidays, and the pesky double gift giving the kids seemed to always squeeze out of their parents, Mattie and Doug gaining a few extras that sent the slumbering man back out to the big box stores for last-minute shopping along with the rest of the unwashed hordes.

⌀

Margaret sat there in appropriate position, head tilted downward, hands cupped one over the other on her lap; her mother and father would approve. Not praying really, more like she was thinking things through. It went about like this. She could give her husband something he wanted, or at least had wanted, and he wouldn't be able to retreat into the ambivalence he was so good at without embarrassing the spit out of himself in front of his kids and her parents. What is more, he probably hadn't gotten so dreary he'd let that happen. *But who knew really?* Okay, it would be good dinner conversation, no doubt. *Go for it for a change.* She gave a quick update about how she was working on a piece that had to do with the Arab labor movement protests and the poet Yassine Lotfi Khaled, and how her husband had come across a poster in the subway backed by an underground group called TMZ; then she looked him directly in the eyes, though as usual they seemed distant. "TMZ stands for Temple Mount Zionists, how about that, Frazier?" she said, and what the hell, why not pull out all the stops. His name left a strange aftertaste on her tongue, like old black olives gone soft or something. She cut into her pork tender, slid the piece onto her fork.

⌀

His jaw dropped. Mostly, what he heard was "Frazier," and his name sounded like music. It also wigged him out he cared so much, now that she'd finally said it. He no longer wanted to see the antiques and fine modern art mixed with pieces from the old world on the Mandts' walls, the crystal candelabra in front of him, the rosewood table etched in gold leaf, the fine china, and with his eyeglasses on the end of his nose, he couldn't see any of it very well. For what seemed so long now, he hadn't had to see anything clearly enough to remind him of everything he'd been running out of the plains of West Texas to catch up with for most of his life—the things that before learning his little trick, he hadn't wanted to see once he did. To write something that might get published, he consorted with the elite, who didn't want to hear anything true, or at best patronized it as long as the work didn't threaten change. Why else had he married Margaret, co-joined with all this? Just take a look around, or rather don't start that. His slumbering was blowing a fuse. All this righteous indignation could be nothing more than a mental pretzel-twist to justify fleeing the velvet prison for some cozy bohemian bungalow, for Anastasie. Who would he rather have call him by name, the French artist or Margaret? Maybe it was as simple as that; he relished the way Anastasie said just about anything. But wait a second, give Margaret a chance. She was making a step his way, and his name sang in her voice like a Springsteen song, which to be honest wasn't the sonorous likes of Edith Piaf, but sure held its own—so middlebrow America wanting to be in the trenches. Margaret had lowered herself to this level by marrying him, you had to give her that. Besides, all Anastasie and he had going was an Internet relationship.

The Comrade and Lydia, Margaret, even his children seemed to be staring his direction as if waiting for him to pass the steaming bread beside his place setting, or say something for heaven's sake. They hadn't asked for the bread, or if they had, he'd missed it. Their eyes looked like a fleet of flying starships from outer space. He needed to get himself together. Margaret had said something about TMZ, he felt fairly sure. The words on that hateful poster in the subway, the Muslim woman being carted off to jail, came to mind one after the other. This was working, settling him down some. He genuinely cared about learning more on this TMZ stuff in a familiar slumbering sort of way, as though taking a favorite old down parka off the hanger before stepping outside into a winter storm. He could wrap himself back inside a solid slumber with talk of politics and social justice. "What was that name again?" he said to Margaret, noticing the way her upper lip curled up almost sensually as she chewed her pork.

✑

She had no idea which name he was after, the organization's or his own. Both had been hard to say in the first place. Had his prolonged silence been another of his backwoods ways of displaying cynical sophistication, proving once again his hold on her and her family? Her parents couldn't bring themselves to smash someone who had come so far. That would be unseemly. They'd wait for him to make a move, and then nibble around it at the edges. God, she felt ashamed of being so much like them. She loved that her husband wasn't. Maybe she should cut him a break and give up his name again, but then her parents would wonder what was wrong with her, with her marriage. Margaret's blood hummed. She was becoming stiffer than them! "Temple Mount Zionists," she said.

✑

Despite his desire for slumbering in this train of thought, his heart sank a little. He'd partly hoped she would say his name another time. "That sounds nasty," he said. "Like one of those interfaith doomsday groups that want Israel to start WWIII."

"Humph, 'interfaith,'" the Comrade interjected. "Zionists never cared about religion, just land."

"Agreed, with the early Jewish Zionists," the slumbering man said, "but they're more and more Zionists, both Christian and Jew, who justify state-sponsored terrorism with mangled religion."

"That's a little strong, don't you think, calling what the homeland is doing 'state-sponsored terrorism'?" Lydia said. She took a sip of wine.

⌁

"Not at all," Margaret said. "TMZ, I'm discovering, has government connections in Israel." *Why am I saying this? Why did I bring up something I shouldn't be talking about to begin with?* She couldn't take her eyes off Frazier's loose bangs combed to the side halfway along his forehead, his take-it-or-leave-it goatee. Right now, she would've loved to have on a tie-dye T-shirt and bellbottom jeans. Rebels with a cause. If he would just ditch that perpetually bewildered expression he'd picked up somewhere back.

⌁

The slumbering man almost looked through his eyeglasses at Margaret. She was actually taking up for him at this table, something that hadn't happened since when? before he had stopped writing, before slumber set in. He wanted to ask who in the Israeli government had ties with TMZ, but that would be pushing for too much in front of her folks. It could wait until they were alone. That didn't keep him from eagerly counting on her parents to go on with this, carry the old Harvard and MIT balls so to speak; Margaret needed to come out and play in the muddy sandlot where he lived, or at least the slumbering man longed for her to.

"The far right in Israel is going over the edge a bit, Margaret," the Comrade said, his tone falling testy. "But a sovereign country has a right to protect itself without being so duly labeled, don't you think?"

She looked at her father with the expression of a deer in headlights.

Come on, Margaret. The slumbering man counted five Mississippis as he took a bite of broccoli chard and swallowed it down, but she still looked the same. The only difference being, on the third second her eye had twitched again. It was time to help her out of the middle of whatever two-lane highway she had gotten stuck on. "Yeah, and how many unofficial official nuclear warheads does Israel have on hand? Isn't it about 180, Professor Mandt? When will they be protected enough?"

"You know that can't be talked about openly," the Comrade said.

"And that's why my wife can't tell you anything more about her work; it's confidential."

⌁

Margaret wanted to melt into Frazier's opening heart, though felt as though she had her hand stuck in a freezer door that somehow wouldn't open. She nodded her agreement.

"After dinner we should go pay your grandfather Mandt a visit," Lydia said, as if to Margaret and the entire table, obviously trying to change the subject.

"No, I don't want to," Margaret said without thinking. All right, they always went over to her grandfather's on these weekends. But he was one of the crazy ones in the family, one of the manic-depressives. It was like walking on eggshells too much of the time when around him; you never quite knew what may happen. And right now, no matter how hard she yanked and tugged, she could not seem to get her hand dislodged from that damned freezer door.

∅

This was another first, thought the slumbering man, her turning away from going over to her grandfather's. Something was going on with Margaret, something big. Maybe this was the right moment to draw out the thing stuck in her craw, stuck in their marriage. "Why?" he said to her.

She looked daggers at him, which he couldn't see well, but felt the blade.

There would be no counting down by him this time. She was disappointing all of them, and he would wait her out. Her eye twitched, two times back-to-back. "Why, Margaret?" he insisted.

"You're making your children nervous with all this, Frazier," the Comrade said.

The slumbering man knew his father-in-law was right. He also believed he, Margaret, and the kids may never get better without her answer, and when would he get another chance like this one? The longer their stalemate went on, the less well it set with him to see her squirming like this. *Screw this, it's over.*

"I never wrote my novel because of his insanity." Her voice cracked.

"Now look what you've done," Lydia said with disdain to the slumbering man.

He ever so slightly tilted his head back to look through his lenses at Margaret, while extending an arm over the food, a request for quiet. "You think because your grandfather was a crazy artist, you have to be afflicted to create?" he said, softening his tone.

Margaret nodded, then looked down at her lap. "Something like that," she muttered.

"This should be done in privacy," the Comrade said, pronouncing it pri'-vah-sea.

Ignoring him too, the slumbering man went on. "For every Virginia Woolf there's a Harper Lee, Margaret. For every Anne Sexton there's a Maya Angelou; for every Hemingway or David Foster Wallace, there's an Updike or Steinbeck; for every one crazy author, there's, I don't know, a hundred sane ones."

Finally, Margaret's eyes met the slumbering man's again. "Thank you, Frazier. You're right. I know you are. But I don't think I'm ready to tackle it quite yet."

"Maybe sometime, then. Maybe sometime." Imperceptibly tilting his head back once more, he looked over the top of his slender reading-glass frames. The gold etching around the rim of the dinner table became a flat line, as if on a hospital monitor when the life goes out of someone.

CHAPTER EIGHT

I was writing poetry as nimbly as an alley cat by 1937, had completed three short stories, one featuring each of my father, mother, and brother, who had never been found. Over 150 good pages had been also penned in my novel weaved from the fabric of that terrible night in our home three years ago, and the great dissident souls there. Osip Mandelstam had been given reprieve to self-exile his family in the Russian village of Voronezh at no small measure, I believed, because of Pasternak's pleas after his friend's capture to Nikolai Bukharin, the editor-in-chief of Isvestia newspaper. Some of the others were still missing, "disappeared," however, most remained strong in the push to make the communist experiment a better one. The active search in the dissident community for my family had faded. All in all, this had been good for me. Here in Peredelkino life moved as slow as my healing, my opening up, so I didn't feel rushed.

Pasternak had read some of my work, and loved it, even admitted I responded well to his editing notes, over which I felt elated he took this interest in me—ugh—make that my writing. But Pasternak had also indicated he wouldn't help me get into writers' school unless I toned down my frontal assault on the system. I knew he thought it would otherwise get me killed; of course, this kind man never went so far as to tell me that. Not to get the wrong impression, he would fall into dark moods from time to time, mostly after dead ends or corners he wrote himself into, mixed with getting more bad news about the Goat-faced Murderer's purges. His writing style had gotten simpler, truer to everyday Russians, and more people were reading him. "But not enough to make a difference," he would say. Enough to keep us from the purges, I tried to convince myself. It was strange, I cared about keeping Pasternak, Miss Zinaida, Yevgeni, and myself safe as a family, a pack of sorts, but left to my own devices, there was little reason to pen anything other than the bare truth with only names and identities changed. Someday I would have to leave them; otherwise, the slowness and freedom of Peredelkino would suffocate me as if relentlessly pressing a pillow over my face. I was coming to know this too. It usually had the effect of allowing me to cherish time with him more and more.

Today, the cherry trees bloomed and the sky was blue; here and there fluffy clouds floated by, casting shadows over us. Maybe best of all, the rains of early spring had ended, and the mud had turned back to red clay, as he and I walked a well-trodden pathway into the village of Peredelkino. He reached over and held my hand, though in a solid, fatherly manner. My heart fluttered with impish delight anyway. We were on our way to shop in the town center's market for vegetables, legumes, maybe some freshly caught trout. Just he and I, for Miss Zinaida was severely with child, and the two-mile or so walk into town would have been too much for her. Yevgeni had been left to his piano practice, which put a bounce in my step. I had been writing when Pasternak asked me to join him. Simply put, he loved his son, no doubt about that, but on this fine morning, he chose me alone.

Beside us on the dirt road, every so often a car whirred by, most of them heading into the village. Hopefully the people in them wouldn't buy up all the trout or best produce before we got to market. Only a few people around here had a motorized vehicle, and most of them seemed to be in use. Pasternak could've driven us in his handsome GAZ M1 gray sedan. What's more, hauling our stuffed-full rucksacks back home would be a doozey. With my hand in his, I nonetheless preferred the walk. The sound of locked-up tires scuffing over the dirt behind us gave me reason to shoot a look over my shoulder. A black sedan swerved close by and stopped, while I pressed against Pasternak. The rear compartment's passenger side window rolled down, and suddenly we were looking at a long-faced man, easily older than Pasternak, with sunken jowls and wild, bushy black eyebrows. His hair had almost entirely gone the way of his younger days, never to return. "Get in the car, Boris," the man barked.

Pasternak's expression darkened. "You can clearly see I am with my young friend on an outing, Vladimir," he said sternly. "We can meet at the dacha after our shopping. You can join us if you'd like."

"Sign this and you can be rid of me now." Bushy Eyebrows held a piece of paper out the window.

"I already told you in Moscow that I would not."

"Your name could be on one of these next if you don't."

"And yours, huh." Pasternak stared him down.

"Take your time." Bushy Eyebrows smiled with nicotine- and coffee-stained teeth. "Go have your fun at market. I am not leaving Peredelkino until I get your agreement in writing." He rolled the window shut, and dust spit out behind the tires as the black sedan drove away.

Pasternak's hand had gone all clammy, and so had mine. I held on tighter as we started walking again. For what had to be the better part of a mile, we spoke of nothing. When we got to the street heading directly into town center, Pasternak instead led us down a narrow lane, little more than an alleyway really. "Where are we going?" I said.

"To visit someone who must be told what is happening."

"And just what is that?"

He stopped walking and looked me directly in the eyes. "If there is anyone in Russia who deserves to know, it is you, young Katya.

"They want me to sign in support of a firing squad for two men I know to be good Red Army commanding officers, but are being accused of anti-Soviet activities. It's getting to where anyone that says anything against Stalin's madness is done away with."

"And you obviously refused to go along with it."

"Yes, but they are here at my home now applying more pressure." He passed a hand through his wavy dark hair, which glistened benignly in the sunshine. "I just don't know anymore."

I thought of what I might do to save my mother, father, and brother...myself if the situation were reversed. But would I commit others to die? Then again, the accused would probably die no matter what I did. "Who are we going to see?" I said.

"My friend Osip Mandelstam has a, well...a love child by a woman, and they live here in Peredelkino. I look in on them from time to time with Osip and his wife having been sent away. I let him know how they are getting along. Anyway, with this, I...I need to know if anyone has approached them."

"Okay, then."

He looked in every direction, and so did I; then we moved on. The black sedan was nowhere in sight. The two of us no longer held hands.

Gray concrete "people's" apartment buildings lined both sides of the narrow lane, each unit having one small window and a rotting wooden door, raw and unpainted. A rat ran in front of us; I all but stumbled while Pasternak took a loping stride right over it. Partway along the block he turned in front of a door, and I came along beside him. He knocked with a knuckle twice gently; then we waited. This place reminded me of how my family lived on the other side of the Urals. The sameness spreading through Russia for its workers, their slow decay, seemed as though some sort of long factory conveyor belt would dump every one of us, sooner or later, into a tiny concrete box no one may ever get out of. Feeling eyes on us, I glanced over at the window and a boy inside quickly moved away. He looked to be about my age. As the door swung open, surrounded by shadowy darkness, this slender lady stood on a bare slab floor with wisps of red hair falling out of a loosely swirled bun along her gaunt, hauntingly pretty face. Her deep-set almond eyes showed the faint look of surprise at seeing Pasternak, and of something carved inside her, chiseled in stone. She didn't acknowledge my existence, but I didn't hold it against her. "Hello, Vika," Pasternak said. "May we come in?" She nodded, then moved aside. Before we entered, Pasternak introduced us, and she smiled shyly, shaking my hand with the delicacy of feathers. I gave her my name, then called her Miss Vika, at which she promptly said, "No, please, only Vika." I decided I liked this Vika.

There was a kettle stove in the middle of the room with its flue going through the ceiling. Hovering near the stove were two dilapidated straight-back chairs, and over against the wall stood a folding metal card table with two even shabbier chairs. A sink beside a small countertop rose to just beneath the window, which let the only light into the apartment. Hanging from the ceiling, a solitary bare bulb confirmed my belief that they got electricity catch as catch can. What had to be the boy's disheveled trundle bed and sometimes divan was over close to the far wall, and off to the side of it a doorway into probably her bedroom and the bathroom. The boy must've gone in there. Pasternak along with Vika sat down at the table. I hesitated for a moment, unsure whether to pull a chair over and join them, before taking a seat beside the stove. Pasternak may have thought me worthy of these proceedings, but to tell the truth, I felt like an eavesdropper. On looking over at them, I noticed a couple of food stains on Vika's wrinkled beige gingham dress.

"Boris, just say it straightaway, what have they done to Osip," Vika said, her expression unwavering, though suddenly even more papery.

This told me Pasternak's unannounced visit itself had already delivered the darkest message in the room.

"Nothing new, that I know of, but they are pressing me harder." He pursed his lips for a long moment. "Maybe I shouldn't have come."

"Why did you?"

"With this happening to me, they may be turning up the heat on Osip. Things are getting so bad for all of us. I thought you could use a friend if they had also paid you a visit today."

"What kind of heat?"

"On Osip, I don't know. They could always change their minds on house arrest and send him to a gulag."

She shook her head. "What are they doing to you, Boris? That's what I want to know."

The furrows in his brow got more severe. "Yes, maybe it's me who could use a friend."

I looked away for a moment, feeling spurned. I could be a friend to Pasternak when he needed one. Earlier he'd as much as said I was up to the task of handling this interlude. Right now, though, I envied Vika's knowing crow's-feet, would've traded her my ripening womanhood.

He told her about Vladimir Stavski, the chairman of the Union of Soviet Writers, the man from the black sedan, being in Peredelkino, and that Stavski didn't intend on leaving without Pasternak's signature in support of death sentences for the two comrades in question. "If I don't come around to their way, they may not leave without me," he said, at the end.

"What are you going to do?" she said.

"What would you do, Vika?"

Pasternak is *wavering,* I thought. He couldn't be human without having second thoughts about not signing what they wanted, but the better question he hadn't asked: What would Osip Mandelstam do? Or rather what had he already done by refusing to recant his poem? Mandelstam hadn't sold his soul to the devil, that's what. This poor woman had been beaten down so far. Had Pasternak on purpose come to someone who would agree with condemning those two innocent men, other than possibly Miss Zinaida or Yevgeni? Did he crave permission from another human mouth that wasn't directly underneath the guillotine?

"I love Osip, you know I do. And I loved him more for not letting them break him." She reached across the table and touched her fingers to Pasternak's. "But to be with him again, I would let the others go if I had the chance now. Maybe you could negotiate his release for your signature."

The creak of the bedroom door opening, and I looked that way. A slim boy with an aquiline face, smooth skin, and a curly shock of brown hair walked into the room. Pasternak and Vika held each other's wanting gazes. "If in your place, my father would not sign it," the boy said flatly. At that, all eyes went on him. "And I'm still proud of him, Mother."

The fiery sheen in his black eyes I had only seen once before, in Osip Mandelstam's the night he was arrested. No way Pasternak could see Yevgeni in this magnificent boy, full of craziness and courage, but by the love of Abraham, I wanted him to. I didn't know whether the boy changed me, or I already had been cut whole cloth from the same bolt of fabric—and would spend many years afterward trying to decide which it was—but I stood up and walked over shoulder to shoulder beside him. "Don't sign, Pasternak," I said.

"Oh, dear Oleg," his mother said. "I'm so sorry, but you will someday come to understand."

He shook his head.

I kept my eyes fixed on Pasternak.

"If I could be as brave as your father and my friend Osip, for even one day," Pasternak said, "I would be blessed."

"And your writing would be more honest," Oleg said.

Begrudgingly admitting it to myself, I agreed.

The trapped light in Pasternak's eyes dimmed further. "Yes, you are probably right," he said.

No, I didn't think he was angry with Oleg, or patronizing; as a writer, Pasternak believed him. My writing felt as necessary as breathing, and Pasternak's did for him too. In that way he and I were birds of a feather. "We better be going to market before all the good stuff is sold out from under us, don't you think," I said. Everyone seemed to like my suggestion; Oleg returned to the bedroom, Vika nodded, then kissed Pasternak on both cheeks in the Russian way, and he indicated giving some thought to her plea over negotiating Osip's release. From the laconic tone when Pasternak said this, I didn't think he meant it—or was I trying to send off in flight an angel with broken wings?

✍

It wasn't until we placed Swiss chard and a few handfuls of Brussels sprouts into our rucksacks at market that Pasternak and I spoke of anything other than what items looked fresh or particularly bruise-free, and I had no intention of going first on airing thoughts which had swirled like dust devils in the silences between us. "You don't think much of my performance with Vika and Oleg, do you?" he said at last, then paid the vendor for the chard.

I continued looking over the Brussels sprouts in a basket; kindness for both of us seemed to call for this. "I understand more than you probably think," I said. "This is your family, and not mine. What would any of us do when in the breach?"

"You were 'in the breach,' as you say, when you became the keeper of Osip's poem, and in another way you found yourself there again in Vika's apartment." He put a hand on my arm, and our eyes met. "You exonerated yourself beautifully, Katya."

"The Stalin Epigram" was in the trunk at the foot of my bed. It gratified me that Pasternak had never asked to make sure the poem remained in good care, or to take responsibility for it himself. Then again, there was this matter of the breach, of standing up for the contents of the poem. "Thank you, truly. But you won't send me to writer's school unless I do things your way."

He smiled knowingly. "Let's go see if there's any trout left nice enough to take home." While we walked slowly along the rows of tables and baskets toward the vendor with her trays of iced fish, he went on. "Katya, I will not put anyone in harm's way to make a point if at all possible. I will find a way to get the message across another way."

"Live to fight another day, huh."

"To write another day."

Why did he always do this to me, melt my big fat literary heart at the most infuriating moments possible?! "Okay, all right, but what if the clearer word, the less nuanced, is what is needed for change to happen?" I said.

"Sometimes it is. And this is worth sacrificing for."

Now we were getting somewhere. "That's how I want to write."

"I know, I know." He stopped, and we faced each other again. "That's why there is Osip and Katya, and then there is Pasternak." Pausing, he touched the tip of his finger to the end of my nose. "I'd like to think we need one another, and the people of Russia and the world need what we have to say."

I actually agreed with him, though felt both flattered and troubled, as though heading off for the summit of a massively tall mountain you were unsure about trekking up in the first place. I was the greenhorn in this expedition. Would there be enough oxygen to stay alive at those heights? Even still, I couldn't bring myself to say I'd been impetuous and wrong in my demand of him back in the apartment. "I'm honored," I said instead.

We walked over to the trout, and all those dead fish staring walleyed gave me the shivers. I usually didn't go squeamish around the delights of carnivores, happened to be one myself. In the places of two larger fish splayed before us, I pictured the executed bodies of those Red Army officers I had never met. It was complicity in death, not concern over eating or being eaten that racked through me.

Pasternak gestured at one of the two fish. "That one looks good, and the one beside it, yes," he said.

I nodded stiffly.

"Fine." To the vender he said, "Wrap those two in paper for us, would you?" Returning to his perusal, he quickly added, "And what about this one and, let's see, that one, there?" He indicated them.

I hardly heard his question. "What are you going to do about signing that paper, Pasternak?"

For a long moment he looked directly at me, then swallowed hard. "I suppose we won't know until I'm 'in the breach,' now will we?"

We stood there as if looking into each other's eyes for what he should do, and believing there may well be two vastly different answers behind them.

"I suppose we'll just have to see." He winked. "So, do you like those fish, or should we make another selection?"

As much as I wanted him poured into me, and me into him, I felt at this moment we were solids, not rivers. "They're fine," I said.

While the fish got wrapped in newspaper, then handed over to him, placed in his rucksack, and paid for, I looked absently over the market. These were country people mostly, inhabitants of the valley who had no compunction to hoist flags on summits. They left that to the poets. I found their mundane goings-on intoxicating for this very reason, dull familiarity. Besides, I would throw up if I looked at the fish again.

By the time we left the market, our rucksacks were full and heavy slung over our backs. We had picked up more vegetables, some rice, lima beans, and a paper sack full of yummy cashews. I even got him to buy a bouquet of white and purple tulips mixed with yellow button daisies that now stuck out of my carry bag. He had particularly brightened at this selection. There was a certain kind of firmness to our gaits, determined sadness, as we walked back home. We both knew we were in a calm before the storm, but into this brief respite we had the moxie and audacity to bring a little beauty. There had been no more talk of trouble. The closer we got, the shorter the distance left, the more I realized we carried no flags to stake conquerors' claims on any mountaintops. We, too, were people of the valley, bearing tulips and daisies, and our mighty pens, instead of guns.

When Pasternak and I came round a final bend in the pathway, we spotted across a wild rye grass field that black sedan parked in front of the dacha. Without a word, we hastened our pace, the rucksacks slapping our backs with every stride, arms pumping. I wanted to run to make sure Miss Zinaida and Yevgeni were all right, unharmed, not cuffed or bound and gagged or something. I glanced over at Pasternak, and his eyes had narrowed like a hawk's, telling me he had similar concerns, but also the age, experience, and well, the God-given makeup to maintain his composure even now, especially now. He was right: we needed each other.

We took the six steps two at a time up onto the front porch; then Pasternak opened the door and led the way inside. Something dark, probably a Rachmaninoff piece, came from the piano. We walked out of the foyer along the hallway toward the great room, and I glanced into the music room as we passed by, spotting Yevgeni alone, playing away. He didn't pause, or as much as acknowledge us in any way. For the life of me, I couldn't understand how that boy could be lost to music at a time like this. But I felt heartened he was okay and didn't have a minder. As we entered the great room, my eyes went to Miss Zinaida, who sat erect on the divan, holding a cup of tea over her bulging tummy from the seventh month of pregnancy. Across from her in an ornately carved chair sat Vladimir Stavski. The back of his bald head looked sinister in its smoothness.

He took a sip of tea, then faced us with those wild, bushy eyebrows. "Hello, Boris," he said. "Will you join us for tea?"

Ignoring him, Pasternak set the rucksack down and went over next to Miss Zinaida. "Are you all right?" Pasternak said.

She shook her head. "His men are ransacking the house."

Pasternak's expression reddened as if with anger, and he shot a look at Stavski. "How dare you force my wife to have tea with you while your goons have their way with our home!" he fired gutturally.

"Those that will not cooperate with the people's government fall under suspicion." Stavski took another sip of tea, then set the cup and saucer on the cocktail table between him and Miss Zinaida.

That's when I noticed the typed letter lying on it. At the bottom of the text was a blank space above his typed name, space for Pasternak to add his signature. I heard the growl of furniture being shoved across the floor, the thud of books or such falling down that came from Pasternak's writing studio and, my God, was it also coming from my bedroom?! Mixed in with Yevgeni's insane piano concerto, I must've missed this until now. A fist balled in my chest. My writing was every bit as damning of the Goat-faced Murderer's regime as Osip Mandelstam's, and then there was Mandelstam's poem. All of it, everything, was in the trunk at the foot of my bed.

"Call your men off," Pasternak commanded.

Stavski slipped a pen from a pocket inside his jacket and extended it toward Pasternak. "Not unless you sign on, Boris."

Pasternak looked at the pen as if it were a poisonous snake coiled to strike. He said nothing.

"And on the contrary, Zinaida and I have been having a marvelous discussion," Stavski went on. "She agrees with me, thinks you should be onboard with us."

"Is it true?" Pasternak said to Miss Zinaida.

"What else is there to do now, Boris," she said, and it certainly wasn't a question.

A bookcase or the like crashed down in the ransacking, and Pasternak began looking toward the archway with his studio beyond, but as our eyes met, he went no further. His expression opened, almost boyish, and his strong jaw set rigid as the most battle-ready veteran warrior. He was asking me for something, I felt pretty sure of it. Or were the only two writers here simply witnessing the destruction of our lives and our work, for this brief moment, together? Partly, I wanted to run into my bedroom and throw myself over my stories, my unfinished manuscript, Mandelstam's "The Stalin Epigram." And if it were possible to be in three places at once, I would've also tried to protect Pasternak's *Doctor Zhivago*, his poems. "Even if they kill us, they will not stop us," I said, my words coming as if from some small pebble breaking apart in me that had to be a million years old.

"You are just a young girl," Miss Zinaida said.

"She is much more than that, and you know it," Pasternak said, looking at her again.

"Yes, she is Katya Ivashov, daughter of her purged parents and sister to her purged brother," Stavski interjected.

"What do you know about that?" I said to this awful man, my legs suddenly trembling.

Pasternak moved in beside me and put an arm round my back. His strong grip kept me from buckling to the floor.

"I know it's true, and I know if we find what their rebellious progeny could be writing in the tutelage of the great master Pasternak, it could be true for you too." He looked directly at Pasternak before going on. "Of course, if you sign, Boris, we will leave promptly with what we came for."

"Don't sign, Pasternak," I said, for the second time today.

In one motion Miss Zinaida took hold of the letter and grabbed the pen out of Stavski's hand. She pushed herself up off the divan, then walked the few feet to Pasternak and me. "Save us, Boris," she said, holding the pen and letter directly in front of his face.

"I cannot sign it," he said evenly.

She stiffened. A purple vein that had risen in her forehead throbbed.

Pasternak took the letter from her and crumpled it into a ball, then let it fall to the floor. "I'm sorry, Zinaida," he said hardly above a whisper. He went to put his other arm around her, but she screamed and threw herself down on the floor. Immediately, Pasternak went to one knee, and still she would have nothing of his efforts to comfort. She flailed herself away.

I thought of their unborn child being battered against the hard floor, of my dead mother and father, of my brother, and when I looked at Stavski again, I thought of why. Breaking and running, I went to my bedroom. The door was wide open; a man looking underneath my mattress shoved it onto the floor. My trunk had been opened, its contents strewn across the room. A quick look around told me my manuscript and stories, my journal, were not in the rubble, and I also didn't see Mandelstam's poem. They could've gone underneath the bed, or be underneath the tossed mattress or something, but it didn't seem likely. I felt hot breath from close behind that had the smell of garlic and stale cheese.

"Have you got anything?" It was Stavski's voice.

I couldn't turn and flee without him grabbing hold of me, so I ran over and stood with my back against the far wall, as far as I could get away from this monster. It felt as if I had lined myself up for a firing squad.

Stavski chuckled morosely at me.

I spit toward him, the hawk landing on my exposed bed slats.

"Nothing," the ransacking man said.

Without another word, Stavski tilted his head sharply toward the way out, and just like that they left.

I lowered myself until sitting on the floor with my back leaned on the wall, then held my knees close to my chest. *Nothing.* The word would not leave me. *Nothing for family, nothing for Russia, nothing for my writing, nothing of a future, NO THING!* I started rocking back and forth slightly, wondering what it meant for Stavski and the ransacking man to have gotten nothing from my room when nothing that I cared about seemed to be left here.

Footsteps clomping along the hallway more loudly as they neared caused me to instinctively clamp my knees tighter against my breasts. Pasternak entered the room and came over nearby. Lowering to my level, he put a hand gently on the side of my head. "They're gone," he said. "They're gone." It took several long moments before I could let go of myself, and when I finally did, we hugged for the longest time.

He moved out of the embrace and smiled warmly. "I'd like to show you something," he said.

I agreed, and he assisted me to my feet. "How are Miss Zinaida and Yevgeni?" I said.

"She is in bed resting. She'll be fine. And Yevgeni is unharmed."

"Good. What do you want to show me?"

He sort of mischievously held a finger over his lips.

I followed him into the music room, where Yevgeni had stopped playing. Now, Yevgeni stood beside his piano bench, with its top open. "I'm glad you are all right, Katya," he said.

"Thank you. And you, you're okay?" This was a little hard for me to say after all that crazy playing he'd done.

He nodded. "Why don't you come over here and take a look at something."

In no mood for his games, I knitted my brow.

"Go ahead, Katya," Pasternak said.

As I walked toward Yevgeni, he gestured at the compartment for sheet music underneath the open seat of his piano bench. In it was my neatly stacked manuscript, and next to it lay Pasternak's *Doctor Zhivago*. I could hardly believe my eyes.

"Your journal and 'The Stalin Epigram' are in there beneath your manuscript," Yevgeni informed.

I could've kissed him; I did kiss him. We laughed nervously. "I thought you'd gone crazy," I said.

"Evidently the bad guys did too."

It took us the rest of the day to straighten Pasternak's studio and put my bedroom back into some semblance of order. Miss Zinaida remained in her and

Pasternak's bedroom with the door closed. Pasternak, Yevgeni, and I cooked the trout, steamed rice, and made a huge salad together. Miss Zinaida didn't come out for dinner. The three of us missed her company as we ate and talked with the ease of released captives. Nothing was said about our predicament. We spoke of music interchangeably with poetry, in literary terms rather than political, all the while looking at one another past the tulips and button daisies I had put in a vase and placed on the table as a centerpiece. That night with my head on the pillows, and still hurting beyond words over the news of my family, I prayed Stavski had been bluffing about their deaths, though I didn't much believe he had been. As exhaustion began overtaking me, the quieter my thoughts got, I recalled how much I had enjoyed kissing Yevgeni. But then, I couldn't stop tossing and turning and actually fall off for sleep, until into my mind's eye slipped the image of the rangy, darkly handsome, aquiline-faced Oleg, Osip Mandelstam and Vika's son.

CHAPTER NINE

The stoutly poured Beefeater gin and tonic needed the lime, so he hooded the green wedge with a cupped hand and squeezed it by the other, sending a long squirt of juice into the tumbler that also drizzled his fingers—which he promptly licked. The slumbering man called his brand of gin only when meeting Buckminster, not as in Fuller, the dead philosopher genius, as in Ross, who at NYU had been his roommate, the slumbering man's, not Fuller's. Upgrading the gin was an adolescent macho thing that because of when they met couldn't go by the wayside. Buckminster's folks had named him after BF because they were hippies in a Vermont commune trying to change the world by example, rather than with words or art or commerce, or had it been by smoking the hillsides' harvests of pot? The slumbering man had never been quite sure. If they had still been hanging on to the sixties there, he would probably join them. Ever since Margaret had hiked up the skirt on her fear of manic depression, he had drawn closer to her pain, to her, as he'd been drawn to Anastasie in the pain of her art. The rub was that Margaret's gray eyes went from dull to anxious, depending on her mood, whereas Anastasie's ice blues gleamed, at least that's the way they were etched into his memory. He had not been able to resist sneaking looks through his lenses at Margaret when she promised to visit her grandfather, and at other times on the ascent or descent of her emotional range when she briefly hit a sweet spot of effortless grace—really sort of Audrey Hepburn-ish. These nice moments were so fleeting it sometimes felt like a cruel game, though he knew this was just Margaret. She seemed to be making half-empty commitments to herself as much as to him about pushing through to her issues. He had quickly retreated and not asked anything more of her. Turnabout being only fair, he would otherwise have had to get into his near erasure of his upbringing. When was the last time he'd visited his parents, walked into his family's closet of skeletons? It had been years. Calls a couple times a month he always made, the excuses of why Christmas was out and so was Thanksgiving had worn thin. Maybe he needed to put on a skirt and let the wind blow it up on his stuff some. Would he then be able to connect with Margaret better, or at least understand her reticence? From time to time she volunteered information on the poet Yassine Lotfi Khaled being recruited by peace activists to help with a planned civil society uprising in Tunisia. Sadly, this was the level of intimacy they could hold for any period of time, political accord. He had to admit, it was better than before their trip to Boston. With Anastasie he had kept up the Internet communiqués intermittently. They had established no momentum in getting to know each other, no rhythm. They were playing cat and mouse, using art and poetry as their code language, though he still had written nothing new. This left him both comforted and threatened, relatively safe for the marriage, dangerous for the heart. How did one woman transform pain into verve for life, and the other not? How could he?

With almost a full month of passing days since they had visited Margaret's parents in Boston, he had tried to shake off this nagging question, but it still persisted. More and more he wanted to see Anastasie and look into her eyes for an answer. You couldn't do that through the Internet, still shots simply not measuring up for the task at hand, and streaming video would've been creepy to ask for. Besides, he wanted to talk with her in person and mine for that nugget of wisdom. But lowering to a clandestine meeting would taint himself into misunderstanding with Anastasie, and possibly with himself. To elevate lust over their honest-to-God deep connection would be a confession booth, rosary-bead-wringing sin, or at least a Christopher Hitchens malfunction of reasoning. So, he wanted to have a couple of drinks with a friend and get some bad advice. What was wrong with that, please and thank you? Then there was his wildcard; in one of Anastasie's texts, she had indicated frequenting this place.

It hadn't been easy coming here for more than the obvious reason of walking his marriage out on a razor's edge. He hadn't sat at the Star Bar in Chelsea Hotel since that time two years ago, when Buckminster had been left high and dry after being found out by the two women he'd been seeing at the same time. Or the idea had been to see them at not quite the same time, but that had failed dismally. Other than that night, he'd turned his friend down, or they'd met at some other watering hole. The ghosts of Mark Twain, Arthur Miller, Thomas Wolfe, Simone de Beauvoir swirling round with the likes of Janis Joplin, Jimi Hendrix, and Jerry Garcia—all of whom had lived here at one time or another—seemed too alive to have time for art no longer produced when it had the chance, and for the slumbering man. They hadn't stopped until they died, as in being six feet under. *I'm getting a head start on stopping*, he failed to convince himself.

Nonetheless, it had been a natural to meet here, this being his freelance photographer friend's favorite bar. "An artist's ass snatch," Buckminster had so ineloquently put it. Whatever. Buckminster had just returned from the Middle

East with microchips full of pictures from the West Bank Palestinian territory, Egypt, and he'd even made it briefly to Tunisia. The slumbering man knew where the conversation would start, for the purpose of possibly avoiding his friend's bad relationship advice altogether. He actually remained interested in the Arab labor-backed protests and the oppression of Yassine Lotfi Khaled's "Tunisian Muscle," and the plight of the poet himself, but in a detached way that kept his blood pressure from rising. Bringing the tumbler to eye level, he swilled the clear liquid around, ice cubes clinking as though from a Bond movie, and then he took a long draw off the G&T. The doubly distorted view of Buckminster through the glass made him look long and skinny as he neared the bar. He spit out part of his drink with a chuckle. Lowering the tumbler, now Buckminster looked to him as the blurry, blubbery blob of diabetes waiting to happen that he was. His orange and white paisley tie seemed like a slice of pizza or something, he had it tied so wide and short. It pointed to his frontal bulge, an arrow indicating the way to uncouthness. The slumbering man sat up a little straighter on the stool. "I'm glad to see you," he said, meaning it. Buckminster would be selected every time in casting calls for West Texas trailer trash. It felt familiar in a Hitchcockian kind of way, scary but totally make-believe. His friend was in fact wicked smart and creative.

"I'm glad to be seen." The big guy's rear end lapped over the stool as he sat down. "How's the blind man doing?"

"Listening to Billie Holiday in my mind, not drunk and not laid yet." He had been called the Blind Man by Buckminster since getting his fake reading glasses. Buckminster thought he was farsighted, which was fine enough to get this nickname out of it. His friend was the only person who wouldn't call him by name that he preferred having it this way.

"Married guys usually get one out of two, but not both. Sorry, pal." Buckminster ordered a shot of Cuervo Gold tequila and a slice of lime with salt from the bartender.

Yep, the slumbering man felt right back in small-town Texas, but as a neurotic mess like Woody Allen or a character in some Peter Carey novel. "No worries. I think my marriage may be falling apart." What the hell did he say that for? Maybe because across the room over Buckminster's formidable shoulder, he spotted Anastasie's unmistakable hurricane of blond hair, her candle-like, tall, slender body alight.

"Oh, man, I'm sorry." Buckminster pulled at his tie, loosening its already loose knot farther below his neck. "You're isolating again, aren't you?"

The slumbering man looked at the blur of his friend again. "Why pick on me?" he said, more testily than he would've liked. Buckminster still knew him too well. The more things changed, the more they stayed the same sometimes.

You couldn't develop intimacy over in a corner all by your lonesome. "Can't Margaret also need to do some Jungian dream analysis or acupuncture or something?" That was better, a lighter tone.

"Uh huh. Who is she?"

"That's my point exactly. Who is Margaret? I don't know."

"No, Narcissus. Who is she, as in the other woman?" His plump lips spread into a smile, or maybe a smirk. "Remember, you're talking to the king of swing here."

The slumbering man fought against looking over at Anastasie again. He wanted to know who she was talking to. "Bucky, have you ever been touched by a woman at a place more at your essence than your staff? Seriously, I want to know."

"Are you kidding?" He took his shot of tequila, then shook some salt on his hand, squeezed the lime over it, and slurped it off. "I've read about such things, but they always seem to go all Anna Karenina, bodies slashed in two underneath a rolling train if you know what I mean."

"Always, like every time?"

"I can tell you this much; you won't know unless you go home to Texas and make peace with your past. Margaret could be your leveler, or whoever you think is now, maybe she really is. But you can't know yet."

Buckminster was at least partly right, he thought. He hadn't gone home much in college, and Buckminster had felt that to be strange. His roommate liked to say back then, "My family is all screwed up together, pal. It's love on a stick, and you should get you some of your own." But the slumbering man's family told him he would never amount to much. That he was selling out by going off to school in New York. He didn't want to abandon them. It was probably why his novels dealt with everyday people, the strugglers, the voiceless. "How do you know through the years I haven't gone home and had come to Gandhi talks with my family?"

"You would've started telling me about your marital woes with what is blocking you from passing Intimacy 101."

"I never fail to underestimate you, Bucky."

"A sheep in wolf's clothing." He laughed out loud.

The slumbering man took another long drink from his G&T, then gestured with the tumbler toward Anastasie. "The tall blonde talking to that guy with the knit hat pulled down over his ears like a bagman is the other woman."

Buckminster took a rather lengthy look at her before facing him again. "I know her, Anastasie Moreau. She's an avant-garde painter. Pretty good at it, and pretty hot."

"Just how well do you know her, Bucky?"

"Not in the biblical sense. Don't get worked up. I hang out with other artists. She's nice, love her French accent; seems perpetually pained about something."

"That's what I think levels me, that and she seems to have made some sort of peace with it."

"Of course, Narcissus hasn't asked her about how she does that."

The slumbering man shook his head, taking only a sip of his drink this time.

"To hell, I say, let's ask her over and get right to it," Buckminster said.

As his friend raised an arm as if to wave her over, the slumbering man grabbed on, stopping it inches above the bar. "All we have is an Internet relationship really. Let's let her come to me if she wants." He raised a conspiratorial eyebrow at Buckminster. He had no problem going over to Anastasie, didn't want to go all machismo on her; it was Bucky he wanted to sell this approach to.

"Good man." Buckminster then asked the bartender for a shot of Cuervo Gold Especial, an upgrade of an upgrade. "Take things at a snail's pace," he went on. "Never works for me, but through these hazy eyes plied with alcohol, even I can see how it would for you, my good buddy."

"Right, right." The slumbering man felt a pang of something like shame rise from a part of himself that had been crippled long ago, and quickly swallowed it back down as if sucking back a bitter lugee of phlegm. Avoiding adultery was not the only reason he kept Anastasie at a distance. Maybe Buckminster was right; he needed to take a trip back home to Texas. For now, changing the subject would have to do. "So tell me, in your travels to the Middle East, what did you find out about the uprisings brewing in Arab civil society?"

"There's an old intellectual by the name of Clifford Odeon, one of the guys who invented nonviolent resistance, who's training community organizers in several Middle Eastern countries how to be effective with full-blown revolutions. He lives in Marblehead, Mass. His lieutenants are on the ground over there."

Maybe that's whose book Margaret is editing? "Do you know anything about the poet Yassine Lotfi Khaled from Tunisia, or a group called the Temple Mount Zionists?"

Buckminster took another shot of tequila along with the pageantry of the lime squeeze and salt licking. "The poet knows some of the Muslims who quietly back the TMZ, which is really just a Jewish and Christian hate group."

The slumbering man took a long moment to collect his thoughts. "Jihadist Muslims who would like nothing better than for another world war to occur— am I fly on this?"

Buckminster nodded. "You are a sharp nail, blind man. The thing of it is, the poet is pure as the driven snow. He wants peace and democracy; that's why he's being pressured by the Tunisian establishment and the jihadists, caught in the crossfire if you will."

"Where is he?"

"Hiding out, God knows where. The scuttlebutt is, only Clifford Odeon and a very few others know of his safe house. The good Lord knows, I tried to get a picture of him and failed." He slapped the bar with a meaty hand. "But I am a pig who never stops thrashing in the mud."

The slumbering man inwardly winced. Khaled needed protection, not exposure. But his friend's self-assessment he knew to be correct—of being a bovine in the dirt. This was as far as he could go with him without getting into a red-faced clash of wills. Until this point in their discussion, he had been oddly aware of feeling like he did when talking politics with Margaret, her sideways technique of not having to go more meaningful places with their relationship. Admittedly, he was in on the same scam, as he'd just changed the subject in this way on his friend. But that rather simple read on things was falling away like shifting sands that left an Us as big in the bar with him as, well, Bucky. Margaret remained closed down to protect herself, and he spewed his guts to the world in his writing until that had stopped. Now, they both were silently askew to their inner selves, and needed to head back into their families for discovering straighter, truer paths. He had Bucky to thank for this knowledge too. He shot another look over Anastasie's way, and she quickly looked back at the guy with the knit cap. She had been looking at him. It was time to lose Buckminster. "You live an exciting life, Bucky. Isn't it about time for you to go help one of your hatched-out-of-wedlock offspring with his or her homework?"

Buckminster's normal chalky expression dimmed while his eyes sort of flowered from dark holes, like early spring redbuds rising above wounds in stark branches. "You know, I may do just that," he said, then tilted his head Anastasie's direction. "Use a rubber ducky, blind man. I always do."

The slumbering man didn't think Buckminster had sired any issue and, what's more, wouldn't want to drive that sharp of a blade into his friend's heart. Buckminster's mixed emotions were surely over him being asked to skedaddle by an out-of-the-closet peacenik, the act in itself a reminder that discerning underground justice could hold a candle to the flame of Bucky's sometimes ham-fisted photojournalism. The subject had been a long running thorn between them, which thankfully wouldn't be taken out of their hides with tweezers tonight. They paid the barkeep and said their let's-not-make-it-so-long-between-next-times. As Buckminster made way for the door, the slumbering man stood from the barstool, with his hands smoothed the T-shirt that had on its front the

Fab Four in their prime—who seemed to be hiking up his moderate paunch—and then sporting a rather cool, if he thought so himself, three-day stubble beard, he took his hoodie jacket off the barstool (he had been sitting on it) and headed toward Anastasie. Taking a quick look through his lenses, he saw she and the guy in the knit cap were locked in an intense exchange. *Boldly go where no man has gone before.* The theme from *Star Trek* played in his mind as he stepped in beside her. He chuckled inwardly. It wasn't good for him to spend much time with Buckminster.

"I don't know how long take you come to me." She kissed him lightly on both cheeks.

"Me too." He wondered whether she meant tonight in the bar, or ever since they had fallen into their Internet relationship. He was already feeling it again, the leveling, the rightness of being with her.

"This Bernard," she introduced her friend. "Bernard, this Frazier."

He had signed off with his name in emails and texts to her, but hearing her say it French style felt as if enjoying a picnic with her amidst a field of lavender in Provence, poetry to the prose of his life with Margaret. He darkened with self-disappointment at making the comparison between the two women in his life. It had been wonderful when Margaret finally said his name again, and yet so familiar. While he shook Barnard's hand and exchanged greetings, she without another word walked over across the bar and sat down at a table with two chairs, as though to say, "Only one of the two of you will be joining me." Bernard told him he was a visual artist who used found items in his work, old pieces of wood, tin cans, hubcaps, buttons, and the like; then he asked what kind of stuff the slumbering man wrote. While explaining he hadn't written much lately and what he had penned was more Steinbeck than Hemingway, he could not help but keep glancing over at Anastasie. She seemed to be carefully not making eye contact with them, looking down at the table, fiddling with a napkin. One of the times he looked at Barnard again, he could've sworn the knit-capped artist had been eyeing his wedding band. Bernard didn't appear to be gay, but one never knew.

Then Bernard said, "Not that you don't seem like a nice enough guy, but she told me she's falling for you, and I don't like it one bit."

Why would any man other than the lucky one? he wanted to say, though thought better of it. No doubt remained now, Bernard didn't like the fact she was dangerously close to consorting with a married man. Maybe he was her friend, maybe a would-be lover? The thing of it was, the slumbering man felt that way about her too, wanted to protect her from himself, and he felt that way, in reverse, about himself needing protection from her. A conundrum, closed loop, some sort of black hole opened up between the bar where he and Barnard stood and the table across the room with Anastasie at it. Just as he looked through his lenses again, she locked eyes with him. Usually it was when he purposefully distorted the world around him that it seemed to take on special effects, out-of-focus tinsel auras, purple and yellow Van Gogh night scenes, but right now he and Anastasie seemed to be pouring waters from their souls into each other; he could see the blue currents run with something more here and now than in his mind's eye. The fear almost entirely left him. He was looking through eyes of love.

"You'll have to excuse me," he said to Bernard.

When he sat down in the chair next to her, she said, "You no hide now, Frazier."

"No, Frazier's not hiding." There were a million things he didn't know about her, and he thought of how wonderfully maddening they would be to learn one by one over the oncoming fifty years or so.

"Why call by own name? You, you, not outside yourself."

"No. I'm not." He smiled warmly. "With you it feels like I'm me, but not other places. I haven't thought of myself as me in a long time." His words were water, a river flowing between wide banks, uncontrollable, though not out of control.

"I must go to France, and you must not follow me."

"I know." He felt almost certain they would never kiss passionately, never make love all day, the next, and the next, and into the next week. This was the kind of love that didn't threaten marriages; it transcended them. The most wonderfully tragic kind of all, it had to be.

"Write me."

"Always."

She reached in her carry bag and came out with a pen, then scratched out an address on a napkin and handed it to him.

He looked at the PO Box address in Marseille, the south of France.

"I must go before cry," she said.

She seemed to know if they touched now, they would become inseparable. He no doubt did.

His eyes stung with tears. "Good-bye, Anastasie."

"Good-bye, Frazier."

He did not watch her walk from the Star Bar out into the blustery New York night. For the longest time he considered the address, wondering whether he would have the resolve not to go after her. At last, he carefully slipped it in his wallet for safekeeping in his jeans' back pocket.

On leaving the bar he didn't know where he would head. It was unseasonably crisp, so he zipped his jacket and raised the hoodie to cover his head. He walked the streets for over an hour, until going into a Duane Reade to make a small purchase. Ten minutes later he sat down at a picnic table in Central Park. The night aglow in white light, undistorted, he gazed skyward. Finally, he took the newly acquired fifty-cent Bic pen from his jacket pocket, and the napkin out of his wallet. He turned the napkin over on the side without her address, then began penning a poem:

> *Under the full moon*
> *a squall line blown*
> *in by a black norther*
> *cuts the sky in half,*
> *and you are walking*
> *the edge of clouds.*
> *I can't tell whether*
> *you're coming nearer*
> *or going away. Maybe*
> *it's just a midnight*
> *escape to Marseille*
> *without a care in the*
> *world, no thought of me.*
> *In a moment the cottony*
> *firmament takes the form*
> *of a heart with an archway*
> *over it, and I can no*
> *longer make you out.*
>
> *So I draw these inky clouds*
> *with words to keep you close.*

At the end, once he was happy with it, there were a few cross-outs and rewritten lines. It took reading the words over three more times before the title came, and then he wrote above the poem's opening:

Still Here

CHAPTER TEN

Spring had given way to summer with the cicadas' cackles and stultifying humidity that made the air stink of scythed wheat which hadn't made it onto wagons and, instead, fermented among the fields—all of it reminiscent of a slow decay that had settled over the household. Pasternak had joined Miss Zinaida, Yevgeni, and myself in becoming concerned over our likely arrest. We had too much to lose with our grand piano, epic manuscripts, tea service, and fine extended family, oxymorons of Russia that softened us; this feeling was palpable between the dacha's walls, while so much of the populace went hungry, had lost loved ones, or gotten separated from them. It had the effect of making me burn with lust for Oleg, the boy uncorrupted by my smart poetry, cut off from even his father's surname. That, and his wizened eyes and strength he seemed to gather from picking up the shattered pieces of being the bastard to a father he idolized though had only been with a few times, then holding them as if in his open palms for all to see. My virginity had been kept, but like a fraying thread. A couple times a week, I had taken to waiting till just after dusk before slipping out my bedroom window to be with him. His mother Vika actually seemed relieved Oleg and I were together. But then, she had deteriorated with consumption, the other horse of the Russian apocalypse. Opening my bedroom door a few inches, I checked to make sure lamplight gleamed from the crack beneath Pasternak's studio door, indicating he remained occupied with his pen, paper, and thoughts. Miss Zinaida never came to check on my homework when done in my room, or to tuck me in bed, her way of making it clear I wasn't from her chromosomes; and Pasternak and Yevgeni hadn't once darkened my doorway, for they were, among everything else good and decent, gentlemanly. Dressed in a billowy white blouse and pantaloons that made me look not much different than a genie let out of the bottle, in less than thirty ticks of the clock, I lowered myself into the bed of roses right outside my window, and then carefully closed it. A thorn pricked my calf, causing me to bite my lip to stay quiet. When I turned to go, a flashlight suddenly flared. "Hello, Pasternak," I said.

"You shouldn't be sneaking off without anyone knowing where you're going," he said sternly.

With the beam in my eyes, I couldn't be sure, but I thought Pasternak failed to hold back the thin hint of a smile. "I suppose there'll be locks on the windows by tomorrow afternoon." I smiled more sheepishly than I would've liked.

"Enough comrades are getting locked up these days. I don't think we'll take such extreme measures." Lowering the flashlight, he extended his other hand and assisted me out of the roses. "Nice outfit. Oleg should like the way you look tonight."

A tinge of being sweet on Pasternak returned. "If only there was a way to be two people at once." I sniggered. "How do you know about Oleg and me?"

"It started with noticing the only place the roses are droopy happens to be directly beneath your window." He winked mischievously. "I'm glad you two are an item. He's a good young man who inherited his father's mettle."

"I agree. Now that this is out in the open, why haven't you been over to look in on Vika since we were there in the spring? She has gotten much worse."

"I don't want to draw the goon squad to her. They have a man tailing me pretty much every time I leave the dacha."

I thought for a moment. "If they are watching me, they don't seem to mind me visiting Oleg and Vika."

"My thoughts exactly." He reached in his jacket pocket, came out with a folded piece of paper, and handed it to me. "I've wanted to get her a copy of the letter I sent off right after we received that unwelcome visit by Stavski and his men. Go on, read it." He shined the beam on the letter.

> *Dear Honorable General Secretary Stalin,*
> *I am a humble servant of the people's government, of the Communist Party, and of the ideals of the 1917 revolution. Myself and every member of my family, including our houseguest Katya Ivashov, hold Tolstoyan convictions that have been proven by our activities in every aspect without fail. I am a writer and not a judge of military tribunal; therefore it is beyond my capabilities to determine the innocence or guilt where it concerns Iona Yakir and Marshal Mikhail Tukhachevsky. As I believe you will understand, I do not have the benefit of testimony or evidence presented in their trials. This leaves me unable to be of help to motherland Russia on this issue, of which I will always rise to help when I can be of service.*

Also, I would like to see my friend Osip Mandelstam.
Now, I know sometimes he goes too far in his criticism, but he
is a stalwart of the people and for what you do to serve them. I
believe his recent poem "Ode to Stalin" is a personal apology
to you for his earlier indiscretions. If you agree with me in the
main, I ask that you grant him and his wife a vacation permit
to come to Peredelkino this summer.

Your and the people of Russia's servant,
Boris Pasternak

As I came to the part about Osip Mandelstam, my hands shook. Pasternak
was braver than I thought. Yes, the letter played up to the Goat-faced Murderer,
maybe my hands quavered partly over the use of this unforgiveable tactic, but it
also pushed him on the issue of Mandelstam, not as far as Vika had wanted,
though probably far enough to anger Stalin. "No wonder you're so concerned
we're done for."

"I deduced that after not signing on to the death sentence for those two
comrades; what would it matter to grab his neck a little more," he said, his
expression turning overly owlish.

It was as if Pasternak wanted to be done with this, and sensed what he'd
said wasn't enough. "Why haven't they moved on you, really?"

"They're suppressing my work in Russia, which would give them clearer
sailing, but my writing has made a name for myself in Europe and even some in
America." He shrugged. "Why make waves with powerful foes, I suppose?"

I kissed him on the cheek, just the one so he would know there was more
admiration in it than the normal custom of touching both sides. Did my lips
linger there a little long? He smelled like the green woods, old enough to believe
in and teaming with fresh life. We were alive and well by walking the thinnest
of wobbly lines. "Maybe I should go back inside and get the original of 'The
Stalin Epigram' to share with Oleg. I think he'll be disappointed his father wrote
that 'Ode to Stalin.'" Those last three words tasted like bitter garlic on my
tongue.

"Maybe you should." Pasternak raised the window with hardly a sound.

I climbed back inside, got the poem, and then this time through he lifted
me over the roses onto clear ground. I wanted to kiss him again but refrained.

He kindly reminded me to avoid exposing myself any more than necessary
to Vika, with her highly contagious illness. I told him I would be careful, and
not to worry, but didn't think it did much good. We said our good-byes; then I
walked into the Peredelkino night, still purple in newness. The stars seemed too

far away to convince me of their worthiness, for all the poetry they made it into. These were times for stanzas of black dirt and quicksand.

The farther I made way along the winding path, the closer I got to Osip and Vika, to their rarely-powered-light-bulb-and-sparsely-stocked-cupboard poverty, the more it felt like going home. Not a home I had ever lived in before, the one that held the heart of Russia now. In Osip Mandelstam's poem and Pasternak's letter, I carried the story of what obdurate militancy does to culture, to artists, the last truth tellers to fall, but crumble they do. Oleg and I had the dubious vitality of no longer so ignorant youth on our side. Inspiration drawn unaware of prospect for a better future, really, something more like the opening fist of becoming. We were forces of nature, not of Aristotle's logic or Christ's logos. I quickened my gait. Maybe I would make love to Oleg tonight.

On nearing their apartment, I set my eyes on the candlelight that shone dimly diffuse through the small window. In times past I had taken a rag to it with little success. Greasy smoke of cooking meals had permeated the glass's pores indelibly. Faintly, I felt cheated of something, maybe just one clear flame in one clear window. I knocked on the door twice, then went inside. "Oleg," I called out.

"In here." His voice came from the bedroom.

While walking toward the distinct stale cheese pungency of infirm, I saw him seated on a chair next to the bed, and using a washcloth, he gently dabbed perspiration off his mother's face. I stopped directly beside him, slipping "The Stalin Epigram" and Pasternak's letter in my pantaloons' pocket. We said nothing to each other. Vika's skin had turned the pale yellow of jaundice; her eyes were rheumy and flared as if staring into all seven levels of Dante's purgatory. With a touch of my hand against her arm, there was no shred of doubt left about her burning with fever. She coughed, and it sounded like a shaken sack of nails. The only doctor in Peredelkino spent most of his time in the bottom of a bottle of vodka. He had been over to examine her a couple of times and came up with the profound suggestion of getting some fresh air and sunshine. Oleg had told me that on both visits, the doctor's breath smelled strongly of alcohol and rice. Pasternak and his family always went to Moscow for their medical needs, but for people like Vika and Oleg, there was no use in that. Without special permission comrades were restricted to receiving medical attention in their local district. "I'll get ice and chill more water," I said evenly, keeping a stiff upper lip.

He nodded and met my eyes like a lost little boy, his dark expression searching even darker regions. "There's still some ice left in the box," he said.

Vika was failing, we both knew it. She had never before been this bad off.

Quickly, I picked up the tin bucket beside him and walked out to the sink. I dumped what little water was left in the bucket, then filled it about three-quarters full. On opening the fridge's door, I saw the block of ice had been chipped away to almost nothing, and otherwise had turned into a puddle on the shelf. I reached in and got the slick stump, then set it on the countertop next to the sink. The ice pick lay there from earlier use, so I took it and then began jabbing lightly, mindful not to waste any chips onto the floor. With each stroke I fought against going at it furiously to kill the tuberculosis in Vika, the cancer of Stalin's Great Purge that murdered my family, the sucking up in Pasternak's letter, nothing more than slow poison. But all I had, like everybody else in Russia it seemed, was one little melting piece of ice. Use it for anything other than to break the fever spiderwebbing from your soul if not also from your lungs, and you'd die before much changed for better or worse, one way or the other. Many corpses walked the streets of exile—such as Osip Mandelstam. When there was nothing but shavings left, I whisked them into the bucket, and then returned to the bedroom with it.

The cool compresses applied on Vika's forehead, neck, and face seemed to help, as her groans turned to whimpers, and she finally fell off to sleep. Some wheezing remained in her breaths, but the rise and fall of her chest had settled considerably. Cold shivers had given way to hot flashes that turned her skin cochineal red before she began sweating the fever out. Maybe tonight was not her night to become the kind of corpse buried in the ground, or capped in a vase as ashes. I began breathing easier myself. The thing of it was, though, Oleg's expression still held the look of that lost boy.

"She's going to be okay." I said in an undertone what he needed to hear, eternal truth, which the facts betrayed.

His wry smile told me he appreciated the lie of a philosopher.

I held his hand, and on touching his skin a wave of tingles washed over my body. For the life of me, he almost always awakened my Aphrodite. "I've got something for you," I said, tilting my head toward the main room.

"Okay," he said, also using a low tone. "I could use a nice surprise."

As I led us into the other room and over to the table, I felt Oleg the boy needed to know the part about Pasternak attempting to arrange a visit from his father, but it would take Oleg the man to withstand learning that his dad had written "Ode to Stalin." For the longest time we sat across from each other watching the candle in the copper base between us flicker, as if with a single tear of flame falling upward. I waited for him to regain at least a little of his edge, a hint of the reclusive, revolutionary gleam in those dark eyes. But he just kept staring dully at the flame. Finally, I reached over and squeezed the fire between my thumb and finger; then I shoved the base over to the side and it fell to the floor. It was time to love a boy into a man and, for that matter, a girl into a woman. Candlelight from his mother's room came through the open doorway, turning us into shadowy silhouettes. Things went all wet in my southern patch. "I love you, Oleg." The words slipped out for the first time. They sounded right in the charcoal air.

I lay on my back across the table, reached up and found the buttons on his shirt, then began unloosening them. He kissed me, his head the opposite way than mine; then he slipped my blouse off. "Take my pants off," I said softly. He walked around to the other side of the table and slowly pulled them off; then his pants came down too. He stood while we did it. It hurt, then it got easier, then it hurt again. The loose girls at school had warned it would be sort of violent, but that wasn't the way it seemed with Oleg. He moved slowly, considerately, stroked my hair while we found our way around each other. At last, he moaned as if with delight. A few seconds later while he still moved inside my V that hugged his hardness tightly, a bolt of lightning shot through me, and I said, "Oh God, oh God, oh God," but make no mistake about it, this wasn't a prayer. Or maybe that's just what it was.

As I experienced this first afterglow there next to him, my spirit seemed to be smoke in the room that breath by breath I took back into someplace beneath my lungs—until another "Oh God" escaped my lips. A splinter stuck into my bum. I held back a chuckle, both amused and embarrassed to be on the tabletop like a flounder served up for dinner. The sliver of wood easily came out pressed between two of my fingernails. We got down off the table, groped around until finding our clothes, then slipped them on. When I replaced the candleholder on the table, Oleg struck a match and lit the wick. He had gotten into his pants but not his shirt. His bare, sinewy torso glistened with sweat in the soft candlelight, and those dark eyes were once again sure as a falcon's.

"You have me, Katya," he said, in a low, masculine purr.

This time my smoke poured out as if flowing into him. "And you are set free."

While he put his shirt on and buttoned it, I sat down at the table again.

"I should go check on Mother," he said.

"Please, there's something I'd like for us to do while she still sleeps." I gestured at the chair across from me.

He sat down and scooted it closer in. "Whatever you have in store can't be as good as what we just did."

"Far from it." I took a long breath and exhaled slowly. "I have good news and not-so-good news." Truly not having a feel for which to disclose first, I slid a hand into my pocket and carefully extracted his father's poem along with Pasternak's letter. "I will not apologize for Pasternak." I slid the letter to Stalin across the table.

Oleg's eyes narrowed as he read. Finally, he folded his hands over the letter. "I don't believe my father would write such shit as an 'Ode to Stalin.' It is a fabrication in his name."

"You could be right. But even if he did, he was forced under torture. You know he was." A pit formed in my stomach. "I'm so sorry, Oleg."

He shook his head. For the second time tonight, Oleg intently stared past the candle's flame at me. This was no boy, nor my lover, but a dissident, a revolutionary burning brighter than any teardrop of fire ever could. "I am going to tell you something, Katya, that I have not been able to say to anyone, even to myself most of the time."

For a long moment his eyes drifted absently back down at the letter, then met mine again. "A friend of my father who visited him in Voronezh came to see us awhile ago. Not Pasternak. Anyway, he told us my father attempted suicide rather than sign a renouncement of 'The Stalin Epigram.'

"Ask yourself, would Osip Mandelstam write any other poem in the name of the Goat-faced Murderer?"

Now, I shook my head. "Definitely not." I unfolded "The Stalin Epigram," with its cross-throughs and rewritten lines, and handed it to Oleg. "That's the original," I said. "Your father gave it to me the night he was arrested."

His taut jowl rippled, but as he looked over the poem, his expression relaxed. "You never told me. It's wonderful you have it. Why you?"

I told him about the night my parents were disappeared and Mandelstam arrested, how he believed Stalin wanted the original of the poem to destroy in public enough to keep Osip alive and force him to deliver it. I apologized for not going into details sooner, and explained that night was simply too painful to relive very often. Then, I said, "How do you feel about telling your mom of Pasternak asking for your father to get a vacation pass to come here?"

"It would lift her spirit, but what do you think the probability is of the vacation actually happening?"

"I'd say it's more like a possibility."

A hacking litany of coughs came from the bedroom, then a guttural moan. "Oooollleeeeeg." Vika's broken voice felt like fingernails on a chalkboard.

"I don't think she could take the disappointment of it not coming through," he said to me as we stood up.

"Maybe not, but right now, I say anything that could brighten her a little is a good idea."

Without another word, we walked into the bedroom. I went over to the shelves next to the bath and grabbed a clean washcloth, while Oleg went to her side. When I got with the two of them, it was clear the fever had returned. As I dipped the washcloth in the bucket and wrung it out, I noticed the water had gone tepid. There was no more ice. With me gently wiping her face, she reached up and grabbed my wrist, bringing the cloth to her mouth. She coughed some more into it, and then spit up phlegm. I stiffened a little, for this was a good way to catch the disease. Vika was usually careful not to place Oleg or me in any more of a compromised situation than necessary. At this stage, she must've been losing her senses. Partly, I wanted to yank my arm free of her. Then, as if most of what little strength left in her drained away, her grasp withered to nothing. On moving the washcloth away from her mouth, I winced. It had turned red with her blood. Oleg and I locked eyes, his face having fallen waxen. "Please tell her," I said.

He looked at his mother again, as though measuring what time she had remaining to live.

"Go ahead, it's okay," I persisted.

One glistening tear, a sad diamond, fell from the ridge of his cheek onto the sheet. He wiped his eyes with the pad of a hand.

"Your father loves you, Oleg," Vika rasped. "Go to him when I'm—"

"He's coming here, Mother," he interrupted. "Boris Pasternak asked Stalin to send him."

At that, her almond irises outshined the angry bloodshot capillaries ravaging the whites of her eyes, though with an intensity of an entirely different kind—something like a fiercely delicate light of hope.

As Oleg looked at me once more, he laughed nervously.

I kissed him on the lips, and held on to it.

From the bed there came another groan. Vika raised an arm and touched both of our faces at the same time with trembling fingers.

✍

It was late, almost midnight, as I walked along the dirt drive toward the dacha. From rows of olive trees on both sides of the lane, moon shadows lay across the ground like entwined bodies, bringing to mind our silhouettes as we made love. The place on my face where Vika's touch had landed still seemed hot from her fever, though it was her blessing of Oleg and me and her desire to see Osip once again that must have actually heated this spot. Yellow lamplight came through Pasternak's studio window. Sometimes he wrote late into the evening and, on top of this, tonight he probably stayed up for my return. A lucky break, for there was something I could hardly wait to liberate him with, but like Socrates sentenced to death by hemlock, freedom may not be won until we drank our cups down. To be sure, I didn't put much stock in merely biding time for life to begin after death as most Christians do; I would live before dying like a good Hebrew. Mazel tov. Besides, the self-proclaimed polytheist Socrates did that, and with no small amount of gusto. What could I expect from a Jew-cum-probable-secret-Christian such as Pasternak? A fence walker. I fought against the tears stinging my eyes, bravado a sheer sateen veil over sadness for Vika being terminal, over what it would be like for Oleg going on without a mother, and as always over the hole blown through my heart at the deaths of my father, mother, and brother. Osip Mandelstam had to be brought out of exile if I had anything to do with it. And maybe, just maybe, I did.

Pasternak would be shaken by my news that Mandelstam had attempted suicide. What is more, if Pasternak could be persuaded to go so far as threatening to make a public allegation that Mandelstam's poem "Ode to Stalin" was a work of the state's, and the people were prepared to circulate the original of "The Stalin Epigram" should any more funny business occur around us or Mandelstam, then leverage, like a pulley and chain, could lift the iron curtain long enough for allowing Vika's lover and Oleg's father to escape underneath. At least, that was the plan.

I changed course from heading toward the rosebushes and my bedroom window on noticing two shadowy figures in Pasternak's studio, one seated behind the desk and one in front of it. Miss Zinaida rarely went into his studio, and Yevgeni could be counted on for sawing logs in his sleep at this hour, but you never knew. If she were in there with him, what I had to say would have to wait until I could get Pasternak all to myself. Why complicate things with her reticence? But if Yevgeni were speaking with his father, then I'd go for it. Yevgeni wouldn't have the stomach for my ideas, but he didn't have enough sway with his father to foil them either. I sidled up next to the window and moved my line of sight ever so slightly clear of the sill.

Pasternak's expression appeared grave, his jowls sunken and gaunt. He listened intently to a woman I had never seen before who had ears too large for her haggard, slim face, a telltale sign of starvation; this, and the simple black cotton dress, worn shiny in places, which hung on her emaciated body like a gunnysack. Her lips moved fast at an angle; a protruding Adam's apple bobbed in fits and starts. In many ways she looked older than Pasternak, though all in all not really. There was something about those crescent eyes, the even arcs of dark eyebrows just above them, a widow's peak in her otherwise carelessly tied-back tussock of brunette hair that told me she once had been maybe not full-on beautiful, but alluring, sultry even. I never before had been able to size up a woman in quite this way. It seemed natural after having sex with Oleg. Yes, that made the difference in so many other ways I couldn't articulate, and felt stirring like the crickets, beetles, and God knows what plethora of creepy crawlers having their way amidst the rosebushes under cover of night. I turned my ear close to the glass.

"Efron is involved with a group of expats who're trying to prove their loyalty to Stalin by going after Russian defectors all over Europe." Her husky voice scraped across ravines in her throat that most likely had been carved by years of smoking and vodka. "We must return to Russia, Boris. The police in Paris are on to Efron. It is only a matter of time before they run us out of the country for good.

"Will you recommend my application be accepted for a job at the Soviet Literature Fund's canteen?"

"Stay in Paris, there is no work for poets here," Pasternak said flatly.

"Are you saying you won't help me?"

A long silence fell over me that seemed to be mocked by cleeking crickets and the whirr of moths coming toward light. Glancing through the window, I spotted Pasternak with his head in his hands. Finally he looked at the woman again, and I went back to listening closely.

"I will try and help if that's what you want, but you should know what happened earlier this evening at the meeting of the Writers' Union in Georgia," he said. "Our good friend Paolo Iashvili, under pressure to support trumped-up charges of treason against Titsian Tabidze, walked into the room and blew his brains out with a hunting rifle."

"Oh my God," the woman gasped.

My thoughts spinning, I put a hand against the side of the dacha to steady myself on suddenly rubbery legs. Paolo Iashvili and Titsian Tabidze were great poets who had knelt at the Bolshevik altar to write a few propaganda pieces. But they hadn't bowed down enough. Both men were friends of Pasternak's; he'd spoken of them often. I had met them in our home in Moscow among the gatherings of artists and writers and dissidents. I wanted to go inside and give Pasternak a hug, needed one for myself. Stalin yanked at the thin, wobbly line we all walked until it snapped into pieces too small for balancing on. No, Pasternak could not be expected to re-approach the Goat-faced Murderer on the matter of freeing Osip Mandelstam. Even if I could get Pasternak to do it, drinking Socrates' hemlock would follow more certainly than ever.

"Should you decide on returning to Paris, I will send you translation work when I can," Pasternak said.

"Okay, thank you. We are pariahs there, too radical for the French and the expat Russians. Little work comes our way."

"You're welcome, Marina. For God's sake, convince Efron to stop participating in hate activities against Trotskyites and maybe the French will back off him."

My blood hummed. This was Marina Tsvetaeva, the wonderful lyric poet who criticized the Russian revolution not for its purposes but for its ruthlessness. She had gone into self-exile in Berlin, Prague, and evidently now Paris. I remembered something about one of her two children dying in an orphanage because she could no longer care for it. She had from time to time been the talk of our dinner tables, both my parents' and Pasternak's.

"What happens when there is no place for a poet and everything you are is poetry?" she said.

"Keep writing what's inside you in a way they won't kill you over but is also the truth," Pasternak said in a defeated tone. "That's what I try to do."

In my mind I recited her poem "I Know the Truth":

> *I know the truth — forget all other truths!*
> *No need for anyone on earth to struggle.*
> *Look — it is evening, look it is nearly night:*
> *what will you say, poets, lovers, generals?*
>
> *The wind is level now, the earth is wet with dew,*
> *the storm of stars in the sky will turn to quiet.*
> *And soon all of us will sleep beneath the earth,*
> *we who never let each other sleep above it.*

Without thinking, I pushed my hands upward against the window, but it wouldn't budge.

Pasternak and Marina Tsvetaeva looked my way with frightfully dark expressions, though Pasternak's quickly brightened a little. He walked over to the window, then unlatched the lock and slid it open. "Good to see you made it home safely," he said, extending a hand. "Come on, let me help you through."

"I've been listening," I said. "I'm so sorry for you both, for your friends, for all of us."

On getting inside I faced Marina Tsvetaeva. "I'm Katya Ivashov, and it is such an honor to know you. I'm a poet who one day, if ever writing half as well as you, would consider myself fulfilling the hugest of dreams."

"I write for you, then." Her ouroboros-like smile delivered Russia's deadly predicament.

CHAPTER ELEVEN

"If you gonna be a square, you ain't a gonna go nowhere. Hey mambo, mambo Italiano..." Grandpa Mandt sat in a rocking chair on the front porch that spanned the length of the unvarnished gray wood bungalow, rocking back and forth, slapping bongo skins held between his thighs, while he sang some calypso Jewish-Russian-American version of Dean Martin's "Mambo Italiano." The loose coils of white hair that fell just below his ears gave him a Rasta relic look, thought the slumbering man, who found himself amused to the point of looking through his lenses at him and tapping a foot to the beat. Good-natured, rascally squinted eyes above Grandpa Mandt's slimly sharp nose and thin lips, along with his triangular, narrow head bobbing atop the rest of his wiry self, made him seem fiercely fragile, a sort of negative Photoshopped print of youth at the age of ninety-plus-who-knew. Easily, most sixty-year-old men had more geographically wrinkled skin and liver spots than him. One of the few hints of his moribund season in life were those scruffy-bearded, sagging jowls, brought about no doubt by the pull of gravity and the weight of a widower being the inferior animus bitches they were. With him falling short of breath partway through the tune, Grandpa Mandt's singing stopped.

So did the slumbering man's tapping foot.

Grandpa Mandt set the bongos down next to himself, then gestured toward the rented Chevy Volt Margaret remained inside at the curb. "She thinks I'm crazy, but you don't, do you, Mr. Constipated Author?"

The slumbering man didn't know quite what to make of Grandpa Mandt having called him this ever since he'd spilled the beans on a visit here a couple years ago about a "writing sabbatical"—that until penning the poem inspired by Anastasie last week had felt closer to what he imagined Hemingway's slow undoing in Sun Valley, Idaho, must've been for the great author: forced retirement after losing your faculties for much more than writing. He recalled telling Margaret for every Hemingway or David Foster Wallace, there's an Updike or Steinbeck who were sane artists in the end. But then, what did that make the slumbering man? He looked at her staring through the windshield out toward the ocean straight ahead, petrified to have the talk that waited with her grandfather. In some ways, he reasoned, she ignored what made her tick, whereas he knew too much about the existential futility of time and culture, even of people. All you had to do was take a look at Grandpa Mandt; that's where we were all headed in the best of storybook endings. A soundly fly denouement. The old man had his highs and lows, but the good news was he *had them*. So then that settled it, the slumbering man wouldn't be bothered by Grandpa Mandt's nickname for him; it was true, and held a hidden compliment to boot. Constipation passed with a slug or two of Kaopectate...*except in the most extreme cases.* "Maybe people trying to be sane are driving themselves crazy, Grandpa Mandt."

The old man nodded by way of agreement. Turning increasingly sober until looking his age, he gazed off toward the ocean. "You've got to be crazy not to be religiously melancholic," Grandpa Mandt finally said.

"Looking for God in the pain," the slumbering man said.

"And with the foolishness of bongos."

"Sort of shoving joy up in hell's face, are you?"

"Or in Margaret's and yours." Grandpa Mandt massaged his temples, as if trying to soothe terrible old memories. "It's about living between opposites with whatever amount of grace we can open ourselves to."

Now, the slumbering man also looked off toward the ocean. Out here at Windmill Point in the little town of Hull, Massachusetts, on the tiny slip of Nantasket Peninsula, it was as if Grandpa Mandt needed close proximity to the end of the earth. Sought the ebb and flow of the tides, the rough seas and the calm, the unabashed lacking domesticity of the water stretching forever on three sides. Gulls circled and dived for mackerel in the shallows; a rogue wave slammed into the concrete bulkhead that rimmed the point, sending spray thirty or so feet into the air. Then, it was as if it had never happened. The water looked almost like glass. "I'll see if Margaret is ready to talk with you."

"You do that." Grandpa Mandt placed the bongo skins between his legs again and then, using the tips of his fingers, tapped a slow and rhythmic ballad without words.

As the slumbering man walked off the porch and through the yard, it felt as if Grandpa Mandt played to ancestors or something old, maybe to the Wampanoag who first looked upon these waters before European pilgrims arrived, bringing peace at the end of musket barrels. Over inside the car Margaret still sat there like a statue, but she had wanted to come here and face her past. He hadn't talked her into this. When they had driven onto the causeway to the peninsula, she pretty much froze up and hadn't said another word. Where was the grace between opposites, between her and her grandfather, her and her unwritten novel, her dark worry that never seemed to rise to playing bongos or singing in the shower, or for that matter between his all but lost lyricism and Anastasie's...what, *religious melancholy*?! By the time he got a little over halfway to the car, he looked over the top of his lenses yet another time. The lime green Volt instantly became furry and almost spherical like a big kiwi; Margaret's face turned into a featureless orb.

He tapped on the passenger window, and she looked at him while lowering the glass. "So," she said in a languid tone.

"I believe he's been playing the bongo or singing most of the time since we drove up to determine whether you can handle his eccentricity, and in some strange way it's part of how he wants to help you work through things."

"It's like he's protecting something from me, warding me off or something."

"Maybe not capriciously. Maybe until we can handle his madness, we're not ready for sanity." His own words sounded too much like a parrot of the isolated old man's shaman-esque wisdom. What had Grandpa Mandt even been talking about, really?

"That makes about as much sense as me coming out here expecting to learn something from a crazy old coot," she groused. "Why can't you or anyone in my family be anywhere near normal?"

"Maybe there is no normal except that mythical place we whirr by on some pendulum we can't let go of." He gestured toward Grandpa Mandt. "At least your grandfather enjoys the ride when he can."

"Maybe we should just go. This was a bad idea."

He leaned through the open window until she almost came into focus. "Your novel is probably all wrapped up in the conversation you and your grandfather need to have, and the thing of it is, a key to whether I write again or not could be too."

She said nothing; maybe her brow knitted.

He ached for her to be his Kalliope of prose, his Euterpe of poetry, his Terpsikhore of song and dance, his muse, but his mind's eye kept giving him Anastasie. "Our marriage may depend on you talking with him, Margaret."

"Jesus H. Christ, Frazier, are you serious?"

"I'm afraid so."

He opened the Volt's door, and she stepped out.

As they headed toward Grandpa Mandt, the air between them—infiltrated by gull caws and those finger taps on the bongos that floated by like glimmering dandelion fibers—could've otherwise been cut with a knife.

"How can I do this for me when I'm doing it for you too, for us?" she muttered to the slumbering man as they walked up the three steps to the porch.

"Be honest and don't cheat by holding things back," he said quickly under his breath.

"Stay with me," she said, her tone rising almost pleadingly. Her eye twitched violently enough that the slumbering man easily spotted it.

He had no ready reply. He'd planned on sitting this out at a coffee shop so she could talk more openly with her grandfather. Or to be completely honest, he wanted to spare himself falling on the needle spires of her mess until, and unless, she polished some more rough edges off them. The thought had crossed his mind of trying to locate Clifford Odeon, the nonviolent resistance guru who lived in nearby Marblehead that Buckminster had told him about. The man may be in the thick of supporting the persecuted poet Yassine Lotfi Khaled. But this made him nervous to even mull over for very long, didn't feel like slumbering at all, quite the contrary. Besides, if he found something out about Khaled or plans for Middle Eastern revolutions and started in on Margaret over it later, from the look of her, she'd probably go into meltdown. And if he left for the coffee shop now, the craggy outcroppings of her inner discord, for today anyway, would likely remain unsmoothed. At last, with a nod in her direction, he sat down on the steps, and she took a seat in the rocking chair next to Grandpa Mandt.

The old man went into a flourish of playing that would've made Mongo Santamaria sweat in his Cuban loafers. Then, resting his hands on the bongo skins, he looked Margaret directly in the eyes and said, "Congratulations, my lovely peony."

✍

Her grandfather was an aphrodisiac for her soul, Margaret's Orpheus, to be clear not her Eros, when on one of his highs. But times like these with him couldn't be trusted. He rarely answered his phone, which made most trips to visit him feel as though you were reaching into the bottom of a Cracker Jack's box to come out with glorious Apollo or darkly grim Hades. You never knew which. Sometimes he'd be curled in a fetal position on his bed, smelling funky from days of not showering, unable to rally in the slightest and be with his family. Other times in the middle of a roll, something would come up in his tortured psyche and he'd seconds later transform into Pluto, abducting Persephone, taking her to the underworld. That is, when Margaret had fallen for his candy to begin with. Even though Frazier had gotten him to answer the phone before they came, and warned him this trip was for the purpose of going deep with her, that they'd left the kids to stay over with friends for the weekend, what was he really trying to convince her of with his showy music making? She reached over and thumped one of the bongo skins with the back of a finger. "Congratulations for what," she said, "that I would've been willing to sit in with Kerouac, Ginsberg, and the other beatniks? I was too young for Haight-Ashbury, Grandpa."

"Thank the God of Abraham." He chuckled, setting the bongos aside again. "The truth is, until you can balance your demons with your better angels, you'll never be able to write the novels you've got in you."

"Please forgive me, but your life hasn't been too 'balanced' if you will," she said testily.

⌀

The slumbering man's hands began hurting, he had clutched them together so tightly. Margaret and her grandfather's conversation had the makings of being a short one. Both of them burned such short fuses so much of the time. If this day fell apart on him, maybe he'd do something crazy, manic even, and hop a jet to go find Anastasie in Marseille. But then, how could he bring himself to do that when he couldn't find a way to relax his grip? *Balance, what a knee slapper*, he thought, his cynic taking over.

"From your perspective, Margaret, maybe." The old man rocked in his chair. "Rock with me, won't you?"

Reluctantly, she complied.

Saying nothing to one another, this went on for what had to be over five minutes. At first, Margaret rocked overly fast, then she slowed down to a snail's pace, and finally she found herself absently rocking right along with her grandfather, back and forth, back and forth, back and forth, feeling almost as though she was a baby held in her own arms.

⌀

Meanwhile, the slumbering man daydreamed of flying across the ocean, landing in the south of France, sharing poetry with Anastasie in a brasserie over a bottle of Bordeaux wine.

Without changing the cadence of his rocking, Grandpa Mandt broke the silence between them. "My family was one of thousands that came out of Stalinist Russia with only one survivor. Most of the dissidents never got out of the country alive."

Margaret audibly sighed.

The slumbering man looked through his lenses at both of them, whose watery eyes were locked on one another. Their dark expressions held the same timeless age. He let go of his fisted hand and placed his palms on the step.

⌀

"I'm so sorry, Grandpa." Her voice shook. "And Nana, her family too?"

"Yes, your grandmother and I were the only two that got out."

Margaret's thoughts careened through her past. How had her grandparents, with all that anguished humanity, raised such a prude as her father? Because it sure as hell took her stiff father and mother to raise her into the uptight mess she'd become. Her grandmother had sent her letters throughout college she returned unopened, all of them. She had wanted no part of a woman's advice who would stay married to her derelict old grandfather. Bile rose in Margaret's throat and she swallowed it back. So much for all of her Gloria Steinem routine with blinders on, not the feminism, the tunnel vision over male-female relationships. She had no idea where to start with her grandfather. "Why hasn't anyone told me until now?" she said.

"This is too much until my granddaughter was at least able to sit down next to a crazy old bongo player and ask for help." Grandpa Mandt smiled knowingly. "And don't blame your father," he went on. "When there is such tragedy in a family, one either embraces it or runs from it to stay sane."

"It's too long of a marathon for me," Margaret said. "Will you tell me the whole story?"

"Your grandmother did that in letters to you."

"But I never read them."

Grandpa Mandt worked hard to push himself unsteadily up out of the rocker and onto his feet. "Please come with me, Margaret," he said. "There's a surprise in the attic for you."

She stood up, then leaned over and kissed him on the cheek. His breath smelled of mincemeat pie, and those unruly whiskers scratched her nose along with feeling something like a tangle of moss against her lips. Margaret hadn't been affectionate to her grandfather since she was a little girl. When the two of them walked into the house together, she felt almost weightless. Pausing, she glanced back at Frazier, and he blew her a kiss. In a couple of minutes, as she positioned the stepladder, pushed away a plywood cover, and then climbed through the open hatch into the attic, she may as well have been Lucy Pevensie stepping through the secret wardrobe into the land of Narnia. The old dust-covered wooden box her grandfather had just described to her, and she now approached, held another world—hers.

∅

As the slumbering man blew Margaret a kiss and she disappeared inside the house with her grandfather, he felt himself gaining a wife and losing Anastasie. In a game of tug-o-war with himself, some unseen rope looped round his heart and pulled more and more taut, until nearly snapping. If he gave up his muse now, no telling how long it would take for Margaret to make enough peace with her past to be that to him. But then, in some ways she was his muse already. They both needed to write. They both were shut down. Maybe he should get on a jet to Texas instead of France, and make peace with his ye ole family of origin. And maybe he could enter into the great Sufi poet Rumi's garden on the far side of the Garden of Eden, where he could appropriately have these two women in his life. He felt the rope not go slack, but it eased off some. *Balance, maybe?*

If he didn't do this now, what happened later may well come out sideways. Balance was not something he had much experience in. He walked inside the house and went into the kitchen, where he spotted a spiral notebook and pen on the countertop near the phone. He took the pad and pen, returned to the porch, and then sat down in Grandpa Mandt's rocker. He slipped the poem he'd written out of his wallet and reread it. Then, the slumbering man began writing on the pad:

> *My dear Anastasie,*
> *I hope Marseille is taking good care of you. Please let me know what's going on with you.*
> *I wrote you a poem called "Still Here," which I'm also sending you. It's the first thing I've written in years. Simply, you are my muse. Read the poem first, please, then open your mind and read the rest of this letter.*
> *You would probably really like my other muse, who happens to be my wife. Her name is Margaret. She is starting on a journey that if she stays on it (and I believe she is going to) will lead her to write things as good as the books you will write or anything I could ever pen. I don't know how this is all going to work out. Somehow I know you will gift different things from Margaret: they will all be diamonds, yours white, hers yellow, but diamonds just the same. Who knows, maybe I can throw in a few agates or something that will help the two of you. I'm not talking about us having a sexual ménage à trois. This is about creating in the face of all the crap. A wise old bongo player I know calls it religious melancholy. We create hope alongside God in our art.*
> *Bonjour and yours always,*
> *Frazier*

Carefully, he tore this page from the spiral notebook, then folded the letter and refolded the paper with his poem on it. He slid them into his wallet and replaced it in his jeans' hip pocket. The old bungalow gave off a couple creaks and groans, as Margaret must've been stepping on beams up in the attic. He was proud of her, he loved her, needed for her to find the truth that would set her free and help show him the way, their marriage the way. Not quite knowing how he would present this letter to her, the reality of Anastasie in their lives, though resolved not to mail it along with the poem off to Marseille without peace between him and Margaret over doing so—he stood up and walked toward the ocean. When he got onto the beach and stared out at the vast, calm water, with sunlight playing tricks on tiny waves as if tossing shiny quarters from the sky, the slumbering man let out a primordial howl. Seagulls continued with their caws and occasional dives for lunch, not seeming to notice him in the least.

✍

Margaret had passed a hand across the wooden box, and dust billowed, causing her to sneeze. The air was close up here and held the moldy smell of exposed roots after a hard rain. It was too dark for reading the letters in this corner of the attic, so she had lifted the box and carried it over into a fan of sunlight coming through a small faux second-story window. Somehow this needed to be done alone, and a shout-out to Grandpa Mandt that she was okay and would be up here for a while had sent him amiably back onto the front porch. She sat on a beam with her feet against the next one over, her eyes fixed on the unopened box. As a child and as a young adult, she had been close with Nana. The two of them would walk along the beach on Windmill Point and collect shells. Even with the tiny chipped shells, Nana would find something wondrous. Margaret kept them in jars atop the dresser in her bedroom until she went to college. She had no idea what had happened to the shells. In her mind's eye, she pictured her and Nana watching porpoises play in the surf, or simply allowing the sun time to set. After a while something would spark in Nana's blue eyes, and she could be counted on to recite a couple of her own poems, also pieces written by Keats, Auden, Pasternak, Shelley, Mandelstam, Tennyson, Whitman, and others. It had been during these times that Margaret surreptitiously began harboring thoughts of becoming a novelist and poet.

And this secret had come to feel dirtier and dirtier the longer it went unspoken. The Comrade would tell her she could be anything she wanted to be as long as she made a living at it. He gave her four years of college on his dime, and anything else would be on Margaret's tab. It wasn't so much that she would've minded taking student loans to fund the Iowa Writer's Workshop Masters of Fine Arts program when she had gotten accepted, but by then the Comrade and her quietly dutiful mother had convinced her she would probably go down the tubes of manic depression as a starving artist. "Just look at your grandfather Mandt," the Comrade would say, "and that should tell you how careful one needs to be." Being the old-school socialist patriarch her father was, he didn't bother considering Nana and her wonderful poems. In the end, Margaret had written the University of Iowa and told them thanks but no thanks. The only way she had kept from falling into depression and staying there in NYU's creative writing program was by telling herself that she would go into the business end of the literary world, and then someday, once she became financially secure, she'd write and Nana would be her first reader. Her muse.

When she had told Nana about her plans, her grandmother became so upset that their walks on the beach, the shell collecting, the poetry recitations never happened again. Margaret would show her, and returned Nana's letters unopened. Then, Nana died of breast cancer.

Margaret lifted the top off the box, and the letters lay scattered this way and that, filling the inside almost to the brim. There had to be over a hundred of them. Seeing them all together gave her atavism the feel of bees swarming round a hive, each bit of concealed information ready to lead a frenzy of stinging. It would've been easier to read the letters with a week or so between the next, as Nana had had the wisdom to time them for Margaret during her attendance at NYU. Maybe she should take it slow now; there was no reason to rush through them, other than the pesky little chore of saving her marriage before it disintegrated into a million pieces like the dust motes that surrounded her in the attic. The words *Return To Sender* stamped askew in red ink on the envelopes brought to mind the old Elvis song of the same name. Odd, what you could think of when confronting your own schadenfreude. She took a letter off the pile and looked at the postmark, which indicated it had been sent during her sophomore year. Something kept her from opening it. These letters needed to be read in the order they had been written. Nana would've wanted it that way. Her grandmother had told a story with them, she felt pretty sure of this. Or maybe Margaret was projecting herself into the contents of these letters. With a sigh she tossed the envelope back on the pile. What did it really matter where the truth lay between these two possibilities? She and Nana were so much alike.

Twenty minutes later the 132 letters (Margaret kept a mental tally) were arranged in chronological order. She leaned back against a truss beam, then opened the earliest postmarked envelope and slipped the letter out. Even back in Margaret's freshman year of college, Nana's script had that angular shakiness that came with old age. But from the start, her message poured onto the page something vital like Hebe's ambrosia.

> *Dear Deceived Darling Margaret,*
>
> *It is not your fault. Until you question everything you have been taught by your family, religion, the state, your friends, everything, you will remain old. Yes, we start young, and quickly become old because of fear that gives off an appearance of the need for safety. The only safety there is lies in taking risks. Everything else is death.*
>
> *Find your muses. No one can get along with just one because nobody carries all the attributes of God. Become someone else's muse. Your grandfather, who you think is*

meshugeh, is mine, and so is the man who introduced me to him, and so is a woman who showed me how to love purely and with abandon—which is morality at its highest calling. Look around you, everything is recreating itself or creating something entirely new all the time. My family and your grandfather's family were killed during the Russian purges, but because of it we learned to let flowers grow out of our wounds. We were always escaping, moving toward reconciling our stories. The other way to treat a wound is sure suicide, which can come slow or fast, but it is non-sacred and so it is the opposite of creative. Give it some thought. You may find I'm not just a fossilized old Jewish lady, and you don't have to be a fossilized yente. Let it out, and let others help you let it out. You are a writer, Margaret, but you must find something worth writing about. More about how to do that later. The matzah ball soup is boiling over, so I'll sign off.
Shalom and love,
Nana

As Margaret replaced the letter in the envelope and put it back inside the box, she felt herself somehow cheating inside her own worldview for comparing Grandpa Mandt against Frazier, and for the first time seeing Grandpa Mandt as more desirable. After everything Grandpa Mandt and Nana had been through, because of it, he was her muse, and she his. One didn't have to have a live person whispering in their ear; a live spirit would do just fine. Grandpa Mandt's bongo playing and showing his granddaughter the way to her own Pandora's box testified to that. Then again, Frazier *had* brought Margaret here. If he just weren't always so damn existentially cool. Where were the flowers coming from his wounds? She needed to see them, needed a muse, but believed she may well be 131 reads of Nana's letters away from having one or two or three muses for that matter. *Did Nana have a lesbian affair? Whatever.* Along the way Nana found the inspiration she needed to overcome. What had her marriage with Frazier really been through that could profoundly shape them, Margaret pondered, the choice to live in West Village instead of up the Hudson in some suburb to keep the kids more connected to a diverse community? What a bunch of ne'er-do-wells they were when set beside her grandparents. She replaced the top on the wooden box, and then called down for help getting it out of that attic.

⌀

The slumbering man had watched bubbles along the edge of gentle waves that rolled in cover his sneakers, then pop into thin air, until feeling as if he were retreating off the edge of some adrenaline-producing high board, and going down the ladder he'd climbed up to dive off a low board, or better yet just simply sitting down beside the pool with his legs dangling in the deep end of his need for Margaret and Anastasie, waters the color of jade, delicious apple green and lapis blue, his subconscious archetypes meeting theirs like the sinuous line where the Atlantic and the Indian oceans come together. This image kept flashing in his mind while he walked from the beach back to visit with Grandpa Mandt on the porch. Many years back he'd flown over these bodies of water on a trip with a group from NYU to work with Missionaries of Charity in Calcutta, India, the organization Mother Teresa had started. He'd been scholarshipped to go, and the work he'd done with the dying there made him a better writer, a more fragile human being, maybe more caring, plus, where those two oceans met had been captivating enough to stay with him, and this seemed to hold the strength and the mystery of what was happening to him now, why Margaret wasn't ready to see the letter he'd written Anastasie. It would feel like infidelity to her, but that was too easy. A certain kind of infidelity lingered underneath the surfaces of both of them, behind the line of their meeting places, and this was true every moment they didn't dive down into the depths to find out what thrived below. In fairness, Margaret was up in the attic hopefully finding more out about her deeper waters. The conversation had remained light between himself and Grandpa Mandt, and then Margaret called out for help.

With the letters from Nana safely inside the box, Margaret lowered it down the attic's open portal.

With the letter to Anastasie safely in his wallet, the slumbering man took the box from Margaret and then carried it out to the car.

On saying their good-byes to Grandpa Mandt, tears welled in Margaret's eyes as she kissed his cheek this time. She thanked the old man for opening up the family to her.

Seeing this wetness through his lenses inspired the slumbering man, a betrayal to his creed that for once he wished would disappear like bubbles from waves.

Quietness settled between them once inside the car.

He took this to mean she wasn't ready to talk about the contents of the box. As they drove away from Windmill Point with Grandpa Mandt's bungalow shrunk to the size of a dime in the rearview mirror, he broke the silence. "You are my muse, Margaret."

She felt her eye twitch again. It was almost as if he'd read Nana's letter. "But not a very good one, huh, Frazier?"

"You're plenty good." *Now that Anastasie is around.*

Yeah, it takes more than one, doesn't it, and you obviously don't have another or you wouldn't be the way you are, she thought but didn't even come close to saying. "What about me?" she went with instead. "Where's my muse gone?"

"I've been away for too long. I'm sorry, Margaret, truly, I am. Maybe I can make a comeback." He gave her a half smile, though inwardly grimaced. Would the woman he loved require more than one muse?

CHAPTER TWELVE

The Blue Goose tavern's bar—pockmarked from shot glasses and beer steins set down on it with the hard release of workers over spending some of what little wages they had earned tending fields or street cleaning or such, those lucky enough to have gainful work that is—stretched out on both sides of Oleg, to the right of me, and Yevgeni to the left. Who could blame the bar's patrons for giving alms to liquid spirits? Stalin's purges had only gotten worse, and Pasternak had told me there was reason to believe the Central Committee of the Politburo had adopted a secret policy of isolating entire communities from rations to let them starve. There simply wasn't enough food being produced to feed Russia. As far as I was concerned, the men and women in here were heroes one and all. Oleg had gotten on with a grower tying bales of wheat and loading them onto flatbeds for transport to the thresher factory and granary. Yevgeni earlier today had returned to Peredelkino from music conservatory in Moscow for a short summer break. Good toward him, playing music into our mass grave for benefit of the buried, their families, and the gravediggers alike. Yes, good toward him. Continually noticing the smooth skin of Yevgeni's fingers and the roughed knuckles on the back of Oleg's hands, while we drank from our steins and talked, a poem began forming in my thoughts. What is more, Oleg's tapping boot on the barstool's foot-rail, and his puckish smile, helped me compose it.

After Vika died, almost a year ago, Oleg hadn't shed a tear in mourning until realizing his father Osip wouldn't be granted the "vacation voucher" Pasternak had requested of Stalin even to attend her funeral. Oleg's dry eyes were those of the devastated in shock, I had thought then, and he cried from the view across inward desolate plains that once held the faint hope of being populated with family. Having been schooled by Vika before the last of her illness prevented it, Oleg had ever since given up formal studies. Besides, we were eighteen now, and the great university was out in the streets, alongside coworkers, in the taverns, not by way of any classroom. Most everything taught through the academy had been decomposed into communist party dogma. Oleg had dried his eyes and unleashed a courageous sense of humor that kept us, along with our small part in the dissident counterrevolution, more alive. Just take tonight in this tavern, as he still tapped out a quirky polka using his foot, and then with my wink he added going at the beat with his hands on the countertop. The poem in my mind—being one of those edgy, tinsel-eyed ditties you couldn't tell for sure on which side of the line it fell, outright delirium or some sort of compulsive sanity impossible to hold without obsession—drew to a benevolent end. To be bold enough to say so, I felt pleased that my poem made room for the polished and the bohemian among us. For Oleg, Yevgeni, and a young writer called me.

And tonight, there were important reasons I wanted us to pull together with more than a little solidarity.

While waiting for Oleg's performance to wind down, I took another draw off my ale, and then said to both of them at the same time, "Pasternak has been so down since finding out his author friend Titsian Tabidze was arrested for anti-Soviet activities that he hasn't been writing most days. We've got to cheer him up, do something to get him un-stuck."

"Why, I do believe my sweetness has got herself pining away over her older, what do you writers call it, love interest?" Oleg laughed lightheartedly, and his expression showed genuine concern for Pasternak, at least that's what I wanted to believe his set jaw and widened eyes indicated.

"You know her too well, Oleg," Yevgeni said, flashing a smile. "I'm glad the beautiful and mysterious Katya is your lady and not mine." He clinked his stein with Oleg's, and the two of them took hearty drinks.

"Eat your heart out, Yevgeni." I shook a cigarette out of the pack we had been sharing that lay on the bar, then placed it between my lips while facing Oleg.

He struck a match and lit the fag. "I adore you," he said. Then, Oleg gave me a penetrating look over his eyebrows.

Without a word as to what both of us knew to be true about my writing, I blew a smoke ring that floated away over our heads. "Seriously," I finally said as it fully dissipated, "he's turned down my asks for writing another letter to Stalin seeking your father's release to visit here. You can hardly blame him for wanting to lie low and protect himself and his family. I feel awfully for his predicament, I really do, but nonetheless…" My voice tapered off.

Oleg slid a finger along the rim of one of the gouges in the bar's surface, then moved it to another. His eyes fell distant.

"Bringing you into this is nothing short of shameful, my dear Oleg," I went on. "Truly it is. But I've tried everything I could think of on my own."

"You do want to see your father, don't you, comrade," Yevgeni said.

"Yes, but Pasternak obviously doesn't like me enough to try the Goat-faced Murderer again on this," Oleg said. "He only wanted to help my mother."

"That's not true," I said. "He was for us seeing each other from the start, Oleg. He's not picking on you. His funk is equal opportunity."

"Pasternak also hasn't sent a letter of recommendation to the Soviet of Literature Fund to help Marina Tsvetaeva get a job there. She wants to return home from exile. After her visit with him here last year, she went back to Paris and promptly sent a letter asking him to go ahead with it. He told me how 'paralyzed' he was to help. He used this word, 'paralyzed.'"

"Look, you know I think we're all damn well eviscerated," Yevgeni said. "That's why I play the piano and don't get involved with politics. But I'll go to my dad with you two. You should see your father again, Oleg."

The young man who held my heart nodded almost imperceptibly.

"Does that mean you'll go with Katya and me to talk with my dad?" Yevgeni persisted.

This time Oleg's head noticeably moved up and down.

When I had decided to bring Yevgeni along tonight, I wasn't sure whether he could be counted on, though I believed we would need his assistance to help ourselves and Pasternak. A man as great as him simply could not remain paralyzed, not if I had anything to do with it. "Thank you," I said, looking Yevgeni directly in the eyes. Why did I love the terribly pained young man rather than this one, who had a capacity more often for joy? Settled, good-natured ways, not so much using humor as a tool of overcoming. Because I was more familiar with anguish, maybe because any happiness Oleg and I set to flight, although we were always partly scuttled by our erased families, went further, soared higher whenever it happened. Or were we just better equipped as underdogs, mutts, and that was the sum of it, nothing else really? I chuckled bitterly. A thought such as this must've birthed Marxism. I was Oleg's in no small measure because he harbored no envy toward hierarchy. His workingman's hands, his unyielding honesty were the weaponry he brought to the revolution.

"My father will die if he doesn't write, and he must come forward for his friends in order to write again," Yevgeni said.

"My sentiments exactly," I said. "What better time to talk with him than now?"

We quickly finished our ales and paid out.

When we went outside it was a moonless, pitch-dark night, with cloud cover smothering the stars. I heard footsteps behind us as we walked along the road out of town centre. The three of us were the only pedestrians ahead or on the other side of the street. On glancing over my shoulder, about fifty meters back I spotted a shadowy figure lean against the pole of a streetlamp. She or he looked away from us, down toward the pavement. I took hold of Oleg's hand and held on tightly.

"There's someone keeping an eye on us," I said.

"Makes me feel right at home." Yevgeni took a long drag off his cigarette, then flicked the butt onto the pavement. He snuffed the tiny red glow underfoot on his next step.

Oleg let go of my hand and put his arm across my shoulders, bringing me in closer. "I'm not keen on drawing the secret police to Pasternak," he said. "Maybe we should do this another time."

"Believe me, they know where he lives," I said.

"Let us not forget, comrades, we're already eviscerated," Yevgeni said with a chuckle.

We kept walking toward Pasternak's gray GAZ sedan, which he'd let Yevgeni and I take into town, and that had been parked at the end of the lane Oleg lived on. None of us looked back.

On arriving at the car, Yevgeni opened the driver's door, and Oleg opened the passenger door to let me in before himself. The footsteps from earlier returned at a more rapid pace, eerily sounding something like Oleg's carefree boot taps on the barstool. Yevgeni got in behind the steering wheel and started the car. "To hell with this, let's go," he said. Oleg and I shot looks toward the footsteps and, as if emerging from the proverbial abyss, a disheveled male in baggy dungarees and an ill-fitting tan shirt came out of the darkness; yes, it was clearly a middle-aged man who now stood before us. My word! His skin had gone sallow, his tuft of wavy hair had grayed and receded high up his forehead, the shoulders bowed as if carrying the weight of Russia, and there were those black eyes; no doubt, this was Osip Mandelstam.

He held up a hand. "Sorry...for stalking...you," Osip Mandelstam managed between gulps of air, obviously winded.

It was as though Oleg had turned to marble, a statue with furrowed brow and raised eyebrow. However long since he'd seen his father last, I did not know exactly, though we'd talked about it being when he was a young boy. Did Oleg recognize him for sure? The mastiff expression of Osip Mandelstam with his eyes intently fixed on Oleg told me the father needed no reminder of his son. For a brief moment the face of my dad flashed to mind. A fist of anger clenched in my chest, and I uncurled its fingers one by one. Partly, I longed for my dad to appear out of sheer darkness like some apparition. This redness toward him didn't seem right, but somehow felt good. Maybe I was really madder at the abyss that held God or nothingness. What have you, it amounted to the same void either way for me right now, but not for Oleg. I stepped beside him and again held his hand, gently this time. "It's okay," I said softly. "Your father has come to you."

Oleg's dark eyes brightened like shimmery garnets, moonbeams in a night sky, as he looked from me over at his dad. Relaxing slightly, Oleg rocked on his feet, as if not knowing whether he was waiting on himself or his father.

"You look fine, very strong and becoming, indeed," Osip Mandelstam said.

"Thank you, sir," Oleg said, his lips hardly parting.

"I'm sorry for the loss of your mother...of Vika." Osip Mandelstam's voice cracked.

None of us said anything. Yevgeni turned off the car's motor as if out of respect, and the silence between us only thickened.

"Thank you, sir," Oleg said at last, in the same manner as before.

"Yes, well, I don't suppose you want me to hug you, so I won't."

Oleg gave him another insipid thank you.

Osip Mandelstam looked my way. "My, how you have grown into a fine young woman, Katya."

I nodded my appreciation. "Your 'Stalin Epigram' is still safe and sound with me."

"I always knew it would be." A flicker of the old fire rose in his expression when he smiled.

And from the heat in my cheeks, I'd say in mine too, as I returned his smile. "Yevgeni and I should go and let you two do some catching up," I said, looking at Oleg once more.

He shook his head, then set his eyes on his father again. "We were just leaving for a visit with your friend Boris Pasternak to press him on helping get you released for a trip here, but now that you're here, you should come too. It seems he's all but quit his writing, and could use some encouragement."

What else could Oleg do to make me fall more in love with him? For the life of me, I had no idea. "That would be a good thing, Osip," I said.

He visibly stiffened.

"Is that a problem, Dad," Oleg said, his tone tinged with the sardonic.

Father and son stared each other down, though more with a curious lack of understanding than anything approaching vitriol.

"Nadezhda...my wife, is with the Pasternaks."

Oleg laughed nervously, shook his head.

A slight grin or Osip Mandelstam's lips pursed, I couldn't tell which. "Maybe it's time she meets my son."

Yevgeni started the motor again.

With a look at Oleg, I tilted my head toward the car.

He nodded by way of agreement.

As Osip Mandelstam bent down at the waist to get into the car's rear compartment, Oleg reached over and placed a hand on his father's shoulder.

Evidently, there had been something more Oleg could do to cupid my heart. And he'd just done it.

On the empty space next to Osip Mandelstam sat the shapeless Leviathan of everything unspoken, unlived between father and son. It was as if the beast's dour breathing took over the inside of the car. Oleg pressed his body against the door, and I sat between him and Yevgeni on the front bench. Yevgeni hummed Mozart's Piano concerto #17, no doubt to soften the air, but it had the disconcerting effect of bizarrely timed gaiety—sort of like how the piece's composer lived the majority of his adult life. I elbowed Yevgeni in his ribs. The humming stopped but Yevgeni, the minor Mozart doppelganger if you will, gave away not so much as a knitted brow to suffering consternation.

Oleg's eyes were intently set frontward along the headlamps' beams, which petered out into the black night. When the car turned onto the rutted dirt road snaking all the way to the dacha, the beams began lurching up and down and sideways. As we neared our destination, I imagined Oleg's thoughts jostling round like these cones of light. The beast still heaved away; nothing had been said for the entire ride. I partly wanted to break the silence by starting a conversation between Oleg and Osip, but feared doing that would be pressing overly hard, possibly emasculating to both of them. Maybe something less direct, a little nudge, could set just the right amount of Mozart free in Oleg? Now, I elbowed him lightly in the ribs.

He noticeably exhaled, and then glanced at me, flashing a tiny conspiratorial grin on the way to looking his father directly in the eyes. "Did you write 'Ode to Stalin,' or did they have someone else write it in your name?" Oleg said.

"I wrote it and other poems in support of the Goat-faced Murderer, but it wasn't the torture that made me do this." Osip Mandelstam cleared his throat. "It was the thought of never being able to see my loved ones again, my children, unless I cooperated."

"Maybe I should be happy they tortured you." Oleg's voice turned steely though laced with fissures, like the famously flawed statue of Lenin in Leningrad. "Otherwise, who knows when I would've seen you again?"

"I cannot disagree," Osip Mandelstam said flatly.

"My God, Oleg," I said. "You forget who you're talking with." I held a bottomless knowing of honoring my parents and brother by not caving to Stalinism, but to be fair, it amounted to my own hypothetical contrivance. I had never been tortured or imprisoned. I felt my words landed too harshly, for I had also never been an illegitimate child. As if there were such a debauched category of humanness. I swiveled partway around and placed an arm across the seatback, fixing my eyes also on Osip Mandelstam. "You should've visited Oleg and Vika more often when you were free."

Tears rimmed his eyes, then a rivulet trickled down his chalky face. He didn't make an effort to wipe it away. "Poets often live conveniently and call it freedom's struggle," he said, and with that, looked only at Oleg. "I'm sorry, son."

Oleg's foot tapped on the floorboard a sad, slow beat, nothing like his polka back at the Blue Goose. "Is it necessary to be that selfish to write the truth?" he said, in a disarmingly vulnerable tone—as though even if the answer were yes, he would understand.

"I wouldn't know for sure." Osip Mandelstam rubbed his shoulder as if having muscle cramps. "Lev Tolstoy had fourteen children and lived to see five of them die. A father should never outlive a son, I can tell you that."

"No, I suppose not," Oleg said, and then looked frontward again.

Tolstoy losing so many children to death probably tore him apart and made him a better writer, I thought. Anna Karenina had been published when he was almost fifty years old. Osip Mandelstam wasn't quite that old yet; he still had plenty of writing left in him, plenty of time to connect with his son. Then again, maybe too much damage had been done for Oleg to fit in his father's shoes well enough to accept his apology, or maybe accepting it wasn't necessary, or maybe he'd just done that? Suddenly, I felt so ignorantly young. On placing my hand on Oleg's knee, his foot-taps stopped. Even this had probably been a mistake; all I wanted to do was provide some comfort, not stifle him. Something cryptic in Osip Mandelstam's claims haunted my mind: If I had to make a choice between romantic love and one of my children, what would I do? Could I ever write again?

"How long will you be able to stay in Peredelkino?" Yevgeni said, glancing back at Osip Mandelstam.

"Ten days, depending."

"Plenty of time for you and Oleg to get to know each other better," Yevgeni said.

"I hope so," Osip Mandelstam said.

Oleg and I locked eyes, our identical expressions giving away what had to be a singular thought. It may well depend on how things go with Nadezhda Mandelstam.

"What the devil," Yevgeni said, and the car shuddered to a stop.

All eyes went frontward, and my throat fell dry. In the headlights on the front deck of the dacha stood Pasternak together with long-faced Vladimir Stavski, the thuggish head of the Union of Soviet Writers. Pasternak's expression looked hollowed out, defeated. Flashlight beams came through the windows on both sides of the car. Shielding my eyes with a hand, I saw it was Stavski's goons, the same two who had ransacked the dacha. They demanded that Osip Mandelstam get out of the car. The great poet rolled the window down, then said, "I have a vacation permit to be here, signed by the minister of prisons."

Stavski laughed out loud. "We have orders from Stalin to deliver you to a gulag in Siberia. Or you can produce the original of 'The Stalin Epigram' and go on with your vacation." A grunt from the hole in Stavski's face below his bushy eyebrows and pointy nose. "You shouldn't travel so far into Stalin loyalists' territory, my old friend."

Osip Mandelstam spat toward Stavski, the foamy ball falling benignly short of its mark.

"Why not give it to him?" Oleg said to Osip Mandelstam.

"Because I've seen you again, and know you will be fine."

"I forgive you, Father. I admire you. I always have."

"I know."

In seconds the goons had Osip Mandelstam out of the car and in handcuffs. A slight waif of a woman with blond hair cut boyishly short, who I took to be Nadezhda Mandelstam, walked out of the dacha and onto the deck, followed by Miss Zinaida carrying little Leonid in her arms. Nadezhda Mandelstam called out Osip's name in anguish. Miss Zinaida stood stoically beside Pasternak, who put his arm around her back. Osip Mandelstam told his wife he loved her. Right before one of the goons stuffed him in the back of a black sedan, Osip Mandelstam shot a look at Pasternak and said, "Start writing again, Boris, and keep writing."

Oleg gently but firmly placed his hands on both sides of my face and looked into my eyes. "You too, Katya," he said.

None of us would see Osip Mandelstam another time.

The next morning Pasternak sat at his writing desk again, working on *Doctor Zhivago*.

And I sat at my little desk, working on my novel after having been away from it a suffocating, long spell. I had stopped writing soon after Pasternak turned away from his work. Inexplicably, I hadn't had the heart for it.

CHAPTER THIRTEEN

The slumbering man flipped through his and Margaret's mail; a window envelope from West Village Plumbing, probably containing a bill for having the kitchen pipes Roto-Rootered a couple weeks ago—theirs, but his fault for too often dumping leftovers down a drain sans the food waste disposal; a subscription renewal for *The Paris Review*—his; a flyer from Jefferies clothing boutique promoting a fall trunk show—junk mail, at least from his POV; a letter from the literary organization PEN—hers; and nothing with French stamps on it or a Marseille postmark. He'd come to heading home from his office early enough to pick up Mattie and Doug from their afterschool piano and tae kwon do classes, and still arrive here before Margaret. Today he'd situated Mattie in her room writing a short story for homework, and Doug in the family room playing Wii Rock Star. All of this to safely check for a response from Anastasie. It had been over a month since he'd sent his letter off to her without getting anything in return, not so much as an email with a smiley face, or a fist giving him the middle finger, or the plethora of responses that could've fallen in between. Had Margaret intercepted Anastasie's snail mail? Probably not. Margaret had actually been warming to him more since their visit with Grandpa Mandt and bringing home the box of letters from her grandmother. Exactly why he hadn't gotten up the nerve to talk about his letter to Anastasie with Margaret before sending it. Oddly the better his marriage got, the more he had felt some sort of immediacy to mail the letter to the French artist. What had he been thinking in proposing to Anastasie that two women poetically share him? Anastasie had to have suitors out the wazoo. She needed an asexual, emotionally intimate relationship with a married man about as much as she needed another cheap-shot pop graffiti artist entering the fine art market. *Right?* Time was a Trojan horse for him and the lovely French painter, along with forgetfulness of mind and the stony toughness that came with being a lone wolf artist or writer. All of which it seemed conspired to trick their need for long-distance muses into complacency.

He walked into the bathroom and stood before the mirror. With a hand to his face, he studied its roundness, and his stubble beard, which looked a little too much like peach fuzz. His thinning brown hair had lightened into some freaky stained yellowish streaks, probably from chemicals in the shampoo and slight early graying. A wild stalk of eyebrow jutted upward and out like a lightning bolt. He kind of liked the look, so decided to show restraint rather than plucking it. Not bothering to suck in his paunch, he set the mail beside the sink and grabbed two hands full of stomach. The short man staring back at himself would need to lean on the Philip Seymour Hoffman vibe—minus the drug overdose if you don't mind—to have any chance of turning whatever he and Anastasie had into a physical thing. *If in fact* anything *remains of us?* This thought sort of ran from his mind through his body and down his leg, like Greek soldiers clambering from the Trojan horse in the middle of the night, or like warm piss, take your pick. Troy was falling to the enemy. No, he couldn't let that happen this easily.

He would write another poem, or maybe even a short story to highlight his Philip Seymour Hoffman-ness, and then he'd send it to Anastasie along with a photo to remember him by. That's what he would do!

Letting go of his stomach, he made way for his tiny desk with his laptop computer on it, which was pushed against Margaret's equally small desk in their cramped study. His half of the room had books scattered and stacked most everywhere; her side had plenty of bound literary missives too, on floor-to-ceiling shelves, and neatly ordered alphabetically by author's last name. With a couple of finger taps on the mouse pad, he called up a Word document, then poised his fingers over the keys, as if about to play Thelonious Monk's "Round Midnight." But no words came. He made a finger sweep and a few more taps on the mouse to stream Monk's music on iTunes.

For the next several minutes, he stared at the white page. A black cursor winked at his duality, or his incompleteness, or both. His thoughts spun.

He needed some inspiration, authenticity, Jungian archetype balancing or whatever, not trickery or battle plans, and he also could use some structure, like all the spines of Margaret's books aligned evenly, level. This whiteness—that ate him alive and at the same time purified—could only be so in the midst of blackness, even a little slip of it. The cursor began feeling more like a slit in the universe from which flowed through the pushed-aside memories of all that was good about him and Margaret, one after the other. He didn't want to hurt her, and he couldn't bring himself to give up his fantasy over Anastasie. Somehow, that was impossible. Now, the cursor blinked a curse and a blessing, one then the other. How could he come clean with Margaret about the French artist, get Margaret's hippie-chick free-love acceptance when she was instead more like...who, the steady Emma Jung? Certainly not the way he'd read that Carl

Jung had mentally browbeaten Emma into reluctantly accepting his mistress, Toni Wolff. Jung had bludgeoned his wife with poetry. Frazier's poetry and prose would have to be better than Jung's, then, perhaps more along the lines of Keats. Quixotic, these thoughts were. Margaret would divorce him, or would she? His brain slowly became bereft, taken over by the numb, flushed-out feeling that made up the bulk of slumber. Finally, he quit trying to impress Anastasie or convince Margaret, and something came; his fingers moved on the keys.

> *Dear Anastasie,*
>
> *Your silence is an albino, scary and one I want to ostracize to a place where only albinos live. Then again, maybe the albino is my friend for I am writing something that feels like poetry. Maybe you being there and me being here is better than us being in the same place together. If we were close, I fear I would spend most my time finding you, and not me. The page would remain white, not blackened by my confusion and fits of clarity. So I write again after a long hiatus, though somehow more for me than for you. I hope you don't mind. I think I will keep writing you letters, and don't feel obligated in the least to return them. Unless you really want to; then I suppose I'll have something else to write about.*

He paused, lifting his fingers above the keys. This would be better transcribed onto nice stationery in his own handwriting, and he would do that. But he had at last gotten on a roll with his writing, and that felt fabulous, like riding the back of some great white whale as they went for a swim in the ocean, diving underneath the surface and then returning above in plenty of time for filling their lungs with air. Partly, he wanted to tell her how much he longed to hold her, to kiss her, to make love with her. But, "Yes," these fine things would be better suited for the pages of a journal, something he hadn't kept in years. He typed again, in a flurry.

> *I hope you are all right, and my intuition tells me you are.*
>
> *Bonjour and yours always,*
>
> *Frazier*

He set the laptop aside, then took some stationery and a pen out of the middle drawer. Carefully, he rewrote the letter, not changing a word. With that done, and the page folded and slipped into an addressed envelope, he opened a side drawer. It took rummaging through some green magazines about urban gardening, and a stack of particularly memorable *Harper's* and *Sojourners* publications he'd stashed, to uncover his old leather-bound journal. He took it out of the drawer, opened it to the first clean page, and then began writing once more.

> *Harmless secrets set me free! I want to make love with Margaret! I want to make love with Anastasie! I want to make love to the page! Where is my story? I don't have to know, but it would be nice to have another novel in me. I wonder what Margaret is finding out about her writing by reading her grandmother's letters. Maybe we can help each other find our novels?*

He sketched the curvy shape of a woman, voluptuous like Margaret.

A knock on the doorframe and he looked over at Mattie, who stood there holding a few sheets of paper.

"Can you help me with my story, Dad?"

"I'd love to," he said, looking at her through his lenses. "After working with Mattie I'll play some Wii with you, Doug," he called out loud enough for his voice to carry into the family room.

"Great, Dad!" Doug hollered back.

Frazier closed his journal, then shut down Thelonious Monk on iTunes. "Come over here and show me what you've written, darling."

✍

Margaret sat at her desk in front of her laptop staring at a blank Word document, as the slumbering man walked into their study and kissed her on the neck. "I had the same problem earlier today," he said, glancing through his lenses at the computer screen. "Couldn't get anything onto the page."

She reached back and cupped her hand behind his neck, then brought him close and kissed him on the lips. It was a juicy, full-mouthed kiss, with a little flick of her tongue on the release. "I'm glad you tried to write something," she said. Her sad smile didn't match up with the kiss.

"*Did* write something."

"A story, a poem, what?"

"I got back into my journal, and just let it flow." He felt guilty for wanting to what? save his marriage by not saying anything about the first thing he wrote this afternoon, the letter to Anastasie? Or was he mostly interested in holding his and Margaret's sexual buzz? The kids were in bed asleep on a school night: coast clear. The growing cucumber in his jeans gave him the answer.

She bit her lip. She said nothing.

Had Margaret in fact intercepted a letter from Anastasie? "Please don't hold back on me," he said, feeling quite paranoid. He leaned in to kiss her again, but she only gave him a slim-lipped press of the lips.

"They're no shortcuts. I simply can't fake it anymore."

"I don't blame you. It's just that she touches some place deep inside me, Margaret. I'm sorry."

ⵥ

Suddenly, Margaret couldn't breathe. "I wasn't—" She stopped to collect herself a bit. "I can hardly blame you for having an affair, Frazier," she managed.

He shook his head, then looked her directly in the eyes. "I'm having a muse, not an affair."

"At least not yet, I hope."

This time it was himself who had nothing to say.

Find your muses. No one can get along with just one because nobody carries all the attributes of God. Become someone else's muse. These sentences from Nana's first letter to Margaret whispered in her mind. She lowered her eyes, no longer able to hold Frazier's steady gaze. "Maybe you won't have an affair, if I can heal enough to be a good muse for you along with her," she said.

"I've told you before, you're a plenty good muse," he said, meaning it more than ever. Had he heard Margaret right...*along with her*?

"Not a very, shall we say, prolific one." She gestured at the blank page on the computer screen. "Who is she, Frazier?"

"A modern artist, a painter, and a very good one."

Her eyes drifted back down toward her shoes. "Maybe having her to inspire you could help you hang in there with me until I get unstuck creatively and can be better for you."

Gently, he reached over, and then with a finger against her chin guided her face until they looked directly at each other again. "I love you," he said.

Tears glistened in her eyes. "Me too."

"I'm sorry you had to find Anastasie's letter," he said.

Her brow knitted. "I didn't find any letter."

"Then what's with 'no shortcuts' and not 'faking it'?"

"That was over me cheating on Nana's advice concerning writing." She gestured at the blank page on the screen again. "I couldn't get anything started because it was me who took the shortcut."

He arched an eyebrow. "What?"

"So you thought..." Her voice tapered off.

He nodded. "Sort of caught myself red-handed."

She wiped off her tears, then kissed him again, laying on another good one. "Don't go anywhere," she said. "Maybe I'm a pretty damn good muse after all." She got up from her chair, then walked from the study toward their bedroom.

For an embarrassingly long, extremely odd moment, he wondered whether she kept a gun tucked underneath her side of the mattress.

In less than thirty seconds she returned to her desk, sat down, and laid a handwritten dispatch on its surface. "This is the most recent of Nana's letters I've gone through." Using a hand she positioned the yellowed missive so they both could easily read it.

> *Dear Margaret,*
>
> *Live life, my sweet granddaughter. Do not spend all your time behind a desk with pen and paper, pontificating about things fabricated out of whole cloth. You will create characters that way, not people. People we remember. Characters become caricatures we laugh at or cry crocodile tears over, and then they vanish from our minds. Fiction is the exploration of deeper truth, not a pack of frivolous lies.*
>
> *So how do you do this writing with purpose that will also entertain? How do you know what to write? Start keeping a journal and write in it every day. Rain or shine, puking in the bowl or dancing in clover. From your journal your story will find you. But you must get started living!*
>
> *And always, always try to change the world dramatically by what you write. Make it a better place. We need it to be.*
>
> *Shalom and love,*
> *Nana*

The letter's final admonishment may as well have had hands that reached out and pulled him toward slumbering. How could he, a hardly published author, change anything, much less something huge and important—for his words, even back when he'd written regularly, rarely got out of the memory chip in his laptop? But then, writing in his journal had given him the feeling of tossing rocks at the wall of a certain kind of injustice toward himself. The word *neglect* came to mind. It had been good to throw the rocks; he couldn't deny it.

✍

Margaret had unraveled into a mess, making it hard for her to concentrate on rereading Nana's letter. She wanted to meet this Anastasie; something about Frazier bringing another woman into their lives was giving her the Frida Kahlo tingles or something. Who would've known, leastwise herself? Don't get the wrong impression, her druthers were to have her husband's sole attention. Until reading some of Nana's letters, *that* surely hadn't gone anywhere, she reminded herself. Yes, the worst kind of aloneness came in the ways of a distant marriage partner. They both had been guilty. She glanced over at Frazier's journal, then read again the part of Nana's letter about how your story finds you. Stinging wetness returned to her eyes. She hadn't kept a journal since her days at NYU, didn't know what had become of her notebooks with the recorded hopes and fears of that young woman.

"Your Nana reminds me of one of my favorite Texans, Molly Ivins," Frazier said. "She was always saying most of the battles she fought were losing ones, but fighting them may be the only good clean fun a person will ever have. Something like that anyway."

"Yeah. The great muckraking reporter for the *Texas Observer* who died a few years ago." She blinked back her tears, then gave him a wink. "Frazier, there're some things that come out of your home state us northeastern liberal snobs secretly adore."

He chuckled warmly. "Do you have a journal collecting dust somewhere in this apartment?"

She shook her head. The thing of it was, Nana's letter and the talk of Molly Ivins had given her something she wanted to write about. She looked Frazier directly in the eyes. What she had in mind for airing out in her journal didn't have to do with Anastasie or her unwritten novel or being Frazier's muse or him being hers. These subjects all seemed too raw and embedded in some open wound to spill her guts over, for now anyway. "Maybe I'll go out to a Duane Reade and get me one," she said.

"I want to buy it for you if that's okay," he said. "The village bookstore should still be open, and they'll have a nicer selection."

"That would be lovely, Frazier." Maybe in letting him go some, she would get him more to herself. Right now, it sure felt like it.

✄

In just under an hour, he returned with a dark blue macramé-covered notebook with hummingbirds embroidered on it. He knew Margaret liked hummingbirds. She sat at her desk editing some manuscript with a red pencil. When he set the journal down next to the papers, she gave it a long, intent look, then passed a hand over it as if wanting to feel the macramé's texture.

She smiled warmly at him. "Thank you, Frazier." He couldn't have done a better job of picking a journal out for her.

"I'll leave you to it, then." With that, he went into their bedroom, put on his loose-fitting PJs, and then slipped underneath the covers. He turned on the bedside lamp, but instead of picking up off the nightstand Steinbeck's *Of Mice and Men* and reading from where he had left off, he stared at the ceiling. His thoughts flowing, he took off his glasses and laid them aside. Everything above went creamy. Would Margaret and Anastasie actually coexist in his life if the beautiful French artist ever contacted him again? Did he want that to happen? At first blush it felt exciting, but not particularly inspiring. There was a reason polygamy hadn't gone over so well in the western world. Women were HMUs, High Maintenance Units, one and all. But then, so were men in their own way. Just look at him, what a piece of work. So be it. Margaret opening up to herself certainly held promise. He hadn't stared at the ceiling contemplating a peace-love-&-incense-burning future with her since…well…since he had been writing regularly years ago. For that matter, him opening up to himself held promise. And how scary right-on was that letter from Nana? He partly wanted to ask Margaret whether he could read Nana's other letters too, but thought better of it. Not to tamper with a good thing. No, not to tamper. He wondered what Margaret was out there in the other room journaling about.

✑

Margaret put her red pencil down when Frazier had left her alone in the study with her new journal, and in doing so she stopped editing the manuscript that would expose the Tunisian poet Yassine Lotfi Khaled as working closely with organizers in the United States to set afire revolutions in the Middle East. All they needed was an incendiary incident to start things off. They were going to be nonviolent revolutions, at least the behind-the-scenes leaders in the US were doing their best to organize with these principles as sacrosanct. If she went forward with this project, if the book came out, everything could be scuttled. It hadn't bothered Margaret so much before, but lately she had a harder and harder time with the vote for tyranny she may be casting. And the harm she may be bringing down on the head of Khaled. This is what she needed to journal about. Opening the blue hummingbird notebook, she felt a jolt of adrenaline, something that had an element of risk to it. "Let's go get 'em, Nana," she whispered. She took a pen from the desk's middle drawer, and then began writing.

> *I feel so lousy. Frazier is so much better of a person than me. I couldn't have cared less about the poet and the work being done to free the Middle East. Well, not really, I just didn't want to get involved. Let someone else do the dirty work of stopping injustice. But what if Nana is right? No, I believe she is right. I must make a difference with my work, or at the very least try my best. Okay, so will I actually sabotage this*

*book? Can I? The publishing house would just put someone
else on the project if I resign or purposely screw it up.*

She tapped her pen on the page, thinking. Something about having Anastasie in their lives made facing into this a point of no return for Margaret, and quite possibly for her marriage. Frazier, the cad and the poet. The forgotten husband. The overwhelmed man of goodwill. She loved him. Yes, she did.

Maybe there is a way...

It was the ellipses she'd left on the page that troubled her while she walked from the study into their bedroom. *Good*, he still had the light on, but he wasn't reading; he just lay there staring off into space. "Frazier, are you okay?"

The sound of her voice brought him out of his trance. He put his glasses back on properly, not supported by the end of his nose, then leaned on an elbow and met her eyes. "I haven't been this good in quite some time."

"Can we talk about something?"

"Anything, anything at all."

She sat down on the end of the bed. "You know that poet named Khaled who's been on the run after writing the poem that got the Tunisian government after him. Well, I know you haven't been happy with my, shall we say, cold and detached involvement in the project related to this. For what it's worth, I'm ashamed of myself." God, she was talking overly fast but couldn't seem to slow down. "Are you too disappointed in me to talk about this?"

"No. I like what I'm hearing, Margaret." He scratched his disheveled hair. "Please, take a breath, chill, and tell me what you're getting at."

She did what he suggested, then continued, "The book I'm editing was written by an informant on the inside of the nonviolent resistance training group here in the US that's working with Khaled and others across the Middle East to organize revolutions in several countries. I've told you some of the basics on this before, but anyway, the author won't give up his identity until the publication of the book. We communicate through encrypted email. I don't know what group he's on the inside of. Oh, man, I'm talking too fast again."

She took another long breath and exhaled before going on. "I think if you and not me, because the author conveniently told them who I am, went to the TMZ, that Judeo-Christian-Muslim hate group you had the dustup with in the subway terminal, they'd probably divulge who the nonviolent leaders are. They can't stand real peacemakers. Then we could work with the good guys to expose the informant. I could help them draw him out with what I know about him, what his tastes are, how he thinks."

He sat up and leaned his back against the bed's headboard. "We, as in you want my help." It wasn't a question.

She nodded. "I know we've both been sort of out of it for a long time, but well, as crazy as it sounds, yes, you're the only one I know who is good enough of a man to do it." Taking hold of his foot under the covers, she mischievously jiggled his toes. "Other than probably Grandpa Mandt, but he's too old for this sort of thing."

He smiled broadly. "Flattery will get you everywhere."

The light stayed on as she got in bed naked, Frazier already having taken off his PJs. He kissed her ear, then whispered, "I know what group Khaled is being protected by. I even know who the man at the head of all the organizing is. He lives in Marblehead. My journalist friend Bucky is on this. He's trying to get to Khaled for an interview."

"We better get there first." She slapped him on the ass.

He mounted her.

This was going to be fun!

CHAPTER FOURTEEN

The End. With a swirl of relief and regret, I keyed those words on the handsome Moskva typewriter Pasternak had given me as a bribe not to marry and move in with Oleg, at least not until finishing my studies at university in Moscow. If my acceptance had been anywhere other than the School of Writers, I wouldn't have taken Pasternak's lagniappe and left. There was the thick haze of Soviet propaganda and censorship to bob and weave through at Writers School, though undeniably, I learned from some of the best Russian poets and novelists. Pasternak had assured me that at the coffee shops certain professors would lead the way in samizdat, the reconstruction of truth, the rewriting of redacted literature, and he had been right. Dissident writers did their real work in these places during evening hours. Of course, you had to be careful of infiltrators, agent provocateurs, Stalinist snitches. Oleg had not wanted me to go away for the school year, but I had another love affair whose pull was too strong to resist—my writing. Oleg and I sent mail to each other regularly, and his letters had sustained me until I could get back home. It felt good being near him these past two and a half months in Peredelkino for the summer of 1941. Pasternak and Miss Zinaida had been pretty lax about me spending any time I wanted at Oleg's apartment. Or rather, Pasternak had from time to time privately asked me to be careful and not get pregnant by making sure Oleg always used a rubber, whereas Miss Zinaida had remained tight-lipped about the entire subject. Nevertheless, much of the time I stayed at the dacha working, often with Pasternak intently at his writing right down the hallway in his studio. A different kind of lovemaking than mine and Oleg's heat, which so easily changed places with tenderness, but as the typewriter keys fluttered, oftentimes so did my heart. Inwardly, I harbored it being that way for Pasternak too. When would I ever get over this father figure secret love? But to be fair, in my two academic years away, it had changed into something similar yet, subtly, and in an important way different. What to call this, though? I slipped the piece of paper from the roller and placed it on bottom of my loose manuscript. My first completed novel!

I felt profound satisfaction, but it hadn't been this way from the start.

There was so much to write about in Russia. The question had for the longest been what to choose. I tried to emulate Pasternak by writing of unrequited love in the throes of sweeping history, as he was doing with his still gestating and closely guarded *Doctor Zhivago* (that is, as far as I could tell, he kept drafts from anyone other than me). But my version came out sappy and overwritten in the amorous parts, and thin while overly broad with history. I simply didn't know enough up close, in my authorly bones, about Tsarist Russia and the birth of communism, and for that matter, with romantic love and losing it, or finding it too late. No, I had to write something I knew of firsthand infused with great richness. We live on an earth that is round, not flat, orbiting a star, and like humankind gaining this understanding, it's the memories and zeitgeist that kept circling back on me, instead of floating off sideways into infinity, from which I cut this novel. Call it the literary pull of gravity if you will. I did, out loud, one night when watching a beautifully sad sunset over the Urals, and at once I knew what to write. The story I couldn't get rid of in my mind. The one about my parents and brother being killed by the Goat-faced Murderer, and all the dissidents who had let a young spitfire girl belly up to the table with them exchanging ideas, daring to write truth and take action in the streets, while other kids and most adults whistled through denied nightmares of Siberian gulags or worse, until it became too late to indulge in such mental gymnastics. My account of this was fictionalized, names changed, not to protect the innocent, really. Who could've done that in those days?

I picked up my manuscript, turned it right-side up, and then headed from my room. My bones felt kind of hollow; my feet set down lightly on the floor, making a feathery sound with each step; all those black words had wings, and they carried me toward Pasternak. God, I ached for his approval. *Stay open, Katya,* I told myself. He does know a little bit about this stuff. From inside his studio, I heard the clack of his Moskva's keys. He'd gotten one for himself when buying mine. My first taps with a knuckle on the door landed so softly, I couldn't hear them. Harder next time, and in a few seconds, Pasternak opened the door. His eyes went to my manuscript, and with a warm smile he looked directly at me. "It's finished," I said.

"I knew you had it in you," he said.

"Well..." I hesitated. "The first draft's complete."

"You've polished it as you went along?"

I nodded.

"Then it should be an enjoyable read that only requires some fine-tuning." He held his hands out as if reaching for a newborn babe.

My entire body felt absolutely weightless now. Pasternak had not asked to see this manuscript before. It had been started at school in Moscow, but worked on all summer here. I had wanted him to read each chapter, let me know whether I was on the right track. He'd volunteered to look at partials of my short stories and poems in the past. All he had said at the start of my novel was "I bought you the typewriter, but you have all the equipment you need. Now go write." He had made no promise to ever look at it. Straightening my spine, I handed him my work. "You spending any time with this at all means more than you know to me."

"You're welcome, but you're wrong." He shook his head. "Someone taught me how to be a better author than I should've been. I know what this means to you." Leaving the door open, he turned and walked over to his desk, then sat down. He moved his manuscript aside and replaced it with mine. As he began reading, I eased into the chair across from his desk. Over the next fifteen or twenty minutes: a nod of his head, possible tensing of the crow's-feet at the corners of his eyes, a strongly exhaled breath, a clear shake of the head, thank God another nod—I studied Pasternak's every wilt and tittle.

"What do you think?" I finally said.

"It's good, Katya. It's really good."

A wave of gooseflesh washed over me. My book was not like life—a story has a beginning, middle, and end—and I wanted this moment to last forever. "You think so, really?"

"Yes, really." He smiled with some sort of reserve. "There's someone coming over for coffee, and I'll need to get back to reading your manuscript later. So, if there isn't anything else?"

I began to stand up but stopped short, then pertly rearranged myself in the chair. "Pasternak, why didn't you read my chapters and tell me what you thought? I've kinda felt exiled to Siberia."

He looked me directly in the eyes again. "From going over your shorter pieces, I knew you were ready to be nudged from the nest. Besides—"

Maybe I am a bird. I failed to hold in a chuckle.

"What?" He arched an eyebrow.

"Oh, it's nothing. Please go on."

"If you talk too much about your story with others while in process, it can easily become theirs and not yours. It is your unique intimacy with your characters and their circumstances that moves us."

I was flying! "Then I want the world to read it!"

His face rippled as though from a bolt of tension. He folded his hands on top of my manuscript. "It's too hot, Katya. Publication of your story should wait until Russia finds herself. You wouldn't survive it now, or you'd become like—" He stopped himself briefly. "I'll tell you what, Marina Tsvetaeva will arrive here any minute now. I would like for you to join us, and Katya, take a good long look at her situation. I don't want it to become yours."

The marrow rushed back into my bones like fire, and all my heaviness returned with vengeance. There would be no defying gravity. I felt angry with myself as much as with Pasternak. It had often crossed my mind during the writing that what was going down on paper contained good-sized portions of, well, the truth. But each time I crossed through something to tone down my prose, it made me sick to the stomach. So, I quit with the self-censorship. Maybe I simply was too young and should heed Pasternak's advice. Or maybe I was more like Osip Mandelstam and Oleg, or for that matter Marina Tsvetaeva. I looked out the window absently just as a goshawk flew from a tree. "I accept your invitation," I said, without looking at Pasternak.

"Good. Are you aware they have imprisoned Marina's husband Efron, and her daughter Alya for espionage?"

I nodded, wishing to be with the goshawk. In fact, from the coffee shops in Moscow, I had learned this and much more, including that Pasternak's poet friend Titsian Tabidze had been secretly executed while in prison. I didn't have the heart to tell Pasternak. As recently as last week, he had told me Tabidze was doing time, and he'd written a letter to Stalin urging his clemency. Pasternak the funambulist, with his friends below and the Goat-faced Murderer above, like a demented god, ready to pluck him off the high wire at the blink of an eye, bosh.

While we went to the front door and let Marina Tsvetaeva in, then escorted her into Pasternak's studio, it was all I could do to keep from gaping. She had been emaciated and haggard when I met her here over three years ago, and the two other times she'd visited when I happened to also be in Peredelkino. On those latter occasions she'd reminded me kindly of what she'd said when we first spoke, "I write for you." Now, she couldn't have weighed ninety pounds; she had shriveled, her facial skin a series of ravines and tributaries connected to dry riverbeds. Pasternak held her by the elbow and guided her into the chair I had just earlier sat in. I stood in front of the window, hugging my arms close. He moved his chair from behind his desk so there would be nothing between himself and this withering poet, and then he sat down. She looked at me as if wanting to smile, though unable. From here on, I write for you, I thought. "It's good to see you again," I said.

Almost imperceptibly she nodded, and then fixed her dead eyes on Pasternak. "I am going with Valentin Parnakh, a damn good poet, and you know this, Boris..." Her voice tapered off. She waited keenly, as if summoning enough strength to go on.

No birds chirped outside. Pasternak sat there patiently. I lowered my arms to my sides. Her neck and head shook. At last, she continued, "Valentin and I are leaving for Chistopol tomorrow to apply for jobs with the Literature Fund.

For the last time, Boris, will you send me with a letter of recommendation?"

The color slowly drained from Pasternak's face until he fell totally ashen. "I cannot, Marina, I'm sorry. Please, let me explain."

Her head trembled more violently. She said nothing.

"Stalin stood in front of the Politburo and said, 'Let this cloud dweller be,' speaking of me, taking me off the secret police's hit list after I wrote him a letter urging the release of Titsian Tabidze," Pasternak went ahead. "That same afternoon, I got a call from the Goat-faced Murderer to tell me if I ever put him in any position of compromise again, myself and my family are as good as dead."

"Will you off the record, nothing in writing, call some high-muckety-muck friend of yours that works there, and help her?" I said.

He looked at me with eyes of a caged man. Our gulag had no bars, not yet anyway. "Zinaida would leave me if she found out, and I cannot lie to her about something of this magnitude."

Thank the Almighty that Miss Zinaida, little Leonid, and Yevgeni were out at market. Who knows what would've happened otherwise. "Give me a name of someone you trust there, Pasternak," I said, my tone suddenly piercing.

"There is no one left to trust. We're all too afraid, and rightly so."

"A name of the best man or woman you know there!" I demanded.

"Why, what good would it do?" he snapped.

He and I stared each other down. Of course, he knew why I wanted the name.

Marina Tsvetaeva struggled mightily standing from the chair. Without another word, she walked toward the doorway. I went to her side, and even though she moved unsteadily, this older poet remained with her dignity. A little space separated us, as I stayed at the ready to stabilize her if need be.

"Think about what you're doing, Katya," he said, his tone turning plaintive.

"Maybe thinking too much is exactly the wrong thing right now," I said evenly.

As we made our way outside and over toward the waiting car, with who I took to be Valentin Parnakh behind the steering wheel, Pasternak came onto the porch.

"We can go over to my home and figure out what to do from there, what do you say?" I said to Marina Tsvetaeva.

"That would be lovely, dear," she said.

"The man you can most trust at the Literature Fund is Viktor Pechkin," Pasternak said.

I faced him and said, "Thank you." Yes, it was time to move in with Oleg.

Valentin Parnakh stepped out of the car, came round the other side, and assisted Marina Tsvetaeva into the front passenger seat. I got into the back compartment.

Pasternak waved.

I waved back.

The car pulled away.

As Marina Tsvetaeva explained to her friend what had happened inside the dacha with Pasternak, I soberly looked on this woman in questionable shape to handle a job of any kind. The rawboned Valentin Parnakh, with his thin mustache and oiled black hair, was vaguely familiar, maybe having been at some of the dissident literati meetings I'd been in. Momentarily interrupting her, I gave him directions, at once squeamish to call Oleg's apartment my home again. It was as if the car rumbling through potholes in the rutted lane jostled me not away from my desire to live under the same roof with Oleg, but also into the feeling of something ending—perhaps a kind of innocence I always reclaimed in the dacha. I wondered whether the inspiration to my writing would fade that came with knowing Pasternak was hard at it nearby in his studio. My baby, the manuscript, had been left with him. I felt the uncomfortable pull of its umbilical cord. For sure he would still read it and give me edits. I wonder, really? My smoldering anger over how he'd treated Marina Tsvetaeva burned through these thoughts, but in the glow of dimmer embers. Why call on this Viktor Pechkin at the Literature Fund for help with Tsvetaeva in such bad shape? Why risk so much for a probable non-starter? No denying it, Pasternak had a point in refusing her. What if the job ended up being for Valentin Parnakh alone, when he and Pasternak weren't even close enough for Parnakh to come in from the car to make the case for assistance? Yes, I would have to get to know Valentin Parnakh. When we parked the car at the end of the lane where the apartment was located, another thought came, in a hiss. Had I lost my cool back in the dacha mostly to justify moving in with Oleg?

With a slower cadence, as if winding down the agonized monologue with Valentin Parnakh, Marina Tsvetaeva said, "I will no longer be able to take care of my son if I don't get this job. I've used almost all the money Efron and I had when they took him away from me." She let go with a hacking cough. "The pittance that it was."

He turned the motor off and looked her way. "If only one job is offered, it will go to you, Marina."

She coughed again. "Nonsense. If there is a single place, it goes to who gets it. I would not give my job up to you."

"For you yes," he said. "For me no." He now fixed his eyes on me. "Thank you for helping us. We have no other options for work.

"They stuck Marina and I in Yelabuga, where there're no jobs. We can only move to another region if our services are specifically requested. No employer is doing that without a push from the higher-ups."

I liked this man. "I'm so sorry, and you're welcome," I said, too noncommittally. Even if we could get an audience in front of this Viktor Pechkin, and even if the failing poet could perform in a job, without Pasternak we had no lever with which to push.

"They want me and my boy Mur to starve," Marina Tsvetaeva said, fixing me with a glare. "They think Efron and Alya told me too much about being Stalinist double agents in the dissident community, and with the expats in Paris. The two of them told me next to nothing."

There had been rumors in the coffee shops about Marina Tsvetaeva's husband and daughter being moles for Stalin. With things coming apart at the seams, many people were doing things just to stay alive another day, others out of conviction. I had read enough of Marina's poetry to know she would never stand against Russia, or sell out those who criticized Russia's faults. And now, looking into her cavernous eyes, something more than belief in her claims stirred inside me; the whirlpool of this woman's desperate need spun with mine, swilling it faster and faster. Most Soviet writers lived in Chistopol, where the Literature Fund headquarters was, the ones who hadn't ticked the Goat-faced Murderer off too much. Tsvetaeva and Parnakh had obviously done so. I knew several authors who were seeking jobs at the Literature Fund who lived in Chistopol. The waiting list was long even for those in Stalin's favor. "Whatever happens with the job at the Literature Fund, you and Mur will always be welcome in my home," I said. "We would take care of you both best we can."

Her expression didn't ease off, but the glare turned into a look of intense gratitude. "Thank you. Who do you know other than Pasternak who can help me and Valentin with this Pechkin?"

A pit formed in my stomach. "Let's go to my home, and see what my fiancé Oleg thinks about this. He has good ideas."

With a knitted brow, she looked at Valentin Parnakh again.

"Oleg comes from good stock; he's Osip Mandelstam's son, am I right?" he said, glancing at me.

I nodded.

Marina Tsvetaeva shrugged. "Do you know anyone who is close to Pechkin, Valentin?" she said.

He shook his head.

"Okay, then." She lowered her tone to almost a mutter. "Let's go talk with this young man of 'good stock' whose father got himself killed by the same people that we want help from."

Without another word, we got out of the car, and I led them toward the apartment. When we arrived on the porch, I faced them. "Let me talk with Oleg for a few minutes alone, please."

Both of them stared me down with the look of craven wolves, or lost sheep, I couldn't tell which. They said nothing.

I knocked on the door and in seconds Oleg opened it. When I introduced Oleg to them, his eyebrows arched. "I know of your poetry and like it very much," he said. "Both of you would make my father proud."

"Thank you," Marina Tsvetaeva said. "I knew your father well."

"And so did I," Valentin Parnakh added.

"What gives me this pleasure?" Oleg said, glancing from them to me, his expression turning serious.

"They have nowhere else to go for help," I said.

After getting them seated at the table with glasses of water, Oleg and I headed into the bedroom on my request. I told him about me leaving Pasternak for him, and of Tsvetaeva and Parnakh's grave situations. I felt like a semi-loved girlfriend delivering the unwanted news of being pregnant with his child, as he looked at me without giving away any emotion. "I'm terribly presumptuous and terribly sorry," I said at last.

He smiled almost boyishly. "And I'm terribly happy to have you as a roommate." He brought a finger to his chin. "Where would you like your typewriter set up? Here in the bedroom, or maybe better out in the living area so you can get away from my snoring."

I, too, put a finger to my chin. "Maybe in the other room, so we won't knock it over having our funnies."

We held each other and kissed. Underneath our bliss coursed the pain for what awaited us in the other room. It was palpable in our hungry clawing, our connection with the deprived, the oppressed. When we separated, Oleg placed his hands gently on my shoulders. "Are you willing to pass a good forgery of my father's poem 'The Stalin Epigram' to help them get jobs?" he said.

"A good one, maybe, but how?"

"My handwriting is almost identical to my father's."

A chill ran down my spine. All four of us could end up in gulags over this. "Yes, yes, Oleg, I'm willing."

"Can I do most of the talking out there?" he said.

"Okay, but we must leave Pasternak out of this, even with Pechkin, especially with him."

He nodded by way of agreeing.

I mustered a smile. Russian men were the best, and mine was the best of them all.

We walked out of the bedroom, then went over and took seats at the table with Marina Tsvetaeva and Valentin Parnakh.

"Well?" Marina said incredulously.

"We will go with you to visit Pechkin," Oleg said. "I'll tell him the original of my father's poem 'The Stalin Epigram' will be delivered once both of you are given employ, and a contract that says you cannot be fired for any reason."

"I'd rather die than give the Goat-faced Murderer your father's magnificent poem," Marina Tsvetaeva said.

"But your son," I said. "Think about him."

"I am."

I shot Oleg a knowing look.

He held my gaze. "It will be an almost perfect forgery," he said.

"It hardly matters," Marina Tsvetaeva said without hesitation. "Mur, and Efron and Alya for that matter, must know I didn't give up our souls to Stalin in some act of trickery that will nevertheless be used to demoralize our comrades. They will think it is the original."

I felt myself becoming more like her.

CHAPTER FIFTEEN

Dear Anastasie,

I envy you the freedom of being a working artist who pays the bills from your art. I continue schlepping through bad manuscripts at Flying Pens to squeeze the eagle. No novel yet, but there is my regular journaling. Sometimes it explores not what we've left behind, rather the moment of eternity we created in each other. Just this morning while walking to work I saw a young couple easy in love, hugging, chatting each other up, kissing, and I had that moment again. A few days ago, I spotted a black-masked, yellow-throated warbler migrating south, and had the moment. A couple of months back, I read a letter from a deceased woman, a writer who had been a Jewish refugee from Russia during the Stalin years, and the moment returned. Every now and then I get it on penning a really great sentence. Anyways, it's not like having a series of moments; I'm having the continuation of an instant that lasts forever.

I feel myself coming out of hiding sometimes, for my journaling is bringing forward a story. I'm experiencing this story firsthand, and it is heartrending and exciting—even could be important. I want to stay grounded in the pain, honesty, and restorative justice of your art as I write; otherwise, the greed for something sensational could take over. I do not want to become some plot slut and forget to develop the people in my story. So, I view your art on your website to remind myself where my center is. My better angels are in your pieces, Anastasie. I must find something more in my story before it becomes my next novel. There has to be encounters in it with this moment of eternity.

I'm tempted to tell you all about it, though somehow think it's too early for that.

At this point, he came close to asking how things were going for her, had she, too, been having their *eternal moment*, but that would be either crazy or pitiful, or both. Anastasie still hadn't returned his letters. It felt weird enough writing to someone gone from his life. She probably had moved on with her heart, given it to another man. *Humph.* As if the slumbering man ever had her heart in the way one can keep it, like she had his. He jotted down a sentence about having noticed on her website that she was having a gallery show in Paris later in the month, wished her well with it, then signed off and prepared an envelope. He had several times caught himself daydreaming of them together in Paris. Each time he'd told himself there was enough money in his and Margaret's bank account to buy a roundtrip ticket, or one-way. No, it was easier to keep looking over the top of his lenses, with everything safely distorted. In any case, he and Margaret had gone into some kind of steroidal slumber since working together on the problem of the missing poet Yassine Lotfi Khaled and Clifford Odeon's preparations for something big happening in the Middle East.

The trip to meet Clifford Odeon in Marblehead at his Badshah Khan Institute for Peace Studies had been surprisingly easy to arrange. Before their visit, the slumbering man had gotten from the Internet that Odeon had been nominated for the Nobel Peace Prize twice, and thrown in jail for civil disobedience more than thirty times, some with MLK, Dorothy Day, and the Berrigan brothers. He had found Odeon to be a bright-eyed, lanky curmudgeon with thinning white hair, who carried the kind of soft-spoken fight in himself that he wished he had. He had asked what animated him, and Odeon said, "A conscience set free by making peace with those who shaped me incorrectly." The slumbering man had tried pushing the comment aside. To be honest, he wanted Margaret or Anastasie or his writing or some sophisticated combination of all three to light his flame and keep it lit, but these brush fires burnt themselves out, even the raging ones, like Margaret's and his Greater-Than-Ever-Sex that brought them closer, until he couldn't accept her new openness, would find ways to distance himself, which just made the sex all the better, titillating him, as if watching themselves do it from across the room; really, just fixing his eyes on him and Margaret in the mirror atop the chest of drawers. When these encounters wound down, he got up to write in his journal or thought of Anastasie or of becoming a superhero who saved a democratic revolution in the Middle East from ruin on the inside, uncovering Clifford Odeon's mole. In a way, he used the French artist to buffer himself against blossoming intimacy with Margaret. Yes, it was true, but why did he do it? Neither woman deserved as much. What is more, the visions of grandeur about playing a part in some Middle Eastern uprising always left him feeling small and insignificant—stupidly mainstream American. Texan. With all the Up-Against-the-Wall-Redneck-Mother, cowboy-boot-wearing, gun-toting, hat-tipping clichés intact. There was no two-stepping around the fact that returning home tugged at his psyche more and more lately. His family lay in wait, hunkered down, and the slumbering man had long ago set out to fly. Would they break his already damaged wings, irreparably crush them, if he went back home, or worse yet, grind his spectacles underfoot?

God, if he could only do something with actual depth in his writing, or something useful in helping Clifford Odeon and Khaled. But then, Odeon had indicated he always took precautions against moles in his organization. Only he knew of Khaled's whereabouts. Odeon had said it could be helpful for Margaret to slow play her edits. When the slumbering man had asked why, Odeon replied, "We can prepare for nonviolent revolutions, but we cannot make one happen. That takes a spark no one can control."

"You are close then," the slumbering man had said.

Odeon shook his head sharply. "We are prepared. Please, do nothing more than what I've asked."

With that, their meeting had ended, and so had any hope for the curtailment of slumbering. It was this circumlocution of thought that had driven him to pen Anastasie another letter. He didn't expect her to answer it, but if she didn't, maybe he would buy a ticket to Paris? Maybe he would. He placed her letter in his satchel, then stood up from his desk. He walked into the mailroom, but instead of placing it in the outgoing bin, the slumbering man headed out of the office. Once down on the street, he felt better, all the bodies, all the shapes and sizes, colors of skin, Brooks Brothers suits, hipster jeans, tie-dyes, ear piercings, the smell of sweat, out-and-out BO, and the scent of Chanel No. 5. This was New York, the place he once believed held the most vibrant heartbeat, where people went to fulfill their dreams. Now, he purposefully couldn't see the glimmering-eyed ones doing just that, and the dim-eyed ones who were in between dreams or broken to the point of no return. This sea of humanity, even if they accomplished what they set out to do, were fish swimming waters poisoned with mercury, poisoning themselves—success in this strong current meant failure. Who had time for moments of eternity in New York City? *Tell me, do you?* he almost asked the nearest person. Without those moments, how could anyone make a difference that mattered, didn't pollute your soul or the planet into…well, insignificance? Slammed with blood-humming claustrophobia, he didn't react and push his way through the throng; he simply flowed aimlessly with them, or maybe he would go over to Union Square. You could always count on something going down there, a good protest, at least someone holding a mike who would shout down authority, call for transparency. Truth.

He dropped the letter in a mailbox on the street corner, then turned and went against the flow of people. The cold, sunny day blew a sliver of wind down his neck, and he adjusted his muff, buttoned the topmost button of his parka while moving more into the middle of the mass of people to shield himself from the weather.

As he neared Union Square, he heard the unmistakable thumping beat of street drummers who used the undersides of plastic tubs. He stopped and took a long breath on entering the grounds, as if the crisp air could purify. A group with signs and banners that had gathered over in the northeast corner of the park chanted, "B of A be a real bad ass! Return our homes!" He thought of his sister Felicia, her and Derek's two kids, his nephews, the spiraling interest rate on the smoke-and-mirror mortgage they could no longer make the payments on. With the drought in Texas, Derek couldn't graze enough cattle on their small ranch to keep an income anywhere near bill-paying level. "We can make taxes or our mortgage; we can't cover both anymore," Felicia had told the slumbering man when they last talked about a month ago. The foreclosure sharks were circling just outside their door. He found himself walking over to the outskirts of the protest, Bank of America's red, white, and blue logo so big on the building just across the street, even he could make it out. How long had it been since he'd gotten off the bleachers and gone down on the field for anything? Over the last several years on coming here, he'd sunk to people watching, a voyeur for writing material that never came, slumbering while seeing clearly. He would usually sit on a bench and look over the top of some book through the lenses of his glasses. Discreet. In control, with his conjured magical realism at the ready with the tilt of his chin, a flick of the eyes. He knew it was a mental trick, but what the hey, this got him through some of the rougher times. Today, though, his legs felt sort of disconnected underneath him, almost with a mind of their own. That was something new.

Directly beside him, a slender young woman with wispy, long, dishwater blond hair, too intriguing not to look at in focus, held a sign his way. Her saucer eyes reminded him of the clarity of purpose in Margaret's look, and the open honesty of Anastasie's.

"Here, you can have this one, I've got another," she said.

He chuckled on reading the sign: *The first time a corporation is executed in Texas, I'll agree they are people too.* "Made especially for me," he said and took it from her. "Thanks."

She gave him a throwaway look and went back to the chant, raising a hand on each recitation.

He joined in, using an almost conversational tone. Maybe it was the good energy throughout the crowd along with the little jump-start from the young woman, or Felicia and Derek getting screwed by their bank, or the big ideas of Clifford Odeon, but whatever stew cooked in him, pretty soon he chanted as loud as the rest, holding a hand in the air too. He was thankful for this confluence, for losing his reluctance though not all of it. The atmosphere phosphoresced, like protests back in college. Those times, he'd had a closed fist right along with so many of the others. Now, the militancy in the crowd soured him considerably. He recalled something Clifford Odeon had said about the namesake for Odeon's peace institute—Badshah Khan. This man had been a devout Muslim of the Khyber Pass in Afghanistan, and a leader of the Pathans, a tribe in the same mountainous area which the U.S.'s "war on terror" targeted as the most radical hotbed for fomentation of violent Islamic jihadists. But in the 1940s Badshah Khan had joined with Mahatma Gandhi and challenged his troops to transform into an army of nonviolent peacemakers. Khan made the case that no matter how fierce of warriors his men were, the British occupiers would crush them with superior firepower. If Khan's troops stood firmly without spiking violence with more violence, should they get fortunate enough to win India back, then they would have a chance to construct a society not based on killing. A murderous cycle could be broken. It took more courage to attempt something as ambitious as that. Either way you could end up a casualty. As long as Badshah Khan remained alive, his army of thousands fought without arms, and the Brits gave up India (including what is now Afghanistan) instead of falling to slaughter them. Of course, there would always be those who claim Gandhi needed the militant organizer Bagha Jatin, and Martin Luther King needed Malcom X. Or that India was well on its way of collapsing economically, and the Brits wanted out. Better yet, as President Obama said on accepting the Nobel Peace Prize, global terrorism couldn't be successfully dealt with using the principles of Gandhi and King. What seemed as clear as this cold December day, however, was that most people cherished operating from their lowest common denominators. As soon as King and Gandhi and Badshah Khan had died, everything went to hell again. The slumbering man's palm remained open, over and over again rising high.

Over the next twenty minutes, the crowd grew until hundreds were behind him and on both sides. Without a bullhorn command, like a flock of ravens, they all began moving onto the street toward the bank. A caravan of black vans and SUVs with heavily tinted windows and no indentifying marks rounded the corner of Broadway and East 17th Street. In Kevlar vests police troops, holding batons and Plexiglas riot shields, piled from the vehicles. They shoved their way between the protestors and the bank building. Out the backside of a couple of larger vans, mounted police clambered their horses onto the street, then moved in. Slurs came from the crowd at the police. The smell of fear and righteous indignation blanketed everyone like thick urban smog. He spotted mendacity behind some of the officers' squinting eyes and a number of the protestors' glares too, but not in the blond woman's expression still by his side. Someone threw a rock, and the bank's window shattered. Tear-gas canisters fired into the crowd. People cried out, hacked coughs, and instinctively the slumbering man used his muff to cover his mouth. One of the protestors on the front line slumped to the ground. Through gray haze, the slumbering man noticed a yellow canister next to the downed protestor's bloody head. Several people from the crowd moved toward the injured young man, others stood their ground, some scattered. The cops nearest the casualty rocked on their feet, stood back, gave people room to tend to him. Spurring their horses, the mounted troops compelled the equines closer. A brown mare neighed loudly and reared up on her hind legs. More rocks, more tear gas. The slumbering man met the young blond woman's troubled, clear green eyes. "Lock arms with me, will you?" he said.

She nodded and did so.

A heavily tattooed twenty-something guy with Mohawk hair and a chain dangling from his jeans' belt loop laced an arm through the slumbering man's other arm, then locked on. A round-faced man in a suit and tie did the same with the young woman. The signs held by her and the slumbering man fell away. Spontaneously, this line of cojoined, gasping protestors became a huge, fast-growing, nonviolent snake. In their seething, venomous barrier, which separated the horses and riot squad from the injured comrade, there were no pacifists, it occurred to the slumbering man. Just a bunch of folks like himself, trying to do the right thing, who weren't hair triggers for a fight.

With a look along the line, he saw police handcuffing protestors, all of whom refused to break the human chain. Some began lying down and going limp, other than with their interwoven arms. The cops must've realized what they were doing further galvanized the chain, held it together with plastic zip-cuffs, because they stopped manhandling people. A small group of the most buff, thick-necked SWAT teamers conferred. The slumbering man steeled himself. From his earlier days of public street actions, he knew whatever the heat decided wouldn't be good for his side. Tear gas jabbed ice picks into his watery eyes, and from the looks of everyone here without gas masks, they, too, cried but weren't sad. The SWAT men broke huddle and went to the prone protestors who had yet to be cuffed. They jabbed them with nightsticks, leveraging the clubs between their arms, separating them. A gray-bearded man with long white hair in a ponytail, and still physically fit, moved in behind those on the ground. In one motion this man lunged at a SWAT teamer, shoving him off a protestor. Immediately, the graybeard was pummeled into a heap on the pavement by two SWAT teamers. White-shirted cops spewed orange streams of pepper spray onto the cuffed protestors' faces. A SWAT teamer waved the cops off, but they ignored the command. Like dominos, more people lay down. As the young man in the Mohawk lowered, the slumbering man released his tattooed arm and remained standing.

"Whose side are you on?" the blond woman said to the slumbering man, her expression twisted with skepticism, bordering on betrayal.

"All of ours," he said and shot a look past her at those standing locked arm in arm. "But flopping will only goad the heat into doing harsher things. Not too cool unless we took a vote on going down." He gave her a wink. "And there doesn't seem to be time for that, does there?"

"Okay, so what do you suggest?"

Without another word, he slipped his arm out of hers and extended both arms in front of his body, wrists pressed together.

Her freed arm fell to her side, and she kept her other arm locked with the man in the suit and tie.

A cop approached the slumbering man and said, "What do you think you're doing?"

"Going peacefully and cooperatively to jail. We've made our point."

The cop rammed his nightstick into the slumbering man's midsection.

He doubled over in searing pain, then managed to raise his arms frontward again.

"I'll be damned," the cop said. "The peacenik is too much of a girlyman to fight back." He strapped plastic cuffs around the slumbering man's wrists.

Frazier said to the blond woman, "Don't mouth off."

As the cop took him away, the slumbering man volunteered, "The way you guys are handling this, I can hardly wait to see the nightly news. We win. But the thing of it is, the banks are foreclosing on cops' homes too."

Shoving the nightstick across his perp's chest, the cop stopped him. "It's the talkers who try to escape." One of New York's Finest cinched the cuffs so tight it made his wrists bleed.

Before rounding the corner where police custody buses awaited, the slumbering man looked back at the protest. The young blond woman had been cuffed and was heading his way in tow by a cop. She seemed unharmed. Protestors were being pepper sprayed and clubbed. Some held their arms out standing upright. Another bank window had been smashed. People pushed against the Plexiglas shields. Holding reins by one hand and by the other nightsticks, mounted police rammed horses into activists. The polished black batons glistened in the sunlight, like exclamation marks. What nauseated him as much as anything were the cops with video cameras, recording it all. Yes, both sides were getting what they wanted, at least for today.

He walked to the police bus, looking over the top of his lenses. He sat down between a heavily balding Happy Buddha in a T-shirt that had written on it *Jesus Was A Nonviolent Peacemaker*, and a skinny fellow wearing slim black jeans with a hoodie indicating *Make Tacos Not War*.

The opening licks of Iron Butterfly's "In-A-Gadda-Da-Vida" sounded from inside the slumbering man's chinos, and he managed to wrangle his iPhone out of a pocket between two fingers. Unable to get the phone to his ear because of the plastic cuffs, he set it in his lap and tapped the speakerphone icon.

The music stopped and Margaret said, "Frazier, my God, I saw you at the BofA protest. They're covering it live on TV. It's on right now in my office. Are you all right?"

How should I answer that? "It depends. Can you get bail money together and go to the city jail in the next hour or so?"

"Yes, of course, how much…oh, never mind." A pause. "Frazier, I know it's a strange time to bring this up, but I had one of those, well, life-changing moments."

Happy Buddha and Make Tacos Not War stared at the phone, and so did the slumbering man. He could've warned her she spoke to all those around, but something more than curiosity tugged too much to stop the conversation. "That's funny," he said. "I've been thinking about a defining moment too."

Now, the men on either side of the slumbering man fixed their eyes on him.

"Wow, really," she said. "When we have time I want to hear all about it."

"This probably won't make much sense, but I read another of Nana's letters this morning. Then, I realized the Khaled story is my story. I'll write a novel about it and—"

A cop walking briskly along the aisle grabbed the phone.

"They confiscated my cell, Margaret!"

With a finger tap the cop ended the call. "We'll bag and inventory this. You'll get it back on your release."

Happy Buddha shook his head, told the slumbering man it was a sorry move to cut off an obviously menopausal woman before she got all her say in. Make Tacos Not War smiled nervously.

The slumbering man shrugged. Actually, he was relieved their call had been aborted. The time it took Margaret to write a novel should be longer than any wait Clifford Odeon expected for breaking the story. Would it bring delay enough for a spark to happen that could ignite a revolutionary fire in the Middle East? Or better to snuff the flame altogether if things over there couldn't come off with more promise than the BofA protest? No, but how to revolutionize revolutions themselves? *Ugh*, damned grandiose thinking. There was something more he needed time to mull over, though; it had to do with the frenetic, assured quality of Margaret's tone. He couldn't find any eternity in it.

With a jolt that rocked everyone inside the bus and turned Happy Buddha's belly to Jell-O, they headed toward processing at the jailhouse.

✍

Margaret clutched her cell phone as if strangling it would bring Frazier back on the line. She was relieved he was okay, not one of the injured protestors. *Right?* He hadn't mentioned anything of the sort, and his voice had sounded fine. Here in Harper's employee lounge, the newscast coming over a flat-screen TV she'd watched the flash report of the protest on, already had returned to regularly scheduled programming, some daytime reality stay-at-home-mom show featuring a young child who had blown up with welts over an allergic reaction to penicillin, all while the kid's anorexic mother with a butch haircut contemplated her sexuality on signing for a Fed-Ex package—the deliverywoman's large breasts and full lips giving the mother second and third thoughts. *Who writes these things?* Margaret inwardly groused, immediately realizing she was misdirecting anger like a ventriloquist can make you think it's the puppet on her knee doing the talking. She wanted to tell Frazier of her revelations about writing a novel. Needed to. She felt their marriage hung by the thin thread of her burgeoning though embryonic creativity. She found herself competing with this Anastasie, this French artist, for Frazier's heart. And especially today she knew she'd have to move outside the three-point line and sink some long buckets to come from so far behind. What a thought. Go figure. She loved the Knicks. She had come in here to get a break from the intensity inside her office, the marathon game of basketball that had gone on all morning called her life. Hastily, she made her way out of the employee lounge, down the hall, and back into her office to gather up Nana's letter and her tote bag, shut down her computer. By the time she entered her office, she had an edgy delight over Frazier needing her help. But the sudden pinging behind her temples told Margaret this was no way to play the game.

Or was it more from returning to face what lay in wait here? Something more than a marathon game really, more like a vampire and the cross to drive it away, put a stop to Anastasie's fangs sinking into her husband's neck, if not his penis. *Yet.* But then, what did she really know about Frazier and this woman's relationship other than the precious little he had shared? She stared at her computer screen, which had on it an avant-garde black-and-white painting of the book *The Grapes of Wrath* with John Steinbeck's name in freehand cursive letters across the bottom of its cover. The vampire's joo-joo. This was Frazier's hands-down favorite piece of modern American literature, *and* the featured artwork on Anastasie's website's homepage! The Frenchwoman's newest piece, its description indicated. Way too close to home for chalking off as innocent coincidence, Margaret felt sure. She had earlier this morning for the first time Google searched to find out about Anastasie—who had hundreds of entries covering her life and work, gallery and museum showings all over the U.S. and Europe, mostly favorable art critic reviews, some of which Margaret read or scanned—and then she had split time between gawking at this piece on her computer screen and reading, then rereading another of Nana's letters. The cross. The missive still lay on her desk in front of the computer. But could she hold it up and drive away this black magic, the very intimacy she didn't know how to get at with Frazier? Did she have it in her to go that far? Could she learn how? If not, Anastasie Moreau (finally, Margaret knew the Frenchwoman's full name) was no vampire. The avant-garde artist would be better for Frazier, or at the very least complete him. Would Margaret be able to win him back, or share him? Sometimes secretly she could sort of channel a gypsy Woodstock-er or something, but not today. She was simply a wife, wearing a mask of confidence like the anonymous protestors so often sported these days, a hard layer of protection all too comfortably adorned on the only person in the world selected by the universe to bail her husband out of jail.

Her eyes drifted from the painting to Nana's letter, and she read it once more:

> Dear Margaret,
> Your grandfather is my rock and he makes me want to sing, qualities hard to find in one man. Today he played the bongos between paying bills. He'd write out a check to cover the electric bill, then slap out a tune. He'd pay the phone bill and play another. When he paid the mortgage he went into a really nice Latin beat. I called him Ricky Ricardo. Why, when we were a bit younger and living in San Francisco, he placed the first daisy in the gun barrel of a policeman's rifle after a bunch of them arrived to try and clear us out. They failed. Even the young hippies waited on your grandfather to go first. He had organized a protest to end the war in Vietnam. It gave me courage to smile while I placed my flowers in those guns. He is so much better at structure than me, at being loose while doing something serious and important. He sort of blossomed into being this kind of man. I always saw it in him; he just got more comfortable in his skin as he went along. His life is a wonderful poem. I believe in you, Margaret. You will spend your life with a man not too different than your Grandpa

Mandt.

Okay, now that you are probably writing in your journal regularly, look for the things you know of firsthand that have great richness in them. Don't set out to write an epic before your time, and the funny thing is, in doing that, you may just write something of epic proportions, my dear. Look for those instances in which you want to go one way but instead you go another. These are the times you find out about your essence. Always go down the authentic road, the one you choose in an instant after trying your best to talk yourself out of it. Find a writing mentor for your novel, or mentors. Choose carefully, and make sure they choose you carefully. It could be me, but I have a hunch you'll need more time to start writing earnestly than I've got allotted on mother earth. Don't get enamored with writers writing to get published, and of course, don't become one yourself. The best work is fresh and often breaks down walls erected by the business of publishing to make the buck. Don't be patient, be passionate, and get with a man who helps you sing your way through the long droughts filled with rejection letters. Keep your story as tightly held as your journal until it's ready for the world. This will keep your power in the secrets of your pen.

Shalom and love,
Nana

As she shut the computer down and *The Grapes of Wrath John Steinbeck* artwork blinked off, Margaret wondered whether Nana had been wrong. Maybe Anastasie Moreau could turn Frazier into a man who made *her* sing, but not Margaret. Frazier's bohemian ways she could see all right, but he stumbled through life in a daze that couldn't make flowers grow in a desert, or break a drought. Maybe she would go visit Grandpa Mandt again and ask how he'd blossomed. Maybe she would. She refolded Nana's letter, then placed it carefully back in its envelope and put it inside her tote bag. Then, she headed for the jailhouse.

⌀

Across Manhattan inside the police van, Frazier looked over the top of his lenses and panned his fellow prisoners, most all of them blurry, some of the ones farther away appearing furry, just the way he liked them. For no apparent reason, he lifted his plasti-cuffed wrists and began tapping out a syncopated beat on one knee, then the other, back and forth, with the palms of his hands. Jazz, or was it the blues?

CHAPTER SIXTEEN

"It's the only way a Jew boy has more than a rat's ass chance of keeping himself out of the Goat-faced Murderer's purges, Katya." Oleg looked out the grimy little window over the sink in our apartment, as if unable to meet my eyes and say this. "And what's worse, if Hitler and the Nazis win Russia, the rat will have no ass at all. Our kind will be killed on the battlefield or gassed and dropped into mass graves." He chuckled morosely. "Hell of a choice, if I do say so myself."

Hard to disagree with. "You think they'd take you presently?" I fingered the stem of a white rose tilted away from me in a drinking glass that was next to my typewriter on the table I sat at across the room. Oleg had retrieved my typewriter, but not my manuscript, from Pasternak's dacha while I was away in Chistopol. Oleg hadn't known that on my going in haste with Marina Tsvetaeva and Valentin Parnakh, my manuscript also had been left behind at the dacha. At my delight over his caring act with my typewriter, we'd made love before talking about the trip.

Now, he kept looking out the window and gave no response.

I felt sure of the answer to this question, and he couldn't think otherwise. Yes. The Red Army had already reclassified deferment statuses on many of our friends. Diabetic seizures no longer kept you off the front, flat feet, bandiness, or extreme nearsightedness, to name a few.

For several pregnant seconds Oleg and I weighed his decision whether to come off injured reserve status—achieved for his "nervous problem," as the Red Army's examining physician had called it—and volunteer for combat duty anyway. This so-called diagnosis he'd worked deftly to get, by acting bloodthirsty, then tearing up and laughing in alternating intervals while at marksman testing over a year and a half ago, in the fall of 1939, right after the Nazis went into Poland, and Russia had a wave of conscriptions for the Red Army. It hadn't been easy to get passed over for active duty, but the thing of it was, once he got in front of the army doctor, who could hardly be seen as an expert of mind disorders, Oleg had fallen sullen and couldn't pull himself out of this state for the longest time. They thought he was faking it, so they tossed him in solitary confinement for a week. The bare fluorescent light tube was left on all the while, and they fed him crackers and water once a day, along with meting out good thrashings on picking up his food tray. When they finally reexamined him medically speaking, all Oleg could do was shake like a leaf with the kind of look in his eyes that must've made them concerned he could lose it in the heat of battle and get some of his comrades killed. Oleg had confided in me all of this, also that the truth of it had been, he felt enraged at his country for going to war to protect for all intents the Stalinist purges and the starvation regimen of peasants. Add to that the Red Army torturing him, and he'd wanted to fly across the room and strangle that fat-faced doctor with gray skin, obviously from the man's carcass rarely throwing off a shadow in the light of day.

But things were different now, worse, much worse if that was possible, as just a couple months ago the Nazis had invaded the motherland in something called Operation Barbarossa. Hitler ignored the Molotov-Ribbentrop Nonaggression Pact signed with Russia, which also included secret provisions for the Nazis and the Red Army to share the spoils of Poland. It had been in the coffeehouses in Moscow that I learned about the divvying of Poland between my government and the Nazis. The pit that formed in my stomach on those occasions had too often re-intensified on hearing other stories of the Goat-faced Murderer ordering hundreds of thousands of Poles to concentration camps in Siberia. At least, that would no longer be a blot on our collective Russian souls. The Germans earlier this summer had driven Russian troops from the area of Poland the Reds occupied. Oddly, out-of-control activity of the revolution's polymelian birth defect—multiple arms grown out of the beast's body to grab hold of people and purge, purge, purge—could be slowed only by the other nation inhabited with millions transformed into monsters who had even less use for Jews.

Outside the window Oleg may as well have been looking at German troops storming the lanes of Peredelkino. If not upon us right now, they were advancing rapidly out of the perimeters of the country toward Moscow. Everyone in Russia knew this. The state-controlled newspapers made sure of it. Stalin was using the situation to galvanize Russians to fight. We were losing hundreds of thousands in battle, millions it would turn out to be. Sitting still, staying put was a silent death march. "In a world gone mad, you are brave to be reluctant to take up arms, my love," I finally said.

He turned round, until facing me. His eyes had that familiar look of a hawk, but they were watery and the whites had gone geographic with red capillaries. "I don't want to leave you alone," he said.

Don't get me wrong, I didn't care for him going away to fight in a war bereft of righteousness on all sides. Oleg and I could simply protect our little corner of the world until they came to take it from us. Separate us from each other. Then we'd fight them. That was worth dying over. Us! I stood up and walked over next to him. I slipped a tissue out of my skirt's pocket, then wiped wetness off the ridges of his strong cheeks. "Whatever you decide to do, it will be a courageous act," I said. My mouth went dry. There was no answer I wanted to hear.

"This battle will never be won with guns," he said.

"Then don't use one unless you must to remain alive."

He nodded unsteadily. "Maybe I will try to lie low, act crazy again, even crazier than before. Then, hopefully I'll be able to stay here and protect you." A pause as if thinking. "It's ideas we must reclaim, and we must create new, good ones that reshape Russia. Katya, your stories do this. They must get published and read."

My dear Oleg right before my eyes worked out his dichotomy of love for a woman and love for his countrymen, even for his country. A reason bigger than Us suddenly floated in the air, and it smelled sweeter than had the fragrance of the white rose, for it included us, enveloped our dreams, not Stalin's or Hitler's. But the dryness persisting in my throat told me Oleg had to be free to make his own decision. "Don't worry about me, Oleg, or my stories. Besides, how would they get published in Russia as things are?"

"You must write them anyway, and when the time is right, Russia will read them."

Now, tears filled the rims of my eyes. "It will be hard to write with bombs dropping around our heads." If not on them, I dared not say. For bad or good, utterances written as well as spoken eerily had ways to make things come true, humans' affinity for self-fulfilling prophecy being a big part of why I punched the keys of my typewriter and all. Or were we simply too young and foolish to stop trying to shape Russia into a better place? Unable to hold Oleg's intent, unanswerable gaze, I looked absently away. Steadfast, the rose sat pertly atop its stem, but somehow in my heart the flower turned yellow and wilted. "Will you go?" I said at last, hardly above a whisper.

Oleg turned and peered through the window again. He said nothing.

I pictured Vasily, then Andrei and Konstantin, followed by Nestor, all friends killed in battle; they appeared as the last time I'd seen them alive: proud, smiling, smug with a glass of ale in hand, depressed, whatever, in their everyday dissident authenticity. Gone, they were all gone, and would never come back to plot a better Russia, to complicate and sweeten my days and nights, or Oleg's. No, I didn't want to lose Oleg that way, to a ditch with a bullet piercing his lungs, or his throat slit by some rabid Nazi, or by a young German man, the reluctant warrior used as a pawn like so many Russian men...and just a nod of

Oleg's head away from him becoming another diminutive chess piece too. Then again, had our friends figured out ways to avoid military service, would they have also skirted the purges? Would the two of us? Or would we simply be starved out like Marina Tsvetaeva?

The sting of this possibility remained fresh, as I had returned only four days ago from our demoralizing attempt to get Marina Tsvetaeva and Valentin Parnakh jobs with the Soviet Literature Fund. The first day in Chistopol, Marina and Valentin filled out applications, turned them in to the receptionist, and we sat in the spartan waiting area until they asked us to leave and closed the office. Several times I'd insisted on speaking with the man Pasternak had said would be our best bet, though not a good one at all, for someone amenable to hiring them, Viktor Pechkin, but this Pechkin never showed himself. On the second day, Valentin got hired on as a doorman. Marina would have nothing of him refusing to take the job, though he would've if for a moment he thought they might otherwise give it to her. That Valentin made clear. In his interview they told him the position would under no circumstances go to Marina, and what's more, he would be held responsible for getting it and then turning it down. Torturously, Marina never spoke to anyone other than the skinny-assed receptionist, who told her in drab monotone that her application would be taken under consideration in "due time." Due time! Anyone could look at Marina and determine this was a commodity in short supply. It had been all I could do to restrain myself from formally implicating Pasternak, using his name to attract an audience with Viktor Pechkin. But getting the Pasternaks or myself exiled or purged hung in the air like a knife. The receptionist coolly had told me shortly after we arrived that people with the Literature Fund knew I was Pasternak's writing protégé. Every time a door opened and someone walked into the reception area, I half expected it to be the horrible Vladimir Stavski, head of the Union of Soviet Writers, and his goons, coming to take me back to Peredelkino and confront Pasternak for supporting the pariah of pariahs, Marina Tsvetaeva. Instead, I had taken the train back home, and Valentin had driven Marina to Yelabuga. What could she do there but wither away along with her son? Valentin was now back in Chistopol opening doors for the literati. Good for him, truly. Ha. Far as I recalled, Survival of the Luckier never appeared in Darwin's or Marx's writings.

"It's Pasternak, and he's got someone with him."

The sound of Oleg's voice brought me back to the present. He walked from the window over to the front door, then opened it. As Pasternak entered with a grave expression, I thought it probably had to do with my deciding to leave the dacha and move in with Oleg, or his displeasure over my failing to help Marina Tsvetaeva get a job, or disappointment in the quality of my manuscript or something, that is, until this waxen-faced, handsome young man with narrow shoulders and a sunken chest who looked to be about Oleg's and my age stepped beside Pasternak. The young man rocked on his feet shakily, as if he may collapse onto the floor any second. Pasternak introduced us to Mur Tsvetaeva, Marina's son. Not extending a hand in greeting when Oleg held his hand out, Mur's lips cracked open slightly, as though it was impossible for him to be happy in the least.

"Please, please, sit down," I said, gesturing toward the table with the white rose on it, our only table. Quickly, I went over and lifted my typewriter off it, then set the typewriter onto the floor. I drew Mur and Pasternak glasses of water from the tap and brought the drinks over to them. While pulling a chair from near the kettle stove over to the table and sitting down, I noticed Oleg walk over and lean against the countertop in the kitchen. Clearly, he needed some space between himself and the rest of us. I could feel him still inwardly churning from the question of his service to Mother Russia, to me, to his truest self. Or were the hairs bristling on my nape as much over my own future, with or without him staying here? I met Mur's troubled gray eyes. "I'm terribly sad your mother didn't get a job in Chistopol; maybe I could've done more to help." Pausing, I glanced at Pasternak, whose expression gave nothing more away. "I'm sorry for not getting to talk to a man named Pechkin that could've hired her if he wanted to."

"It doesn't matter," Mur muttered. "My mother said you people could help me."

I shot a look at Oleg, who had gone from pensive to pasty, the whiteness of darkness and dread. I must've looked the same way. He nodded slightly or tilted his head toward Mur, I couldn't be sure. "We'll help you if we can," I said, more vagrancy in my tone than I would've liked.

Without another word, Mur slipped a piece of paper out of his shirt pocket, unfolded and placed the note on the table, then turned the writing to face me.

I read the almost perfect cursive script:

> *Dearest Mur,*
> *Forgive me, but to go on would be worse. I am gravely ill; this is not me anymore. I love you passionately. Do understand that I could not live anymore. Tell Papa and Alya, if you ever see them, that I loved them to the last moment—*

My eyes flooded, making the words unreadable. I used the same tissue I'd wiped away Oleg's tears with to soak up enough of mine to go on.

> *...and tell them I found myself in a trap.*

I wanted to say something, but no coherent thoughts came. Not only my mind, my emotions and spirit, too, were swamped, sloshed around aimlessly looking for answers to questions that didn't exist—as Oleg had done at the window most of the morning. It freaked me out about Oleg having faked it with the army doctor by acting crazy until he became crazy, sort of, anyway. Sometimes your boat sank so fast you were on the bottom of the black ocean before anything could be done about it.

Oleg brought a chair over and sat down beside me, his hand then laid gently on top of mine. The electric, searching expression in his eyes indicated he needed comforting as much as he hoped to lift me from the depths.

I turned my hand over and gave his hand a good squeeze, a signal I was with him even as he probably silently chided himself for not having insisted on going forward with the forgery of "The Stalin Epigram" to help Marina Tsvetaeva secure a job.

"Mur already knows Zinaida and I would have him stay with us, but Marina told him you said that you would help him if and when the time came," Pasternak said in a miserable tone, looking directly at me.

I would've taken Pasternak's hand in mine too, had Oleg and myself not been so fragile. Everything about Pasternak gave away that he blamed himself for not doing more to help Marina. We were all swamped. I hadn't told Oleg of my promise to bring Marina and/or Mur into our home, so Oleg's head moving up and down along with a squeeze of my hand didn't lift me, but righted some of my listing in this strong current. I looked at the white rose again for several seconds, and then met Mur's eyes behind the flower. "Yes, of course, you can live with us for as long as you like," I said.

"By all means," Oleg said.

Mur nodded. "Thank you." His brow furrowed until those thick onyx eyebrows that looked so much like his mom's almost met. "But I do not have a work permit that's good in this district..." His voice tapered off. "I don't have one at all; the Goat-faced Murderer's people revoked it."

The next minute or so passed by cold and walled-off as winter, but the heat of August surrounded us outside.

Pasternak cleared his throat, then finally said, "Maybe it's a blessing in disguise not to have regular work, Mur.

"Stalin needs troops to fight the Nazis more than he desires to purge dissidents. But I'm afraid he will act with impunity on young men, and old, who he sees as sitting on the sidelines. Despite the Goat-faced Murderer's methods, the war could bring us together and end the purges. I am hopeful of this." Pasternak's tone took on some verve. "Once Hitler is pushed out of the motherland, we will be victors and Russians one and all. Even Stalin will have a hard time disputing this."

"Too much Russian blood will have been spilled for him to take any other position—is that what you think about this poet gone mad, Stalin?" Oleg said hotly.

Pasternak nodded. "Something close to that."

"Humph," Oleg grunted. "You're a Cassandra."

"We must try to do what seems impossible for anything good to happen," Pasternak said.

Oleg opened his mouth but came up short of saying anything.

"Three days from now I'll be heading to Moscow for deployment in a munitions factory. I asked for a field command, but my bum knee kept me from getting it." Pasternak looked at Mur again before going on. "If you come along I could probably get you some choice in the kind of duty you'll have."

"I want a Maxim-Tokarev machine gun in my hands, and to be on the front lines." Mur's eyes flared like burning coals in a funeral pyre—his own.

"You hate the death of your mother more than the Germans," I said without thinking. "Get hold of yourself."

"Yes, you're still in shock, Mur; be reasonable with your request for service," Oleg said. He slipped his hand from mine. "Pasternak, I admire your courage," Oleg added.

Pasternak indicated he was only doing what most anyone would do, then placed a hand on Mur's shoulder. "Your mother wanted you to live. You must only fight to stay alive and keep Russia alive."

"Certainly," Mur said, though his eyes still sparked with the nihilist lust of Keres.

With this undertow of war pulling Oleg, Pasternak, and Mur away, a tsunami above washed me onto some desolate shore. What if Oleg's so-called honor drove him to the front lines? He wasn't a killer. That's why he'd gone into a hole of depression with the army doctor after shooting at targets, much less human beings. Should he survive the battles, Oleg may well return to me a living dead man. Unable to abide this, I created my own little Homeric fantasy: If Hitler's troops could quickly get to Moscow and assassinate the Goat-faced Murderer, and then the Red Army rebound to defeat the Germans, now that would be making Pasternak's impossible-possible come to pass. An end to the purges and war, indiscriminant killing, at least for many years.

As it was, though, assuming we Reds wound up the victors, Stalin wouldn't miss a beat recharging his purges. Pasternak should know this. In the end, he and I were poets, and Stalin was a poet gone foul. What would be left of me without poetry after for so long drinking it down as water from a wellspring?

I would become like Mur or Marina Tsvetaeva or, God forbid, Stalin, the Goat-faced Murderer himself. Disdain, like the metallic taste of a coin, filled my mouth. Pasternak walked such a fine line in never full-on confronting Stalin that he couldn't, or wouldn't, intuit how far gone things were for Russia.

I looked Oleg directly in the eyes once more; then another of the tsunami's waves crashed. These would be the hardest, most necessary words I'd ever spoken: "You must go with Pasternak."

"I fear you're right." Oleg's lips pressed together tightly.

"What kind of service will you ask for?" I probed.

He thought for a long moment, then a little nod as if giving himself permission. "Field medic."

I forced a slim smile. "Good choice, my love." I fixed my eyes on Pasternak again. "You'll save more Russian lives by completing *Doctor Zhivago* and getting the world to read it, instead of making bullets."

"I will make bullets for now. *Zhivago* wouldn't be publishable anyway, probably not for a long while."

You'll never know unless you attempt to get it into print! I fought against blurting.

"In fact, Katya," Pasternak went on, "you'd do a better job of keeping out of harm's way until this war is over by working with me at the munitions plant, maybe serving as a nurse in a Moscow hospital or the like."

We both knew my scholarship to Writer's School in Moscow kept me out of civilian conscription to provide for the military, but it wouldn't keep me from the purges or exile. A petal fell off the rose onto the table, and the gyre of my inner ocean stilled some. "I will write, and try to get my stories published. This is how I will do, how did you say it, 'what seems impossible for something good to happen.'"

Pasternak carefully lifted the petal and held it in his open palm. "Then I'll give you edits on your manuscript before leaving for Moscow," he said.

I had wondered off and on whether he would do this since I'd left him to fend for himself with Miss Zinaida and Yevgeni. "Of course, you will," I said. I picked up the petal and brought it to my nose, then slowly inhaled its dewy perfume. "And if you'd like I'll still be your first reader on drafts of *Zhivago*." My knowing inflection carried something like the delicate renewal of a dying rose.

CHAPTER SEVENTEEN

Anastasie walked across the expansive minimalist gallery with her art on the walls, and her creamy face blushed tiny plums, a rising of sultry stars, as she stopped directly in front of Frazier. They drew each other into an embrace. Her small, pert breasts pushed against his chest. Spiders crawled from his heart all the way to the tips of his fingers, the pads of his feet. On resting his head on her shoulder, he glanced down her slender back and noticed that no wedding band encircled his ring finger. What's more, eyeglasses weren't perched on his nose and he could see perfectly well. *This has to be a dream*, he told himself.

"You take care of where love is not before come to me," she said in her delicious French accent.

They kissed passionately, almost cheesy given the circumstances, French style, their tongues plunging into one then the other's mouths. The longer they explored the inside of their throats, the more he fell self-conscious. It wasn't that he minded his and Anastasie's PDA amidst the crowd admiring her art; the tantalizing spiders swarmed him more and more, and each of these tiny creatures had eight legs. He hadn't ended anything with Margaret, best he could remember. Wasn't she on her way to get him out of jail or something? And even though she'd sounded too heady when he'd called for help, definitely her not having come from the black electricity that gave him the all-overs now, she had excitedly divulged her idea for a novel centered on the Tunisian poet Yassine Lotfi Khaled. *Yes.* That was part of what bothered *and* enlivened him. Even in his sleep it still did. Margaret may start writing! But she was stealing his subject matter, at least a major thread of the story that had been incubating in his mind. Maybe they could work together on it? Momentarily, the spiders stood motionless. There would be no collaboration unless Margaret could unleash this feeling in him. And him in her.

As they came out of their kiss, Frazier met Anastasie's sapphire eyes. "I'm here before I should be," he said.

"You arrive good time. I am true?"

"Awake, I love Margaret and you."

"In dream things made right."

Weirdness to the extreme, Frazier fairly lucidly reasoned at this sort of Jungian dream analysis going on between them. Perhaps truer love coursed through veins of the swarming spiders, and could never amount to anything but misty fog between himself and the flesh-and-blood women in his life. Compared to this, waking reality held too much history as well as prospects about the future for spiders to spin webs glistening with the dew of his hot blood. Maybe a more transcendent knowing in the awakened subconscious could be mined from the cavern of sleep. "We're in Paris, are we not?" he said.

Anastasie nodded.

"Can we take a walk along the Seine holding hands?" he went on. Surely, he couldn't be held accountable to what might happen after that in some dream.

Lacing her fingers with his, she said, "But first I show you, I've going deeper with words. It become art."

As Anastasie and Frazier made their way across the room, her fans stepped aside, clearing a path. On the last of them parting, he stopped and squeezed her hand a little harder than affectionately. Before the two of them, on the wall, hung a large canvas of charcoal and black airbrushed bold lines with swirls intermingled among fragile, haunting shadows. The piece all at once drew you in and sent you away. The image was roughly the shape of a book, and the cover had written on it *The Grapes of Wrath by John Steinbeck.* His grasp of her hand eased, though he continued to hold on. "I suppose the fact I've never told you how much this book matters to me means you got this information, shall we say, from the universe," he said.

She smiled warmly and took from her gabardine's front pocket his wedding band. She brought his left hand up between them, and then slipped the ring onto the proper finger. "The right time for our love started way before you and Margaret were married," she said.

Somehow he knew Anastasie meant the kind of love madly, wisely scurrying those spiders, if not shared between the three of them, knowable by learning some language without syllables or letters. "Our love," as the French artist had put it, must be available for everyone who dared to question *why* while traversing shadowlands. *Wasn't it?* "It's a shame the best we can do is try to put down what it means to be human in words and pictures," he said, with a gesture at her painting. "No offense intended, just the opposite. Your work is hauntingly strong, Anastasie."

"It's not the best we can do, but it may be all we can do while conscious," she said, ignoring his compliment.

They left the painting and went outside. It started to rain when they crossed Quai Voltaire to stand along the bank of the Seine. This overused icon for romance couldn't be topped, Frazier felt more than thought while looking at gentle waves in the water, hearing them lap against the concrete bulkhead. As a faint awareness of pride in the quality of this dream came to him, the river turned to stone. Without another word, they went over and lay down on its surface anyway. Hard and uncomfortable, this was no place to leave each other, or awaken from alone. Raindrops became pebbles falling from the sky, as if pinging marbles dropped from the failure of Freud's id. More than "basic instincts" or "pleasure drives" fell from this Paris dreamscape, and rose from the recesses of Frazier's together with Anastasie's psyches—seemingly, the mystery of creation, or love itself refused to be pelted to death.

"Your wife, Margaret, is here for you," Anastasie said, suddenly in a man's muffled tone, as though coming through a PA system with a short in the amplifier. Frazier held an arm across his face to shield his eyes from the falling pebbles, and took a look around. Margaret couldn't be spotted anywhere. Anastasie said it again, in that same masculine voice.

Slowly, hypnagogia replaced his semi-lucid dream state, until his mind fell fuzzy, he felt his eyeglasses resting on the end of his nose, and the scratchy PA system clarified. He recognized the voice as that of one of the protestors he'd been jailed with, Donny Johansson, the rotund fellow with the *Jesus Was A Nonviolent Peacemaker* T-shirt on. The slumbering man opened his eyes and looked on Donny's round face directly over him. The Seine River of stone had morphed back into the concrete floor of their cell that he'd fallen asleep on in utter exhaustion.

"The cop came by and told me you'd be released into your wife's custody as soon as you woke up." Donny chuckled, and his jowls jiggled. "Hope you don't mind, 'cause I shook you pretty good a few times and you still wouldn't snap out of it. You must'a been having one hell of a wet dream or something."

Being behind bars with political activists never failed to bring a few of the good guys into the slumbering man's life. It had been years ago, but some of the best fun he'd had involved trading stories with fellow civilly disobedient detainees. Come to find out, Donny was a human rights attorney who represented several of the prisoners cleared for release at Guantanamo Bay, Cuba, but, nevertheless, were being held indefinitely. Even more endearing were the jokes Donny had told, none of them political, all of them self-deprecating: chubby people have sex lives too, or exercise is overrated, or who cares as long as the bar stool doesn't crumple to the floor underneath one's weight. He reminded the slumbering man of his good friend Buckminster, only with better values, a big man comfortable in his formidable bulk. "Or something." In one motion the slumbering man grasped Donny's hand, and the big man assisted him onto his feet.

First the slumbering man then Donny called out for a guard to come, but all they got in return were echoes of their voices off the jailhouse's metal walls.

"The acoustics are perfect," Donny said. "Sort of punk rock reverb."

The slumbering man bounced his eyebrows Groucho Marx style, then in a righteous, gravelly, nasal semblance to Bob Dylan broke out with "Maggie's Farm." Before the end of the first line, Donny added his off-key baritone and, pretty soon, several inmates joined in. In the cell across from the slumbering man and Donny, the tattooed young man with a Mohawk who had locked arms with Frazier in front of BofA, sang the loudest of all. The slumbering man wondered whether the young man held any animosity toward him for being a non-flopper out in the streets. They hadn't said a word to each other since being locked up in here. At the end of the song, the young man smiled broadly, which to the slumbering man looked as though his mouth was full of white foam, or vanilla cake.

"Mind if I lead us in the next one?" the young man said.

"That seems right," the slumbering man said, before anyone else had a chance to respond.

They sang David Rovics' "Behind the Barricades," and then went right into a newer Rovics tune called "Who Would Jesus Bomb," a satire about so-called Christians killing without remorse for "peace." No matter if you hadn't heard the songs before. Those singing half a line behind added to the reverb rather nicely, it occurred to the slumbering man. Finally, a beefy, no-necked cop came ambling along the cellblock, and the song immediately turned into cheers sprinkled with jeers. The cop faced the slumbering man and Donny's cell, then nodded toward the end of the hall. The door of steel bars slid open.

"Frazier Pickett the Third," the cop said in a disinterested tone.

"That's me." He and Donny verbally exchanged email addresses, assured each other they would stay in touch. "Do you have someone working on getting you out of here?" the slumbering man then said.

"A lawyer friend from church," Donny said.

As the slumbering man stepped into the hallway, the cop took hold of his arm. Looking through his lenses at the young man with the Mohawk, Frazier said, "Do you have someone coming for you?"

The young man shook his head. "That's okay, man. I don't want to give them the pleasure of getting hold of my bail money. I'll do the time."

Years ago that's what the slumbering man had done when locked up for civil disobedience. Once or twice Margaret had been right there with him serving a week or so of time. He was glad she would be out there for him now. He missed her, and he wanted to give Mattie and Doug hugs, then tell them all about being a jailbird for justice.

The cop tightened his grip on the slumbering man's arm, then led them toward the cellblock's exit. A smirk came across the slumbering man's lips as he heard the young man in the Mohawk start the inmates in Woody Guthrie's "This Land Is Your Land." The chorus was a cacophony of keys and pitches, and everyone sang on time with the lyrics.

Less than ten minutes later, he signed for his sequestered belongings, a belt, wallet, thirty-two dollars in cash, and his iPhone, which he received in a manila envelope through a chute below double-paned glass with chicken wire that had a far from unattractive, if severe, woman in a blue uniform behind it. He pushed open double doors and walked into the receiving area. The doors made a gear-grinding sound on closing. Spotting Margaret across the room, he slightly tilted his head back to look through his lenses again.

Extending her arms, she walked toward him with a luscious smile on her naturally pouty lips, not at all unlike Anastasie had come for him in his dream. Her full, round breasts pressed close against his chest. When they embraced, he set his eyes on his wedding ring, and even in the bad fluorescent light, it gleamed up at him from his finger. He'd always liked his and Margaret's simple gold bands. "Thanks for bailing me out."

"I'm proud of you, Frazier."

Easing his head back just enough, he kissed her. Her fleshy lips didn't feel cheesy, and they didn't need a French kiss to probe one another. Their truth had millions of words for the past, and none at all. The spiders ran wild in him. "Let's go home," he said.

"Maybe not so fast. I got a sitter for the kids." She winked. "Besides, there's something happening across the street I think you'll want to be a part of...make that, we'll both want to."

As they went outside the police station, Frazier spotted across the street in a park twenty or so of the protestors who had been in Union Square. A few of them wore bandages on their arms or heads, and several of the signs calling for justice in one form or another were bent or torn, and they'd been leaned against trees together with the backsides of park benches.

"They're the lucky ones who have people with the means and desire to bail them out of jail," Margaret explained. "They're here as a welcoming party for those getting released, and in solidarity for others still locked up."

"Wonderful, yes, let's join them," Frazier said. He noticed a couple of picnic tables set up with drinks and potluck food containers, replete with plasticware and paper cups. At another table, in front of laptop computers sat four people, one of whom happened to be the slender, young dishwater blond woman who had been next to him at the protest. He felt relieved to see her free. Partly, he wanted to introduce himself and Margaret to her, come to know her name. She had helped inspire him to get back into street action, and he was grateful for it. But the fact that Margaret wanted to be here, had obviously checked this scene out before entering the jailhouse, along with her what? full-on emotional availability reminiscent of their college days, kept the spiders tickling his insides. No, he would not make the introductions. Better not to tamper with this…this…*eternal moment.*

The young blonde raised an arm high and waved at him or—

"Hello, Margaret, good to see you come back here with my buddy at the protest," the young woman called out.

"Hi, Sophie." Margaret returned the wave, walked toward her. "Come on, Frazier, maybe they could use a couple of writers at the media center."

"Yes, maybe they could." He already felt alphabet characters sparking from the tips of his fingers through the laptop's keys that would compile letters to editors. Reports that would change the world for the better, even a little bit.

Sophie gave Frazier a warm smile as they shook hands and exchanged names. "I'm glad you're all right," she added. "They roughed you up something awful at the protest. What you did took the heat off me and showed me the way. Thanks."

"You're welcome. It only hurts on the inside and outside." He wasn't kidding; the cop's nightstick to the gut had blown his stomach up into one massive bruise. But he tried to hold himself without favoring the injury, mostly for Margaret's sake. The air suddenly fell riddled with holes that stippled his breathing. Margaret wouldn't be able to help herself from hovering over him. He didn't want mothering; the slumbering man needed a partner in getting the word out about the protest and its ongoing aftermath—precisely to oxygenate himself out of slumber.

Margaret gingerly placed her hand on his shoulder. "God, Frazier, that's terrible. Let's take you home and let you lie down, or maybe we should go to an emergency care center and get a doctor to take a look at you."

Every spider in his body pulled their legs underneath themselves. He looked over the top of his frames, and the park, the picnic tables, the people including Sophie and Margaret went smudgy and distant. His mind's eye returned to the dream about Anastasie, her art connecting so intensely with him, their eternal moment turning to stone. He partly wanted to blame Margaret for it. Why couldn't she stay connected with him long enough for the good stuff between them not to harden so quickly into rock? Maybe he would take her aside and spill his guts about the dream. Something had to crack them open before they could determine what lay inside. But was now the time? No, it just had been a dream; Anastasie hadn't contacted him. He only fantasized about her art as an ode to his beloved John Steinbeck's seminal contribution to literature, and the slumbering man's soul-map to common people, their dignity showing him the way toward his own. Quite possibly, he reasoned, the dream had been about his love affair with himself. And little more, if anything. It would be downright mean to slay Margaret with that dream, his poetic narcissism or whatever. The slumbering man knew he'd done it again. He felt alone.

✍

Upon placing her hand on Frazier's shoulder, Margaret had felt his deltoid tense unmercifully. Why couldn't he just accept a little TLC, not have to suck it up and act impregnable at times when he really could use some help? The closer they got the farther away she and Frazier became...make that *further* away (the odd thought flashed of Ken Kesey's Merry Pranksters riding around the country in his psychedelic bus named *Further*, because they were on a philosophical and spiritual trip more than a physical one). Maybe she would confront Frazier right here and now about getting so intimate with the French Artist that he "inspired" her to paint his favorite book by his favorite author. The boiling current flowing through her veins cooled and sort of turned to gray water as she mentally put the quotes around the word *inspired*. What was this about? Of course, she had failed her husband in never having done something as honestly cool as that for him. Maybe her novel could be the very thing, but she couldn't bring herself to take him aside and share her ideas about it. Not now. There would be a better time than this. Besides, the gray water turned black when she considered writing her novel for him more than for herself. *I can be such a narcissist when I think of actually authoring something. Maybe that's why I don't ever do it.*

"I want to stay here and help for a while," the slumbering man finally said.

Margaret removed her hand from his shoulder and managed a slim smile. "I'd like that too." She could've kicked herself for her tinny tone.

✍

Sophie and the salt-and-pepper-beard professorial-looking man beside her were all too happy to surrender their posts at laptops and catch some pizza or a cold cut sandwich and soda over at one of the food tables. "It should be pretty self-explanatory what to do," Sophie said to Frazier and Margaret, with a gesture at the laptop's screen. Then, the young blond woman and The Professor stood up and walked away. Mild embarrassment slivered through Frazier as they sat down. Without sharing another word, he knew Sophie and The Professor wanted a break from them, and Margaret's lowered gaze told him she understood the same.

The slumbering man looked through his lenses again, at the screen. The communications system was a Linux open-source piece of work that impressed him right away. All four laptops had been linked to a single "Media Peace Room" (versus a War Room, the slumbering man mentally noted) for

"Operation Get The Word Out On Bankster Bullies." Every letter or interview already sent to news outlets appeared on a list in real time. Another column contained media sources that hadn't been contacted yet. There were tabs for sample communiqués and proposed interview questions to ask protestors, the police, or bystanders. In the upper left portion of the screen was a live feed split between the exit for the jailhouse and the park. Frazier noticed himself and Margaret on the streaming video. The upper right area of the screen had what looked to be reruns of local news coverage of the protest, along with a live feed to CNN. A chop-top gold 1967 Cadillac with classic giant wings rolled across the lower portion of the screen with a message on its side panels: *Start by telling your story*. With a finger sliding across the touchpad, he positioned the arrow on the winged Caddie, and then gave it a click.

A blank page came up with the cursor blinking for the text to begin. He looked over the sidebar of media outlets where articles had already been submitted—*The New York Times*, *The New York Daily News*, *The New Yorker*, *The Boston Globe*, *Washington Post*, etc., the usual suspects for any self-respecting, enlightened activists to approach. Switching over to perusing the list of untapped sources, he almost chose the *Denver Post* for no particular reason, and then came close on *Sojourners Magazine*, a sympathetic progressive publication he often read. Possibly because of his love of slumber, or lingering tension with Margaret, or some legitimate writerly itch that hadn't been scratched, or a combination of all the above, on and on he scrolled into more obscure publications; until his eyes stopped on *The Mudville News*. This was the Monahans, Texas, newspaper he had grown up with and his family regularly read. He began typing:

> *Your longtime good neighbors, my hardworking brother-in-law together with his loving, also hardworking wife, and my sister, Derek and Felecia Samuels, are close to having their ranch foreclosed on by the bank because of a fraudulently represented mortgage they were sold down the river on by some boys and girls wearing tight-fitting suits, if you know what I mean. Which having grown up myself in Monahans, there's no doubt you are certain of my drift.*
>
> *Now, I'm way up yonder in New York City, and I'm glad I'm here, because day before yesterday at Union Square I got beat on by police and then thrown in jail along with a bunch of other good folks who took to the streets carrying signs and singing songs in peaceful protest of Bank of America's shenanigans. I know many readers of* The Mudville News

don't think much of us northeastern liberals, especially
transplanted ones like me, but I believe you will agree we are
all in this together. It's time for a moratorium on foreclosures
of these funny money mortgages.
  Here's what happened more particularly....

Frazier hadn't laid something down as fluidly in so long he couldn't remember the last time. These people he knew, and by just putting things out there—truths below facts of the protest, and the authenticity of small-town Texans—he felt himself creating magic. By staying close to the ground, he flew high. Writing about big things in a small way had been missing from his work. For the first time he admitted to himself, in the past he'd written about little things in a little way, endearing, earthy, but where was the audience for this? Damn few readers could fit inside his desk's bottom drawer, the crypt for his old manuscripts. He put the finishing touches on the piece, and then gave it a once-over. On a couple of red underlines from spell check he accepted the changes, and other than that his editorial felt like pure sex. He clicked on the Send button; then with a swooshing sound from the laptop's speakers, his article was gone.

Leaning back on the bench, he looked over at Margaret, who went at the keys of her laptop with something akin to passion, and a puckish grin. Had he ever seen her quite like this before? She had the verve of the girl he'd protested with in college, but the wizened creases in the lines cresting alongside her mouth, the hunger in her gray eyes told him she burned with some kind of new fire.

✍

When Margaret had sat down at the laptop, she made up her mind to quit stepping all over herself with Frazier, and for that matter with her own self, their marriage, and just let it rip, at least for a while. Then, see how things went. It had scared her not to outline her story, think it through before starting in. She'd wanted to hate Anastasie Moreau's spontaneity, which could be seen by anyone, even a fool, in her art. The truth of it was, she wished to be more like her. That's when Nana's words from her last letter had come to mind like some postscript not for Margaret's article, but her future: *Look for those instances in which you want to go one way but instead you go another. These are the times you find out about your essence. Always go down the authentic road, the one you choose in an instant after trying your best to talk yourself out of it.* With that, she'd taken a slow breath, pushed her ample breasts out, and started attacking the keys.

Margaret felt as if she was having an affair with the page; her heart thrummed, the words came easily. She'd gone with submitting to the *Chicago Sun-Times*, as it probably had the largest readership of any outlets still available.

Go right to the top, that's what the Comrade had told her since she was old enough to remember. And grabbing the hem of Paul Revere's proverbial blue coat, she took her revolutionary words to the American people, well, the residents of Evanston, Illinois, and the surrounding area anyway. All of the facts were right, and her comparisons to patriot mythology, the call to be mature, nonviolent, evolved citizen activists, not simply flag-waving simpletons, brought her message alive…but something human was missing. If only she had been at the protest and in jail with Frazier. She needed to know these people, and she only had old memories of the student protests she'd been in. His bumbling, dumbling stroll through life brought him to Union Square right on time, Margaret told herself. Her business suit day at Harpers, her getting the kids to school and picking them up on time, had kept her from putting the words down that by Rocinante's ass she knew Frazier could get onto the page. If and when he ever went to write, which of course he was doing right now. No, he couldn't write for her. She had to do that. Inwardly she stiffened at the thought of him becoming her literary mentor, a muse, maybe, but not that. Tears welled in her eyes, and she blinked them back with little success. She kept pressing the keys.

𝄢

Seeing rivulets trickle along Margaret's cheeks drew Frazier closer to her. In his experience, until you made yourself or someone else wet, your writing went lacking, pure and simple. Flying with your pen was one thing, crying another entirely. He used to make Margaret sob with his best stuff. Granted, his *Mudville News* article wasn't at that level, though near enough for a little soaring above treetops. "Stay with it, Margaret," he said. "Your emotion is good for the page." *And for us!* The rock of them together flowed water like a newly cut amethyst geode. It sparkled, and the thing of it was, Frazier still looked through his lenses.

"Damn." She laid her palms over the keys, while setting her eyes intently on Frazier. "I'm such a top-down writer…a top-down person. All this blubbering is because I need to go deeper, not because I am."

"You already are by knowing that, wanting it," he said, using a soft tone. "Plus, you're probably being too hard on yourself." He gestured at her screen. "Mind if I take a look?"

She shook her head unsteadily. "But I don't think I can take any literary criticism right now." She turned the laptop to face him.

Her opening line reeled him in like a Rio Grande catfish snared all the way down to the gills. She started right in with the riot police going ballistic on protestors. This was good, real good, offices held accountable at city hall and Homeland Security he didn't even know existed. She also dared to take shots at the FBI and CIA possibly being on hand filming everything, Big Brother style.

Then came the allusion to patriots, as in the American revolutionaries were a bunch of ragtag working people and gentleman farmers, whereas the BofA protest held the beginnings of a 21st-century patriot stand—because the banks were taking us all down, those who worked for a living, and the poor, that is. Not the boys and girls weekending in the Hamptons. He looked over the top of the screen at her and noticed she'd wiped her tears away. "You're teaching me," he said. "Thanks for sharing this, really."

"Okay, okay." She held up a hand. "I can take a compliment." A pause. "But I wish I could write human beings like you do." Then, Margaret said something she hadn't planned on at all. "Do you think you can wait for me to learn how?"

In succession and then all together, he thought of the stone river, spiders flushing in the dream of Anastasie and reality of his wife, their water-filled amethyst cracking open. "You are ahead of me and I am ahead of you." He felt as if his words were flowing from the geode. "You are behind me and I am behind you. Therefore, there is no race to catch up in; there is cooperation and admiration between us, or a self-made illusion it seems."

✐

She thought for a long moment. Anastasie was no figment of the imagination, but somehow Margaret and Frazier were really talking, not without the Frenchwoman, beyond her, over her shoulder to each other. No, Margaret wouldn't bring up the painting of *The Grapes of Wrath*, not now anyway. What's more, Frazier was such a frigging poet; the beauty of his words sent something without a name tingling through her entire body. "I've been afraid to look from the bottom up, and you've been afraid to look from the top down," she finally said.

✐

He let those words sink in, rolled them over in his mind. The *Mudville News* article sort of haunted him now. On making surprising, yet somehow all too familiar, sense of things, he said, "I need to visit my kinfolks...and stay there until I can tell them it's okay, that I can look from anywhere and still love them...tell myself."

She smiled warmly. "I think I would do well to try that with my family."

He shrugged as if to say, "Who would've thought?" Then she did too.

Out of the corner of Frazier's eye, he noticed the section of her laptop's screen streaming CNN live fill with what looked to be tens of thousands of people in the streets. He moved the arrow onto the sound icon for that feed, clicked the mouse pad, and then turned the laptop so both of them could see it.

A CNN newswoman's voice came from the computer: "Here in Tunisia as a result of the self-immolation of a street vendor named Mohammed Bouazizi, who set himself on fire in protest of the harsh dictatorship of President Zine El Abidine Ben Ali, a largely nonviolent protest of thousands taking to the streets is occurring…"

Frazier and Margaret locked on each other with saucer eyes, then looked again at the screen. It seemed neither of them could find the right words for this, and their thoughts were spinning.

The broadcast continued, "The army is moving in. There are casualties already, and no one I've talked to can give me a number of dead or wounded. The protestors are calling this a revolution. They say they aren't leaving the streets until their demands are met. They want the current government to step down, a dissolution of the political police, dissolution of the RCD, the ruling political party, release of political prisoners, and they want democratic elections to be held. More people are coming to the streets all the time. This looks serious."

Frazier and Margaret looked at each other again.

"The spark," he said.

She licked her dry lips. "I hope the poet Yassine Lotfi Khaled is okay. He's probably over there lighting matches."

He smiled, though with an expression of concern. "Bottom up, huh."

She nodded. "Would you like to collaborate on a book about it?"

"Yes, but not until I get back from Texas."

This time, she nodded a bit stiffly.

He waited for her to say something about paying another visit to Boston and her family, or getting closer to the poet, or the people of Tunisia, those she would write about. But Sophie and The Professor returned for another turn in The Peace Room, and nothing was said by Margaret about this, or anything on how they might create a book that could make a real difference. Instead, she let on with excitement over getting something written and in the hands of a good "industry player" like her beloved Harpers.

⌀

Inwardly, Margaret felt herself ignoring Nana's advice about not chasing your literary tail to seek a publishing deal. Time was of the essence now. Yes, time was of the essence.

⌀

When Frazier got to LaGuardia Airport and stood in front of the kiosk showing international flights, he took a good long look at departures to Paris, all the while fingering his e-ticket to Midland International Airport. Maybe he had arrived early on purpose, maybe not; at any rate, he had a couple hours to make up his mind before missing his flight to Texas. He wouldn't check his bag onto the plane quite yet.

Ten minutes later while sitting in an airport bar with a half-drunk Beefeater gin and tonic in front of him, on his iPhone he navigated to Anastasie's website. The screen flashed up her painting of *The Grapes of Wrath by John Steinbeck*.

CHAPTER EIGHTEEN

Snowflakes swirled outside the window of my room at the Writers Building in Moscow. It seemed as if the city sat underneath some vector of an hourglass that curved outward and upward into the gray sky, with frozen white sand falling, falling onto incredulously sublime linen sheets—two-faced Janus's cold bed for looking into the future and the past, or for a dual-headed Babylonian bird of prosperity, Mammon Ra, tamed only by Jewish wealth hoarders as far as Nazis and Stalinists were concerned—but whatever one's druthers, Lavrushinski Street was hidden below, frozen through to its cobblestone bones. The longer it snowed, the more chances increased that German troops would not make it all the way to Moscow, may just lay down and die before killing Oleg or Mur or Pasternak or Yevgeni or Miss Zinaida or even one more Russian. Hitler had pushed his boys beyond most of their food rations, had marched them through the soles of their boots and rotten socks into frostbite. The longer it snowed the farther it kept Oleg away from me in the battlefield, and the bitter cold or a German bayonet could kill him too. Word had it our troops were more aptly built for these winters if not better outfitted. Truth of the matter, our boys were freezing to death and starving too, though at a little slower rate; what food there was came from Russian silos and corrals—which were still mostly controlled by Russians—and locals readily provided shelter for our troops. But more of the time, our boys were in the harsh elements, chasing down the Germans or retreating to recover from high casualties and lick their wounds. The Nazis had stooped to put trainload after trainload of German Jews into occupied Russian villages, and sent many of them in military uniforms without ordnance onto the front lines, to be slaughtered. If it stopped snowing and the Nazis made it here, Stalin may or may not fall, but one thing for certain was fierce anti-Semitism would converge on all Jews, German and Russian. We would be dead; nothing of this war and our government's activities had convinced me otherwise. Pasternak could no longer even get his poetry sympathetic to our military in print. He'd indicated on his last visit with me that the editor-in-chief of Pravda newspaper told him to publish him now was a question of "high politics." If

Stalin was going to lose millions of good Russians in this war, win or lose, why not get rid of his liberal intelligentsia, pain-in-the-ass Jews. All that, and more, I feared should the hourglass's sands of time run out too soon, or last too long. I cannot tell you how much of this December morning I'd spent staring absently through my window at the falling snow, when the knocks came on my door.

"Who is it?" I called out, standing up from my writing desk.

"Solomon Mikhoels. Some of us are having a meeting in the lounge, and we wanted to invite you."

Solomon Mikhoels...what on earth was the prominent Yiddish actor and director doing here at the Writers Building? I'd never before known him to darken these doors. I liked him well enough, would cross paths with him at the coffeehouses every now and then. Besides, he'd been at the table in our home the last time I'd seen my parents and brother alive. Solomon the dissident organizer, and a ruddily handsome one at that. I walked over and unlatched my door, then opened it. He was unshaven, and his eyes had dark half-moons beneath them. "Good, thank you," I said. "I'll be along shortly."

As I went back across the room and lifted off the desk a large brown envelope containing my manuscript, all polished and ready to go to the publisher—as if there existed one in Russia which would give my work the time of day—it ate away at my insides that a strapping man like Mikhoels wasn't out on the front lines alongside Oleg. For the last several months, other than blatant state propaganda, not only the written word but plays and films hadn't gone anywhere either. Muzzled, artists who otherwise questioned the state may as well pick up guns, or a woman like myself could go make bullets alongside Pasternak in the munitions factory. Yes, this meeting better be the start of something that had a good go at making a positive difference, or what else was there to do but join Pasternak? My arms felt like sausages hanging from meat hooks as I walked over and placed my manuscript underneath the mattress. Once out in the hallway, I locked the door, then headed downstairs.

When I entered the lounge, I stopped and panned the gathering. On two sofas and several chairs arranged in a big circle sat well-known poets Itzik Fefer, Leib Kvitko, the novelist David Bergelson, Emilia Teumin, an influential editor who had also been at our home that night long ago with my family; there were others I'd met but didn't know well, a few I had no idea of their relevance, and Solomon Mikhoels, who on making eye contact with me stood up, gestured at one of the sofas with an open seat next to Itzik Fefer. I had admired Fefer's work until, even before the war, he started writing pabulum, often published in the state's oracle magazine, *Novy Mir*. Smiling sort of sorely at bald-headed Itzik Fefer, with his round face and spectacles made of circular lenses, I sat down. Solomon Mikhoels floridly introduced me as the daughter of heroes for the dissident movement, Dimitri and Marfa Ivashov, and as the bright writing protégé of Boris Pasternak. Ugh. Actors could really pour it on when they wanted to. He piqued me more than a little by going on in some sort of avuncular tone that we'd known each other since I was a little girl brash enough to be at meetings of dissidents and great thinkers.

"I am a woman now," I spoke up.

He held up a hand of surrender. "Yes, forgive me, that is perfectly clear to see," he said, dropping the paternity from his voice. He said a few words about each person here, even those he knew I was familiar with.

Then, he got down to business. "We're here to discuss forming the Jewish Anti-Fascist Committee. As you know the Nazis are closing in on Moscow. They're no more than a day or two away unless the Red Army can stiffen resistance." A pause, as if to let that sink in. "Quite frankly, our army is out of money. The committee will write and speak in a language most all the world will sympathize with, including and especially American and European capitalists. They need Russia to beat back the Germans in the worst way. Simply put, we'll raise funds from Jews and capitalists worldwide to end Hitler's Holocaust."

Partly, I wanted to ask whether Pasternak had been invited to this. It would be right up his slew. But I needed to be here on my own merits, not as merely some conduit to the most influential Russian writer of them all. If the latter ended up being true, you wouldn't find me as a card-carrying member of the Jewish Anti-Fascist Committee. I liked what was being said, though; maybe we could make our pens and our mouths count for something that saved lives during war. Better to just listen for now.

"Not a bad way to keep us out of Stalin's purges, at least for the duration of the war," Emilia Teumin said. "We can purchase our safety with Stalin, but it cannot be on good intentions alone. He'll want to see the cash."

"Agreed," Itzik Fefer said. "That's just it, and I've already received fat checks from Jews and some of their capitalist friends in America."

Nods all around. And from one of the men introduced as a medical doctor: "That should buy us the time we need."

For what? Did this so-called committee care anywhere near as much for saving the lives of others caught in the Holocaust's crosshairs as protecting their own skin? And what about our troops? They'd hardly mentioned them. The people here I knew had always been principled, stalwart dissidents, if bowed by Stalin's purges, but the war was twisting them back behind ideals and passions. Their eyes were tired, their voices too.

"We're out of time unless we prop up our troops with winter coats, sock warmers, and canned rations for the rest of winter, and not to forget munitions," the poet Leib Kvitko said. "For the life of me, I have a son on the front."

I straightened my spine. "And I Oleg, my lover, Osip Mandelstam's son. This is better talk. Help for the here and now."

The hiss of a leaky coil in the radiator, the roll of thunder like a snare drum solo, a cough and a couple sniffles as a result of colds brought into the room made the silence without words heavier and darker, large enough to swallow us all.

"Yes, the here and now," the novelist David Bergelson said at last, "but also the there and then. Without a story with a good ending, we won't make it through the first chapter."

I smiled inwardly at our Janus. "As in Stalin must be neutralized by how good our work is," I said. "And we must tell it to other Russians and the world, so he would embarrass himself too much to purge us." My good feelings fell as tired as the eyes and voices in the room. No, it was we who desperately needed a story to believe in.

"To some extent, I agree," Bergelson said. "Mostly we must make our own future by getting the Jews of the world to pressure Stalin into submission. Bring America and Europe into moving militarily on the Goat-faced Murderer if he moves on Jews in Russia."

My thoughts spun. I came up with no answers, no improvements for this grandiose plan, though I had an inkling where we could start, test our mettle if you will—save some of the German Jews, be an underground railroad for them or something.

The doctor who had spoken earlier said, "We should create enclaves in areas Russia controls that Russian Jews relocate to, and that we also bring German Jews in Nazi-occupied regions and those stranded on the front. At first we call the German Jews POWs to satisfy Stalin. But later they would help make up enough of a population to gain the international support needed."

The doc was good, real good.

"How do we convince the Red Army to capture instead of kill these German Jews?" a woman university professor named Lina Stern said. "They're under pressure from Stalin to shoot them. Prisoners are expensive to keep alive."

"Every young Jew serving in our military would take them alive, and many others who know right from wrong too," I said. Anyone who can make out the difference between two-headed Mammon Ra and a common yard crow, I almost added, but instead went with, "Starting with Oleg Mandelstam."

"Stalin won't get the money unless he allows them to be taken as POWs," Solomon Mikhoels said. "It's as simple as that."

Nods around again, then more of the terrible wordlessness. We all knew if we succeeded, Jews would be sitting ducks, all rounded up, for Stalin's whims.

"Everything we say or write must focus on anti-fascism," Itzik Fefer said. "We must put our Russian dissident commentary aside for now."

David Bergelson guffawed darkly. "The censors are not only disallowing anything worthwhile from getting published, they're disappearing people even for trying."

I pictured my manuscript in its envelope. Pasternak had made detailed editing notes, of which I'd tended to with almost reckless abandon. My story had been chamber music, but now it rose and fell and soared to crescendo like a symphony. The Jewish Anti-Fascist Committee was correct: My book was being smothered underneath my mattress by the arthritic, though relentless, hands of the Goat-faced Murderer's Russia. Queasiness overtook me at the thought of the only chord played over and over these days.

Suddenly, howling air-raid sirens pierced the air like needles.

Sighs and gasps came from several at the meeting.

"Why now, just when we're getting somewhere?" the doctor said.

"To the basement like good little boys and girls," Mikhoels said. "We'll continue there."

All of Moscow had been through randomly timed air-raid drills for the past two weeks. Without further delay, the Jewish Anti-Fascist Committee members gathered their pens and notepads, then began making their way out of the lounge and along a hall, toward stairs that went belowground. Some of my fellow student writers who lived in rooms here, along with staff, also headed toward the basement.

When I got partway down the corridor, through the sirens, batwings beat dark whispers that quickly escalated into swarming thrums—overtaken only by my pounding heart. For the first time I heard Nazi Luftwaffe propellers, the groans of their engines. This wasn't practice!

An explosion shook the building, and a framed photograph of Osip Mandelstam, Albert Einstein, Titsian Tabidze, Paolo Iashvili, Marina Tsvetaeva, along with Boris Pasternak, all standing in a cozy group just outside the Writers Building, fell off the wall, its glass shattering across the floor. The committee members hustled forward, staying in almost perfect single-file. Itzik Fefer, directly in front of me, stepped on the picture, glass crunching underneath his well-polished black shoe. I picked up the photo, then moved outside the line, brushed shards off the glossy print with a hand. Einstein and Pasternak remained alive, but not the great poets Mandelstam, Tabidze, Iashvili, and Tsvetaeva. It struck me that all of them refused to hide in bunkers and pray away what could've been their final moments, and what's more, four of the six had met just such moments trying to make a difference till the end. Another explosion rocked me against the wall. I heard a sledgehammer drive into the building's roof.

There couldn't be anyone who wasn't insane doing such a thing. *What's going on? Am I losing it?* Once again, a deafening thud came from above. It probably wasn't shrapnel; I didn't believe the building had been hit directly. *My God.* Bombs had landed up there without detonating!

...

Yet!

I grabbed Leib Kvitko's arm, and he fell out of line, while fixing me with an anxious grimace. "Please, let's go to the roof and take the undetonated bombs away from the building," I said, breathing hard now; my chest rose and fell. "They're probably too heavy for me to lift without some help. I think there're two bombs up there. Even state broadcasts warn that many times they explode later."

He pulled his arm out of my grasp. "Let's hope for duds."

I watched him catch up to the end of the line, and then with Leib Kvitko's broad back and quick legs, the last of our committee disappeared down the stairs. No other residents or staff members were in the hall. Everyone in this building whose instincts had driven them toward the basement evidently had gone for it. The photograph still called out to me without words. I stared all those in it down, as if looking into a mirror I felt unworthy to hold.

"Katya, come with the rest of us. What you want to do is too dangerous."

It was Solomon Mikhoels's voice, and I locked eyes with him. His fair expression and knitted brow held nothing but care and concern.

My lips trembled. I stayed put.

Yet another explosion, maybe two or three blocks away, shook the Writers Building's windows.

Excruciatingly long seconds passed between us, and then he reached for the doorknob. "It must be closed for the safety of all below. Won't you come with me?"

I shook my head. "It's too dangerous to stay in the basement even if I don't make it off the roof alive." For my soul, I almost added. But if Mikhoels needed to be told that, no way he'd figure it out for himself quick enough to come along. I turned and ran the other way. Up five flights I took the stairs two at a time. Finally, I pushed the door to the roof open and stepped outside.

A cold blast of wind gave me shivers, and here I stood dressed in dungarees, a cotton blouse, pullover sweater, and saddle shoes. My harsh weather parka and goulashes were in my room, but maybe I would use the iciness to quicken the senses, get through this. The air smelled musky and spoiled like rotten eggs in a butcher shop or something; smoke billowed from below. Across the street, an apartment building had a hole blown in its side. People's screams from over there sang a startlingly inescapable death-cult harmony with the sirens still blaring. Golden streamers of a few antiaircraft rounds from rooftops of buildings none too close by streaked the gray sky. Overhead, wings of the Luftwaffe squadron spread out like geese flying south for winter, just as free as you please. It had stopped snowing, and the Writers Building's flat roof was a blanket of whiteness dotted by several black holes. My breathing made harmless fog that went to nothing as I intently looked on each one of them. I now hardly felt the frosty conditions; the war made my blood flow thick, as if through a furnace. At the bottom of at least two of those depressions lay unexploded bombs.

Having noticed a shovel leaned against the wall just at the stairwell's exit, I went back inside and got it. I propped against a wall the photograph of Mandelstam, Einstein, Tabidze, Iashvili, Tsvetaeva, and Pasternak. It would be kept from getting destroyed in the work I had ahead and, besides, they'd be looking my way.

Once outside again, I walked slowly toward the nearest dark hole. On nearing it, I reached carefully down through the snow, using my other hand to hold the shovel above, so as not to clip a bomb with it. I felt around until coming upon something jagged and rough. It felt more like rock or a piece of concrete. Maybe some debris from the apartment building across the street actually had made it up here? My already knotted stomach turned over on my hand making contact with metal. Inch by inch, I made a painstakingly slow, circular motion with that hand, at last clearing away enough snow to make out a chunk of the apartment building that had been torn away along with its iron rebar insides. Checking out the next two holes went more smoothly, as a piece of wooden window frame and a leg from a dining room chair gave no cause for alarm. A sliver of hope crept in: maybe there were no unexploded bombs up here. That's when I bent down and fondled the smooth metal nose undoubtedly of a shell casing. Winter roared back at me like a lion. I shook like a leaf, but somehow my blood still ran hot.

I set down the shovel in thick whiteness and noticed it made its own dark depression. When I finished moving snow outside a ring of about three feet with the bomb in its center, my fingers no longer had any feeling. Cupping my hands over my mouth, I blew into them over and over, but the numbness didn't budge. Everything about the task ahead seemed too much for me. I didn't have a clue just how volatile this thing was, where to touch it, where not to, much less the strength to transport it downstairs and then into the trunk of some car for taking to some field in the countryside well away from any humans. This tungsten steel teardrop-shaped missile had to weigh over a hundred pounds. Maybe that flywheel canister on its tail contained the detonator. I rubbed my hands together until generating a little heat. I hadn't come this far to turn away now, and wasn't about to curl tail between my legs and head for the basement to once again beg for help. No. I picked up the shovel again, then carefully stepped in front of the bomb's nose. If it's too much for you to lift under control, things would be safer leaving well enough alone, I told myself. In my mind's eye, I dropped the bomb, setting it off, and, as if in slow motion, the Writers Building crashed in on itself. Ever so slowly, I slipped the tip of the shovel's blade underneath the shell's snout. Then, farther underneath until only the flywheel appendage remained free of the blade. Taking care to apply pressure evenly with my hands, I attempted to lever the handle downward; the bomb held fast like a stubborn monster in its sleep. Now, I leaned over the handle with my upper body to put more weight on it, and the bomb lifted some, though more wobbly than I would've liked.

An explosion nearby that again shook the Writers Building mightily. I watched in horror as the shell casing bounced completely off the blade. My skin prickled all over, my entire body coursing with adrenaline. "God of Abraham, let it be a dud," I said out loud. With that, I slid the blade back underneath the bomb, and then lifted death off the ground. My legs shook as I sort of lurched toward the stairwell door, keeping my eyes fixed on the projectile and the white snow a few feet ahead. Once over next to the exit, I shimmied halfway around and backed through the doorway. On facing frontward again to take the stairs down, I momentarily looked at the photograph against the wall of Mandelstam, Einstein, Tabidze, Iashvili, Tsvetaeva, and Pasternak. Their eyes seemed to follow my movement.

Rest breaks as often as necessary, I reminded myself, and then made it onto the first step successfully enough. Good. They could be taken one at a time. As I stole a glance down the stairwell, there seemed to be a million steps left.

All of a sudden, shoes slapping on concrete came from below; the sound got louder and louder.

"Help!" I cried out. "I've got a possible live bomb! I need help taking it away!"

"We're coming, Katya! Just stay where you are!"

Could it really be his voice, or was I simply falling apart? "Pasternak!"

"Yes. I'm on my way!"

Without another word, I leaned my bum against the wall, then carefully lowered the bomb onto the platform directly above. I slumped to the ground, spent and trembling.

In no more than ten seconds, Pasternak emerged from shadows in the dim lighting with a knapsack slung over his shoulder, and Solomon Mikhoels right on his heels. Pasternak smiled, though his brown eyes looked pained.

I knitted my brow, wanting him to be proud of me. "Did Solomon call you?"

Pasternak nodded. "You're very brave, Katya." His eyes went to the bomb, and he slipped the rucksack off his shoulder. "Mind if I take a close look at that little Fraulein?"

The lines in my forehead deepened. "Are you kidding? Be my guest."

He went to one knee directly beside the bomb, laying the rucksack next to it. "Yes, she's a SC250." He opened the rucksack's flap and reached inside. One by one he came out with a big wrench, needle-nose pliers, wire cutters, and a long, skinny punch sort of looking device, setting them side by side on the floor.

"You really do know what you're doing," I said, truly impressed.

Pasternak nodded again. "At the munitions factory they not only teach you how to make bombs, they also show you how to take them apart." He glanced at Solomon Mikhoels, then set his eyes on mine again. "I need one helper, and Russian chivalry says that should be Solomon. Please wait for me in the basement with the others, Katya."

Pasternak's fatherly expression made me see red. His eyes, which seemed to hold all the tortured love of Russia, disarmed me just enough to hold my cutting tongue. "If it's just the same, I'd like to stay," I said.

Now, Pasternak's brow carved ravines. "Earlier today I got word Mur Tsvetaeva was killed in battle. And Yevgeni is switching his education to become an engineer, so he can have skills more acceptable to the military than music. He's itching to fight." He massaged his temples. "I can't lose you up here on this roof."

I swallowed hard. "And Oleg, have you heard how he is?"

He shook his head. "I check with his commander a couple times a week. No news is probably good news."

"His letters get to me less often."

"Everything's harder now. I'm sorry, Katya."

"It is. And, Pasternak?"

"Yes."

"I can't lose you up here on this roof. I'm staying." Before giving him a chance to respond, I shot a piercing look at Solomon Mikhoels. "You can stay if you like, but don't you think I've earned the right." My almost guttural tone change implied an underbelly: Solomon, do you really want Pasternak to know how you let me come up here alone in the first place?

Mikhoels and I stared each other down.

His face tightened.

I held my hands out steady in front of Pasternak. "Let's see, Solomon, who has the nerve for this work," I said. "Show your hands."

"You're incorrigible." Mikhoels chuckled. "Just the way I like my revolutionaries." He looked at Pasternak. "I actually believe she'll be better at this than me."

"I know when I'm beat." Pasternak handed me the needle-nose pliers, then picked up the big wrench. "Give me those when I ask for them," he said. "And there's some chance I'll ask you to clamp a wire with them, okay?"

"All right, then," I said. "Let's do this."

"God speed and good luck," Mikhoels said, then was off down the stairs.

As Pasternak directed his full attention on dismantling the bomb's casing, I once more looked at the photograph against the wall, and said a little prayer about calm and clarity. For when Pasternak had mentioned me possibly securing a hotwire, my hands had begun shaking ever so slightly.

For the next several minutes, he worked on the bomb with the elegance and precision of a surgeon until it lay open with the nose off, and yellow, white, red, and green wires exposed that snaked their way off a small fuse box or something. He asked for the pliers, which I gave him. Then he said, "Talk to me, please. It helps me stay calm." Glancing at me, he winked. "This kind of work will make you a wreck, huh."

I returned his smile, nodding my agreement. "Let me guess, they don't always connect the same color wires to the same resistors."

"Yep. And the tricky bastards change the placement of the resistors too."

I bit my lip.

He reached in with the needle-nose pliers, went for the red wire, then switched to the white. "Keep talking," he said.

"Are you going to join the Jewish Anti-Fascist Committee?"

"Sort of. I'll write pieces for them using a pen name. Work behind the scenes on things."

I thought for a long moment. The people of the committee may not have come onto the roof with an impetuous young woman, and, in fairness, only Pasternak had the training needed to be up here. Yes, there were many ways to show one's courage. "You think Stalin will eventually come down hard on the committee."

He wiggled the white wire with the tip of the pliers. "Or the Nazis, have your pick."

"Are you still taking a break from *Zhivago*?"

He nodded once more. "It's the hardest thing I've ever done." The pliers' tongs opened and then clamped on the white wire.

"I've completed your edits on my novel. You really helped me. It just kills me it can't be published in Russia now."

He chuckled as if at the irony, released the wire, then leaned over and kissed me on the cheek. "Start another novel without delay," he said.

"I will."

"Cutter, please."

I handed it to him.

I wasn't nervous at all when he snipped the white wire.

CHAPTER NINETEEN

Sinuate, purple and gray clouds, like a huge river risen over its banks by way of deluge, veiled the Boeing 737 from sight of those on the ground thirty-five thousand feet below; but then, no one he knew would be watching for the plane, thought the slumbering man with a ping of sadness. Looking out the window at the opaque current helped separate himself from all he didn't want to set eyes on—even through his distorted, slumbering peepholes—though, at the same time, he believed a close look was needed to get unstuck, if not with the women in his life, then for *John the Baptist's* sake, with his largely unimagined next manuscript. He always turned to religious allusions the closer he got to Texas. *Scary.* Or was he afraid of himself, and weirdly drawn to the endless river distancing him from having to decide anything? Other than for all the carbon this jet spewed across the sky, he would've loved circling up here until he got the desired answers from Anastasie, or Margaret, or his inner muse. Let the cosmos take its own sweet time in making the decisions for him, while he flew in the belly of this metal bird, and floodwaters drowned his unanswerable questions below. But not so long as Christmas Eve, four days away, he'd promised Mattie, Doug, and Margaret to be home in time for the holiday. Admittedly, the slumbering man already looked forward to being with them.

Margaret had worked late into the evenings getting her novel started in the two days since the BofA protest and before he'd left for Texas. They would prepare dinner and eat with the kids; then she had headed for her writing desk. On that first evening, she had come home from her job at Harper's with exciting information drawn out of her source, the nameless mole in Clifford Odeon's Badshah Khan Institute for Peace Studies. Over the Tunisian uprising the mole had been sort of schitzy, partly cheering the people on, partly critical of them without better leadership in the streets. Margaret had smelled a big rat around the mole slighting this nonviolent uprising. Frazier had sorted out some of the complications with her; for one, the U.S.'s power elite, possibly getting what they wanted in the ouster of a noncompliant dictator of Tunisia, couldn't bring themselves to be for the common person. The "fascist wannabes," as she'd called them, must see themselves as knowing better, always. Margaret was documenting the mole's inconsistencies to build a character around him in her "fictionalized" account. This guy had told her to keep one eye on Tunisia and the other on Egypt. Things could spread quickly in the Middle East. The slumbering man had thought her brilliant if still too driven, rather than inspired. But what did he know, he had told himself. There were plenty of ways to create likeable, believable people in books. Unearth deeper truth. Margaret even had volunteered she was being "humanized" by Nana's letters, and felt the power, at least for now, in the letters, was better nurtured in her if not shared. Nonetheless, Frazier had sensed, by her ending several of their conversations before they were done to "get back with her novel," that she was hiding something more than the contents of Nana's letters. Margaret could be a killer author, but could she reach him in his darkest recesses? Did she desire doing so enough to grow that much?

Whatever. He had his blue plate special full with what lay ahead between him and his family. He envied their hardworking, hard-playing, loyalty-to-the-end love; their speaking in a few words what he couldn't say in an entire novel, their unbidden need to keep things basic. Maybe his family's penchant to live simply meant they operated at maximum capacity, full scope. Why had God given him such an overactive mind to compare his relative deprivation? *Bullshit.* He'd just float along, or fly along, or swim along in the river, or drink G&Ts the rest of the way to his destination. No more gradualism when troubled, following the rabbit trail of *Anastasie.* As soon as he inwardly said her name, he felt cheated by his upbringing, the Bible Belt across his backside. Why shouldn't he honor the awesome serendipity that had occurred between the two of them? It didn't mean he had to commit adultery. Having a muse didn't have to lead to other things. His folks would agree marijuana wasn't a gateway drug to heroin or crack. It made connect-the-dot logic, of the Monahans, Texas, *Mudville News*, mixed with NYU existentialism sort.

Looking through his lenses, he read from his laptop on the seatback tray for what had to be the twentieth time an email he'd sent Anastasie before leaving the bar in LaGuardia Airport:

> *I perused your website because I miss hearing from you.*
> *If the art on your homepage is a message to come to you in*
> *Paris, please give me a sign, a smiley face, anything.*

He had finished the email using what he'd said to her in his dream:

> *I suppose the fact I've never told you how much this book*

matters to me means you got this information, shall we say,
from the universe.
                                                                    —Yours always, Frazier

Just like every time before, his blood thrummed. He yearned for her answer—not received as of when he'd been instructed by the flight attendant to shut his laptop down for takeoff—and he dreaded an answer from her. The slumbering man believed in Margaret and him, ultimately, eventually. It would be far out if he had some Acapulco gold rolled in a doobie, to light up and toke on once in the rental car. Ah, the vicissitudes of being near the border in West Texas. It made you think cosmically funky thoughts. To go to Paris would be devastating in freedom; to not go seemed all *Prince of Tides* on the causeway of whispered regrets. If Margaret and he were together in Texas, would she smoke a joint with him like in the good old days, before she'd gone so professional? Why had he asked Anastasie for another sign, when she'd already given him one? Psychically, anyway. Surely, the French artist would blow some refer with him. Or could either of these relationships get so right all that he wanted was a natural high? How long had it been since he'd smoked pot anyway? Six, no, seven years. Truth was, he didn't like it much; Mary Jane gave him the giggles for a few minutes and dulled his senses for days.

Dappled light flashed through the window. Then it became dusky in the cabin, telling him the plane was descending through the cloud layer. A public address announcement came from the captain to fasten your seat belt, and that they'd be at the gate in fifteen minutes. Out the Boeing 737's window on IH20 far below, cars looked like bark beetles, eighteen-wheelers centipedes, and, as the slumbering man continued descending toward Midland International Airport, in front of airplane hangars or walking to and from office-warehouses, the antlike people got bigger, more human, though he inwardly shrank, or rather rode some kind of time machine, taking him back to his teens, even before, when he'd eaten dust carried by high West Texas winds going to the Pick-E-Pack to get his pop cigarettes. For beer Pop would've sent Novella, his "Old Lady," as Frazier's mom was affectionately called by Pop and, make no mistake, by no one else, leastwise in Pop's earshot; otherwise you would've gotten one of Pop's "belt whuppins." Of course, his Old Lady, and only her, safely called Pop her "Old Man." Most of the kids had made that error no more than once, for she'd take a switch to you good, boy, yes, she would. The slumbering man's folks were post-revolutionary products of the late sixties, but not the nonviolent, flower-child type—the Che Guevara, gun-in-your-hands type. They'd run some weed out of Mexico until they got busted when Frazier had been just old enough to remember the anxiety in their home over whether

Moms would get a probated sentence in exchange for Pop pleading guilty and doing some time behind bars. One year later, when Pop got out of county jail, the countercultural uprising had ended in their household. Now, the slumbering man's folks pretty much wanted to be left alone and make retirement in a few years. Pop had worked himself into the job of rig foreman for a local oil drilling company that lately had been doing "sissy work," as Pop called it, fracking gas wells in the Permian basin. Moms took her braided-silver-and-black-hair self to "facilitate" children at Monahans' one and only Montessori establishment, aptly named Our Way Texas School & Liberty Laboratory. It kept students through eighth grade, though recognized no formal classes. Sort of quirky, redneck hippie in its approach. No wonder, thought the slumbering man, he'd always been the most bohemian guy of his straight buddies, and the most straight arrow when around artist/writer friends. The result, he never could be completely at home, not with his family, or Margaret, or in his fantasy about Anastasie. Wherever the slumbering man went, he took along the other half of himself that felt as unique as a flower child in the West Texas plains, or a cowboy among iconoclasts. He needed to feel less unique, or at least uniquely one person with different facets, yes, and comfortable in his skin, more integrated. Maybe that's why he hadn't gone to Paris, wanted out of New York for a while, and as the plane's wheels sat down hard on the runway, why he again looked absently over the top of his frames into God only knew what the future may hold over the next several days with his family.

Thirty minutes later, heading along a magnificently lonely straight-as-far-as-the-eye-could-see farm-to-market road in the rented Ford Taurus—which reeked with pinewood air freshener and made him consider just exactly what concoction of carcinogenic chemicals was being consumed—the slumbering man really would've liked a joint to blow. As he'd gotten back in wireless range at the airport, still there had been no email response from Anastasie. She probably thought him some sort of Sedona-Vortex-Channeling-Boulder-Sitter, way too esoteric to waste her time on. On the call to let Margaret know he'd made it inside Texas safely, she had actually acknowledged he was doing things in the right order, and her the wrong, to get clearer with family before taking on a big writing project. Her vulnerability had drawn the slumbering man closer to her, *and* sent a wave of guilt washing over him. "But how do you break through to the Comrade and Lydia?" she'd said. "By then, the Tunisian revolution would be over and largely forgotten, my book old hat." The slumbering man couldn't disagree, yet continued to believe there were no shortcuts to knocking down creative blocks that kept your writing from being more human. Otherwise, you could be on time, and no one would read you. A subject he had become something of an expert at. In his mind's eye, he scored a joint from his high school classmate and small-time pusher, Rudy, just like old times. Where was Rudy when you needed him now? A sardonic smile spread on Frazier's lips. At least he wouldn't put himself through reentry with Pop and Novella, no; first he'd hitch up his brown corduroys, snug the laces of his lime green Converse All-Stars, and avail his urban post-college-boy persona, in all its ingloriousness, to Derek and Felicia. As he turned the Taurus onto the red clay washboard ranch road that cut through flat-as-a-pancake plains all the way to the horizon, he wondered whether purposely trying to piss off family by his manner of dress, distance himself from the get-go, held any purchase with reconciliation. No way he could put on un-faded blue jeans, a silver-tipped belt with humongous brooch buckle, boots, and a cowboy hat for the occasion. What the hell, Derek and Felecia wouldn't respect him if he did. They knew Frazier better than that, and they loved him anyway; well, for sure his sister did, and his brother-in-law adored her. When he'd called to set up this trip, Pop and Novella as well as Derek and Felicia had received the idea with open-armed Texas hospitality. One of the good parts of living in hard country, these folks, without question, fed passers through, even gave them a place to stay the night, before slitting their throats at the slightest deviation from custom. On balance, outsiders often could be un-American, even terrorist sympathizers. Frazier wasn't quite in that league with his family, but then he damn sure hadn't asked them what they'd thought about his op-ed in the *Mudville News*; better wait until they were eyeball to eyeball on that subject. He rotated the radio's audio knob, and a local classic rock station, playing Lynyrd Skynyrd's "Sweet Home Alabama," blared. The slumbering man didn't sing along.

Rooster tails of dust chased Jenny and Pooh Bear, Derek's Australian shepherd and German shepherd ranch dogs, as they ran about the length of a football field toward the Taurus from over beside the house. Frazier stopped the car long enough to roll a window down and receive a couple of slobbery licks across his cheeks, stroke the dogs' necks. It was cool the dogs remembered him so well. Up ahead he spotted Felecia walk through the front doorway onto the screened porch of the two-story structure with wood siding badly overdue for a coat of white paint. She waved at him, and he returned it. Maybe Derek was out working cattle, the slumbering man told himself, the thought immediately falling as dry as West Texas desert sand. He wasted no time in getting out of the car and walking over next to his long-legged, sinewy sister, with freckles like sprinkled wheat spurs on her skin. She looked great, standing there with her salt-and-pepper hair cut in a no-nonsense style with bangs in front and wedge behind, hadn't aged a day in the three years since he'd seen her last.

"You're a sight for sore eyes," she said.

"Kind words, indeed," he said, patting his more than slight paunch. "You haven't gone to the dogs, *much*, yourself." He winked. "Wanna race? Maybe you could finally beat me." Felicia had always been a tomboy, the athlete in the family. When they were growing up together, she'd won enough medals and ribbons in track and field events to entirely cover one of her bedroom's walls. But she had never won a friendly footrace between the two of them. Frazier secretly believed she'd always let him come out ahead.

"No thanks. I only run five miles most mornings. How about you?"

"I even quit walking to the mailbox to check for rejection slips on the books I haven't written."

"You poor, tortured artist." She kissed him on the lips. That's just the way they did things in his family.

He hugged her, breathing off her skin his own smell, sort of pond water and green reeds close to the bank at early morning. "What did you think of my op-ed in the *Mudville News*?" he said.

"I liked it; give me a mountain to climb and I'll scale it, may as well be the bank. It sure as hell feels like our mortgage is Mount Everest."

"You could've been a writer, sis."

"Starve half the time, and plunged into cavernous thought the other half, no thanks."

"How about Derek? What did he think about my article?"

She gestured toward the front door. "He's in there pouting over it right now."

"It, or me being here?"

She laughed nervously, glanced away. "We abide differing opinions in this household."

Gooseflesh rippled along his arms, down his legs. "Maybe that's what I've come here to find out."

While they retrieved the slumbering man's things from the car and got him settled into the guest bedroom, their talk centered on Mattie and Doug, and her and Derek's kids, Dwight and Johnny (as in, namesakes Yoakam and Cash). Finally, Felicia put on a little-too-wide smile and asked about Margaret.

"We're doing better," the slumbering man said, more tentatively than he wanted.

"Kid brother." Felicia chuckled. "Your Old Lady is harder to live with, if you can believe it, than I am."

He smiled. "She's drawing about even with you."

"Good, good, let's go find Derek."

"Okay, but I'd like to say hello to Dwight and Johnny first."

Her brow knitted. "They're out riding horses. They'll probably ride till sunset."

And not here to greet their uncle? That was odd; he'd always gotten along well with her kids. "They spend a lot of time on horses these days, do they?"

"Yes, well, things aren't too cheery around the house."

"Stupid question, sorry."

As they headed along the hallway, the slumbering man looked once again over the top of his frames. The wild boar's head, mounted above the doorway that emptied into the den, seemed to open wider its fanged mouth.

Keeping his eyes set through the floor-to-ceiling windows that framed their spread outside, Derek greeted Frazier, then gestured at a small refrigerator next to the rough-hewn mesquite bar, and said, "Get yourself a brew if you want." In his dark brown leather chair, Derek held a Lone Star beer. Felicia made a deft—"I'll let you boys enjoy your beers in peace"—First-Lady-of-the-Ranch exit.

As the slumbering man grabbed a Carta Blanca and snapped the top off in a wall-mounted cap opener, he smiled inwardly. True to form, Derek had on the western outfit Frazier had rejected wearing while in the air. But it was right for Derek, who looked wind-chiseled and tawny, well fed on his cattle's beef (the slumbering man had taken a quick peek through his lenses). He sat down in a chair identical to Derek's that had a table with carved longhorns on its surface in between them, and then took a sip of beer. Because they were indoors, Derek's brown Stetson lay on the table. Frazier's brother-in-law took a draw off his Lone Star. Their bottle-tipping duel went on for a good bit, nothing being said by either of them. The desert plains dotted with cactus, ocotillo, sage, and cattle looked to the slumbering man sort of like a huge yellow and magenta background dribbled with greens, black, and browns, which brought to mind an Esteban Vicente abstract expressionist painting. The longer they sat there drinking, the more it settled over him that understanding at least something of the drought Derek fought against day in and day out, the underfed livestock, the dust, would be essential to have a clue what to break their silence with—so he came out of intellectualized-art-critique hiding, and looked through his eyeglasses in earnest this time. The wooden fencing had to be higher dollar than barbed wire, and more humane on cattle and wildlife, thought the slumbering man. A rusty water tank sat out there at about five hundred yards, its windmill turning in the wind, filling it with life. Derek had built a large shade shed next to the tank, where several cows huddled at a feeding trough. The house needed repair, but not Derek's ranch; he kept it in fine working order, best he could, yes, best he could. Here and there most of the cattle stood languid in the bright sun as it fell low in the sky on this chilly evening. Neither was there enough room at the feed trough for them, nor probably enough feed. "I should've called and given you a heads-up on my article before it got in the paper," the slumbering man said at last. "I'm sorry, Derek."

His brother-in-law took a long draw off the beer, then made a popping sound with his lips. "You were only trying to help."

They continuously looked out across the ranch.

"It would'a been nice if I could've gotten my story together to tell people around here myself, that's all," Derek added.

More sipping for quite a while.

"You want another beer?" Derek finally said, pushing himself out of the chair. "'Cause I'm getting another."

"Thanks." Frazier nodded, took a last swig off his brew, then placed in Derek's outstretched hand the dead soldier.

When Derek handed over the fresh Carta Blanca, Frazier looked him directly in the eyes. "Is there any legal way to keep the bank off you that hasn't been looked at? Because Margaret and I would pony up the money for it. Of course, I'd have to talk with her, but I'm sure she'd want to."

"I can't take your money." Derek squinted his eyes, and his tone fell gravelly. "You're not rolling in dough."

Another man would've tiered up, believed the slumbering man, and it wasn't over finances or the lack of them; he looked on a kind of prideful finery that carried Derek through harsh winters, long, searing hot summers, that mended fences, kept the windmill well oiled, stoicism that gave Felicia something to hang on to, but wouldn't dare accept help. Frazier took a long draw of his beer, then said, "I haven't written a novel in years; I'm sinking as a writer, Derek. I'm here to see if making peace with my family will keep me from going down with the ship." He took a long swig of beer. "Maybe we can help each other." As soon as those last words rolled off his tongue, he got all tangled up with something like an inborn *need* to assist Derek and Felicia. There had never been anything he could do for them, ever. The bookworm of the family had always been its unspoken weak link.

Derek eyed him for a pregnant moment before sitting down again. Then, they went back to sipping and staring out the window, except the slumbering man returned to the view of that Esteban Vicente abstract painting.

"Don't tell Felicia about this conversation," Derek said, his tone once again sturdy and even.

Inwardly, the slumbering man winced. But dishing out some feigned patriarchy couldn't be the worst of sins, especially if it meant breaking through to Derek. "I know what you mean, and don't *you* say anything to Margaret." Of course, Margaret was fifteen hundred miles away, and she and Derek hadn't spoken since three Christmases past.

Derek reached out with his beer, and the slumbering man did the same, their bottles all but touching over the longhorn table. "Deal," said Derek, smiling conspiratorially. "But in no uncertain terms, I won't accept money from you. So quit working me on that."

They chinked glass against glass.

There probably wouldn't be a better moment than this, the slumbering man's instincts told him. "Man to man, would you let me help you using something else?"

Derek tilted his head inquisitively. "You've got my ear."

"Before you say no, hear me out. In New York Margaret and I have some friends in the media, newspapers, magazines, TV reporters, these sorts of avenues. Maybe, just maybe, I could make your and Felicia's story a national one. Put so much pressure on the big bank that holds your mortgage, they'd have to renegotiate on acceptable terms with you guys.

"Now, I know you hate publicity, but Derek, let's face it, I've already let the cat out of the bag with the only people you give a flip about, your friends and neighbors. I won't kid you, it's a long shot." The slumbering man held up his beer as if in salute to the ranch. "Deal?"

Derek sat back in his chair and looked absently out the window again; he held the bottle in his lap with both hands.

Outside it appeared to the slumbering man that two brownish paint drippings moved in haste toward the ranch house. Tilting his head back to take a good look through the lenses, he spotted Dwight and Johnny riding their horses like the wind. He held in saying "Do it for them," but kept his bottle raised in honor of everything good about Derek. Fixing a look at his brother-in-law again, Frazier noticed wetness in Derek's eyes. Immediately, he lowered the beer.

"Deal." Derek lifted his Lone Star a few inches, didn't take a drink off it. "But I'll need to talk to Felicia about your idea. Get her sign-off on it."

"Yes, Derek, I understand."

CHAPTER TWENTY

We spoke loudly over the noise.

"Who cares which insane mustachioed dictator eventually declares victory in this war? It's about death and nothing more. I only think of Oleg." A rush of horridly hot wind filled my mouth, not nearly as charring as my inner furnace, already at the boiling point over the jabber-y monologue, which I'd had little choice but to endure, on the balance of power shifting back to the Nazis after Mother Russia had so miraculously pushed them from Moscow, now almost two years ago. *Balderdash!* My husband had been MIA for six months. "I must know whether he's alive!"

"Yes, do pray Pasternak brings you good news." Solomon Mikhoels kept his eyes fixed on the road measled with potholes ahead of his old rattletrap R71 Russian remake BMW motorcycle. "Sorry for going on a bit much about the bigger picture. Awfully insensitive of me to lay that on you right now."

The sidecar bounced me around like a ragdoll tossed back and forth by budding Jewish princesses, an unwanted imagining of bored imperial darlings at play before the revolution, or more accurately like some Wiccan riding a broomstick in high turbulence. I may as well have been a witch stripped of occult powers. Before Pasternak left a month ago on the Red Army train to Grozny, I had pulled most everything from the fruit basket of my intellectual witticism and feminine wile, short of offering up the apple of my naked body, in trying to convince him on the idea of taking me along to the front, tell his Stalinist minders I was his attaché and, anywhere he went, so did this young woman. Pasternak had refused to bite into my offering that juicy red Astrachan. I didn't much blame him and, to be fair, I held no animosity that would last over a few seconds more toward Solomon Mikhoels, who had for the most part deftly nibbled around the edge of my overly ripe fear. He'd graciously agreed to take me to meet Pasternak on his return to Moscow. "Provide some moral support," is how he'd put it. Since that day of removing the bombs off the roof of the Writers Building, when I'd come to question not Mikhoels's commitment to the dissident community, but his inner salt, I had actually come to greatly admire him. A gentleman, if also an impassioned leader in the Russian Jewish underground, and God knows there weren't many of us left to our own devices in Russia. Our kind either fought in the war like good little soldiers, or had been shipped off to Siberia, or found themselves in one of those godforsaken modern-day Pale villages just waiting to be rounded up by Stalin, or happened to be of the "lucky" few who could help Stalin, or embarrass him too much if moved on—as in Pasternak along with his family, and perhaps his young writing protégé. Mikhoels and the poet Itzik Fefer had recently traveled to the U.S. and England, successfully coming home with carpetbags full of money for Stalin's war effort. What's more, Mikhoels and I had worked together in the underground to help German Jews shipped to Russia for slaughter get fake Russian papers and quietly set them up to live in one of the countryside villages where homeland Jews were being relocated. Who could blame Solomon for getting a little long-winded over his political concerns, particularly now? Things had gotten so complicated and tenuous plus, unlike myself, this handsome hunk of a man didn't have a lover to obsess on. I didn't think he liked guys. He enjoyed female amorous interests most anytime he desired partaking; then they'd just one day soon be gone from his life. What have you... Solomon Mikhoels had never hit on me, and I'd not seen or heard of him making moves on any woman with a steady man in her heart. For him, there were simply too many free birds flying the air. I looked over at him, hands gripping the handlebars loosely, his eyes steadfast and maybe having fallen more melancholy, but then he could just as well be squinting from the road grit and the gale-force wind kicked up by our ride. "Thanks for understanding," I said.

He nodded, seemed to force an unsure smile.

Seeing the tenuousness in his expression and no longer able to have it as my own, forbidden fruit, kept way down in the bottom of my basket, suddenly lifted words from my gut and not my head. "If Pasternak hasn't found Oleg, I'll get to the front with the help of the Jewish underground or something! So help me, God, I'll find him!"

Solomon set his jaw, kept his eyes on the road. He said nothing.

Over the next several minutes, the wind howling by cut wetness in my eyes, but it wasn't the culprit of grief at all; the essence of my tears came from a well filled by the aquifer of Oleg and me. Glancing over at Solomon again as he turned the motorcycle into the train depot's parking area, I noticed his eyes had gone watery too, and wondered whether this was from the wind, or some internal storm.

It took a moment to lose the jouncing of the road still inside me, once Solomon stopped the one-off BMW. He came around to the sidecar, then gave me a hand out—which I squeezed knowingly before letting go. Without another word, we walked briskly into the terminal.

The marquee for arrivals indicated the train coming in from Grozny ran on time. As we neared the platform next to the empty tracks, I was struck by the preponderance of military personnel and lack of civilians. The Red Army controlled the rail lines, with armed men in uniforms who stood at the ready in clusters every ten meters or so. War seemed to create a boon for travel; before that it was the Goat-faced Murderer's purges sending Russian citizens to the Urals. When would Russians come here en route to visit family, or go on holiday in the country, or God forbid, to ski the tall mountains? The terminal's huge iron archways, its majestic high ceiling with lights dangling from wires like stars floating in some galaxy, held the stuff writers and artists sought to capture glimpses of in their work. The romantics, those insisting on someplace better against all evidence to the contrary. The destination of railcars better left unknown, or at least vague. They mocked my inability to write something new. And I hardly cared. I wanted certainty, the cold, hard fact of Pasternak's warm body, blood flowing through his veins, walking off the next incoming train. An un-mysterious message delivered, a journey with no allure, unimaginative. Uncreative. And the very thing that sparked something inside me, this whispered hope of stealing art back from a culture bent on destruction. But first Pasternak needed to tell me Oleg was okay.

Beyond the archways in the middle distance, a sad, lonely whistle, and I spotted white steam pour from the engine's smokestack.

"C'mon," I said to Solomon, and we walked toward the far end of the platform, toward the train, maneuvering our way through military personnel and a few others in street clothes.

In a couple of minutes that seemed to be hours, the cranky iron maiden rolled to a stop in its bay. I set my eyes on each passing window in the "revolutionary leaders'" car, and then the "people's" cars. At first, my spirit lifted a little at Pasternak not accepting privilege, but the more windows went by without his ruddy face and wavy dark hair showing itself, the more I fell back into darkness. Maybe his berth was on the other side of one of the cars. Some of those passengers now stood grouped in the exit compartments peering out the windows, casually saluting comrades or waving at those here to meet them. But then, Pasternak wasn't particularly inclined for this sort of fanfare. A good thing no platform existed on the other side of the train. If he got off at all, I would know it.

"Your friend in the military brass assured you Pasternak would be on this train, didn't he?" I said to Mikhoels.

"Yes, but Katya, I'm sorry." He held his hands up. "Things change rapidly on the front."

I nodded my understanding and closely espied those disembarking. Over the next several minutes, the flow of people slowed to a trickle, still with no sign of Pasternak. Of course, he could've gotten caught up with something benign that delayed his trip home. But what if this wasn't the case at all? Finally, no one other than the brakemen and engineers were getting off. Mikhoels's words of warning turned over in my mind. "Who could we call to find out if Pasternak is okay?" I said to Mikhoels.

"I tried before leaving my apartment to give you a lift, and the lines in and out of Grozny have been destroyed."

"Are you saying that..." My voice tapered off. No one was leaving the train. It slowly transformed into a black serpent, the windows scaly speckles of skin; everything started spinning. My knees buckled, and an arm looped round my waist, breaking my fall. "I cannot...lose Pasternak...to the war too," I hardly managed.

As my inner gyrations slowed, with our faces no more than an inch apart, I looked into Solomon Mikhoels's hazel eyes. Even now they glimmered. I partly wanted to slap him, and hold on to him tightly. I did neither.

He released his hold.

I steadied on my feet again, surprising myself by being able to give him a half smile. Then, over Solomon's shoulder I spotted Pasternak struggling with his trunk as he clambered down the train's three steps and onto the platform. My smile broadened and vanished just as quickly. I ran over to Pasternak, then placed my hands on either side of his waxen face. The stubble from his scruffy beard prickled my palms. "You need a shave."

His lips parted slightly, and nothing more.

"What took you so long?" I went on. "You're the last one off or something."

"The trunk is loaded with books. I waited for the aisle to clear before attempting to lug it out here."

"Full of books?" I raised an eyebrow.

"I gave readings of my poetry to the troops and to the people of Grozny. They gave me their books to bring back to the Moscow library."

"Why?"

"When bombs are almost constantly falling and troops are firing at you while raiding your home or place of business or your military bunker, the mental space for culture is erased. They wanted to send their books away from the front, to someplace they can be put to use."

"And Oleg? Tell me what you know about Oleg." I suppose waiting this long to raise the subject of my husband was on purpose. I trembled with fear of Pasternak's answer.

He swallowed hard. "Maybe that should wait until we're alone."

"He's gone, isn't he?" I said, my tone falling almost hushed. "Oleg's been killed." I began pounding my fists against his chest.

For a long moment he just stood there with his arms at his sides and let me have at him. He said something my frenzy wouldn't allow me to hear. In one motion he raised his arms and took hold of my wrists snugly.

Tears flooded my eyes, and he went blurry. I oddly may have felt a little comforted by this effect; it was impossible to tell for sure or deny it out of hand. One thing was for certain, though; I wanted everything to melt away like a harmless nightmare.

"I don't know, Katya," Pasternak said, using a measured tone. "No one knew anything for sure about Oleg."

"But someone knew something," I said flatly.

He nodded almost imperceptibly. "Please, this is not the place to speak of this."

"Okay, okay." With my blouse sleeve I dabbed my eyes. "Where shall we go to discuss it?"

"How about the lounge at the Writers Building?"

I nodded my agreement.

A military orderly walked over and gestured at Pasternak's trunk. "We have a car and driver for you, Mr. Pasternak, with instructions to deliver you directly to quarters near the munitions facility here in Moscow."

Eerily, it was as if the military had been listening in on our conversation, or at the very least kept an extremely tight leash on the great writer.

"That won't be necessary," Pasternak said. "I've already arranged transportation."

"I have orders, sir."

"And I'm not in the military, so I don't have to follow them."

"Jews like you are sent to the gulags every day, sir," the man said, his tone turning bitterly sardonic.

Florid color returned to Pasternak's face, and his eyes narrowed ever so slightly. "Solomon, will you give me a hand with my trunk?" he said, not taking his eyes off the orderly.

"Yes."

"Thank you."

Pasternak and Mikhoels took hold of a handle on each end of the luggage, then lifted it. The three of us began making our way along the platform toward the terminal and the exit.

Feeling eyes on us, I glanced over my shoulder. The orderly spoke with a man whose jacket's gold epaulets gave away an officer's rank. They shot a look at us, then resumed their verbal exchange. The officer seemed none too happy.

"You have room for me in your vehicle?" Pasternak said.

Solomon chuckled. He explained we had come on a motorcycle with sidecar. We then went outside, where Pasternak hailed a taxi. Pasternak and Solomon waited for the cabbie to get out and open the rear compartment; then they placed the trunk inside and closed the hatch. Pasternak folded into the cab's backseat and left the door open, an invitation for me to join him.

There was so much I needed to find out, and at the same time didn't know whether I could bear up under. I didn't want to be alone with Pasternak for this, or was it I appreciated Solomon Mikhoels' help and concern to the point of feeling torn between the two of them? I trusted Pasternak explicitly to care for me. Who could've asked for more from a mentor and, well, a father figure? He'd given me away to Oleg when we got married on Oleg's first furlough home, seemingly so long ago and yet just yesterday. The only other man who had held me as securely as my dear Oleg proved himself moments ago, when I collapsed into Solomon Mikhoels's strong arm. What is going on with me?

"I'll see you both soon, I'm sure," Mikhoels said, then leaned over at the waist and set his eyes directly on Pasternak. "I want to discuss how we can get more Jews to relative safety, now that you've been to the front."

Pasternak assured him they would talk.

Then Solomon looked at me, and his almost blithe mouth yet droopy eyes carried some strange recipe of sadness and expectation, as though he were a man who understood intimacy, acted it out without pretending, really, on stage and screen, but had experienced very little of it in his own life. "Good luck; I hope you locate Oleg," he said.

"I know you do, and I appreciate it."

When I bent over to get in the car, it started to rain.

Solomon Mikhoels let out a clipped but seemingly genuine laugh. "Oops," he said. "Unbecoming at a time such as this."

The rain began thawing something frozen in my chest. Holding a finger up between Pasternak and myself, I said, "Please don't take this the wrong way, but I'll see you at the Writers Building."

He looked over the top of his eyebrows at me. "Let it rain, kid."

I straightened myself and faced Solomon. "Take me with, will you?"

He smiled warmly through droplets falling from the soupy sky like diamonds and needles. "Why, sure."

I closed the car's door; then the cab drove away.

While we walked toward the R71 Russian remake BMW, I said, "I need you there to talk about all this with Pasternak. Thanks."

"Glad to be of service."

"Solomon, that's not entirely correct. I want you with me." I hated that he had held me. Only Oleg gets to do that.

∅

The rain had been kind to us, letting up as we made our way to the Writers Building, persistent enough, though, to turn my thaw uncomfortable, adequately forgiving to somewhat free my mind, which hurried to reclaim its troubles. Solomon tried cheering me with a song from one of his plays about picnicking in the rain. When he noticed that wasn't doing much good, he quieted. As the rain stopped and our faces dried, his cheeks remained wet from tears for Oleg and me. I inquired about them, and that's what he'd said. By our arrival a few patches of blue sky had opened, portholes to the sun that seemed no more than pinholes, as everything conspired to shrink my hope, freeze me over again. Pasternak had had to wait in the lounge for me to shower and change clothes, and while Solomon Mikhoels toweled off and put his dungarees and flannel shirt through the dryer down in the basement. Not wanting to make Pasternak endure any more loss of time than necessary from the folly of our ride over, I moved like a rabbit or a bad ballerina getting dressed. Now, in the creamy peasant dress Oleg had given me on our first anniversary, I walked into the lounge. I had gotten here before Solomon Mikhoels. Somehow that was just fine. Pasternak stood with his back to me at a window. My sandals made the sound of feathers landing on the hardwood floor as I walked over, pulled a chair out from the butcher's table in the center of the room, and then sat down. Maybe I could turn myself into a phoebe and fly out the window. But the panes were shut.

Pregnant silence filled the room, save for my anxious breaths. At one point I opened my mouth to speak, yet nothing came.

Pasternak turned and faced my way, his expression even and true—a gift for me—as revealed by one slight quaver of his chin. "I came upon a badly wounded Russian infantryman in a little makeshift hospital at Grozny. This boy saw Oleg last, the only one who did I could find." His Adam's apple moved up and down like Sisyphus's rock trying to escape his throat. "I'm afraid I've failed you, Katya."

I shook my head. "What did you learn from this 'boy,' as you call him?"

"I'm sorry, you're right. Innocence has been abolished." He walked over, then sat down in the chair beside me. A pass of his hand over his face, and then he looked me directly in the eyes again. "The young man's name is Grigory Vale...or was; he died before I left the front."

My heart sank into my ankles. For the loss of this Grigory, and what more he would never divulge. "Did you find out everything he knew about Oleg's...disappearance?" I couldn't bring myself to use any other word for what may have happened to my husband.

"Grigory was very bad off, had lost a leg and part of his abdomen. He could only talk in a couple of whispered sentences before drifting off into fitful sleep. I saw him once and came back the next day, but—

"He told me when he had gone down in a firefight with the Nazis that Oleg was clearing injured comrades and taking them to cover behind some bombed-out buildings. He carried off the injured soldier right next to Grigory, but the Nazis had cut off his line to cover. Oleg had no choice but to head into the worst of the fire serpentine with the soldier draped over a shoulder."

I pressed my hands against the table, rocked over it like some Hassidic at the Wailing Wall. "How far did Oleg make it?"

Feeling a hand on my back, I glanced that way. It was Solomon Mikhoels's. I began sobbing.

He took his hand away.

"No please...leave it there," I said between heaves.

With his hand pressed firmly, gently against me again, I stopped rocking, gulped back my crying until it slowed considerably. Then I locked eyes with Pasternak. "What else did Grigory tell you?"

"The last thing he remembered on that battlefield before passing out was thinking this crazy medic would surely come for him next."

"So did Oleg make it through the fire?"

Momentarily, Pasternak pursed his lips. "Grigory fell into sleep before I could press him on that. I asked all over Grozny, military, civilians, the hospitals and medic outposts." A long pause. "I even went to the mass gravesites and spoke to undertakers, if one can call these people that. No one else knows anything. I'm terribly sorry, Katya."

I shook my head vehemently. "Oleg is alive."

Pasternak's eyes widened. Solomon Mikhoels sat down in the chair on the other side of me, never lifting his hand off my back.

"I'll call in all my chits with the military until we find out something if at all possible," Pasternak said.

"Thank you," I said, then met Solomon's eyes. "You and I know safe houses for Jews in Grozny. We've talked with these people in our work."

"I'll make some calls as soon as the phones get back up there," Solomon said.

I reached back and took hold of his hand, then brought them onto the table between us. "Will you take me to Grozny?"

Hesitancy flashed in his expression, same as when he'd gone down into the basement of this very building that day it had been bombed, when Pasternak and I defused the fuselages. I attempted to let go of his hand, but didn't seem to be able to.

I shot another look at Pasternak. "Will you take me?"

"You know I would, but I'm too high profile to go underground without making it a near certainty we'd be spotted, tailed, and apprehended."

I nodded my understanding. Really, I already knew this to be true but hadn't wanted to face it. And getting caught in Jewish underground operations surely landed you in the gulag.

Solomon firmed his hold of my hand.

I shifted in my chair and measured him. The trouble, his weakness had all but vanished from his face. It wasn't that Solomon didn't have a high profile, he did, but the actor was a master of disguise. I'd seen him pull it off on missions with the underground. Nothing this dangerous directly at the front, but nonetheless effective. "You must take me," I said.

"Of course."

I took a deep breath, then exhaled slowly. Still, I couldn't let go of his hand. If that happened, Oleg would most certainly be dead.

CHAPTER TWENTY-ONE

Earthy musk, purple haze potpourri, which only really primo pot scents the air with, hung round their heads in a thick smoke cloud. In spite of this frigid day, they kept the Taurus's heater off, windows shut, not losing any of the "*good thang*" to AC filtration. Just like they'd handled their toke-and-drives back in high school. Frazier took a long hit off the torpedo, and then held it toward Rudy, who sat in the passenger seat, his baggie of ganja between them on the console. The slumbering man's old friend had plumped up some as had Frazier, and Rudy's full, bushy, fire engine red beard challenged the slumbering man's murky desert mud goatee-with-jazz-dot. A muted gray and rust colored knit cap down over Rudy's ears, which otherwise stuck out like batwings or something, covered his burr cut red hair. His deep-set eyes always seemed to be in some sort of Cheech and Chong squint, even when not high, which if his scam came down anything like it used to, then he went around straight much of the time. Rudy Carver had both feet firmly planted in these sprawling hardpan plains, no beating-around-the-shrubbery, citified rebellion going on with him. Refreshing. Although, mildly embarrassing for the slumbering man's dualities. As Rudy took his turn with the joint, he shuddered, zipped his green to darker green camo jacket close under his chin. Frazier's navy blue down parka over a sweatshirt and T-shirt did the job from the waist up, but in blue jeans his legs were icicles. He could hardly believe Rudy had a wife, three kids, two dogs, a cat, a bevy of chickens, and forty acres to keep up with. Rudy and Ellie sold "conventional" produce at farmers' markets over the weekends. Turns out they organically grew tomatoes, green chile peppers, and habaneros on all but the five acres farthest from the road. Back there, Rudy cultivated the Big Bend Blond they were burning down.

All those years ago his and Rudy's toke-and-drives after classes had been Frazier's MO for preparing to spend the rest of the day with his parents. He had phoned them earlier today to set up this visit, and the call had been chilly with Pop. He'd headed over alone to face them, but the closer he got the more Frazier felt low in his stomach the shattered glass of his upbringing—until he may as well have been a teenager again. That's when he'd decided to track down Rudy. No more putting it off now. Well, make that an hour or so more. The gas gauge indicated a hair less than a quarter of a tank. They had headed out to the back roads three-quarters full.

Rudy blew a snaking stream of smoke from his mouth, then said, "I'm getting the munchies, dude."

Frazier laughed sort of like a popcorn cooker blowing its top, then, keeping a hand on the steering wheel, reached in the backseat and brought back a jumbo bag of Frito's corn chips. "Here." He tossed the bag at Rudy. "Add some cholesterol directly to your veins. Open it up and dig in, but don't take them all. Oh, there's a can of bean dip back there too."

"Cool." Rudy passed the joint to Frazier, then retrieved the dip.

The slumbering man's lungs were sore from lack of practice, though no way Rudy would find out if at all possible. The next drag went down hot, sweet, and like fingernails carving a gorge along his throat. He suppressed a coughing fit.

"You and Margaret get high together all the way up there in NYC?" Rudy said, between cramming his mouth full, chewing, and swallowing down the swill.

Holy cosmic cherubim, the slumbering man didn't want to answer. "Not really."

"How do you cope with all the unmitigated crap, man?"

"I, well, slumber."

"How does that work?"

"I'm pretty much blind with myopia but have reading-style glasses so no one will know unless I want them to. Most of the time I look over the top of my lenses."

"Damn, Frazier, it's that bad. Tell me something real."

Over the next several tokes and handfuls of corn chips, all the way to the clean-as-a-whistle bottom of the bean dip can, the slumbering man talked about his marital and writing woes, though didn't say anything about Anastasie. He and Rudy hadn't been around each other enough to know whether Rudy would blow him off as a friend for considering an extramarital relationship, and Rudy didn't seem like the kind of man who'd understand the slumbering man's nuanced muse explanation. Frazier finished with a flurry over Margaret's and his different angles on writing about a Tunisian poet named Yassine Lotfi Khaled. Pot being the truth serum it is, he was pleased to know he cared this much about writing anything, anything at all.

"Wow, man, I've been following that shit closely," Rudy said.

"You've been following the Tunisian poet's plight?"

Rudy shook his head. "The hope for the world, for something resembling actual democracy, for a nonviolent revolution that could actually work, which the Tunisian people are giving us all one huge-ass teach on."

The slumbering man took another long hit, exhaled. "Damn, Rudy, honestly, do you think things here have a horseshoes' and hand grenades' chance of changing for the better because of what's going on over there?"

"Are you kidding? I campaigned hard for Obama in '08 because he said he'd do things differently and for the good of the people, but it's just been more of the same inside ball. I've been depressed too, man." He gave Frazier a slim smile. "At least I've got the guts to *really* get high in dealing with it."

"Ruuuudy," Frazier said, as if tossing a Slinky at his friend. The slumbering man had seen too many writers, artists, and publishing house people go down the tubes on their drug of choice. In fact, his own slumbering was a pretty good indicator to tread lightly with the wacky weed. There'd be no AA or NA in his future if he could help it. But that was him, Frazier, the slumberer. Willie Nelson, Edgar Allan Poe, and, say, Andy Warhol did pretty well and still got high, if it had taken a toll on their—how to put this?—physical features.

"Whatever, Frazier. If I had the money, I'd go over to Tunisia and get in the streets with those good people."

"You would, truly, do you think you'd go?"

"Without a doubt, man, wouldn't you, Mr. Leave-Me-Behind-in-Monahans-Progressive-Radical-Commie-Pinko-Fag?" Rudy laughed out loud, took another toke off the reefer.

"Ouch."

"You used to be in the streets, man. You gave me the big teach, sort of a hero for the townie if you will. No really, ask yourself, what do you care about enough these days to take action on? You're the only Spiderman I know. The one that got away."

"Baby steps, baby steps," Frazier said. "Hand over that joint, will you?"

Rudy did.

Frazier brought it to his lips but stopped short of taking a hit. There was a better way. He pulled the car over to the side of the long, straight blacktop road to nowhere *and* his folks' place. Giving Rudy back the torpedo, Frazier said, "Why don't you take the wheel for a while."

His friend readily agreed.

They got out of the car and changed places.

As Rudy drove on, the slumbering man looked over the top of his lenses, and everything turned into a dream world.

✍

Twenty or so minutes and some almost too groovy cosmic banter with the slumbering man's toke-and-drive buddy later, Rudy stopped the Taurus in front of a padlocked metal gate for Frazier's parents' two and a half scruffy acres fenced by barbed wire looped around wooden posts well on their way to decomposing into the earth. Glad he had backed off the Mary Jane, Frazier tilted his head to use his eyeglasses.

In bib overalls, gray T-shirt, and bulky working boots, Pop sat on the lone lawn chair in front of his shop, a rusted-out metal shed with weeds like Medusa's hair all around it, the place's overhead door broken, hanging catawampus by a single hinge. By the time Pop got home from that dawn-to-dusk job out on the oil rigs, there wasn't enough left of him to keep the place up, and on weekends he needed to recoup enough to do it all over again, a beer in hand and some ball game on TV. Pop's arms were folded almost defiantly across his thick chest, his heavily sweat-stained Poncho Villa sombrero low on his brow.

A slight smile came to Frazier's lips as he looked, just beyond the shop and a precariously leaning carport, at the little two-bedroom, one-bath adobe house he'd grown up in. A line of red, pink, and yellow blooming rosebushes on either side of the front door went all the way to the corners of the house. Moms had planted them from twigs. In his mind's eye Frazier saw himself as a kid "helping" her get them started with his little plastic beach bucket and trowel. The yard in front of the house always stayed nothing more than a thin layer of West Texas dust, as vehicles came in near the bushes to park. A water hose lay on the ground in front of the rosebushes. Moms had been keeping them going.

Frazier had hoped having an almost fully self-anesthetized Rudy as wingman may be a good idea, the innocuous observer on stage left who held things together some just by Frazier's folks not wanting to create a scene that would get back to people in town, but now that he was actually here, the slumbering man had better go in solo. "I've got this."

"You sure, man? Your dad looks pretty righteous."

"No, I'm not certain. Why don't you have a beer or two at the Eagle's Nest?" He got a ten-dollar bill out of his jeans pocket and held it toward Rudy. "On me."

"I should be paying you." Rudy took the money.

A cloud of ganja poured out of the car along with the slumbering man. Pop sniffed the air mightily, then shook his head. As Frazier walked over and rested his forearms atop the gate, Pop slowly pushed himself out of the lawn chair and began making his way toward him. The slumbering man looked over the top of his lenses again. "Nice to see you, Pop. Looks to be you're still getting around nimbly."

"Mighty fine." Pop inserted the key in the padlock, then turned it. "Let me take a good look at you; hardly remember your resemblance."

"My 'resemblance'?"

"To your mother. You never did look much like your handsome Old Man."

Yeah, and you probably like it that way, Frazier fought against saying. "Uh huh. I noticed the rosebushes are in full bloom."

"The Old Lady does like her pitter-patter."

"About the only beauty this place has, she's nurtured it."

With a hand Pop gripped the gate.

They stared each other down over the top of it.

"You about to open this thing up, or hold it shut on me, Pop?"

"Haven't quite decided yet."

This wasn't what Frazier came here to do, dive into an emotional knife fight, slash for slash, stab upon stab, that they'd gotten so good at, weirdly somehow as if playing washers or throwing horseshoes on Sunday afternoons, just about the only fun activities his family had joined in on together. With that thought, it became important for Frazier to know whether Moms and Pop still played. Without this good thing and the once a week night out at dinner, the only remaining ritual would be their family's knife fights. And what could you do with that other than bleed one another out—make slumbering people?

Looking through his lenses again, he glanced over beside the shop and spotted iron stakes and cut-down PVC pipes that when in junior high school he'd helped Pop set in the ground for those games, shoes and washers lying here and there. "Please let me in," Frazier said at last.

"I do suppose you've come a long way to see us." Pop swung the gate back.

Without another word, Frazier walked over and began gathering up the horseshoes. Carefully, he positioned himself just behind the near stake, then took a hard look at the other one. His first toss came to rest a few inches right of the stake and dead-on with distance. His next shoe clanked against the iron rod, then spun round it like some Cirque du Soleil acrobat.

Pop came alongside him and said, "Your mother is expecting you inside the house."

"I know, and I'll get to her soon enough." Frazier winked. "Bet you can't beat me at a game."

Grinning slyly, Pop took a long look at Frazier's ringer. "Bet me what?"

"A six-pack of Carta Blanca for the winner, and—"

"You're on," Pop interrupted.

"There's something in it for the loser."

Pop nudged his sombrero back a little, squinted at Frazier. "What are you up to now, son?"

"Whoever comes out on the short end of the stick has to tell Moms her roses are a thing of beauty they've secretly enjoyed for as long as they can remember."

"I don't know, I ah…"

"You've already accepted the bet, Pop."

His dad grinned for no longer than a nanosecond. "Oh, hell, let's get on with it, then."

While looking once more over the top of his lenses, the slumbering man's next toss fell over two feet off the mark—he somehow felt sure of it.

Pop rubbed the horseshoe against his overalls, took aim, then let it fly. "There, take that. Easily inside your shoe."

Frazier made another wayward toss.

From hearing the cluck of his father's tongue, he figured Pop's throw bested him again.

As they walked the distance between stakes, Pop said, "You a normie, son?"

"How do you mean?"

"Your eyes got more red in them than a Rand McNally road map." Pop picked up two horseshoes, as did Frazier. "There're people who can handle the stuff and people who can't," Pop went on. "Normies are people like your friend Rudy who can moderate their use, carry on their lives in good fashion." Pop stepped in behind the stake. "They're not flighty in their everyday lives."

Like me you mean! Frazier's blood flowed like a Rio Grande valley flash flood.

Pop's horseshoe clanked against the far stake.

Frazier looked through his lenses again, took dead aim, and then covered Pop's ringer. "What do you think makes the difference between an addict and a normie?" the slumbering man said.

"Hell if I know…just the way they were hatched, I suppose." Pop stepped in behind the stake again, shuffled his feet into better position.

"Do you think being 'flighty' as you say, becoming an addict, has anything to do with the way you were raised?"

Pop grunted, then tossed his shoe every bit of three feet past the stake. "Don't blame me for your misbehavings."

"Before today I haven't smoked weed in years."

"Good, then."

"Not good. I'm not a normie, Pop."

His father locked eyes with him. "You're not up there in *New York City* (those three words came like spit nails) shooting up horse, are you?"

"No, I'm a slumbering man. I have a hard time caring about anything, and when I do I don't do anything about it. I've gone all but legally blind, though I don't use my eyeglasses most of the time. It keeps me high, tuned out, in a way that somehow I make it through the day."

"How did things come to this?"

"Maybe it's the way you say 'New York City.'"

"And look what happened to you up there. You could've had a good life here. There's nothing wrong with hard work of hands."

"Or of mind."

Pop's expression twisted, but his blue eyes remained true. "You're the one who went for big dreams; even if you haven't accomplished them, they're yours and they're big."

"I swear, I think you're a little jealous of me."

"That does it. This game is over." Pop dropped his horseshoe onto the ground, sending up a puff of dust that went to nothing in the cold breeze. As he began walking away, Frazier stepped directly into his path. They blew foggy breaths onto each other's faces.

"No, it doesn't do it, Pop, and nothing is over that I came here for."

"And just what is that?"

"Your blessing." Where were these words coming from? "I don't think I've got a dust devil's chance of becoming a normie without it."

Pop looked downward, kicked another puff of dust with his steel-toe boot. "I don't know how to do so," he said, all the spit and vinegar gone from his tone.

Pop's body was in the shape of a question mark. How hard had Pop's life been to have calluses over his soul thicker than the ones on his hands? "But would you like to?"

Pop nodded slightly, or a gust blew the sombrero's brim down and his head simply followed.

"I've got an idea. Please, don't go anywhere on me," Frazier said. He walked over to the rosebushes, and then broke a stem off that had a large, well-formed yellow blossom. When he came back, Pop still studied the dirt down round his boots. As if presenting the national book award to John Steinbeck, or a diamond drill bit to a rig foreman, Frazier moved the rose several inches below Pop's face. "Just look at it," Frazier said, softening his tone. "For a moment don't think of how hard your life has been, or Felicia and Derek's, or mine and Margaret's, or how hard you worked for Moms and us, or how your big revolutionary dreams haven't come to pass just yet. Close your eyes until you see all of your grandkids." Pausing, he gave Pop a few seconds. "Go ahead, it's okay. Close them."

Pop did so.

"You see them?"

Pop nodded.

"Now, open your eyes and look at the rose."

Pop did this too.

"Isn't it beautiful?"

Again, Pop nodded.

"Say it, Dad."

"It's mighty pretty."

A wave of gooseflesh prickled Frazier, not from the cold weather. It was his blessing. "What do you say we go inside and let Moms know how we feel?"

Pop's third nod came. "Give me that thing, will you?"

Frazier handed Pop the rose.

The two men made their way toward the house.

As they walked inside, the screen door loudly slapped shut behind them. Moms didn't rush through the doorway that separated the kitchen from the "TV room" to give Frazier a hug and a kiss on the lips, with her bittersweet expression giving away she fiercely loved him, though felt miffed over how long he'd stayed away. The small hole opening in his chest—like a cigarette snubbed through paper, which sent embers out larger and larger—told Frazier he'd come to expect Moms' greetings more than he'd realized. He heard her busying herself at the sink, clinking silverware under faucet water. She couldn't have missed the sound of the screen slam.

On them entering the kitchen, Moms showed her back as she filled a long-snouted yellow pitcher with water. Still the bohemian with loosely tied graying hair, though more of a pear-shaped figure than before, Moms gave the ivy spilling from a clay pot on the windowsill over the sink a good drenching.

"Hon," Pop said. "I've got a something for you."

She set the pitcher on the countertop, then used a dishtowel to wipe sweat or maybe tears from beneath her eyes. "You talking about our boy being here?"

"Not entirely," Pop said as she turned and faced the two of them.

Her troubled eyes went from Frazier to the rose and back again.

"Hi, Moms." Frazier smiled unsteadily.

She wistfully reached for him, but then her arm fell to her side. "So glad you're here, Frazier. Sorry for the shape I'm in."

"What's wrong?" Pop said, his tone thickening with concern.

"I just got off the phone with Felicia, and Police Chief Brody earlier today told them that sometime between now and tomorrow noon, his men will evict them by force if necessary."

"They can stay in what used to be Frazier's and Felicia's bedroom, here with us," Pop said without hesitation. "It'll be cramped, but we can put down sleeping bags for the grandkids. Things are going to be okay."

"No, they're not!" Moms snapped. "Derek has loaded his shotguns; says he's not leaving." She glanced at the rose again. "Oh, I shouldn't have raised my voice at you."

"I'm loading up my Browning twelve-gauge pump and going over there to stand with Derek," Pop said. He shot a look at Frazier. "Can you get Rudy to bring your car back here pronto?"

Frazier nodded. "Why?"

"To fetch Felicia and the grandkids, then bring them here to safety. Derek and Felicia are down to one Dually Ford truck. I figure he may need his only means of transportation should he decide somewhere along the way to bail out."

"But you'll have your truck."

"Once I get over there, I'm not leaving until the police and the bank back off for good."

Frazier's face tightened. He believed Pop, admired his recklessness in a way. Looking Moms directly in the eyes, Frazier said, "You're the only one who can talk some sense into Pop."

Her already red-rimmed eyes filled with tears again. "Sometimes you have to take a stand for what is right."

The weight of all three of them being more alike than not fell heavy on Frazier.

Pop held the rose toward her. "I've secretly always liked your flowers."

She placed her nose into the womb of the blossom and took a long, slow breath. "Be careful, Melvin."

"I'll probably be home before dinner. So-called *Police Chief* Chapman Brody doesn't want anything to do with me. Known him since kindergarten; he's a bully that always backs down when somebody bigger than him shows up."

"It's probably suicide," Frazier said. "This Brody will come with others. Besides, if you don't go over there, Derek is the type who'll likely back down."

"He ain't—" Pop's jowls turned blotchy and purple as if with anger.

"What, a chicken with his head in the clouds like me?" Frazier saw blue stars.

"Old Man, don't grace that with words," Moms said, then intently looked at her son again. "You're the one born for verbalizing, Frazier. You're a good boy, a writer, not a fighter."

Strange as dust devils on a still West Texas afternoon, Frazier's mind careened through his and Moms' literary history. It had been Moms who turned him on to books. Moms, named Novella by Frazier's grandmother, a woman who incessantly read pulp fiction romance. Moms caught up in Heller's *Catch-22* '60s, and now a survivor of them. Left to her devices, Frazier would've written best-selling antiwar novels, but he never quite imagined on paper, or in person, effective nonviolent resistance for change. Major story lines in two of the three manuscripts on the bottom of his desk drawer. "If you haven't noticed, I'm a grown man. Have been for quite a while."

"I've noticed," Moms said.

Pops raked his teeth over his lip.

Frazier's next words would need to be dandies. "Let me make one phone call to see if Margaret can put the *New York Times* and CNN or other biggies onto Brody together with Derek and Felicia's bank. That kind of media will stop what's going down better than two men with shotguns.

"If I succeed in getting the coverage, then you and I go over and talk Derek down. If not, then I'll stand with you guys after clearing out Felicia and the children."

"I've got another gun in the case. You can use one of those."

The stars turned red. "I'll not be using a weapon."

"Talk about suicide," Pop grumbled.

Frazier extended his right hand. "Do we have a deal?"

Pop made no move to accept it. He said nothing.

"C'mon, Pop. Malcom X and King shook hands, figured out what they could do together."

"The *man* has a point," Moms said.

Now, Pop's eyes went from his wife of forty-plus years to the yellow rose and back. At last, he shook Frazier's hand. "This ain't horseshoes," Pop said.

"No, it's not." Frazier took his cell phone from his jeans pocket, then speed-dialed Margaret.

His blood ran cold when her voice mail greeting played. "It's an emergency here, Margaret. Pop and Derek are taking up arms against the police unless we get some media coverage from major outlets calling for a reprieve on Derek and Felicia's foreclosure."

"*Get* a reprieve," Pop interjected.

"Yes, achieving concrete results to stop the bank," Frazier went on. "You know some of the right people to get this done." A long, orchestrated pause. "Yes. Yes, I understand. So this *can* happen." The line bleeped off. He studied his folks' expressions to make sure they harbored no suspicion, and continued without missing a beat. "Your sources are chomping at the bit for this kind of stuff. Wonderful! Call me back as soon as you know who's going to take the story.

"What? Uh huh. Everyone's okay so far. Pop and I are about to go over there. Yes, well, ah, I'm afraid I've committed myself to stand with them. No, nonviolently. I have some tricks up my sleeve that could work to diffuse things, but as you can see, we need your help. Yes, I love you too. Okay, and just tell Mattie and Doug that I love them, will you? Okay. Bye." He pressed the End button.

"She's a better woman than I thought," Moms said.

"I'll get my shotgun; it's in my shop." Pop turned on his heels, then began walking from the kitchen. "It may be too late to help them by the time some story gets out."

"That's not a good idea!" Frazier called out as Pop disappeared through the doorway.

His folks' landline rang, and Moms immediately put it to her ear. "My goodness, Felicia, hello. Things are changing fast over here. You are? Good. That's the smart thing to do. Get yourself and the kids over here, honey."

Frazier asked for the phone and Moms complied. "Sis, please let me speak with Derek."

"He may not agree to come to the phone," Felicia said.

"Tell him he agreed to something between us that could save your property, and I want to know whether he's come through on his end." If Frazier's hunch was right, Derek's pride had kept him from approaching Felicia on going after media coverage.

"What is this idea of yours?"

"I promised Derek it would be between himself and me only."

"I'll take the phone to him, and don't worry, he won't have a wife left if he doesn't talk with you about options."

When Derek got on the line, Frazier said, "Margaret has agreed to take your story out and is contacting sources as we speak. Please bring your family over here and give this a chance to work?"

All he heard over the line was Derek's raspy breathing. "Thanks for not totally embarrassing me with Felicia," Derek said at last. "But I don't see why I should leave until the story does some good."

"Ask yourself, brother-in-law, do you really want this to go down—you and Pop with guns, and me as your human shield—because we're coming over. This news goes out with the three of us holed up like crazy men harboring death wishes, the outcome is probably not going to fall to your family's favor."

More belabored breathing. "But if we leave, they can just take the place. Wouldn't it look better for the cameras if we stayed put, stood our ground without threatening use of weapons?"

Pop walked into the kitchen again, this time carrying a shotgun, his peepholes ablaze.

So were Frazier's eyes, for everything good his bloodline had in it. "If Pop and I come over there, we're not backing down one iota, Derek, and just so you'll know, Pop's already got his Browning twelve gauge."

Pop cranked the shotgun's pump action. "Lock and load."

"Do you catch our drift, Derek?"

"Damn, you guys are more off your rockers than me."

"So what's it going to be?"

"Felicia is already loading the truck. I suppose we'll be over there shortly."

It wasn't until hanging up the phone that Frazier realized his armpits flowed rivers down his sides, and his shirt stuck against his back.

Pop opened the shotgun's breach, and then worked the pump action to spit five shells out. He pumped it dry once for good measure. "Malcom and Martin at their best together." He beamed.

"Right on, Pop."

"You spoke of having some 'nonviolent' tricks up your sleeve to cool things off. Do you think for a moment they would've worked without me having your back?"

They just did, Frazier wanted to say almost more than anything. "I'll let you know once this is all over."

"I have to hand it to you, kid." Pop gave him a man-friend slap on the back.

"I hope Margaret comes through," Moms said.

Pop smiled warmly at her. "Don't kill our buzz, Old Lady. It's as good as the Maui Wowi we used to smoke."

Frazier chuckled more nervously than he would've liked. "How long has it been since you got high, Pop?"

"When I went up the river over the stuff. Don't want to give the U.S. government any more of my time behind bars, if you can imagine what I mean."

"I believe I can." It seemed to Frazier he could very well be turning into a normie. Suddenly, he knew what he wanted more than anything, to get Margaret's agreement on helping with the media story, and then assure his toke-and-drive buddy that Monahans was Rudy's territory; Frazier's next places of interest would be Tunisia as well as Egypt, where according to Margaret's mole in Clifford Odeon's organization, the second distillation of the revolution fermented even now. His townie friend could not give him the big teach on nonviolent action for democratic change in the Middle East, and Frazier just leave it at that. Actually picturing Spiderman, he smiled inwardly.

"I better rescue Rudy from the Eagle's Nest," Frazier said. "Call him to come get me, then I'll run him home. I'll come back here to spend time with everybody."

"You going to light up with Rudy?"

"No Pop." *I'm going to tell him I am in fact "the one who got away," but am no longer running so hard, arms pumping as furiously as you pumped your shotgun's action, T-shirt flapping in my wake.*

"Why 'no'? You won't be a normie until you can answer that question with integrity."

"Because I just kept you, Derek, and myself alive." *No matter what the cops do, or the banksters, or the media, or even Margaret.*

She would think him clever and brave for doing what he'd just done, right? Margaret had been trained from a young age to stand with family who accepted her with reservations—hers and his—he was abundantly clear on this much. Who could know what Anastasie would think of him at a time like this? History with Margaret meant something, not just the passing of time, but trust, at least to more of an extent than with some muse he hardly knew.

Right now he wanted to love on Margaret, to write a great story with her. That's why travels to Tunisia and Egypt would come soon. After spending Christmas with Margaret and the kids, and taking leave of absence from Flying Pens. He shuddered inwardly. This was beginning to feel like cold turkey. Could he avoid slumbering for such long stretches? Maybe he should go to AA for slumberers.

Then again, Margaret might fall furious with him for implicating her in all of this with Derek and Felicia, asking her to call in chits she'd spent years amassing in New York.

Possibly Pop had it half right, being a normie required more of a certain type of stuff than the slumbering man could manage. Frazier felt like a shaman at the altar of some fire-and-brimstone Monahans, Texas, Southern Baptist church. Nowhere to go except back inside himself, to a place you could rightly call *integrity*. If only he more often listened for this native drumbeat amid the din. Then maybe he would be a normie of another kind.

CHAPTER TWENTY-TWO

Grozny stank with munitions sulfur and the musky mold of rubble; yellowish, sickly dust kept my nose stuffy, that is until mixed into fluids my body produced to ward all this off. Then I intermittently drizzled the ravages of war from various orifices—the nostrils, the eyes, I pissed it out—but never as fast as it came at me. Solomon Mikhoels and I hurriedly walked along Pervomayskaya Street, the bombed-out office and apartment buildings seeming like skeletons, macabre dollhouses, many with outer walls and roofs no longer there, or shredded into random juts and fangs of rebar, plaster, and concrete. To keep ourselves intact it was necessary to step over or beside detritus and potholes indistinguishable from ordnance depressions. We had transformed into patrons attending some dark symphony composed of a brass section trumpeting staccato machine-gun fire punctuated by kettledrum blasts from tanks' main guns. On Pasternak's advice over how to increase the probability of managing our way through this hellhole based on what he'd learned from his recent trip here, we were now Dr. Nestor Spalko and registered nurse Isidor Krabava-Spalko, with papers to prove it that had been flawlessly created by Jewish Anti-Fascist Committee underground loyalists back in Moscow. Nestor and Isidor, comrades in the Red Army eager to go where the action was and medical attention urgently needed, spouses, inseparable. That story and our made-up orders had gone over well enough with Red Army personnel dispatch in Moscow. Solomon placed calls to safe houses here before we left home, and no one had known anything of my Oleg's fate. In what remained of this city, there must be other Jewish sympathizers who would know something, or maybe just some local Russian with a good heart, I'd frequently told myself to keep from sinking too low. Solomon and I had been getting familiar with the guard detail's habits at our quarters in a requisitioned house just behind the front, their cigarette breaks, when they tended to quiet down for long periods, possibly dozing off in the night. Then we'd slip away to find Oleg or gain at least some clue about him, and return to quarters before being noticed missing. If too little downtime from the guards presented itself, we'd be forced to escape, then find another way back to Moscow once our real work was done. So far we didn't know enough about the guards' routines to execute our scheme, and this kept me on pins and needles. But right now my anxiety-spiked adrenaline had little to do with that. While playing doctor and nurse the previous two days here, we had visited with the injured, got to know their cases, dressed some wounds, things that we could wing. Today, the head of the makeshift field hospital had scheduled Solomon for a string of amputations and me as his OR assistant. It sure as hell was time to kick in plan B! Problem was, our military escort walked tightly alongside us, his assault rifle held across his chest, an index finger extended over the trigger casing. Command didn't want to leave one of the few physicians and nurses they had on the front uncovered. As we turned and headed into the hospital beneath internal archways laid naked to the world by Nazi shelling of what had been the actual Grozny Opera House, I placed a hand on Solomon's arm, stopping us, then slid the fingers of my other hand along his tie. "You look awful, darling," I said. It was true, his face had gone flaccid, his eyes strident. "You need a pick-me-up before such a grueling sequence of surgeries."

His brow furrowed. He said nothing.

There we stood, Solomon in his powdered hair and glued-on powdered bushy beard and mustache, me in a fire engine red, wavy, long wig and black rim spectacles with unaltered lenses. He looked ten years older and distinguished, and I don't quite know what kind of woman I resembled. The train ride had gone fine, at night him sleeping on the floor and me in our berth. And he'd been a perfect gentleman here in Grozny, going outside our quarters while I got ready for bed. He had curled up on the floor here too. Now, I winked at him, and then faced our military comrade, who looked somewhat confused and very serious, still at the ready hairpin-trigger-wise. "I need five minutes alone with my husband." I winked again. "To steady his hands, if you know what I mean."

The soldier's face tightened.

"Trust me, comrade," I went on. "You can guard our door. It'll save lives in the OR, I promise."

Without waiting for a response from our escort, I grabbed Solomon's hand and led him toward a bathroom I'd used once before. The sewerage had clogged, water no longer flowed through faucets, and yet I remembered a shattered window that opened to an alleyway behind the hospital/opera house. The things that stick in your mind when attempted escape was inevitable and at the same time seemingly impossible. Who knew, maybe no Red Army personnel would be in the alley, and then we could dump our disguises and simply walk away as ourselves without anyone noticing the famous actor. Entering with Solomon and quickly closing the door behind us, I held my breath less from the stench than the terrible odds against our success. Yesterday, I had caught a whiff of tobacco coming through the window.

He feverishly scanned the place, and then began massaging his temples. "Now what, my little sex kitten?"

"You should be so lucky." I walked over underneath the window, then climbed onto the sink, placing my feet on either side of the bowl. I slipped a few jagged pieces of glass out of the frame and quietly set them on the countertop. With my blood humming, I peered through the window one way, then the other. At the end of the alley, where it connected to a heavily militarized street, two soldiers stood talking, their weapons slung over their shoulders by leather straps.

"Anyone out there?" Solomon said.

I told him about them, without taking my eyes off the army guys.

"How's your throwing arm?"

Shooting a look at Solomon, I raised an eyebrow.

He held a good-sized shard of glass extended toward me. "Distract them, Katya, or would you rather me give it a toss?"

I pictured myself as a kid, bookish as I was, hurling the ball nearly half the length of the field at runners during games of Lapta. "A bit of the closet tomboy, I'm afraid." I took the glass from him, reared back and gave it a good throw into the bombed-out, roofless office building on the far side of the alley. The soldiers exchanged more words, brought their rifles to the ready, and took off in the direction of the shattered glass. Solomon and I dropped our disguises on the bathroom's floor, then shimmied through the window one after the other, me first. The fall was gentler than I'd expected, just a couple meters really. We landed on our feet.

"Let's find a place to lie low till nightfall," he said in an undertone.

I nodded my agreement. We would do what we could to avoid Solomon getting spotted on the streets of Grozny, probably not by any of the newly conscripted members of the Red Army, oh, maybe some of the officers who'd seen him on the grand stage in Moscow. The famous actor had explained aboard the train that he'd been here several times, though never to perform at the Opera House, but before everyday people in the streets with a troupe he led of younger upstart actors. Early on they did comedic satire pieces about the Czarist regime, and after the revolution went so bad, they turned their plays against Stalinism. They would often grab up their props and small wooden plank stage, then scatter in every direction possible when members of the Militsiya or Red Army showed up with guns aimed at the performers. Some of them had been sent to gulags for a time. When he'd told me about this, I offered to write one-acts for them, and was delighted over Solomon's reply: "I've been waiting for the right opportunity to inquire of your generous talents for our little ragtag group." Behind his glimmering eyes over these plays, this subversive poetry, I had seen the stuff that inspired peasants, and me; there truly could be egalitarian community someday, somewhere, call it communism sans the capital C.

Without another word, we ran the opposite direction of the heavily militarized zone toward a somewhat less occupied cross street, veering away from the hospital/opera house. Once on the cross street, we slowed to a walk. My chest rose and fell with troubled breathing even after I no longer felt winded. Tracers of ordnance lit the air like fireflies while artillery explosions shook the ground, and then a couple of blocks away, their muddy clouds of fire rose. The Mephisthophelean concerto of this war gave all devils at least some cover, I supposed, including us. Only one other person in civilian clothing was out on this street, an old man with a badly curved spine, and he was on the far side of the road, his eyes cast downward.

In seconds three soldiers rounded the corner ahead and came our way. I fought against bolting, Solomon and I scattering as he and his actors had. Mikhoels' determined pace didn't falter as we passed them by. When we got to the avenue of the building at which I'd hurled the shard of glass, I glanced that way, and two-thirds or so along the block just outside the building stood those two soldiers who'd gone to search down whoever caused the disturbance. One of them spoke into a walkie-talkie.

"We may have the perfect love nest to hole up in," I said. "Keep walking and keep your eyes frontward not to draw attention." I explained to Solomon if the soldiers were calling in the building as all clear to their superiors, then it was somewhat reasonable to think when the posse comitatus went out after us, it wouldn't bother with that place. I ended with, "We can circle back once giving those two soldiers a little more time to go their own way."

"Flimsy," was all he said.

No more than the distance of Pasternak's dacha's lawn ahead, or maybe the length of a Lapta field, a fireball cratered the street, knocking us flat on our backs. Rocks showered down, smoke billowed. Rolling onto our stomachs we swiveled our heads to the side, and I looked directly at his sooty face with raccoon eyes. "You got a better idea?" I said.

He bared his teeth.

A smile or a grimace, I couldn't be sure. "Anything broken?" I said.

"Don't think so. You?"

"Who knows, I can't even feel my teeth chattering."

We stood up, and I headed back the way we came, Solomon walking beside me without protest. *Faustian redirection, indeed.*

When we turned onto the street with the shattered-glass building on it, I immediately noticed the two soldiers were gone. At the same instant we started running again. Once we made it to the front of the building, it became clear this wasn't ruins of office suites or apartments but an old church, its spires like broken bones, its copula now the patch of blue sky directly overhead, as if God mocked the yellowed air of destruction that hung close to ground. A Loving Creator outsmarting Beelzebub, I sort of needed to believe. Remembering how Pasternak just before dinner went through an almost undetectable genuflection, I did the same now. We walked into the only room that still had a ceiling, and it happened to be a small chapel. There were breathtakingly beautiful Byzantine frescos on the ceiling of Talmudic figures I recognized, Jacob, Moses, Sarah, Rebecca, and there was Jesus along with some New Testament characters I wasn't too sure of, Saint Paul or the disciples or something. For a long moment I tilted my head back and drank in the purple, gold, and forest green brushstrokes, beige and Nubian skin tones, age lines in the plaster skittering across the figures, an insistence of something spiritual, here in this moment of all times. Stealing a glance at Solomon, he had joined me in, well, what else to call it other than art appreciation? Anthropology that had the ability to suspend the clock, elevate hope for no good reason, illogic arising as a brighter truth. No requirements to become a member of this congregation—humanity's. I had no idea whether we would find Oleg, but in a way we had located where he was, where all of us were. I leaned against a wall and then slid down on my haunches. Solomon did likewise against the opposite wall. "Pretty flimsy for sure," I said.

His smile had a sparkling, starry quality set against his almost totally blackened face. "It'll have to do."

We sat there for the longest time, not exchanging another word, and then a bomb shook the building. It wasn't a direct hit, but close enough to crumble plaster off the ceiling, as if heaven itself blew apart and fell on us in thousands of tiny colored splinters.

Solomon crab-crawled over next to me, where he put his hands against the wall right above my head and curved his body to shield mine.

"No, I want to see it," I said without thinking.

He didn't move. "See what? I'm trying to keep you alive."

It became hard to breathe, though not because of a lack of oxygen. "I must see what's left of it." I shoved at his chest, but found myself only strong enough to barely budge him. "Will your Russian machismo not let me choose how to die?!"

At that his hands came away from the wall. With a sad and apologetic expression, he held my gaze for a long moment. Finally, he sat down beside me.

I looked up at the ceiling again. It took awhile for the chalky dust to settle enough to see anything else. Then, slowly, as though out of Peredelkino autumn fog clearing for an Indian summer day, the frescoes reappeared. All of them were fine, the age lines having deepened and cut some new tributaries, Jesus' brow now gave off several white furrows, and Moses' robe had gotten ripped, but otherwise the paintings were positively splendid. In a way I couldn't explain, better.

As the ferocity persisted outside with the putrid fragrance of war, some kind of unseen demon infiltrating this chapel, I kept my eyes fixed on the paintings. Eventually, I leaned against Solomon's side, and he placed an arm across my shoulders.

My mind occasionally wandered to thoughts of who if anyone performed the surgeries we had obfuscated. Did any of those young men die but could've lived? At times I would cut my eyes at Solomon, noticing whitish calcium lines on his face where tears had flowed through grime.

Like this, we waited for the cover of darkness.

✑

A cloud-blanketed night poured down on Grozny like tar, eerily sticky in quiet, viscous enough to suck up the war for a few hours with blackness so complete it shrouded the moon and all the stars. The fickle electricity was down, flickers of light coming from candle flames in windows here and there. Solomon had told me out of this muck sometimes fell bombs from Nazi air raids. Huh, I supposed we were lucky tonight, as the two of us made our way toward the first safe house Solomon wanted to check in with, the hub of communications for the Jewish underground here. Occasionally, a troupe of Red Army soldiers on night patrol could be spotted by the orange tips of cigarettes. The ones who didn't smoke became spooks; maybe you'd hear their boots clomping but not often. They knew to move like phantoms in staying alive. There were no civilians out. A formal curfew existed, though Solomon had been told it wasn't enforced. If you were crazy enough to go outside at this hour, the troops weren't about to risk moving from the tar into simple nighttime to protect you, get you back inside. Nazi snipers came out on lunar rotations too. We walked close beside buildings, or from tree to tree, but mostly the blackness provided our cover, that and our measured, soft steps.

Solomon touched my arm, then indicated a nearby large oak. We moved underneath its canopy and stood next to the trunk, which was wider than us both. We looked up into leaves and branches, but the indigo in spaces between them made it impossible to make out any sniper who might be perched up there like one of the plentiful crows in Grozny.

Using a low tone Solomon said, "The safe house is three blocks away. It'll be darkened for our arrival." He glanced at his wristwatch. "We'll approach from the alley. If I sneeze, that's the signal something isn't right and we'll not enter."

I nodded my understanding. "What does the house look like?" I said hardly above a whisper.

"It's best you not know."

Somehow the night got blacker. A crow cawed in the tree, giving me a start. I slipped my hand in my gabardine's pocket and fingered the photo of Oleg. "Let's go."

Five minutes later while we walked up wooden steps of the modest A-frame house, a curtain fell across a window near the back door, and then the door opened. Without a word a shadowy figure that brought to my mind's eye a fire hydrant, probably a woman, extended an arm and motioned us inside. Solomon and I followed the fire hydrant along a hallway, me sliding my hands against the walls on both sides so as not to bump into them. A door opened and the three of us walked into a windowless inner room well lit by several candles. Six people sat around the room: three middle-aged, ample women on a sofa, and in straight-back chairs were two slim, sharp-eyed thirty-something women next to a man with a peculiarly wrinkled face, maybe from having been on fire. A map with red, yellow, and blue pencil markings lay open atop a coffee table. The elderly, curly-gray-haired lady who had led the way shut the door, then faced Solomon and me with a warm smile. Her skin was creamy, rosy in places, and her eyes round, the nose wider, closer to her face. This helper of Jews didn't appear to be of Hebrew blood. So much the better, further incognito, more loving if you will. A wave of gratitude washed over me, along with a pang of shame for judging her heritage without knowing her.

"Solomon," she said as he kissed her on both cheeks.

She returned the gesture, and he said, "Mika, you old communist, so nice to see you again."

My goodness, this had to be Mika Vodovos, one of the founders of the Jewish underground originally from Moscow. After having lost her husband, Rudolph, a Jew, to the Goat-faced Murderer's purges, and her getting spared because of renouncing under torture her Orthodox Russian Church upbringing, becoming one of the "assimilated gentiles," she had almost immediately thereafter taken up the cause of saving Jews. Everyone associated with the underground knew her story. Few had met her. Mika Vodovos kept a very low profile. It didn't surprise me in the least this woman chose to place herself on the front. Communist sans the capital C, I thought as Mika Vodovos looked directly at me. Her blue eyes shone brighter than most teenagers' eyes, and they danced mischievously in the candlelight.

"You must be the lovely Katya." Instead of getting the expected Russian kisses on cheeks, she extended her arms and placed a hand firmly on each of my shoulders. "We are all here about the business of locating your husband."

My mouth lost its wetness. "Thank you so much."

"It is our pleasure." Mika Vodovos indicated chairs for Solomon and me, and then the three of us took the remaining places. Just the right number of seats; a well-planned gathering.

She introduced the others as "head of households" for the safe houses in and near Grozny. I had spoken on the phone months ago to one of the younger women called Tilda, and this settled me a little, connected me more, though their courage made me feel small. Mika Vodovos went on to say that regretfully no one in the underground knew anything about a young medic named Oleg Mandelstam. They had checked all their sources and gone into the field searching firsthand.

While she continued, a fist grabbed my heart and squeezed the blood off; I began getting swimmy in the head. Why are we here! I partly wanted to scream.

Then she said, "Sometimes the Jewish men dispose of their Red Army ID, give out assumed names. It makes sense if you think about it. Jews are being gassed by Nazis and rounded up for ghettoizing or worse by Russians, and after being subjected to such awful carnage on the front, others are simply through with war.

"If you have a photograph of your husband, that may help tremendously."

The room spun as I presented my photo of Oleg to Mika Vodovos. I straightened my spine. They would not know of my deterioration; for Oleg's sake, they must believe me to be as strong as him. There were grumbles and murmurs as they probably passed the photo from one to the other, and then the man's clear voice, Peterov, wasn't that his name? "I nursed this boy back to health." I could hardly trust my ears. But in my head, everything began slowing down.

"Please say that again," I said at last.

Peterov did just that.

"Was he injured badly?"

"Yes, but he got to where he doesn't look any worse for wear than, Missus, if I do say so myself, me."

I could've kissed this heavily scarred curmudgeon, so I stood up and walked over to him, then planted my lips on one cheek after the other. Where he'd been burned felt smooth as silk. Now, I saw him with 20/20 vision. "Where did Oleg go?"

He cleared his throat. "You may want to sit back down for this."

"Just tell me. Is he alive?"

"He was when he left about three months ago."

Obediently, I returned to the chair. My lips quivered, and I no longer cared whether my vulnerability showed. "Go on, will you please? I must find him."

He nodded, smiled wanly, and then handed the photo to Mika Vodovos.

She studied it for a long moment before meeting my eyes again. "Oleg is using the name Dimitri, my dear. He is one of those who is through with war."

My papa's name. "He never wasn't through with it," I said.

She wetted her lips. "Yes, well, we got him to an underground outpost for Jews, but he left in the night. He believes Jews are heading for slaughter by congregating together."

"I believe this too." My interjections weren't helping.

"Your Oleg has been missing for nearly two months."

If he weren't in distress, he would've contacted me! "Can you get me to this...this place Oleg is no longer?"

"Yes, but the underground railroad is extremely treacherous. The outpost is in the Urals, three days' travel from here if things go fairly well. I must tell you, they almost never do."

I returned her gaze with eyes every bit as intense as hers, though mine were desperate with life, for it, no puckish quality whatsoever—such affectation may as well never have existed.

Solomon Mikhoels said, "I'll come along and help you find him, Katya."

My skin crawled. In the entire world I only wanted Oleg and me. "Okay," I said.

CHAPTER TWENTY-THREE

"You two gave us the best Christmas present ever!" Felicia said in an excited tone with noticeably rounded vowels, so much so the slumbering man couldn't tell how much of it may be a performance for the sake of her kids, her husband, or all of them.

Looking at the laptop's screen while this Skype video call streamed Derek and Felicia, Frazier and Margaret sat on stools at their kitchen countertop that doubled as a bar. His brother-in-law's out-of-focus large head and sister's slender face brought to mind tan butts of copulating reindeer, say, Donner and Vixen, surrounded by something like glittery, glowing red, blue, yellow, white, and green snowflakes—which must be lit-up ornaments that all but obscured a rural-West-Texas-hang-everything-you-can-get-on-the-tree-save-for-the-kitchen-sink spruce pine. "Ha, ha, ha," the slumbering man sort of pithily sang, "happy Xmas."

"Yes, well, seeing you with big smiles and in your home is a wonderful present for us," Margaret said. "All the gift we would dream of receiving from you guys."

True enough, his sister and brother-in-law hadn't sent the not-to-exceed-five-dollar presents to Mattie and Doug, as was a holiday custom. One of which Margaret pulled the slumbering man's ass out of the fire while he'd been in Texas by arranging their end of this gift exchange for Dwight and Johnny. But then, thought the slumbering man, who could cast aspersions after the armed showdown with police that Derek had come a gnat's eyelash from getting into.

"Hi Uncle Frazier and Aunt Margaret." Dwight and Johnny's voices came through the laptop's speakers. "We're so glad you got those TV people out here with cameras and microphones to keep the bank from kicking us out," Dwight added, probably him anyway. The slumbering man felt okay about it being the older boy's slightly huskier voice, not sure though. He hadn't been certain of much since returning from Texas to New York. The kids seemed like two small reindeer glancing at the screen as they crossed and went out of sight, call them Blixen and Rudolph with one of their noses flashing rosily, or had it only been a blinking red bulb? You know the kind; if one shorts out, the entire string goes dark. The slumbering man shot a look into the family room to make sure the lone strand of twinkling white lights on their measly little fake tree still dazzled, and they did, well, at least the bulbs remained on. Up against the Texan's his and Margaret's Christmas for Mattie and Doug somehow paled, and it came with confusion only a comfortable sophistication breeds: that of strivers, chattering liberals, do-talkers, and the even more benign do-gooders, certainly not radicals for social change that amounted to anything with legs. For starters, the Hanukkah menorah, in its entire candle-burning glory, sat on the mantel above a permanently dampered fireplace, having been years ago shut down by city ordinance. More and more things seemed crimped off down to almost nothing here. It had been like pulling teeth to get Margaret to share with him about the miraculous feat of convincing a senior *New York Daily News* reporter that a story in Monahans, Texas, was worth the time and expense. The reporter then landed on the front page this killer-sad photograph of Derek, Felicia, Dwight, and Johnny standing on their front porch with an unadorned Christmas tree between them and the house that had been slapped with eviction notices across the front door and windows on the day before Christmas Eve. Most of the major news organizations had jumped aboard with the story, and Margaret, to her credit, had insisted it be put in writing in return for the *Daily News's* exclusive head start that she get the interview with a Credit Suisse executive in his Manhattan office. She'd asked him whether he could "enjoy their idyllic, snow-blanketed Connecticut weekend place with family gathered round a fire inside when his bank's foreclosure proceedings on Derek and Felicia's home at the eleventh hour had locked them out of such a merry little Christmas of their own," that's how she'd put it. Then she gave the suit a set of papers, informing him the stroke of a pen would stop "at least this one especially immoral act because of its untimely violent aggression out of millions Credit Suisse had in the mill." The exec said he'd take it under advisement with legal counsel. On the morning of Christmas Eve, Derek and Felicia's home had been spared, for the time being.

It was this that had tumbled the slumbering man down into heavy slumber. He didn't have the heart for explaining to Felicia and Derek the short-term nature of the bank's reprieve. Maybe he would tell them after the holidays. Or he and Margaret could pull another rabbit out of the hat for them. At any rate, with nothing short of threatening divorce, he had forbidden her to do anything with Derek and Felicia other than "the kind thing" of lying about this. She'd argued as though hammering nails into his forehead, "the demands of ethics" together with "treating Derek and Felicia like the adults they were," and then she finally agreed to remain quiet around the issue, though sent him to sleep on the couch. The slumbering man hadn't looked through his lenses since. What destination was home for him in reality, physically, metaphysically? Not Texas any longer. Where then, if not heading toward his roots? Maybe that was no longer possible; he'd accomplished all he'd come for concerning Mom and Pop. Okay, he still had his sights partially set on Tunisia and Egypt, but with him and Margaret further away from collaborating on a story about civil uprisings brewing in the Middle East and the poet Yassine Lotfi Khaled's role in all of it, the two of them without a hat or rabbit to pull out of it, lately Spiderman-social-justice activism held less cachet. So that left him here, and in this place the couch embarrassed him with himself, Margaret, Mattie, and Doug. Its waiting on him in silence seemed to boldly play some opus as if amped up through the Bose speakers flush-mounted in the walls for surround sound. Don't be fooled, this was a rococo melody darkly inspired by the warm and fuzzy holiday season he'd until this year faked it through and enjoyed in portions, as if entering anterooms of compartmentalization to protect himself one from the other. There was somewhere else though, an inner place he'd begun frequenting again—Paris, Anastasie—that called him like the blue night-light across from the couch he fitfully slept on, a single beam that faintly flickered into his slumbering eyes. In this thin exile, as insignificant as the width of a wall separating him from their bedroom, yet seemingly impregnable in its vastness, the night-light was turning into his north star.

When Mattie and Doug came alongside him and Margaret to visit with their aunt, uncle, and cousins, something slowly tethered the slumbering man to an undeniable goodness about Christmas and Hanukkah, not the gift giving, or celebration of faith, or even reconnected family ties. Maybe it had to do with the thing Margaret had put in the bank executive's face that jarred the guy into doing something better than he had in him. The slumbering man felt the pleasing gravity of having his family together in their home, how fragile that was for Derek, Felicia, Dwight, and Johnny, as well as for himself, Margaret, Mattie, and Doug. He thought about not being with Anastasie, and the underground Tunisian poet's isolation at this very moment. The aloneness of so many who gutted it up to get through the holidays, and those who didn't give a rat's ass about them. As the Skype call wound down, he said simply, "A very merry Christmas and happy Hanukkah to all," and meant it.

As the others said their good-byes, he realized his inner demons had diverted him from much of what they'd talked about, though from their upbeat, ingratiating tones, he felt sure Margaret had lived up to her devil's bargain with him.

In his slumber, her sort of impressionistic face made his next endeavor slightly less difficult. "I feel badly for all but forcing you into the position of helping them save their ranch and not getting into whether it will stick, or else I'd..." His voice tapered off. Mattie and Doug remained within earshot, but that wasn't so much why he'd stopped. Oddly, he pictured a tomb for his family in some graveyard, and his name being the only one etched in the stone. The year below his name was 1978, his date of birth, and ellipses were in place of his death. He could hardly wait for nightfall and the onset of insomnia. Without his particular type of instability, the slumbering man feared there would be no north star at all. "My ultimatum took things too far. For what it's worth, I tried though couldn't bring myself to do this before the call."

"Honestly?" Margaret said evenly.

Looking through his lenses, he glanced at the plastic cross precariously leaning to the side atop the Christmas tree and then at the menorah candles. Finally, he met Margaret's gray eyes with more clarity than any time in the three days he'd been back home. "God of Abraham or Jesus or Santa as my witness, and with a little luck all three and Buddha thrown in for the asking—yes."

𝄐

Margaret didn't quite know what in Frazier's bouillabaisse of tasty ingredients whetted her appetite for him: his seeming humility for the first time since returning from Texas, his quirky sense of humor, or his apology. Whatever it was, she had to admit inwardly that she'd been on some sort of intimacy-hunger-strike with him for far too long. She'd tried to let her anger toward him roll off her back like water, but until now it had boiled as if in a pot on the stove over simmering heat. *A pretty damn slow-cooked recipe for marital success*, she thought. But then, what was one to do? She wanted to stay in a circadian rhythm like the sea tides rolling in and out, or the opening and closing of gazania daisies, or Grandpa Mandt's bongo playing, or better yet, the poetic ebb and flow of Nana's letters. Needed to if she was ever going to write a novel worth anyone's time to read, and Frazier had upset her fragile beginnings with his call for help from down south. No, it wasn't so much the hassle of lending her assistance; Margaret's instincts had been to lay down the pen on her as yet unnamed manuscript and dive right into getting media coverage for Derek and Felicia's predicament. Of course, Frazier and his family had to do everything with junkyard dramatics thrown in, and that had irritated her, though this sort of stuff had also been an anti-intellectual aphrodisiac since she'd met Frazier, exciting, even endearing, in a nutso kind of way—by which secretly she longed to have more of the *Pickett gene*, if you will, for herself. Oh, the stories Frazier had told her about his upbringing, field reports from the edge on his family and, what's a decent way to put it? her direct experiences during the few times they had all been together. Perhaps envy of them had been partly why it had taken this long for her to toss Frazier a crumb; she mulled the possibility. But her redness, at least on the surface, had flared during that interview with the Credit Suisse executive. Undoubtedly it had been a good thing to do for Derek, Felicia, Johnny, and Dwight, for her marriage, and therefore the right thing, but at the same time, it had been wrong for her. Frazier, by having been in the thick of a near firefight-home-foreclosure-eviction lived the messy, bottom-up life that created the stew of genius for writers. The excellent interview piece that nailed the Credit Suisse executive against the wall had only sent Margaret clambering along a stairway to highbrows—decidedly not to heaven—which made the view from the top vertiginous, a precipice to jump from, because up there you breathed only the thin air of global corporations turning people into machines. She felt like a cog in the wheel, albeit a squeaky gear that had gotten some grease for her in-laws, lubrication which would quickly dry out as if it had never been applied to begin with. Unless Margaret could really get more of what real people went through, come down and stay down, at least for a while, long enough to finish her book, then the letter of Nana's she'd read while Frazier was out of town would surely haunt her all the way to the grave. She recalled its most indelible lines:

> *Love is sweet at times and brutal at others, not immoral or amoral, but above and below morality. You make up the rules as you go. At the same time there are eternal truths that cannot be violated without heartbreak. You rarely know which is which. It's so hard to find someone who has expanded themselves enough to gift their beloved air to soar in and earth to stand on. This person will free you to be a feeling human being and a better writer. You must free him for him to be capable of freeing you...*

"I'm sorry for relegating you to the couch, Frazier," she said at last. "I've mostly been mad at myself and took it out on you. Struggling to get my novel going is the most of it."

✍

"Yes, it's too bad my family's emergency interrupted your flow," he said more testily than he would've liked. It's just that his and Margaret's relationship felt like a merry-go-round ride too often set to cacophonous music, round and round you went to where nobody could hear well enough to make out the announcement for your depot, *or see it.* He threw in his slumber to boot.

"That was uncalled for, please forgive me," he went on in a softer tone. "Easy to blame the other for poor writing habits. I've done it to you the other way around." He partly wanted to walk over next to her and do the makeup kiss and hug, then maybe slip her his tongue, grab her on the ass. It had been an awfully long time on the couch and in Texas away from their conjugal bed, and Mattie and Doug were now occupied with a computer game and an open book in the family room. But Frazier going to Margaret would mean heading the opposite direction from Anastasie and the blue night-light, his north star of late, a constant if only in his mind, this muse that didn't have to carry the daily load. She was ephemeral, fire and ice, burning or sculpted to his liking, distantly written into the slumbering man's poetry without pages yet, somehow, all too close. So he just stood there unmoving, arms at his sides, eyes once again set over the top of his lenses.

✍

Why are my feet as heavy as if stuck in cement? Margaret asked herself. She wanted to go to him but needed him to come to her. It was the next part of Nana's letter that called for this test; well, not actually, if she were as fully a woman as Nana had been, there wouldn't be this stupidly inadequate pop quiz over her and Frazier's love. What is more, Frazier wasn't her cold-fish father, who hadn't adored her enough. And she was a woman who could think her way through these Freudian pits. Still, Margaret also simply stood there, in her mind turning over Nana's words, which sounded like some heavily scratched vinyl record underneath the needle of a phonograph player with the audio blaring monotone:

> *This kind of love can sometimes be enjoyed with more than one person, but probably other than at the same time, though not always. Be creative and never give up on love. Without a kiss, a naked body to share, a muse to open the mind and heart, there is no flying then landing on solid ground, no literature, no poetry at all, no celebration of God.*

Did this mean she would have to allow that French artist, Anastasie, into their lives? Was it why she and Frazier couldn't move together right now? Could Margaret ever be enough for him, him for her? Maybe she was already too late to have him all to herself. Or that was a pipe dream anyway, as Nana seemed to indicate with her muses and lovers and such. *F- this!* She should never have started reading Nana's letters! There was until this moment an unthinkable reason why she had rejected them when in college, not having to do with turning away from her family's manic-depressive artists but over the fear of being a sane artist, a writer who stunk at the craft and now was also a failure at marriage, and life itself. Put it this way, what Nana demanded of her may be too much, too open and messy, too morally corrupt, or perhaps too pure, uncontrollably wild in the moment, like the universe, or maybe even like God.

The air thickened between them into an eerie, unseen fog.

Margaret's tongue pushed against her palate so hard that it tasted coppery. Her eye twitched.

The thing of it was, Frazier, in his slumber, could nearly see the haze between them. More so, it rolled over him as if coming off the East River. He felt suffocated.

Margaret sat down on a stool in front of the laptop again. Quickly, she typed in Anastasie's website address, her fingers landing hard on the keys. When the French artist's homepage photo flashed into view, she lost her breath. The artwork of John Steinbeck's *Grapes of Wrath* had been replaced by an avant-garde graffiti spray-painting of a Paris street café with the outline of a man and woman sitting at a table and gazing blithely into each other's eyes. She swiveled the screen directly at Frazier, managing, "It's you and her, isn't it?"

✍

He dared not look through his lenses, didn't have to really. The unfocused artwork on the laptop's screen even the slumbering man could see wasn't a loose depiction of his favorite book. No good reason seemed to exist for asking his wife whether she'd been on Anastasie's website before; of course she had. "You give me too much credit, Margaret."

"Yeah, um, her last featured painting was—" She interrupted herself. "Oh Frazier, I don't know whether to divorce you or ask that you introduce me to her." A pause. "Or both."

"For the record, I was as shocked as you were Anastasie did a piece on Steinbeck." A pit formed in his stomach over him using the French artist's name with Margaret.

"So you *are* in close contact with her." Placing her hand on her forehead like a protective visor, not to shield the sun but to hide her tears, Margaret cried. In no more than three seconds, she wiped her eyes with the pad of a hand, and then once more intently met Frazier's eyes. "Wait on me please, and I'll be better inspiration."

The pit in his belly turned into a large stone, unpolished by stream water or desert winds, jagged as if having been left alone, retaining its original twisted shape in a vacuum for eons, a moon rock. Yes, the slumbering man needed a muse—or muses—every bit as much as Margaret somehow seemed to. And more than ever he knew this wasn't something that could be put off for some distant days. The stone in his gut had to be carefully ground down, rounded, eventually buffed for a high sheen, maybe purposefully left rough on its most craggy side. Otherwise, not oxygenated, the stone gets heavier, no going sideways allowed; you couldn't ignore this law of nature forever. He'd tried and failed miserably at giving up on writing right along with love, true love that is, authentic prose. "We need to write our novel together now," he said in an emphatic tone, gushing and turbidly mixed with desperation.

∅

On hearing his proclamation she immediately knew he was right. Something about the honesty in his voice and that seeped through the creases in his brow touched her own inner adoration-hate affair with the idea of actually letting him close enough to be her muse, or find out he would fall short of it, or she would. If either of the latter two painfully real possibilities happened, then nothing would be left of them other than being Mom and Dad to Mattie and Doug. That surely wouldn't cut it for her and Frazier, or the kids. Parents had to show children what affection looked like. In her mind's eye she pictured her cold-fish father beside her dutiful mother, and it gave her a shudder. Ignoring Frazier's suggestion for the moment, she said, "What did you learn that was most helpful about being with your folks?" Besides, he'd gone to Texas looking for answers that ran in swift currents. It was somehow required of herself and, by God, of Frazier, too, in the worst and best of ways to snare their own delicious, juicy New England lobster or what was it they fished for down in his Lone Star state, big, fat, bottom-feeding catfish or something of the sort. Yes, Margaret understood from too many years of treading water that the ocean between them was great, but could it be exciting to swim toward the other side anymore, ever, even for a little while here and there, enough? Her face flushed hotly with perturbation at herself, at Frazier and what was left of them. She had no interest in merely *enough*! Why did he just stand there like a marble statue, staring her down?

∅

At first Frazier waited with bated breath for her response over collaborating on writing, and then, when she tried to change the subject, he felt bamboozled by her immaculate skill for erecting walls faster than they could be knocked down. What is more, he had learned in some aspects too much and in others too little from his trip back home to pick something out as its MVT—most valuable thing. Nevertheless, if he could give her what she wanted, then maybe they could get back to tackling something creative together, at least make a stab at that happening with her rather than through his unanswered letters and emails to Anastasie together with the waning fantasy of the French artist signaling her affections for him through her homepage. It was the redness overtaking Margaret's expression, not altogether unlike a cluster of Derek and Felicia's fuzzy Christmas lights on the screen just minutes ago, that triggered something in him, a familiarity with anger, expertise with it born in Texas long ago that had palpably changed over the last few days. His blood coursed like white water as he worked through whirling, though sort of oddly elegant thoughts, which began fitting together more and more nicely as they slowed. "I'm no longer mad at my mom and dad for raising me the way they did." He chuckled mercurially. "Maybe now I can be mad at other people until I get tired of blaming them for me tuning out."

✍

It seemed to be her turn to give him a wistful snigger. Margaret believed him, though until now she had been accusing him more than her parents for her constipated ways. Yes, she had. She felt as if all of Nana's letters were bound in some unpublished book and each page read, *Take responsibility for your happiness. Not everyone in your family is a prig.* She would have to finish writing this book for herself like Frazier had been doing for himself. Margaret admired him and was angry with him for holding up a mirror in front of her face. "I should visit my folks until I'm no longer red because of them so much of the time," she said.

He smiled almost warmly. "Some day, some way all this could inform your writing and mine, Margaret."

"Recovery through the pen." She returned his smile by kindly parting her full lips.

I'll start by going to Tunisia and Egypt if necessary to locate the poet Yassine Lotfi Khaled, get him to open up to me for our book, for the betterment of humankind, he fought against blurting out. It wasn't that he'd set his sights too high; any writer worth his or her salt ought to go for broke. Frazier instead realized any flight to those destinations would likely have a layover in Paris, and right now that didn't seem like such a good idea: his lingering resentment at Margaret told him Anastasie could be all too comfortable shelter from the storm. "You want to work together on the book?" he said.

She nodded almost shyly.

Over the following few quiet seconds, save for the sound of Doug playing a video game in the other room, the slumbering man's anger turned for the better part indolent, the kind of discomfort you might just be able to walk away from entirely. "Where should we start?" he said.

✍

Margaret's reticence came from the other thing that stoked her anger at Frazier since he'd returned from Texas all wrapped up in his family's woes, him having nothing left over to help her work out her problems with the militant, hard-core, religious Zionist, not to leave out racist, TMZ's attempts to thwart yet another Middle Eastern poet, a Qatari named Mohammed al-Ajami, so she hadn't bothered trying. Irritation flitted every which way inside her chest like a sparrow that had flown inside a glass house and was now trapped, banging against windows again and again, determined to return to its natural habitat. Even her thinking of this book as a joint project sent the sparrow's wings flapping more furiously, its tiny body thudding harder into Margaret's. Maybe saying something, opening her mouth, would set it free. "Things are changing rapidly with the story; it's hard to know where to begin anymore," she said at last.

⚘

Her tone all at once took on an almost feral quality, frenetic just under the surface, professionally detached without the polish, Frazier reasoned. Where had her bashfulness gone, or had he misread her comfort for this project, and her agreement to do it had been filled instead with meekness under the weight of what she'd misperceived as some sort of emotional blackmail to save their marriage rather than Frazier's actual passion for the writing? Or had she mostly gotten it right with him? Hell, in a way, it would be okay if they couldn't work together without pulling each other's hair out by the roots. Then possibly, just possibly, he could get with Anastasie before it was too late. Suddenly he felt as if he were a wounded wild boar, one of those animals frequently hunted down in the West Texas desert, some kind of beast anyway, cornered before the kill. "Why don't you update me on recent developments," he said flatly.

She swallowed hard, and then told him about Mohammed al-Ajami coming under attack in a TMZ media campaign to have him imprisoned in his home country of Qatar for breaking a couple of draconian laws concerned with "insulting the Emir" and "inciting to overthrow the ruling system." As the charges sought after by those warmongers came out of her mouth, so did the sparrow, flying up into blue sky. Margaret knew without a doubt Frazier was the one person she should share this with. "All of it over another dissident poem," she said incredulously, shaking her head in disdain. "The Temple Mount Zionists are becoming the literary police." Margaret reached over and took hold of Frazier's hand. "We can't let that happen."

"Not if we can help it." The slumbering man felt the wild boar slip between strands of barbed wire and run away, limping but not severely enough to prevent escape. "What's your involvement so far?"

"I went to PEN's Writers in Prison committee with the poem and the crap on TMZ's website about it. PEN assured me they would push back through legal and diplomatic channels.

"I'm probably one of the first to get hold of the poem in the States. The mole in Clifford Odeon's organization turned me on to it. Looks like I've pissed off him and the TMZ by taking it to PEN."

Frazier knitted his brow. "Are you still slow-playing your edit of the manuscript the mole wants to get published?"

She nodded. "He's getting more and more antsy though."

"Uh, huh. Has he threatened you in any way?"

"He's too slick for that. I'll probably just be taken off the project someday soon. I don't think it will cost me my job, but if it does, so be it. Farrar, Straus and Giroux has been after me to make a move for some time."

"A change could do you good."

"That's the way I look at it."

"You do, truly?" He smiled crookedly.

"Maybe you're rubbing off on me more than we realize."

"Indeed." His smile faded into an expression of concern again before he went on. "How do you know something you've done bothered TMZ?"

She let go of his hand and gestured toward a window at the front of their apartment. "I take it the two guys in the blue Camry parked across the street are members of that esteemed group. They've been on my ass since shortly after PEN published on its website my article lambasting TMZ over smear tactics directed at both Yassine Lotfi Khaled and Mohammed al-Ajami that also, and more dangerously, incites broader violence. I gave it the headline 'Radical Fundamentalist Christians, Jews, and Jihadists Partners in Religious Terrorism.'"

The wild boar began walking with an even gait. "I'm proud of you, Margaret." Frazier walked over to the window, slightly parted the blinds, and then looked through his lenses at the Camry. His eyes narrowed as he spotted the two TMZers—Mutt and Jeff—one nearly a foot taller than the other even while sitting in the car. He was sure; these guys had been stationed at the subway billboard that condemned Khaled's poem "Tunisian Muscle" and Muslims in general.

When he finally turned from the window, Margaret stood across the room holding a piece of paper. She must've gone and gotten it from her desk while he'd been transfixed on Mutt and Jeff. "Is that what I think it is?" he said.

She nodded again. "al-Ajami's poem is called 'Tunisian Jasmine.' It's a goodie." She walked over and handed it to him.

Just looking at the poem gave him pause. This felt like déjà vu or something close to it. The actual shape of the piece struck him as familiar. He went over next to the computer and set the poem down on the counter. Attentively, he began reading:

Tunisian Jasmine

Knowing that those that satisfy themselves and upset
        their people
tomorrow will have someone else sitting in their seat,

knowing that those that satisfy themselves and upset
      their people
tomorrow will have someone else sitting in their seat,
for those that think your country is in you and your
      kids' names,
the country is for the people and its glories are
      theirs.

Repeat with one voice, for one faith:
We are all Tunisia in the face of repressive elites.
We are all Tunisia in the face of repressive elites.
The Arab governments and who rules them are, without
      exception, thieves
Thieves!

The question that frames the thoughts of those who
      wonder
will not find an answer in any official channels.
As long as it imports everything it has from the West,
why can't it import laws and freedoms?
Why can't it import laws and freedoms?

He loved it, could see why the powers-that-be and the crazies had it in for the Qatari poet as much as they did for the Tunisian poet, and he hated that. Senator John McCain's media sound bite over the Tunisian uprising possibly metastasizing into "cancer that could spread across the Middle East" came to mind. *When exactly had democracy become a diagnosable disease?* With all of this, the form of 'Tunisian Jasmine' still dominated his attention. "Margaret, if you have one handy, please get me a copy of Khaled's 'Tunisian Muscle'?"

"There's one in my files, why?"

"I want to check something out about the two poems. It may be nothing at all."

In seconds she returned from her study, and then laid Khaled's poem beside al-Ajami's.

"What is it?" she said.

"Give me a minute."

Line by line he didn't read them against one another; no, he compared the spacing of verses, the indentations, use of capitalization or lack thereof, the punctuation, the number of stanzas and verses in each stanza. They were parallel poems to the tee. He looked Margaret directly in the eyes. "al-Ajami is closely connected with Khaled, probably sending him and others in their underground movement a message with 'Tunisian Jasmine,' consciously or not. No way to know for sure without..." His voice momentarily tapered off. "Where is al-Ajami, do you know?"

"He's a student at the University of Cairo." Immediately Margaret wanted to edit out these words as though taking a red pen to a manuscript. No matter that she and Frazier were laying down some nice unwritten prose of their own, this path went through Paris.

Unable to hold her gaze, Frazier diverted his eyes, though he was also unable to do anything other than keep in his peripheral vision the laptop's screen, which still had on it Anastasie's ogling couple at the street café. His loins burned too brightly for him to get on a flight with a layover at Charles de Gaulle Airport. He simply would have to let Anastasie know he was in town, at least for a few hours. But how long did it take to strike the match that may well burn down his marriage? He looked directly at Margaret again. "Maybe the best course of action is to bring the fact that these two poems match up in structure almost exactly to the attention of Clifford Odeon," he said. "See if he knows or can help us decode what these two poets are saying to one another or their followers."

It felt to Margaret as if the sparrow flew down from the sky and this time landed on her head, all the while chirping a love song for her and Frazier. No need to decode its meaning. "A motley idea if I do say so myself." She leaned over and kissed him.

He was glad it was her lips pressing against his and not the French artist's.

"And maybe I'll have time to drop in on my folks long enough to lose some of my anger towards them. Extract the ole corn cob from my butt." She winked.

He returned it. "Let's just hope your parents or Grandpa Mandt aren't about to lose their home to foreclosure."

Margaret kissed him again.

Frazier slipped her a little tongue.

CHAPTER TWENTY-FOUR

Mountains spread before us like spirit fathers joined hands in some Kievan Rus ring of friendship, the late afternoon sun backlighting their broad shoulders, also turning the thin cirrus clouds into magenta, purple, and gold pastel plumes that floated aimlessly across this hazy, pre-gloaming sky. Wild grasses and alpine trees gave way to nude terrain at the uppermost regions, nearer the peaks. Stretching my arms overhead, I lent myself permission to savor a couple of slow, lung-filling breaths of pristine air.

Solomon and I stood at the edge of verdant high-country fields surrounding the outpost, good for growing broccoli and cabbage in prime season, switching over to Brussels sprouts in early winter, until the long, hard freeze set in. I knew this agriculture from time spent during my childhood with the part of our family that lived among these Urals and worked the land. People were out tending these fields, harvesting, weeding, carrying baskets of produce. Goats roamed near a two-story farmhouse that had a stream of smoke rising from its chimney. Not far from the house, pigpens abutted horse stables and a wooden barn that suffered bowed sides like a case of the mumps. Solomon carried a duffle bag across his back, and I an overstuffed knapsack. All told we traveled light, though he had insisted on putting some of my things in his bag to help with the load. I liked that he had, and didn't plan on letting on it was so. My bones pinged, as if uncoiling wire from a tangled mass. We'd been cooped up on the journey here for the better part of five days.

Come to find out the underground railroad was no actual railroad. It involved us taking ride after ride in old jalopies over rock-strewn, washboard roads that often went to nothing. Courageous souls—peasant farmers and college professors; communists, czarists, and anarchists; Jews, Christians, agnostics, together with out-and-out atheists—were the engineers, the engines, of this odd train. You would travel until getting a few kilometers from Red Army checkpoints, where the driver took some side road until way into backwoods forest. Then, you got out and hiked a machete-cut trail with little cairns of piled stone every so often, showing the way that bypassed the checkpoint and ended at your next awaiting car and driver. Brilliant, to be downright honest. We had been warned by every one of our drivers that Stalinist patrols regularly located the trails and lay in wait to capture or oftentimes kill—depending on their mood any particular day—Jews attempting to pass. New routes continuously must be cut for this fluid locomotive of justice to have even a ghost's passageway. Yes, it was a wonder any of us made it this far, that Oleg had.

With the help only of a crude pencil-sketched map provided by our last driver—no more cairns or cleared swaths to indicate the way—we had walked for over ten kilometers to arrive here. The driver wouldn't come any nearer the compound with a vehicle. Now I reached in my peasant dress's side pocket and came out with the map, checked it one last time, then ripped it into tiny pieces, as I'd been instructed to do by the driver. "This place is so remote it's believable the Goat-faced Murderer's secret police don't have it in their crosshairs." I opened my hand and the breeze sent asunder the paper shreds.

"Yet," Solomon said.

As we made our way between rows of cabbage toward the farmhouse, I unsuccessfully shunted aside no delicate amount of redness at Oleg for having taken off from this compound. Even though there were no phone lines here, messages passed through the underground, and Oleg had told no one where he intended on heading. That couldn't be altogether true; he loved me too much to just fade away. Someone here had to know something that would lead me to him. Maybe he'd left a clue rather than being forthright about his destination, something only I would understand. Besides, it was almost as if he knew I would come for him by adopting my father's name for his alias. I mulled other possibilities until an icy shiver ran down my spine. *Maybe Oleg somehow found out Solomon's "yet" is coming any day and decided to leave in haste!* I quickened my pace and, without complaint, Solomon kept up with me.

On nearing the house, I noticed at the three steepled windows across its second story that two women and a man held rifles trained on Solomon and me. Who could blame them for taking nothing for granted? We walked onto the porch that spanned the place's front, and then Solomon knocked on the door.

In a few seconds from behind the door, a man said, "Who's there?"

"Katya Ivashov-Mandelstam and Solomon Mikhoels," I said.

"What era are you from, Katya?"

"Suzdalian." I gave him the password Mika Vodovos had whispered in my ear back in Grozny.

"And you, Mr. Mikhoels, your era?" the man said.

"Muscovite, I'm afraid." Solomon winked at me.

I almost managed to smile inwardly, a little grin really, not having known of Solomon's, what to call it? completing-the-loop password. With two ancient Russian societal epochs just declared, and the other all but eternally provided by the Kievan Rus friendship ring of these Urals, the door finally opened.

A round-faced man with a thick brunette mustache and eyebrows introduced himself as Oscar Ramkivich, whom Solomon and I knew to be the outpost's coordinator. He seemed kindly, and asked us in, explaining most people slept in tents out behind the house, but we would be treated as guests, which warranted mats on the floor inside. Over tea across from the fireplace, we got right down to the issue of Oleg. Oscar Ramkivich added nothing new to what we already understood.

"Who did he befriend here?" I asked my first and only question.

"Your husband worked hard in the fields, but at night he stayed mostly to himself." A pause, as if thinking. "Sometimes he would play the spoons on his knees with Anton. They're both musically inclined." He set his teacup down on the side table between our chairs. "Anton is probably finishing up his work right now. You can have dinner with him in about an hour half past."

I, too, put my teacup on the table. "I'll find him in the fields now if you'll be nice enough to point out Anton."

"Don't know exactly which part of the farm he's on, but we can go out to the porch and, with some luck, I'll spot him."

With that the three of us stood up and went outside.

The outpost's coordinator panned the fields, and then placed his hands on his hips. "I'm afraid my eyesight isn't what it used to be, sorry; with this low sun I can hardly make out one from the other."

"Please tell me what this Anton looks like," I said.

Solomon began to say something, probably to slow me down, and I waved a hand dismissively.

Oscar Ramkivich described an overtly slim man who on first impression appeared gaunt and even more sullen than the others, though, Ramkivich added, Anton Yashkin often found something to make him smile in the little things of nature or people's oddities.

I thanked Oscar Ramkivich, then looked at my fellow sojourner. "This is something I must do alone. I trust you understand, Solomon."

He nodded thoughtfully. "If Mr. Ramkivich and I see Anton return from work, I'll come find you and bring you to him if you like?"

"Of course you will," I said, using a softer tone.

Once fifty or so meters into the broccoli crop, I glanced over my shoulder, and Oscar Ramkivich had gone back inside the house, but not Solomon Mikhoels. He stood there keenly scanning the farm, a hand held at his forehead to shield the sun.

The first person I came upon in the fields was a slender, young woman hunched over just as all the others wielding short-handle hoes at weeds that seemed to have snuck underneath the plants' leaves, like voyeurs looking up skirts. With one hand she held a broccoli shoot off the ground and, with the other, she chopped into spiderwebbed wild growth that had tiny yellow flowers. Then she pulled out its roots. "Hi," I said, taking the picture of Oleg out of my pocket again. "Sorry to intrude but I'm looking for my husband."

She straightened, looked at me from underneath a floppy-brimmed gardener's hat, and then began rubbing the small of her back. Her close-set green eyes and daintily symmetric nose juxtaposed with skin below her high cheekbones well on its way to turning leathery passed as code for bygone felicity. "It's not a bother." With the short-handle hoe she indicated the photo. "That him?"

I showed her the snapshot. "His name's Ole—he goes by Dimitri."

She took a long look at it. "I don't recall seeing him. As handsome as he is, I would've noticed." She smiled demurely. "No offense."

"None taken. When did you arrive here?"

"A couple months or so ago. You lose track of time."

Exile certainly didn't take long to disorient. What's more, this grinding work wasted no time in having its way with you. That's why my folks had left the Urals, and why I only came back to visit the grams—until now. The hair on my wrist bristled. I awkwardly couldn't take my eyes off this pretty young woman whose code was being further broken: Did her circumstance foretell my future, that is, if Oleg couldn't be found? How would I care enough about anything to return to Moscow or Peredelkino and again put pen to paper for dissident samizdat or my own prose and poetry or even to help Pasternak with *Zhivago*? "He had left by then," I finally said. "While here he befriended a man named Anton Yashkin; would you happen to know where he's working today?"

"Anton, yes, he's over there." She gestured toward the adjacent rows of cabbage.

"Thank you. Pardon me for not introducing properly. I'm Katya."

"Olesya. I hope you find him." All at once she bent over at the waist and crouched using her knees. Then she slashed down with the hoe into another weed.

As I walked away, stepping over row after row of broccoli, Olesya said gutturally, "An odd duck, that Anton."

I didn't look back.

On making it into the cabbage, I stopped and looked over the rows. Everyone was bent over and most of them were skinny, making it hard to tell the men from the women, except for the few "large-boned" ladies and those whose hair wasn't in a bun under their hats. I tapped one then the other on the shoulder and said, "Anton?" but several failed to respond, and those who did weren't nearly as spindly as called for. At last, I spotted this reed in coveralls five rows away. It had to be the diminutive Anton. If a strong wind came up, it almost seemed he could get blown away right along with the dust. I leapt over the rows and sidestepped between field workers until next to him. Instinctively, I lowered down on my hands and knees. "Anton," I said to this man about Oleg's and my age with red, splotchy, and otherwise grayish, taut facial skin, somehow not burnable in any normal kind of way by the sun, or maybe he stooped most of the time when outdoors. Unshaven, his whiskers sprouted like under-watered saw grass clumps spaced far apart, yellowish near their roots, turning browner toward the ends.

Without a word, he continued slinging his short-handle hoe rhythmically, as if to some inner song.

I began pulling weeds from around a cabbage plant. Their stems broke off in my hands above the roots in this thick black soil good for clinging to.

"What are you doing out here tool-less?" He leaned over and used his hoe like a surgeon to uproot the stubble I'd left, tamping down the dirt without leaving a trace of having violated the earth. "Fine enough." He laid his implement down directly in front of me, then finally met my eyes. "I'll get another shorty from the shed. Use this one."

He stood up and I did too.

"Anton, I'm Dimitri's wife. My name's Katya."

Blushing, his gray skin went almost as crimson as the blotches. "Sorry you're here and he's not. He's a good spoon player, percussion man par excellence."

"Thank you and, yes, Oleg can do much more than merely hold a beat. Do you know where he went or why he left?"

"He didn't say."

"Anything. Anything at all."

Anton shook his head. "Sorry."

My arms and legs went rubbery, and I slumped to the ground, though tried to make it look as if I crouched down right along with the rest of the workers. I picked up the short-handle hoe, lifted a cabbage shoot, and then whacked at the ground beneath a huge weed pod. My hands stung and arm muscles pinched with every stroke into the heavy turf, but I dared not stop. It didn't feel good, or satisfying, nor did it make me realize I was still alive. I pictured Olesya over in the broccoli, and my arms kept moving. A lightning bolt of pain shot through my lower back that caused me to pull up and wince. Then I resumed my numbing assault.

After what seemed the longest and yet no time at all, when the sun began falling behind the Urals and their long shadows moved over the fields, I was still going at weeds with my short-handle hoe. That's when I heard the clear, unmistakable whistling of Vysotsky's "Ballada O Lyubvi." Looking that way, Anton worked beside me again with his own short-handle hoe. Until now I hadn't noticed he'd left and returned. Almost all of the other workers had gone in for the evening. "How can you make music at such an awful time for me?"

"Sometimes there isn't anything else left."

I quit hoeing, looked him directly in the eyes. "You're the kind of man my husband would've liked. His real name is Oleg, did you know?"

Anton nodded. "He told me when he left this place."

"You were with him when he left?!"

He nodded again.

"Which direction did he head?"

Anton indicated northeast, over the Urals' peaks.

I fixed my eyes on the farthest mountaintops. Something other than dullness returned to my heart, not hope, but a gritty will to go onward. "Are you sure he went precisely that direction?"

Looking along his arm and pointed finger as if through a sightline of a telescope, he said, "Yes. Why?"

"Dimitri was my father's name, and my husband chose to become Dimitri, and my grandfather's name is Dimitri, and Oleg knows Dimitri and the rest of my family live in the village of Mashinska." For a moment I brought a hand over my mouth. "Do you know where that is?"

"Just on the other side of those mountains, Katya. But do you really think he could've made it over?"

The ice-capped, barren ridgeline no longer looked like a Kievan Rus ring of friendship, that was for sure. Shoving his question out of mind, I said, "What did he take with him, Anton?"

"A backpack stuffed with rations and water." He held up the short-handle hoe. "And one of these."

"Then that's what I'm taking too."

I kissed him on one cheek, then the other.

"Katya, it's getting dark, come inside or I'm coming to look for you!" Solomon called out from the farmhouse.

"Be right there!" I hollered.

It was as if the mountains' long shadows were fingers, threatening to clamp round my throat as we made our way out of the fields, and in spite of the Urals that may have already taken Oleg, I whistled along with Anton the Russian love ballad.

∅

"Getting on the other side will be next to impossible." Solomon paced one way, then the other beside the kitchen's long food prep table. "If starvation doesn't get you, frostbite probably will. Be reasonable, Katya."

Without so much as glancing at him, I slipped inside my knapsack two baguettes. Already packed away were canned peaches, salt-pork jerky, and a large jar of water. "Oleg wouldn't have left here with a death wish, and neither am I. Even if you're right about making it over the pass, there're thousands of caves in those mountains. Oleg may be staying in one of them." I hardly believed this, but couldn't bear my mind's eye looking upon Oleg's skeleton picked clean by lemmings, wolverine, Arctic fox. "Maybe all I'll find are his bones." My voice cracked. "And that will have to be enough."

"Please come back before nothing more than bones is left of you. I won't be able to wait here forever."

I moved one arm, then the other through the knapsack's straps, centered it across my back along with a wool sleeping blanket tied to the bag with twine. Then I took hold of the short-handle hoe I'd brought in here and leaned against a chair. On my way out of the room, I paused in the doorway, but there was nothing left to say to Solomon.

Stepping into morning sunshine warmed my face, which the air chilled. I tugged at my knit cap, lowering it over my ears. No music remained to whistle or hum into my bewilderment, only the mechanical crunching of my valenkis on the dirt between rows of produce. My breaths gave off puffs of steam that came with more rapidity as I made it beyond the farm into rocky, bramble-of-thorns terrain amidst dense alpines, everything sloping deceptively upward toward distant bases of mountains. Inwardly I bemoaned not having a compass. The jagged peak at the pass to Mashinska began looking like all the others, that is whenever they showed themselves between the trees. It would be unlikely to get lost and walk in circles in this forest, but you could easily end up on some mountain to nowhere.

A hawk from a low branch flapped its wings into a bass drum sound and flew directly at me, only swooping upward as I hit the ground prone. It cawed almost like a human's outcry. Sitting up, I shot a look to see if the creature would head back for the bounty in my knapsack. The bird had vanished. I squinted, then momentarily rubbed my closed eyelids. Was my vision playing tricks on me? Several hundred meters away a freakishly thick-torsoed person or something sort of flickered between tree trunks. Maybe it was a deer or elk, though they don't walk on two legs. A bear could, but only for short distances. I fixed my eyes on the opening in the trees just beyond where I last saw the moving shape. It flickered again between trunks, and this time I noticed a splash of orange over olive green, the colors of a shirt and pants I'd seen before leaving the farm. "Solomon!" I called out.

"It is I, my lovely comrade! Where in these blasted Urals are you?!"

I quickly got onto my feet and raised my arms overhead. Crisscrossing them continuously, I recited one of my longish nature pieces in the loudest tone I'd ever used to perform my poetry, or for that matter anyone else's. By the time I got to the last stanza, Solomon, with bulging backpacks over both shoulders, stood before me, so I gave him parole of a sort by dropping the verbal literatim. "For a moment back there, I thought you were the hunchback of Notre Dame." I smiled. "Thanks for coming."

He nodded his you're welcome. "Maybe with enough food and water, we can make it to Mashinska."

"I'll partake sparingly."

"We must."

The next three days relentlessly brought more of the exhausting, burst-blisters-on-bottom-of-my-flat-feet climb. When either one of us lost confidence in the landmark peak showing the way, the other would point it out, oftentimes with a little hesitation though never admitting doubt. As the sun began to set each evening, we'd locate a cave, tie up our knapsacks to a high, sturdy limb after taking out enough rations to have dinner, and then we'd collect fallen branches and twigs to start a fire. On entering the caves, I couldn't help myself but to search around for bones while holding my short-handle hoe at the ready. "Just seeing if there're any hidden beasts about to devour us," I'd joke with Solomon, who proved kind enough not to point out what a sad case I was, looking for Oleg's remains without a clue. Each morning my rucksack got precariously lighter and lighter, and we weren't at the base of the Urals yet. The mountains were near and far. In this topography, which kept getting more treacherous, you couldn't cover much ground in the space of a day.

Two moons and suns later, five days in now, we arrived at the tree line, an altitude of which going above didn't allow for life. No caves to be found up here, and no food in our backpacks. But for a crater lake about one thousand meters below, we would've run out of water too. Once we made it onto the saddle of the pass, a cold, howling wind cut like knives. There existed not one thing to divert or quiet it. First Solomon, then I, retched, though threw up nothing other than a little water. At last, we looked on the village of Mashinska far below in the valley. All downhill, and that was damn fortunate. From the looks of us, there wasn't anything left to go higher. Absolutely nothing. Neither said what we had to be thinking: *No way Oleg would've made it this far.*

His single knapsack of food and water and a short-handle hoe had to have proven woefully inadequate unless he'd killed his fare with superhuman adroitness. In lower altitudes Solomon, using my short-handle hoe, had taken down a couple of rabbits and marmots, but up here they simply didn't exist. And you had to navigate this no-man's or -woman's land for days. Mashinska was too far away, still. How would we get there alive? I sat down, hardly caring anymore.

For the longest time we shared only the deafening wind. Midday passed, and dark afternoon clouds ripe for a snowstorm floated toward us. A stalk of lightning fired from the thunderhead, then another.

"If you don't think you can go on, I'll place your arm over my shoulder and we'll get down that way," Solomon said raggedly.

"You're in no better shape than me."

Ignoring my observance, he said, "I'm not going to blow smoke that Oleg is down there with your family awaiting your arrival. You and I both know they most likely would've contacted you by now if that were the case."

"They don't have phones and the mail is decrepit around here. What's more, Oleg may want me to come to him without the censors opening letters that give his location away."

"You're pulling straws out of the stack and calling them needles, Katya. Let's go."

"He's not down there!" I started bawling.

Solomon sat down next to me and placed a hand on my back. He said nothing.

God, I hated his pity. "What if I said I'm staying here?"

"I'd stay with you."

"How long?"

"Forever."

His tone carried finality and sureness I'd never before heard from him, an inviolable sweetness. "I'm not ready for this, Solomon." Finding out about Oleg awaited below, along with my peasant family, who loved me but didn't understand my Moscow, dissident, literary ways, and there was something more I felt utterly ill prepared to face, not now, probably never.

⌀

The first four days at Mashinska, I lay in bed and mostly slept. The straw-filled mattress covered in white linen sheets may as well have been a puffy cumulous cloud, it felt so good after the hard, rocky soil my back had endured. Mama Ivashov each morning, noontime, and early evening had brought me a bland version of shchi, her Russian cabbage soup with every scrumptiously fresh ingredient from the family's collective farm. At first, I had had a hard time getting down any food and water, but that slowly gave way to recuperation. It had been hard to hold my tongue on asking about Oleg, but any attempts would've surely been rebuffed, a setback for opening up, truth coming out. With our family the "We" of those gathered in any particular place, always considered a precious gift, had to be honored before "I" needs could be met. *The communist revolution should learn from the peasants rather than rule them,* I thought more than once while talking myself into at least a modicum of forbearance. Besides, I needed the rest. Until now. Early this evening there would be a huge feast that included my dad's side of the family and my mom's, the Grishins. No more than two kilometers from here, they had their own collective farm, hardly more than subsistence really, in seasons fortunate to get some favorable weather providing just enough harvest to satisfy the Stalinist crop quota mongers. All of the collectives around here struggled like that. I got out of bed and walked toward my bathwater, noticing it steamy a bit above the tub, thanks to Mama Ivashov having done the boiling over a fire in the kitchen. In that hot fog Oleg's handsome, aquiline face, not burnt from the war, appeared like an apparition. With each step I lost patience.

Thirty minutes later I was greeted with hugs and Russian cheek kisses from grandparents, aunts, uncles, first and second cousins, along with others so distant that the dark features and green eyes of our bloodline gave out almost altogether; and then I got a nice hug with Solomon. It was our first time together since arriving here. He'd obviously been on the mend too. Other than for the dark half circles beneath his eyes, he seemed back to his comely panache. Coming out of our friendly embrace, I took a good, long look at him, trying to remember us actually getting down the mountain. It was no use. The last thing I recalled was passing out about two-thirds of the way on our descent. Solomon must've carried me for the balance of it. "Thank you," I mouthed.

"You're quite welcome." He gave me Russian kisses.

As we all sat down at picnic tables that had been set end to end outside the little house on this lovely evening bathed in soft, angled sunlight, piquant smells of roasted pheasant, buttery yams, garlic Brussels sprouts, spices of saffron, thyme, fresh ground peppercorns, salt, and most thankfully of all, no more cabbage of any kind wafted over us. We spoke of the six children born this past seven years since my last and only visit after Mom, Dad, and my brother, Radko, had been disappeared. Two girls and four boys. All but two of them liked playing lapta; one of the towheaded boys was a reader already, and one curly-headed little girl had taken to drawing. Between warmhearted chuckles, Grandpa Grishin extolled about someday losing these two young ones to my and Solomon's fancy Moscow ways. Yes, the "We" here worked its magic. My impatience hadn't evaporated into thin air, as had the steam coming off my bath along with Oleg's image, but the unself-conscious conversations going on all around somehow salved the gaping wound in my soul. Thoughts of whether their silence on Oleg could be because they never received my letter about our marriage with a photo of us included and that he himself never made it here, which had been swimming round my head as though still trapped in the small tub with me, now seemed to float out to sea and back on more of a tidal rhythm. I would find out what they knew or didn't know soon enough, or maybe way too soon. Squirming on the bench, I shook off that horrible possibility, though not entirely, and then started a conversation with Uncle Maksim about the quality and quantity of wool he'd sheared this season. Three extended exchanges with others at the table later, as sunset flared into colors of the renaissance, the tide rolled back in, dark, and with high swells, as if the looming moon already had its way with me. Nonetheless, I stayed in this slack water until dinner wound down, guests going inside to help with cleanup, or have a smoke away from the table, others forming a ghost story circle with some of the younger kids. Conspicuously, Papa Ivashov hadn't gone for a smoke with the other men; he picked at a wedge of strudel pie. I stood up and walked the distance of two tables, then sat down beside him. "I simply must talk about Oleg," I said evenly.

He laid his fork on the saucer, and then using a napkin dabbed crumbs from his mouth and a few that had fallen on his infrequently trimmed gray beard. One of his brown irises looked off walleyed, the other fixed directly on my eyes. "A couple months ago some of us out hunting near the base of the pass over the Urals found your husband in pretty bad shape. The picture you sent helped us identify him once we got him home." He passed the napkin over his lips again, as though needing time to sort out troubling thoughts. No flecks of piecrust remained anywhere on his face or in his whiskers.

"Oleg enjoyed working in the gardens once he got better," Papa Ivashov went on. "Not much of a hunter though." He seemed to force a little chuckle, then turned serious again.

"Not many people come here to work that weren't born here, Katya. When the Stalin men visit, they look for new workers and check them out thoroughly.

"Oleg hid from them successfully, until the Stalinists threatened a young lad, your cousin Tekla, with torture if he wasn't forthcoming on everything he knew about the people of Mashinska that might be 'in the least pertinent' was how they put it." He held up a hand. "Don't blame Tekla, my dear one. He's merely a boy."

I wanted to strangle my distant cousin! "What did they do with Oleg?" I already felt sure of the answer, but had to eliminate any possibility he got away.

"They took him to the gulags."

My thoughts became awash. Those places were black holes. Few ever found out anything about comrades the Goat-faced Murderer sent away, or worse, had secretly executed by firing squad. I had friends that it took years to learn of their deaths behind those walls, Pasternak's friends too. Once in a great while dissidents would get word out. Even if I could make that happen, I would die to know of their terrible treatment of Oleg; literally my heart would almost certainly stop beating. Word never came of one's pending release, not unless they got sent away after some high-profile show trial. Even then it was rare. If Oleg were ever let go, or my love escaped, he'd know where to find me. Yes, he would. That much I could do: stay put. "He believed I would come here looking for him, didn't he."

"He felt convinced of it."

I laid my head on my grandfather's shoulder and sobbed salty tears, water for a black ocean.

✍

In the strangest way I also enjoyed the work, perhaps because Oleg had. Swinging the short-handle hoe brought pain and progress. Sore joints, aching back, bloody palms, and plump Brussels sprouts, cabbage, potatoes, onions and the like. Other than out in these fields where I mixed my despair with black dirt, I had pretty much sat in a chair next to the lone window in a bunkroom behind the house and kept watch for Oleg or Stalinist patrols. None had come yet, and it had been nearly a month. Though word had arrived from close-by villages that patrols were making the rounds once again. My appetite no longer held sway, nothing tasted good, but you had to eat something to carry on like this. The waiting fermented hopelessness like cheap, rotgut vodka, which I'd taken to more and more often. When drunk late in the evenings, I'd sometimes walk outside and look at the moon and stars in their double-image fuzziness, and my numbness seemed to find fellow unfocused, not some sort of cosmic friends, but what? cohorts in misery. The only thing that held enough sway to make me question what I was doing happened to be Solomon Mikhoels. He, too, had stayed, worked right alongside me until I told him I needed some space to sort things out for myself. I didn't want to keep Solomon away from his acting or playwriting or his role as leader of the Jewish Anti-Fascist Committee, or the underground, which, now we knew so indelibly, helped Jews escape the Nazis and the Stalinists. The price extracted from others for him waiting on me felt too high. I'd hoped his social justice and artistic passions would overtake his feelings for me, at least provide some balance and get him back to Moscow. So far, not so good. Right at this moment, Solomon slung his own short-handle hoe at weeds in the potato patch no more than twenty-five meters away. I couldn't let the Stalinists come and take him away, pressure someone else to rat him out. Could I? I wouldn't much care if that happened to me. Oh, I planned on going into hiding when they came. But who knew, if apprehended maybe I'd end up closer to Oleg.

I looked over at Annah in the row of cabbage across from me. During dinnertime and on breaks, she loved to gossip, which meant she knew things. Her hoe went more furiously than normal at chopping weeds. Hurriedly, she pulled their roots up, then tamped the soil. "Any update on when the Stalinist quota keepers are going to get here?" I said.

"Tomorrow. That's why I'm trying to get up my count of cleared ground."

The more weeded rows, the better the cooperative's chances of getting paid its fair share of rubles from the quota brigade. I swung and cleared with more vigor, all the while increasingly weighted down with something more than the rigors from this specific brand of communist farming.

Finally I stuck my short-handle hoe's blade in the ground, then stood up and walked over next to Solomon. "The quota police are going to be here tomorrow, have you heard?" I said.

He nodded, glanced over, and gave me a wink, never stopping his work.

"Are you trying to force me to leave with you by staying unless I go too?"

Tossing a weed aside, he looked me directly in the eyes. "You are a smart one. Too expansively talented to farm and do little else for the rest of your days, although don't get me wrong, working the land is a noble pursuit. The simple fact is Russia needs you near the center of things in Moscow, Katya."

It felt as though slight disappointment rode bareback on a stallion of guilt that bucked me over caring at least a little that Solomon's comment didn't include amorous reasons. A couple of days ago, I'd watched an equine get saddle broken in a corral right across the way, and whatever was happening in this field was going on here and now.

"If Oleg comes back to Mashinska, your family will contact you," he went on. "A code could be arranged to get past the mail censors. It's okay if you leave presently."

"Because you want me for yourself and hope he never returns," I said, vomiting the words.

He stood up and his face was inches from mine. "I love you. There's no denying it."

This sentiment coming out of his mouth, rolling off his tongue, brought a sour taste in my throat. "Saying that is cruel."

"Yet it's true," he said, softly as the gentle morning breeze. "True enough that if you and Oleg can be together, I want that for you."

I opened my mouth to lay into him some more, but somehow stopped short of it.

No, Solomon absolutely won't leave without me.

CHAPTER TWENTY-FIVE

Silently and tumultuously he versified everything around them, the poet in Frazier unabated now, set loose in his confusion, instinctively in search of harmony just when that felt all the more remote. The wind outside was so cutting, their rented Volvo shook, seemed to almost quiver spasmodically, and an ice-sheet covered black water beneath its ledge, hiding, no, holding down, suppressing the edges of the bay from what otherwise would be lapping whitecap foam that smiled at the sky, even this leaden dome, gibing with authentic joy the sunny eternity above the firmament, just by being itself if given the opportunity, nothing more, no chip on the shoulder or anything, responding only to the moon's pull and rush of air, the spinning, ever spinning earth rubbing against its atmosphere like the centrifugal force of silence inside the car, roping Margaret and Frazier to their own oppression, with freedom somewhere just out of sight and unreachable, or perhaps, for no logical reason, attainable, should they keep twirling round faster and faster until breaking through, as if everything told him so much more was frozen inside themselves that needed to be thawed after winter passed. But in most ways they had been in a land without changing seasons, one long, cold stay in this nameless, frozen tundra region since, well, honestly, since long before they were married, at least as far as he was concerned and, now, while they crossed the causeway into Boston, Frazier had the thought of a madman, to open the door, jump out, and fling himself from the bridge. Oh, it wasn't that they didn't have their coming together and drifting apart, but there was always the ice-sheet, the gray sky, the fire of the sun that occasionally burnt a hole in the ledge and ignited hope or sex; however, at some reptilian level, sweaty and clawing, as though they wanted to destroy each other, mangle making love until the sacred, poetic ideal, from the Bible's Song of Solomon to Blake to Shelley to Keats to Ezra Pound to W.S. Merwin, to his and Margaret's puny selves, became unrecognizable, the farthest thing from intimacy. It left them worn out and distant, not closer together, in open water. He simply couldn't take it much longer. Something had to give between them. But what, really? God, he wished he could more consistently live out loud the whore always roaming around inside himself as honestly as his friend Buckminster did—anywhere nearly as well would do quite stupendously—hook up with Anastasie to make him every bit the prolific literary figure that she was an artist, juggle a mistress and a wife to fill in his gaps. Problem was, he all the while had this nagging feeling a godforsaken angel or something wouldn't let go, almost as though to suspend the gravitational swirl toward something pure and good he had little to no actual, practical experience with. It sure as hell wasn't because he was that nice of a guy. If Frazier could shake the angel, he most definitely would. Glancing in the rearview mirror, he caught a glimpse of Mutt and Jeff staring through the blue Camry's windshield three vehicles behind. The two TMZ idiots had been following him and Margaret from the moment they walked out of their apartment in Manhattan, on their way to pick up the rental car at the severely cramped Hertz lot—where he almost rammed the damn blue Camry while backing onto the street.

These pregnant silences between them had started about a week ago, soon after Margaret shared a draft of her manuscript's first chapter with him. Frazier had to give her credit, Margaret's prose was terse and moving, powerful and, in a way, lyrical, Hemingway-esque, but that's where his praise stopped. When read carefully the content came from a bourgeois heart, prejudicial and mean-spirited like Philip Larkin's most honest poetry. It was as if Margaret wanted to hide or deny this part of herself, and it seeped out of her pen onto the page despite every effort. She would praise her character based on the Tunisian poet Yassine Lotfi Khaled over his "heart for the people" and "courage to publicly be in solidarity with them under such dangerous circumstances for writers of truth to power"; then she turned around and wrote doggerel such as, "Why take these risks for people who can't read what he was writing?" She may as well have called them rabble, unworthy, ignoramuses. Truth was, from what he'd read in *New York Times* reports and watched on broadcasts of *Democracy Now!*, the people—who had taken to the streets of Sidi Bouzid after the death of the food-kiosk vendor who set himself on fire in protest, Mohamed Bouazizi, and now, this outpouring spreading to the streets of Tunis, the Tunisian capital—were a cross section of society: doctors, engineers, professors, activists, farmers, peasants, yes, most of them were locked in extreme poverty, and that's what their revolutionary movement was all about, going up against a dictatorship that starved the people into what Frazier would call wisdom, albeit certainly not of some highbrow literary type. Whatever. This wasn't a project he could work on with her, yet that's exactly what he had continued doing. He'd given Margaret compliments on her first chapter, a few stylistic editing comments, left it at that. And now they were on the way to pay Clifford Odeon an unexpected visit to see what else they could uncover for "their" story.

Why had he ever left Texas if all that held store for him was being the apologist? Keep his truest feelings to himself, or inside his novels on the bottom of a drawer, or water them down to the point of copacetic exteriors and bowed souls, his and hers, for not telling the truth about timeless values could never be love. Sure, fibbing about little things and keeping his truest feelings toward Anastasie under wraps until he figured out what he was going to do about his French muse was offering a sort of kindness to Margaret. But he was so shy at crucial moments he just let things fester. It left you stuck in purgatory with no way out except some unseen trapdoor to Hades. Until recently he'd hoped for a ladder to appear leaned against an open skylight. Maybe the fall all the way back to his roots in Monahans was too breathtaking to chance. But in all honesty, he'd escaped the first several rungs of purgatory, his upbringing. His recent trip home had revealed that much. Hadn't it? More likely, what he wanted from Margaret, fantasized in getting from Anastasie, was what he didn't have the courage to say and do for himself. Simply put, his authenticity didn't mean enough to him, and Frazier knew it.

✄

Margaret sat in the passenger seat staring absently out the side-window at the turbid sky, and then her eyes locked on a lone steamship going headlong into it, until at the horizon grayness swallowed the ship whole. The sudden hollow feeling beneath her ribs came as a dark twin sister to the emptiness already there. She didn't know how there could be any more humongous of an opaqueness inside her, but obviously it was vaster than you could get in touch with on your own. A strange thing: She no longer felt as alone, quite so misunderstood, as when she and Frazier headed out this morning. Margaret partly wished she could board the steamer with her twin sister and go off into the sky. To be fair, she'd been exiled within herself ever since a week ago, when Frazier doled out such pitifully tepid support for her manuscript's first chapter. For sure he was a good writer, his edits had been heady and right on; it was what he didn't say, the dimness in his eyes as he spoke with her about her draft that had just done her in. She had told herself over and over their marriage certainly wasn't perfect, but they were getting better, together, as a couple, and that was enough, all you could expect, though, now, Margaret no longer could fill the void even a little with this mantra. It just slipped right out of her brain like vapor that inexplicably went through the window and then floated out toward the horizon, became part of the smothering sky.

Her eye twitched. *Shit! Here we go again.* She couldn't get in the same county as the Comrade and Lydia without going sort of bonkers tense, and seeing as Grandpa Mandt's bongo-playing, peacenik advice had gone down with the gifting, or dumping, of her grandmother's letters, depending on how you looked at it, she may as well include him and Nana's ghost too.

A shriek came out of the backseat from Doug, followed immediately by Mattie blurting, "You're such an un-fun bookworm!" and instinctively Margaret pointed a finger like a blade, in one motion raising her arm and twisting her body around to face the kids, but then she slowly curled her finger alongside the others, didn't utter the admonishment to get Mattie and Doug back in line that had risen in her throat like some flying fish breaking for the surface in Boston bay. Mattie elbowed Doug in the side together with shoving her Game Boy digital device in his face, which made Doug turn toward the door and press his paperback against the window. "Leave me alone; quit being a big fat bully!" he snapped, furrowing his brow as if determined to remain in his story. *How different these two are*, Margaret thought. It was hard to imagine how they came from the same gene pool, were raised in unchanging urban liberal live-and-let-live zeitgeist with all its contradictions, keeping safe distance from the really messy systematic oppression in stop-and-frisk territory over in, say, Jamaica, Queens, and then there had been no shortage of lefty prejudicial judgment toward the straights, the squares—all of which had been dealt out by her and Frazier in substantially equal portion. Yet, the children were so different. Okay, yes, Doug often liked playing digital games, but he was her sensitive one who would never push Mattie or anybody else into doing something they weren't interested in. He thrived on reading, and his drawings were exceptional, liked sports, was a pretty decent midfielder in soccer, also ran up and down the court like a deer in basketball, played hockey in a way that highlighted skating skills and stick handling, finesse being his forte, not much on hard body checking. Doug would linger at the breakfast table on school mornings just to carry on conversations with his mom but didn't much care for being late for the first bell, which Margaret was ashamed to admit to herself she had manipulated to shut down some of these morning talks, as impatient as Mattie, just more skilled in how to get her way. Her little girl could hardly sit still at breakfast or at most any other time. She liked things orderly, her paintings never going outside the lines she had sketched for them. She, too, played soccer, as a striker, a goal scorer, voraciously competitive. She liked being hugged by Margaret but only when no others were looking, whereas Doug seemed to feel this way as well but simply couldn't restrain himself from putting an arm around Margaret's waist and giving her a squeeze before heading off to the schoolhouse or at any random time he needed some affection. That was it: Doug needed affection and Mattie only wanted it. Her son was moody, her daughter driven.

"Give your brother some peace and quiet, Mattie," she finally said, then shifted back around and looked out at the gray sky again. *Genetics*, the word sort of stuck in her mind like the seemingly unmoving cloud cover. Her kids were young, just getting started in art and sports and life, but how much would they change over the arcs of their existence? How much had she? Not much really. Maybe all this personal growth Margaret was trying to accomplish by understanding her family's stuff amounted to little more than one big fat cover-up for a hopelessly mismatched marriage. Why put herself through it? Then again, Frazier did seem, not different, since returning from Texas, just a little more comfortable in his skin. But he was the moody one and she the driven. Maybe Frazier was only going through another of his *phases*. Why confront her parents and Grandpa Mandt for family secrets, known or unknown, even to themselves, if she was hardwired to bowl right over or through things, onward and upward, find adventure in accomplishments and those relationships that could get off on doing well, not for merely survival, but to thrive, be happy at least some of the time? What other choice did she have really? None. She wasn't fine with the way she was, but she was fine the way she was. The thing of it was, among everything else, could she ever lose the fist in her chest that balled any time she stood in front of some inner mirror looking at herself naked like this? Something she knew for certain, Margaret hated looking in the mirror enough not to do so very often. Or was she mostly tricking herself, building a case to not share any more of her novel with Frazier, because he'd devastated a very sensitive part of her? Something artful, not blossoming, emerging, budding, and now she was a barren tree again, thanks to him.

"I give away too much power to you," she said, swiveling her head toward Frazier.

He made a quick backward, forward chicken-neck move in astonishment, keeping his eyes fixed on the road ahead. "I've been thinking it's more the other way around."

"Who knows with your moods? What I want to say is, my novel is off to a good start no matter what you really think."

Your *novel now, and not* ours… She may as well have slapped him. "Yes, it is," he said, measuring his words carefully.

"There you go again, patronizing me."

The stinging in his cheeks turned into this burning flush of guilt, worse than his initial anger, far worse, a prison cell he always walked into willingly, locked the door behind himself, and then tossed the key to some gaunt gendarme, all smiley-faced, toothless, and evil. But this time, inwardly, Frazier held on to the key, commanded the guard to step away. The man's smile got wider, a slice of watermelon across his face. Frazier wasn't actually hallucinating, he *felt* what was happening into this true story, creative nonfiction. The gendarme reached through the bars and grabbed the key, then walked away laughing. Frazier pressed his face between two columns of cold steel, inwardly screaming, "Come back here and open the door! We both know I should've been released a long time ago on time served!"

"But you're a lifer, the system needs you," the guard said, facing Frazier again. "It's not fair; it's not supposed to be." Ha, ha, ha. With that the man turned and left the shadowy corridors of Frazier's mind.

The only way out was to break out! "The truth is, your writing is inspired in its clarity of purpose," Frazier said out loud. "Sneakily poetic in the most effective way. I have to say, though, Margaret." Pausing, he looked her directly in the eyes, yes, through his lenses, no slumbering permitted to gain his freedom now, as well as hers for that matter, possibly, hopefully. Their joint writing project seemed a last shot at putting things not back together, but together for the first time in a way that could last, the stuff of soul mates. Really? Come on, who was he kidding. "You're still too top down, overly celebratory of hierarchy as if it were inherently better than collective wisdom of the community or individual, let's call it folk knowledge. It's like you've got this blind spot." He swallowed hard, set his eyes along the highway once more. "And I don't know if you want to get rid of it."

⌀

Or can! Margaret winced at the thought. *Genetics, genetics, genetics,* the word inwardly went off as if coming out of some echo chamber. "I understand it in my head, just not in my heart so much, I suppose," she said. "Please forgive me, Frazier, but I don't know if I want to see if I can work things through with my family."

"Then I also don't see any reason for us to go to Clifford Odeon together as a team. Even if you're so kind as to reinstate me," Frazier's tone took on no small amount of sarcasm, "I don't want to work with you on this project as things stand."

"Stop arguing in front of us," Mattie said from the backseat.

"I'm trying to read," Doug added.

The fist in Margaret's chest became a hand holding a chisel trying to carve its way out. Now they'd gone too far, brought the kids into their own private chaos, something that never happened between the Comrade and Lydia during her upbringing. That home was solid, stable, you could count on it not shaking on its foundation, but then what hadn't gone on in front of her so often left her alone in some dark room. Better that than taking the kids down with you, making them like sparrows from a shabby, wind-ravaged nest...sort of the way things in Frazier's rearing had been for him, who, to his credit, had agreed to never argue in front of the children and until now had held up his end of the bargain not perfectly, but very nearly. Problem was, Frazier's face had gone all puffy red, as if drunk with anger and perplexity, maybe a hint of shame too. That last part, if true, would be just like him to get superiorly complex on her. Shooting another look at the kids, she grimaced at noticing Doug's twisted expression, his protruding eyes staring a hole through the paperback's pages, clearly no longer doing something that could be called reading, more like clutching at words as though each one was a rung on a long rope to just about anywhere else. And Mattie, to Margaret's amazement, had lowered the Game Boy onto her lap, and she looked at Margaret knowingly, with a familiar, sad slit of a smile. The smile they had only shared before on those rare occasions when Mattie, in her room alone with Margaret, reached out for tenderness.

"Your dad and I are sorry for going rad on you guys a little." Margaret, too, smiled sadly; then she fixed her eyes on Frazier. "Aren't we?"

✍

He tried nodding by way of apology but couldn't bring himself to do it. Their children weren't shallow characters in one of Dr. Seuss's rhymes, *Green Eggs and Ham* or something; life was messy, more like a Chekhov short story, pretty much take your pick, "The Lady with the Dog," "Ward 6," "The Kiss," "The Story of a Nobody." Maybe they hadn't done Mattie and Doug any favors by raising them mostly Margaret's way; maybe his need to be the slumbering man even before he'd fallen upon the technique, his secret weapon for slumber, a fuzzed-out world, had kept him from adding nearly enough of his touch in their family and, in fact, that had cheated all of them dearly. Sure, they'd exposed Mattie and Doug to the West Village, which brought its diverse relationships, but they hadn't talked to them about these things. Besides, once he opened up with his dad and mom back in Texas, as hard as it had been to get the words out, things started getting better. He didn't have to glance in the rearview mirror to know Doug was for all intents and purposes curled into a ball on the backseat and Mattie had put on a strong face, a mask, or would as soon as she regained composure, which never took long. Now that milk had been spilt in this car, he and Margaret needed to find a way to clean it up in front of the kids, show them how to repair the circle from brokenness to wholeness, or at least try. Otherwise it was time to turn the Volvo around and head back to Manhattan. That would be too much of a sacrifice on way too many subjects. What's more, he thought sardonically, it would confuse to no end Mutt and Jeff. Okay, first he had to release some of his red on, so Frazier took a long breath and then exhaled slowly. Nothing much came of it. Had he not been driving, the world would've gone blurry over the top of his lenses.

For the next several minutes, they drove on, coming down off the causeway, losing sight of the ocean while they maneuvered through the tedious Boston streets, the gray sky getting lower and lower, heavier and heavier, until it seemed to rest its weight on top of the Volvo, crushing in on the Margaret and Frazier Picketts. Family secrets, what remained unsaid, Frazier thought and Margaret, as unquestionably as the day is long it seemed, couldn't begin putting into words, ground you into the earth, made neurotic messes out of yourselves and your kids. So what needed uttering? A lie must be named but the right one. The novel they were struggling to work on together was a lifeline, a conduit of cooperation, but it in itself wouldn't heal them. And how much could a person be expected to meet another's expectations by making peace with family of origin? In fact, Frazier's reasoning went, there was a language without words, a great connector, maybe the only one really, the weightless feeling he'd experienced with Anastasie and never at that level with Margaret. No, even it wouldn't be enough. You had to share similar directions, similar, what? values, maybe, or at least have the ability to bring them closer together, and therefore the thing pressing down on them all in this car had to be the lack of true love. With that you'd want to go onward; without it, you'd just have to let the roof cave in on the entire family while you all sat in your seats at some eternally damned traffic light giving everyone the red eye. There eventually wouldn't be the strength in your soul to do anything else. The best you could hope for would be to put it off for another day, at some other intersection; all the while the black clouds filled with water evaporating from your pain and resentments until bursting. Because they were all in the car together and this was happening, he found the stuff to go this far in; otherwise, alone with Margaret, there would've been a way to forget the generations, put scars on his kids they'd one day make desperate pilgrimages back home to come to grips with. He had to inwardly admit, her reticence wasn't entirely off key, or in a certain way not much was wrong with it at all: If Frazier spoke truth at their cores in front of the kids, the roof would, most assuredly, fall in on them.

"I apologize to all of you for being so harsh on Margaret," Frazier said at last, glancing intently over at her for a long moment. "Mom and Dad have to see if we have what it takes to work together on writing a book, and we will, I promise, do that while loving you guys to pieces, and learning how to love each other better." *No matter if it's not enough to sustain our marriage.*

∅

From the thickness in Frazier's tone, his watery eyes, Margaret knew what he didn't say. A lump rose in her throat, the deadly, bitten apple off the tree of the knowledge of good and evil. "Yes, we will," she said at last. "And maybe it's a good thing to drop Mattie and Doug at my folks before visiting Clifford Odeon, so…" Her voice tapered off. "So I can have some time with my parents when we get done with our work. That is if you would be up for that, Frazier, though I totally understand if you're not." Damn her husband, and love him. Only bringing the kids into it could make her give up this much—what was the word for it? A shamefully bitter one crowded its way in front of her spinning thoughts: control. Swallowing down the apple, she turned again in her seat toward the children and said, "Would that be okay with you two?"

"Whatever, okay," Mattie and Doug said almost at the same time. Then Mattie went back to playing something on the Game Boy, and Doug—still with a little of that horrified expression, but only a trace, wasn't that so?—resumed reading his book.

Without another word, Frazier made a right turn at the next intersection, en route to the Comrade and Lydia's brownstone. He lowered the window, then extended an arm and made a sweeping motion forward, signaling Mutt and Jeff the slight change in plans. Whatever. Quickly, he shut the window. It was cold outside.

✍

Clifford Odeon seemed almost too happy to see Margaret and Frazier as he showed them into his office at the Badshah Khan Institute for Peace Studies. He talked faster than the time before Frazier had visited him, together with doing something else noticeably different. Odeon lit up a fag, then proceeded to puff on the thing like an existentialist not entirely at peace with his philosophy. It creeped Frazier out a little, and from the knitted brow Margaret flashed him when Odeon looked intently at the cigarette while snuffing it in a heavily smudged ashtray atop the little oak table that they sat around across from the peace guru's modest but cluttered desk—Frazier knew she shared similar sentiments. The ashtray reeked of stale nicotine. Clifford Odeon's teeth only had a tinge of faded yellow, off-white really, those of a regular smoker long ago who had recently gone back to it. The dry, hacking cough Odeon fought against made Frazier wonder whether the downfall had occurred in the last few days, a tender, un-calloused throat indeed. Odeon complimented Margaret on her "astute sense of parallelism" by covering Yassine Lotfi Khaled and Mohammed al-Ajami, the "two resistance poets' persecution" in her recent article, and he had been keen to learn she was just getting started on the novel, "good timing for not uncovering the organizing in the Middle East quite yet." Frazier was struck by the fact Odeon hadn't mentioned the poems themselves that had caused all the ruckus, as if possibly wanting to avoid the subject of their content altogether.

Now, Odeon lit another cigarette and looked directly at Frazier, then Margaret. "I'm sure you didn't come here simply to soothe an old man's soul. So then, to what do I owe the pleasure of your company?"

First, Margaret told him the mole in his organization had passed al-Ajami's poem to her in advance of the Emir of Qatar's severe reaction to it, which Odeon met with a wave of his arm, sending a stream of cigarette smoke between them, a line in the sand, as though this information he both considered a fait accompli and a rudeness for Margaret to have acted on it without consulting him.

"Is that everything you have," Clifford Odeon said pithily.

Margaret shook her head, and then shot Frazier a glance.

He reached into the inside pocket of his winter parka and came out with copies of "Tunisian Muscle" and "Tunisian Jasmine," then laid the poems side by side on the table. Giving Clifford Odeon a knowing smile, Frazier said, "If the mole knew what the signal was in these identically structured poems, he wouldn't have given them to Margaret, or he would've told her what it was to screw things up for the movement by her reporting on it."

Momentarily Odeon's eyes widened, as if he was both surprised and impressed by Frazier's skill. "But you want to know, and why should I tell you?"

Margaret churned, a dark dance going on between her inner intelligentsia bourgeois gunning for a career-saving exposé or maybe even a Pulitzer, and her ideals for a badly needed grassroots revolution. But more than her journalistic ambitions were on the line. Her marriage was too; she could feel Frazier's breaking point palpable and in the room with them. *Why did we even come here?*

"Because those who want you to fail will figure this out and tell their own destructive version of what the connection may be." Frazier leaned forward, across the line. "We could break a story designed to keep the heat off whatever it is you're trying to accomplish. It may just be what the movement needs."

Odeon took three puffs on the fag in rapid succession, then nodded thoughtfully. "And for that you'd want an exclusive on the story when it's in the movement's interest for the truth to be told to the public."

"Yes," Margaret said flatly.

The peace guru cut his eyes at her. "And why should I trust you."

"Because I'm not entirely a capitalist pig journalist looking for a scoop at any cost." Uncontrollably, her eye twitched.

❧

A sure thing she felt conflicted over how much she meant this, Frazier thought, though Odeon with some luck may interpret it as an indication of a comrade's conviction. The slumbering man looked over the top of his lenses, while the peace guru's pale face along with thinning gray hair turned into sort of a glowing egg. There was nothing else that could be done now.

"I'll think about it; I'll mull over your offer." Clifford Odeon stood up and gestured toward the doorway. "Thank you for coming to me with this."

It felt to Frazier as if they were being rushed out. As they said their good-byes together with *you know how to reach me's*, and then Frazier and Margaret made their way along a long hallway in the old row house toward the exit for the Badshah Khan Institute for Peace Studies, Frazier's thoughts spun. The old peace guru was clearly savvy enough to know a high-powered journalist's ambition usually trumped all reason and sanity for publishing restraint, even a woman who had enough empathy to go to PEN with her findings. Why wouldn't Odeon want to hash things out more now, control the message at least on the most important things to him? And there was something else that gave Frazier a chill. In the middle of winter, closer to death, you can find the cross, or go right past it into meaninglessness. Which were he and Margaret doing? Could she ever get that twitch to go away, level her eyes and burn a hole through the ice, a woman at peace with herself, a woman free of, not only post-traumatic stress disorder, PTSD, brought on by her family's stultifying weather pattern, but just as much pre-stress traumatic disorder, PSTD, if you will, her own personal snowstorm falling from marbled clouds of split-off-ness. *Choose a side, Margaret, please!* He swallowed down these hissing words, a squashed callout for her mea culpa and, in a way, his too. In spite of everything, he could've shared more of the load in there with Odeon, insisted on not leaving without a way forward together. Too often the slumbering man let others do the dirty work whenever possible, or even when it became impossible. The chill coursing through Frazier intensified. He had contracted the same PTS/PST disorders as Margaret, but not from one long northland freeze after another until they all seemed to run together, as she had, instead, by way of some insidiously spontaneous, though all too familiar, low-dipping arctic jet stream that froze his family solid, only to be quick thawed, a kind of recurring shock treatment, in the almost unbearable Texas summers.

All of a sudden Margaret gasped and stopped walking.

"What's going on?" the slumbering man said.

"Look out the window."

He complied, tilting his head back ever so slightly to look through his lenses. His friend Buckminster was out there in the street next to the curb with another guy, and both of them were talking to the TMZ idiots who had been tailing him and Margaret. If anyone barged in on a mainly nonviolent revolution and mucked it up with his ham-fisted reporting, it would be Buckminster, Frazier understood at a cellular level. Reason or peaceable protestation wouldn't have any authority with his indefatigable college buddy. Quickly in succession, he pictured himself at the BofA protest, then this black man about his age, a member of the ANC, lighting a fuse to blow up an apartheid regime electrical plant, something he'd seen in a documentary. There was a time to hold your arms out in front of your body and go to jail in civil disobedience, and there was a time for creative sabotage of the powers that be. Inside Frazier the storm cleared. Maybe he was glad for the opportunity to go up against Bucky. Illustrate that his slumbering, lie-in-the-weeds-like-a-water-moccasin style could strike every bit as lethally as Buckminster with that almost perpetually fanned-out king cobra neck. In the struggle for peace and justice as well as with the fairer sex, yes, inescapably, an old friend, a close friend, came with this hedonistic spade. Womanizing for Bucky may mean a harem or at the very best serial monogamy, and for Frazier a French muse/mental mistress together with a wife. Or maybe the slumbering man wanted to change his style, choose, get off the fence, and be a better husband to Margaret. A little better anyway. Find a way to *do something* that didn't perpetuate violence in the winning or losing. Maybe that was also it, Frazier thought.

"You think that other guy with Bucky is the mole?" he said.

"I'd put money on it," Margaret said.

He took hold of her hand. "Let's go out the back door, what do you say?"

"But what about the story—" She came up short as if catching herself before going on. "What about the poets, the movement for real democracy if Bucky gets the reins with Odeon on this?"

"Going out the front door will only make him try harder for a scoop, that's what I think."

She squeezed his hand agreeably.

Unable to help himself, he waited a long moment for her eye to twitch, or something, but her gaze remained steady.

He led her back down the hallway, and when they arrived at Clifford Odeon's office, Frazier tilted his head that way; Margaret gave him a nod back. They entered the peace guru's office again.

Taking the phone away from his ear as if a bee had stung him through the handset, Clifford Odeon said, "What?"

"Your mole and a longtime friend of mine named Buckminster are talking to the TMZ goons who followed us here. One or both of them are probably working with or using the TMZ as informants. Bucky will play all sides against the middle for a story." Frazier returned Margaret's earlier squeeze of the hand, looked her directly in the eyes as he continued. "But you can trust my wife with the movement." He looked once more at Clifford Odeon. "When you're ready, you'll contact us, I'm sure of it."

With that they headed out the back door, and then walked three very cold blocks to a coffee shop, from which they called a cab.

"Let's go to 1226 Blanchard Street in Boston, please," Margaret said to the cabdriver.

"I'll call Hertz from your folks' place and let the company know someone will need to pick up the Volvo from where we left it, and I'll rent us a different vehicle," Frazier said. This would cost a bundle, the huge cab fare from Marblehead back to the city, and double rental cars along with a sure penalty for leaving the Volvo stranded. No question, Frazier reasoned, that was better than facing down Buckminster, the mole, and the TMZers to set off more of a feeding frenzy on the poets, on the fragile Tunisian uprising and its encrypted next moves.

Margaret nodded thoughtfully. "Okay, it should give me some good time alone with my parents for a long overdue talk."

He shrugged. "Maybe so, if you feel up to it after all this. No worries if you don't." Her words were gentle snowflakes falling on cedars, evergreens in Frazier's forest.

CHAPTER TWENTY-SIX

The war had been over for three years and then some, and I hadn't seen Oleg for nearly four, all that time me working the fields and staying with family at Mashinska, not living really. A certain kind of barren irrationality set in, waiting on Oleg to come, when I knew he was still locked away, or dead. Communications were sparse on the Siberian side of the Urals; nonetheless, Solomon and I had managed to get encrypted messages by way of mail to friends in the underground, asking them for assistance to locate Oleg in some gulag. We received letters in return from time to time that at first I read with bated breath, but eventually came to dread their arrival. With each passing month of getting no news back about Oleg, the soil of my soul turned more and more fallow, no crop rotation, one day like the other, little to irrigate it with other than the goodhearted simplicity of the peasants, cups of vodka that delivered me to the fuzzy stars and restless sleep at night, and then there was Solomon's solidarity, him refusing to leave Mashinska until we finally agreed he could better help find Oleg by returning to Moscow. In the looks of our eyes, when we seldom allowed them to meet in just this particular way, we recognized, though didn't dare bespeak it, the bigger problem for Solomon staying longer could be spotted in his inner fields that had also fallen fallow, this good man awaiting my amore, which simply could not be harvested. I had to hand it to him, holding fast for eighteen months, never once trying to take advantage by consoling me on his breast, which I would've been weak enough to fall for more often than one should care to admit. No, Solomon had simply been with me, taking a patient bearing, with an honorable agenda practiced honorably. And then he was gone. So be it.

For the rest of the time, there was only the work, the peasants, and the vodka. Without trying to, the peasants taught me that one day turning almost identical as the other could be somewhat spiritual, a trickle of water of a sort to keep me going, for on those days no one got an inadvertent hoe across the foot, or came to fists or hair yanks over the prize of a woman or of a man, or fell in the fields from heat exhaustion or heart attack, all of which the community too often suffered. Of course, my family did what they could for me, serving up bounteous affection, including me at every meal and the occasional fete, but after a while their unconditional offerings only dried me up more, reflected back too much of what I'd once had with Oleg, and then lost. No, I was no longer a child or a daughter—only the itinerate granddaughter, niece, cousin—my home was no longer here; this was not the kind of love I could accept much more of without breaking into pieces, like a clod of dirt tossed on the ground, becoming a thousand disconnected grains, identity lost, until the rains came to make mud once more, reform me into something that held together, wet and sticky, even becoming solid again with the right amount of delay to dry out, but, not to fall emaciated for yet another time, the precipitation must deftly repeat itself. During my stay at Mashinska, this kind of weather never came. Nothing like it. In short, God didn't use His or Her hands, or His or Her breath, on me.

The long train ride back to Moscow had felt like a desperate grasp at survival, mine more than Oleg's, to be honest. What could I do to locate and free him that amounted to anything? Nevertheless, I had to try to do something more for Oleg than waste away in Mashinska. Maybe being around poets and authors at the Writers Building would hold me together some, give me a few ideas or inroads to find him. But after arriving there, it didn't take long to figure out most of them were nothing more than menches for Stalin, mere propagandists. Being around them made my stomach turn, and what is more, most of the hearty, dissident souls in the Jewish Anti-Fascist Committee had been carried off in railcars to be jailed, or disappeared. Waves of guilt washed over me now and then over not seeking out Solomon, who was still around Moscow and maintained his apartment, according to the poet Peretz Markish, one of the lucky ones in the JAFC who by going far underground had also avoided Stalin's ratcheting up of the assault on Russian Jews. My visit with Peretz, arranged through a comrade at the Writers Building, had taken place in some rat-infested basement of a condemned hospital. No more holding court in coffee houses for our kind. Perhaps Solomon was too high profile to be sent away, too famous internationally, like Pasternak. Whatever, I was glad Solomon was okay. And the fact I felt so reticent about looking him up, while somehow pulled to do just that, told me I had no business seeing him. Too much awaited me in Moscow and clearly not enough. The afternoon of my third day there, I boarded another train for the short ride to Peredelkino, none too soon.

When the train got close enough to the little station house for me to sense its impending appearance, and while urban clutter gave way to rolling countryside, dotted with elm trees, maples, alongside the occasional live oak, blessed with what would otherwise be my enjoyment of this resplendent summertime verdure, instead, an eerie rawness of inchoate poverty rushed in, as if I were suddenly one of the leafless top branches on some old oak that, moments ago, I had noticed death inching up the trunk, wide tongues of it turned the color of ashes. My grandfather had tried to gift me money he'd buried in little jars near his house, like canned preserves or plums or something, which I had no choice but to accept, though under condition it would be a loan repaid some day soon, albeit interest-free. That may as well have been a million years off in some imperial life I had no desire to reincarnate into. Truth be told, only a few measly rubles remained in my purse, enough to buy a meal or two, but not cover a room at the inn, or even come close to paying the "abandonment fee" on Oleg's and my apartment. That would have to wait. Besides, under the guise of "continual property usage" laws, the hale and hearty "people's government" had, no doubt, long ago confiscated our place and assigned it to some other lot. If I could get on my feet with work, then maybe there would be a future here, even though I hardly wanted one. Whatever grievances the government had against me for my dissident opinions and for going after Oleg years ago, I hoped for no really good reason would have faded with the end of the war; therefore, I could get a work permit under my actual name and not some alias fixed up properly by underground friends. But there was something other than that I would use my rubles for. A couple minutes after the train pulled into the station and I got off, at the cashier inside I exchanged some of the money for coinage. I walked over to the payphone on the far wall in the lobby and slipped in its slot some of the kopecks, enough to make a two-minute call. I had to think for a moment to recall Pasternak's phone number.

He answered on the third ring with a reserved "Hello."

"Pasternak, it's me, Katya."

"My God, it's wonderful to hear your voice," he said, his tone brightening. "How are you?" A pause. "Where are you?"

"I'm okay, I guess." It wasn't a complete lie, as I, too, felt lifted by talking with Pasternak. "I'm at the train station in Peredelkino."

"When can I see you?"

"The walk from town to the dacha is a delight. I'll be there before you know it."

"No, no, you mustn't," he said, something darkening his words. "I'll fetch you; stay where you are."

This was no heartfelt extension of assistance or an attempt at lessening the time between us or, for that matter, even paltry obligatory etiquette. Believe you me, if there was anywhere else in this town for me to take refuge that provided a roof over my head, I would've gone there right now. "Thank you but I'll walk, and that's that."

"I'll come get you, Katya; I won't hear of anything else."

"It's a nice summer day; I'm off. Bye."

Truth was, I needed the walk as much to think some as because of my flaring chutzpah over not wanting to fall prey to whatever black snake coiled round Pasternak. Had the war and the increased intensity of the Goat-faced Murderer's purges after the war bowed him, brought intractable changes; had it all, a confluence of things I understood and others I probably never would even be made aware of, turned this great man brittle? The voice on the other end of the line hadn't come from the person I knew who helped me look for Oleg through the underground, who made me his one and only writing protégé, who, well, loved me and I loved him! Then again, he did seem like the real Pasternak on taking my call, simply reconnecting with me, learning I was nearby and for the most part, anyway, all right. It would be only natural for him to be apprehensive, having not seen or heard from me for all those years, hmm? Yes, it would. Being boldface honest, I sure as hell was anxious over meeting up with him again. And this condition sharpened me in a way I liked: fire in the belly, like some mischievous old friend returning who knew me when I had the sensibility, the naïveté, to be puckish, this inner phantom coming out of dormancy or whatever it was that pushed my buttons, certainly proved more animating than the cold gray grief mixed with fear I had lived with since Oleg left never to return.

As I made my way along the main road, which curved up ahead toward the dacha, a yearning overcame me to head down the narrow street of Oleg's and my apartment, a spirited quest to reclaim something, if only a memory of the life together we started there, all too brief, filled with sweetness, lust, and pain, the death of Vika, the loss of the man I loved to the insanity of war and Stalin. What I wanted most was just one immensely satisfying look at the rickety little table we had made love on, a chance to watch the candle's flame burn again, if only in my mind. Maybe the current occupants would be kind enough to let me browse around inside.

I rapped with a knuckle on the door of our apartment, and then stood there on the porch, waiting for someone to come. Another rap came with more stillness that passed as slow as the sultry summer afternoon. Finally I knocked once again. All along only the cicadas' clacking up in the maple trees greeted me. I walked over to the small window over the kitchen sink and looked in. A greasy haze clung to the glass, as it had when we lived here, but it was so thick now that I couldn't make out anything inside. I tried picturing the room, a chair or two beside the wood-burning furnace, the countertop and cabinets, the doorway to the bedroom, the table with the candle on it, but all I could do was put empty words together for these precious and pitiable contents; no images would come. Shakily I placed a hand on the window, which was covered by a wet film, this season's tears, as locked out and sad as me.

Pray God there still remained this one other treasure here for me that wouldn't actually require entrance to the apartment. I looked one way, then the other along the lane and didn't see any activity, save for a cat watching me from a windowsill across the street, certainly no police, and the residents had to be at work, school, or inside their homes. I walked over in front of the porch, then slipped off my shoulder the knapsack with my few things in it, and set it on the ground. Wasting no time, I shimmied beneath the underside of the porch raised almost a foot off the ground on the apartment's pier and beam foundation. I counted slim lines of light coming through spaces between the wooden slats until coming to the fourth line, the place I had buried it. Then, I clawed the dirt with my hands, again and again, until I felt the round metal top. A few more quick digs down around it, and then I lifted the glass jar. Rotating it underneath a strip of light, I could hardly see through the jar's murky brown surface from soil pressed onto it but, make no mistake, the original of "The Stalin Epigram" was in there.

Once back outside, I sat on the lowest step up to the porch and went at the stubborn jar, trying to open it. Sweat beaded on my forehead; my hand began hurting I gripped the top so firmly. Nothing, it had rusted against the glass, and I simply wasn't strong enough to break the bond.

I don't quite know how long I had been on that step failing to have any success with the jar when the pithy rustling of tires rolled over this street with chuckholes like chicken pox, although, along with the noise I raised my head. Suddenly, my heart seemed to do something like leave my body and crawl into my knapsack to join my one change of panties and peasant dress. This wasn't the resident of my and Oleg's apartment coming home, or the police on patrol, no, it was Pasternak behind the steering wheel of what looked to be a spanking new GAZ M1 ocean blue sedan. His previous GAZ, at least the one I was familiar with, had been gray. Things change but most often not much or enough. Pasternak obviously was still so important to the Stalinists that they let him live high in these terrible times. An insider, outsider. Really now, could one be such a concoction without having been mostly bought off? Nevertheless, when he smiled, his eyes danced with flecks of God and, not the devil itself, but easily some minor fallen angel or another, his entire expression conveying the weight and depth and obstinacy of a poet, a rebel, and, yes, one smooth operator for the truth. As I returned his smile, genuinely finding it within me to do so, I hoped during my absence he hadn't become too smooth by half. Without a word he got out of the car parked right in front of me and walked round its front. Standing there before me, I realized that his hair had thinned along with silvering some, his jowls had fallen slightly, and he was skinnier than I would've liked to have seen him, just this side of gaunt really. "Pasternak," I said.

"Sweet Katya." He reached out a hand. "Want some help up?"

I took hold of his hand and we brought me onto my feet. I brushed some dirt off my skirt and blouse, then picked up my knapsack and slid an arm through its strap, though kept hold of the jar, not putting it away in the bag.

"I drove up and down the road to the dacha, until I began to think you may have changed your mind about seeing me. I even went inside the train station looking for you. Finally, it came to me where you were." Pasternak lowered his chin. "I'm so glad my instinct was right."

I knew what he meant: The Stalinist goons have long memories, and I could've been apprehended and taken to the death trains. "Can you protect me here, at least for a while, until I can figure things out a little?"

"I'll do my best."

"That's good enough for me." I'd never been more aware of being with someone who walked such a fine line that kept him out of the purges…and perhaps his protégé too. "Thanks, Pasternak, truly, thank you."

"It's not necessary to thank me and, you're welcome." With a tilt of his head, he gestured at the jar. "Not that it's any of my business, but what do you have there?"

"It's the original of 'The Stalin Epigram.' I hid it here before going away to look for Oleg." I held the jar toward him. "It seems the top's stuck on. Do you mind opening it?"

He took the jar, looking at it with a certain fascination. "Some of us tried to retrieve things from your apartment to protect them once you didn't return. Nothing of importance was there. I'm sorry, Katya."

I nodded my understanding.

"We figured the Goat-faced Murderer's goons had already taken what they wanted." He gave the top a good twist and it came off. With a warm smile, he handed me the jar. "It's been in your keeping and so it shall remain."

My heart raced as I carefully inched the poem free of the container. The paper had yellowed so, I felt afraid it may well come apart in my hands on unrolling it.

"Go ahead, it's okay," Pasternak said almost tenderly. "Osip cared only that his work last as long as it could be of some use. I'm sure he would've wanted you to unroll it rather than the poem stay obscured until the paper and ink turn back into dust."

Without another word I very slowly sort of peeled the paper off its own backside, until I was looking at the whole of "The Stalin Epigram." The ink had smudged some; nevertheless, each magnificent word of truth against the ravages of Stalin and Stalinism were readable. Pasternak stepped in behind me and looked over my shoulder at it. My eyes filled with water until the poem's words all ran together. No matter, I had already read it.

"It's why we've carried on together," Pasternak said. "And why we continue."

I knew he meant us, him and I, ever since that night this poem came into my possession at my parents' home, as well as, in a way, all of Russia, especially the dissidents. I couldn't bring myself to meet his eyes, for surely I would just start sobbing. "I think you're right." I painstakingly replaced the poem back in the jar. He handed me the lid; I gingerly screwed it in place, and then placed the jar in my knapsack.

"Shall we go then?" he said.

"Yes, there's nothing more here for me now." I waited for Pasternak to lean over while getting into the car before wiping the tears off my cheeks with the pad of a hand. Then I, too, got in.

He drove to the end of the street, where we turned right onto the main road, instead of left toward the dacha.

"Where're we headed?"

Pasternak looked me directly in the eyes, and for several excruciatingly long seconds didn't say anything. The car swerved into the oncoming lane, yet he didn't seem to notice.

I clutched my knapsack to my breast, as if that would do any good. "What is it, Pasternak? You're scaring me."

"I'm sorry, I'm sorry." He set his eyes back onto the road ahead and righted the car into its proper lane. "We're going to my mistress's house, simply put. Her name's Olga." This time, he didn't so much as glance at me. "Please don't judge me harshly."

"She's taking me in?"

He nodded. "I've talked with her and she's expecting you. You'll like her, I'm sure of it."

How could I warm to the woman who corrupted this man I held so loftily, the man who taught me through his writing and his ways to love inviolately, so I could love Oleg the way I did? Yes, Pasternak had picked up with me where my parents left off, and to be completely forthright, and then some with his particular genius and sensitivity. Of course, Miss Zinaida was a hard case a good bit of the time, but still, why not divorce her if true love lay in another's lap? It fell on me like bricks why he'd been reticent to have me out to the dacha when I called from the station, and would have nothing of it now—with all this going on, Miss Zinaida must be beside herself. It was all too much like that manuscript of his, *Doctor Zhivago*. Was he losing his literary mind, his human one, confusing the two, or was he somehow breaking through to his destiny, if there was such a thing? "Oh, my dear Pasternak," I said at last, suddenly and unwontedly picturing ruddy Solomon Mikhoels in the fields working alongside me in Mashinska. But then, the image wasn't entirely off-putting I had to inwardly admit. That is, if destiny happened to be real, and larger than Oleg and me together. The rims of my eyes filled with water again, and I blinked away tears for yet another time. Damned if I'd let Pasternak see me that way over this. He might misconstrue my meaning, or get it spot-on. "I'm sure I'll like anyone you care so much for," I added.

It was getting dark outside now, and candles atop saucers and ensconced by little glass vases in groupings of two or three lit this Olga's apartment on Potapov Street with a buttery sheen that sort of flirted with you, as if to say, "No artificial illumination allowed, a poet, a vamp lives here." A tapestry that looked to be from India hung on a wall over the white linen divan, and an Afghan rug weaved with indigo, bloodred, and gold swirls lay on the floor underneath a coffee table which looked to be made from old African tribal masks. Set on the table was a hardbound copy entitled Selected Works of the wonderful Hungarian poet Sandor Petofi, and I noticed beneath the author's name Pasternak credited as the book's translator into Russian. No other art or family photos held station here, and if it weren't for the shelves from floor to ceiling on the far wall overfilled with books stood up in rows along with others stacked sideways on top of them, the place could've been called minimal or something. As I stood there beside Pasternak taking all of this in, the empty spaces together with the adorned, my mind opened, though my heart clamped. No, I didn't want to be seduced or inspired by the occupant of this apartment, the creator of this mood. It was quite enough to share Pasternak with Miss Zinaida, a mostly predictable stoic, Czarist-era holdover, but the woman who lived here had more of my touch, that is, if I had a handsome, shall we say, pragmatically mature comrade to put me up and keep me, with freedom to travel the world to find such subtly tasteful accoutrements as these. Inwardly, I almost chuckled over the conclusions I could jump to like a schoolgirl playing hopscotch. Hardly anyone without risking his or her life could get outside Russia's borders these days. Nonetheless, Pasternak had opened the front door with his own key, and I still stung from having been put through such a clichéd icon of untoward intimacy. Where was his mistress anyway!

"Olga," Pasternak called out.

No response came.

"Maybe she got intimidated by the prospect of me." This time I did chuckle.

"Nice to see some of your spice return."

Yes, I had to agree with him, being here in Peredelkino was already doing me some good. "Thank you, old man," I said very nearly lightheartedly, then turned serious again. "You may want to check the other rooms, make sure she's okay, or maybe she just stepped out for a bit."

Pasternak's brow knitted and as quickly relaxed. "It's probably not anything like that," he said, then looked through the doorway to the rest of the apartment. "I will be a tree, if..." His voice didn't taper off, it just oddly stopped, as though the partial thought was somehow also whole.

The sound of a door opening and closing, and footsteps came toward us, until there she was in the room with Pasternak and me. It seemed she filled the darkness between the shifting candlelight, evened out everything around us almost ethereally, this somber beauty who did not glow like unadulterated loveliness does but, instead, drew you to her like the swill of smoke that refused to dissipate, curvaceous, melancholy with those half-closed eyelids, her shoulder-length dirty blonde hair in soft, wispy curls, and full lips that almost smiled in their natural state, inviting me into a commonwealth of sadness and yet joy too. Something about me wanted more of what she had, against my better instincts, or maybe rather from whatever lurked around repressed inside me that needed releasing; either way, I felt I would, somehow or other, get something invaluable from staying with her, even if it turned out to be for only a few days. Without so much as a flit of doubt on my part, this woman, Olga whatever-her-family-name-happened-to-be, was so understatedly fresh and open-faced that whatever I needed to learn could not be kept undisclosed for long, even if she preferred such a tenor between us or, perhaps, especially if she did.

"You must be Katya," she said, extending a hand as forthrightly as any man. "I'm Olga, pleased to meet you."

I shook it more firmly than most young women would, proud of the calluses from wielding my short-handle hoe out in the fields that now rubbed against her smooth skin. "I hope I won't be too much trouble."

"My home is yours." Her azure eyes widened almost imperceptibly. "You're as lovely as Boris said and, well, we are all in trouble."

The what? inevitability in her tone told me this was no flip generality; something specific lay behind the admonition.

"I'm sorry for the delay in coming out to greet you," Olga went on. "But Boris and I have this lovely verbal signal before I show myself to anyone other than him."

"I didn't think she'd be that, shall I say, careful on meeting you," Pasternak said to me, then set his eyes on Olga again. "Sorry for not sticking with the program entirely, my love." He began rocking on his feet as if anxious to make a move he didn't want to make, or possibly bolt out the front door and leave, something of the sort anyway. Where was it coming from?

"It's quite all right," Olga said. She then offered me a glass of vodka or water, of which I chose the benign option, for fear whatever the inevitability in the room with us like an ostrich with its head buried in the sand may bring could just as well send me on a drinking binge. This wasn't self-imposed exile on the other side of the Urals; here, I would actively try to locate Oleg. Keeping my wits about me was paramount.

While Pasternak went to pour her as well as himself a vodka, Olga sat down on the divan, languidly patting the seat cushion beside her. "Katya, please, let's get to know each other a bit; although, from all the things Boris has told me about you, I feel we're friends already if you don't mind me being so presumptuous."

"It's not even near a problem." I looked her directly in the eyes. "You seem magnificent, and I do want to get to know you well. But has Pasternak spoken to you about helping find my husband…has he told you Oleg is in some gulag probably under a false name, lost to us all?" I hadn't meant to be so direct, but if my instinct was right, this subject held no inconsiderable lack of footing as, in fact, being the ostrich, the inevitability. Pasternak hadn't said anything to me about Oleg, and not for lack of opportunity. He would've gotten word from Solomon Mikhoels or others in the underground about what happened to Oleg in Mashinska. And he would've acted on it, unless he had really changed, and his soul had been burnt too badly from Stalin breathing down his neck, the decimation of his dissident friends, the war, a stifling marriage.

Olga sat back against the divan, her eyes darting toward the doorway Pasternak had gone through. She said nothing.

The ostrich burrowed its head farther down, having a sharp beak, indeed.

I just sat there awaiting Pasternak along with her, determined for my silence to speak my resolve.

He walked back in the room, and as he handed Olga the tumbler of vodka, she said, "She wants and deserves to know, Boris."

My increasing sense about the fine quality of this woman also seemed to be right.

Pasternak straightened almost as if taking a blow on the chest. They both took long draws off their vodkas. Finally, he nodded his understanding, then pulled a chair against the wall over to just across the coffee table and sat down.

"Please don't be a poet right now; be my godfather, Pasternak," I said.

"I had hoped to let you get settled in some before broaching this subject. I'm sorry; I can see that was a mistake. Nonetheless, I wanted you to hear this directly from me." He set the tumbler down on the table. "It seems over two years ago Oleg killed a guard in the night, and then slipped out of the gulag in that guard's uniform. No one has heard from him since."

It felt as if my world turned upside down. Nothing made sense. If Oleg were alive and free, he would've come to me, or gotten word to me! "How sure are you of this information?"

"Very. A high-level Stalinist who's secretly a dissident sympathizer that I grew up with told me." He grimaced. "Oleg was kept in solitary confinement in a separate cell from all other inmates from the day he was apprehended. The Stalinists knew he was Osip's son, so he got special 'protection.'" Pasternak made quote signs with his fingers. "No one associated with the underground in the gulags could locate him."

As he spoke, each word seemed to come in slow motion, long and dragged out. This was too much, simply too much to bear. "Why didn't you tell me sooner about this, talk with Solomon and find out where I was?"

"Solomon told me where you were, but I had to wait until you came to me. They would never have let me travel across the Urals unwatched, without a minder. It would've meant your death and mine."

"I wouldn't have cared if I died!" I snapped, unable to think clearly at all now.

CHAPTER TWENTY-SEVEN

The rental car broke down on the way to their appointment, and they got a cab ride back here; that had been Margaret and Frazier's story met by the Comrade's stony stare and Lydia's caring, shrewdly matriarchal eyes. It was as if her mom was always in control, or vying for it, all the while acquiescing to the Comrade being her front man, Margaret thought. How would she ever crack her parents' code? And what would be on the far side of it? While Frazier and her dad had gone to get another rental car, she asked her mother about what made people crazy on the Comrade's side of the family. Margaret knew this was sort of cheating, a way to avoid her father's disdain, or God forbid, shake him into truth telling, and what would that be like? Would it unravel too much of their family myth? Something in her fought against talking with him because she liked all this structure; it gave her a clear path to trod, if not meaning, if not the openness to have a marriage any more alive than her mother and father's, well, not *not alive*, for the Comrade and Lydia loved each other, that had always been clear; they just did it in such an archaic way.

True to form, when questioned, Lydia had said things like Margaret should be proud of her father for giving her such a wonderful upbringing only one generation removed from her father's family escaping Stalinist Russia. But when Margaret pressed her to put meat on the bones of the mental illness and the plight of being refugees, Lydia once again fixed on Margaret those wizened eyes, deadened by generations of Nordic feminine wile maneuvering inside patriarchal domination, and simply said, "You'll need to ask your father about those subjects."

Just then the Comrade and Frazier, having presumably returned with another rental car, walked in on her and her mother around the island in the kitchen. Frazier looked at her in her entirety and that was unnerving. No, it wasn't just her love for him that he needed and, by God, love for the people Margaret unquestionably felt, even as strongly as Frazier, she believed, but Margaret could shut the door on everyone so fast in her heart, just like she was futilely trying to do with Frazier right now. Perhaps it was a good thing not to be able to hold on any longer, let that old balloon she so often was haunted by go and enjoy the jaunty flight as air whooshed out its stem, all the while reminding herself that her feet were firmly planted on the ground. She wasn't inwardly riding that F-ing balloon into oblivion, but to her very humanity. That was the idea anyway.

Without a word other than hello between her and Frazier, Margaret diverted her eyes to her father and then her mother. If this were all about genetics, she should let Frazier go now, once back home get on www.lawyers.com and fill out paperwork for filing a divorce, the nice and tidy 21st-century amicable kind. Frazier didn't deserve this and neither did she. Thankfully, or just as much not, Frazier went into the TV room where the kids were, gathered them up, and then left for a "drive along the oceanfront." He must have sensed the end of the road nearing for them, too, and wanted to buy a little time, give her the space to talk freely without Mattie's and Doug's hot little ears in the next room.

Asking the Comrade and Lydia to take seats on barstools at the island along with her was harder than running from the TMZ and the FBI or CIA or NSA or whoever the mole worked for, more difficult than leaving Clifford Odeon without an understanding on how to help the poets Mohammed al-Ajami and Yassine Lotfi Khaled and what they were communicating about freedom and participatory democracy. But it wasn't because she didn't care as much, not at all; Margaret had shut the door to protect herself the only way she knew how, like her mother and father did so easily. Their deadpan expressions and vacuous eyes told her this much. A hot stream of bile rose in her throat. Who cared whether Frazier's friend Buckminster got the story, and not her, on the meaning of the poems to the movement. The putrid, sulfur taste on her tongue informed her of something else: The movement's success mattered to her every bit as much as the outcome of this visit with her parents, or at least almost nearly as much. All of this came from the same air that had been interminably pent up in the balloon no longer tied off in a knot.

In certain ways Margaret had been preparing for this over many a season, ever since her college days really, formulating things she wanted answers to from the Comrade and Lydia about her family. But there was always something to hide behind: marriage, having children, raising them, juggling a fast-track career, and, for too much of the last several years, living with Frazier's tuned-out-ness. She hardly remembered she'd put these questions together right along, because they quickly had turned into polluted air and were blown into the balloon, its thin, rubbery skin, a placenta of sorts, holding in the confusion, though not the paranoia over something very ominous bursting inside her at any moment. That feeling she secretly cradled in her belly like a bastard baby, ever growing, insipidly insidious, this blob of emotions too awesome to admit to herself, much less Frazier, before now. Needing something to help her get the first words out, she recalled Frazier had told her about getting higher than a kite with his towny friend, Rudy, almost directly before doing this with his parents. She felt badly over the look-down-her-nose admonition she'd given Frazier for subjecting himself to the "derelict influence" of Rudy. What is more, all her old friends had polished themselves to pristine sheens in mostly highbrow post-graduate programs and/or the holding together of their "fine" families, and besides, come to think of it, so had her newer friends in the literary biz or on the New York charity boards she served on. The eclectic West Village, where she and Frazier and the kids lived, suddenly seemed like mere window dressing, not a real community she'd joined in with, become an actual member. Plenty of the artists or writers or gypsies or fools who lived there would share a doobie and a real conversation with her if offered the chance. Right this moment, she would've given pretty much anything to have just such a friend as Rudy and a solid hour to cruise around in his El Camino. The thing of it was, all Margaret's questions had left her, as if in some tarnished halo swirling round her head, a Saturn ring she couldn't quite grab hold of.

For the love of hominy, just say something!

"Dad, Mom, I need to ask you some questions so I can make sense of stuff, important stuff, at least for me, but I don't want to hurt you, or push you into pain, so please, please, let me know if I'm taking you to places you don't want to revisit. Do you mind too much?" Oh crap, she had gone all the way back to being a twelve-year-old in front of them with a less than stellar report card, or in her bedroom with clothes strewn on the floor, or any number of other dastardly behaviors.

"What sort of 'stuff,'" Lydia said.

"Family history," Margaret said.

The Comrade's eyes momentarily narrowed. He said nothing.

Stung with anger, Margaret fixed her eyes on her father, her adult-self returning to the room. God in heaven, she and the Comrade could be so much alike. "I just don't understand how you guys can be so different than Grandpa Mandt, than the artists in our bloodline," she said evenly, working hard at not jumping him with an attitude. "How do you think that is?"

"Some God makes bankers, some lawyers, some artists, others thieves," the Comrade said.

"It's all genetics, then?" Margaret said glumly.

The Comrade and Lydia met one another's eyes, as if checking on their mutuality of instincts, and then they both nodded.

"It may cost me my marriage. Not that I think either of you are purposely lying."

For the longest time there was only the sound of the central heating system flowing through floor vents, the hissing of a pot of water for tea Lydia had going on the stovetop.

Margaret fidgeted with a napkin, determined to wait her parents out.

Lydia got up and poured tea for herself and Margaret, along with a bourbon neat for the Comrade, and then sat back down.

Slowly, her father's expression softened almost imperceptibly, his eyes coming to life, even glimmering slightly, or was this only Margaret's wishful thinking? He took a sip of whiskey, looking Margaret directly in the eyes. "Environment probably plays a big part too," he said without the usual puffery, or whatever it was, in his tone.

Lydia almost choked on a sip of tea, and then put her hand over the Comrade's hand, which rested on the granite island just short of his tumbler.

"It's going to be okay," he said, with another intent glance at his wife.

Margaret's fidgeting with the napkin eventually tore off its corner, as if slitting open a bag of the Greek goddess's of truth, Aletheia's, corn chips, each one a different question. Which chip would she select first, or was it better to simply grab a handful and toss them up into the air, see which ones the Comrade went for, if any, God forbid? Taking a sip of tea, she spilled most of the cup's contents all over the napkin, turning it brown, and with that, a bloodbath came to mind. "How did your environment in your upbringing affect you, Dad?" she finally said, swabbing the wet countertop with a sleeve of her shirt. As she waited for his reply, Margaret balled the soggy napkin in her fist.

Her father's brow furrowed, and then he passed a hand over his face, as though both searching inwardly for an answer and looking for a way to wipe it away altogether. "It too often made me feel all alone, almost a surrogate husband to my mother. She'd talk with me about her ups and downs, I'd pay all the bills, take her to the doctor, my, she was such the artist, the writer of stories that would change the world, while, to be fair, she also had this peculiar interest with the mundane."

"Nana leaned on you during Grandpa Mandt's manic or depressive episodes," Margaret said.

Her father nodded.

"What else strange did he do or not do when like that?"

"Oh, I must say, a lot of the time my father was a charming, intelligent man, full of conversation and laughs, a fabulous bongo player and singer who brought music and art into our home, but other times he'd talk for hours on end about overturning the Goat-faced Murderer, that's what he and your grandmother called Stalin, right along with their revolution of dissident music and prose." Her father closed his eyes for a long moment, as if looking back into his childhood. "It was as if they'd all but done it singlehandedly. And of course, there wasn't a successful counterrevolution in Stalinist Russia.

"When Dad got really sick—"

"Horace, why go that far?" Lydia interrupted.

Margaret felt loved by her mother, the way you'd love an adolescent.

"Our daughter wants to know, so she gets to know." The Comrade took another hit of bourbon neat before going on.

"Your grandfather sometimes wouldn't sleep for days, we'd pull him out of hole-in-the-wall bars at all hours, and he fooled around on your grandmother with other women."

Margaret's eyes got big as saucers, although, mercifully, there was no twitch. "Do you think Nana contributed to Grandpa Mandt's illness by staying with him, a sort of tacit approval of his philandering?"

"You do ask good questions." Her father smiled sadly. "Genetics or environment, take your pick, I couldn't say."

Margaret unfolded the napkin, spread it smoothly onto the countertop. The stain was simply brown tea now. And yes, Aletheia, approvingly, had entered the room and sat down on the fourth barstool. It was as if her father needed to clear the air not only for her, for himself as well.

The next twenty minutes may as well have been an evening at the symphony listening to Bach and Mozart with a surprise appearance by Duke Ellington and Ella Fitzgerald, their conversation rising and falling with detail and depth, Margaret and her dad striving for crescendo, then riffing old-school jazz, Lydia even becoming if not supportive, accepting of this tête-à-tête, with father and daughter tasting freedom unleashed, family secrets scored to some looser harmony, imperfections laid bare and found starkly beautiful, liberation, the kind all great music and poetry pulls off, redefining individual relationships, and therefore culture, Margaret elegantly reasoned and gave herself permission to do just that. What had she earned an MFA at New York University and married the sensitive writer Frazier for if not to be able to thread thoughts such as this? But it was more than fancy intellectualizing to avoid the fear of repeating family mistakes with Frazier: In feeling the full range of this messy song that was hers, raw and unfiltered, along with her parents, she no longer had to worry about hitting every note in tune.

At one point her father explained that the escape from Stalinist Russia by her grandparents probably sent Grandpa Mandt into his manic-depressive state, and the death of his beloved wife years later pushed him over the edge more and more often, he missed her so. Things had fallen tender between herself and her mom and dad, even Lydia giving her a conspiratorial smile, surprisingly feminist in the timing of its understanding. Her parents' respect for how hard her grandparents worked side by side to save Russia from itself before being forced into exile inspired Margaret to recite some lines of poetry from "Tunisian Jasmine" and "Tunisian Muscle" in sort of a medley:

> *"The workers who toil will be heard in the streets*
> *with entire bodies*
> *the muscles that will outlive the corrupt government.*
>
> *For those that think your country is in you and your*
> *kids' names,*
> *the country is for the people and its glories are*
> *theirs."*

Then she told her parents this was happening today in the streets of Tunisia, with everyday people standing on the shoulders of all the peace-loving revolutionaries who came before them, like her grandparents. Something strange was happening to Margaret: She felt there was in actuality no "them," only us, we the people, all are have-nots and haves in more than one way or another, all were ordinary citizens, in need of a people's movement, if you stray too far to the right, you come toward the left, and oddly enough, if you stray too far to the left, you drift toward the right, a participatory democracy of the soul. Some borderless community, starting with herself, Frazier, Mattie, and Doug, her parents, grandparents, together with all other scared human beings hiding behind masks everywhere, trying to keep it together for the kids or something. No sitting down, there was too much work to be done until all stood barefaced before one another, or at least in the privacy of their own tents.

By the time the whiskey tumbler and teacups went dry and their talk wound down, Margaret could hardly wait to get back together with Frazier. But she decided not to call him on his cell phone. No, she'd sit here with the Comrade and Lydia and enjoy the snow that had begun falling outside the kitchen window. Maybe they'd talk about the illness some more, but she didn't think so. Perhaps they'd discuss poetry or her novel or her parents' bridge group or her mother's docent work at the holocaust museum or her father's latest academic research on Russian history or how the kids were doing in school. It didn't much matter which, and right now, this meant everything to Margaret.

∅

A lone gull coasted with wings extended, flapped them several times, then simply rode the frigid wind some more, out there a hundred yards or so, where the ice-sheet extending from the shore met gray waters that reflected the sky, melding everything above with the sea and the earth, and somehow Frazier felt there was no escape. Had he abandoned Margaret or gifted her the necessary anonymity to speak freely with her folks? If something in his experience held any indication of a remotely satisfactory answer, well, he'd gone in solo and done pretty well with his mom and dad in their big talk, his bumbling humility and slumbering intuition even coming in handy. Hadn't it? Maybe he should've hung around to sort of facilitate things back in Boston. *No thank you.* He looked one way, then the other along the shoreline, trying to spot more gulls, but there wasn't even a second one on Windmill Point.

Why had he brought the kids here anyway, to Nantasket peninsula, with Grandpa Mandt's home only a few blocks away? A million miles from Texas. No more land on which to distance himself from most everything, only the vast Atlantic Ocean before him, an end of the line of sorts for a mammalian lacking a waterspout. Well, not exactly, there was the ice-sheet covering black water below, turning it that colorless of all colors, the lack of color to be technically correct. Empty, and full of secrets. He partly wanted to walk out onto the thin white crust, and then reach his hand through any number of holes in it, until he came up with a remotely satisfying answer, or got frostbite, or fell through this precarious ledge. The thought made him shiver as much as the cold. Instead, he picked up an abalone shell, reared back and skimmed it on the ice. There were thousands of them scattered across the beach. Setting his eyes on Mattie and Doug, who were holding hands, his in a blue glove, hers in a red mitten, Frazier reached up and snugged his parka's hood around his face as winter rushed back in. The kids had skimmed some shells too, giggling like birds chirping, but now they stood there with cheeks as flushed as the pigment in Mattie's gloves. Teeth chattering, they both stared holes through him. If this seaside adventure even for a moment had been fun, it wasn't any longer. He was going all *Sunshine of the Spotless Mind* on them.

"I'm sorry, guys, for keeping you out here this long, sort of got carried away."

"So, can we head back to Gramps' and Grams' house now, where Mom is?" Doug said.

"Let's get inside the car and let the heater run. I'll check my cell phone and see whether Margaret has called to let me know she's had enough time to enjoy her mom and dad without us around to bug them." He smiled and it was so cold his lips hurt. "What do you say?"

Neither Mattie nor Doug nodded or said another word; hand in hand they simply made their way for the rental car, another Volvo, this one silver.

As Frazier followed them over to the car, in his mind he couldn't let go of the kids' stares. Somehow in both of them, he was looking at himself at that age.

Margaret had not called or texted. They always say the longer juries deliberate, the better chances are for acquittal, whoever "they" were. He kind of dared himself to be hopeful for Margaret, for their marriage, and surprisingly for something he needed out of her family's story, whatever it was behind their tight-knit togetherness, the likeable imperfections if, for no other reason, because, once exposed, they could all just be poor slobs together, but there was something else, the symbiosis, whatever it was that couldn't in a hundred blue moons be called love, that brought him and Margaret together, kept them bound. The instability flowing from their equally intense eyes that made him slumber, her a perfectionist and—an unwanted intrusion he wasn't ready to give up, may never be—which also made Anastasie his muse. How would this manifest in Mattie's and Doug's lives, for it is what haunted him from their stares? Yes, the looks out of all their eyes were the same, and out of the Comrade's as well as Frazier's father's, of course, that's right, his dad's was also identical, and there was another…

He looked over his shoulder at Mattie and Doug in the backseat. "Buckle up your seat belts."

As the kids did so, he went on.

"I haven't heard from your mom. We're so close to your great-grandpa Mandt, it would hurt his feelings if he ever is told through the family grapevine that we didn't stop by."

Doug shrugged.

"Do you think he'll play the bongos for us, Dad?" Mattie said.

"Let's find out."

In less than a minute Frazier stopped the Volvo on the uncurbed street's shoulder in front of the old unvarnished, gray-wood bungalow, which seemed as if some nimbus cloud full of secrets had fallen onto the ground. The three of them got out, tottered on their feet a moment or two, and then leaned forward, sort of pushing their way through the howling wind toward the little house. To Frazier the veranda seemed barren, lonely, the two chairs seats pillowed with snow, an undeniably pretty, though all but sinister warning: It was no time for bongo playing out here. Wouldn't be for a long while. With a nearly sideways gust, off the seats tiny white tufts swirled—just as quickly disappearing. Frazier held Mattie and Doug by the hands, one child on each side of him, and being careful with every footfall, they took the four creaky, iced-over steps up onto the deck. He gave the kids' hands a squeeze, then let go. Using a knuckle, Frazier rapped on the door.

It opened a couple of inches along with this slip of darkness, as provocative as any leggy, bowery hooker's dress slit, an invitation that costs. Frazier had never before paid the price. "Grandpa Mandt," he called out, using a singsong tone.

Nothing came through the crack except more blackness.

"Maybe he's not home," Doug said.

"Or maybe he's in there dead." Mattie's voice shook.

"Grandpa Mandt," Frazier called out again, this time a bit more forcefully. Nothing.

Frazier pressed a hand against the door and it swung open. No lights seemed to be on anywhere in the bungalow. As he walked inside Frazier flicked a wall switch next to the door and the overhead domed-glass fixture in the middle of the room remained dark. It was downright cold in here. The fireplace across the room held a sad heap of gray ashes. Frazier went over to a window, then, with his hands, opened drapes yellowed from tobacco smoke that had once been cream-colored or white. Dull winter light poured in. He looked back across the room at the kids, who now stood in the doorway almost like ice statues, frozen in trepidation. "Come in and take a seat on the sofa or something," he said. "It's going to be okay."

He immediately wanted to take back this inane attempt at comforting them. Patronizing his kids only made them more afraid. They were small; they weren't stupid. Frazier walked over in front of Mattie and Doug and then lowered himself until his eyes evenly met theirs. "I'm sorry you're having to go through this, but I've got to see what's going on with Grandpa Mandt," he said.

Mattie nodded her understanding, but still with a troubled expression.

Doug's brow knitted intensely. "I don't want to go inside."

Frazier looked him directly in the eyes. "Pal, I would like for you to be with your sister while I take a look around. Will you do that for me?"

"I'm not afraid," Mattie said.

"That's great," Frazier said, suddenly thinking on his feet like a boxer. "But it's always nice to have another in your corner."

She gave Frazier a quizzical look.

Her confusion was better than some other alternatives, he supposed, setting his eyes once again on Doug. "What's it going to be, pal?"

"I'll do it," Doug muttered.

With the kids sitting side by side on the sofa in the main room, Frazier walked along the hallway toward Grandpa Mandt's bedroom. On passing by the small bathroom with its door open, he looked in, and then on his right he scanned the kitchen; both rooms were still and lifeless. When he arrived outside the shut bedroom door, he paused and steadied himself. Frazier tapped on the door with a knuckle, then louder. Getting no response again, he entered the room.

On the bed the pillows and sheet were mottled from the impression of a head and body, the spread thrown back. The pall light came through a window. Quickly, Frazier walked over, then folded back the louver doors and looked inside the little closet. Nothing inhabited it but a few well-worn, dusty plaid shirts and dungarees, a pair of boots and some moccasins.

Just next to a corner of the room beside the bed, another door seemed to open to the outside. *God forbid*, Frazier thought as he went over to it. He turned, then pulled the handle inward, and immediately, a blast of cold hit him. Squinting his eyes behind his fake reading glasses, the slumbering man watched Grandpa Mandt in astonished horror. The old guy was out there on a little screened porch in nothing but a bathrobe, his thinning white hair blowing this way and that. He tipped the long spout of a blue plastic pitcher into the base of a potted plant, maybe a eucalyptus, then another, probably a small lemon tree, Frazier couldn't be sure. Of course, the plants were skeletal in winter, as well as were the three or four other potted fauna on the porch. What is more, the pitcher didn't have any water in it. Grandpa Mandt was irrigating them with nothing at all.

"Grandpa Mandt," Frazier said once again, almost sternly through the wind's whine.

The old man faced him with the exact bewildered look out of his eyes Mattie had given him earlier.

"What are you doing out here like this, Grandpa Mandt?" Frazier went on.

The old man lifted the pitcher a little, then said, "And how about you, did you bring my granddaughter back for another visit?"

"No, it's me and the kids this time."

"My great-grandchildren are here." A smile trembled across Grandpa Mandt's lips.

"Mattie and Doug are in the den." Frazier walked beside him, then grasped his elbow and placed his other hand on his back. "Now let's get you inside before you catch your death of cold." *If you haven't already.*

The old man nodded, and then his eyes slowly lowered as if he was checking himself over, for the first time in a long while realizing what kind of shape he was in. "They can't see me like this," Grandpa Mandt finally murmured.

"We'll go into the bedroom, let you get yourself together some first."

As though returning fully to reality or the present or something, Grandpa Mandt began shivering as furiously as the little windblown potted trees.

Once inside, Frazier guided Grandpa Mandt over to the bed, where the old man sat down and Frazier lowered himself beside him. Now Grandpa Mandt looked at him almost childlike. "For the life of me…"

"It's going to be okay," Frazier said for the second time in twenty minutes, but this time he had no misgivings whatsoever. And he'd never been more unsure of anything.

Sitting there with Grandpa Mandt lost in something that felt to Frazier like too much freedom, he pictured Margaret as if she had simply let go and wrote her novel, and another, and another, with heart as well as abandon, her bongo playing, if you please. Would she end up like this old man? By giving him what he wanted most? Her unbridled humanity. *This isn't right*, he told himself. He should be solely concerned for Grandpa Mandt right now, though, however hard he tried to push her out of mind, Frazier couldn't help but see Margaret in this selfsame darkness. Absently, he looked through the window into the gray light, the bruised silver sky. Maybe living your life with too many juicy adjectives leaves one like this, he thought of the old man, of Margaret and, yes, also of himself. But then, look what happened to the sparse-prose Hemingway. He shuddered inwardly, not so much from the chill in the house. *Get hold of yourself; you're losing it, and somebody has to keep it together here.* He again looked at Grandpa Mandt, who hadn't perceptibly moved. Seeing them—Margaret and Grandpa Mandt—as free as he wanted to be was just too raw and revealing, as if simultaneously standing before God and the four horses of the apocalypse or something of the sort anyway.

All of a sudden Grandpa Mandt's expression brightened, gold flecks in the old man's hazel irises sparking like fireflies. Grandpa Mandt looked penetratingly into the slumbering man, not so much as if reading his mind, more with wisdom and intuition that may only come with manic depression, Frazier felt more than reasoned.

"I'm not sorry you found me this way," the old man said. "So much of it is a choice. Margaret is making hers, you'll make yours, and I made mine long ago."

Frazier had no doubt; these were lucid words, open and vulnerable, not defensive, ones that came gently, almost like an outstretched helping hand to a fallen Samaritan. He cleared his throat. "How did you make your 'choice'?"

"So, you think you want to understand something that's hardly understandable?"

"Yes."

"I'll do this for Margaret."

"It'll be for me as well."

"I know." Grandpa Mandt smiled weakly. "I suppose then, in a way, it's for my great-grandchildren also." The old man gestured toward the closed door to the hallway. "Mattie and Doug out there in the house?" he said as if remembering it.

"They're in the den biding time, but I believe they'll be okay for a while longer."

"God bless them. I haven't had what it takes lately to get the electric bill paid, and I'm not talking about money." Using a hand, Grandpa Mandt smoothed his scant, unwieldy white locks down on his head. "There's some dry wood, kindling, and matches beside the fireplace. Why don't you stoke a fire for Mattie and Doug, and then come back for our talk, son."

Frazier hadn't wanted to leave the room and risk deflating the momentum between them, but Grandpa Mandt was present and in the moment enough now that it would probably be all right. "Only if you promise not to go back out to water your plants." Frazier winked.

"You never know with us crazies, but I promise." This time Grandpa Mandt smiled wider, showing his liver-spotted gums above two fairly nice rows of tobacco-stained teeth still in his mouth.

Most likely not dentures, Frazier figured, by way of a few of them having gone missing here and there. Who would have fake teeth with holes in them; it wasn't a question.

Less than ten minutes later, he left the kids sitting cross-legged on the floor cozying up next to a good fire, bored out of their minds, but on the whole compliant when he'd explained that Grandpa Mandt was okay and the two of them needed to have an adult talk. Now, he tapped on the bedroom door again, and Grandpa Mandt asked him in. As he entered, Frazier held an even gaze on Grandpa Mandt rather than letting out a big smile, a dignifying decision, for in one of two chairs across from the bed, Grandpa Mandt sat dressed in dungarees and a tartan shirt, his hair neatly combed.

The elder gestured at the other chair, and Frazier walked over and sat down on it.

"Rather surprising, isn't it?" Grandpa Mandt said.

"Indeed, and immensely satisfying."

Grandpa Mandt laughed out loud. "Well, that's the way this stuff works sometimes, poof it's gone, once you come out of the trance." He raised his hands, turning serious again. "At other times it's the devil to come back from. If you've got it, you don't have a choice whether to live with it, only how."

A pregnant silence filled the air between them.

Frazier leaned forward in his chair. "Please go on."

Grandpa Mandt seemed to think for a moment, and then nodded as if giving himself permission to continue. "You can take drugs and regiment yourself mercilessly, like my son, Horace, has done. Hell, you can become a pillar of the community like that." The elder looked out the window as if reliving his own son's painful choices. "But you may not have very many original thoughts. Your artistry will tend towards mimicry." Setting his eyes on

Frazier again, they were now almost steely. "But it seems those particular afflicted ones can then take on academia or business or popular, commercial art like a Trojan. There's no cultural advancement or social justice in that, believe you me."

"And you made the choice to stay free," Frazier said.

"Messily creative." The old man brought a hand to his mouth and gave a raspy cough.

Frazier wondered whether it was more from his smoking habit, or having traipsed around outside in a bathrobe and slippers. "How do you manage really?"

Grandpa Mandt went on to explain that it didn't get very bad until the war and directly afterward. Back then in Russia, they had opium, electric shock treatments, and a quick straightjacket for folks like him. Now and again the old man took long pauses before launching into more details and, understandably so to Frazier, as Grandpa Mandt confessed extramarital affairs he'd had when in manic phases. And there was his music and his art Grandpa Mandt lit up over, along with his wife's writing, without living fully and unencumbered by "apothecary, no more than the least possible daily structure, and going underground as much as possible to avoid the soliloquy of the state's apparatus, their lives would've been nothing more than status quo mortar for making bricks of calcified shit." That's how Grandpa Mandt in a flourish had put it.

And to Frazier it sounded like great jazz at the Village Vanguard or what? yes, something Anastasie would say, or communicate through her art, and like Margaret was trying to find the chops for. He couldn't deny her that, didn't want to. He was beginning to understand that making peace with your family of origin wouldn't heal you, though it might set you to flying despite the odds against it, that you may have aerodynamically anemic bees' wings, which weren't supposed to have lift for your body's weight, but did anyway, inexplicably, and only for the diehard contrarian, the rebel, the improviser at all times, the bongo player, the unrelenting flappers; anything else underestimated what wings you had, ensured you'd sentence yourself to being subhuman, automaton even, if you didn't get your meds just right. He thought of Margaret right now across the bay attempting to make peace with her parents, or at least their story. He was so proud of her but there was more. For a glorious wave washed over him that could only be called love. Honestly, at some wondrously harmonic depth he'd never before felt for her. If they kept this up, their suffocating, predictable symbiosis, his slumbering even, may just be left behind, and they would be bees, not to stop there, honeybees, the kind Emily Dickinson just had to write poetry about so often!

"When you put it that way, there doesn't seem to be much of a choice,"

Frazier said.

Grandpa Mandt chuckled. "It's desperation all the way."

Frazier nodded his understanding, and almost immediately his buzz began to dissipate.

Steadily, Grandpa Mandt kept looking at him with those kind, wizened eyes of an old man and a mischievous youth all in one. "What'd you come here for, really?" the elder finally said.

"To be honest, I'm trying to save my marriage before it disintegrates into me having an affair," Frazier said, surprising himself. Somehow falling closer to Margaret also made him feel further away. What's more, Grandpa Mandt's extramarital dalliances didn't seem like freedom, or maybe so, albeit, a kind without good love, lacking integrity the old man espoused to so preciously hold dear, that Frazier desperately wanted for himself. And then there was all that talk about opium and electroshock and straightjackets; let's get real, psychiatry had come a long way since then. These modern, heavily degreed drug dealers had to have gotten better at the mix. Who said you couldn't be properly medicated and freer for it today? Certainly not this old guy; he wouldn't know. But still…there was something about Grandpa Mandt's fragile clarity that would be better off without outside tampering influences if at all possible. Something about Frazier's as well, and he knew it down to his marrow. "How did your marriage survive them, Grandpa Mandt?"

"My dear Alice was unfaithful without really being unfaithful because she'd been made a straw widow, but as a young man I couldn't accept it. You put that together with the stress of the war and my mania, and, well, it took some years for me to come to my senses." He looked out the window again before going on. "In short, she understood."

Not having the slightest idea what a straw widow was or how one could philander without doing so at the same time, Frazier, nonetheless, had heard enough about this. Nothing Grandpa Mandt had said would change the fact that Margaret would not understand, and he couldn't blame her for it, not one bit.

"I can see by the blood draining from your face you really do want to stop short of having your affair," Grandpa Mandt went on. "And seeing you're here having this chat with me, I can also tell you want to do more than save your marriage; you want it to inspire you. Am I correct?"

Frazier nodded almost mechanically.

"Okay, good." Another long pause as if the old man was trying to work something out with himself. "There's something I've been meaning to give Margaret once she finishes reading her Nana's letters, but I'm going to give it to you to read first under the condition that you'll also wait to hand it over to her until then."

"Fine, I think, but why are you doing this?" Frazier said.

"Because the both of you need to understand why my Alice understood me. Then maybe you can do the same for yourselves. Besides, our art is our best part and, don't get me wrong, that includes our children. They're God's art through us, just like everything else we produce if we're improvising like human beings. I want you to know that too. See some of it firsthand."

The elder pushed himself out of the chair and stood up on spindly legs before Frazier. "Come on, follow me." With that the old man shuffled out of the bedroom and partway down the shadowy hallway, with Frazier in tow. Grandpa Mandt gestured overhead. "Now go up in the attic and bring down two or three of the canvases leaned against the wall." He reached in his pocket, then came out with a Zippo lighter. "You can use this to see up there." He handed it to Frazier.

"But I thought you wanted me to read something of your wife's," Frazier said.

"You need to see some of my art too. How else are you going to judge whether I was right to stay off the opium?"

"Good point," Frazier said, with his tone turning tentative.

On Grandpa Mandt's direction, Frazier got a stepladder from the kitchen closet and then placed it underneath the attic's slat door. With the faint light of the Zippo's flame, he climbed up and slid the door aside. Once hunched over standing on beams in the attic, he looked around, but everything turned to darkness within two or three feet.

"They're over against the wall on your right," the old man called up to him.

He felt his way over until the flame illuminated a fraction of one canvas, a dove flying with what looked to be Russian peasants riding its wings. Passing the light slowly across the painting, he made out the scythe and hammer underneath the dove, and then the caption: Russia Is the Dove, Not the Flag Under Stalin. His eyes widened with wonderment. He'd seen this print before when studying Russian dissident art at NYU. It was one of the iconic pieces of the underground movement at the time. And it had been signed Anonymous, as this one was. The next painting had been similarly popular, a fist in Stalin's face with the caption: How long will it take you to purge all good Russians? Carefully, he wedged the canvases under an arm and then made his way back over to the portal. On handing them down to Grandpa Mandt, Frazier said, "So you're the famous 'Anonymous.'"

"Afraid so."

"Kids, Mattie and Doug, come here please," Frazier called out while descending the stepladder. "I want to show you something that made your grandpa famous and helped people through some very hard times."

In the shadows of the hallway brightened only by the Zippo's tiny flame, Frazier gave Mattie and Doug a proud rundown of the artwork and what made it so important. They both giggled at the story, and looked on the paintings with ambivalence. Even so, they weren't too young to start becoming little bees, Frazier felt sure of this.

Once he leaned the canvases against a wall and Mattie and Doug returned to the fire's warmth, Grandpa Mandt stood there in the hallway holding a stack of papers, a manuscript? The elder must've gone and gotten it while Frazier was enthralled celebrating Grandpa Mandt's art with the kids. "This is what you want me to read and then pass on to Margaret?"

The old guy nodded as he handed over the papers to Frazier.

On passing the Zippo flame above the top page, Frazier saw that the author's name underneath the title of this story, called simply "My Long Journey Home," was Alice Mandelstam. Not Mandt. With wide, almost pleading eyes, he looked again at Grandpa Mandt.

"We changed our name on escaping the Russian purges to come to America," the elder volunteered.

Mandelstam...Mandelstam... Frazier reached into the recesses of his memory. "By any chance are you relation to the great Russian poet Osip Mandelstam?"

Grandpa Mandt nodded again. "He was my father."

"And you never told your children or your family."

"There was no reason that wouldn't endanger them." Grandpa Mandt's eyes had fireflies once more. "Until now."

"Was this ever published?"

"It was too hot to publish at the time it was written. Once Alice learned English, she translated it into her new language, but still no one would touch it in the West. She had eight other unpublished manuscripts." He smiled. "My Alice was a warrior for truth and peace."

"That's a shame none of her work got into print," Frazier said, feeling the stunted career of another worthy author turn his face red with indignation.

"In some ways yes, in others no. She wrote for the love of writing, and left the outcome to God." Now, Grandpa Mandt put a hand on Frazier's back. "Alice tried to change the world, but instead she changed me and a few others who knew her well that read her work."

The redness seeped out of Frazier, replaced almost instantly by gooseflesh, as he set with the tenacity of Alice. Whatever quality her writing held would have to wait to come through in the reading. But there was one thing for certain; Alice Mandelstam had already become another of Frazier's muses.

CHAPTER TWENTY-EIGHT

Autumn always passed like a fast train between the summers and long winters in Peredelkino, though it seemed as if God had decided for such a short stay, this little season would be a joyride for those desperate enough or courageous enough, take your choice, to open their eyes and actually see it—which for most of the people who lived around here was next to impossible, as their own all too fleeting opportunities with poetry (and I don't mean only words written down on paper) along with the ever present dark gravity of Stalinist Russia kept their heads down, eyes inches in front of their feet, and, yet, for me the gold and orange and red and purple leaves, the crisp air that with gusts sent them wafting to the ground as if by way of providence and chance mixed together, yes, also a sun day by day softly lowering its angle on all of us, had more and more become necessary to gift my soul, oftener than I would've cared to. I took no small amount of solace in the branches that were being stripped, for their skeletal spindles would gain foliage again in spring, yes, most trees' roots went sufficiently down into soil, spiderwebbed underground to make it through the coming freeze. Whatever it was that grounded my feet on the path I trod seemed to be loosening far beneath me while, at the same time, clinging on harder.

Every time Pasternak came for a visit with Olga and myself, we would share a meal together and then they'd go into her bedroom; it didn't matter if it were breakfast, dinner, or suppertime, this routine took place. I supposed he could only steal away from Miss Zinaida when circumstances allowed, if you catch the meaning. After our mealtimes together, I had to get out of that apartment. The squeaking bed and cooing that came through the wall was simply too much to stomach. I hadn't had sex in so long, and how could I ever entertain it again really? Oleg had taught me how to make love. My nipples and his member being up, which happened delightfully often, also had to be accompanied by our spirits being unfettered, even in the slightest diminution, toward each other; otherwise, we'd almost always pass on doing the deed. On those rare times when we ignored the importance of this, there were regrets. This made any other way to sup the nectar of sensuality seem quite pedestrian, if you please. Not that Pasternak and Olga weren't making love as opposed to simply having sex. From the looks of things between them, they were bound in some sort of tortured bliss. What more could two Russians hope for these days? Ugh. Besides, my old puppy love for Pasternak just would not give up and die a natural death. A considerable amount of unfounded jealousy spiked. So, I'd take these walks, down the road toward Pasternak's dacha, but never getting in sight of it, rather heading into the rolling terrain and forest off to the east, just before the road curved. As it were this nice afternoon, I headed out of the forest and back up the road. Pasternak and Olga had had enough time to do what needed doing and collect themselves by now. Something that felt overly ripe drove me to return to the apartment before Pasternak left. No slinking away allowed. My God, I was unhappy with this matchbox-size life of mine.

On entering the apartment I heard water running from the faucet in the kitchen and headed toward the sound. As I stopped just inside the doorway, they asked how my walk had gone and would I like some water, to which I replied "okay" and "okay." Pasternak handed a full glass to Olga, who still had the telltale rosiness in her cheeks, though other than that they both seemed unscathed, casually dressed artists, him in dungarees, walking boots, and a pullover brown herringbone sweater, her wearing a long-sleeve gray peasant dress that dipped at the neckline to proudly present just the right view of her ample buxomness. I always felt like such a waif around Olga.

When Pasternak held out a glass of water toward me, he said, "I keep looking in on the writing materials I gave you, and it seems they're not being used."

"Well, you're right about that," I said. What was there to write about other than their love affair? I simply couldn't bring myself to fictionalize the loss of Oleg, and Pasternak and Olga's sordid goings-on, which hardly seemed off-color the more I thought about it, well, I needed more convincing or something to interest me in a story about clinging Russian souls in all probability going down with the ship. Sometimes there existed a fine line between poetic prose that drew one in, gripped the reader, and melodrama that fell apart at the seams. What is more, the alternative, penning nonfiction, held little sway with me. The deeper truths, that's what I wanted to mine, or it would be better to stay away from caves altogether.

"Katya, you've been here nearly four months," he said. "I believe it would do you good to write again."

In the broadest sense, of course, he was right and, maybe, in the narrowest too. I took a long drink of water, stalling.

"If you're not yet ready to do that, I could give you some of the translation work Boris brings me to check over and edit my drafts," Olga said.

No, I was a writer, if a dormant one, and a reader, having gone through much of the fine literature on Olga's bookshelves—at least I hadn't stopped with books—but I wasn't some copyeditor, especially not for her work, this luscious and admirable woman who happened to be better for Pasternak than me for one reason and one reason alone, our age difference. Which also meant for most every other reason imaginable: cultural changes they'd experienced I could only read about, bucketfuls of wisdom and poetic living born of those particular pieces from Russia's past, oh, and not to forget the reality of our different lives today, right now, which already shaped our futures like iron rebar, something hard and unbendable, yet equally unknown! Let's face it, I knew nothing of going from Czarist balls to communal living; I just knew the dismal aftermath of revolution, which, come to think of it, gave me no small amount of godforsaken, wonderful humanity to bring into this room with them. "Thank you for the offer, Olga; I'll keep it in mind if that's all right," I said at last. "But maybe I will get back into my writing sooner rather than later."

"Sure, the offer will remain open." She smiled warmly, her always-sad smile.

Her relaxed graciousness made me feel defeated, ashamed for having my persnickety self to carry around.

"I've got something for you that might just make it 'sooner,'" Pasternak said. "Please, let's go take a look at your writing space, Katya."

What can he show or tell me in there that can't be done right here? I thought. But getting away from Olga's dominating presence, only and unfairly because she glowed as naturally as her beloved candles, for now, appealed.

"Trust me," he said to Olga, while leading me toward the tiny nook of a space I stayed in underneath an enclosed stairway that went to the apartment above.

A bunk bed fit just underneath the slant of the stairway's underside, a ceiling that almost daily I bumped my head against. Barely outside the recess for the stairway, screwed to the wall were three clothes hooks, from which hung my nightgown and bath towel. I took off and put away my hooded jacket on the available hook. At my back, nothing more than a slim ledge, really, served for my writing desk, as unused as it was uninviting. When I turned halfway around, I was facing Pasternak, no more than a couple of inches away from him actually. Blackberry tobacco from the pipe he'd taken up since I'd been away was on his breath, a smell so agreeable it almost seemed edible. Inexplicably, I didn't know whether to kiss him or slap him. "What's going on, Pasternak?" I said, sort of as a means of protection for both of us.

Without a word, he stepped aside, gesturing at my writing space, which had been obscured by his frame.

Immediately, I spotted a stack of papers, a manuscript, with the words *Doctor Zhivago by Boris Pasternak* centered on the top page. My mouth went dry. "Is it finished?" I managed.

"It's still a work in progress that I'd like you to look over and give me your thoughts on," he said, now using an undertone. "Will you do it?"

"Yes, yes, of course I will," I said, as if my words were suddenly coming from the glory of the autumn fire up in the trees as well as falling onto the ground all around me in the forest.

He opened the little drawer on the underside of my writing ledge, and then brought out my pen, inkwell, along with a few sheets of paper. "For taking good notes," he said, one by one laying the materials beside his manuscript.

I nodded shyly. "When did you start writing on it again?"

"Some time after the war ended." A momentary open-mouthed pause. "Right after I met Olga actually."

"I'm so happy for you." I meant this in every aspect, including the literary and the amorous ones.

"Let's keep this our little secret, shall we? Olga would get jealous from a literary standpoint."

I nodded again, this time more confidently. With that I threw my arms around him, hugging him like the blessed godfather Pasternak was to me, had been ever since I once, in a moment of horror, became a very needy thirteen-year-old girl.

🍂

Snow covering the landscape everywhere indiscriminately displayed itself a foot high or more along the maples' and oaks' bare branches as well as the feathery green limbs of alpine spruces, weighing them down until some of the weaker appendages had broken off and fallen to the ground, while, undeniably, also turning all this outside my nook's little window into a kind of white magic that, as I lay on my side atop the bed peering through icy glass, carried me not away in my mind to better times of winters past, as I had spent far too many hours inwardly reconfiguring to no avail other than endless grief, but rather, for a welcome change, my thoughts were transported to reminiscent scenes in Pasternak's imaginary Varykino and Yuriatin, starkly magnificent places in the Urals during awful times, these two north poles of love pulling at his protagonist, Yuri. All of this and so much more Russian alchemy Pasternak had created in his manuscript. It was not finished by any means. When last reading this story, years ago before the war, it, of course, had been significantly less developed, just as I, for then it was mostly my teacher in writing, another arrow in the muse's quiver and now it had become some sort of highly credentialed instructor in real, honest-to-God living, also more, a mirror of my course, truth that ran as hot and pervasively as blood throughout my body yet, still, beyond my wherewithal. You could know what blood is, but you would never become intimate enough with its elements and construction to create blood, poetically or otherwise—unless you had been there from the beginning. With this latest draft I had written and then rewritten the closing chapters in the privacy of my head several times. Who would Pasternak have the beloved, sensitive, and brave Yuri end up with, his wife, Tonya, and their children, or his mistress, Lara? What would ultimately happen to Yuri, caught in the crossfire of revolution, him believing the best in both the reds' and the whites' ideologies, renouncing the worst? This character probably had what it took to become a giant figure. I mean Yuri seemed the soul of Russia herself and, therefore, how much of our future could this one literary human reveal? Regardless of the outcome for this book and whether Russia, together with the rest of the world for that matter, may or may not do the math on it, blasphemy would be the only appropriate calculation, should Pasternak's *Doctor Zhivago* ever find itself trivialized as some mere fabulist's prediction, as is so often the case with verbose fiction writers' flights of fancy. No, while reading and rereading the manuscript over and over these past three months, I had come to believe it rose from the voice of a sage, a prophet.

The familiar sound of Pasternak's key turning in the front door's lock brought me back to the present. I had come to enjoy these visits, even though the severe cold kept me inside through our meals together as well as his and Olga's lovemaking. The two of them seemed right for each other; it was a shame all this sneaking around, timing being such a cruel master, or was there something as good, albeit different, between him and Zinaida that I simply did not understand?

As I got down off the bed and smoothed my sweater, then the pleats in my brown corduroy pants, I listened to footsteps that told me Olga was coming to greet Pasternak from her study, where she'd been working on a translation. They called this apartment The Shop, as Pasternak kept Olga busy translating foreign authors into Russian, and, I suppose, it also provided a flimsy though plausible cover for their affair to anyone who considered it for the better to ignore, namely Miss Zinaida. So far she'd not stormed in here calling their hand. On the times Olga was caught up finishing a section of her work, I would get to Pasternak first and then we'd banter in undertones about things such as how he was chomping at the bit to get my editing notes on *Zhivago*, and then I'd tease that I was literarily playing hard to get, but this encounter would not occur today. Too bad. I felt myself getting closer to articulating to him something of substance on his manuscript.

I stopped on entering the sitting room because Pasternak and Olga were in a spirited discussion about her translation of a Bengali poet by the name of Rabindranath Tagore, whom I didn't know much about; however, I'd read some of Olga's other translations, which were admittedly lyrical and nuanced. When we had talked about them, she shared that this work was more like an actor putting her interpretation into a script on stage or screen, than similar to writing something of your own. I liked that way of looking at it, which gave me one more reason to feel Olga Invinskaya and Boris Pasternak were a great pair. And right now, they were in no way disappointing. They took this conversation into the kitchen and all the way to the dinner table. It finally wound down in a decision they would collaborate on Tagore.

Mutual muses, I thought.

Pasternak reached in the inside pocket of his jacket and came out with a card, then laid it on the table in front of me.

A work permit with my name on it for a position in the little Peredelkino library.

"I finally finagled it," he said.

My stomach churned, though it wasn't that I didn't appreciate what Pasternak had done, or want the work. God knows I'd been after him to arrange this without me having to go into the bowels of Russia's bureaucracy. A dissident who had been across the Urals and back looking for her "deserter" husband could well not make it out of government offices in anything other than shackles. I felt rising in me like a geyser the betrayal of Oleg working with his hands in the fields, and me wielding the short-handle hoe alongside peasants in Mashinska. "Thanks for doing this, really, Pasternak, but I've told you I want an agricultural work permit."

"But do you insist on it?"

"No, but after a while, I'll suffocate in a library."

"What better place for a writer?" He gave me a quizzical expression. "Besides, you love books."

I wanted to dive into the fact his *Zhivago* was written from the full mosaic of life he'd lived, not from books, but that would come too close to betraying our agreement to keep my involvement with it secret from Olga. And this, too, added pressure to the spewing geyser; after all, Olga and I had come to treat each other as equals; why couldn't Pasternak allow that? Things change, yes, they do! When I opened my mouth, I had little idea what would come out. "Creativity doesn't have to come as literary masterpieces to be just as impactful as something that at first glance seems small. Take placing an alfalfa seed in a neatly troughed row of earth, covering it with dirt, and patting it down, and then seeing its green stalk in spring."

"I must say, as usual, you make a damn good argument." Using a hand, he cupped his chin, sort of like Rodin's *The Thinker.*

I fought against chuckling at the sight of him.

"It truly is better for one's writing than being in a laboratory," he added.

Inwardly I beamed and probably outwardly too. "Yes, well, I'm glad that's settled then."

"Before I leave, I want to talk to you about another story." He smiled knowingly. "The one you've been working on all by yourself in your room."

Zhivago, I knew it! How could I deny him now? "I think I'll have something for you to look at this time."

"Wonderful," he said.

"I'm glad you're getting back into your writing," Olga said.

I couldn't bring myself to look her in the eyes. "Oh, it's nothing much so far, actually."

"It's enough for you to show Boris. I'd love to see it if you're okay with that?"

I locked eyes with Pasternak. Maybe he nodded almost imperceptibly, but it looked more like a hard blink of the eyes, the guilty kind that jostles your entire head.

"He's been my writing coach for so long; these early drafts I can only share with him." At last, I met her eyes. "I'm hope you understand."

Placing her hand over mine, she said, "I do indeed. Boris is my first reader too."

You couldn't find a hint of jealousy in her tone or manner.

And neither was there in mine as I thanked her and then lifted my permit from the table, also thanking Pasternak, who promised he'd try to get me into working the crops.

They left for her bedroom.

I went to my nook.

Sitting at my writing ledge with pen, ink, and paper in front of me, there was nothing I could tell Pasternak about his novel. I strained for words, anything, but whatever came seemed forced, contrived, trite. Finally, I gave up.

Then I wrote: *You're in the next room over, making love to at least one of your true loves, and I'm in love with a dead man.*

It was the first time in my heart I left out the possibility of Oleg being okay, missing, trapped, surrounded by the Red Army, holed up somewhere. And then, was there any chance he could return to me but hadn't because of the unspeakable? No, not even a speck.

I balled up the sheet of paper with those words on it, and tossed it onto the floor.

✄

Hearing a knock on the front door, I suddenly gripped the spatula like a sword at the ready. My omelet sputtered in the skillet on the stove, as if sniggering at my weaponry, its impotence, and mine, if even thinking about going up against any red legionnaires who may be outside the door. Pasternak and Olga were in Moscow presenting their translation of Rabindranath Tagore's book of poetry; they had decided on staying through the week, and today was only Wednesday. Besides, if returning early for some reason, they'd just use a key. No one else ever came to this door, absolutely no one. Was it Miss Zinaida finally here to clean house on Pasternak and Olga's love nest, unbelieving of whatever story he'd presented about heading to Moscow? Pasternak covered his tracks as deftly as a minx; the collaborative translation of Tagore would be published only with Olga's name on the byline. He would most assuredly avoid newspaper and TV interviews, as he'd successfully done before when with Olga in public. No one outside the Moscow literary community who didn't do a considerable amount of digging would ever know the two of them were together there. But then, if nothing else in my memory of Miss Zinaida before the war remained insightful, she had seemed to hold some inner spade in a way that it would only be put down with her corpse in the grave. I was flummoxed she hadn't yet made her way to the Potapov Street apartment, actually. Maybe she wanted to have the initial groundbreaking while Pasternak and Olga were away, unearth some of what they would otherwise bury too far down to ever reach, no matter how hard Zinaida dug in the soil of them. Something I very well would do if in her place.

Another knock.

I turned away from the stove, almost comically not setting down the spatula. My feet wouldn't take me any nearer the front door. A key rattled in the lock; then the door opened. *Pasternak and Olga?*

"I will be a tree, if..."

It was Solomon Mikhoels speaking Pasternak's secret signal for Olga. Pasternak or Olga must've told it to him. They wanted him here. No Red Army goons could force him to say that. What is more, Solomon would give his own life away before he'd bring them to my doorstep. Yes, he loved me that much and, as for myself... I shoved aside the rest of this thought. Time had not diluted my penetrating connection to him, in a certain sense, unfortunately, and, well, I didn't know whether it was from the rush persistently hanging on around the imminent threat of outsiders, or these feelings over Solomon bubbling up, probably some swill of the two currents, but, in some primal way, I was more alive than at any point after my return to Peredelkino.

Lowering the spatula at my side, I began walking toward the sitting room. When I got there Solomon stood just inside the doorway with a leather sheaf held by one hand and, by the other, what looked to be a framed painting, impossible to miss the wide smile spreading across his lips. Yes, this dear man was here in all his rangy, sharp-featured handsomeness, together with those intensely dark artist's eyes, as if on a constant search for the marrow of life, not to forget, their kindness.

"I come bringing gifts of sorts," he said spritely.

"Whatever they are, you're the best present of the bunch!"

"You may've spoken hastily once you see what I have here." He placed the sheaf on the coffee table and leaned the artwork against a wall. "There's more."

"More?"

"The best is yet to come. I've got it in my car—don't go anywhere." He turned and hustled outside, in seconds returning with his arms full.

"Is that what I think it is?"

"Uh, huh, I believe so."

I don't remember whether I ran or floated over beside him to look over this Moskva typewriter held so it faced me, the same model Pasternak had given me long ago, the kind I wrote my early stories on as well as my one completed novel. I punched the Γ key and it stuck, then the Φ with the same result. With that I tried several other keys, which worked perfectly well. Without a doubt this was my typewriter.

The smell of char and a thin stream of smoke came into the room from the kitchen. "I must turn the oven off, but I'm bursting with questions and can hardly wait to see what my other gifts are. So you don't go anywhere."

By the time I returned, he had sat down on the divan, having placed the Moskva atop the coffee table between his sheaf and the book of Petofi's poetry, which always could be found there. As I joined him on the divan, our thighs touched, sending a tingle through my body; as nonchalantly as possible under the circumstance, I adjusted my leg a couple of inches away from his. Solomon's eyes glimmered as if with new snow in sunshine. I was glad over this chemistry, also scared of something more happening while I still wore my wedding band. I didn't want to take it off, wouldn't regardless of whatever amounts of body heat fired between Solomon and me. I felt sure at least of this much. "Before we get into your other tidings for me, please explain how you came by my typewriter." I gently placed a hand over my heart. "I never thought I would see it again after leaving it behind at our apartment to go in search of Oleg."

"I'm sorry you've been separated from it for so long. I would've liked to have gotten it to you sooner." He passed a hand through his salt-and-pepper, wavy hair.

"Years ago, before your and Oleg's apartment had been turned over to other occupants, some local members of the underground managed to get it for safekeeping. A little while after I returned from Mashinska and it became no secret in underground circles I'd been all that time with you there, your typewriter was brought to me."

"And you've had it all this time."

He nodded. "I've been waiting for you to be ready for it and, what's more, for me."

"I haven't been writing anything. Why do you think I'm ready for a typewriter?"

He chuckled warmly. "Because Pasternak looked me up in Moscow and insisted I come. He said you could use some encouragement; that was how he put it anyway. I hope you understand, I simply couldn't turn him down. If I should go—"

Interrupting, I placed a hand on his knee. "No, stay...for a while longer." I removed my hand. "In the interest of full disclosure, I spent a few days in Moscow on returning from the Urals; Solomon, I just couldn't bring myself to see you then."

"When I was told you'd been at the Writers Building, I surmised as much."

"You are a dear for not rushing in on me here back then."

He shrugged. "See what I mean. I needed Pasternak's nudge to come."

"Yes, I need his 'nudges' too." My eyes went to the leather sheaf. "Does that contain what I think it may?"

"Well, the boys surely wouldn't just abscond with an old typewriter from your place and that's that, now would they?" He reached over and picked up the sheaf.

It was all I could do to contain myself while he undid its tied-off straps. In one motion he slipped a stack of papers out of it and handed them to me. Using my thumb, I quickly shuffled through the pages. Yes, here it was in its entirety, my unnamed novel. The story of my family and its demise to the purges, of losing everything and pushing on anyway, someway. Hopefully convincingly laying out this was no way to run a world revolution. A treasure if to no one else but me.

"Oh, my great and good God's mercy" was all I could think of saying. I laid the manuscript on the table, and then hugged Solomon, at first like an appreciative friend, but after a few seconds more as you would a lover. I kissed him all along both cheeks, around his eyes, on his mouth, his full-lipped mouth. The slats over the chutes that held back my dammed-up waters lifted, setting my river free. Needless to say, the painting or whatever my other gift was would have to wait. I stood up and then held both my arms out toward him. He took my hands while rising onto his feet, and in seconds we were in my little nook. Thoughtfully, he didn't mention our cramped quarters; in fact, from the sad and sanguine look in his eyes, which seemed to carry all of our past together with a future that didn't exist beyond right now, I realized something: He must feel the same way about my narrow bed—in it our bodies would be closer together, even after making love.

⸕

This must've been a dream, me lying on the bed in my little nook with Oleg to one side and Solomon to the other, if for no more reason than the space in actuality wasn't wide enough for three. Even in this subconscious haze, I felt other demons visiting, like Oleg being here yet not truly here. But everything seemed very real: the funky smell of our sex and sweat, those cold, wet spots on the sheet beneath me, their bodies pressed against mine. Oleg and Solomon slept in nakedness above the covers, as if spent beyond orgasms and afterglow, their chests rising, then falling rhythmically to some metronome, inward and universal, maybe because unlike Orpheus with Eurydice, who hadn't made it out of the underworld with his lover intact or himself, we lucky ones got to become distinct beings again, no longer lost, eternally diving back into the womb, or onto the phallus; yes, this Greek tragic myth and my own, I was aware of too. Don't get me wrong, we hadn't had some sordid, orgiastic ménage a trois, at least it didn't seem so, for no guilt, poetic or otherwise, and no tares over splitting myself between two men, set heavy in my heart or between my legs. Somehow it was as though I'd made love with them at the same time, not as two men, but one. We had done something right with God and with our souls. I simply had to find out whether this inner knowing would carry over into my waking up.

My eyes opened to flickering candles I'd lit and placed on my writing ledge for us. Of course, only Solomon lay next to me. We were snuggled close together under bedcovers that at the same time felt like a safe, warm cocoon and a partly empty place. Half of my masculine wholeness, or the likeness of a sort, had suddenly gone missing; call it the essence of Oleg. I turned my head sideways, and Solomon's beautiful face was right there, so I kissed his cheek softly. His lips puckered a little, then relaxed. Plenty of the rightness from my dream remained here in bed with us: I was in love with Solomon. Recalling how tender and strong he'd been, with just the most wonderful touches, together with our joint orgasm during our actual lovemaking, unquestionably, I trusted Solomon's feelings for me had blossomed even more. Besides, he slept so serenely now. Somehow, though, we still weren't alone. I looked the other way at the candles, and in hardly any time at all, their flames took me to Oleg. I pictured the time when he and I knocked a candle off the table while making love on it. Tears flooded my eyes from the waters of different wells, Oleg's, and the other, Solomon's. This wetness was salty and pure, and it stung. Using a corner of the sheet, I wiped my eyes, and they filled right back up. How could I go on like this with Solomon and a ghost? I needed time to think or pace or just get away from the both of them for a while. Careful not to disturb Solomon, I folded back the comforter and sheet and slipped out of bed. I took my robe off the clothes hook, then put it on. Heading out of the nook, I glanced over my shoulder to make sure Solomon remained asleep, just as well he not see me like this.

I lit candles in the sitting room, and the artwork Solomon had brought with him, my other gift, caught my eye. It was a print of a painting that had a Russian tank taking aim at peasants working the fields. Its caption read: *Comrades, we're blowing you away for your own good and the Motherland's.* The print was signed by Anonymous, in small cursive writing down around the lower left corner, almost as if the artist didn't want to be associated with this piece at all. On closer inspection, the letters seemed almost contorted, maybe because Anonymous didn't want anyone doing a match on their handwriting that would uncover their identity. Smart, if I said so myself, and what's more, it did for a few moments take my mind off the uncomplicated men complicating my life. I resumed my pacing, and my thoughts went to Pasternak and Olga together with a pang of almost envy. At least Pasternak, Olga, and Miss Zinaida were caught in the middle of a flesh-and-blood love triangle. Any one of them could change things if he or she wanted to, but then love doesn't really change, does it? Certainly Pasternak wasn't staying with Miss Zinaida out of some moralized obligation, playing the martyr, no, that could never be him. Who did he love more, Miss Zinaida or Olga? Who did I, Oleg or Solomon? Making a choice and going solely with it was necessary to avoid slighting someone you cared the world for even while with them, or not, all the time, twenty-four hours of every day! I sat down on the divan and absently churned this conundrum over: *Oleg isn't here any longer, not really, how do you know, yes, he is, he's somewhere and he loves you, no he's not, he's nowhere except in some mass grave, you're being stupid and callous, go with Solomon and stop looking over your shoulder...* But then there seemed to be eyes in the back of my head. For no particular reason at all, I picked up off the coffee table the book of poetry by Sandor Petofi and opened it. An inscription in Pasternak's handwriting was on the page across from the first poem:

> *Petofi is magnificent with his descriptive lyrics and picture of nature, but you, lovely Olga, are better still. I worked on him when I first came to know you. I was translating both of you. If you'd like, read the poem on page 38. Petofi seems to know my feelings for you all too well.*

Without hesitation I turned to that page, and immediately felt answers were somehow coming soon, a few of them anyway; words from God seemed to pour through this poet for me in this time and place. In short, time stood still. Yes, I supposed, every good and alive relationship needed the perfectly deft and apt signal. Before this moment I had thought it nonsensical and silly. I reread this wonderful little poem, which just may also be the biggest I'd ever read:

> *I Will Be A Tree, If...*
>
> *I will be a tree, if you are its flowers,*
> *Or a flower, if you are the dew,*
> *I'll be the dew, if you are the sunbeam,*
> *Only to be united with you.*
>
> *My little girl, if you are the heaven*
> *I shall be a star above on high,*
> *My little girl, if you are hellfire,*
> *To unite us, damned I shall die.*

Oh, without a doubt, Olga was Pasternak's Lara in his manuscript, and Miss Zinaida the shadow holding them together, for without the hellfire of their predicament, this kind of love that would bring you to write such a poem or a novel like *Doctor Zhivago,* or anything worthy of awakening my long-hibernating pen, would have to be apothecary ground from this crucible.

At last, I had an editing note for Pasternak. I stood up, then went over and blew out the candles. Quietly, I walked into my nook, slid open the drawer, bringing out of it pen and ink along with a sheet of paper that I set on my writing ledge. Usually I sat on the edge of my bed to write, but not wanting to jostle Solomon, standing up would do just fine.

> *Finish* Doctor Zhivago *with a flourish! In your novel and in life be with the one you most love in the worst of times and at least a few of the best of times, but, should you love two just as much, with everything about you, if in different ways, then God help you. No, truthfully, there is nothing better to bring you and your readers to the divine!*

Yes, this is what needed saying. Not a word would I change.

I blew out the candles still flickering on the ledge, and then slipped back in bed beside Solomon.

                                        ✇

Two weeks later while I was packing for a trip to Moscow to be with Solomon, Pasternak once again used his key in our door and then spoke that hauntingly beautiful poetic signal. This time, to bring me the news Solomon had been run down in what was supposed to be an automobile accident. One in which the driver rolled the vehicle over his body and back, over and back, over and back, crushing him into pulp. Of course, it was Stalin's secret police who did this. They had already jailed or disappeared most of the others on the Jewish Anti-Fascist Committee, and finally, they'd assassinated its leader. For years to come, all the rest of my life actually, I would from time to time wonder whether Solomon bringing me my typewriter and especially my dissident manuscript had embarrassed the Stalinists for letting such items escape their destruction when before taking over my abandoned apartment they had had the chance. Gave them just enough additional reason to act when they did on Solomon.

What's the difference, really?

Now, my beloved red comrades had made me both a straw widow with Oleg, and the better-known kind with Solomon. That good and courageous and fiercely kind man and I had been married, all too briefly, in our hearts.

CHAPTER TWENTY-NINE

Frazier slowly, even begrudgingly, turned the final page of Alice Mandelstam's manuscript, *My Long Journey Home,* and then set it atop the four- or five-inch stack of papers he had already read. Tears welled in his eyes, as much from the story's vastly universal humanity, populated by such well-crafted individuals somehow plumbing deeper depths, as that it was beautifully sad and courageous without one indulgent thread, leaving you to ponder so much by offering no nice and tidy answers inside what had become this full-blown love affair between the slumbering man and Alice's prose. Something that, truth be told, ran counter to the art of slumber, looking over the top of his lenses at will, in control, tuned out or in, rather than sticking with the frigging plethora of gut-wrenching paradoxes until they brought a kind of joy beyond hope, not in need of it. Crazy and aware enough to allow absurdity to actually take place instead of the rationally predictable near certainty of our decline, each individual and all of us together, caught up in the necessity of the capitalist machine fighting it out with socialists or communists, take your pick among disconnected, disconnec*ting*, power-hungry systems, their grand distraction to community building, to Pete Seeger, B.W. Stevenson "Shambala" brotherhood and sisterhood, the idyll knocked off balance just enough not to pursue it, which sooner than later takes down the planet, including all that lived on it, save a few microbes eating off dead ashes, a horrible new start. Yes, in slumber you could miss the magical doors opening to walk through, the realest moments ever, all out of focus, just some fuzzy flickers of light that came and went. How many of these doorways had he not walked through so far? Alice Mandelstam's book was just that profoundly challenging and superb. The kind Frazier started out reading as a page-turner, hardly able to put down, and then, somewhere about halfway through, he changed and read at a snail's pace, taking all the time he could without losing the feel for it, because he didn't want this to ever end.

In a way he didn't think it ever would. He opened his Moleskine notebook and got a pen from his desk's drawer.

Is Alice, Katya?
Just how autobiographical is this book?

He tapped his pen on the page a few times before making more notes.

Katya has the heart of a peasant while having the
lyricism and sophistication in her writing of someone like
Tolstoy or, yes, Pasternak himself.

The pen tapping came more rapidly this time. He'd read *Doctor Zhivago*, the book so prominently on display within Alice's manuscript; the audacity she had, writing of such proximity with greatness…or the right to and, therefore, her relationship with Pasternak had been accurately represented. Alice had married Grandpa Mandt, who was actually the son of Osip Mandelstam, a close friend of Boris Pasternak's. Frazier's course in Russian literature when at NYU had touched on the friendship between Osip Mandelstam and Boris Pasternak, okay, so quite possibly Alice had been close to Pasternak too. Now, he thought through for what had to be the umpteenth time his conversation with Grandpa Mandt after the old man righted himself from watering potted plants with air, especially the part about differences in how Grandpa Mandt and his son, the Comrade, handled their manic depression, one living into the strong winds of it, the other finding shelter in the form of upper-middle-class polite society through heavy doses of prescription drugs.

Margaret was cheated of her peasantry, has to think her
way to it, doesn't know it by heart, can't possibly the way she
was raised, but her "togetherness" sure has saved my
unpublished, non-writing, non-literary agenting, anemic
social justice activist butt!

On rereading this notation, the words "can't possibly" brought him up short. Maybe there was something beyond hope for Margaret and him, the magical thinking that when she reads this manuscript, her grandmother's spirit, the glorious full scope of it, will seep down into her soul the way the book had affected him, although, sort of from the opposite direction. Without losing any of her sophistication, she wouldn't be able to keep from letting her inner peasant become a big part of her, and he would become a more fully involved sophist, a non-slumberer in the thick of things, while keeping a hold on his Texas trailer-trash soul, the closest thing being reared in the good ole U S of A probably has to a peasant's life anyway. Something he'd never been more at home with inside this household. What's more, *Doctor Zhivago* had been his mother's favorite film. He had watched it at her side growing up a couple dozen times if at all. There was another affair of sorts he had become clear on: In a way his mother was Pasternak's Lara too. Yes, wouldn't you know it, this clearly less than rational vision for his and Margaret's future held purchase with the loco transplanted Texan in Frazier. But when would he ever find out whether Margaret had finished reading all of Nana/Alice's letters? He'd promised Grandpa Mandt not to hand over the manuscript to Margaret until then. Something about all this shaman-esque thinking, or whatever to call it, told him if he got going too fast, went out of order, plenty of things could fall apart, including his marriage.

He closed his Moleskine and placed his pen across the top of it. He then opened a side drawer, where he set down Alice's manuscript on top of his three novels. It felt as if he'd forced Alice's spirit into some prison cell with his own, and then shut the door willingly on them both. What else could he have done? Margaret would be home from work soon, and the novel needed to be out of sight. She never snooped around his old manuscripts. He couldn't blame her, just the same, what a shame. Doug and Mattie were in the family room supposedly doing homework, and by the hush outside the study's door, it seemed things were going just fine in there. Besides, there was something he wanted to fiddle around with. Using his laptop, Frazier typed into the rectangle portal for accessing the Internet www.lenscrafters.com. In less than ten seconds, he clicked on a link for normal-sized eyeglass frames. Uh huh, he liked the black Frank Lloyd Wright lookalikes, and come to think of it, the John Lennon round grounds were pretty fly too.

The front door of their apartment opened and shut.

"Hello, my dearest loved ones," Margaret called out in a jolly tone.

She had gotten noticeably more comfortable in her skin since her visit with the Comrade and Lydia, and Frazier's debrief of his time with Grandpa Mandt. "Nice to have you home; I'm in here." He did everything he could to match her congenial cadence. Without any hesitation, he logged off the LensCrafters website.

"Frazier, I think I've broken the code to al-Ajami's poem, 'Tunisian Jasmine,'" she said on entering their study. "If I'm right he's in huge trouble." She sat down at her little desk right across from his.

Imperceptibly tilting his head back, he looked through his eyeglasses directly at her. "Does the mole have knowledge of this?"

"He knows I'm on to something, but so far he's drawing the wrong conclusions."

"How big is it?"

"Fat man at the dock huge."

The hairs on the back of his neck bristled. "Impactful enough to make the difference for the next phase of the Middle Eastern revolution's success or failure?"

"Al-Ajami's future, probably not the revolution's, though the mole is all over me because he thinks what I'm working on could be bigger than it is." Margaret's eyes flared fierily, her thoughts seemingly sparks hardly contained behind those gray irises.

Strikingly, her expression almost matched how Frazier had imagined Katya at critical moments in *My Long Journey Home. Could Margaret's peasantry be breaking through some?*

"But isn't the worth of this poet's life big too!" Her voice shook as if with conviction.

"Is each grain of sand spooned into the bucket of restorative social justice important?"

"I hear you, my poet."

"Clearly so." He managed a smile, which would've been easier had the next question not needed asking. "How much does the mole know of whatever you've got on this?"

"Not any more than I want him to know, which isn't much. He's all tied up with thinking I've figured out the location of the key planners for the Egyptian uprising." She raised a hand. "The guy obviously believes it's going to happen any day now. He's pretty vehement about stopping it, Frazier."

Mattie and Doug's lighthearted laughter from the family room came through the door and into the study.

Eerily for Frazier, this brought to mind two of Emily Dickinson's bees buzzing round a hive about to be torched by the apiarists themselves. He wrestled against blurting something close to, "Damn, Margaret, whoever the mole works for, rest assuredly, plays for keeps. By engaging this game of bait and switch with him, you very well may have just put yourself and our family at great risk!" Some blend, to what portions he couldn't be sure, of his barn-door-stubborn Texas peasant together with the radical soul of Alice Mandelstam's novel held too much sway over the slumbering man for that. He stood up, then walked over to the window and looked across the street. Sure enough, Mutt and Jeff inside the blue Camry were right where you could count on them to be. Late that afternoon, when Frazier had gotten home from Flying Pens, he checked and the two TMZers hadn't been over there by the curb. Probably they'd left him alone for a while to stick close to more imminent prey, Margaret, he reasoned now. Facing her, Frazier said, "If you want to tell me what's going on in more detail, that would be really cool."

"I could use your help." She pouted an inducement. "Besides, aren't we working this story together?"

"Like two grains of sand outside the sandbox." He smiled ephemerally and sat back down across from her.

She opened the satchel she had come into the room with, and then brought out some papers. "Take a read of this," she said, handing a couple of the sheets to Frazier.

It was a document stamped across the top *Confidential—Status Orange*. Someone using a thick black marker had redacted much of it. From what he could make out of the text not marked through, Hosni Mubarak, Egypt's president, had an illegitimate son by the name of Baruti Rahotep. This Baruti had been traveling to Omaha, Nebraska, over the past year, and his trips had increased in regularity the last two months. The name of the organization Baruti spent time with in Omaha had, of course, been redacted. Frazier set the papers down on the desk and met Margaret's eyes again. "I guess for a Muslim who can have as many wives as you like, Mubarak is one dandy extraordinaire." He chuckled.

"Yeah, of course you know most Muslim men are down to one measly wife these days." She flashed a sharp smile.

"Hurray for at least some measurable decline to patriarchy on steroids." But was her comment a barb out of concern over him and Anastasie? he inwardly questioned.

She handed over another paper, a copy of Mohammed al-Ajami's "Tunisian Jasmine." "My curiosity got piqued when on one of our phone conversations, the mole—he says his name's Gary by the way—made a snide comment about the part of the poem that goes 'for those that think the country is in your kids' names, the country is for the people...' He said, 'It's not for all their kids, not the bastards' bastards anyway.'

"That's when I started digging around, asking questions of Egyptian insiders HarperCollins could put me in touch with. It didn't take long to find out about Hosni Mubarak having sired his beloved Baruti Rahotep.

"A son out of wedlock trying to get an inheritance by gaining his father's eye. This is the theory I went on to file under fast-track status using the Freedom of Information Act with the Department of State. I was surprised I got that so quickly." She gestured at the redacted document.

"You are quite the Sherlock Holmes," Frazier said. He massaged his brow, rereading the redacted document, then the poem. "Okay," he finally went on, "so what am I missing? How does Baruti Rahotep fit in to the work you're doing?"

"You know whose headquarters are in Omaha, Nebraska, besides Warren Buffett's Berkshire Hathaway?"

He placed a fingertip on the blacked-out space directly underneath Baruti's destination in Omaha. "This organization's."

"Splendid, Watson, just splendid. That would be the home offices of the Temple Mount Zionists."

Frazier's jaw dropped. "And they're zeroing in not on the planners of whatever's about to break in the streets of Egypt; they're going after al-Ajami directly, and they'll just see if they might get lucky on the others being with him. Am I warm?"

"You're on fire. Gary the mole doesn't know how al-Ajami's poem is calling forth the revolution in Egypt, but he damn sure believes it's doing just that. Of course, this part of the message in al-Ajami's poem you figured out with the parallelism between it and Yassine Lotfi Khaled's 'Tunisian Muscle'."

Her expression darkened as she went on. "If Baruti gets back to Cairo before we get word to al-Ajami to move to another safe house, well, you see..." Her voice tapered off. "They've located al-Ajami and want Baruti to do the dirty work of taking him out."

"How sure are you of this?"

"It's more than instinct and less than proof. I decided to confront Gary the mole with the possibility his people had located al-Ajami in Cairo and were just waiting for the right time to move on him. And Frazier, he hesitated too long and then was way too adamant in his denial."

A grin slipped onto Frazier's lips. "'The man doth protest too much, methinks.'" He quoted a line from Shakespeare's *Hamlet*, taking the liberty to switch genders.

"You got it, babe."

He thought for a long moment. "How do you know Baruti's in the States now?"

"I simply called TMZ up and told them I was Mr. Baruti's secretary, and my computer went down along with his meeting scheduler. I asked the woman on the line if she would be so kind as to confirm our meetings for this week, and to my all but wet-between-the-legs surprise, she put me on hold for a while, then did just that. Baruti leaves for Cairo day after tomorrow."

Frazier shook his head in astonishment. "You're amazing, truly."

"Don't give me too much credit too fast. My contacts in Egypt through Harpers won't touch contacting al-Ajami with a ten-foot pole."

"Yeah, well, they tend to disappear people who do things like that over there rather handily." Pausing, he looked absently out the window for another long moment. "After what happened at Clifford Odeon's office the last time we were there, do you think he'd take our theory seriously enough to contact al-Ajami?"

She shook her head. "He's not even taking my calls anymore. We were wrong about him needing a distraction story from us to keep the revolution from being thwarted in its next moves."

"Well, Holmes, we can't get everything right." He picked up his pen once more and tapped it atop his Moleskine, almost as if beckoning his notes on Alice Mandelstam's novel to help him now, but more knowing that in Alice's time as well as his and Margaret's, when hitting rough spots, you'd have to do some improvising. "Margaret," he finally said, "it's probably time to contact my worstest, best friend in the world, Buckminster, don't you think? He was recently over there, and I'm sure any number of the pikers he hung out with in Cairo would be obliging to help for a not too inconsiderable sum of greenbacks."

Her brow knitted. "Can Buckminster be trusted?"

"For an exclusive byline on the story with us and all follow-up pieces, yes; otherwise, not on your life."

She stared him down. She said nothing.

He could almost see her peasant go back underground. God, if only Alice's book could be given to her right now. "How close are you to being finished with reading all of Nana's letters to you?" he said, surprising himself.

Her eyes narrowed. "What planet are you coming from now, Frazier? And for the record, that's hardly any of your business."

"Yes, sorry." He crisscrossed his hands in front of his body like a referee waving off an incomplete forward pass. "Never mind, never mind." A long breath that he slowly exhaled through his nose. "Do you have any better ideas on who to contact to help al-Ajami, Margaret?"

"Other than sharing our story with the devil himself, no, I suppose not."

Thankfully she referred to it as "our story," as in hers and his, Frazier thought. "Bucky it is, then." He picked up his cell phone off the desk, and then tapped speed dial entry #3.

✍

Frazier's friend Buckminster wasn't completely the fallen angel of death, Margaret thought, waiting for the call to be answered, or not. Certainly Frazier wouldn't leave a voice message of any detail, unwanted eyes already being on them; why not assume listening ears too? Anyway, she had to give Buckminster at least this much good juju. He sort of deserved it, always being in their marriage's corner with, how did he like to put it? "You guys are my *American Idol* grand champion couple, proving just by being your overly challenged selves at intimacy those who muddle along together, stay together," something of that Norseman turkey-bone-slathering nature, give or take a pronoun or infinitive particle. Besides, she regretted having stiffened so unbendingly at

Frazier both over the idea of reaching out to Buckminster and his inquiry about her progress with Nana's letters. All this unshakable contemplation of "making peace with your family of origin" had ramped up to almost the OCD level since the shrink—who she'd had a first session with on the rebound from that talk with her folks and Frazier's hair-raising account of his time with Grandpa Mandt—told her "quite a bit of work" would be necessary to determine just how much of her "disconnected need to eradicate cognitive dissonance" could be rectified with psychoanalysis or prescription drugs. They'd come upon a strategy to start with a medium dosage of Paxil and a referral to a good psychologist. She hadn't set an initial session with this person, a Dr. Frida Buttertart, but, if the woman's name meant anything, then Margaret almost looked forward to it. You had to laugh, then again maybe better cry; either way, who could beat a head doctor with six degrees of separation from Frida Kahlo and a great pastry? It almost constantly nagged at Margaret that she hadn't informed Frazier about seeking professional help. And now, even with the antidepressant flowing through her veins, she couldn't make her right leg stop rapidly bouncing up and down, as if she were a sprinter in the blocks just about to bust a one-hundred-yard dash or something. *Answer the phone already, Buckminster! No, what a stupid way to run a race like this one.* Especially when she had done so well, gotten herself centered, or drugged just right, to carry on with Frazier such important interchange about the poet Mohammed al-Ajami's precarious fate, that is, up to the moment she lost control of the situation. She clamped a hand over her right thigh, with little impact on her nervous leg until, at last, Frazier said, "Hello, Bucky, my good man. What snake pit are you in at this time in history? I've got something for you it's probably not a motley idea to talk about over this phone connection."

"Go for an encrypted line," Margaret mouthed without making a sound.

Nodding his agreement, Frazier also mouthed, "I'm making it his idea." In a couple seconds he said into the cell phone, "Yes, I'm sure it's worth it for you." Another pause, and then, "I'll wait like a teenager for her first date to show up at the door." He ended the call.

"He's calling me back on a safe line, but, boy, is he hot under the collar. I've already compromised him some."

Well, he sure as hell had no problem compromising us with Clifford Odeon, Gary the mole, and God knows who else! She fought against letting this fly, instead pressing her tongue against the roof of her mouth. "Good work. Getting us on a secure line is the important thing."

No more than the first note and a half of Iron Butterfly's "In-A-Gadda-Da-Vida" sounded from Frazier's cell, and he took the call. "Yes, yes, I know, I wouldn't have called unless it was something that important. Hey, I want to put you on speakerphone so we can bring Margaret in. No, no, she's in this up to her neck. I'm not endangering her unnecessarily. I would never do that."

Margaret found Frazier's end of their exchange demeaning, the kind of patriarchy she would, with little doubt, end up purchasing her shrink and Dr. Buttertart their next round of home improvements by way of fees to unravel in her, and yet it was also undeniably sweet, in that West Texas, love your momma, wife, and apple pie way. A brand of reverse feminism the Comrade and Lydia didn't know how to put out there, but on her recent big visit with them, bless their clam chowder, her parents had managed to do some of it New England style.

"Hi Margaret, how's the woman of my dreams?" Buckminster said over the speakerphone.

"I'm simply giddy over putting a Pulitzer Prize-winning story in my husband's best friend's lap."

"Uh huh, and you're too savvy to do that without needing something that could get the city dogs chomping into my ample ass."

"Yes, well, I know you're already circling the wagons with the big dogs, Gary the mole's bosses," she said. "And you probably have somebody feeding you info out of TMZ, and just to add one more compliment to your exemplary, shall I call them, skills?"

"Please do." Buckminster laughed out loud.

"You've probably got Clifford Odeon eating out of your hand now instead of mine." On saying this, her tone lost any hint of sarcasm.

"Whatever in the world are you talking about?" Buckminster said.

"Margaret and I were in Odeon's office when we spotted you outside talking to TMZ members who we call Mutt and Jeff because they follow us around everywhere," Frazier said hotly. "You were also extremely chummy with the guy we call Gary the mole." Their friendship could withstand a lot of things, but not lying. Frazier would not abide that.

A long pause on the other end of the call, nothing but a little intermittent cyber static coming through.

Frazier and Margaret put index fingers across their shut lips at the same time.

"Yes, well, it is rough all over, but I am sorry you were the ones who got hurt," Buckminster finally said.

Together they had accomplished the near impossible, namely, getting Bucky on the defensive, Frazier reasoned. What is more, he was actually enjoying this, already fantasizing about Margaret and him writing the piece, staying with it until they got the right number of grassroots people in the streets, poetry, and international powers-that-be shenanigans into it. "From here on out if we agree to go forward together on this, the three of us are a team, Bucky. One of us gets 'hurt,' as you call it, the others get them out of trouble, up to and including taking a bullet for them if necessary," Frazier said.

"Then make it worth my while because, as you can imagine, with my contacts around the subject of what's about to happen in Egypt, I'm days away from breaking something huge." A short pause. "There's probably a Pulitzer in it for me, Margaret."

"Let me guess," she said. "Your story will be one of those *New York Times* propaganda pieces that exposes the revolutionary leaders or, if not that, because you don't know where they are, you'll incite their followers to rat them out by scaring the crap out of them over how close the CIA, or paramilitaries backed by the CIA, is on coming down on them. How'd I do?"

"Brilliantly," Buckminster said. "Not exact but close enough for hand grenades or government work."

"What if I told you our piece will be bigger than that," she said. "Because it will expose the people you're following around and the nations they work for, directly or indirectly, as bald-faced liars and cold-blooded assassins in time to stop the killing. People right out of Orwell's *1984* exposed for championing democracy while strangling it behind their backs. Only this time it will be put out there in full view for all to see."

Another long silence on the phone, except this time you could hear Buckminster's all but labored breathing.

A good sign Bucky's sweating out a decision, Frazier thought.

Margaret took it that the big perv may very well be getting off on the power trip. *In Bucky's mind, either way he wins, right?*

"I'd say our stories are of the same magnitude." Buckminster ended the delay again. "Toss a coin as to which one to work on."

"For your illegitimate children's sake, Bucky," Frazier said. "If you're right and it's all the same how much coverage these stories could garner, then why not do the right thing. Tell the better truth."

"It would be fun to work together on something. Tell me what you've got and what you want me to do."

"If it keeps with what we've already told you, then no backing out on technicalities," Margaret said.

"You're too good," Buckminster said. "Agreed."

Margaret and Frazier told him everything they knew about the poets Yassine Lotfi Khaled and Mohammed al-Ajami, the signals in their poems calling the revolution to Egypt, the cry for help in al-Ajami's "Tunisian Jasmine," the TMZ's dark movements with Baruti Rahotep, Gary the mole's bad poker face on all this, and the assassination that would come down without

Buckminster's soliciting help from friends in Cairo to take al-Ajami to a new safe house. For Frazier, his and Margaret's passion and sensitivity in relaying all this felt something like folk dancing together at one of those fetes with Katya and members of her family in their home village of Mashinska from Alice's book. And their sophistication proved them every bit as deft at storytelling, mining some deeper truths, as Alice Mandelstam or Boris Pasternak. Of course, he may be just a tad biased, but what was his and Margaret's little *Dead Poets Society* good for? If an author couple couldn't think of themselves as fabulous, then who else would, really?

✍

Margaret felt relieved al-Ajami might live, and to tell the truth, also that her story would not be trumped by Buckminster's. Yes, she had something good to tell Dr. Buttertart. She'd call for an appointment as soon as she got some time to herself.

✍

One more thing, Frazier was certain if Buckminster had decided otherwise on working together on this, especially after Margaret and he spilled everything to him, their friendship would've been over. Fortunately, it was not the case.

✍

"No news outlets will take our story other than a couple of radical leftie blogs, *TruthDig* and *Truthout*," Margaret said, her expression flushing splotchy and red. "They're good web publications, but what I can't stand is we're just singing to the choir." She took a bite out of her bagel with a thin spread of cream cheese and then chewed it hostilely, almost as if ravaging meat off the bone of some animal killed with her bare hands. Her morning cup of coffee had gone cold, still sitting there full to the brim on her and Frazier's kitchen table. But could you blame her really? Margaret, Frazier, and Buckminster had been at it hard, submitting the article that exposed the TMZ along with clandestine U.S. government involvement spying on and infiltrating with agent provocateurs and saboteurs the nonviolent revolutionary organizers in Egypt and the U.S., including Clifford Odeon and his Badshah Khan Institute for Peace Studies. There was some sweetness besides the obvious, and rightly so, thought Margaret, because in the article herself, Frazier, Buckminster, along with some unnamed friends of Buckminster's in the Egyptian underground democracy movement had been put forward as being responsible for thwarting the assassination of dissident poet Mohammed al-Ajami, getting him to a new undisclosed location before Hosni Mubarak's son, conceived out of wedlock, Baruti Rahotep, could get to al-Ajami. Of course Rahotep had gone into hiding or been disappeared by the now defunct regime of Mubarak. Margaret had no idea which and, quite frankly, held little curiosity over what had happened to this guy. Her head had been spinning from other things: The uprising had been incredible all across Egypt, truly it had. Who would've thought between it starting in Cairo's Tahrir Square on January 25th that three short weeks later on February 11th, Mubarak would be thrown out of office? Egypt had a long, rugged road to travel in setting up the kind of participatory people's democracy the protestors demanded and were now attempting to get on its feet. The heavily U.S.-backed Egyptian military, with many of the same people leading it who had done Mubarak's heavy-handed bidding that kept Egypt for the past thirty years in an "emergency state"—translate military martial law meted out with impunity—had installed themselves as the "Provisional Authority" negotiating with the Revolutionary Council. Yes, Egypt had a long way to go and was just getting started. All this made Margaret proud and, at the same time, frustrated to no end. Her little band of merry pranksters had had a hand in all of this with their article as well as getting Mohammed al-Ajami smuggled out of Egypt and into his home country of Qatar. But secretly, in a way even to herself, she didn't know whether what most animated her was the further good that could come out of their work should the article ever get mainstream media coverage or her parched thirst for recognition, for a Pulitzer, oh, face it, at the very least a few "atta girls" from colleagues when around the water cooler at HarperCollins.

⌀

Frazier sat across from Margaret at the table, fascinated at her all but furiously chewing that piece of bagel. He'd just this morning taken a call from a *Democracy Now!* producer asking for an interview with himself, Margaret, and Buckminster. They would still be "singing to the choir," as Margaret put it, but that show had a huge following. It would've been exciting if Margaret weren't quite so ravenous over wanting more coverage for their work. Secretly he, too, had been disappointed over the lack of interest by corporate media sources but, honestly, not surprised. Instead of throwing his digestive system into a frenzy, he had gone back to Alice Mandelstam's novel several times and reread sections of it, all the while remembering Grandpa Mandt's revelation that Alice had written nine manuscripts during her lifetime, none of which got published because they had been too politically hot. All this was particularly troubling for him now, because he'd been so pleased with the ebb and flow of him and Margaret doing the article together. Her research had been every bit as savvy and thorough as his, if not more so. That certainly wasn't worthy of a newsflash, but something else had stayed with him as delightfully persistent as a front page headline for their story in the *New York Times* most assuredly would have: Margaret's prose remained to the point and terse, but it had steadied, lost most of the sharp edges, and in its strident, cohesive, as well as admittedly humane truth-telling, took on a poetic quality he had not picked up before. He had added the powerful florid metaphor here and there, paid homage to Nietzsche and Tolstoyan philosophies of transcending war and imperialism, along with a touch of stinging satire. Together they had made the piece sing. Why couldn't that be the thing that sent them into some sort of passionate sensuality eating their morning bagels, or better yet, into the bedroom like, well, Lara and Yuri, Katya and Oleg, Pasternak and Olga…like great lovers? Frazier bit into his bagel and cream cheese, then chewed it slowly. The slumbering man enjoyed making her wait, never for a moment throughout this morning looking through his lenses. In a way he'd been waiting most his life on the soul mate he'd found in them writing the article together, and also on all the people blinded by ambition to pass him by like bulls charging past some matador's red cape, Frazier always deftly sidestepping the beasts, swooshing the cape free of their horns at the last moment. Now that's some grade-A slumbering. Sadly to him, he had become too much of an expert.

"If you're not going to say anything about our work getting for the most part passed over, then I'm off to work," she said.

"It's sort of a drag, but I don't see it as that big a deal." He shrugged. "I'll get the kids to school."

✑

She looked him directly in the eyes. "Frazier, why can't we keep the good mojo whenever we're lucky enough to get some going?" Margaret meant it. What was she doing wrong, or him, or both of them? Maybe she needed to double down on the Paxil or go to two sessions a week with Dr. Buttertart, or maybe Frazier needed some of her drugs.

"I don't really know." He took a sip of coffee and swallowed it down, the hotness against his throat somehow giving him more courage. "But your writing was really wonderful in that article, and any time I've brought that subject up, you've sidestepped the whole thing. Been too busy to get into it any more than a quick 'thank you, darling.'"

She almost choked swallowing down another bite of bagel. He had nailed her, that's for sure. She'd even talked to Dr. Buttertart about the reticence to discuss with Frazier her writing, which no one needed to tell her was her best ever. What's worse, she'd loved working on the article with him. It had almost been like great sex at times. And that, Dr. Buttertart had told her, was precisely the problem. Margaret was afraid of intimacy with a man, and so she kept her distance and poured her angst over the isolation into her career, her kids, the previously stiff writing, anything but her husband. Not when it really counted, and Frazier snuck in close. Her head doctor had suggested the problem came from her father being "shut down emotionally," and so Margaret was both mad at him and afraid of him, the detritus of which got dumped on Frazier as though taking out the trash daily and he was the landfill. "I've been seeing a shrink and a psychoanalyst" was the only thing she could think of to say. "I'm sorry I haven't told you. It started right after seeing my folks and you telling me about your time with Grandpa Mandt."

⌀

Frazier's thoughts reeled, not that he was upset, sort of oddly relieved to know this; at least something was working to some extent. In point of fact, Margaret had started smoothing out soon after that last trip to Boston. He smiled warmly. "I'd say keep it up. Whatever you're doing is helping with us and your writing."

"Thanks, really." She swallowed hard again, this time without a bite of bagel. "Do you think taking mood-altering drugs is bad?"

He opened his mouth though no words came. Barely adjusting his eyes, he looked not through his lenses but at his reading-glass frames. Finally, he met Margaret's eyes again. "We all have our drugs of choice. Some of them are just more obvious than others," he said. "If they work, fine enough; if we can heal our minds and hearts enough not to use them, then that much the better, I suppose."

"Instead of changing society and relationships to make them less dog eat dog and more understanding, less stressful or whatever, they change the human beings." She smiled sheepishly. "It all seems kind of nuts to me but, Frazier, I'm taking Paxil." There, she said it. Margaret took a sip of coffee, quickly spitting the cold black liquid back into her cup.

How could he get bent out of shape about this, or happy, for that matter? Something about her confession left him dead to rights if just with himself, and he was in no mood to slip off his glasses and let her take a look through the lenses. Not anywhere close. "It's okay with me. And, Margaret, you don't have to tell me anything that doesn't feel right to divulge."

"Thanks for saying that too."

"It's only fair."

Momentarily she looked at him askance. Without another word she stood up with her saucer and cup, then went over and put them on the counter next to the sink.

Frazier was glad she didn't ask the question begging in the room like an infant in need of breast milk: What was his drug of choice? He, too, stood up, then walked over beside her. "I hope you have a good day at work," he said.

"You too."

They kissed sort of like two pieces of cardboard touching.

⌀

Pinging with insecurity about herself, about them, Margaret gathered up her shoulder bag and was gone out the door. *Yet, somehow we're making progress, aren't we?* she told herself on the sidewalk en route to catch the subway. Until now this morning, and really since her last appointment with Dr. Buttertart almost a week ago, she hadn't thought once about Frazier and the French artist, Anastasie.

✍

Being the recipient of Margaret's chippy little kiss only assuaged some of the guilt Frazier felt over allowing her Paxil confession to stand without one from him about slumbering and all; this, along with him letting her leave without mentioning anything about *Democracy Now!*'s interest in their story. *Whatever, life not only must, it will, "muddle on."* He chuckled inwardly at using Bucky's favorite euphemism for his and Margaret's, what to call it, perpetual marital status? as he walked into the hall. Looking through the doorway into Doug's bedroom, he spotted Doug on his bed reading a comic book and still not dressed for school. "It's time to move, buddy," Frazier said. Without waiting for a reply, he faced the opposite side of the hall and tapped on the bathroom door, behind which he heard the shower running. "Mattie, please hurry up in there." The kids had a good twenty minutes to finish getting ready along with eating a little breakfast and still avoid heading out for school late, so Frazier headed into the study and sat down at his desk.

He opened his side drawer, then lifted off the top of his manuscripts Alice's *My Long Journey Home.* Placing it beside his laptop, cell phone, and Moleskine notebook with a pen on top, he looked at one, then the other of these items like a cat fascinated with sparkly objects or something: He could email Buckminster and inform him of the *Democracy Now!* gig; he could return the call to the show's producer, or text Margaret an apology for holding back, or... Oddly Frazier couldn't put words with his attraction to Alice's manuscript. It seemed to sit there in direct contradiction to the promotion of their story, or at least to the almost obsessive hunger for its dissemination which Margaret and Bucky too often exhibited. His eyes drifted over at his unpublished manuscripts on the bottom of the open drawer. Back in the day he had tried to sell them for so long that they became shopworn, yes, he had. And now they were keeping awfully good company. Silent to the world, in darkness, where all mysteries really worth solving must be grappled with. Deeper truths are always at first too fragile to hold in sunlight and, many times, for generations to come. Frazier was channeling poetic inspiration or whatever you want to call it. God, he loved when phrases flew into his mind like white doves in the night sent from muses past, present, or future. How else could you explain this kind of head-trip? No, these whispers would not be contained by time. What had the one complete letter from Nana/Alice to Margaret that she shared with him awhile back said about this? The words flowed easily, water from some black river: *Do not spend all your time behind a desk with pen and paper pontificating about things fabricated out of whole cloth. You will create characters that way, not people. People we remember. Characters become caricatures we laugh or cry crocodile tears over, and then they vanish from our minds. Fiction is the exploration of deeper truth, not a pack of frivolous lies.*

Frazier picked up his pen, opened the Moleskine notebook, and then jotted down:

> *Nor is it found in nonfiction facts manipulated for an agenda, but rather in the poetry of ordering them, and digging in the dark dirt around their roots, adding just the right music that makes you want to do something about the truth.*

Now he could put words to Alice's manuscript. It was as if a force of nature guided his hand across the page.

> *Katya and Solomon Mikhoels are sympathetic people because their extramarital affair was made acceptable by the impossible circumstances brought about with Stalin's purges. Yuri and Lara's affair is beloved because they were trapped in the ravages of war together. Isolated! Would these couples have been together in more peaceful times? Is love good enough on its own to be sympathetic, with no external justifying "facts" around to gussy it up? Could it stand the morally and humanly clarifying test of fiction?*

This feeling of gliding with his pen hadn't visited Frazier since, well, honestly, since writing his letters to Anastasie and, undeniably, also a few times here and there when adding creative touches to his and Margaret's article. It struck him that for the first time in a long while, he no longer pined inwardly for return letters from his French muse; mainly he just wished he could get in her hands a copy of Alice Mandelstam's magical novel. Live up to something they'd said to each other shortly after meeting for the first time that seemed indelibly engraved in his psyche: "You will write your books," Frazier had said. "You help me" had been her reaction. Then he promised her, "We'll help each other." Nothing seemed better right now to fulfill his part of that pledge than to share with her *My Long Journey Home* along with his notes about it.

But no matter how hard he tried to make a decision to do just that, package it all up and send it to her in Marseille, he couldn't stop some other inner voice, talking himself out of doing so, because it would be wrong to share the manuscript with her without Grandpa Mandt *and* Margaret's permission, because he would never ask Margaret for anything such as that, and truth be told, he did not know himself whether true love on its own could withstand the test of really outstanding fiction, be lifted from the pure snow at midnight like a broken icicle fallen as a result of the daylong sunshine's deceptively placid warmth.

Staring out his window at wintertime in the city, a row of partly sheared-off icicles clung to the windowsill. Not a drip of water fell from them. Steadfastly they remained here, alive, if you will, even though torn and deformed by earlier melt. The other part of them had joined the snow cover, becoming part of its long, slow journey back to the Hudson or East River, and then out to sea. Water no one could hold in his or her hand.

Frazier began recalling one by one all of the correspondence he'd written Anastasie; his poem "Still Here," penned after she left for France; the letter about whether she'd be up for being in a merry trio of muses with him and Margaret; the one claiming it was better for her to remain nonresponsive in France, for if she were here in New York, he'd not be able to stay away from her or get any writing done; another very wonderful one, perhaps the main reason the exploration of this subject in fiction needed to come through for him, his letter explaining the eternal moment they had shared that both lasted forever and was gone in a second, and also informing her of him getting closer to finding his own story because of that glorious and torturous feeling; and finally there was this one specific text, which by now seemed almost trite, of him fishing around for whether her artwork put up on her website was an invitation for him to come to France and be with her.

No, muses weren't chosen, nor did they choose you. They were part of everything. Fallen icicles. Inescapable, if in the past, present, or future, a few of them ended up hanging from your sill. Indeed, as much as Frazier having written these letters to Anastasie, they'd secretly been missives for Margaret too; in fact, in the darkest, most illuminating hour of fictional truth, they were also letters to Alice.

CHAPTER THIRTY

In the end our typewriters kept our souls from becoming so bowed that without as much as a murmur, we gave up and died. Yes, I was sure of this for Pasternak and me. Even during those years the Moskvas just sat there on our desks collecting dust, their keys untouched, at least they held the faint promise our life-giving words might rise once again. You couldn't silence this unwritten poem without taking up a sledgehammer and crushing these truth-seeking devices into nothing more than clumps of metal. It must be said, while I found myself still in shock over Solomon's assassination together with the impossibility of shaking off Oleg's absence—which took over every day with something like endless drops of water from a soured source falling onto me stripped naked, eyes pinned open—Olga Ivinskaya was taken away by the Goat-faced Murderer's thugs right in front of my hysteric protestations in our apartment. She had then been given a kangaroo court trial that sentenced her for all intents and purposes indefinitely to the gulags. It was about trying to get her to rat out Pasternak's dissident beliefs, activities, plans, and, of course, they would've settled for complete fabrications that discredited the great writer, anything sufficient to justify getting him out of Stalin's way once and for all. Pasternak and I knew her silence on these matters would win her the hellish prize of torture and solitary confinement. After that, with the years turning as slowly as decades, writing anything was simply out of the question.

When in Peredelkino, which was most of the time, Pasternak two or three times a week would visit me at the apartment, which neither of us had the heart or sense of humor to call The Shop anymore. He looked the devil, had fallen even thinner if that were possible, more gaunt, and his movement took on a kind of lethargy, as if every one of the pockets in his clothes had been filled with sand. Early on we tried talking about literature or the possibility of taking writing up again, but those topics led to nothing more than our watery, red-rimmed eyes. So we had switched to talking about benignities of how Miss Zinaida, Yevgeni, and Leonid were getting along, which couldn't be called marvelously or dangerously by any means, or about my work in the potato and alfalfa fields, something which probably had saved me but I could experience as hardly more than dull routine, a subject I only wanted to talk about for so long. No, in some macabre way it was better to speak of the atrocities, perhaps because we could no longer cry over these things, that part of us already rotted through and through, diseased members no longer able to respond with pain over what had been unflinchingly terrible and relentless for so long.

And when would it ever end? After killing Solomon they jailed the rest of the Jewish Anti-Fascist Committee members, then they tortured them, and finally they lined thirteen of the fifteen of them up against a wall and shot them down. Ever since my childhood, so often spent hanging close to my parents' dissident community gatherings in our home, I had known these courageous people, now senselessly dead: the poets Peretz Markish, David Hofstein, dear and fragile Itzik Fefer; Leib Kvitko, the physician and onetime colleague of my father's at Botkin Hospital Boris Shimeliovich; Benjamin Zuskin, who replaced Solomon to direct the Moscow State Jewish Theater as well as Solomon's people's street acting troupe; there also was Professor Joseph Yuzefovich; journalist Leon Talmy; editor of Eynikeyt newspaper Ilya Vatenberg together with Ilya's wife, Chaika Vatenburg-Ostrovskaya; and the lovely and multilingual Emilia Teumin, editor of the International Division of the Soviet Information Bureau. Of the two others, Solomon Bergman fell into a coma and died in prison before the Goat-faced Murderer got a chance to put him before the firing squad, and the medical scientist Lina Stern was the only member of the committee who avoided the bullet. She had regularly brought to those meetings at my parents' house delicious chocolate chip cookies she made herself. Lina Stern was not released from the gulag, not in 1952 when these executions took place anyway.

The insanity got worse if that were possible. Many more of those who had once been physician friends of my parents got swallowed up in Stalin's paranoia around Jewish doctors purposely letting high-level officials in the red government die on operating tables or wither away in hospital beds. Who knows whether there was any truth to this in a few isolated cases? Pasternak and I had asked around in underground circles, not finding one shred of credence to Stalin's so-called "doctors' plot," and then there was more to consider: The medical professionals I knew would never get involved in something like this. Dissident doctors valued their own integrity enough to practice the art of medicine for much higher reasons than death-dealing against their enemies. My father, Dimitri Ivashov, if he had been alive for this, and thankfully he was not, simply could not have stooped so low. He would've taken his own life or stood before a firing squad first. I felt sure of this. However, one silver lining appeared on the backside of this black cloud, and that came when Dr. Viktor Abakumov, who had been a ringleader rounding up for arrest and exterminating the Jewish Anti-Fascist Committee, got snared in the doctors' plot himself and then sent away to the gulags.

When a stroke took Stalin on March 5th in the year of our good lord and savior 1953, church bells didn't ring throughout the land; they had been silenced right along with everything else. But a tiny little bell in my chest did chime. The first note of music I'd managed for any reason in years. You could have said my work in the fields had a certain rhythm, the song of dirt bringing life, which back in Mashinska I had been able to sing at times, but not here, not after everything that had happened and not happened; now there was always this empty, hollowed-out rhyme about it. What is more, Stalin, the madman and sociopathic killer, was replaced by Nikita Khrushchev, the idiot and loud-mouthed pig. The days in Russia sort of went from opaque blackness to steel gray. You could palpably see your own and every one of your countrymen and women's soupy depression. I didn't even try to tell myself things would get better now.

Lo and behold, that turned out to be a mistake.

One early evening later that year, I walked into the apartment after a day in the potato rows, and there she was almost like an apparition! Olga Ivinskaya sat right across the room on the divan reading Sandor Petofi's book of poetry. As if a gift from the clouds or something, she was flesh and blood here in her home, The Shop. Yes, I suddenly could call this place by its real name again. She had lost weight and her skin had yellowed, which I'd seen occur more often than I cared to admit with those released from gulags, but Olga's high cheekbones and swanlike neck still brought elegance along with her anywhere she happened to be. My knees shook, and I put a hand on the wall to steady myself. "Olga," I said this wondrously gratifying name.

She lowered the book and looked directly at me with those keen azure eyes.

No, they haven't broken Olga.

She tried to say something, but tears came in place of words.

A much better communication, I knew this in some place far behind my eyes.

She wiped at the wetness on her cheek with the pad of a hand, then replaced the book on the coffee table and stood up.

Still without a word we walked toward each other, stopping no more than six inches apart. For the longest time we looked into each other's eyes, seemingly not seeking out the past or some hint of our futures; rather, this one moment meant everything, and the next one and the next. At last, we hugged tightly, though not overly so, just right actually, in a way it could very well be the two of us would never let go. Then, the most wonderful thing happened. I, too, found my tears again. Her wavy hair inadvertently wiped some of them away. The longer we stayed like this, the more I came to believe we would not discuss what had happened to us during our time apart. "Does Pasternak know you're here?" I finally said in a soft tone.

She nodded slightly, gently. "He's coming as soon as he can get away from the dacha."

I came out of our embrace and our eyes met again. "He'll be beside himself with delight."

Olga smiled, her expression opening like the moon. "Do you really think so? It's been so long, Katya."

"He pines for you." I giggled like a damsel. "I'll light the candles, get the right ambiance and all. For what it's worth, we should skip dinner together so the two of you can get right down to business, if you know what I mean."

This fine woman, who stood before me with as much right to her bliss than anyone I could think of, actually blushed. "Does he now?" was all she said.

"Yes, honestly, he pines away like a puppy." Not to hold her at bay or anything of the sort with her tweaked modesty, I turned and walked into the kitchen, where the matches were kept in a cupboard. With them and a striker in hand, I began lighting candles, starting with those in the sitting room. To get herself ready for Pasternak, Olga had probably gone into her bedroom, which I could not have been more pleased to have long ago decided not to take as my own.

On walking back into the kitchen to put the matches away, I spotted mottled flaxen light coming from her writing room, an area where I hadn't lit candles. Unable to tame my curiosity, I headed that direction, stopping in the open doorway. With her back to me, she sat there at her table with pen in hand, dabbing it in an inkwell and then putting it to paper. Yes, Olga's writing something! Her Moskva typewriter sat on the table beside her stationery just the way it had on the day she'd been taken away almost five years ago. It was ready for use, as each week when I had wiped the dust from my Moskva, the towel had been put to hers too. A couple of times I had even changed out our typewriters' carbon ribbons. Nevertheless, as sure as the rotation of the earth, Olga was carrying on as I'd known her to always prefer, that is, writing her first draft out by hand. Transfixed at her doing something so blatantly courageous after everything she'd been through, and that felt like another all but forgotten relic, my own writing, a kind of literary voyeurism fluttered over me not too dissimilar as the flirtatious candlelight. Not wanting to disturb her or be found out, I rolled my shoulders in to sort of shrink myself and used a feathery step for backing away.

"Is that you, dear Katya?" she said.

I stopped in the hall just out of her sight, willing my anxious feet not to bolt for my little nook and turn me into some dreadful fugitive on the run. "Yes. Sorry for being a peeping Tom." I managed to walk back into the doorway; Olga had swiveled in her chair to face me. "It's just that, I suppose, you're doing something that has been too much for us to attempt around here..." I simply didn't have what it took to finish this sentence with during the whole time you've been away.

She smiled knowingly. "There is no art, no writing when the iron fist of oppression steals love from you. It proves too much in the gulag, I can assure you, and so it also seems in Peredelkino, isn't that the truth." This was not a question but a statement of metaphysical reality.

I nodded, still unable to summon more words, and determined not to loosen tears. I mean, she had returned to her lover, but what was there for me? As we looked at each other, staring down these awful or wonderful truths depending on which side you stood, some crazy desire came over me to blow out candles all over the house and place myself in this evening's gloaming along with its eminent promise of darkness—which sneaked through slits in the window blinds like a band of burglars. But why perpetrate that on Olga too? The utter absurdity of this consideration brought a slight upturn to my lips. Despite everything else about my circumstance, being close to love alive once again between Olga and Pasternak somehow made it dimly more accessible in my own heart. One single candle flame, whereas, for so long, there had been no light at all.

"Come here, let me show you something," Olga said in a soft tone.

As I walked over next to the writing table, she turned and faced her work again. She picked up the piece of paper with her handwriting on it and held it my way.

On taking it I felt the lone flame in my heart grow brighter, warmer, as my eyes went directly to this poem's title:

Why Katya's Love Is Greater Than Mine

Reading it, somehow the fiery sun shone instead of the logical pale moon on the verge of rising outside:

> *Midnight whisper*
> *with no half-life*
> *amplified across Her moonbeams*
> *clear as Timofei Dokschitzer's trumpet*

in noon sun
she waited without taking Pasternak
while I had no choice but to wait,

and on my release a phoebe flies homeward
not needing to be told where to go
towards prose written again and love reclaimed?
Words are her and my bones
our heartbeats
like shafts through a greasy window
burning recompense
dust motes illumined in some sort of random harmony.

Her and my compasses so long felt not needleless
but they kept moving the magnetic poles
and we kept striking matches in the time machine
until at our feet unburnt pine slivers
below spent sulfur tips
scraps
really kindling
for our hearts' and our poetry's bonfire,

this midnight flame even bluer
me a laughing cross bearer
of half-bliss's
sparks spitting from ambers
as if stardust had wings
caught a breeze
called Katya's un-thieving love.

No use in trying to hold in the stinging wetness that flooded my eyes now. Unspeakable to make this long story short, Olga and I more than knew each other to the core; we were sisters of Russia's greatness and her demise, of love bigger than one man and yet most notably found in the one man between us…of the blessed, godforsaken chronology in each of our lives that turned us into crooks and priestesses, both at the ready with forgiveness.

"Everything about your poem is true except the title." My body trembled but not the hand that held her poem before us. "The kind of love you write about is immeasurable."

She looked away shyly for a moment, then intently met my eyes. "You're a treasured literary critic, and whether I agree with your analysis or not, I thank you for giving me a chance at a life again."

It was not enough to hide behind the veil of my love for Oleg that still resided in me as presently as this night, or for Solomon, who I loved something like an infant who had died right after childbirth. No, Pasternak would've been fair to love amidst the ruin of all that had come and not come my way. Who knew, maybe it was the iron fist upon us so relentlessly that kept him and me from opening to one another? Could be Olga was right about that. Or quite possibly Miss Zinaida held the rest of his heart, and that was enough for Pasternak. As I looked the lovely Olga in her sad and hopeful green eyes, there was one thing for certain: My restraint with Pasternak had nothing to do with me being even one iota morally superior or more tenaciously loyal than her.

The sound of a key turning in the front door's lock and then Pasternak called out, "I will be a tree if…"

Olga and I beamed, sniggering with a hand held over our mouths, and then we dropped our hands to our sides and laughed out loud. "Go to him," I said in an undertone.

"Yes, thank you, I will," she also said in low tone. "Take the poem, it's yours."

I pressed it against my chest. "Now go," I said, making a shooing gesture with my arm.

"I'm on my way, dear Boris," she called through the open doorway.

While she stood up and left her writing room, I noticed her expression soften and then her eyes began buzzing with a different intensity than I'd seen come from them before, as if preparing to read Pasternak, measure his feelings for her on first sight. Those sudden spangles in her irises giving away that Olga did not know what answer she'd get.

My heart was aflutter as much over them reuniting as from the poem I held in my hand. The certainty of its contents, of them holding each other in their arms out in the sitting room and, conversely, the mystery underneath these words of hers, behind the closed doors of her awaiting bedroom, all this breathed life into me. For a split second I felt just how alone I was without Oleg's or Solomon's honest-to-God love in the here and now, and for the first time in I don't know how long, I didn't ignore it down inside me. I carried it with me into my nook, where I sat down in the chair at my writing ledge in front of the Moskva typewriter. I slipped a sheet of paper in and rolled it into position. Then, I stared at the page blankly. It felt like looking at a bone in some mass grave. I couldn't help but listen for Olga and Pasternak, giving off a sign, a moan, laughter, the clink of wine goblets, I didn't know what, anything, really, to let me know how they were doing out there. Somehow it would shape what I would do with this bone-page; the blood coursing through my body like an electrical current told me as much. No, just write something, I admonished myself. Still nothing went onto the page. There was the sound of her bedroom door opening and shutting along with, maybe, even giggles, I couldn't be sure by way of them being muffled through the walls, but undoubtedly, these were affectionate noises. I rolled the page down to the middle, the place for a title to a novel. My fingers moved toward the keys and then I came up short. On further thought, I would not use an author's nom de plume. Covering my identity in the body of the story with a fictitious name would be as far as I could take universalizing my work, helping readers, if there ever were any other than close friends, focus on deeper truths rather than some autobiography stuffed with too many deadening facts. This time my fingers made it all the way to depressing the keys, and black ink etched itself into the paper with noticeable solidity, somehow as if the creative act itself was more important than anything about me, as I typed simply this:

My Long Journey Home
by
Alice Mandelstam

I took that page out of the typewriter, then quickly inserted another. Where to go from here?…yes, with a poem, that poem, the one which made so much difference in all our lives. I stood up and walked over next to my bed. Reaching underneath the bed, I took hold of the old jar with the poem in it I had long ago stashed there for safekeeping. Once back in my chair, I unscrewed the top, then very carefully removed the poem and unrolled it. I read it over three times before setting it on the little ledge. With that I continued typing:

The Stalin Epigram

Our lives no longer feel ground under them.
At ten paces you can't hear our words.

But whenever there's a snatch of talk
it turns to the Kremlin mountaineer,

the ten thick worms his fingers,
his words like measures of weight,

the huge laughing cockroaches on his top lip,

the glitter of his boot-rims.

Ringed with a scum of chicken-necked bosses
he toys with the tributes of half-men.

One whistles, another meows, a third snivels.
He pokes out his finger and he alone goes boom.

He forges decrees in a line like horseshoes,
One for the groin, one the forehead, temple, eye.

He rolls the executions on his tongue like berries.
He wishes he could hug them like big friends from home.

This poem by Osip Mandelstam, my father's friend, slapping down Stalin's atrocities, got Mandelstam years in prison, and got my father, mother, and brother killed; nearly got Boris Pasternak, the great Russian poet and author of the most wonderful novel, Doctor Zhivago, *killed too. I was just a young girl when given the original version of it, written in Mandelstam's own hand, to keep safe…*

My words came on and on. Oh, as always writing was like squeezing a lemon from inside my brain, but this fruit was huge with its skin opened, the seeds pithy in just the right way, its sourness the sting of things, adding hard and necessary lines, and not to forget the lush delicacy of so much citrus juice spilling onto the page like sunshine on a cloudless day. I cried, the words were so beautiful and gut-wrenching. My hand slammed down on the writing ledge almost of its own accord. I laughed, though not so loud as to disturb the lovers next door; then I applauded them and my writing. Every so often words spilled out in the wrong order, albeit never the wrong words, so I'd take that page out, insert another, and go about a retype of it, getting things right this time. Some combination of this ménage à trois between the page, the written word, and myself went on continuously as the first chapter unfolded before me. I could feel it going even deeper, coming through with the most sanguine drops, nectar from the rind, if you will, when Pasternak came into my nook and stood directly behind me. He had on a long terrycloth robe and was barefoot.

"I heard the sweet clacking of keys and just had to come see what you're up to," he said, placing a hand on each of my shoulders.

"It's the start of a novel." I smiled, though kept my eyes fixed on the page in the typewriter. "Maybe I'll ask you to edit it someday."

He gently squeezed my shoulders. "Yes, I should have time once I finish *Zhivago*."

I twisted around in my chair and looked him directly in the eyes. They were sparking with life only being with Olga could ignite in him, I felt sure of this. There was no need to ask whether he would dive back into his manuscript right away; that fact was written all over his expression. He reached into the robe's pocket and came out with a piece of folded paper. "I've been carrying this around in my wallet ever since you gave it to me. Until tonight I didn't know whether I liked what you had to say about my work or not."

"And now you do?" If this was what I thought it to be, he had held on to it without making use of it for going on five years, some kind of horrendously long gestation period but, perhaps, worth the wait for a perfectly ripe pregnancy.

"Yes."

"I can hardly remember what sage advice I gave you, Pasternak," I fibbed, almost coquettishly. "Please refresh my memory."

He unfolded the piece of paper and laid it on my writing ledge just in front of the Moskva. I read my own handwriting:

> *Finish* Doctor Zhivago *with a flourish! In your novel and in life be with the one you most love in the worst of times and at least a few of the best of times, but, should you love two just as much, with everything about you, if in different ways, then God help you. No, truthfully, there is nothing better to bring you and your readers to the divine!*

"I really hope you answer that question in your novel." I held my editing note toward him, but when he reached for it, I pulled it back. "You are going to get back into the consistent daily writing schedule that inspired me to take up the pen in the first place, correct?"

By way of agreeing he touched two fingers to his forehead in a little salute. "I have a feeling you'll be trying to answer the same question in yours."

"You're a smart one." A pang of regret resurfaced that he had Olga, along with, for that matter, Miss Zinaida, to share beds with him, and here I was left with no one. I had little inkling whether to envy him this complexity, however, for the likes of such I would've traded away in a heartbeat my particular brand of double-winner widowhood. "Don't you think you should go back to Olga before she starts having ideas come into her head about us?"

He chuckled lightheartedly.

"Now get back in your love nest," I went on without giving him the chance to respond in any other way. "I've got some writing to do." I shooed Pasternak using the same sort of arm gesture with which I had sent Olga to him.

CHAPTER THIRTY-ONE

"Why do you wear those damn reading glasses on the end of your nose all the time, Frazier?" Margaret said evenly, though shuddered inside. It took all she had to get this out there between them, and that's after this morning, for the better part of forty-five minutes, having rehearsed with Dr. Buttertart until getting it down pat. That swear word in her delivery had been added somewhere between the psychologist's office and arriving here in Washington Square Park on this otherwise sparkly September day with a bed of white, orange, and yellow zinnias, the nearby greenbelt, not failing to mention her and Frazier side by side on a bench, all under dappled light, compliments of a huge weeping willow tree and, almost without acknowledging it, the noon sun directly overhead. It was idyllic enough to make you want to puke. Why couldn't it have been rainy or that they'd caught a late summer heat wave? Anything, really, to keep things short and sweet or provide an escape hatch for doing this some other day, a plausible reason for delay to take back to her next $125 session on the couch. During these "head-shrinkers," as Margaret had become fond of referring to the appointments, she had come to understand ignoring the weirdness of Frazier's reading glasses had been, in some way, similar to a wife pushing out of mind a husband's affair with his mistress even though they flaunt themselves almost right in front of her face, which was the analogy she and Dr. Buttertart had hit upon, an awfully inconvenient one at that, Margaret had maintained for a while, but the longer this parallelism's juices inwardly fermented, the more it shook her. And now, waiting on Frazier to swallow down a mouthful of meatball hoagie sandwich and give her an answer to this long-overdue question, Margaret reasoned, perhaps that had been Dr. Buttertart's objective all along, getting her to take not only a hard look at how nicely convenient it had been to let Frazier have whatever quirky secrets lay behind his wearing those silly glasses around everywhere but also his carrying on some F-ing "muse affair" with that French artist, Anastasie. He hadn't mentioned Anastasie in quite some time, though he sure as hell hadn't told her they were no longer in communication either. Yes, Margaret and Dr. Buttertart had made a good joint decision in starting with this question about his glasses before confronting him on the other *thing*, whatever kind of triangle it happened to be, or maybe, hopefully their *thing* had "fizzled out altogether," just like Crosby, Stills, Nash & Young said about their song "Guinevere" on the movie of the original Woodstock concert she'd watched with Frazier a couple of times over the years. It was funny, as in oddly so, the bits that came to mind sometimes. *Whatever.* Right this moment, what she happened to be proudest of, something she'd not discussed with Dr. Buttertart and that refused to be coached or rehearsed away, as it seemed to have a mind of its own no matter what: Margaret's eyes, neither of them, had twitched even once since meeting Frazier for their picnic in the park. Hah, hah, hah. The hidden fruits of therapy, yeah, she would chalk this down to that, sort of as if receiving a twofer item on sale day at Macy's. When would Frazier ever finish his bite of sandwich? Oh yes, she felt sure this was one of his patent-pending stall tactics.

✍

Frazier had a flip thought that all the chewing he was subjecting this bite of Subway sandwich to would turn it into some sort of meatball, red sauce, banana pepper, onion, and wheat bread smoothie down in his stomach, gross, but better than facing completely alone the riot otherwise going on in his head. Stuffing the hoagie in his mouth and tearing off a chunk had been his attempt at not letting out an entire string of nervous laughter or unloosing a slew of defensive snipes at Margaret. Take for example some of the candidates still up for possible release, "I'm such a nerd I always have to be ready or I'll pee my pants if I miss something that needs reading," and, "I went from wearing regular glasses to these reading glasses because my myopia sort of miraculously healed itself," (of course a lie; when his eyesight failed, it descended fast) "however, since you never noticed the change, I decided to keep these reading glasses on until someone loved me enough to care!" Or maybe he could divert things more towards her with, "We all have our hang-ups, Margaret, like your eyes that twitch every time you're about to face down someone who intimidates you, namely here in this park at this moment, none other than the little old bookworm, me, so just let everybody have their own hang-ups, why don't you?" but then, honestly, everything about her eyes remained clear and steady. Besides, deep down Frazier had been expecting this confrontation for a long time, dreading as well as actually desiring it all the same. Not until she spoke the question did he really understand why. It made him feel loved and neglected in equal portion. At least that was something to go on; until now there had just been at some very important place inside him the loneliness and the slumbering. Two old friends he'd brought up from Texas and got even better acquainted with in New York, but could always be found on the wrong side of the tracks in his soul. And, by the love of God, he didn't need any of Margaret's head doctors to figure that much out. He swallowed down the meaty swill. There was one thing he'd be open to right about now: a handful of Margaret's Paxil beans. "It's a trick so I only have to see things clearly when I need to keep myself, you, and the kids safe from harm, like driving or getting on the subway, or on the rare occasions I think it's of any use to know the details of things." He lowered his sandwich to his lap. "Mostly it's because most everything has either regressed or progressed to being FUBAR, fu—"

"I know what FUBAR means, Frazier," she interrupted. "So let me get this right, you're nearsighted, not farsighted." She put a hand to her brow for a long moment. "I just thought your eyes weren't too bad to begin with and you simply didn't want to be bothered with your regular eyeglasses anymore, but you must've started needing reading specs. With you wearing those things around all the time, eventually nothing made sense about it."

"Not bad guesswork, not bad at all, but wrong. I'm almost legally blind." He slipped his eyeglasses off and held them toward her. "Check it out."

She set her sandwich on the bench, then took the spectacles and put them on. Panning the park with the frames high on her nose, she looked directly through the lenses. Everything was distorted into a kind of fantasyland. "Wow, this is awesome," she said in a lilting tone. "It's sort of like the few times on particularly rough days I've taken an extra Paxil…or two."

With that welcome what? permission, he, too, looked over the park, and it made him think of Tolkien's hobbit land. "I call it slumbering."

"Well, it does have its benefits." She took off and handed him back his eyeglasses.

For the first time with her, he placed them high on his nose and looked through the lenses without tilting his head back. No diversion, this damn sure wasn't slumbering. He felt as if all of a sudden being in one of those dreams where you're with people you know and everyone's dressed, but you're naked, running around desperately looking for your underwear or a T-shirt, and for the life of you, there's no telling where those articles of clothing are. "I'm sorry, Margaret," he said, meaning it very much.

"It's okay." Her gray eyes had turned kindly and sad. "I've been part of the FUBAR."

"Thanks for owning that, really."

"It's no harder than preparing a twenty-part recipe for tiramisu flambé after dropping a thousand bucks in cooking lessons with the gourmet chef Dr. Buttertart."

Belching and chuckling at the same time, he folded the sandwich wrapper over the open end of the hoagie he'd barely gotten into. Tossing it like a football, he made a swish-shot into the trash container about twenty feet away.

In a stroke of good-natured bemusement, Margaret arched an eyebrow, then turned serious again. "Why do you think because things are FUBAR we decide to slumber?"

"We feel like we can't make a difference."

"There's got to be more to it than that. It seems like such an unfortunate choice to stay perpetually defeated or something." For a long moment she looked absently at the circles of sunlight dancing on the path at her feet. "Maybe it's because once Obama talked so big, then let everyone down, here at home and around the world really, we just don't see any way out of the mess in time to save ourselves."

"That's probably a big part of it." He glanced over at the trash container now in possession of his hoagie. Something about the direction their conversation was turning made him almost need his unquenched appetite, as if taking by the hand some sister called unmet desire, and she held on for dear life. He'd never thought of Margaret as slumbering before, but it sort of made sense once she took to the Paxil. Of course he was glad over her getting on some journey of personal growth with the help of the good Dr. Frida Buttertart. If only the lonesome cowboy poet inside him could be reined in a little, then maybe he, too, could open to some professional help. Honestly, though, reading a good book or unraveling one of his own stories at a typewriter seemed the best therapy possible for Frazier. And he'd been neglecting himself badly over the past four years, which sure didn't have the ring of a picnic in the park to once more inwardly face. *Now there's a reason for slumbering!* A shitty though real one, for him anyway. Maybe it was the persistently all-American, never-miss-a-full-meal hunger pangs that whispered a kind of way forward to the slumbering man for their interchange, along the line of reasoning that to emerge from slumber one needed the constant push of unmet need, or perhaps it was the slender blonde reading a paperback book who sat on the bench across from them and resembled Anastasie. All this brought to mind the children's pool-depth water Margaret and he were so expert at wading in on the subjects of politics and injustice as opposed to floundering in the deep end of marital intimacy, where they already found themselves up to their necks. Whichever it happened to be that prompted him, or something else entirely, he couldn't quite put a finger on, Frazier, nonetheless, ventured on. "You know, Margaret, I really got a charge out of doing that article with you and Buckminster. It did make a difference, and what's more, we got the word out to others on our *Democracy Now!* interview. That went nicely, don't you think?"

She nodded. "I was so nervous about what Buckminster might say, but he actually came through as someone who cared rather than a baboon straight from the jungle."

"Yeah and ouch." With an index finger he repositioned his eyeglasses high on his nose, as they had slipped down a smidgen.

"Okay, my bad." Now she wrapped up her sandwich and reared back to throw it in the general direction of the trash container. That's when the beauty who looked almost like Anastasie Moreau's twin, from the photos on the French artist's website Margaret had viewed, caught her eye. With an unsure smile, she lowered her arm, then set the sandwich down beside her again. "It's just that I can't help myself from being hard on Bucky; he deserves it so much of the time."

"You're right about that." Somehow Frazier couldn't quite claim he enjoyed seeing things in the park clearly, though for the moment, at least, this was working better than slumber. *Why is this?* he asked himself. There was the day's natural ambiance chipped away at with the throng hurrying through the park to wherever in this relentless city of New York each one of them headed. Quite possibly too little slumber, the overabundance of clarity of purpose, could only be put into balance by the kind of connection he and Margaret were attempting to plumb? And then there was the benefit, simply and inexplicably, of setting eyes on the fruit that needed no words in its fullness, which the slender blonde across the way dangled in front of him just by being nearby, a projection all his own, otherwise a stranger, truly unknown and, for now anyway, his surrogate Anastasie. He noticed Margaret espying her, and a wave of prurient discomfort washed over him, sort of like a sudden onset of the rash you wore long-sleeved shirts to conceal.

"Something else that gives me some hope is how well the Arab Spring is doing," he went on. "I really don't think it's some sort of seasonal activity—better to call it the Arab Resistance."

∅

She nodded her agreement again, though the black butterflies set aflutter in her stomach told her she and Frazier were embracing a good topic and avoiding a more pressing one. Margaret couldn't take her eyes off the woman who reminded her of Anastasie Moreau. "Yes, and what happened in Wisconsin with the push back against killing collective bargaining for public employees of the state, if we're lucky, may just be the start of a United States Spring, the beginning of a resistance movement taking to the streets here," she said.

"If we keep this kind of talk up, maybe I'll be able to get me some appropriate glasses and you'll kick the Paxil."

Margaret met his eyes intently. "Yeah and ouch."

He flattened his hands out on the bench and pressed downward. "Sorry for getting into your business."

"Thanks," she said, but the butterflies were swarming now. In a bassackwards way, Margaret was glad Frazier had opened this door. She would probably never get off the Paxil without going further with herself, her family of origin, and with him. She looked once more at the lovely woman over on the bench. It felt as if God or all the furies in Hades or something had delivered this Guinevere right here to set Margaret churning over the real Anastasie, especially now, while she had Frazier spilling a not so insignificant portion of his guts to her. *Make sure you're well prepared before getting into his muse with him,* Dr. Buttertart's words echoed in her mind. No, she hadn't yet gotten to put such a coming forward together with the head-shrinker, but something told Margaret this was her moment, maybe the most lucid one for delving into this she would ever come by. Or the black butterflies simply carried her away. Something inside her shoulder bag seemed wiser words than any psychologist could ever inspire or bring forward from Margaret. Yes, Nana's last letter would not let her go. Ever since she first read it almost a week ago, she'd gone back and forth on whether to ball it up and eighty-six it in the trashcan. Now, she best not think it through anymore or she'd never pull off what needed doing. In one motion she slipped the bag over her head and off her shoulder, then reached in and came out with it. She slipped the letter out of the envelope and presented it to Frazier. "I need to know which it is with regard to our love." She gestured at the letter.

Without a word he unfolded the yellowed paper. He read it:

> *Dear Margaret,*
>
> *My surname was not originally Mandt, it was Mandelstam. You have the blood of great poets in you! Your grandfather and I had to change it to get out of Russia and stay out of harm's way once we left. You need to know this should you come across any of my novels if they ever get published. There is one I want you to read whether it's published or not called* My Long Journey Home. *It very well may help you find your way home too. Ask to read it and it is your gift from me. If I'm dead by the time you get to it, go to your grandfather for it. If he's dead, then go to the literary executor of his estate of whom my last will and testament requires it be kept for you. Okay, enough of that.*
>
> *I want to share with you the best piece of advice I ever gave anyone who cared to live well or write well. If it applies to you in one way or another, please do yourself the greatest favor you will ever receive and act on it. Here it is: In your novel and in life, be with the one you most love in the worst of*

*times and at least a few of the best of times, but, should you
love two just as much, with everything about you, if in
different ways, then God help you. No, truthfully, there is
nothing better to bring you and your readers to the divine!*

*There isn't anything further I can hope in my wildest
dreams to impart to you of material value.*

Shalom and love,

Nana

✍

Yes, this was Alice's last letter to Margaret, Frazier felt sure of it. And Alice's
parting advice was exactly the same as the editing note in *My Long Journey
Home* she'd written for Katya to give Boris Pasternak on his novel, *Doctor
Zhivago*, and, of course, on his life split between Zinaida Pasternak and Olga
Ivinskaya. On running Margaret's request through his mind again, he realized
she wanted to know *which* and not *whether*. Undoubtedly, she already sensed he
loved both her and Anastasie, and was only confused over how much he cared
for either of them. Anything he may say next could easily be a lie, for Frazier
himself hadn't figured that out. Who knows, maybe it was moot because he
would never see or hear from Anastasie again…but he could not bring himself
to believe love ever became a foregone conclusion or ended, not if it were once
real; then it may as well be the air we breathe. Point in-sort-of fact, he had
immediately fallen under the spell of the stand-in Anastasie still across from him
and Margaret. Of course, his literary self knew together Margaret and Anastasie
represented the whole of feminine archetype, and while you're at it, throw in all
the goddesses of poets, novelists, and muses, but, nonetheless, there also was
this very real person in Marseille, and despite his efforts not to give her abidance
in his soul, even now, he wondered whether there truly were one too many
women in his life, infiltrating his marriage, or could there be a way for the three
of them to coexist spiritually if not physically? If so, did he have to tell Margaret
a truth only for poets? Better yet, was she one, really, at her core? Okay, stupid
question, but could she go that deep when on Paxil? His lowering the letter left
the two of them looking directly at each other. Her wide-eyed, flushed, though
courageously open expression against, for all she knew, a pending onslaught
deserved his very best. Frazier felt his quaking chest tell him as much.

"I don't know which it is, Margaret." His voice shook. "But I'm really glad
it's you I go home with every night."

She laughed, along with tears quickly overflowing her eyes, and then she
laughed again. Margaret hardly cared she was losing it.

He thought better of acting on the instinct to reach over and help wipe
them away, keeping his hands at his sides. Besides, his eyes stung with salty

wetness too, and at the moment, Frazier needed to be left to his own devices. If she touched him, he would undoubtedly break way, way further down.

"You...son of a bitch...I love you for your honesty...even now." Margaret sort of spit the words amid her laughing sobs. "And...the thing of it is...I don't...blame you... Until I got with...F-ing Dr. Buttertart...and the pusher-man...there wasn't enough...of me around...to meet your needs... Oh, Frazier...I don't honestly know...if there's enough of me now." She laid her head on his shoulder. "It's as if Nana...is telling me...it's better to have someone in addition...to you...as a muse...and vice versa."

He put an arm around her and held her close. "I think she's saying life happens, and whatever shape it takes, we need muses to find our way to God." It took several minutes for her tears to stop flowing and her breathing to steady.

"On my last visit with Grandpa Mandt, he gave me Alice's manuscript of *My Long Journey Home* to read first and then give to you, once you'd read all of her letters," he finally added.

She raised her head and met his eyes with almost a naive expression. "Have you finished it?"

"Yes."

"How was it?"

"Truly magnificent, a masterpiece, I'd say. It answers questions that lead you to five more questions."

"About the shape of love?"

He nodded. "How not to slumber around for it or while speaking truth to power."

She smiled warmly. "Maybe we'll get some of the answers we need from her book."

"I sure have, and like I said, more questions than answers." He returned her smile.

They kissed like lovers.

When they came out of it, Margaret first, then Frazier, nonchalantly, as though inadvertently but actually on purpose, glanced across the way, and the slender young woman on the bench had gone.

∅

"So they're ready for me to pick up!" Frazier said with rising inflection into his cell phone.

"Yes, sir," said the LensCrafters eyeglass specialist who at the start of the call had introduced herself as Tonya.

"Drop by at your convenience and I'll fit you with your John Lennon round grounds. They're very Occupy Wall Street if I say so myself." A short pause from Tonya. "Sorry for bringing up politics, but I just think what's going on over in Zuccotti Park is awesome, and I figure anyone buying frames like these may feel similarly. I hope I haven't offended you in any way."

"Just the opposite, actually. They're on to something with the ninety-nine percent getting nothing more than crumbs off the table from the one percent."

"Respectfully, Mr. Pickett, it's *we're* on to something. I hang out at Zuccotti after work most days. Sometimes I spend the night."

With a smile spreading across his mouth, for a moment he held the phone away from his ear and looked at it in a kind of awe over this Tonya. "Maybe my new specs will be good juju that gives me the courage to join you at the park."

"We are the ninety-nine percent, sir."

"Yes, *we* are."

"I look forward to your fitting."

"I look forward to the good juju. See you soon, Tonya." He ended the call, then set his eyes once again on the desktop computer's screen in his cubicle workstation at Flying Pens Literary Agency.

He'd been poring through author queries for literary representation by the agency all morning, and now he began reading the first chapter of a dystopian horror novel in which eating food had been given up for obsessive sex by this society of the future, best he could make out from the synopsis he'd read just before Tonya's call, because in the end this author wants us to grapple with sex being more necessary than food, yet the abundance of orgiastic behavior kills rather than gives sustenance. Maybe it would've been weird enough to catch some publisher's eye if only the writing wasn't so stilted and corny, Frazier reasoned. He looked for books written on about the eighth grade reading level, as unfortunately, that happened to be the sweet spot for adult popular fiction. Don't make them think, spoon-feed them the answers, and keep it surface-level suspenseful, never existential and rarely metaphorical. The problem with this particular writer was he made you think all right, about his, how to put this? flunked-out-of-eighth-grade literary acumen. Frazier stopped reading halfway through page three, then brought up on the computer screen Flying Pens' stock rejection email. You know the one, or if you don't, here it goes anyway: *It is such a competitive marketplace and literary representation is a highly personal choice that, regretfully, we at Flying Pens will not be able to take on your book. We wish you the best of luck in your writing career. This project could very well be right for another agent.* When Frazier clicked on Send for one of these letters, a flash of queasiness always passed through him, and getting this off to Ollie Bryant from Flagstaff, Arizona, was no different. Each and every one of these sad communiqués, in a small way, made him feel as if somehow his own work was getting turned down yet once again too. Not to worry, these slumps usually didn't last long, because his worst writing had been superior to anything he'd come across in Flying Pens' slush pile. Of course he weaved better yarns than this. *Don't I?* Here came the tricky part; to get completely out of these slumps, he'd go into slumber, looking over the top of his lenses at a milky computer screen with black freckles until he no longer felt like such a loser. But how could he do that on this day of all days to curtail slumbering by way of picking up his John Lennon round grounds from the feisty and lovely, dissident LensCrafter herself, Tonya? He attached Ollie Bryant's query package to the rejection letter, and then condemned it to Flying Pens' *Severely Wounded Soldier* file. Hah, hah, hah, but the weak tummy remained. With a flurry of mouse moves, clicks and double clicks, he navigated onto Occupy Wall Street's streaming video at Zuccotti Park. In seconds he lost all self-consciousness of his authorial inferiority complex, and became fascinated with this *General Assembly*, as some facilitator with sharp, walnut-colored eyes and killer dreadlocks referred to the gathering on the Occupy video feed. This large group of people repeated in bursts of a few words the exact message coming from whoever had the floor. The staccato effect somehow captivated you. When something particularly poignant was said—such as right now, with the nattily clad, 1960s Afro-sporting Princeton professor Cornel West expounding, "You people are our best and bravest. To expose the plutocrats and autocrats for the greedy warmongers they are will bring the heat on us. I stand with you. Thank you for giving me a public square to take a stand in."—then the crowd lifted their hands and wiggled their fingers in approval. Those fingertips had undeniable power, sending to Frazier through the computer screen something akin with starlight, our collective bondage wriggling free if only just a little.

He heard his boss's, Maisie Bilkman's, panty hose rubbing against her thighs before she wheeled into his cube. "Are they sending in best-seller manuscripts through YouTube video these days, James Joyce?" she said sardonically along with a gesture at Frazier's computer screen.

Laconically, using the mouse he moved the cursor on top of the red x in the upper right corner of the screen and then hovered there a couple seconds before clicking off the Occupy Wall Street General Assembly. Turning in his chair on rollers as he faced Maisie Bilkman, Frazier looked over the top of his lenses. Honestly, how could you imagine a more perfect farewell performance for slumbering? "Why would I waste my time on such inanity when I can plan the revolution?" He gave her a lazy wink.

She didn't fire off another quip, nothing of the usual fare between them.

On chancing a glance through his lenses, he couldn't take his eyes off her sallow expression. Something was truly wrong and Frazier knew it. "Talk to me, Maisie, what's going on?"

For a moment she brought a hand over her mouth. "Manny Baton choked on a spicy chicken wing while dining at a HotWings establishment and died last night at his table. His head fell into a pitcher of beer."

"I'm sorry to hear that. Really I am." He found it hard not to chuckle at the strange appropriateness in how Flying Pens' only best-selling hack author kicked it. "How can I help?"

She smiled as if forcing it. "Become my next Manny Baton."

"A ghostwriter, no way."

"A signatory writer underneath Manny's name. You know how Clive Cussler or Robert Ludlum's estate churns out all those books with other young writers penning them."

Frazier shook his head vehemently.

"Before you turn me down flat, I've got an offer for you I don't think you can refuse. Manny Baton's books bring in butt loads of money, Frazier."

He looked once again over the top of his lenses. "If your offer doesn't involve enough literary freedom to use at least some metaphor, challenge existential thought a little, not solve everything with sex, corrupted power, or money, than there's not enough cash in your or Manny Baton's bank accounts to buy me off."

Literally, she peered down her nose at him. "Any time Manny tried to get deep, even just underneath the surface, Random House edited it out. I'm sorry, Frazier, but the market simply won't bear it. All the mainstream publishers are in lockstep on this for pop genre books." Dropping the imperious expression, she winked. "But I can make you rich."

"Get behind me, Moloch." He returned her wink. Habitually Frazier tried remaining in slumber but somehow actually preferred seeing Maisie Bilkman clearly for whatever would come of this. Almost all he could think of was the integrity contained on every page of Alice Mandelstam's *My Long Journey Home*, which lay in his desk drawer at the apartment on top of his also unpublished work, all three of Frazier's novels clinging to the same kind of depth and honesty as Alice's writing. Bless Manny Baton's soul in purgatory or wherever it happened to be eternally soaking in barbecue sauce. Yes, there weren't hairs from Frazier's West Texas roots still tangled in red clay soil if his manuscripts hadn't been his best shots at the times they'd been penned, not watered-down pulp fiction, the furthest thing from that. No denying it, he hadn't experienced hardships the like of Alice's Katya and Boris Pasternak and their dissident friends in Stalinist Russia, so his stories didn't contain such blatant injustice. They were subtler, perhaps, because the great American dream was such a deft lie. No, his work always seemed to find a way to wrestle with breaking free of West Texas provincialism to carve out an existential, poetic path for surviving in iconoclast society, his protagonists in one form or another being male versions of Truman Capote's death-defying hick-gone-to-the-city in Hollywood's version of *Breakfast at Tiffany's*, Holly Golightly; and while he was suddenly so much about this business of lifting himself out of slumber, may as well admit something else: He fantasized himself as none other than Holly's true love in the end, Paul Varjak! A tin ring out of a Cracker Jack box to slip on your lover's finger was always better than some garish band of gold when it came right down to the Texas redneck, nut cutting. Of course, in Capote's actual short story, Paul Varjak, who didn't even get assigned a name other than for a time Holly's brother Fred's, was at the end left only with Holly's unnamed cat. It was enough to give you a cold shiver. Finally, Frazier broke the stare-down going on between him and Maisie Bilkman. "I quit, boss."

As if punched in the stomach, Maisie rocked on her feet, but quickly recovered with a smile that did seem quite genuine. "Since your second week here, I've wondered why it was taking you so long, James Joyce."

"Thanks for not trying to talk me out of it, Maisie."

"At least some of us riffraff need to stay true." She shrugged. "I just seem to need more inspiration to do it, so come through for me. I want to see your books on the best-seller racks in the literature section." With a finger she wiped at a tear as if it were a speck of dust. "Get out of here, already. Go write your books or start a revolution or whatever good things you'll do."

"Okay, Maisie, I will." The only part of her directive he felt sure of attempting would be the walk out Flying Pens' door.

He stood up, then extended open arms toward her.

They hugged.

And he almost didn't mind the overpowering smell of her strong perfume. It reminded him of this one particular mother who greeted him at the front door every time he picked up a girl he'd "gone steady" with for a while during high school in Texas. That girl, Trixie, and Frazier had dated for a pretty long time, actually.

✍

The late September sun shone almost with the cheeriness of summertime, although the air carried a crisp chill, autumn, the season for leaves to make final green hurrahs before their gloriously colorful dying and sad fall to the ground, leaving branches bare. Frazier's shoes felt unusually springy on 11th Avenue's sidewalk, almost as if the old leather had been replaced by rubber on his soles and somehow, too, inside his soul; yet, like the leaves loosening their grip on the trees, the glue holding this new wonder material in place wasn't quite dry, not set well. In short, everything seemed to him a metaphor for some kind of state of imperfect transition. He had picked up his new John Lennon round ground eyeglasses from Tonya at LensCrafters, and they looked smart in a hippieish sort of way he liked. In a pocket of his navy blue Dockers, he had his new eyeglass case with the fake reading-glass frames inside. All the way over to LensCrafters, Frazier had promised himself to leave the old frames behind, ask Tonya to trash them. Okay, fine enough, slumbering may very well be begrudgingly going into its own deciduous molting season, but it simply would not die an easy asleep-in-bed-in-the-middle-of-the-frigging-day death.

He headed down the steps to the West 96th Street subway dock. As he got on the Redline and stood there holding a metal pole to steady himself, Frazier began wondering what on earth he would tell Margaret about bugging out of Flying Pens. No question about it, they needed the money to hold things together with their West Village lifestyle. He'd be fine living in Brooklyn's more affordable bohemian arts district, but would Margaret and the kids? He'd get a job waiting tables at some fancy Upper East Side restaurant in the evenings so he could write most days in peace with Margaret at Harpers and Mattie and Doug in school. But would he write in earnest again, really? Serpents in the underworld, it had been so long. *No, squash that thought!* His latest stuff, that article he'd written with Margaret, had sparked with brilliance. Apart from that, truly, a fourth novel it would never make. There wasn't nearly enough of him in it to sustain the marathon of marathons of long-form prose. That project was yet to show up in the nether regions of his mind, as had every one of his novels, with hardly more than a whisper. He had fiddled around with some ideas, but never mind, they weren't good enough. *Trust...trust...trust the muse...and write every day until she comes round...then run with it...* He felt as if he was letting his loved ones down and at the same time showing himself, as well as them, a way to live without slumbering, creatively, authentic, some modern-day Franz Kafka, or Emily Dickinson, or Vincent van Gogh, or for that matter, Alice Mandelstam with her nine unpublished novels. In the most important way, it didn't matter whether you were ever "discovered." What made the difference would be the pages you wrote. He knew that much now, but would Margaret, Mattie, and Doug? Because he couldn't give a flip whether anyone else got this about him. When would Margaret ever finish reading *My Long Journey Home* and come talk to him about it? If she didn't get this picture tuned in after reading Alice Mandelstam's book, what hope would be left she could understand enough to not go all hurly-burly over him choosing his own writing over the money from turning into a Manny Baton clone? Not even this Dr. Buttertart, good as she'd proven herself so far, would likely be able to navigate Margaret through fog that thick.

As the subway slowed for the Christopher Street dock, the one for getting off and making the two-block walk to their apartment, a bunch of people moved closer to the door, but not Frazier. He reached in his pants pocket and came out with the eyeglass case, and then switched out his glasses. With the fake reading glasses resting on the end of his nose, everything seemed "normal" again, fuzzed out, the people's faces flattened Georges Seurat style, Frazier's comfortable, almost psychedelic world of slumbering. The thing of it was, though, the glue had begun to dry, holding the rubber in place better, his soul refusing to stop with the bounciness, at least not entirely. Even so, all in all calling Margaret on his iPhone simply would not do. This news needed delivering in person, if also under a state of slumber. Yes, Frazier knew where he'd disembark farther down the line, at Wall Street, only a stone's throw from Zuccotti Park.

Just before arriving at that exit for the subway, he again put on the John Lennons.

The Occupy Wall Street encampment, for lack of a better phrase for it, maybe "permanent protest," buzzed with activity: To Frazier's right there was a drum circle with peace-loving, mat-haired pot smokers, next to button-down collar clerks, beside an actor in a black turtleneck who Frazier couldn't quite recall the name of, and right in the big middle of the group stood a thirty-something mom and dad, who had his little girl on his shoulder and his older daughter by the hand, everyone involved swaying with the beat. If there had been a transparent wall up between his life with Margaret and his kids on one side of it and this drum circle on the other, Frazier would've been the wall. It was as if he could only tear it down, not his entire being, as in eighty-sixing himself or something idiotic like that, rather, the impetuousness to quit Flying Pens without so much as consulting Margaret, then he, too, could be enjoying this drum circle with his family like the one right in front of him was doing. How could he show Margaret, Mattie, and Doug a better way if he remained a wall? Yes, he'd have to talk with Margaret soon. The longer the wait, the thicker the wall became. Enough already of being so hard on himself, so he took a stroll past Food Not Bombs' tented kitchen, with smells of cumin and red beans mixed with Indian curry wafting from it, and then there was the legal support team's tent, where a couple of attorneys took contact along with citizenship information from folks in case of arrest. From the handwritten sign on their table, it seemed they would help bail you out and/or contact your family, as you preferred. Next was the media tent, with a passel of techies at laptops and a couple of people who were filming behind video cameras on tripods. Frazier became more and more impressed as he meandered along, getting the feel for this place, good vibes. Underneath the medical tent a redheaded fellow with a thick mustache, who wore a white smock with stitching over the chest pocket that indicated *Doctors Without Borders*, tended to what looked to be a college-age young man's sprained or broken ankle. He came to an Information Booth, which had flyers on General Assembly schedules and committee meetings, such as direct-action planning, police liaison, nonviolent tactics, security, facilitation, banners and signs, greening the environment, reimagining government, and then he came to the one on organizing and maintaining a library. He asked a rangy older gentleman wearing a Veterans for Peace T-shirt at the information table where the library was located, and the man told Frazier, "Just beyond the Occupy the Arts group right over there," indicating with an outstretched arm the easternmost part of the park. An area Frazier had not yet made it over to. They had introduced themselves, so Frazier thanked Jorge Sanchez and then headed out for the library. Who knows, maybe he could bring some of the books from his bookshelves at home to contribute to the cause or, better yet, read from his and Alice's novels, if they had a reading circle. He bounced on his rubbery feet blithely again. Come to think of it, he could start a reading group if there wasn't already one going.

As he passed by the Occupy the Arts area, out of the corner of his eye, he spotted someone tall, with this thick shock of almost golden hair, wheat blown sideways, could it be! He stopped walking and faced that way. His chest filled with something like sunshine. She stood sideways to him working on a canvas that had a thousand little figures on the bottom portion of it, and rising from the center of them was this one big fist held in the face of a pockmarked, disease-ridden, obese man in a suit who loomed over the tiny people, the caption *Bankster* beside the man's fat head. It was her, wasn't it, and not the Anastasie lookalike he and Margaret had gotten distracted by that afternoon in Washington Square Park? Of course this was Anastasie; these new glasses of his were immaculately in focus, no tricks or gimmicks of distortion allowed.

Why hadn't she returned his letters, really? What made him stop writing them? Surely in the final analysis, the feelings he held for her now had no boundaries in time. His eyes drifted again to the piece of art she worked on, and the thought came that it gave nothing away to the honesty and insight which Grandpa Mandt/Osip Mandelstam had captured in those dissident icons of Russia, the prints the old man had had Frazier haul down from his attic. As the fullness of her piece washed over him, visually as well as implied, something about the close similarities between Anastasie Moreau's artwork and Grandpa Mandt/Osip Mandelstam's told Frazier whatever her reasons were for not continuing their correspondence, they must be good ones. No longer was he a wall but simply a man again, who stood at a window with light coming through from both sides. As if unlatching the locks that held the frame in place and then raising the glass pane, he looked upon her without any restrictions. Frazier began walking toward Anastasie, though hadn't consciously sent a signal to his brain for placing his legs and feet in motion. The rubbery shoe soles had quieted too, his steps now as incontrovertible on the grounds of Zuccotti Park as he was of being at home with the other 99%ers, romantics one and all, those who'd dare sing John Lennon's "Imagine" and mean it enough to come out here to make that kind of world become more real, even a little bit. Yes, in fact, we needed our utopias to have something worth walking toward.

"Anastasie," he said, on coming up beside her.

She lowered her paintbrush and faced him with those sloe eyes glimmering, her irises like dewy plums at daybreak. "Frazier," she said in that spritely French accent. A warm smile spread across her lips. "You no hide anymore. I like you glasses."

"Thanks for the compliment…and peace out, I suppose." He rocked on his feet, slipping his hands in his pants pockets, with one of them gripping the eyeglass case. It freaked him out to see her this clearly, unfettered by slumber, but it also felt good, as if he were dancing with the ballerina atop the bull in the famous Occupy Wall Street artistic photograph, and doing fine enough to probably not fall off.

Her eyes followed his hands going into his pockets. "Is banana in there or you just glad see me?" she said, gesturing at the bulge in his pants the eyeglass case made.

Or is she looking at my crotch? He took his hands out of his pockets. "Oh, that's a case with my old eyeglasses in it so I can hide if things get too rough."

"It's okay when you need hide, go right ahead. I not mind."

Her words came evenly soft, weighty and light as a feather. He stopped rocking on his feet. "I may at any moment."

"You write?" she said.

"A little stuff that's not too bad."

"Why not more?"

"Maybe I've been looking for my muse."

"And you find her."

He didn't know whether that was a question or a declaration. Nevertheless, he had found his muse in Alice Mandelstam as well as more and more with Margaret and, of course, now Anastasie. Perhaps it was a blessing all three of the most important women in his life were as different as the moon and sun and planets, yet were certainly in his orbit, or perhaps a curse. "I believe I have."

"Then you write novel, yes."

"When it comes, when it comes." If the direction of their conversation didn't shift, he would most certainly find himself changing glasses soon. Her next question could well be "Don't you have any ideas to expand on?" albeit delivered in her irresistible way of speaking, and he would not be able to refuse. This was a subject he did not want to get into. Long ago Frazier had learned that talking about his own creative work in progress brought it a death sentence in the womb. The odd thought passed through his mind, *Then why have I wanted to collaborate with Margaret?* "How about you, Anastasie, are you getting any writing in?"

She shook her head. "When you stop writing letters me, I stop with novel. It only half through."

He dare not ask for a synopsis of it, turnabout of the sort only being fair play. He was her muse too, and he'd failed her. Or possibly the literary gods wanted it so, as in Alice/Katya's absence from love, which made her book just the much richer…as his and Margaret's separateness while sharing the same bed may imbue his novel to come and, yes, Anastasie too, never beside him but, in a way, always with him. He smiled more tentatively than he would've liked. "Maybe we'll both write more now."

"Okay, I think you good on that."

He wouldn't ask her how long she'd been back in New York. Somehow it didn't seem to matter. "I'm going to see if they'll let me lend a hand in the library."

"Right next door to art space, good." She smiled again. "Please, go see what kind trouble you get to. I'll be here paint."

"Yes, it is good, indeed."

They kissed on one cheek, then the other, with Frazier making sure not to let his lips linger on her silky smooth skin. Anastasie smelled of fresh air over a green field early in the morning.

She returned to her canvas and he walked over to the library, wishing he had eyes in the back of his head.

As Frazier stepped just inside the surprisingly well-appointed library tent, with books lined up in IKEA shelving on all three sides, floor to ceiling, a narrow-jawed, bespectacled man, who sat in a metal folding chair, looked at Frazier over the top of the book he was reading. "You're welcome to check something out and take it with, or just sit in here and read." The man gestured atop a card table at a clipboard with paper where names beside book titles had been written in.

From an article in the *Village Voice* a week or so ago, Frazier knew David Graebar, the author of the book *Debt: The First 5,000 Years* that this bookish man was into, to be one of the original organizers of Occupy Wall Street.

"Splendid, thank you. I was wondering if I could help staff the library if you might find another hand of use."

The man slipped a bookmark inside the book, then closed it. "Why yes, good news, indeed. You're talking to the right person. At General Assembly I've been twinkled the head librarian around here." He held his hands up and wiggled his fingers, sending off a little Occupy Wall Street starlight.

Frazier sat down on the only free folding chair of the five inside the tent. They introduced and shook hands; then Frazier said, "I'm a writer."

"I'm an ex-librarian at Manhattan Central Library," said this Stewart Markesh. "Got sent out to pasture before I was ready because of budget cuts. I've written a novel or two myself, unpublished as they remain."

The librarian, whose scruffy beard had tufts of growth partway down his neck, also had almond eyes that sparked with what Frazier took to be intellectual curiosity. "My novels are also, shall we say, not bound."

"Does it matter to you?"

"Not so much anymore."

"Then we're going to get along just fine." Stewart Markesh scratched his beard for a long moment. "You can take tonight's shift if you'd like. It starts at 6:00 p.m., runs to midnight. The fellow who had signed up for it got hauled off to jail around noon for hanging a banner across the façade of the New York Stock Exchange. Legal is getting him out, but NYPD usually makes sure not to release OWS folks until they've spent at least one night behind bars."

"Did the people participating in this act of civil disobedience get roughed up by the police, made an example of, pepper sprayed or something?" Frazier had also read accounts of this type of deplorable behavior by the police.

"No, I don't think so. Not any more than cuffing them and hauling them off in a police van does that."

"Do you know if his action got some media coverage?"

"Damn good at that. Evidently one percenters don't like it put right in their face."

"Magnificent, and I'm on for tonight's shift." Frazier thought that he would have to attend some of the Direct Action Committee meetings, and serve some more jail time if need be to further get this message out to the general public, as many of his fellow slumberers as possible, even if they'd never stooped to using fake reading glasses to accomplish the feat. It wasn't their fault others of his ilk hadn't fallen into knowledge about his secret weapon. Myopia of the eyes there were ways to deal with, and for the mind too, actually, the unvarnished truth.

Frazier excused himself from the tent, and then walked toward a quiet maple tree, along the way glancing over at Anastasie, who still stood there dabbing her brush in paint and going at the canvas with intent concentration. The best part of it for Frazier happened to be no boyfriend-looking person hung around her. He leaned against the maple tree surrounded with empty sleeping bags and pup tents. Most people were gathering at this afternoon's General Assembly. For close to a minute, he remained committed to reaching into a pocket and going after either his iPhone or his fake reading glasses, and totally unsure as to which. Another glance over at Anastasie, and still he saw no sign of a boyfriend. As the "people's mike" started up, attendees repeating some speaker's short phrases that indicated the beginning of the GA, he dug his iPhone out and, without giving himself time to back out, punched the #1 speed dial entry.

On the first ring Margaret answered. "Hello, Frazier, are you okay?"

"Yes."

"Then explain to me why the kids have been left by themselves at the house all afternoon."

"Are the kids all right?"

"Yes, they're fine, it's just that they called me at work because they were worried about you."

He didn't always show up right when the kids got home from school, but would always touch base with them when left alone in the house for any significant period of time. "I'm sorry. Are you home with them now?"

"Uh huh."

"Then please tell Mattie and Doug I'm sorry."

"Okay, but where are you?"

"I'm at Occupy Wall Street in Zuccotti Park."

"Okay, cool, I love what's going on there. Even thought about heading over there myself." A pause. "Will you be home for dinner?"

"I've signed up for the night shift at the library they've got set up."

"So then when can I expect you?"

He looked once again at Anastasie, and wouldn't you know it, no boyfriend even yet. This time he didn't take his eyes off her. As if his gaze sent a homing signal to her or something, she looked away from her painting and over at the library, then scanned the grounds until locking eyes with Frazier. "I'm probably spending the night down here."

"You're wha—" Margaret caught herself, counted to ten slowly as Dr. Buttertart had suggested for these occasions when she got the reds and wanted to control everything within reach or, for that matter, earshot. "I'm sorry, Frazier," she went on at last. "I wish I were there with you. Stay as long as you like." Saint Paul, Mary, and Joseph, that was hard to have said.

"No worries, I love you," he said, definitely meaning it.

"You, me too. Have fun." She ended the call.

Anastasie waved at him.

Frazier waved back. Then headed directly for the library.

Things went well over there on his shift, with him helping people find books by Howard Zinn, Studs Terkel, Noam Chomsky, Cornel West, Chris Hedges, and the classics like Melville's *Moby Dick* and Dostoyevsky's *Notes*

From the Underground, along with Kafka's *The Castle* and *Amerika*, just to name a few. Every so often he'd look over at Anastasie again, and found her either painting or not in the Occupy the Arts area at all. They never noticed each other at the same time again, nor did the dreaded boyfriend, if one existed at all, show himself.

A little after eleven o'clock, while Frazier was checking over the loan-out sheet to make sure all returned books during his shift so far had been marked as such, he heard her voice right next to his ear.

"Frazier, can you check out me Gunter Grass's *Tin Drum*?"

He met her plum-colored eyes and smiled warmly. "Good choice. I think we just happen to have it." It was, no lie, one of his favorite works of literature, perhaps right alongside Steinbeck's *The Grapes of Wrath*. The more he found out about her tastes and ways, the less they needed to talk anything over about their relationship; it was already unfolding better than words could all not often enough manage.

The normal course was for people to get their own selections off the shelves, but he went and retrieved the book for her. "Just sign for it and it's yours." He indicated the clipboard.

As she filled in the information, she said, "Was that your wife on the phone with you earlier?"

"Yes, it was."

"You love her, don't you?"

He craved his fake reading glasses like heroin addicts must crave the poppy. His hands actually shook.

"It okay, Frazier. There enough love to go around."

"I hope so," he managed.

Now she smiled warmly. "If you stay night, we have some extra sleeping bags over in art area."

He swallowed hard. "I'm staying then."

"Good, see you late." She picked her book up off the card table and headed back over to her canvas.

Frazier watched her in mind-blowing, poetic amazement glide like an angel or a sorceress all the way there. He thought of Alice Mandelstam's novel and her final letter to Margaret giving advice about loving more than one person at the same time, and it did him no good. His hands still shook.

It wasn't until a young woman wearing an orchid in her braided, brunette hair came into the library and checked out Tolstoy's short story "The Death of Ivan Ilyich" that his hands completely steadied.

❧

Somewhere around two or three a.m., in the middle of this moonless, pitch-dark night, a cold front blew through Zuccotti Park, awakening the crows that had been sound asleep in the treetops, as well as Frazier. He rolled over in his sleeping bag to face Anastasie in hers, but she was outside of her bag on her knees or something. He reached for his Dockers on the ground beside him, then got his John Lennons, which he'd slipped in a pocket before bedding down. On putting them on, he saw she was only wearing panties and T-shirt.

She shuddered and gave herself a hug. "Can I get with you? It freeze me now," she said in almost a whisper, as if not to awaken the others nearby just outside the Occupy the Arts area on a little grassy knoll.

Without a word he unzipped his bag, and she slipped in beside him. Only wearing boxers and an undershirt himself, plenty of her skin pressed against his flesh, his member stiffening in the bargain.

"It's okay," she said, then turned her back to him and spooned in close.

He gently laid his arm across her chest.

Feeling his heart beat against her back, she cooed.

He barely managed to move his hardness away from her ass.

In not much more than a minute, Anastasie breathed the rhythmic cadence of sleep.

It took Frazier another hour or so to fully doze off. First he had to find more peace within himself on the throbbing question of whether there was, indeed, enough love to go around, but, at the same time, far less than free sex would pass as admissible, not and nurture the wholeness of his loves, his three muses, these petals of the most mystical flower, somehow to integrate them in his soul being the truest form of the red rose's disease, the most primal, the cure. Or would he be better off studying wild purple orchids that thrive only in the stultifying jungles? His last conscious thoughts were again of Alice's farewell letter to Margaret, the part that went: *No, truthfully, there is nothing better to bring you and your readers to the divine!*

He awakened before the sun came up with Anastasie still snuggled in next to him asleep, and his boxers were sticky on his legs from his unconsciously released jism.

CHAPTER THIRTY-TWO

I opened the mailbox out by the street in front of The Shop and reached inside, coming out with my and Olga's post, three envelopes along with a postcard. On flipping over the postcard, with a panorama of Leningrad's Church of the Savior on Blood along the banks of the Neva River on the cover, I looked at the closing signature from Irina, Olga's daughter out of a marriage prior to Olga knowing Pasternak. Immediately, I diverted my eyes from her note's strikingly precise cursive text, as not to read correspondence meant for Olga. Each one of Irina's postcards, which had come more frequently over the past year or so, were like tulip seeds for spring planting in Olga's inner garden, they brightened Olga so, took away some of the recurring dark haunts over the miscarriage with Pasternak's and her child that had happened while she was in the gulag. Irina's first postcard had arrived in mid-June two years ago, the week of Olga's birthday. Before that this twenty-three-year-old unmarried teacher of Russian literature at upper school in Leningrad had been for way too long a bygone casualty of Olga's affair with Pasternak. Thank our stars Irina over time also had been informed of Olga's release from the gulag, as well as her miscarriage, through dissident friends who cared about Irina's mother immensely, and come to find out, Irina did too. I hadn't even met her until six months ago in the fall of 1955, and it was all at once hard and not so difficult to believe I had been living with Olga for going on three years, and most of that time what I knew of Irina came from the faded photograph of her at about age six slipped between the frame and glass of Olga's dresser mirror. It seems Olga's husband had left her and taken little Irina over Olga being too close to the dissident community, unsafe to be associated with. What a catch that guy had been, my word. But not so stupid in a pansy-ish sort of way.

As for matters such as this, or at least in the same ice rink with it, Pasternak himself continued to walk a seemingly endless fine line between his dissident friends along with the rotten, propagandistic Union of Soviet Writers, and he negotiated another wobbly line by keeping a wife and a mistress, something patriarchy held dear, though a few free women had gifted themselves at great cost, such as the late Marina Tsvetaeva, who had dared to have multiple partners, at times men, at others women. Whereas, sadly and perhaps even admirably, Olga Ivinskaya struggled in the tangled web of mistress-hood, its powerlessness over marriage, and sovereignty when it came to seduction, but underneath, all the while, I could see it in her oftentimes distant eyes, Olga knew the best love sets no boundaries. It is chosen freely, because it irredeemably selects you.

For all three of ourselves—Pasternak, Olga, and me—we bore up under the pressure of our and Russia's missteps with our writing. Pasternak had finished *Doctor Zhivago*, and I had read through the entire manuscript. Simply put, he had cobbled together a masterpiece. To be sure I felt a kinship with Olga over her poetry, not only those magnificent words, also her lost-ness, which drove her to the writing desk, just as it did us all, to set her flying like Franz Kafka or something. Yet, Olga enjoyed a safety net underneath the rope, the surety of being caught in some freefall by Pasternak always returning shortly with his "I will be a tree, if..." and then she would feel found for a while, part of everything that mattered; you could see it clear as day in her radiant expression. Of course, I at times fell green with envy. I only had the typewriter and my work in the fields and those frightfully long, empty spaces between the two, no one with a signal coming through the front door. How long could my imagination sustain such fragility? I often wondered.

Compared with Olga, Pasternak, and Miss Zinaida, I supposed Oleg and Solomon and I had been, in a somewhat morbid if also undeniably merciful way, lucky not to have been thrown together in a triangle or, otherwise, have had either Oleg or Solomon lose out to patriarchy's rule forbidding two men share one woman, or to too much freedom should we have ever figured out how to shed the shackles of patriarchy; God knows, we tried to treat each other as equals, indeed we did. My secret: I ached to be with only one man, freely, and unless my heart ever opened again, it would have to be lived on the pages of my next novel, those white bones you could turn into flesh and blood, breathing and loving and dying. The manuscript I had recently completed contained yet even more complicated times than the current together with the relationships they had inspired, certainly not to leave out the selfsame maneuverings of others who happened to be nearby in this random and all the same somehow sublimely ordered universe. If not from them, the dear and troubled lives that had crossed mine, then how else would I myself have learned how to love through those terrible as well as magnificent days and nights?

Yes, I was pleased with *My Long Journey Home* and, what's more, on Pasternak's read of it. He had been duly impressed enough to comment "Your writing hugs the people tighter, more honestly and caringly than my pen ever could." No question, *Doctor Zhivago* held more of Russia's range, top to bottom, than my newly finished novel, but quite frankly, I agreed with Pasternak, my words held more of the peasantry in them. And why wouldn't they, with the whole of my bloodline hailing from the far side of the Urals.

When delivering in person his final draft of *Doctor Zhivago* to *Novy Mir* in Moscow, Pasternak graciously had also taken my manuscript to consider for publication, almost two months ago, more than enough time for the editors to have read through both of them. So, over the last three weeks on my days off, I had watched at the window, and then headed for our mailbox just after the mail carrier delivered Olga or me something. On the other days I came in from the fields and went right to the coffee table to check for any mail of mine, where Olga always put those items beside Sandor Petofi's poetry book. It was unbecoming to myself, this obsession with getting feedback on publication. And I honestly felt it compromising the poems I had written since completing *My Long Journey Home.* They weren't as close to what it meant to be human or connected with nature, a tad too self-conscious. Somehow this traipsing out here to the mailbox as well as first thing rushing the coffee table, like Cinderella awaiting the arrival of a golden slipper, would have to stop. But to tell the truth, I didn't quite know how to stay away from the lure of at least some moderate amount of fame. Trying to dampen this, I from time to time reminded myself that what drove me was regard for my story not to get mothballed like my last novel. Perhaps there was some truth to it, perhaps, but who was I to decide? A writer overlooks flaws in his or her manuscript like a swooner only sees the dark features, his chiseled jawline and not the shifty eyes...the buxom curviness and not the note she palmed his best friend underneath the dinner table. Then, of course, there comes the equally extreme self-doubt with the manuscript, not much different than what it must be like when waking up next to a naked man, yourself naked, and not remembering his name from meeting the night before at some drinking establishment.

I slipped Irina's postcard behind the three envelopes, and the first letter was sent to Olga with no return address. The next one, also for her, had come from the Korean poet Won Tu-Son, who she'd translated in the past as well as more recently. That envelope noticeably had been opened and its flap pasted back down by the mail censors. When I placed it on bottom of the stack, my eyes immediately flashed as wide as the big blue Peredelkino springtime sky; the final letter was for me and in the envelope's upper left-hand corner were typed the words *Novy Mir* along with its Moscow address. With a finger I opened the flap and then carefully took the letter out and unfolded it. There was this. "We are so happy to have had the opportunity to review your work," etc., etc., buttery nonsense, and then, here it came, the death sentence that suddenly turned the sky dingy without need of assistance from some fat raincloud:

> *Your authorship is not in keeping with Soviet socialist*
> *ideals, its collective reality over the individual. Even though*
> *you are the protégé of Boris Pasternak, you certainly aren't as*
> *wise as him, in that your prose is clearly rebellious, whereas*
> *his remains implicitly so...*

I shook the letter at the sun. Pasternak had warned me against getting my hopes up, that he didn't think *Novy Mir* would publish his work, much less mine. Squinting my eyes shut, I suddenly saw glowing stars fill the surrounding darkness more from anger than having stared down the fiery ball above. And in those stars I noticed a dance of sorts, like diaphanous mist going this way and that in the wind, between me and Pasternak, his fine line and my in-your-face prose, more like Osip Mandelstam's "The Stalin Epigram," along with all those other dissident writers and artists and academics and doctors and everyday heroes who had been exterminated by the Goat-faced Murderer's lackeys as if they were nothing more than pesky bugs. I had no desire or, for that matter, the acquired ability to emulate Pasternak in my writing, and, what is more, nothing would make me happier than him being published by *Novy Mir*. In our own distinct ways, we were imagining away the emptiness history had darkly left us to so much of the time, in moments of stillness, really, whenever you could steal a little room to feel and think; invariably too soon you got this terrible book called *Russia's Falsified History & Its Necessary Future* shoved in your face again, one that honest to heaven and hell should never have been published. With the red ink of lies and wonton brutality to bring "peace" already all over Russia's pages, it seemed if Pasternak's, mine, and other dissident writers' much truer words failed to get out, then for all of us, the twisted fantasy of Gogol's simple office clerk, Akaky Akakievich, who got sent to prison because someone stole his overcoat and he had the "audacity" to protest to the authorities, would more and more become our only future. Yes, writers with salt must throw their pebbles at the seemingly unmovable wall in order to stay salty. Somewhat surprisingly I pictured myself not at my writing ledge typing away on the Moskva, but in the dark rows harvesting potatoes. In the end it probably all came down to the most basic elements dealt with forthrightly. This is why what I found in myself by working the fields was every bit as great as the complex written word. Everyone had to eat, but not everyone had to read. Alfalfa and potatoes, in fact, carried all the stuff of poetry that reaches people, sings the cycle of life and death and life again, as much as Tolstoy's or Gogol's or Pasternak's, or God forbid, my contributions to literature ever could.

Nonetheless and because of these findings, I headed out for Pasternak's dacha in a hurried walk, my arms swinging in wide arcs; then I started to run.

Had *Novy Mir*'s answer on *Doctor Zhivago* arrived in his mail today too? If so, my going to the dacha could spoil his celebration with Miss Zinaida or, for another matter, her comforting his disappointment. I mean, how would she react to me showing up unbidden? Not as if an invite would be extended this side of one of my novels outselling Pasternak's or something else equally improbable. The only time she and I had been in the same room together since my return to Peredelkino was over two years ago, when she showed up to give a piece of her mind about never granting Pasternak a divorce no matter how long Olga and he remained together, as Olga lay nearly on her deathbed with internal bleeding. It would've been heartless had Miss Zinaida not softened and insisted on taking Olga to the hospital. No, Zinaida not only didn't want Olga out of her hair bad enough to let her die without professional help, at least a small part of her actually could abide Pasternak having his mistress, that is, as long as he desired Olga and, well, her. The harshest hoopla of protestation had to have come from her Czarist-era social refinement, which had worn down to just a thin, artificial film. It had quickly melted away on coming to grips with Olga's real need for help, which, together with the way Zinaida later in the evening brought Pasternak to Olga's hospital bedside and then went out in the hall to give them some time alone, was how I came to learn all this about Miss Zinaida. By the time I came to the bend in the road as it turned toward the dacha, my pace had slowed to something below a determined walk; maybe this admittedly hot hat reaction to come here had been a mistake. There was nothing Pasternak could do about my rejection letter, and I wouldn't want him to finagle something with *Novy Mir* even if he could. What I wanted was his chest to press my head against and have a good cry. But don't get your hopes up for that with the likelihood of Miss Zinaida's stern eyes leveled on you. The only thing that conspired against my chickening out was springtime. It abounded everywhere with greenness, a background on nature's canvas colored in with the pink and white apple trees in bloom and the purple lilac limbs, reminiscent of Wassily Kandinsky's watercolors, all of this kind of painting over enough of my reservations to walk on. The sparrows and phoebes seemed to be singing a light ballad, just sad enough to make me feel as though with friends. Thank God, I had slowed down some; otherwise, this season's so necessary artistry would've been overlooked.

Pasternak and Miss Zinaida sat in two of four unvarnished wood chairs around a low, marble-top table on the porch stretched across the front of the dacha. A pitcher of iced tea was on the table along with two partly drunk glasses, and there, next to the pitcher, probably lay *Novy Mir*'s letter to

Pasternak, open over an envelope. The soft breeze made a panel upturned at one of the two creases in the letter quiver. I walked up the three steps onto the porch more confidently than the hanging bat inside my chest would've made her approach. Wisely, she always waited for cover of nightfall to venture from the cave. Pasternak stood up and smiled knowingly, while Miss Zinaida remained seated, though I couldn't tell whether her lips narrowed in tautness or with a slight smile of her own. My eyes went to the letter again, and now I noticed a third yet empty glass beside it. The bat dug her claws more securely into the underside of my breastbone.

"Welcome, Katya, we thought there was a chance you'd come by today," Pasternak said.

"Or Olga," Miss Zinaida said flatly.

The bat flapped its wings.

Pasternak gestured at the chair across from them, and as I sat down in it, he settled into his chair again.

"Tea?" Miss Zinaida lifted the pitcher.

I nodded. "Thank you."

Keeping her eyes fixed on mine, she poured my glass, the yellow and green flecks of her irises sparking with what I took to be genuine hospitality together with the part of her held prisoner by Olga enjoying some freedom, at least for the time being.

"It's so nice to be here with you. I've missed this place so." I took a sip of tea and swallowed it down. "I've positively despised not having more of a relationship with you, Miss Zinaida, and of course, Yevgeni. I hardly even know Leonid. How is he? How are you all?" There, I had said this. It felt right, as the bat seemed to be dozing off to sleep.

"Yevgeni is all the successful engineer in Leningrad." Miss Zinaida moved her glass in a circle, swilling the tea. "He can be a little too busy for visiting his parents sometimes. Leonid is in school, and he's good with the books, like you were, Katya." Her eyes went to the letter on the table.

Its contents could wait for now. I leaned a little forward. "And you, Miss Zinaida, how are you?"

"Glad to be alive in the spring, but, you know, I like autumn best. It seems to me that's where life begins, when all our good intentions and not so good go back into the earth and prepare to become something useful again."

"That's quite beautiful." Yes, Miss Zinaida did somehow seem to hold our crazy and elegant cycles of life together, not with any illusion of staidness or boring predictability, rather by her own poetry, this enduring adaptability. I loved her; I needed her. Glancing at Pasternak, I caught him beaming at his wife. Of course, he, too, loved Zinaida, wouldn't think of being without her. The great writer wasn't just stuck here at the dacha between forays with Olga at The Shop and when they snuck out of town together now and again, not anything of the sort. If Olga was the almost continual blossoming of spring for Pasternak, Zinaida was the lush green turf that provided so much of the oxygen.

"Yes, well, today of all days Boris could use another author to talk with who also hasn't sold out to the mindless chatter that passes for Russian literature." Miss Zinaida reached over and took Pasternak by the hand, though her eyes hardly left mine. "I'm glad you're here, Katya." She smiled like some sly cat. "I took the liberty of reading your manuscript before Boris took it with him to *Novy Mir*."

I suddenly felt disrobed. "You don't think it's too scandalous of your actual life?"

She waved a hand between us. "Are you kidding? You've done nothing but good work. Anyone who lets a writer near should know she or he is fair game for book material."

"If I would've asked you about using you as a character beforehand, would you have said yes?"

She shook her head. "Most certainly not."

"Well, you don't have to worry for now anyway because *Novy Mir* turned down my book."

Snugging her grip on Pasternak's hand, she said, "Then you're keeping good company."

At that I met Pasternak's shimmery, dark eyes, betraying none of the disappointment in him that had been having its way with me. With his free hand he made a thumbs-down gesture. "It seems I'm not a good enough socialist to get my latest work published in Russia either."

"I'm so sorry, Pasternak."

"Please, there's no need to be."

I just had to ask, "How can you not be beside yourself right now?"

"Because the writing of it was my balm."

"And that is enough for you?"

"It seems it will have to be."

No, no, no! Novy Mir had muzzled a genius's transformative word for all in Pasternak's *Doctor Zhivago*. His book had reached its hands into the dirt and unearthed Russia, not one smidgen less clearly had he revealed it than those red copper- and iron-laden ridges of the Urals which in early spring showed themselves like veins between the green trees in the valleys, throbbing with the blood of both the ages and of now. "Pasternak, we'll just have to get *Doctor Zhivago* out through the underground, turn it into the best samizdat ever," I said, using an insistent tone. As soon as the words flew from my mouth, I realized they were as much for his work as mine, but how to bring that up in front of this great man who had just been muzzled, shunted aside? Unbelievable, simply unbelievable when you got right down to it.

He took a long, slow swig of iced tea, then set the glass on the table. "I'm not too sure about doing that," he finally said.

"Why withhold it from Russia?"

He smiled almost slyly this time. "Because you'll put your *My Long Journey Home* out right along with *Doctor Zhivago*, and I'll simply be overshadowed."

All three of us laughed out loud.

"I'll get you a copy of Boris's book before he changes his mind," Miss Zinaida said, letting go of Pasternak's hand. She took another quick sip of tea, then stood up and walked into the dacha.

"Isn't this turning into the most lovely day," I said to Pasternak.

He leaned back in his chair and looked over the fertile grounds everywhere in front of us, bees dipping their stingers into apple blossoms, willows weeping all the way down to blades of grass, a ladybug lighting on his sleeve and as quickly gone. "I like the heat of summer best," he said at last.

"Yes, me too. It makes things grow with strength and steadfastness if at all, almost as though because this honeymoon exhausts itself by taking part in so much…splendor." I came close to saying "sex."

☙

"There is a man in Leningrad who wants to meet you, Katya," Irina Ivinskaya said. "His name is Sergio d'Angelo. He's in Russia on a visa as a journalist for the Italian Communist Party."

"Why does he want to meet me?"

"He got hold of your novel by way of a copy I circulated through samizdat, and he loves it. He tells me he's confident of being able to help you get it published in the West, in Italy, perhaps also Europe and the United States."

"How well do you know him?"

"Sergio splits his time between Leningrad, Moscow, and the rural provinces. He fits in easily with the higher-ups as well as everyday people. He's the kind of person you enjoy having a few vodkas with. I've read some of his articles in Italian leftist newspapers, and they sort of have the same kind of hinted-at dissidence Boris Pasternak's work leans toward. He seems for real…I don't know."

"Okay, I suppose. When can he come to Peredelkino and talk things over?"

"I tried getting him to agree to come here with me on this trip, but he insisted the meeting be held in Leningrad with just you and him."

For a moment it felt as if the summer sun overhead had become a wintery

King Grossman

cold, yellow moon. "Let me think about this some."

"Certainly, that's fine, please just let me know something before I leave to go home tomorrow." Irina's eyes went from me to the table of produce just on our right. "Aren't these asparagus lovely?"

"Yes, they are," I said, hardly noticing the vegetables. My thoughts seemed to enter a labyrinth, all narrow pathways with tall hedgerows. Yes, despite my brief lunar eclipse, my blood hummed over the possibility of my actually being published, becoming an author rather than merely someone who writes stories. But I hardly knew Irina if you got right down to it. She had seemed nice enough, together with true to the dissident movement, on her two previous visits in Peredelkino to spend time with her mother. During her last time here a few months ago, when I told her of my plans to circulate through samizdat in Moscow my novel, *My Long Journey Home*, as well as Pasternak's *Doctor Zhivago*, she had insisted on taking a copy of each book to do the same with in Leningrad. I had agreed because, after all, she was Olga's daughter, and all of my literary contacts happened to be in Moscow. Had I been too hasty, overly credulous of Irina? Could it be she was jealous of my and Olga's closeness and wanted me out of her mother's apartment, seeing me as some sort of thief of her daughterhood, or the like, or something completely different of which I had no inkling? Irina had from the start seemed a bit, not quite stiff, but you could say demure with me as compared to the way she forthrightly got along with Olga. And hadn't Irina been almost a little too eager in letting me drop the discussion for now while also pushing for an answer before she left? Still, all in all my instincts told me she was simply trying to help out a writer whom she liked the work of. Who knew, though? Not to be overly prudish or reckless, I mean, years had passed and Stalin had died, but my status as a potential or actual threat to the state followed me around like a shadow impervious to the dark of night. Even so, of course, I had come to believe I was safe in Peredelkino as well as when staying with a few people who had been dear friends of Solomon's in Moscow, but there was no way before today I would've traveled to places where Stalinist holdovers with grudges to settle—and there were plenty of them scattered all across the country in Khrushchev's regime—could get their hands on me without any of my close comrades around to keep them at least a little honest. Call it paranoia if you like, latent retribution such as this happened each and every day in Russia. The purges had ended, though not the misuse of gulags for holding political prisoners. But then I had to admit, it made some sort of sense for this d'Angelo to arrange a clandestine meeting. Getting my manuscript out of Russia would be a feat, indeed. The Foreign Affairs Ministry or whoever controlled this kind of thing wouldn't in a million years willingly let it happen. Not even Pasternak himself could get something like that approved for his own work, much less mine. I'd never heard of it happening since the revolution with any Russian's literary work. Not once. Besides, just face the facts, on my two trips to Moscow to generate interest for my and Pasternak's novels through samizdat, I hadn't come up with a sole literary critic willing to give either manuscript so much as a casual read. Dissident scholars and poets and artists in the coffee shops could hardly put the books down once they got their copies, taking to them like they did to good vodka. Although other of my and Pasternak's friends who were close to publishers ran too big a risk of being sent off to the gulags for trying to get into bound print these manuscripts state censors had already shaken their fingers at through those *Novy Mir* rejections. How to blame them, really? What's more, I had come to terms with this limited success of only our comrades reading the books—that was good, you know, the most joy came from writing them, and all—until this fine early afternoon, here, walking the aisles of the produce market with Irina. Come to think of it, she had maneuvered me out of the apartment with Olga so we could talk alone, safely in a public place. Did she not trust her mother, or was she protecting her from potentially hot information Olga didn't need to have? Because if she lacked faith in Olga, I would have nothing more to do with Irina on the subject of my book and, for that matter, on very little else.

We came upon a long table full of spices piled in mounds on platters: cardamom, saffron, nutmeg, cinnamon, vanilla, and others; the tangy intermingling with the softer, melodious aromas that went up my nose somehow emboldened me just enough more for doing what needed to come next in our conversation. We purchased our spices and placed the little paper bags half full of them in our knapsacks; then I asked her to accompany me to the perimeter of the market. Once we were a sufficient distance from others not to be overheard or eavesdropped on, I stopped and she followed suit. "Why'd you bring me here, away from the apartment and Olga, to talk about this Sergio d'Angelo?" I said, looking her directly in the eyes.

"Oh, that's simple, Mom would want Sergio to get the Italians to publish *Doctor Zhivago* ahead of your book. That's if she could stomach the thought of what may well happen to her and Pasternak if Sergio was actually successful."

"And what are your feelings about it?"

"I'm trying to convince you to publish instead of working through Olga to get to Boris Pasternak, yeah. I don't want my mother in harm's way any more than she already is as his mistress."

"Such a nice daughter, and thanks so much for thinking of what may come of little ole me, first or second in line."

"Oh, forgive me, of course if you go to Leningrad and your meeting with Sergio goes anywhere, then you, too, are in danger." A stream of her long, wavy brunette hair fell in front of her face, and with a hand she flipped it away, her eyes unwavering from mine. "I just thought you would be up for the ride."

It was as much the verve in which she tossed her hair out of the way, that sort of parched-mouthed thirst to keep our intense connection unbroken, as it was the clarity of her words, all the remnants of politesse suddenly gone, the way she treated Olga; this is what made me believe in Irina Ivinskaya. Finally, she and I were flying together, but I feared right into heavy wind shear. "I think my and Pasternak's books should be published come what may. But if you're right about Olga, I would agree with her on this: *Doctor Zhivago must* be first in line."

Irina shook her head. "Sergio will have nothing of that. He explicitly told me not to have you or Boris Pasternak waste your time on doing anything other than what he asks. It seems the Italian publisher he's representing will have it no other way than *My Long Journey Home* getting out first."

"And does this publishing house have a name?"

"He wouldn't divulge it."

"A real scholar and a comrade, huh." I wrinkled my nose as if something stunk. "I'm not entertaining one moment more some shadowy proposal that from its inception puts me, my soul, at odds with the man who taught me how to write, my muse. Besides, it simply makes no sense for whoever this publisher is to not first get the big-name Russian author's work into the hands of western readers before the nobody's. It isn't like my story is better than Pasternak's, just different."

"Sergio thought you would probably come to this decision, and if you did, he asked me to request that you bring with you to meet with him the original of Osip Mandelstam's poem 'The Stalin Epigram.'"

Gooseflesh rippled along my arms and legs, while something like black widow spiders crawled beneath my skin. The audacity of this Sergio to presume to know how I would respond! But he'd gotten me right, in fact, too accurately so. It was as if he knew something at my core... And then what of the poem? I hadn't told anyone other than Pasternak and Olga about still having possession of "The Stalin Epigram," though, to be completely honest, below the spiders, in my blood flowing like river rapids, there was this other truth: Oleg would know in his heart I never let that poem go, should he still be alive. "Of course, d'Angelo didn't tell you why this poem was so important to him," I said at last, ignoring her implying the meeting would occur as if some foregone conclusion.

"No, he didn't say." She held up a hand. "I just figured any number of Italian communist dissidents would love to have the original of the poem that got under Stalin's skin the most of all."

"Why would d'Angelo or you ever think I have the poem?"

"Anyone who cares to knows Osip Mandelstam had been with his son, Oleg, and you just before being taken away to the gulags for the final time. You are Oleg's wife, really, Katya; if the original still exists, who else would have it now?"

Irina's expression remained intense and clear, in short, unwaveringly authentic. I appreciated that she referred to me as Oleg's wife, not his straw widow. "And d'Angelo is just the kind of operator who would test this theory out if I turned him down," I said, just when a plump magpie alighted on a nearby maple tree's branch and began squawking, almost as if d'Angelo's pesky spirit had suddenly arrived to defend itself. The bird didn't seem to have any intention of relenting, so I lifted my voice as I went on. "I mean, at that point, what does the guy have to lose?"

"Good thinking. I think, in the flesh, Sergio does seem sort of smooth, but not a bad guy, Katya." Pausing, Irina seemed to take measure of me. "I do hope you at least come to Leningrad and see for yourself, make a more informed decision what kind of person he is. Your book is too, well, necessary not to get published because you simply didn't show up. Besides, in the long run you would also be helping Pasternak."

"You're right as much as wrong, Irina."

She tilted her head inquisitively.

"I'm going to Leningrad, but I will help Pasternak in the short run."

"How on earth so?"

"By not agreeing to work with control freaks."

The furrows in her brow became even more noticeable.

"Come along, Irina, if you'd like. I'm going to talk with Pasternak."

"Right now, at his dacha?"

"No better time than the present. Of course, I'll understand if you want to pass. Miss Zinaida does have some pretty nasty claws when they're extended. And all this may bring out the beast in her, if you know what I'm getting at." This was an allusion to not only the publishing discussion but also Pasternak's mistress's daughter showing up anywhere near the dacha.

Irina's slim, savvy smile told me she understood this jungle ahead, that we would pass through its lush green edge into darkness just on the off chance of finding a little light in a swarm of fireflies or, perhaps, by rubbing sticks together to make a fire.

"You'll mess things up for yourself and Pasternak," she said.

"I have no intention of doing anything of the kind."

Not allowing a beat for yet another retort, I turned and headed for the dacha, with her at my side. On taking each and every one of our steps without further protestations, Irina more and more became my friend.

The summer sun and thick air made the windows across the front of the dacha perspire. Right as I went to knock on the front door with Irina at my shoulder, another magpie lit on a windowsill, or was it the same bird from the outdoor market? It turned halfway around and looked at me, the tips of its tail feathers whisking across the glass, which in their wake made this translucent arc, a colorless rainbow. Yes, for what lay just ahead, it would be up to us to add the spectral colors. Otherwise, we were bound to stay in some alternate reality of only blacks and whites, as stark as every magpie's ever hatched two-tone-ness, those dove's and crow's feathers all in one creature. An impossible convergence if it weren't for this obnoxious species proving us wrong. The thing of it was, almost eerily, for this one rare encounter, a magpie refrained when near humans from cawing its head off. Irina began raising an arm as if to shoo the bird but, with a frown from me, pulled up short. Somehow all three of us were in this together. At last, I rapped on the door using a knuckle.

Miss Zinaida opened it wide and stood in the middle of the entrance, as though the girth of her whole body was a turret in front of the castle called Pasternak. "What brings you here?" she said to me almost brusquely, then eyed Irina with this incredulous expression.

"Through disseminating my and Pasternak's manuscripts as samizdat, there's something a-brew on getting them published," I said.

"I see." Miss Zinaida's eyes flared as if with genuine interest, though she didn't budge from the doorway. She looked at Irina again. "And you are?"

Irina straightened her spine. "I'm Olga's daughter, Irina."

Miss Zinaida's face fell sallow and yet her eyes blazed, another improbable convergence. "No, no…not here, you don't just have your way at this house." Her voice sort of crackled, as if the words came from some radio with terrible reception. She began closing the door in our faces.

"It's Irina's contact who's willing to publish our books," I said rapidly.

The door stopped, leaving a space wide enough to see only Miss Zinaida's red eyes and pulsating nostrils.

Irina shot me an icy look that the door kept from Miss Zinaida.

Okay, I was being liberal with the truth while not telling a lie. What have you, I felt badly for Irina, but there was nothing I could do to soothe her just now.

"She didn't want to impose herself on you or Pasternak," I went on. "I talked her into coming because without her involvement there is no *Doctor Zhivago* in print, unless you and Pasternak have got some other publisher lined up."

"Oooooh, sometimes I hate my life," Miss Zinaida sort of groaned.

"Months go by where I can't stand mine either," Irina said into the door.

As if being stalked by a cat ready to pounce from high grass, I made sure not to lock eyes with Miss Zinaida and possibly incite her further. Maybe the door opened a hair, I couldn't be certain.

"What's all the ruckus?" It was Pasternak's voice from behind Miss Zinaida.

The door opened wide again and Miss Zinaida said to Pasternak, "Your mistress's daughter...for all I know she's yours together, thinks she can get you published. Her name's Irina if you don't already know, Boris." Miss Zinaida made an arm motion as if ushering a princess into some Czarist ball of the past. "Do come in, dear, oh, and by all means, you too, Katya."

Now it was Pasternak with an odd convergence, his expression screwing up as if he was the cat's prey under attack, while his mellow brown eyes may as well have been looking on some newly born kitten. "It's nice to see you again, Irina, please, do come in, the both of you," he said without any of Miss Zinaida's dripping sarcasm.

Just as we walked inside, I gave the magpie a wink. Holding fast, maybe even still looking at me, or over my shoulder at the silvery, sun-faded grounds for a dragonfly or some such to snatch right out the air, dinner, this crow/dove made not a peep, nor flew away. A quick lift of a foot against its feathery underside to stand on one leg and that was all.

Pasternak led Irina and I, with Miss Zinaida in tow, toward his writing studio. He asked Irina and I whether either of us cared for a glass of water or tea and we declined. As he sat down behind his desk, he gestured at the two chairs across from it while looking directly at Irina and me, not so subtle of a hint that Miss Zinaida give up the eagerness on this discussion and go about some other business, for there wasn't another chair in the studio. Not much of a bother, Miss Zinaida nimbly went and got a chair out of her sewing room. In little more than a flash, she sat in this chair next to me, Irina on the other side of me. A glance at Irina, who sat there almost elegantly erect with her hands folded one atop the other in her lap, told me she was a much cooler customer than myself. I squirmed. Pasternak's eyes went from me to her, then back at me. It was my move.

"It's about getting both our books published in the West, starting with Italy and going from there," I said.

Pasternak's brow knitted. Twisting in his chair, he looked absently out the window.

"One of Irina's acquaintances through samizdat in Leningrad is secretly trying to find just the right Russian works to smuggle out of Russia, I'm afraid," I forged ahead. "His name's Sergio d'Angelo, an Italian Trotskyite communist it looks like. He wants to start with *Doctor Zhivago* and *My Long Journey Home*."

Irina shot me another cold glance.

At least she didn't correct the order in which I'd presented the books. Not yet, anyway.

"I don't know, Katya," Pasternak finally said, without looking away from the window. "Assuming everything that needs assuming is fine, this is a capable and reputable publisher…" His voice tapered off, and then he looked me directly in the eyes. "I wrote my book for Russia."

"It seems the only way to get the kind of work we do to our comrades is to have it come back in from the outside," I said.

He nodded thoughtfully, sadly.

"Don't listen to that tripe, Boris," Miss Zinaida said. "This would mean ruination. Our entire family could end up in the gulags."

I fixed my eyes on her. "Don't forget me, and Irina, and Olga." The words just came; I couldn't help myself.

Miss Zinaida's cheeks flushed crimson, as if just beneath the surface, she ached to lash out with an "I couldn't care less about the three of you," but knew if she did, Pasternak may well pursue this opportunity—or life prison sentence—on indignation alone.

"They want to publish my book first, but I won't hear of it," I continued with Pasternak. "*Doctor Zhivago* has the best chance of getting back to Russia in a big way."

He nodded again.

"She's just using you as a guinea pig, Boris!" Miss Zinaida fired. "Let her be the guinea pig, for Christ's sake!"

"We may only get one chance at it," Irina said.

Was this Irina's own righteous anger trumping her heretofore meticulous logic? Whatever the case, thank the saints in heaven. It was time to shut up for a while. Let things sink in.

The longer we sat there without more words exchanged, the better I felt about Pasternak, who had quit with the distant eyes and was right here in the room with our probable history in the making; though, all the while, the worse Miss Zinaida got, pacing behind our chairs and wringing her hands.

She stopped walking and looked poisoned darts at Pasternak. "I'm calling Olga to find out just how she feels about this suicide mission."

He recoiled in the chair as though taking direct hits. "I…ah…didn't know you had her phone number."

The convolutions people say at times like this, I told myself.

"There're plenty of things the genius writer is shielded from," Miss Zinaida said.

Pasternak pushed himself away from the desk and stood up. He looked darkly over his eyebrows at Miss Zinaida. "Please let me be the first to talk with Olga about this."

"Not on your life!" Miss Zinaida walked out of the room. In seconds you could hear the clicks of the rotary dial coming from the phone-nook in the hallway.

Pasternak stood there fragile and steadfast, like Michelangelo's marble David, which at any moment could melt, turning into an ice sculpture if subjected to more direct summer heat. Just open a window and it would undoubtedly happen, I couldn't help but think, along with the onset of the magpie's incessant cawing. An electric fan in the corner of the study miserably cooled us.

As we listened, every bit the wet-lipped, lurid eavesdroppers, to Miss Zinaida fervidly and, in a way, dancing along the edge of a cliff while discussing the life-and-death stakes with Olga should Pasternak allow *Doctor Zhivago* smuggled out of Russia for publication in Italy, it became obvious Miss Zinaida was too wizened to dare disparage myself or Irina in building a bridge across those two women's own personal chasm.

"Yes, I thought we would agree on this," Miss Zinaida said. Then, "Uh, huh, right, Irina and Katya are in with Boris now trying to talk him into it; of course, those young women believe in their literary cause, so you have to admire them, but not let them have their way under any conditions whatsoever."

Placing his hands on his writing desk, Pasternak guided himself back into his chair. He looked at Irina for a long moment and then he and I, with intent and wanting eyes, stared each other down. Not a word was uttered between us and, noticeably, we didn't once blink.

"Yes, a perfectly wonderful idea, Olga," Miss Zinaida said. "I'll drive over and get you right away. Bye."

You could hear the phone all but slammed down into its cradle. There were footsteps on the wood flooring, followed by the back door being opened and shut. Finally, the car groaned to life and then backed out of the driveway, its tires crunching over flint and dirt.

Olga had been after Pasternak to buy a car for her use at the apartment, and until this moment I had not found myself in any way pleased with him ignoring the request. At least for that we would have a little more time alone to hash this out.

Breaking away from our stare, I looked out the window and through the sweaty glass the blue sedan heading along the road into town appeared to be something alive, big and hairy, a water buffalo or perhaps a cow, until it quickly passed through a remnant of the translucent rainbow like a shiny sapphire jewel flaunted in front of peasants. That blasted magpie, still perched on the windowsill, seemed little more than a shadow with two shades of gray.

"How much do you love my mother, Boris Pasternak?" Irina said. "And don't pass me so much as an ounce of dung."

I looked at her, and she held on to the arms of her chair tightly, her eyes boring into Pasternak's.

"As much as any man can love a woman," he said unwaveringly.

"Then you must make your decision before she and your wife return," Irina said. "Even though she wants to be Zinaida's ally in this, my mother will not be able to withstand it. She loves you too much. End this dreadful argument between them before it starts, please."

"You're fortunately as well as regrettably probably right; I'll do my best." Pasternak keenly met my eyes again. "How do you feel about me taking the initial opportunity away from you, really, Katya? Even if this is possible."

"I accept the likelihood you'll pave the way for me far better than I could ever do so for you, and I'm not talking here about either of us being any sort of guinea pig."

"Who gets to publish, who gets to perish as an enemy of the state?" Pasternak massaged his temples.

But there was more about this going first that wedged itself in my mind, something Irina had said: *We may only get one chance at it.* Of course, she was correct; the risks were myriad for failure, most everything having to go right to pull off even one publishing success, much less two back to back that came out of Russia this way. It still made absolutely no sense why d'Angelo had insisted I inaugurate things. That's when this other thought blew in like a gale force wind: *Without knowing it, could Irina have been talking about me as much as Pasternak's or my books?* I pondered this from every angle I could think of. "We can both go first, I'm sure of it," I said at last.

"What now?" Irina said almost derisively. "There is my trust and, well, pride of reputation with Sergio I would appreciate you not walking over quite so happily."

Pasternak may have let out a slit of a smile or a tiny grimace, I couldn't tell which.

"Hear me out on something, please." Yes, it was my turn to stiffen my spine. "Sergio d'Angelo asked for me to bring the original of 'The Stalin Epigram' to Leningrad; you know that, Irina, but Pasternak doesn't. Anyway, earlier Irina and I had surmised any self-respecting Italian communist publisher would love to get the poem as booty in dealing with me, so why not float the idea if you're Sergio? But from the trail of our conversation, now I'm convinced there's more to it than this.

"Through d'Angelo Oleg is sending me a message that he's alive!"

CHAPTER THIRTY-THREE

With this feeling Katya and Oleg had become permanent parts of her inner being, Margaret placed facedown on the rest of the manuscript the final page of Nana/Alice Mandelstam/Mandt's novel *My Long Journey Home.* Her love for Frazier was as timeless as Katya's was for Oleg and Solomon, or Pasternak's for Miss Zinaida and Olga or, while she was at it, Yuri Zhivago's for Tonya and Lara, wasn't that so? At least Margaret wanted it to be, and, at the same time, she harbored resentment over Oleg, lost to war, the gulags and foreign exile, or not, aware of the affair, or oblivious, every living moment having to share Katya's heart with Solomon Mikhoels, and Miss Zinaida doing the same with Pasternak and Olga—Tonya with Yuri and Lara—just as Frazier shared his heart with Anastasie Moreau…though spared his body…probably, so far, anyway… God, Margaret was glad the French artist lived far away. A hardly noticeable pang of guilt landed in the pit of her stomach that she preferred denying, though couldn't, not entirely.

Who were more tormented, the ones having the affairs or their betrayed? Which were more animated to press on and unabashedly live their convictions, to create their art, write their books, as well as, yes, tend the gardens of their households, their souls? She got out of bed and walked over to a window, then pulled the string that raised the blinds. Tilting her head upward, she looked for the moon, but the night sky was all faded into an artificial gloaming by the lights of New York City that obscured celestial bodies, cheated Margaret of the universe. A glance at the Boze clock/radio/CD player beside the manuscript on the bedside table told her it was 3:37 a.m. She simply wasn't used to sleeping without Frazier next to her, and had little desire to kick the insomnia. That would be too comfortable, too numb to them, their marriage. If it weren't for Mattie and Doug, she'd head down to Occupy Wall Street at Zuccotti Park and join Frazier right now. What a thought, because everything she did or didn't do in some way or another almost always came around to the kids, tending the garden she and Frazier had tilled throughout everything else, or they too often "slumbered" through, as Frazier called it, letting their family go to weed.

When would Frazier buy some appropriate eyeglasses? When would she get off the Paxil? As soon as Margaret asked herself these questions, they seemed the wrong ones. How could she and Frazier, without ruining what they had together, keep muses in their lives to avoid thicker lenses, stronger doses? Now that was the infuriatingly better subject to explore, just like all those wonderful characters in Nana's novel had done at their own fulfillment together with peril, not much differently than the way she and Frazier were stumbling toward together as well as apart. She walked back over to the bed, turned the reading lamp off, and then lay down on Frazier's side of the mattress, placing her head on his untainted pillow.

On closing her eyes she almost immediately pictured Frazier all bunged up after she got him out of jail for his civil disobedience at the BofA protest; then her mind's eye flashed on the news clip she'd seen of Occupy Wall Street protestors getting pepper-sprayed directly in their faces while corralled behind orange police tape. Why this head-trip of tough outcomes now, in the middle of the night? Was Frazier all right? It made no logical sense, but Margaret felt something changing between her and Frazier, something not necessarily bad or good but, nonetheless, powerful enough for her to sit upright along with switching a light on again. She scooted over on her side of the bed and picked up off the nightstand her iPhone. She had checked it earlier several times, and still no calls or texts had come in from Frazier since the one late afternoon that he'd let her know of being at Zuccotti Park. She hesitated on dialing his number, as he would surely be pissed getting awakened at this hour for nothing other than her anxious whim. By her stars, there was good cause, though; Margaret knew this as much as she knew *My Long Journey Home* to be an outstanding literary work, even if it happened her reasoning couldn't be put into words. *Dial him before you change your mind again*, she told herself, and then did just that. On the first ring, his phone answered and sent her to his voice mail greeting, a sure sign that he had turned it off. She left a short message asking him to call her, that she simply couldn't sleep and wanted to hear his voice, not giving anything away about her intuition. She took more than a little pride in the fact that she hadn't lambasted him for having his iPhone shut down in the event of an emergency with her or the kids. Cha-ching for Dr. Buttertart's efforts to chill her out some. Margaret could take care of herself and the kids just fine one night alone, thank you. Okay, fine enough, she'd already made friends, if you will, with her sleeplessness, so why not do something hair-raisingly courageous, one of the worst and best things a writer could possibly do: put a really great manuscript such as Nana's up against some of her own work, compare, cry, and learn or, with a little luck, lull herself into heavy eyelids.

She took the manuscript with her into her and Frazier's study, then sat down at her desk. In seconds Margaret brought up on the laptop's screen her severely unfinished work of fiction more than loosely based on the poets Yassine Lotfi Khaled, Mohammed al-Ajami, the TMZ, and, as odd as it was spine tingling, what it had in common with Nana's manuscript: the role of dissident poetry in peoples' movements. No, in the big picture the fruit hadn't fallen far from the tree, she thought. But Nana's words flowed like tributaries into rivers that went to the sea, and came back as big drops of clear rain from thunderheads, washing things clean, muddying others, as if touches from some she-god herself. It wasn't that Margaret's writing fell less than poetic or insufficiently layered for opening your mind to questions beyond the text. It gave as much room as Nana's for reading between the lines. In certain passages Margaret's terse, to the point, progression both excited and moved the reader where she intended taking you. There could be no sidestepping, nevertheless, something went missing from her work that hadn't been lacking as much from the recent collaborative article with Frazier. Now she made a couple more clicks on her finger pad and brought up on the screen beside her manuscript the piece she'd written with Frazier about the nonfiction goings-on with these same poets and the burgeoning Arab Spring. She bit her lip. As far as she knew, Yassine Lotfi Khaled had since the successful revolution in Tunisia resurfaced there safe and sound, whereas Mohammed al-Ajami remained in the underground of his home country Qatar, tentative as she understood this protection to be from checking with sources through Harpers and a friend of hers at the *New York Times*, as well as with, yes, how could you avoid him, really? the one and only Buckminster Ross himself.

As she read her and Frazier's joint article, it was almost as if she were taking it in with new eyes. His prose had the freedom and easy diversity with point of view similar to Nana's and all his own, them getting inside their characters as though inhabiting their minds, sharing hardships along with joys in their skin. Until now Margaret had thought his metaphors, nuanced parables, and earthy sense of humor were simply God-given gifts which she somehow lacked, but that wasn't close to being right. In this article she had opened some inner gate at least a little way, through which her writing crossed the tight boundary of her safety zone, expanded, wandered with purpose beyond her capabilities, and with that came no small amount of Hemingway-esque poetry. Before this piece the only thing her writing had had in common with the great writer was his macho terseness, sadly, without the freedom he allowed himself; thus, it all too often came off, for lack of a better word, bitchy. She could admit this to herself now because of the feeling that Nana's literary blood flowed through her veins. It wasn't just the others who were poets. Margaret Valarie Mandt held the sinew and sonorousness of a Mandelstam! All she needed to do was keep the gate open, walk through it herself as well as with her writing. Damn, that was a scary thought.

She closed the file on her and Frazier's article, leaving only her untitled manuscript on the laptop's screen. For a long moment she placed her open hand atop *My Long Journey Home*, which sat right next to her computer, as if channeling Nana's spirit off those pages into, not her mind really, more like her entire body. Her head took on a fullness without words or ideas, what would've been called overwhelm brought on by the insomnia, but this wasn't open to some sort of armchair diagnosis. Frazier and Alice and Oleg Mandelstam—aka Nana and Grandpa Mandt—their essences as artists dwelled inside her now, nothing given away to Kalliope of prose, Euterpe of poetry, Terpsikhore of song and dance; yet, inexplicably, they all melded together as Margaret, her own muse.

She created a new file named Rewrite, then placed a copy of her manuscript into it. Without thinking too much, she began typing:

> *At first, the work of the poet Yassine Lotfi Khaled seemed nothing more than another routine editing project, but only because of my antiseptic humanity. The real article was right there inside me, an in-patient at the lightless hospital that smelled of alcohol and safe distances of which I'd checked my soul into. Little did I know in helping this poet stay free, I would be freeing myself.*

Yes, wonderful, these were Margaret's opening sentences now. Who knew where the words came from and why care? They fell onto the page messily and true. She shivered inwardly with knowing they were exactly the right ones.

As she went on, reading and deleting and adding to her story, along with sparingly using the urbane metaphor, only when nothing else would bring the depth of understanding or feeling home—such things as ice or steel or concrete of the frozen, immovable, imperial interspersed with parched desert sand and oases of nonviolent revolution—with all this Margaret swung the gate of her literary pen open wider. Every now and then she caught herself stiffly writing word by word, or going over and over a sentence before giving herself permission to put the next thought down, and, the beauty of it, she would take long breaths and exhale them slowly, all the while keeping a hand again on Nana's *My Long Journey Home*, that is, until she felt more daylight reappear between the gate and the fence. Then she'd once more let the words flow, okay, to be perfectly honest, not as freely as Nana's writing seemed, though surely well enough to get a smile of her grandmother's from somewhere on the far side of the morning sun now rising over the tops of buildings outside Margaret's window. As time went on and the number of rewritten pages mounted, she found herself aching for more clarity and depth in this jangly elegance of words, the kind, if not of similar style, Frazier and Alice had in their writing. Not to fret overly much, this happened to be the most marvelously exhilarating literary misery she'd ever experienced. Looking through the window at the purple dawning as if with orange hippie fringe along the hemline of a sixties sarong, Margaret said out loud, "Please show me more."

Instead, the alarm clock in her bedroom sounded. With a satisfied smile at her manuscript while working the finger pad, she shut down the file, then got up and walked away from her laptop and Nana's novel.

"Mattie, Doug, it's time to get moving," she called out in the hallway outside the kids' doors. Right when she made it into the bedroom and tapped the button to desist the alarm's all too obnoxiously soothing chime, Margaret heard the front door open. Thank heavens Frazier had come home. More than a little she missed him, wanted to talk with him about her writing, could use some help getting the kids to school, and not to be misunderstood, Margaret felt lifted by Frazier having improvised this overnighter at Occupy Wall Street, a non-slumbering activity par excellence.

Without delay she walked from the bedroom and headed along the hallway toward the foyer. Stopping in the doorway, she first noticed Frazier's new eyeglasses, John Lennon lookalikes; then, to be expected, there were his crumply, slept-in clothes and disheveled hair. His expression had fallen almost waxen. In short, he looked like hell warmed over, a twenty-first century dissident against The Man. She felt tempted to compliment him on giving his drug of choice—those fake reading spectacles—a rest, but wanted to let him bring that news on his own terms, just as she wouldn't want him going all starry-eyed should she pass on a Paxil refill. Oddly, he simply stood there. She went over to him and gave him a kiss on the lips, which also strangely seemed tight-lipped. Then again, Margaret could easily cut the boy some slack; he may have been through more than one would know at the protest site.

"How did things go out there?" she said.

ᘓ

"Inspiring, truly. The whole place feels like participatory democracy as it probably was practiced when they invented it in Athens, Greece, only better. That was a men's-only public square. This one has everybody in it." *Fabulous, I somehow got that done despite this frigging pit in my stomach.*

Of course what he had to say was hopeful, but his tone didn't match the message; the word *bedraggled* came into Margaret's mind. "Is something wrong, Frazier?"

Bull crap on Monty Python himself. She just had to ask that, didn't she? There would be no lying for Frazier; he was up for withholding the grisly truth about certain things, although with no out-and-out tossing away the integrity he and Margaret had managed to erect into something like a seemingly fine and, for the most part, sturdy house—unless you knew where the fissures in its foundation were. "Yes," he said flatly.

"I knew something happened to you; it came almost like a premonition in the middle of the night." She now looked on him knowingly as well as with concern. "Did the police move on the encampment? They didn't rough you up again, did they?"

He shook his head. "Nothing like that."

She placed a hand gently on the side of his face. "What happened, Frazier?"

Okay, here came the harder part for him, deciding which debacle to go into: meeting up with Anastasie Moreau again, quitting his job at Flying Pens, or the heartbreaking phone call he had received just this morning from his sister Felicia in Texas. Surely all of it would have to come out soon enough, though the wizened innocence, some kind of reclaimed freshness he'd never quite seen before with such unrestrained openness in Margaret's clear-eyed expression gave him even more pause than, how to put this? the already notable quantity he had entered the apartment with. If more of the time she met him with this what? absence of conditions? he felt coming his way right now, then maybe he would've quit his job long ago to write full time and could stay away from Anastasie enough not to move into Zuccotti Park and share a tent with her. Margaret's countenance was, quite frankly, almost eerily similar to Anastasie's when she had let him know it was okay if he needed to dip back into slumbering now and then. The pit in his stomach began changing from black guilt to the blues, some kind of enlightened sadness, could it possibly be, with him and Margaret moving away from rights and wrongs, toward something that needed exploring more, going for whatever in all its nebulousness this was between them? Perhaps it would be better to deal with other people's problems for the next bit, and, if lucky, in the process he and Margaret might gain a little more confidence some of the scales shrouding their inner eyes were falling away. Or was he merely throwing some last-minute Hail Mary to try and save them…make that him? With him having had right out of the blue not come home, maybe she'd simply taken an extra Paxil or three to help her into the day and happened to fall upon the perfect dosage, if only it weren't so damned unsustainable. What is more, this stuff about Margaret experiencing some sort of portent, quite possibly around the time he'd let Anastasie in the bedroll with him, refused to leave Frazier alone; yes, it was freaky, in spades.

"Felicia and Derek's ranch has been foreclosed on," he said at last.

"What!" Crow's-feet cut further into the sides of her head while she lowered her hand from his face. "Are they out of their place already?"

He nodded. "They have all moved in with Mom and Dad."

"In your folks' little place—and don't get me wrong, it's a nice place—they must all be on top of each other."

"Felicia and Derek are planning on getting an apartment soon. He's taken a job with the bank's property management subsidiary to help keep the ranch going until it gets sold off. Felicia told me the job is the one good thing that came from pressing their banker publicly with your article and the coverage it brought to their situation for a while." He chuckled morosely. "A damn humiliating concession to offer Derek if you ask me."

✄

"Yes, it certainly was, those bankster bastards." Margaret felt helpless, a foreign country she'd rarely allowed herself to visit, but it was as though everything that had brought her to this moment, not the least of which being Nana's *My Long Journey Home* newly on her soul, imbued her with an almost crazily inverted strength flowing from some black well of weakness. For the first time in her memory, she could actually refuse herself taking a fast train back to familiar territory, the allusion of power. Besides, it unfortunately was too late to help Felicia and Derek. "But we got them hooked up with a great attorney for their promise to keep us informed before anything bad happened. These things take time, Frazier. Why didn't they let us know something earlier?"

✄

Frazier both hated and loved Margaret's lionhearted tenacity, probably because he wished he had more of it himself, and it was still there in her, don't get this wrong, but her tone held something novel in its intense yet measured quality, maybe less expectation of meddling in other people's business. "Texan pride, pure and simple."

"Well, okay, then, I respect their Texas pride. It makes me want to get over to Occupy Wall Street with you as soon as I can and protest on behalf of Felicia, Derek, Dwight, and Johnny, as well as all of us other ninety-nine percenters."

Frazier's face fell hot and clammy. He wanted Margaret by his side at Zuccotti Park, and he wanted Anastasie there too. Unacceptable to let happen, though probably inevitable. To make things worse yet in another way better, Margaret was right: Such a heartless act perpetrated on his sister's family rendered everything being protested against—nothing left to call it other than out-of-control big capitalism—all the more worth going out into the streets for change. It had become personal irrevocably, in real time, now. "You've got a good point there," he said, sort of off key.

"It's more like a passion." She tilted her head. "There's something more, isn't there, Frazier?"

He nodded slowly. "Maybe we should sit down for this."

✑

With her thoughts searching for possibilities, though arriving at nothing for what was coming next, other than maybe something to do with Frazier's obvious decision to change the way he looked, or make that hadn't looked, at things going on around him, Margaret said, "Okay, but it would probably be a good idea to get the kids some breakfast first." She needed time to think, or settle down some, or slip herself another Paxil when Frazier wouldn't notice. As much as anything there was this rising umbrage over no longer being in the wee hours of the morning free flowing with her novel. By her stars, how had life gotten so complicated in such a few minutes?

✑

Speaking only of the unseasonable cold front that had moved across the city and a couple of other equally inane subjects, they fixed eggs over easy and toast with jam.

All the while Frazier inwardly fought against taking off his John Lennons and setting them on the countertop, just head into some willful, transparent slumbering with Margaret; but then, that wouldn't be slumbering at all. This dark art required deceit, hiding from the world without it knowing. Yes, regretfully, even if he wanted to put on his fake reading glasses, in this state of affairs, they were no longer useful. May as well take them from the eyeglass case in his pants pocket and toss them in the trash. On second thought, he wouldn't dare go that far, for there were other situations, many others he could hardly begin to think of, in which they may still come in handy. *Whatever.* Right now some inescapable experiment of intimacy with Margaret seemed the only way forward.

Once they got Mattie and Doug seated at the kitchen table, Margaret explained that she and Frazier needed to talk something through away from little ears, that the kids should take their time with breakfast and because of this an extra glass of OJ was in it for them this morning. With that Frazier led Margaret into their study. He shut the door, and then they sat down across from each other at their writing desks.

In an attempt to gather at least a modicum of composure and courage, Frazier cast his eyes downward at his desktop. His heart sort of aimlessly beat, as though looking for direction and him unable to provide much, if any, a coy atrial fibrillation. *That's how life outside of slumber really is*, he thought, remembering how things had been years ago before he'd fallen into the habit. You wanted to get yourself together but rarely seemed up to the task. It felt almost like this nightmarish déjà vu together with some new capacity to be more human and humane. No way he could've admitted this much to himself before being caught between Margaret and Anastasie or without having had read Alice Mandelstam's book of, perhaps at its most profound, the destinies of muses. At last, he looked at Margaret, who sat there with more youthful eyes than he'd expected, her crow's-feet all but unnoticeable, one of her hands atop some manuscript. On glancing at it, he recognized a part of the title not obscured by her fingers: ...*Journey Home*.

"Have you read your grandmother's book?"

"Every word of it."

Perhaps this was what he sensed new in Margaret, Alice Mandelstam's novel having a similar effect on her as it did on him. Sort of a conduit to authenticity, a river that flowed through a silent God filled with the waters of your frailty and strength, at once simple as well as complex, understanding, best of all forgiving. Of course, both of them had read great literature with the ability to reshape your life; the thing of it was, this book was part of Margaret's genomes, *and* it also, as if serendipitously, answered his letters to Anastasie, questions he'd never felt safe enough to pose to Margaret until, maybe, now. He went to talk but his words seemed to get stuck in phlegm, so Frazier cleared his throat before giving it another try. "I quit my job at Flying Pens."

Involuntarily Margaret's eyes widened like saucers, but she actually admired him for getting away from that office of endless dead ends. "It's going to be okay, Frazier." She pressed her hand down more firmly on Nana's manuscript. "Just like that?" Surprising herself, she didn't have to force this smile.

"Pretty much so."

She chuckled a tad nervously with fear over their future and hers. "It's good. You'll have time to write full time if you'd like."

He heard her right, didn't he? One gargantuan reason Frazier stopped writing after his third novel failed to get published was the pressure she had unwaveringly applied for him taking a "real job." "I thought I'd balance my work with some moneymaking freelance journalism, while getting going on my next novel whenever it comes together in my head and heart a bit more."

Partly she envied Frazier claiming his freedom, as Margaret was surely heading toward her own, just not quite so impetuously. No, that simply wasn't her way. "Well, you are married to one of the best creative nonfiction editors in the business." She pointed her thumb at herself. "I could help you get some of your articles in front of buyers for magazines and newspapers."

It was hard for him to keep his mouth from falling open. "You're on."

"Have any ideas for your first article?"

He couldn't tell which outweighed the other, his conviction to the Occupy Wall Street movement, or some almost nutty burgeoning desire to find out whether Margaret and Anastasie could be friends, muses together with him, leave sorting out the physical stuff for later. Although he hadn't given more than passing thought as to where to start before just these last few moments, there would be no turning away from his answer. "I'm considering a series of pieces on what it means to be a ninety-nine percenter willing to stay in Zuccotti Park and nonviolently go up against this beast we somewhere along the way turned into. The work would be highly individual and global at the same time, folks versus the machine. What do you think?"

                                                        ✍

"I love it." She meant this enough to want to do some of these type of stories herself. But that would be macking on his idea. No, it was time to find her own way as a wife and a writer. Besides, it would probably make her more mysterious to Frazier. And there was another thing tugging at her, something perhaps more necessary than following her initial instinct to get the kids in school, take the day off by calling in sick, and head to Occupy Wall Street with Frazier. She'd use one of her infirm days all right, but to pay Grandpa Mandt a visit for finding out what she needed to do to unloose herself more, so she could write a novel all the way through that flowed as well as the writing had gone earlier this morning, only without the stingy thinking parts. To do that she would need to be as unchained as Frazier, as free as Alice and Oleg Mandelstam. Right when she removed her hand from *My Long Journey Home*, a wave of insecurity washed over Margaret. "Will you get the kids to school this morning please?"

"Sure. You got something pressing at work?"

"No, I'm taking the day off to see if I can find my own story."

"Want to talk about it?"

She smiled shyly this time. "Maybe I'll pull a Hemingway and opt out of speaking of it before it's finished."

As though intrigued, he leaned forward in his chair. "Not to give your story's power away in the process of making it, huh?"

"Or you could say my power, what there is of it."

"There's plenty, and I feel it gaining momentum."

"Thanks, Frazier, I do too."

Without another word they stood up and walked next to each other. Margaret and Frazier kissed with a new kind of passion, their lips fitting familiarly, as titillating as any time they weren't simply going through the motions, which of course you did as married people. Another thing, this was even different than their detached, hungry sexual comings together; it had something more curved back on itself, this deep, almost still current of amorousness.

✒

As he watched her walk along the hallway toward their bedroom to get ready for her big day, Frazier dared entertain thoughts of a non-Paxil-taking Margaret as well as his fake reading glasses being forever enshrined inside some Dumpster. And he was glad as hell she wasn't coming with him to Zuccotti Park just yet.

"Mattie, Doug, let's go, you're getting the pleasure of your father escorting you to school this morning," he called out.

Frazier would come directly back home and take a shower, change clothes, put a few things to make it overnight in a backpack, get the tent he'd bought for his and Doug's camping trip to the Adirondacks over last spring break, and then head down to Occupy Wall Street. Maybe there would be space available for him to set up camp under that maple tree close to the library, near Anastasie. Perhaps the kids may find it fun to go to the protest for a while after the last of their classes let out. He knew in his bones something huge was about to change in his life—what exactly, Frazier had little idea of. It wasn't an ominous feeling.

✒

Margaret could hardly take her eyes off the lapis blue ceramic urn that once held Nana's ashes, still in its place over on the mantel above Grandpa Mandt's fireplace. Yellow and orange fingers of light sort of weirdly fondled the urn from a modest fire Grandpa Mandt already had going when she arrived just a few minutes ago on this chilly day in the final throes of morning. Ever since her grandmother's funeral more than six years ago, anytime Margaret had thought about this, which wasn't very often, she got pretty creeped out that Grandpa Mandt had brought home Nana's cremated remains and, when asked on rare occasions by some family member, he always refused to say where he'd released her ashes. It had seemed to Margaret just another of Grandpa Mandt's eccentric barriers with the rest of the family. However, as she sat here in the wingback chair covered by fabric swarming in colorful butterflies, which she knew to have been Nana's favorite chair, Margaret felt differently about the empty urn: Nana's spirit remained in her written words, not in her ashes. Alice Mandelstam/Mandt's prose as a reflection of her life was so sadly beautiful and personal, while also being adamantly challenging, Grandpa Mandt surely would have good reason not to share with nonbelievers of improvisational living the secret of her return to earth, if for no more than him finding it abhorrent to make public the final sanctification of his and Nana's kind of love, which somehow endured on its own strength rather than moral platitudes. All this in Margaret's mind and heart transformed the urn into simply some old vase that could use a good dusting. On looking at Grandpa Mandt, who sat a few feet away in his favorite chair also directed at an angle toward the fireplace, she noticed his eyes dart from her to his teacup, as if he was mildly embarrassed over having curiosity about her fixation on the urn. He'd been kind to sit there in silence while she inwardly worked things through some. In fact, he hadn't asked any questions when she called him early this morning to arrange coming here, or since she'd arrived, treating her to his unhesitating acceptance as well as warm hospitality even on such short notice, as if telling Margaret mostly without words, he was here for her in any way that could be helpful, and it was her move to make. "I read Nana's book," she said.

"I know."

"How?"

"You seem more comfortable in your skin than I can ever remember you being. Alice's book can have that effect on a good reader." He chuckled, immediately followed by a cough too weak for Margaret's liking. "Of course, an old man's memory isn't what it used to be."

Yeah, and you don't know about my little friend named Paxil. Margaret pushed such glibly dreary self-talk out of mind. All things considered, she was okay with herself for only taking the one pill this morning, no extras for this visit. "Thank you, Grandpa, and seeing those eyes of yours are as sharp as a hawk's, I get the sense your mind is clipping along in rather immaculate fashion."

They smiled knowingly at the same time, as though over Margaret making reference to the imagery Nana/Alice used in her book for Oleg's alert black eyes.

"Yes, well, anytime you've seen a raven on a tree branch or circling overhead, be sure it's been me keeping my eyes on you."

"I've felt as much, but you must know, I didn't trust you until very recently. I'm sorry, Grandpa Mandt."

Now they smiled a sad conspiracy, as if to let each other know the reason for this was clear: Poetry had skipped a generation in the Mandelstam/Mandt family. No need for an apology from her or him.

"You may ask me anything you'd like," Grandpa Mandt said, looking her directly in the eyes.

Margaret thoughtfully went for a sip of tea. On the way to Nantasket, while taking the subway, train, and taxi, she had gone through how to get into things with her grandfather, and she'd arrived at some questions about Nana's creative process: Had she written regularly or only when inspired; for what duration did she usually write when sitting down with her manuscript; had things flowed on the page better for her in the mornings or later in the day; perhaps was she a night owl; how close to Katya's longer periods away from writing had Nana's actually been; what sort of revisions she made on *My Long Journey Home*; did

Grandpa Mandt have those marked-up papers in the attic; would he share them with Margaret? Although, on all these questions she would like to have answers, Grandpa Mandt's hauntingly crisp expression told her she was being offered an invitation to fly higher above the treetops with this raven, who had star garnet eyes and possibly some version of the Holy Spirit coming along for the bargain. It was as if the light from the fireplace etched white glimmering crosses in Oleg Mandelstam's obsidian-colored irises. Grandpa Mandt's face, wizened by age spots along with a complex network of wrinkles, otherwise looked as she imagined the young Oleg when defending his father's unrelenting dissident loyalty to Pasternak in the book. She set her cup down in the saucer on the small table between her and Grandpa Mandt; then Margaret again met his eyes intently. "Anything, are you sure?" she said.

"Using a little discretion with unsavory details, yes."

She swallowed hard, then said, "What's up with those affairs you had with other women once you and Nana were here in the U.S.? I mean, after reading her book, I understand some things, but mostly I don't know how you could've let your behavior get that out of hand, or how she could've stomached it and stayed with you, much less continued to love you dearly, which there's no doubt in my mind she did."

"Perhaps real love comes when it wants and, just the same, leaves of its own accord." He looked over at the fire, and then stared distantly into it.

Margaret wanted to give her grandfather all the time he needed to locate what he was looking for inside himself. Somehow she felt whatever it was might just help her lose the negative fantasy she'd been having off and on since Frazier had come home from Occupy Wall Street no longer slumbering, which went like this: His new state of being could quite possibly make him no longer willing to lie in the weeds without his French artist, and instead, he'd look her up and become another version of Grandpa Mandt. Margaret said nothing, herself casting her eyes over at the humble little fire.

"Sometimes if you're lucky, love decides to stick around because of as well as despite yourselves," Grandpa Mandt finally said, without looking away from the flames.

"Would you please go a bit more into the 'because' and 'despite' parts of that?"

"Are specifics really much of a concern?"

"I have a feeling they'll help me open up, maybe not make mistakes I otherwise would."

For a while there were only the sounds of a few crackles from the fire and the whining wind moving past his bungalow.

"Love must be cultivated like a garden, written like poetry, painted like art, played like music." Grandpa Mandt once more looked at Margaret, this time with an almost boyish anguish taking over his expression. "Your grandmother did a better job of that than me."

She couldn't bring herself to ask for more, though felt sure she would benefit greatly from his hidden wisdom. The thing of it was, some kind of disparity in age—unassigned to years or chronology—between this wounded boy she saw in his eyes and the old man who could no longer do anything about having had inflicted that pain on himself and others, seemed too much to expect her grandfather to bear for very long. One way or the other, the art of love required no small amount of reading between the lines, and a certain amount of impassivity while you did so. *Indeed, the master is teaching the pupil, perhaps inside both of us*, Margaret thought, though not quite reasoned out actually, something better than that, call it what? divine improv? She reached across the little table between them toward the armrest and placed her hand over Grandpa Mandt's.

His eyes drifted down over at their hands. "I couldn't get my artwork out of the U.S. and into Russia, the only country it was created for. Once they gave us political asylum here, your grandmother and I were kept close watch over. At first I told myself it didn't matter, but it did; after a while I got severely depressed. I stopped painting and turned away from tending our crops." He glanced across the room seemingly at his bongos. "It felt like the only thing I had left to find my song with were those lambskins. I'm afraid that didn't prove to be enough to dance with the muse inside me exclusively, if you will, so I looked to other women, which isn't in itself a bad thing, unless you go too far too fast as I did. All told, I needed more poetry, not more women."

When Grandpa Mandt sort of placated the fact of having other women in his life, Margaret on reflex went to move her hand away from his, though caught herself before making that mistake. There was richness in the whole of what her grandfather had just said that resonated deeply, saved her from becoming too much the Comrade's daughter, shaped by the passed-over generation. "I need more poetry too, Grandpa."

"I thought you would come to that conclusion." He nodded as if congratulating himself as well as Margaret. "And I've got just the thing for you."

Amorphously hopeful, Margaret arched an eyebrow. "Yeah?"

"Quite." He slipped his hand from underneath hers, and then slowly pushed himself up out of his chair. "Come with me, please."

"I can hardly wait to see what you're up to," Margaret said while standing up.

With the chancy steps of an old man heading out with purpose, Grandpa

Mandt led her out of the den, then along the hallway and into his bedroom. He stopped just inside the doorway and gestured over toward the far side of his bed. "I had a young man who's a neighbor of mine bring it down from the attic after you said you were coming today."

Margaret saw nothing that rose above the edge of the mattress other than the wall and a bedside nightstand with a lamp on it.

"Go on, young lady, and see what of your grandmother's is yours now."

Almost breathlessly Margaret walked over and rounded the corner of the bed. Right there on the floor next to the wall, there it sat, this had to be it, Nana's Moskva typewriter! Cyrillic silver letters of the maker's name were centered on its black metal base. Margaret lowered onto her knees next to the typewriter. Most of the white characters on the keys had been worn all but illegible by Nana's fingertips, the П, А, ы, Н, О, and Х keys completely so. She felt along its casing, and then placed her fingers over the keys. Glancing at Grandpa Mandt, who was beaming, she said, "It's clean as a whistle."

"I wiped it down real good once the good fellow got it out of the attic."

Margaret depressed the Г key, then the Ф, both of which got stuck about halfway to the paper cylinder, just as they had in *My Long Journey Home*. On her pushing a little harder, they went all the way down with a couple of clacks, a kind of music she hoped to make plenty of in years to come. Yes, learning the Russian language well enough to write fluidly in it had just become a must-do. And what a gift Nana had given Margaret and Frazier anyway, by through the years having translated her manuscript into an English language version. She stood up and walked over next to Grandpa Mandt; then with tears rimming her eyes along with a lump in her throat, she hugged him like the very real and wonderful grandfather he was, something she hadn't done since early childhood, before the words "manic depression" meant anything to her, which the Comrade and Lydia sometimes used when talking about Grandpa Mandt. "Thank you, thank you so much," she managed, blinking back the stinging wetness. But it was no use. Her chest began trembling and her tears flowed. "I'm…sorry…Grandpa," she got out between sobs.

He kept her close for a little while longer, then placed a hand on each of her shoulders, gently separating them until their eyes met. "It's okay, dear."

"I know, but it doesn't feel that way."

"Yes, though tears are freeing for an artist. We have to know fathoms of sadness before we can know even higher joy. Without these things our art is tiny."

Margaret parted her lips into a slight smile. "And so are people."

He nodded by way of agreeing. "It takes time, believe you me. Go gently, especially when most everyone else is saying hurry up, and you'll not give your passion away."

She laughed almost blubbery, then winked. "I suppose then it may not be the best idea to ask whether you've got Nana's other manuscripts translated into the English, so I could read through them night and day till they're finished."

"That wouldn't be such a bad thing, but perhaps taking them in over time would allow you the room to change along with them. How should I put this? So you may more appreciate their ever-increasing arc of maturity and grace and courage." The elder tried to return her wink, but his eyelid got stuck about halfway down, sort of like the Moskva's Г and Ф keys had.

"Maybe I could read one of Nana's stories between each of my novels, that is, once they're actually written."

"A positively wonderful thought." Grandpa Mandt's eyes became shimmery again, though in a way Margaret couldn't tell whether it was from delight or some underlying sadness showing itself with a thin film of his own tears. "You can take Alice's books with you. They're up in the attic."

The thought came back around that Margaret had shortly after arriving here today, when dealing with the urn empty of her grandmother's remains: *Nana's spirit remained in her written words, not in her ashes.* Grandpa Mandt was offering to give up too much of his wife, even if her words rested quietly unread by Margaret somewhere in the attic above his bed or over his favorite chair or perhaps nearer where he ate his meals at the kitchen table. "How about this instead? I'll come borrow each book from you one at a time when I'm ready for them; then I won't be tempted to go on a binge and read them too soon. I know it'll be more trouble for you this way, but it'll be a big help to me. Besides, that way we could sit down together and talk about each of them to our hearts' content." She smiled warmly now.

"That would be lovely for us to do on all nine of Alice's novels." He gave Margaret a similar smile, though his lips quavered almost imperceptibly.

"I look forward to that, Grandpa."

Wonder mixed with some kind of woe entered the room like the unseasonably cold September wind, yet there were no windows open in the house, just in their hearts, as both of them could not avoid the truth that Grandpa Mandt would also become ashes before his and Margaret's new task was done.

"I have something to ask of you, Margaret, and I don't want you to feel any obligation to do it unless you feel participating would be good for you. Are you okay with this so far?"

His eyes had lost their wetness and so had Margaret's. They looked on each other solemnly, after the storms.

"Yes, we're doing fine," she said.

"Once I'm gone, would you spread my remains with Alice's?"

"It would be my great honor to do so."

For the longest time the two of them stood there wordlessly.

Margaret's entire body seemed to be a shoreline with gentle waves lapping one after another onto it, and then receding so deftly, there was no feeling of undertow.

"Good, then if you'll drive my old Buick and take me along with, I'll show you where this great event will occur." Grandpa Mandt broke the silence between them.

But Margaret could've easily stood there longer looking on her grandfather almost as if for the first time. "How long has your car been sitting in your garage without being taken out?"

"A couple, three years, I don't know."

"Do you think it'll start?"

"I crank the engine up once a week like clockwork. She'll be fine."

"Then where are the keys?"

He reached in his corduroy pants pocket and came out with them.

Margaret was a bit surprised when about thirty minutes later Grandpa Mandt directed her to turn the Buick onto a road heading inland, leaving Mattapoisett Harbor and the seacoast behind. She would be fine with her ashes strewn into these beautiful waters, and felt Nana could've easily requested the same of Grandpa Mandt for her remains. This incorrect leaning gave Margaret pause, not because she'd gotten it wrong, rather over her completely lacking some sacrosanct place; nowhere came to mind for her ashes to be scattered. Most any nice spot would do. The entire universe was God's, but which little corner of it would she eternally cozy up with? Was that even so important? Margaret inquired these things of herself without any answers coming. She escaped this inner circumlocution by asking Grandpa Mandt those questions about Nana's writing process she'd come up with this morning on the way out to Nantasket. He offered what responses he could, finally explaining that Alice over the years had become increasingly protective of how she went about creating art. This actually picked Margaret's spirits up quite well, for she, not unlike Nana, had in fact turned more judicious with Frazier over talking about rewrites of her novel. It made her someone with more distinct definition, she reasoned, less bound by other's expectations, perhaps even a little closer to the sacred, if not with a preferred physical location for this practice just yet.

More and more as they drove on, something else didn't seem right to Margaret. The fancily fenced estates with sprawling manicured grounds kept getting grander, this being the territory of hedge fund managers and corporate moguls, not an area she could imagine Nana would have had anything to do with. She glanced over at Grandpa Mandt in the passenger seat beside her, wondering whether the old fellow's mental faculties were a tad confused and they had gone off course. As she opened her mouth to make a carefully worded inquiry of the sort, he gestured ahead to the right.

"Turn just up there on Ostrich Foot Road."

Grandpa Mandt seemed so confident, which in a way added to Margaret's confusion. While making the turn, she said, "What ever intrigued Nana enough to want to have her ashes left in this neighborhood?" Immediately, she wanted to take back the almost pejorative "ever." Grandpa Mandt surely didn't need to be put through any of her emotional gymnastics.

"Alice sometimes liked to bring the rich and the rest of us together in the most infuriatingly wonderful ways." Grandpa Mandt playfully rapped a few bongo beats on the dashboard. "You'll understand soon enough. We're almost there."

In little over a mile, they passed the last of those audaciously gaudy properties, and directly ahead there was this dense forest in transition to autumn, some trees still having green leaves, others turned red and brown and gold, together with a portion whose branches were already skeletal, all of which spread out on both sides of the road that went directly into the forest's shadowy depths.

"Stop at the sign, please," Grandpa Mandt said.

It took Margaret a couple of looks along either side of the road to spot the little placard tacked to a wooden post that had no wire strung between it and another post. What's more, there didn't appear to be fencing anywhere near the forest. She pulled over onto the grass beside this road without a shoulder and stopped the Buick. Looking through the side window, Margaret read the little inscription on the sign: *Welcome To Sacred Cow Farm*. She scanned through the forest, and saw nothing other than a seemingly endless thicket.

"Alice co-founded the farm," Grandpa Mandt said.

"Wow, right here?"

"Yes. She loved this place, called it her earth poem."

"That's awesome." Margaret again met his eyes, which had turned dark as the sunless areas just inside the forest. "I'm sorry it got all grown over, Grandpa. How long ago did that happen?"

"It's not grown over; this is an experiment in cooperation with nature, trusting that the forest will in return give you what you need."

"But where are the crops?"

"They're protected by the outer forest. The food pests like to eat is almost everywhere in this wild foliage, so the little buggers get so fat and happy they never make it as far as the cultivated areas." He winked, and this time his eyelid performed magnificently, folding all the way over and back. "We'll get to the crops, don't you worry."

"Then where to from here?" Margaret gripped the steering wheel and set her eyes on the road ahead.

"Before we go further, your grandmother herself whittled the inscription on the back of that sign. Perhaps you'd like to read it."

"Of course I would." This was starting to feel like entering one of those too-cool-by-nines bars that had little to no signage in New York City's meatpacking district, only pretty much in the opposite: Here by way of its understated presence, something was opening to Margaret instead of becoming more exclusive. She got out of the car and walked over behind the little placard. Nana's inscription had been carved into the wood with precise letters, though so small that reading required Margaret's extra attention:

> *The culture that has arisen from the forest has been influenced by diverse processes of renewal of life which are always at play in the forest, varying from species to species, from season to season, in sight and sound and smell. The unifying principle of life in diversity, of democratic pluralism...*
>
> —*from* Tapovan *by Rabindranath Tagore*

She brought a hand over her mouth on realizing this quote came from the Nobel Prize-winning Indian philosopher/poet/musician/playwright Nana had included in *My Long Journey Home*, one of the authors with whom Boris Pasternak and Olga Ivinskaya collaborated with in translating their poetry. Yes, Nana had come upon this credo for sustainable living long before Margaret's sometimes so embarrassingly self-important generation invented the term.

"The inscription is brilliant," she said on getting back in behind the steering wheel. "It seems to be this call for insurgency in a revolution that just might come off well."

"Your grandmother was convinced you win it one sustainable community at a time until the vision catches fire."

"I like that, but why not put the inscription on a bigger and more visible sign? It's almost as if Nana wanted to keep it secret."

"She pretty much did. One time I encouraged her to make Rabindranath Tagore's quote more prominent around here, and Alice told me in no uncertain terms, 'Working with the earth is a poem you can appreciate better without words.'" Grandpa Mandt gestured ahead. "There's a dirt road about a quarter mile up there. Take that one."

While Margaret shifted the Buick into drive and evenly pressed down on the accelerator pedal with her foot, she pictured Grandpa Mandt and Nana as the young Oleg and Katya in *My Long Journey Home*, them working the fields of Peredelkino and the underground Jewish refugee farm in the Urals and Katya's family village of Mashinska—never while together and yet always inseparable. They somehow held on to each other through plunging their hands into blackness, turning it over, planting, weeding, taking only what they needed from the ground. By the time she drove onto the dirt road heading into the heart of the forest, Margaret's thoughts went to her and Frazier's several attempts with rooftop gardening at their apartment building. He had built out of redwood some nice-size raised beds, and she'd agreed to help keep them going. They managed to get three motley springtime harvests of turnips, onions, heirloom tomatoes, and eggplant. The thing of it was, every year by summertime she had gotten too busy at work, which would send him further into what she now could name as slumbering, the result being their gardens fell fallow by the middle of June. The written word could set you to dreaming about living in harmony with what sustained you, but it couldn't make the dream come true. All told it seemed to Margaret unless you let your worst sadness in or were both blessed and cursed enough for it to overtake you, only then could you come to understand something about the architecture of sunbeams or the silken veil covering the moon or the yearning to touch at least one colorless rainbow, or how to love the earth and its bounty. This way still felt overly restrained, too much held in her mind, although a mere glance over at Grandpa Mandt told her it didn't have to remain her condition. Whatever else she needed already flowed in their blood.

Just up ahead she spotted fifteen, twenty vehicles, several of them pickup trucks, a couple of Chevy Volts, two or three Priuses, an old psychedelically painted VW van, all of them parked beside trees, no timber having been felled to create a parking lot. She slowed the Buick to a stop between two Ford pickups. Grandpa Mandt said nothing and didn't make a move to get out of the car. Margaret scanned this large, almost circular clearing with several plats of produce. Winter vegetables they would have to be, looked to her like Brussels sprouts, cabbage, potatoes, maybe radishes, several kinds of greens and lettuces. In the middle of each plat were open-air wooden shade sheds that had woven baskets underneath their roofs along with hoes, rakes, iron graters, and tillers. Two tractors sat idle, as this was obviously growing season, probably not time for turning over dirt in any big way. A whole bunch of goats roamed freely, mostly nibbling away at wild grasses outside the plats. A couple of people used shovels to scoop up goat dung and then drop it into large metal containers, which had scrawled in black paint on their sides the words *Free Fertilizer*. Some of the goats were being hand milked underneath the one shade shed on the outskirts of the cultivated plats. A stream cut directly through the center of the circular clearing. Attached by fat hoses to pumps along its banks were metal irrigation trellises on wheels that jutted out into the potatoes, cabbages, and one plat of greens. The other crops were on their own with the soft September sunshine and blue sky. About an even number of men and women, mostly young twenty- and thirty-somethings, filled baskets with items ripe for harvest, others chopped weeds with hoes, and some walked slowly among the crops, using their hands to pick off leaves whatever pests that had made it past the outer forest. *Probably not too many to take out*, Margaret figured. For sixty feet or so encircling the plats, there was this bug-buffer-zone of unplanted, cleared ground.

"This is quite a place," she said. "You must be so proud of what you and Nana started here."

"It was mostly her doing." Grandpa Mandt's voice shook.

She looked at him, but he kept his eyes set on the farm. "It's understandable it would be hard for you to come here, Grandpa."

"I haven't been back since spreading Alice's ashes." He gestured somewhere out the windshield. "I let them loose among the potatoes over there. She loved potatoes. Said they grow so fast and in just about any kind of soil, you could feed the world off them." Grandpa Mandt reached over and grasped the door handle, but didn't lift it.

All the while Margaret waited there beside him, her grandfather seemed stuck in the present as well as the past. "Would you like for me to spread your ashes in the potatoes too, Grandpa," she finally said.

Without a word he nodded.

Margaret partly kept her attention directed at his hand on the door handle, which still didn't move other than for the tremors of old age.

"We can go home now if you'd like," she said.

"Not until you get your hands dirty." With a twisted expression, as though suppressing his trepidation down below some higher calling, Grandpa Mandt opened the Buick's door. "This is for you as much as it is for me."

"What is?"

"You must understand I stopped coming out here except on rare occasions, starting when I had my first affair on Alice. So often she came to the dirt as her muse, and I wasn't together enough to join her in this practice."

Momentarily his words seemed out of step, oddly self-effacing, but in the next instant, they brought Margaret up short. Did Grandpa Mandt know something about Frazier having more than a muse relationship with Anastasie Moreau, or possibly another woman on the side somewhere? Was it that Frazier and Grandpa Mandt had opened up to each other and talked about this on Frazier's last visit? As undeniable as Solomon Mikhoels, the way Nana wrote about him anyway, had been a lady-killer until falling for Katya, Grandpa Mandt had had something move him enough to offer *My Long Journey Home* to Frazier before Margaret. Or could it be Grandpa Mandt knew that love, even true love, invariably would have tributaries like the canals coming off this stream which flowed into the crops of Sacred Cow Farm? Maybe he was trying to tell her it was up to each of us just how you tapped into the most secretive river of all. "Might you be a little more direct on what it is I'm supposed to benefit from?" she said.

"I've been clear enough for anyone who listens with their heart." With that Grandpa Mandt began the arduous process of unfolding his creaky old body out of the car and getting himself onto his feet.

Margaret also got out of the Buick and then walked over beside him. As he righted himself, she slid her arm underneath his. "I'm listening," she said.

"I know that," he said in an almost gruff yet somehow jovial tone.

When they walked onto the bug barrier's open ground, some of the farmers looked over at them. This one older man, wearing a floppy gardener's hat with his silver hair dangling below it, stood up from using a trowel between rows of radishes, and then waved in the direction of Margaret and Grandpa Mandt. "Mandt, you old buzzard, is that you?" the man called out.

"Yes, it is I," Grandpa Mandt hollered back kind of singsongishly.

The older farmer walked over and gave Grandpa Mandt a handshake along with a hug, then introduced himself to Margaret as Ralph Kramer, and by that time almost all the others had gathered in a half circle in front of them. Some knew Grandpa Mandt well, as Ralph obviously did, and others were familiar with him being one of the legendary founders of the farm. Ralph talked about the "miracle" of Alice convincing the wealthy landowner to contribute this forest to his family's charitable foundation, thereby creating an ongoing vision for cooperation with nature rather than using it until depleting it. Then Grandpa Mandt and Margaret got an update on how the farm was, while organic and pesticide-free, still outproducing big agribusiness operations three to one per acre, together with feeding over 150 families. As that wound down, Grandpa Mandt made a motion with his hands as if pushing air downward and asked them all to go about their work in the ordinary way, because he wanted his granddaughter to "see the Sacred Cow in action." Without much delay, everyone complied.

As she and Grandpa Mandt made their way over toward the potatoes, with her arm again laced underneath his, Margaret found it sort of distressingly wonderful that more people loved Nana for her agricultural than her literary talents. Once they stood among row upon row of spuds, Grandpa Mandt zipped his bomber jacket close around his neck. Margaret partly didn't want to keep him long out in this unseasonable weather, though, on the whole, she didn't feel like leaving. The gusting wind seemed to carry Nana's spirit. On looking over toward the shade shed in the middle of the potatoes, she noticed a few short-handle hoes, probably not very different from the kind Oleg, Alice, and their comrades had used in the fields of Russia. She asked Grandpa Mandt to stay put, then high-stepped over the rows to get her as well as him each one of these implements, and then she returned with them.

She went to hand him one of the hoes, but he squinted into the low sun and shook his head.

"This ground is for you now, Margaret; it's too late for me."

"It can't be too late if you're really here to prove something to the both of us."

"Prove what?" he almost barked.

The wind kicked up again, this time along with a huge cloud of dust that swarmed them as well as much of the farm.

"I don't know...maybe that love is unaffected by death or anything else," Margaret said, along with no small amount of grit invading her mouth. Still holding one of the hoes, she got down on her hands and knees, and then began digging out a spidery weed encroaching on a potato plant. She chopped another weed and another, getting into a nice rhythm, one Nana would be pleased with for sure.

"Help this old grandfather of yours get down there, will you!"

Stopping her arm in mid-swing, she looked at him and nodded. Not wasting a moment she stood up. Securing his elbow with her hand, she lowered herself along with him beside the row of potatoes.

Not speaking another word, he picked up the other short-handle hoe that lay on the ground, and with the gusto found in a bongo player getting a good groove on, Grandpa Mandt went at a weed.

With her next swings of the hoe, Margaret began the final stanza of what she felt to be one of her best poems ever, even compared with the breathtakingly raw ones she'd penned at university, and right up there with diving into those rewrites of her novel, or her recent efforts sans words on paper: the family-of-origin work with Dr. Buttertart, her talk with her parents about manic depression being environmental or genetic or both, simply though sometimes unnervingly opening to herself and Frazier more, and not to leave out the mysterious effect of having read *My Long Journey Home*. She thought about all this while working the potatoes. Once she and Grandpa Mandt had done almost everything they came here to accomplish, she smoothed the dirt back over the dug-out places and gathered the uprooted weeds for removal from the crop. Fine enough then, her poem may be closing for this day, but Margaret knew by way of her thrumming blood it was far from finished.

CHAPTER THIRTY-FOUR

Grabbing a knot in this rope and then reaching for the next higher knot, I at the same time clamped my feet over a knot below, making a sort of frog-lurch along the rope. It went all the way up and over the top of this gray concrete wall thirty or so feet tall. I would've said this was the wall separating East and West Berlin, as it looked just like pictures I'd seen of it in books and magazine articles, but every few feet higher, I kept glancing over my shoulder at the landscape of Peredelkino and Moscow and Mashinska at the base of the Urals, all in some sort of mosaic. I had spotted Pasternak's dacha and The Shop, then Vika, my, and Oleg's apartment, which was someone else's now, the potato and alfalfa fields; in Moscow the Writers Building along with the literary canteen which Marina Tsvetaeva failed to get hired on at; also there was my family's compound surrounded by rich agricultural land in Mashinska, together with the imposing and, in a way, protective snowcapped mountain peaks.

"That's it, you're doing magnificently, Katya."

Pasternak's voice came from below and I looked that way, spotting him with Miss Zinaida at one side and Olga at the other. The women had their arms slipped behind Pasternak's back, a joint claim to their man if not an entirely copasetic one. Pasternak waved to me, and Olga blew me a kiss; then Miss Zinaida did the same as her. It wasn't as if Miss Zinaida had matched Olga's kind gesture for me in favor of the dark purpose to merely stay in Pasternak's good graces; the sad smiles on both women's faces told me as much. No, this didn't happen because people were similar or different than you or, for that matter, over relationships bound together in biblical appropriateness. Love grew deep roots and sprouted wondrous flowers from tilled rows seeded with your shared history and hearts, watered by tears and blood. Underneath the ground, in the form of decomposing stardust, which as much as these other things sent up green shoots, the bodies lay of all those unable any longer to wave or kiss: my parents and brother Radko, Solomon Mikhoels, the too numerous murdered poets and dissidents, good comrades I had worked alongside who simply died in the fields while wielding their short-handle hoe. This, until now, inescapable local soil—along with what contributed to life above and below its surface—I was leaving probably not to return.

My backpack along with another satchel with a strap—one bag over each of my shoulders—slumped heavily along my back, but not to disparage. Somehow I knew my Moskva typewriter was inside the satchel and also that in the backpack were copies of *My Long Journey Home* as well as *Doctor Zhivago*; a letter signed by Pasternak and another by me approving publication of our work, neither of which had been given over to d'Angelo; and then there was "The Stalin Epigram." It had been a good idea to wear blue jeans, as with each of the frog movements, my knees scraped against concrete. On making it to the top, I threw a leg over and sat astraddle the wall. As I looked on the other side, Rome sprawled everywhere: the Coliseum, the Vatican with its Sistine Chapel, gargoyle-mouthed fountains, labyrinth gardens. The sun blanketed all this with a honey-colored sheen, and weather on the Italian side wasn't hot or cold or just right; in fact, there didn't seem to be any air at all. I could breathe, but each inhale and exhale felt like a theft of life from Russia.

"Hurry, come on, the literary police could spot you up there, Katya," Sergio d'Angelo called out in Italian.

Fixing my eyes on him, uncannily, in my mind I translated to Russian this language I knew very little of. "But how can you survive over here whether the police take you away or not?" I spoke in my native tongue.

"This isn't hell, don't worry. Things just seem that way from the wall. You'll be okay."

All at once almost unbearable heat descended. Somewhere a magpie squawked. *I must rejoin Pasternak and Miss Zinaida and Olga, head back to Russia, get to Oleg some other way.* Shooting a look that direction, everything was as black as the inside of a cave. There really would be no going back.

As I made my way down the Italian side of the wall, on my cheeks and along my neck tears mixed with sweat. I could hardly wait to get to the pavement and, at the same instant, never wanted to arrive in this foreign place. Looking one way, then the other, I saw no police, only a strangely empty street, other than Sergio d'Angelo still directly below. He was right about one thing already: I could breathe more fluidly with each lurch downward. Reaching out and grasping the rope, d'Angelo steadied it for my final few feet of descent. My shoes hit the ground and immediately I faced him.

"Where's Oleg?" I said flatly.

"Detained."

"By whom?"

"God, for all I know."

"Do you, or do you not, have him in Rome?"

"Sorry, Katya, it's all been about getting you over the wall so those approvals to publish your and Pasternak's books would be Italy's." He indicated my backpack and the satchel. "I'm sure you've got them in one of those carryalls, so unless you want to be a person without citizenship or visa, you should give the documents to me."

Once again I momentarily couldn't breathe, but this time there was no shortage of air. Instinctively I went for the rope and it had vanished, as well as the wall, bustling Roman street life replacing it. Cops in black uniforms emerged from around the corner of a café. On the crowns of their caps in silver lettering were the words *Literary Police.* I ran the opposite direction along that one all but deserted street. The sound of their leather shoes on the pavement increased from taps to slaps, then became thuds. In one motion I slid the backpack off my shoulder around in front of my chest. I opened the top flap, and then began tossing the pages of *My Long Journey Home* and *Doctor Zhivago* to the wind. An updraft caught them and they spiraled into the sky. I took out the two letters and tore them in pieces. As these shreds also headed upward like some kind of snowflakes untamable by gravity or the scorching sun, I stopped running. One of the cops yanked the satchel with my Moskva inside from my shoulder almost at the same instant another slammed me to the ground. While being cuffed with my arms pulled behind me, a knee crammed down into my back. I thought my spine would crack. *Do it good enough to kill me, why don't you!* Then I could be with Oleg. And I would sweetly face him in all my gloriousness and defilement. What a dénouement in reverse. The only document still inside my backpack I hadn't sent to the heavens was "The Stalin Epigram." That I would hand deliver to Oleg if you don't mind, or even if you do. With the ugly noise of something like a large oak branch snapping, my spine split in two.

Suddenly, I awakened in a cold sweat to some sort of long, baritone horn blast.

This place was strangely unfamiliar, the cramped little room in dim light that wasn't even as large as my nook in The Shop, me lying atop a thin mattress with a stiff pillow underneath my head, and the bed which had chipped blue paint all along its metal frame. What was with the little round window? ...no, a porthole, my God, of course, I was on the cargo freighter *Madonna's Pride*, headed for the port of Civitavecchia. Still shaken by my nightmare of worst fears, I reached down beside the bed and placed a hand on my backpack, then next to it my satchel. Good. They were right where I'd put them. I traced the shape of my Moskva typewriter with my fingers over the satchel. While sitting up and crossing my legs at the ankles with knees splayed open like a Cossack, I brought my backpack in front of me. I unzipped the main pouch, and then one by one checked for the contents that had to be inside, for it was I who had packed them, but my still pounding heart would have nothing other than me seeing for myself right now: not the two changes of clothes, Dopp kit, or even my falsified Italian passport under the name of Gina Cometti, rather, the copies of *My Long Journey Home* and *Doctor Zhivago*, those letters of approval for publishing my and Pasternak's novels—his signed, mine not—and the original of "The Stalin Epigram." I thumbed through them slowly, a few times brushing the palm of my hand across a page, as if the smooth texture of the paper along with the slight embossing of black ink made them more real. This calmed me some but not so much, as the nightmare just wouldn't die a natural death in my mind. Should any attention be paid to it, really, even a little? Could my subconscious be trying to reveal anything of importance? I mean, the meeting in Leningrad with the slim-nosed, round-spectacled Sergio d'Angelo, who, along with those chipmunk cheeks, could easily be called bookish and mild mannered, had gone exceedingly well enough to have gotten me this far. D'Angelo's claim then and now seemed imminently plausible that Oleg, after breaking out of the gulag, had made his way to Leningrad—a good place to disappear into, as no one knew him there. And he'd made friends with Trotskyites who helped him get smuggled out of Russia to Italy's communist underground of the same ilk. One thing reddened me every time I thought about it, though—they had made a deal with Oleg to never contact me or anyone in Russia again, and Oleg had actually kept it. At the right occasion the Italians would bring me to him. This was the thin, fraying thread Oleg clung to all that time without it breaking? What the hell, it had been nearly eight years that I almost hadn't made it through without him! Okay, okay, but you had to give this to Sergio d'Angelo: He had risked his neck by way of smuggling me out of Russia, even when I refused to sign the approval to publish me and he had refused to accept Pasternak's letter of authorization for the time being. He had acquitted himself nicely of being Oleg's comrade and good friend, and if any changes in the order of publishing our books came about, d'Angelo had insisted it would be with Oleg's blessing too. I had bucked a little on that, but deep down felt more connected with Oleg for the gesture. Yes, this Sergio d'Angelo seemed a stand-up fellow. Before leaving for Russia he had purportedly promised Oleg to bring me and my work back to Italy ahead of Pasternak's, and I certainly had no reason to disbelieve him. *The nightmare had simply been a bad dream,* I told myself, yet my heart would not completely return to normal.

The horn sounded another time, then quickly once more, and again. The announcement of "astern propulsion," a slowing down, for I had asked the first mate about the signal of landfall approaching, and this triple blast, he'd said, was the best answer that could be given a rookie voyager.

My blood rushed as if pushed through my veins by the power of the ship's mighty propellers, this time not because of some scare from the nether regions of my psyche but in anticipation of arriving at the port of Rome. Sergio d'Angelo had promised me something too, that he'd bring Oleg with him to greet me in Italy. Almost flinging the backpack to the floor, I stood up. In one long step I was at the porthole peering out on this industrial harbor. There were longshoremen hauling bags over their shoulders and stacking them on the dock; cranes lifting huge wooden crates off ship decks, then swinging them over dry land; men reaching up their hands to guide these boxes in safely, tug crews washing down their vessels or mooring them by tying thick ropes off to dockside cleats; and plenty of men with a few women mixed in just milled around, as though waiting for their ship to come in. Where would one find Sergio d'Angelo and Oleg amid this commotion? All the while my eyes went from person to person, my blood slowly thickened, like viscous tar or something. My heart worked harder and harder, though I had less and less spunk. How much had the years changed Oleg? How much had they changed me? Would I even recognize him? Was it possible for him not to want to be with me after so long apart? What would I feel for him, really? Oh, I'd asked these questions of myself before, though they at once seemed pitifully rhetorical. This, now this, was happening.

A flash of white glare turned the porthole's glass into a mirror, and suddenly I noticed my pallid complexion along with mussed hair the color of brown sugar—hold off on the sparkle, if you will—which fell out of a ponytail band like some fountain that spewed every which way on top of my head. What's more, all I had on were panties and a T-shirt. The glare cleared but I still couldn't spot d'Angelo or Oleg anywhere out there. *Madonna's Pride* was now being guided by tugboats in close to its berth alongside the dock. I simply couldn't fail to be on deck at the rail when the ship came to a stop, and with myself looking better than this nightmare-hangover of a mess I was in. I took from my backpack a bra along with a yellow sundress and my Dopp kit, all of which I laid across the bed. First, I laced my arms through the bra's straps and hooked it together. Something a little Dionysian made me push my hands up underneath the cups. My moderate breasts did not fall hardly at all as I let go of them, still retaining some firmness that had been gifted by the springtime of life, if I happened to be bragging. When I slipped on the dress, there was no denying it fit as well as could be expected over my plain figure with minimal curves. In seconds my hair was down below my shoulders, and I stroked it with the brush from my Dopp kit. Using a hand I brought some strands in front of my eyes, and they still didn't shimmer much, though were nice and soft to the touch, almost silky. A pinch and firm pat on both my cheeks to rosy them up, then I put on a pair of sandals. I replaced the brush and slid my Dopp kit back in the backpack along with a Russian-to-Italian dictionary that before falling asleep I'd been going through to learn enough to get past customs. Over one shoulder, then the other, I slipped on my backpack and the satchel with my Moskva in it; my goodness, they were every bit as heavy as in that awful dream. I was done here, but somehow couldn't leave just yet. For a long moment I closed my eyes, picturing Oleg all sharp-eyed and virile, a workingman artisan with well-formed muscles and the kindest smile ever. Okay, this was better. I could meet Oleg again this way, feeling almost like a college girl with a crush on the handsomest boy on campus. I headed out of the berth.

While walking briskly along the hallway past the crew's quarters, I paused briefly to see whether Luciana, who I had worked with on galley duty all five days at sea, happened to be in her room, but she wasn't there. Three doors down I knocked on Perla's, another galley-mate's, door and again nothing. Simply unable to leave this ship without trying to find these women—who had been so patient with my poor attempts at speaking Italian as well as having proved themselves just as much poets of preparing the harvest as my comrades in the fields of Peredelkino and Mashinska—I went down the stairs at the end of the hallway instead of up toward the main deck. I had a pretty good idea of where they would be, having taken myself off the work schedule just this morning. A dockside meal would be served for any of the crew who preferred to eat onboard rather than in port.

On entering the galley, I called out their names, and Luciana stopped chopping onions, while Perla, next to a huge pot of something which smelled of the ocean and legumes, turned away from the stovetop. She held the spoon she'd been stirring with as if unconcerned it dripped her red, tomato-based soup onto the floor. I hugged and gave cheek-kisses to one, then the other of them, at the same time in Italian extending my gratitude along with farewell. Eyes gleaming, they rattled off responses that, to tell the truth, I understood about every fifth word of and, in a way, didn't miss anything. They wished me a "hot bed with my crazy man in love missing my body," or something of the sort anyway, and then the three of us smiled conspiratorially. Of course I had worked alongside most of the others in here, but it was these two women who had reached out so warmly to a foreigner only one rung up from a stowaway. Yes, I would remember Luciana and Perla always. I, not hastily though, surely without letting grass grow underneath my feet, said good-byes to the others, and then made my way out of the galley.

As soon as I arrived at the main deck's railing, this breeze coming up the side of the ship lifted my sundress not unlike a mischievous lover, and I quickly smoothed it down with my hands. Over on my right two men turned handles for spindles of cable that were attached to the pedestrian ramp while the far end of it lowered onto the dock. Still, I saw no sign of Sergio d'Angelo and Oleg. I checked my watch, and it was 5:23 p.m.; the *Madonna's Pride* had dropped anchor over twenty minutes late. Would I have to locate a payphone landside and place a call to the number d'Angelo had given me for contacting him in Rome should problems arise? I mean, I didn't actually know whether he'd gotten here from Russia safely. What if Sergio d'Angelo never made it to the plane he was supposed to have gotten on after I left? If our plans were discovered by most anyone in the Congress of Soviet Writers or Khrushchev's homeland spies before *Doctor Zhivago* or *My Long Journey Home* made it through publishing and found a way into the public spotlight, then there would be nothing that had even a remote chance of protecting Pasternak, Miss Zinaida, Olga, Irina, and, conceivably, even Pasternak's children. I slipped the strap of my backpack off one shoulder and set the bag on the deck, then did the same with my satchel. Alternating the use of my hands, I rubbed the soreness along my shoulders. *Sergio d'Angelo and Oleg are caught in traffic or something, simply running late,* I tried convincing myself. Another updraft lifted my dress, and once again I patted it down. This time the breeze felt like an unwanted grope, a hand of last-minute and infinite sullying…or merely that of some harmless, dirty old man to be slapped down and sent away.

Over the next twenty, thirty minutes, much of the crew walked off the ship and onto shore until, finally, the pedestrian ramp just sat there empty. My arms hung heavy at my sides, as if the Roman god of the sea, Neptune himself, tied them off to cleats like you would mooring ropes, a ship's fixture, unmovable without assistance. One of the two uniformed customs agents who had been checking papers and clearing people off the *Madonna's Pride* looked up at the men handling the pulleys for the pedestrian ramp, and the agent made a gesture for the ramp to be taken up. Clearly there would be no further disembarking before the agents made next rounds. At about half a turn on the levers that raised the ramp, I called out in Italian for the men to hold off for a few seconds. At least that's what I'd intended to say, for one lifted an eyebrow while the other rubbed his back and shrugged—as they stopped the cranking. "Grazie," I said to them, hurriedly lifting my backpack and satchel over each shoulder again. When partway down the ramp, I noticed the customs agents', if not outright angry, certainly more than disinterested stares. *Great, just fabulous,* this foisting on them the nuisance of a straggler while attempting to smuggle myself into their country. What is more, Sergio d'Angelo had assured me he would've "taken care" of my entry through customs as long as I played along with some, at the minimum, bad Italian. If you please, I didn't feel very comforted right now. I made the last long step over the foot or so gap between the dock and the slightly raised ramp and stopped directly in front of the agents, one a slim, dark-haired woman, the other the real article, a tawny-skinned, well-fed Italian man. "Ci scusiamo per l'attesa fino," I said, something like, Sorry for the hold-up. Their fixed blank expressions gave nothing away. "Ho le mie carte." *I have my papers.* I slipped off my backpack and satchel and set them on the dock. Quickly, I got out my passport, then handed it over to the woman.

She read it carefully, glancing twice at me as if confirming my actual face with the photo inside.

"Per favore, posso avere uno sguardo," the male agent said, indicating my backpack and satchel.

"Please" and "I look" were the only words I could translate. I handed him the backpack, and then looked in both directions along the dock. My anxiety turned the people into all but blurs; who knew whether Sergio d'Angelo and Oleg were among them now?

The male agent sort of ham-fistedly brought out some of the papers, then turned them over, as if looking at this moldy loaf of bread that would be quarantined for virulent spore testing.

Did he have any idea what he was actually looking at? I prayed silently to the Almighty, if there was such a source, they were nothing more to the agent than a stack of papers wasted on some little woman's fiction. "Fatto storie." *Made-up stories.* I smiled as if shyly.

He sort of grunted, then looked at the other agent. "E la donna, no?" he said.

It is the woman, no? Even I knew what this meant.

"Si," replied the female agent, handing me back my passport.

The man replaced the papers inside my backpack and then returned it to me. While he gave what seemed to be an almost cursory inspection of my satchel and the Moskva, I put the passport away and zipped the backpack shut.

As soon as I got the satchel and the backpack over my shoulders again, he took hold of my arm, though almost gently, an apprehension of strange mawkishness. "Vieni con noi," he said.

All I understood was the word come. As they walked with me sandwiched between them away from the dock toward the perimeter fence and one of the harbor's metal-gated exits, the man's clammy hand made my skin crawl. Seeing clearly again, as if keenly aware of heading for my own solitary cell, I repeatedly looked one way, then the other for d'Angelo and Oleg. The longer they weren't spotted, the more I fell numb to my future and yet became highly aware of certain things in the past. The gulags had killed Osip Mandelstam but not his son Oleg or Olga Ivinskaya, some horrid luck, because all three of them had hearts of lions along with the deftness of lambs. Torture and incarceration had changed Olga, sobered her, sent her to the typewriter with a special kind of sadness and truth, made her a hungrier lover. What had it done to Oleg? What would it do to me? I wondered whether before my deportation they would allow a phone call back home. If so, Pasternak had to be alerted to the danger every member of our dubious band of renegade literati was in now; yes, that's what must be taken up.

Once outside the gate we walked two short blocks lined with improbable surroundings for a customs processing office, mostly warehouses for shipments in and out of port, a marine supply shop, and on the second corner some whiskey-drinking establishment, where we headed right into the alley behind it. Before I could figure out in my mind the Italian for Where are you taking me, the bookish Sergio d'Angelo stepped out of the driver side of this black Fiat automobile parked behind the pub less than fifteen meters away, and, blessed savior, may as well thank the devil too, from the passenger side Oleg unfolded his sinewy body onto his feet. I fell breathless, speechless, hardly noticing the customs agent letting loose of my arm. Oleg's aquiline face had lines along the curvature of his mouth and underneath his cheekbones, places that had once been smooth, and that curly shock of brown hair had not grayed, just receded some, all of this making him look attractively worn, no, not down, more like severely honed. The sharpness in his black eyes still came from an earnestly wet-stoned blade, though one used more judiciously now, as though rationed according to what had been stolen from him.

He waited for me to start walking toward him before coming my way. He limped noticeably, but not like a gimp. I slowed my pace slightly so neither of us would be required to go more than halfway. As we stopped less than a foot apart, I noticed pinkish geographic skin, the detritus of burns, along his neck an inch or two above his shirt collar, and, not to let my attention linger there, I met Oleg's eyes again. There wasn't any need to smile to show our pleasure, but we did. Our chests rose and fell visibly, a legend for maps buried inside us, showing the way to excitement as well as roads that may not have destinations. Oleg's breath smelled like Russia without the vodka, unimpeded in freshness which brought to mind fog nestled in a valley.

"You look ravishingly beautiful," he said.

"You too."

I placed a hand softly on his face. The breeze picked up and tousled his hair, making him seem young and at the same time old, just the way I felt. Somehow a kiss was not the best thing, and I could see in his sadly alive eyes this was the same for him. I took my backpack off, then my satchel, and set them on the ground.

We hugged until sometime after Oleg's tears soaked the shoulder strap of my sundress, and mine made a dark coin on his jacket.

Coming out of our embrace felt like when the rising sun in the east clears the fog. Yes, I loved Oleg and he loved me, but could we fall in love again?

"Are you hungry?" Oleg said.

"Not so much." It was supper hour, though food was far from my mind. "How about you?"

He shrugged. "Would you like to see my studio, where I live?"

"I'd like that very much." I kissed him on the cheek, letting my lips linger on his warm, divinely etched skin.

He just stood there and accepted it, not blandly, as if partly wanting to and also unready to move toward this kind of touch.

Oleg and I had boarded a slow train.

As the two of us kind of reentered the alleyway outside the tight circle enclosing ourselves, we scanned the area, and Sergio d'Angelo was already in the Fiat behind the steering wheel, while the customs agents had gone their own way. I picked up my backpack.

"The treasures." Oleg smiled knowingly and gestured at the pack.

"For some, pirates' booty."

He lifted the satchel by its strap. "Mind if I help you with this?"

"That would be lovely."

Oleg took me by the hand and we walked toward the car. His fingers intertwined with mine felt better than my kiss on his face, for he caressed me now, in a way, even closer than our hug, less desperate—he could do this much.

When Oleg and I got in beside each other in the Fiat's rear compartment, with me setting the backpack on the floorboard between my feet and him doing the same with my satchel between his feet, Sergio d'Angelo twisted around and said, "Welcome to Italy, Katya."

"It's wonderful to be here."

We spoke in Russian.

"How was your voyage?" d'Angelo said.

"Good. I was treated as any other member of the crew."

"Yes, well, they are our main source of moving certain comrades in and out of Russia. It's tricky business every go at it; I'm glad things went well."

"All except the cold reception from those customs agents. Why didn't you tell me before I left Russia something like that would happen?"

D'Angelo's brow knitted as if with genuine concern. "They didn't tell you they were taking you to us?"

I shook my head.

"I'm terribly sorry, Katya. You pay off who you must, and some agents are more helpful than others it seems."

"Thank you for the apology, really. I'm here and that's the thing, right, fellows?"

Oleg slipped his hand in mine again, this time giving it a little squeeze. "Please take us to my studio, Serge," he said.

D'Angelo's brow smoothed, while from behind those round spectacles, his eyes shimmered as if suddenly looking on the Romans' Venus and Cupid in the backseat with us. "My pleasure," he said, then faced frontward and bounced his eyebrows into the rearview mirror. "My pleasure, indeed."

The trip into the city was long, 120 kilometers on a mostly winding road, and for the first two-thirds of the way or so, Oleg and I talked in turns, catching up a little, that is, between several easy, long silences to enjoy being next to each other as well as get used to it again; though, that wasn't solely the crux, this feeling as much like some relearning of Oleg, his wordless essence or atmosphere: the hawk in his eyes, the artist in his soul. In fact, he told me of having taken up painting and playing bongos. He'd learned the Italian language fairly well, and thusly said enough to lose my comprehension and impress. I told him I would strangle him if he ever volunteered to tutor me in the language, though insisted I wanted to learn it. We began to laugh together. All this made me wonder what Oleg was learning of my truer self. I talked of how good I felt about *My Long Journey Home*, and it would be quite lovely for him to read it but he mustn't feel obligated in any way to do so. He had then smiled warmly and indicated he could hardly wait to "wallow in my book," have a "good, slow read" of it. He admitted Sergio d'Angelo had gotten a copy of *My Long Journey Home* to him, and he'd tried to read it, but getting that close to us without having me here in the flesh simply had been too much to bear. With that, gooseflesh had taken me over for the next full kilometer. I decided not to go into our pasts because that could lead to Solomon Mikhoels, and I simply wasn't ready to cross that bridge just yet. At times during this drive, my thoughts had run away from me on why Oleg also chose against taking us through the gap in his history—too painful, too soon, too amorous with some other woman?—and how could I complain if that were true? Then again, that's just what I'd do, only complain is too genteel of a word for it; turn my insides out in feline agony would be more accurate. He asked about how Pasternak and his family were doing, so I informed him of Pasternak, Miss Zinaida, Yevgeni, and Leonid's general well-being, along with the wonderful complication in their lives of Olga and more recently Irina. I had gone on to say Olga was a muse of mine, a dear friend who helped me "love you from afar." Yes, those exact words tumbled from my mouth before I could hold them back. Fine enough, because I felt better for having set them free. At that Oleg's black eyes had intently met mine, and they held his familiar kind of dark love for me, indeed they had. So why not kiss me? Perhaps because he didn't want to in front of his friend Serge? Whatever the reason, we needed to break our trance or I was about to French-kiss him right there on the outskirts of Rome, Italy. On grounds of my own, lent to by his fragile, quiet virility, I so wanted Oleg to go first. No, it still wasn't the right time, and certainly, this unspoken subject needed changing.

Right then Oleg did it for us, about forty kilometers from Rome, for I had seen a mileage sign just a bit ago, and he did this with what seemed to be deceptively serene, green pastureland inhabited by a few cattle milling about on both sides of the road. "How is Pasternak dealing with the possibility of his book being published in the West?" he said.

"Pasternak and his extended family will find themselves in much more danger inside Russia when that happens than you and I would be in exile with my book on bookstore shelves, yet he wants to go forward with publication." I found myself clutching my backpack's strap. "That just about says it all on the matter, doesn't it?

"Although I have something more to add. It's no secret you and Sergio have wanted me to go first in publishing and, don't get me wrong, in a way that's extremely endearing, but, Oleg, it's only right for Pasternak to be first. There are so many reasons why; in short, he deserves it more than I."

"Of course Pasternak is a great writer, though that's no reason to diminish your work in the least, my love."

Oleg used the word love, *for me, out loud!* "But you haven't even read my book," I said, in a soft and deliberate tone.

"I'm not eavesdropping, it's just impossible not to overhear you two," d'Angelo interjected, keeping his eyes fixed on the road ahead. "I know deferring to Pasternak is something you value highly, Katya, and quite frankly, I also believe you're selling the strength of your book short, which by the way I, indeed, have read.

"Nevertheless, I've been working on the possibility of Pasternak's book being published ahead of yours with Giangiacomo Feltrinelli, the publisher in Milan. There're complications you and Oleg should know about in making a decision together on this."

In the rearview mirror Sergio d'Angelo's eyes briefly met Oleg's and then flashed on mine, before he went on. "Katya, your fake passport will not stand up here in Italy long. The fascists in our government perform regular sweeps to target those with anything unusual in their documentation. We managed to get Oleg actual Italian citizenship, and let me tell you, it meant pulling all the strings we had.

"The communist leadership here will not stick their necks out that far again unless you're published and made into a star author for the movement." His eyes momentarily met mine again in the mirror. "I'm sorry, but you'll need to leave the country soon should you not publish ahead of Pasternak. And, of course, that would present the even further problem of getting Oleg out with you."

I locked eyes with Oleg. We seemed to search each other for our inner maps. On both of them was there a fork in the road with this signpost having plaques in the shape of arrows, Oleg's name written on one and mine on the other, that indicated we go divergent ways? Or had it been all those years of separateness already endured which made us look for answers in lightless places, where there weren't any good replies?

He put an arm across my shoulders and brought me close. "The decision is yours, Katya," he said at last.

"Thank you, dear Oleg, truly." I moved my lips close to his ear and whispered, "I wish I knew the right thing to do."

With a hand on my cheek, he gently guided my face until our eyes met again. "We'll figure this out," he said.

I nodded almost imperceptibly, as that seemed about all I could muster in the way of agreeing. Not to be more confused than over the obvious, without as much doubt as the size of an Italian gnat, I believed Oleg.

He moved his lips toward mine, then ever so slightly slowed his approach, as though accommodating my scars, my soul's limp, so we might meet in the middle for the second time today.

At last I came for Oleg's kiss.

This almost visible circle once more formed around us, inside of which was our entire world.

Several minutes later when all three of us again wordlessly stared through the windshield into the middle distance, my appetite roared back. I made a suggestion to partake in some local spaghetti marinara with meatballs and garlic bread, which was met by stunning approval from Sergio and Oleg. We stopped at a red-checkered-tablecloth little restaurant Oleg indicated as his standby eatery near his studio. I beamed the whole way through Oleg proudly introducing me as his wife to the round-faced proprietors, Luigi and Giovanna Donati, who wore white aprons wonderfully sprinkled with tomato sauce droppings. While we dined and drank Chianti, nothing was said of my and Oleg's dilemma; only the earthy sweetness of working-class Rome had we invited to our table. For dessert we each lit up a cigarette. More than just a little, this felt like the good times Oleg and I had had with dissident friends at the Blue Goose tavern in Peredelkino. He even tapped out a beat on the tabletop.

♫

As Oleg inserted a key into the lock of his studio's door, which came off as charmingly bohemian with its varnish worn down to raw wood, I felt, in a way, something inside myself unlocking too. Until the moment of us walking over the threshold together, our apartment in Peredelkino held my fondest memories as well as some of the hardest ones, and the thing of it was, I no longer retained the key to enter those rooms, savor and heal just by being in them—though, now, here in Rome of all places, the bolt turned and the door opened again. Oleg turned on some overhead lights, then set my satchel down on the floor. You could hardly see any wall surface in the flat for all the dissident Russian artwork signed by the well-known Anonymous. It warmed me that Oleg remained close to our homeland, as if through these pieces calling forth its better angels. The entire place was one big rectangular room, with his bed against one wall, and shelves with foodstuff on them in a small kitchen area across the way; just down from there sat a metal clothes rack full of Oleg's pants, shirts, sweaters, and a winter coat or two; underneath it were a couple pair of shoes and some boots along with a cardboard box probably for his underwear. We would have to give a few of his things away to make room for mine, sparse as they were, or bring in another clothes rack. A commode had to be hidden behind this partition, hand-painted with music notes above a circle of people holding hands, which curiously seemed to be done in Anonymous' outside-the-lines style of bold colors and not completely finished figures.

Over by the stove Oleg brought a flame underneath a kettle. "Will you have tea with me?" he said. "I've got some mild leaves that won't give you a caffeine buzz."

Almost absently I nodded by way of accepting his offer, while slipping off my backpack and setting it on the floor next to my satchel. "Are you personal friends or something with Anony—" My jaw dropped in mid-sentence. At the far end of the apartment, I spotted paints and an easel with a partially finished piece on it that had the makings of a wall much like the one from my dream, only it seemed to be of iron—the Iron Curtain—together with a man holding a flamethrower who was giving this barrier the torch. "Oleg, you're Anonymous, aren't you?"

He turned and faced me, with a finger across his lips and his eyes electrified by sparks made brighter because of those black irises. "Do you like my pieces?" he said sort of lyrically, lowering his finger.

"I love them, and have loved them ever since I came across your art for the first time in Russia."

"I'm glad you think so highly of my work." Oleg a little too quickly went back to setting up our tea service, putting out a glass container of sugar, then slicing a lemon and placing the pieces onto a plate, a modest artist.

This dear man wasn't simply another of my muses, but the one darkest and brightest of them all, a burning star along with the surrounding void necessary to keep itself afloat while holding its relation to all other stars. As I walked toward him, something was happening inside of me: I had dreaded having to eventually confront Oleg with why all those years he hadn't come back for me or at least sent word of waiting on me, to hell with his Italian keepers' demands; however, his being here all along doing this art for Russia, through it, oftentimes when little else could, inspiring me and so many others back home, somehow this erased in my dark soul the need to ask these questions. Yes, Oleg and I had been where we needed to be, and more and more I was coming to believe we now were too. When I came up behind him at the kitchen counter, I noticed his shoulders ever so slightly moving up and down as if he were silently shedding tears. I laced my arms underneath his and across his chest, my chin touching the ridge of his shoulder. "Whatever it is it's okay, we're together now," I said softly.

"Nothing could come close to filling the hole inside me without you, Katya. My art kept me going." With an expression as open as a clear night sky and just as unreadable, he turned his head and met my eyes. "It has been my only mistress, let me assure you."

I inwardly fought against placing myself worse than him, not as stalwart or somehow less moral, for having opened my heart and body to Solomon Mikhoels and, at the same time, felt even more this sense of being where I was supposed to be. *A truly good woman would tell him now about Solomon and me,* I said to myself. Right when I opened my mouth to force this confession out, Oleg turned in my arms and faced me full-on, which proved to be plenty to keep my words hidden, at least for now. He looked so terribly sad and aroused; what's more, his pelvis against mine felt like wickedness given a blessing from God in heaven. I took a napkin off the countertop, then dabbed wetness from the bowls underneath his reddened eyes.

He kissed me with the intensity of a man trying to test his or my love, I couldn't be sure which, perhaps both. With a tender touch, he slowly ran his fingers along one of my shoulder straps, then the other.

Dropping the napkin, I ached with animal lust, trying to find a way to make love, or not. To tell the truth, it didn't matter much whether what was happening flowed from the higher or lower regions of our souls. Maybe the lower was really the higher that simply needed windows opened so the wind could blow through our house freely? *Slip my straps off, will you, Oleg!* I smiled the hungry smile of a seductress.

Oleg's smile happened in a flash, almost like that of a teenage boy nervous over losing his virginity, if not for some sort of tortured pain given away by his quavering lips. His fingertips stopped moving over the straps, just staying in one place at the crest of my shoulders.

He wanted me but needed a little help taking me, right? After all, it had been so long since... A chill coursed through me at the thought Oleg no longer found me attractive, much less irresistible; nonetheless, it didn't much quell my fire. I reached over and turned off a light switch on the wall, and suddenly we were side lit in twitching moonbeams coming through windows at the far end of the flat. My virile, fragile lover stood there over his head in this creamy stream. As I moved my hands to unloosen the top button on his shirt, he clasped his hands over them.

"What, Oleg, what is it?" I said, in little more than a whisper.

More tears flooded his eyes, then began to drop, these glimmering pearls.

This time I didn't wipe them away. "What, please? We can't keep this barrier up."

He murmured something I couldn't quite make out.

"Again a little louder, darling."

He just stared darkly into my eyes.

"I love you, Oleg, truly I do."

His lips spread slightly, as if he couldn't bring another smile, though desperately wanted to.

In a way this seemed enough; his clear black orbs fixed on my eyes told me I was loved.

"My body is so scarred, I don't want you to have to look at it," he said, letting go of my hands.

"Oh, forgive me for being insensitive."

"Please don't be hard on yourself, Katya. You're as sensitive as my bongos played with brushes." Using a thumb, he moved aside wetness puddled on the ridges above his cheekbones. "It is I, not you, that has this problem."

Of course, the ravages of war and the gulags were concealed beneath his yellow and gray plaid shirt and dungarees, unassuming cotton weaves, as difficult to penetrate as the Iron Curtain, which, according to Oleg's artwork in progress over on the easel together with my own dissident heart, must be brought down. I placed my hands on each side of Oleg's face while steadying my eyes on his. "Your marks are already beloved to me, and I will see them only when you're ready."

The teakettle started whistling.

Oleg smiled once more, with the nervousness gone and the pain still there, though more shadowy now, almost as vaporous as the steam mist passing between us.

I arched an eyebrow. "Shall we have tea...then?"

"Perhaps just a cup." He winked.

Without turning the lights back on, Oleg lowered the flame underneath the kettle and then began to serve us, inquiring whether I'd like a lemon slice or a spoon of sugar, both of which I accepted. As he set the teacups on the slim table against the wall with a chair on either end, he said, "Did you bring my father's poem along with you?"

"Yes, of course. I'll get it for you now if you'd like."

"I would, very much."

I walked over and got my backpack, then returned with it. Oleg had lit a candle on the table. Under his watchful eyes, I carefully extracted from the pack *My Long Journey Home*, grimacing at some dog-eared and all but crumpled pages from that customs agent's indelicate handling of it. One by one I smoothed the damaged pages best I could. Oleg offered to help, and I declined, as if these pages were my war wounds I'd just as soon tend to myself. Fortunately on taking out *Doctor Zhivago* and setting it next to my manuscript atop the table, Pasternak's manuscript seemed to be in good condition. I then brought out the two publishing approval documents and set them atop the manuscript of which each controlled the destiny. Oleg sipped his tea patiently. Along with my slipping a hand in the backpack again, my stomach jumped into my throat. If that customs agent had damaged Osip Mandelstam's, my husband's father's, poem, no doubt about it, I would vomit. Maybe that's why I had waited for it to be the last piece taken out of my pack.

I carefully brought forth "The Stalin Epigram," then held the yellowed page in a shivering bolt of creamy moonlight, aided by the candle's flame only a little. The poem seemed to glow. There was nothing the matter with it. I handed the page to Oleg, who nodded his thanks. His eyes shimmered like star garnets as he took it in, a look I had surely only seen once before at this intensity and aspiration—many years ago in Peredelkino when Oleg had made peace with his mostly absentee father.

Enough time passed for him to read the poem over four or five times, and then Oleg set it on the table between him and the candle. "It's amazing you kept it safe all these years."

"Sort of a miracle, really. I got separated from it for quite some time."

He ran a finger along the edge of the paper. "It's funny how things change. Used to be Stalin would kill you or free you to get the original of this poem. Now it seems only rich communist collectors are interested in it."

"I guess they'll just have to eat their hearts out living without it," I said, sitting a little taller in my chair.

He again looked up from "The Stalin Epigram," locking eyes with me. Oleg seemed almost ethereal in the moonbeams and candlelight, caught somewhere between heaven and hell. "Don't get me wrong, I actually admire you for this, but you really aren't going to publish in front of Pasternak, are you?"

Maybe it was our mutual and different scars healing together at least a little, in the same home, in the same life, here tonight, that made me soften my position, I'm not sure; it could've been the yellow moon coming too close, calling me to its barren landscape. "I've thought I wouldn't since the problem of who went first arose, but, Oleg, we're making this decision together. I can't simply expect you to step away from the life you've made here for yourself." I passed a hand through the shadows across his artwork. "The Italians are doing a great job of getting your work into Russia. Who knows how it would be somewhere else?"

His eyes widened, became less infused. "You're every bit the beautiful person I remember you to be, Katya."

"Okay, so your memory's coming back nicely." I chuckled almost playfully. "But what do you have to say about this subject?"

"I can do my work from anywhere, and just like your writing, I'll leave the distribution of it to destiny."

"I don't know, Oleg, your work is already out there making a difference."

"What if I told you I'm more of a bongo player than a painter?"

"I'd believe you, but come on."

"I've already made arrangements for us to leave Italy. I finalized them with Sergio at dinner while you took off for the powder room. All that's left is for us to choose a location."

I placed my elbows on the table and leaned on them. "What kind of arrangements, at what cost?"

His eyes went to the poem once more, oddly as if he was rereading it. Finally, he looked at me again. "The original of 'The Stalin Epigram,'" he said.

One of my elbows fell off the edge of the table.

"The head of the Communist Party here, an old Trotskyite, wants it for the trouble of us messing up his plans to make you a best-selling author."

I shook my head vehemently. "I can't let you do that, I simply can't."

"Katya, please let this poem finally do some good for us. The plain truth is I need to write a new chapter with you. Everywhere I look in Rome, I see my forced exile. I want to make choices together with you for the rest of our lives; let's start with picking a place to start anew."

His words rocked me back in my chair with their music, a sheet right out of Puccini's *Madame Butterfly* or something; why not for the Christians' and the lions' sake, we were in the birthplace of opera. In fact, in some of my most candid moments through the years, I had questioned why I hadn't left with my parents and brother the night of that horrific raid by the Goat-faced Murderer's goons in favor of being the keeper of this poem. At least I would've chosen to die with the people who loved me the most. So many people got killed over this poem, and here I was alive, a hairy ball of shame in my gut for the effort. Then there was also the time Marina Tsvetaeva hadn't let us help her secure a good job with a forgery of it. That cost her life and, yes, arguably, it helped stiffen the spines of dissidents by not giving it over to Stalin for waving in all our faces as a huge humiliation at the core of our efforts. But as Oleg had just alluded, those days in Russia were over. Khrushchev wouldn't send one of his lackeys across the street for the original of "The Stalin Epigram" now.

I picked up the one-page document off the top of my manuscript, and then tore it in pieces. "That's what's left of my unsigned agreement to let Sergio's people publish my book," I said, releasing the shreds, which fell onto the table.

Wetness once again fountained Oleg's eyes, which noticeably returned to glimmering black orbs, as if these were tears of sadness and joy. "I won't ask you if you're sure of this."

"Thank you for that." With a fingertip I rearranged some of the scraps of paper for no particular reason.

He smiled puckishly, then blew out the candle's flame.

Leaving us only in the shivering moonbeams again.

Without another word we stood up and walked over beside his bed, no, make that our bed, stepping around a set of bongo drums on the floor near it. Standing so close I could once again smell his heated Russian breath, Oleg used two fingers to slip the strap of my sundress off my shoulder, then the other one, baring my breasts.

My areolas actually pulsed, my nipples reaching out toward Oleg's chest, his skin.

Gently but not overly so, he cupped my cleavage in his hands, and his breathing came in gusts through his nostrils.

My body became the vibrant night, shooting stars and comets with long tails swirling inside me.

Unable to help myself, my eyes went to the scar on his neck, then back at Oleg's beautiful face.

"It's okay," he said softly.

"I won't ask you if you're sure," I said, in an undertone as subtle as the lunar body casting one side of our faces in shadows and the other in a creamy veil. Keeping to the slow time our love desired, I unbuttoned his shirt: With each opening up of the panels of fabric, I kissed along the scars laced over so much of his torso—as though daring to taste sweet morning dewdrops off a spiderweb shimmering with them.

Once the last button came undone, I slipped his shirt off his body and let it fall onto the floor. Together we took off my sundress and panties; then I removed his jeans and underwear. He put an arm across my back, then lowered me onto the bed with him.

I liked the silence between us, as words would certainly fail, even the L-word, especially it.

Oleg handled me like a precious lilac never to be plucked, as he lowered himself on top of my body, between my open legs. His member going inside me hurt some, but only from my disuse. The moonbeams rushed in.

We made love with the tenderness and intensity of poets exploring Gaia's mysteries and finding them, wondrously, even through our almost mutual orgasms.

In afterglow, I lay with my head on his chest, and we still said nothing long after our breathing became easy and rhythmic again. On glancing up at Oleg's face, I noticed he was staring distantly at the ceiling. I joined him in doing this until I couldn't take it any longer. Our silence was no longer my friend.

"Was it not good for you?" I said at last.

"It was wonderful." He stroked my hair, but with a kind of separateness to his touch.

Has he fallen shy again about his scars? I asked myself. No way was I going there with him, not now, perhaps some other time when we were fully clothed. I tilted my head until our lips were almost together, though it was just like behind the pub at the harbor when we first came close again—this wasn't the right time for a kiss. More for myself than him, I scooted over on my side of the bed, allowing a little space between our bodies.

In a few seconds, Oleg said in an almost anguished tone, "Damn, I'm sorry." He got up out of bed, then walked over to a dresser and took something out of a little package I couldn't make out for the dim light. He picked up something else that quickly brought forth a flame, then lit a cigarette.

It was as if he stood over there like some buttery specter burning a little hole into the dark air, stinging my soul with each puff and thorny red-tipped glow. I sat up in bed, pulling the sheet over my nakedness. "Oleg, being with you is starting to feel like riding a roller coaster that's coming off the tracks."

His cigarette tip flared more brightly again, and then he blew streams of smoke through his nostrils that swirled in the yellow moonlight. "I know about you and Solomon Mikhoels."

The thorn gouged into me. "Oh, Oleg."

He said nothing, only another puff of the cigarette.

I got out of bed with the sheet around me and went to him. "It was an impossible time," I said, looking him directly in the eyes.

"I know. It's just that after we made love, all I could see in my mind was you and him together."

I reached for Oleg's hand, but he didn't respond.

"Please let's sit down and talk this out some," I said.

He nodded his agreement.

We walked over and sat down at each end of the little kitchen table again. I sort of expected Oleg to have wrapped a towel around himself or gotten something to cover up a bit, but he sat there erect with his shoulders almost arched back, as if wanting me to deal with his scarred body in the cold shadows under no influence of amorousness.

I relit the candle on the table. I wanted to see him just as he was, and I wanted him to know it. This was in no way a tough response to his challenge; if something such as that needed to come out, I would've turned on the overhead lights.

"Would you have told me?" he said.

"Yes, of course, I just thought we could use some time together first."

"Well, I suppose you're right about that." He flicked some ashes in a teacup we'd left on the table. "Maybe it was a mistake, but I had Sergio ask around about you in Russia. That's how I found out about you and Solomon."

"I would've done the same in your situation."

He looked off into the moonlight for a long moment. "In my mind I understand you thought me dead, but my heart doesn't quite know how to forgive you, Katya."

"The decision to forgive often comes long before the feeling you've actually done it, don't you think?"

"Probably so, thank you for saying that." His shoulders fell into a more natural roundedness. "The thing of it is, you needed someone, and Solomon was a good man worthy of you."

My soul had no apologies to make, I felt sure, as I'd searched it for them over the years, as well as since we'd been sitting here looking into each other's eyes. "I ache for us so much, Oleg, but I've hurt much more without you."

He took another long drag off his cigarette, and then once more from his nostrils let out a dragon's stream of smoke. "I'm so lucky you're here, Katya."

I wondered whether we would one day be able to say these words again without the fiery tips and pushed-back shoulders and smokescreens...or maybe our intimacy was better nurtured slowly with our egos at the ready to strike out some. Not too close, not too far away. I inwardly shuddered. If I were Oleg in such close proximity with me now, perhaps I'd have an affair with some mistress other than my art just to get even, see whether we could withstand level ground in our thorny garden. Who could blame him for that?

"I'm the lucky one," I said, meaning this more than anything I'd ever said.

Twenty minutes or so later, our breathing returned not to normal, instead, settling into this tired, sweet rhythm after another round of sumptuous foreplay and, not as close as earlier, though still very nearly mutual orgasms. With our heads on our pillows, Oleg and I lay under the covers looking at the ceiling once more, and this time above us, there seemed to be a friendlier creamy void.

"Maybe we should head to the United States," he said.

"Right now I'd go anywhere with you."

We chuckled mischievously.

"Why there?" I said.

"Because they're making citizens out of Russian defectors like hotcakes."

"Um, I see. Just that easy then for you and I to be cooked on the griddle and served up nice and fluffy."

"Not quite, but with a little luck almost."

"I'm still listening."

"Sergio informed me that the Communist Party here has had success helping Russians get into the U.S., but we'd be wise not using our actual surnames to give ourselves some protection from the Russian government retaliating against us. The Italians issued me a passport as Joseph Mandt. If it doesn't bother you too much, we could be the Mandts; of course, we could come up with something else."

I didn't want to be a "defector" with an alias name; it felt like asking me to denounce my entire family or something. All I needed was another place to live, a godparent homeland, if you will. It seemed to be my turn for offering up the silent treatment. Capitalist imperialists needed enemies as well as the communists, and both wanted trophy converts to their dirty religions of power. No cooperative ground to stand on. At least the Russian Reds openly censored and controlled you, whereas the elite of the United States espoused opportunity on their own greedy terms, a compassionless lot when you got right down to it, freedom with mirrors. If Oleg and I went there, I would find people of the crops and make friends, work alongside them. That's what I'd do. Poor people and peasants everywhere probably for the most part extended the same borderless hospitality. Turning my head toward the yellow light pouring in through the windows, I looked into it across Oleg's beautiful, disfigured chest. Him, his tormented and joyous range of being alive and dead and resurrecting right there before us; mine, I knew, were the stories I would tell in whatever form they took, one way or another, again and again, with the moon as my muse, for she gave no dogma, only poetry and fine prose.

"If we go to the U.S., I'll write as honestly about its triumphs and injustices as I did of Russia's in *My Long Journey Home*," I said at last.

Oleg's eyes met mine, as if he were measuring something behind them as well as far away. "Then you probably won't get published there, except for perhaps your current novel."

"Something tells me there's not room in the West for more than one book of fiction offering a fair look at communist Russia, and that will in all likelihood rightly be Pasternak's *Doctor Zhivago*."

"I hope you're wrong, but I get the point." He stroked my hair again, now slowly and smoothly, in an intimate way.

It felt as though the moonbeams flowed these words through me. "If what I must write isn't publishable, so be it."

CHAPTER THIRTY-FIVE

Frazier fascinated himself by clearly seeing his fellow New Yorkers, who of course didn't pay him any mind at all. They had earphones in their ears jamming to music, or books open in their laps, or were texting into mobile devices, some old-schoolers read the *Daily News* or the *Times* or, mostly, they just distantly stared at nothing in particular, even the people nearest him on the subway; to be sure, they were well practiced to pull off not noticing him with the Coleman tent in its carry bag over one shoulder and his backpack over the other. The tourists and those from the heartland here on business, now they'd gawk at you, but the amazement and thinly veiled fear in their expressions let you know they actually thought the whole of this some sort of sideshow; for them it was like being cast right from the street as an extra in an Edward Albee or Tracy Letts off-Broadway play, something you'd tell your children and grandchildren about but wouldn't think of reading these darlings the entire script in all its detail, full of characters with thriving neuroses, the complications of deciding on love or hate or manipulation or honesty or war or peace or isolation or cooperation without the illusion of a playbook, all of it carefully staged so that not much of anything could be reduced to some sports metaphor—call it real, absurd life. But as for those who lived in Manhattan, before the last twenty-four hours, Frazier had known of only two possible approaches: you looked blankly at people who weren't in your immediate circle of family and friends, or you slumbered. One way you pretended you could go to work and come home, perhaps even chase your dreams, contribute to the betterment of the metropolis, and since this happened to be the center of the developed world, you were doing your part in holding out a big juicy apple for everyone, everywhere to take bites out of, all along having this shadowy, hollowed-out feeling you really only walked in high-walled ruts; the other way you knew the ruts were everything and even your dreams were death if they came true. This had never been clearer to Frazier since pushing aside slumbering and heading over to Zuccotti Park for the first time yesterday. He was beginning to learn another way, looking through new lenses that didn't require any kind of special eyeglasses, and to his bemused inspiration, all it seemed you needed was a freely democratic public square to gather in, even if surrounded by cops in riot gear and SWAT-teamers with assault weapons slung over their shoulders.

He felt a rising urge to do something totally outlandish and ask a few people whether they thought it was taking less risk with their futures to stay in this quiet-mouthed routine or to help create the kind of democracy that served the people without being bought off by big money. Were the issues of growing economic inequality and climate change and looming financial catastrophe and the U.S.'s perpetual global "war on terror" big enough? Would they cause sufficient pain and suffering in your own life or those close to you that in all likelihood it already turned out to be less risky to speak out publicly, join the Occupy Movement, and stick with it even if at the cost of your job or becoming a pariah, some sort of modern-day bushy-bearded prophet? Better yet, who on this subway had been evicted because of rising rent gentrification or a funny money mortgage or had gone bankrupt over outlandish medical bills or insurmountable student loans or had been laid off their jobs to "increase productivity"—defined, greed—or worse yet, lost a son or daughter to senseless militarism? If not having fallen prey to one or more of these things, or any number of other systemic debacles, could people in the middle class care enough about others to act on their behalf before there wasn't enough of a middle class to "shake a stick at," as they say in Monahans, Texas? Yes, the 99 percent were locked out whether they knew it or not.

Or was Frazier more jacked up over Margaret having been so pliable, even supportive of his sudden change in direction to write full time, and not for a moment meant for the diminished importance of being just minutes away from again seeing Anastasie? Did it matter which moved him the most toward Zuccotti Park, his heartfelt convictions or his heart? The way things sat with him, he was on the right side of humanity, with love for everyday people as well as for his muses, all of whom were also so easy to despise. Fortunately or not, these almost cross-purposes came naturally for him, and in this order. A regular Diego Rivera with a pen instead of a brush, seemingly forever trying to paint his pictures with words. And that was part of the problem, wasn't it—Diego had the panache of being the world-famous artist, whereas Frazier himself simply lacked that kind of shtick? No, come on, fame took Diego away from the love of his life, Frida, for way too long, way too often. Maybe the truest truth was Frazier simply felt more at home with those burnt children of Occupy Wall Street, folks with little to lose, having been all but crushed underfoot by Moloch.

He got off the subway without asking anything of anyone.

Ten minutes later while he walked into Zuccotti Park, there was a General Assembly under way, and from the people's mike, Frazier heard the subject of state-owned banks versus private banks being discussed. He looked over at the Occupy the Arts area and didn't see Anastasie, but then she was probably attending the GA, as most of the Occupiers were. To his delight, he spotted a small open space over in the shade of the maple tree not too far from the library, and he walked that way. Wasting no time he went about setting up his dome tent, just large enough to sleep two people in a cozy arrangement. If Mattie and Doug ever spent the night down here, he would sleep in a bedroll outside the tent, yes, that's what he'd do. If Margaret joined him with the kids, then she and Mattie could have the tent, and he and Doug would be outside on the ground. It was as if he merely went through the motions of inwardly fighting against running the other scenario, those times without any of his family here. Should Anastasie get cold in the night again, there would be all the privacy needed to find out just what lay in store for the two of them…together with his marriage. At that thought Frazier considered leaving the park never to return, but mostly he wanted to find Anastasie and talk with her, feel her out after having left early this morning with a few pleasant words about how nice and warm they had kept each other inside the sleeping bag as well as his promise to return a little later in the day. Of course, Anastasie must have understood he went to be with his wife. Now he set the last stake in the ground for the tent, pushing down on it with the heel of his sneaker. He took a moment to admire the tent, which almost glistened in the midmorning sun, then headed toward the GA. Scanning the crowd once, then again for Anastasie, he finally spotted her swath of yellow hair and slender face, its rapt attention on the speaker, who was saying something about how public banks loan money to the local community directly from deposits; they don't invest them on high-risk bonds backed by way too many worthless mortgages. Anastasie was here with the other burnt children, Frazier's people, hers too, while Margaret was somewhere else trying to find out about herself. Perhaps someday Margaret would know just who her people were, those afraid of fire or others who, no matter what, ran toward the sun. There were some of those who had been at the BofA protest here, the skinny young man with a Mohawk, the lovely blond Sophie—with whom he presently exchanged waves on their eyes meeting from across the way—and others he hadn't gotten to know at that action but nonetheless had been there; unfortunately, Donny Johansson, the rotund, Christian, nonviolent peacemaker he'd shared a jail cell with, didn't seem to be around. He felt sure if Donny's cholesterol hadn't totally clogged an artery by now, he'd show up sometime or other, probably soon. Frazier carefully walked between the haphazard rows of those on the lawn over next to Anastasie. He smiled warmly at her, and she scooted her behind on the grass to make room for him to sit down beside her, which is exactly what he did.

"Nice have you back," she whispered into his ear.

"Wonderful to be here again," he said in a low tone, meeting her almost lavender-colored eyes. He laced an arm across her back, and she leaned against his side.

They stayed that way until people who had been directly victimized by the banking and mortgage scandal began getting "on stack," the queue for speaking at the GA, to share some of their personal stories—which prompted Frazier to slip from his jeans' hip pocket the notepad and pen he'd brought for just the purpose of getting down on paper the most important parts of these kind of testimonials. As he made entries here and there, quotes that held these people's pain and anger, he realized all their stories in one way or another were his sister and brother-in-law's, Derek and Felicia's story, except the Occupiers whose lives and families had been pillaged by the bankster class understood their power was in numbers, organizing ourselves to nonviolently take to the streets, instead of walking into traps like Derek's near shotgun showdown with the police, Frazier noted. The folks at Zuccotti Park seemed to understand the 99 percent would undoubtedly lose violent battles, if for no other reason than the one percent had possession of the most lethal artillery as well as the draconian laws allowing their use on the people. Between speakers Frazier's thoughts buzzed with possibilities for the novel he had in mind, bringing the stories of rednecks together with peaceniks, his characters emerging from them, to put forward the deeper truth for everyday people of all stripes and persuasions that as long as the powers that be could keep you fighting amongst yourselves with inferior weaponry, you were sure to remain serfs in this modern-day feudal system. Zuccotti Park would be a verdant field providing literary fodder, just as much as Monahans, Texas, other places in the heartland as well. The possibilities were almost limitless. Yes, more and more Frazier could hardly wait to do this research.

When the final speaker had made it through the stack and the people's mike was turned off for the time being, Frazier began going back over his notes, cleaning them up before memory faded in the least.

"You good, Frazier," Anastasie said.

He put a thumb on the page in the notebook to hold his place. "In what way dare say?"

"You know what write about, that obvious."

"Really now, is it?" He smiled crookedly.

She nodded. "I desire write about everything matters to me, so I do nothing but paint. My canvases are snippets only. How to narrow down on something big?"

His thoughts went to Oleg/Grandpa Mandt's "Anonymous" dissident art and the book that told some of this story along with so much more. If only he could share *My Long Journey Home* with Anastasie, maybe it would be a creative beacon for her too, for them, together or apart. But that story was only for Margaret now, unless Grandpa Mandt and she ever said otherwise. No way he'd ask Margaret for her Nana's manuscript to clandestinely lend to Anastasie; just considering doing so felt as if committing adultery of the soul, perhaps worse than infidelity of the bed, the former cruel if acted on, the latter messy, as true as frail. Or was this circuitous rationalizing really just a way to premeditate the murder of his marriage?

"Your paintings can be as important as any novel."

The glimmer in her eyes almost anytime she looked at him dimmed. "To you maybe but not *moi*. Please don't talk me out of write."

Suddenly Frazier felt he was somehow cheating on Anastasie, as though having a sordid affair with the pedestrian, hack-poetic part of himself, caught red-handed in some hotel room naked with this tart, a minor muse at best. His and Anastasie's chemistry had first sparked and then stayed alight over the possibilities in store for them, showing each other the way to their words, a delicate connection with no ulterior motives, seductive in its honesty and vulnerability. If he wanted to end whatever they had between them, probably all he had to do was stay in this cheap hotel room, make another comment pulled from his reptilian DNA. It sure would simplify things as soon as the kids got out of school and he brought them over to Zuccotti Park or if Margaret decided to hook up with him here later today, whichever. But then it couldn't fill the hole in his heart over needing the kind of muse that had traveled from Marseille to New York to join this social movement, an already prolific artist in need of stretching herself with a novel, something not better than, though sort of coming from the other direction than a severely blocked writer setting herself free for the first time, as Margaret so valiantly attempted. Besides, he had no idea how to keep the light in his eyes from being snuffed out should Anastasie's expression remain dark even a minute longer because of him. "Is there a thread that runs through your artwork, something that freaks you out and energizes you at the same time, makes you run from it as well as return to it over and over again?" he said at last.

She gestured at his notepad. "That what you write in there?"

"Yes, it's really about making sense out of how where I come from in Texas brought me to New York, and why I stay here. No matter where I go, there I am, it seems, so I hope to explore the pain and the blind spots and the joy of it all in my novel. I was taking notes on people who got their homes foreclosed on like my sister and brother-in-law down in Texas had happen to them."

"I see what you mean." She paused as if thinking. "I am here because too many artists in France think they don't try hard."

"Why do they think that?"

"They rest heavy on shoulders of great French artists of past."

"So they're lazy, is that what you're telling me?"

"*Oui*, and in New York artists try hard. Even too professional here."

"Okay, now we're on to something."

She shrugged. "So where's my big novel in that?"

He thought back on attending her gallery show just after they first met, the angst in her work, some sort of sadness that simply would not be silenced, and therefore the beauty of it all. "Whatever sent you so far away from home that didn't have to do with your art could well be the heart of your book, Anastasie."

Her eyes widened, then quickly relaxed. "I disguise that in my canvas."

"Yes, I know, but you can't hide in a novel; for that the blank pages are too 'big,' as you say."

She squinted as if looking into the sun even though the orange orb was at their backs. "I must return to the source, this little village outside Marseille if rejuvenate that."

His mouth went dry; was he about to lose her again? "Writers freely go places most people pay big bucks never to get close to again."

"I must think on this one." Her expression softened some before she went on. "Will novel of yours have a person like me?"

"That depends; will yours have one like me?"

"I could not make, how you put it, 'sense' of how I got from there to here without Frazier on my pages."

"Neither could I without Anastasie in my manuscript."

Her eyes again became two fields of lavender in the French sun.

Frazier brought his face close to hers, and they kissed delicately, then with reckless abandon, as if Occupy Wall Street along with everyone in the park had ceased to exist. To him it didn't feel like cheating. Love was a huge novel you absolutely could not go underground in, but of course this was not some book they were reading, or writing.

✄

Why am I doing this? Frazier asked himself, and didn't get a simple answer, but then, he wasn't expecting one. With Mattie and Doug on either side of him, the three of them walked into Zuccotti Park. Right before he left here not more than an hour ago to meet the kids when they got out of school, Anastasie had told him if he wanted to bring family to the park, she would be "happy as clam" over in the Occupy the Arts area working on a canvas; although, her eyes had turned stony, as if in betrayal of her tacitly being his kiss-and-not-tell comrade. No, she kept something much more hidden under these rocks, and all the while he had been gone, Frazier felt it pulling him back here, a vortex amidst her stones. While he and the kids made their way past the Peace Garden—consisting of several raised beds which sprouted winter vegetables along with a makeshift sign stuck in the ground indicating the large plot as such—Frazier wouldn't allow himself as much as a glance over in the nearby arts area at Anastasie. Building this wall somehow needed to be the first move in taking down his other wall, the one between blood family and his new, larger family, the Occupiers. He couldn't let whatever was happening between Anastasie and him sully this place for himself, Mattie, and Doug, bring his children into a mess they didn't deserve. Problem was, with each step he felt this invisible barrier between him and Anastasie increasingly turn his eyes to flint also. The rocks were black, lying rocks. Frazier and Anastasie's thing for each other simply could not be illicit. No, he would have to find a way to stop her from hiding behind her artwork; the boulders must be removed from their eyes or they would surely stumble into some dark river and sink to the bottom, only to stay forever weighted down. Frazier's inner muse as well as his lips pressed against Anastasie's had made music too painfully beautiful for corrupting, and he still heard it, if artificially walled off from her and everyone else in Zuccotti Park—just as at the same time hummed in his mind another seemingly pristine notion: introducing his children to his most real self, a revolutionary in the making, Frazier Pickett III, husband and father (also a man with a mistress?) on some sort of pilgrimage which delivered him here in this particular spot. Would he end up in the movement a bold, stalwart dissident, as Osip Mandelstam had been, or more the nuanced diplomat, sneaky with his words, like Boris Pasternak? Frazier longed for his own Katya to help show him the way, push him to be more bold when he fell back into slumbering, or simply hold him off whenever he went to put on those fake reading glasses again, though for the love of biting the Big Apple, he believed it would somehow take Anastasie and Margaret together to manage the equaling of one Alice Mandelstam/Mandt. He thought maybe this was how Abraham in the Bible had felt on taking his child, Isaac, up to the altar to murder him, sacrifice him to some kind of demon God in which an Orwellian nightmare of Scripture called Himself love. Of course, as it were, God had spared Abraham the killing of Isaac, but until this moment Frazier hadn't understood a thing about why all that macabre drama. It seemed sometimes you had to walk yourself and the issue of your loins directly into the breach for there to exist even a sliver of light revealing what the divine had in store for you, and for those you love. Frazier just hoped he wasn't being guided out of darkness by a host of fallen angels in disguise, their black wings covered over with white silk. In this realm of the soul, even when you weren't slumbering, things remained chimerical, indeed.

"Can I see if they'll let me help over there?" Mattie said, with a gesture across the way at this group of twenty-something artists constructing a plywood home about ten feet by ten feet in size, with solar panels painted on the roof that had thick black Xs drawn over them. A couple of the artists pasted red and orange flames made out of shiny poster board along the bottom on all four sides.

"That's a protest piece," Frazier said. "Not just some cool dollhouse from hell."

"I know that." Her tone turned matter-of-fact, almost the same as Margaret's did in response to Frazier's glib geek-isms, only in the higher octave of youth.

"Of course you do. What do you think its message is?"

"Not sure." Her little brow knitted as if in supreme concentration. "Maybe it's saying if we don't use the sun for electricity, we'll burn up from global warming."

His eyes widened in amazement. "How does a ten-year-old know so much?"

"Mommy talks to me about stuff like that sometimes."

No doubt Margaret did this kind of kickass parenting, but gee gads, what was he, chopped liver? "Go for it, Mattie, though don't just barge in on them. Ask nicely, okay?"

"What do you take me for, Dad?" Mattie took off her backpack and handed it to Frazier, then turned in the direction of the art-house and walked briskly away.

"A girl who'll grow up to be as successful as your mother," he muttered, while watching her arrive over there. She said something to a sharp-featured young guy with his long hair stuffed underneath a bulging knit cap, who smiled and nodded, then handed Mattie a couple of flames and a bottle of Elmer's glue. *Who knows, maybe she inquired instead of instructing him on her participation?* Frazier chuckled inwardly at the thought. Really he was a tad prickled with jealousy over Margaret being such a wonderful parent. For all his sensitive ways with their kids, what had it gotten him?

"But you brought us here, Dad; that counts for something," Doug said.

His son certainly was a chip off the old block at almost uncannily taking on the bigger person's frailty, no doubt feeling guilty over his father embarrassing himself without the awareness of it, just as Frazier had done as a kid, still did in a way: Most everyone over thirty seemed almost clownish so much of the time, yet he was undoubtedly a village idiot of a sort himself, a dissident, a writer. Sometimes he was positive of being under endowed with the capabilities to do anything else. "It counts for I love you." With a hand he mussed Doug's hair. "You want to go check out our tent?"

Doug nodded. "Can we spend the night here?"

"Probably so, we'll see."

The two of them made their way about halfway there, when Doug said, "Hey, that picture looks a lot like Great-grandpa Mandt's you showed me when we went to visit him. Let's go take a look at it."

Frazier's eyes followed Doug's line of sight directly to Anastasie, who stood in front of an easel while painting a bulldozer that had rolled over what looked to be a Palestinian's home. The piece had a caption that read: *Equipment Provided by John Deere & Company, Made in the USA.* Damn, this was happening too soon. But then, with a little luck what the harm? Doug would surely think of Anastasie as his dad's friend, some unthreatening chum. That is, if Frazier and Anastasie kept themselves from ogling each other. "Okay, let's head over there."

"Do you know the lady painting it?"

"Yes, we've met."

As he and Doug walked toward Anastasie, Frazier looked over at Mattie, who pasted yet another flame onto the art-house. A young woman, wearing denim overalls splotched with paint and a red bandanna tied around her head, gave Mattie a warm smile and a nod of approval on the flame. Things were going fine over there, so Frazier didn't have the excuse of needing to see after Mattie for the purpose of delaying, or avoiding altogether, Doug's introduction with the one woman who could quite possibly come between his son's mom and dad. In the instant of setting his eyes on Anastasie again, he realized how little he actually knew her. Would she be stiff with Doug? Probably not, but then, she didn't have kids of her own, at least, not any Frazier had been made aware of. Unnervingly, it was more important to know her better to protect his kid's heart than his own. But wait a minute now, this was Anastasie, who had seen through his slumbering from day one of them meeting, and accepted it as little more than an endearing quirk, who had given him cryptic signals through the art posted on her website that she cared for him…and after a point in time *stopped* returning his emails. For heaven's sake, just yesterday he had expected her boyfriend to show up any moment. Then their kiss, the kiss that somehow changed everything from fantasy to reality, but of what kind? Virtually unfounded paranoia and slumbering went together as nicely as peace vigils and MLK for the slumbering man, who inwardly trembled over wanting his fake reading glasses, which were just over his shoulder in his backpack. Nevertheless, his hands remained at his sides, one of them holding the strap of his daughter's backpack with SpongeBob stenciled on it. He needed to keep clear eyes on Mattie, on Doug and Anastasie, and, for that matter, on the entire park, for it was getting late in the afternoon and Margaret could be returning from Grandpa

Mandt's any time now. She hadn't called or texted Frazier all day: Maybe she'd just show up here. Why hadn't he told her about Anastasie when they were alone just this morning, when he had the chance? Even still, he had no intention of gathering up the kids and leaving Zuccotti Park. Yes, Abraham held a spike over all their hearts. If Frazier bowed out now, for the rest of his days there would only be slumbering—of this one thing he was sure.

Anastasie and Doug got along every bit as well as had Malcolm X and the Black Panthers. Like father like son, Doug also seemed charmed by Anastasie's French accent together with her easy Provençal ways. After Doug told her how much he liked her art because it reminded him of his great-grandfather's, she went so far as to set him up a smaller easel and fresh canvas beside hers.

What had Frazier been worried about between Anastasie and his kids? She was a natural, bless her and, at the same time, spite her for in such short order getting almost as close to Doug as Margaret seemed with him, not really, well, okay, sort of. Whatever, it took a village to raise kids; he fell short of entirely convincing himself of this.

"You may share my paint for protest something, anything you care?" Anastasie said to Doug.

"What is a...um, 'protest'?"

Clueless is okay, Frazier thought. Doug couldn't help being two years younger than Mattie, without having gotten quite far enough along for his mother or Frazier to teach him of these things. *Right?*

"Something not fair to you or others." Anastasie handed Doug a brush.

He just stood there staring at the canvas.

"Let see...is there something hurt feelings at school?" she went on.

Doug seemed to think for a long moment, then nodded. "When Jenny-Lynn peed her pants sitting at her desk, all the kids made fun of her, and since then they stay away from her on the playground and at lunchtime." He bit his lip. "She cries a lot now."

Anastasie smiled warmly. "Protest way they treat her."

Doug dabbed his brush into some red acrylic, and then made his first conscious dissident mark on canvas, then another, and another, until finally he had blood draining out of what had to be Jenny-Lynn's heart. Anastasie helped him clean his brush when he wanted to change to black. He then began sketching out stick figures who were pointing at the heart.

She looked over at Frazier and said, "We fine, if you have other thing to do."

Is it worse should Margaret show up and spot Doug with Anastasie, just the two of them together, or with me here beside them? It struck Frazier that the more horrible outcome would be if Margaret saw him hanging this close to

Anastasie, even more so than Doug being alone with her. That being straight in his mind, he had to admit to himself, there wasn't a good reason to stop this great fun for Doug and Anastasie and, while he was at it, vicariously as a father, for himself too. "Maybe I should check in on Mattie, my daughter," he finally said. "She's doing some environmental art."

"*Oui*, good. Take your time, other artists at work here."

"Yeah, Dad," Doug said, without looking away from his canvas.

When Frazier faced Mattie's direction, she was still going about her business over there just as you please. But then he noticed next to the art-house two men looking past her right at him. No mistaking them, it was Mutt and Jeff! Ancient history he'd thought until this moment. They had quit tailing him and Margaret after the article came out exposing TMZ's collusion with the U.S. government's undercover mole in Clifford Odeon's organization, ever since these jerks' efforts failed to do their part in thwarting the Arab Spring.

He fixed his eyes on them while walking over toward the art-house, noticing their expressions were different than the cocksure, jutted-jaw hardness he'd gotten used to when they'd been following him and Margaret around, especially on occasion when he or Margaret made eye contact with them, which had happened more times than he cared to remember. These guys weren't resuming that sort of assignment, no, Mutt and Jeff's owlish astonishment indicated they found themselves just as uncomfortable to have Frazier approaching them as he was doing it. *So, why are they here?* Those two certainly weren't peace and justice advocates, unless it came at the end of a gun barrel, *pax Americana*. On flashing a smirk at them, Frazier stopped and faced Mattie, who seemed just as enthralled with her project as Doug was with his own across the way. Frazier complimented her on her work and the message it carried. She beamed, said, "Thanks, Dad," and then got right back with using scissors on a large piece of poster board to cut out another flame. When he faced Mutt and Jeff again, they had collected themselves into their all too familiar smugness, with eyes like some sort of jaundiced moonlight coming through slits in window blinds. Frazier walked the five or six feet over to them and said, "You guys are too obvious. No one will believe you're sympathetic to the ninety-nine percent as soon as you open your mouths around here. Why don't you just give up on whatever it is you've got planned for disrupting this movement and leave?" He gave them another smirk. "Otherwise I'm getting on stack at the next GA; I'll tell everyone what you did to me and my family, as well as about the kind of hate speech you support, the sabotage of democracy worldwide, you know, these sorts of things. May as well also do a teach-in on the article we wrote that in part featured you. Remember those really nice photos of you in it? Who knows, you guys may be on the CIA's payroll."

"You think you run us off and it's over, simple as that?" the taller one said.

"No, there're probably agent provocateurs all over this place. But we'll keep ushering them out once they've been exposed." Frazier spoke with conviction, for he had noticed the volunteer, unarmed security detail from time to time surround someone who continuously gummed the GAs by refusing, once their allotted time ran out, to give up the people's mike and get back on stack if they wanted to talk some more, or blocking (vetoing) actions that otherwise had the group's consensus as well as met with the nonviolent social justice values already decided on by the people here. Security did this without so much as laying a hand on the provocateur, moving as a group of five to ten locked arm in arm until the person was outside the boundaries of Zuccotti Park. If anyone showed up again and made similar trouble, they got the same treatment.

"If we can't get this thing to fall apart from the inside, then it's going to get rough on you people," the smaller one said in an almost guttural tone. "I don't know if I'd bring my kids to such a dangerous place."

"He makes a good point," the taller said.

Frazier didn't believe for a moment Mutt and Jeff were directly threatening to harm Mattie and Doug; all you had to do was look just outside the park at the abundance of armed police who were there to "protect the protestors" as well as the "general public," as he'd heard a representative of the cops claim on a recent TV nightly news report. The cops seemed to be gathering strength in numbers day by day like a huge West Texas thunderstorm about to explode with bolts of lightning. "You know, the thing of it is, guys, you're getting screwed by the economic and political system as much as the rest of us. Tell me if you will, when did you get your last pay raises?"

"Now you're getting personal; that pisses me off," the taller said.

"Democracy is personal, and I'm glad I'm showing my kids it's honorable and necessary to exercise our right granted in the U.S. Constitution to assemble in public and redress grievances."

"Why are we even having this pitiful little debate when it's no use?" the smaller said.

"You think we're having a debate?" Frazier chuckled mercurially. "I'm doing research for my next story."

"You don't want to write *that* article."

"Why not? I'm recording everything we're saying on my iPhone with an automatic encrypted backup." Frazier bluffed the techie stuff. "I already have most everything needed for a great story." A pause. "The interesting part will be seeing whether you guys leave now, or cause trouble here and make even bigger fools of yourselves."

The muscles along Mutt and Jeff's jaws rippled. They said nothing.

Frazier chuckled once more, this time with a rising sense of satisfaction. "I swear you guys are going to help me get a Pulitzer yet."

In a few seconds Mutt, followed by Jeff, simply turned and began walking away.

Frazier watched the two men mutter between themselves until they finally stood over near the police barricade. They seemed careful not to talk with any of the cops or make eye contact with them, as if attempting to keep their cover with the Occupiers. *This is primo*, Frazier thought. He all but salivated to write a piece with the aim of helping the movement expose provocateurs, which would undoubtedly come out better if Mutt and Jeff stuck around.

He turned away from them to again watch Mattie work on the art-house, a sliver of fear pricking the back of his neck over her safety. With a glance at Doug, still next to Anastasie painting with purpose, Frazier felt the knife press harder into his skin. Slowly he scanned the park for other children and spotted several, each of them dulling the blade a little. Insanity loomed outside the park, not inside it, though, no getting around it, the ones with guns called sanity insanity. Nowhere was safe, but at least in Occupy you found poetry, art, a Peace Garden, music for some better world, each person here contributing in his or her own way. Frazier set Mattie's backpack on the ground, then slipped his pack off and got his notepad out of it. He opened the pad to the notes he'd taken at the GA earlier on the banking and foreclosure scandal, excerpts of real people's stories. On reading through them, he saw in his mind's eye each of the folks who had shared: a couple from upstate New York who had worked in a paper mill until the mill closed because of clear-cutting the forest to nothing; another man from Harlem who got pushed out of his rent-assisted apartment on technicalities and was now homeless; a single mother who came all the way from Las Vegas, Nevada, with her three kids because her mortgage payment had all but doubled due to mumbo-jumbo fine print in her mortgage... He stopped reading and pictured two other children, his nephews, Dwight and Johnny—as in Yokum and Cash—who were beyond some fear of nightstick or rubber bullet state-sponsored harm implied by Mutt and Jeff against Mattie and Doug, as awful as that would be, and hopefully about as likely as getting hit by lightning for his kids, all the young ones here. Frazier imagined how it must be for his sister's family trying to keep their chins up while living with his mom and dad, Derek humiliated by selling off his ranch bit by bit for the bank, Dwight and Johnny embarrassed and made fun of at school, Felicia hemmed in with nowhere to raise her family properly and little prospect of anything turning up other than some tiny apartment or a trailer home. All these people's hardships as well as their triumphs in pressing on remained Frazier's top story to write, even more so than ferreting out agent provocateurs amid the Occupy movement. It was personal.

He closed the pad and placed it back into his pack. Writing his book would have to wait for now. Maybe he'd turn another journalist onto the Mutt and Jeff story, perhaps Margaret. That story would be more personal for her. But then, you couldn't really choose a story for someone, not if it was going to be the right one for them. If there was anything clear now to Frazier, your story had to find you. Then it would hold on tight.

For several minutes he just stood there watching one, then the other of his children work on their art, and pretty soon this left him once more alone with his thoughts. There still was this huge undone act, partly roped off outside the park with all the insanity, partly trapped inside the barricades, and as long as he put off facing up to it, he'd surely contaminate everything good about himself, this place, the two of them. Frazier reached in his backpack again, this time coming out with his iPhone. He speed-dialed Margaret and got her lengthy, highly professional voice mail greeting in that all too familiar tone of the woman he also knew to be actually getting more vulnerable lately, though, right this moment, her veneer of togetherness loomed larger than ever, almost seeming believable through and through. Of course, this was her "work voice," but sometime long ago too much of it had seeped into the way she talked with him. Before making this call—The Call—he had learned to tell himself that her greeting was just part of surviving in the jungle she swung from vines in. It started and stopped there. The pesky part was, even in the best of slumber, he had had a hard time outright believing that. Now, inwardly owning up to this lie oddly drew him toward the new, more chill Margaret, if she really existed.

There were things he wanted to ask her. Where had she spent the day to, how had she put it early this morning, "find my story"? Did that go well? Where could she be with her cell phone turned off? For God's sake, was she all right? You could rely on her not going dark by phone until the family sat down for dinner together in the evenings, and come to think of it, she often took calls from junior editors, authors, or her bosses again after mealtime. This simply wasn't like Margaret. Perhaps he liked it. Or at the minimum could relate to her better. This happened to be the sort of thing he'd do: absentmindedly let his phone run out of juice or something at a time when she or the kids could need him in a pinch. That is, except for him spending last night with Anastasie; then, he'd turned his cell phone off for the sole purpose of hiding. And that is precisely why he couldn't bring himself to ask Margaret any of the things he wanted to. Until he spoke to her about him and Anastasie, everything else between him and Margaret would have to be put on hold, an impossibility in this ever-spinning world, he knew all too well. He considered becoming a chameleon, going through the motions like most everyone walking the streets of

New York, but he couldn't manage to move toward the world out there, beyond the Occupiers, not if that meant saying good-bye to all this forever or until Anastasie left the movement, which, honestly, he could never wish for her. Feeling the way he did, Margaret would for certain sniff him out in hardly any time at all. What's more, much more, he didn't want to lose what had been going on between them lately. Somehow the sum of his and Margaret's flaws, their emotional dumps on each other, their blocked writing, obsessive fragility, the willingness to face into their pasts, the freedom and courage coming from doing just that, and, yes, their sense of humor emerging again, his and her history as much as their future, gave him at least some hope for the here and now, not to forget considering how good they were in bed, the two wonderful kids they had to prove it. Which is why Frazier said this after the beep: "Hi Margaret, please call me. We need to talk about muses. Anastasie Moreau is here at Occupy Wall Street. I love you." Until the words came from his mouth, he had no earthly idea what they would be, though there was no doubt, things would never be the same.

He made sure the ringer was turned up to its loudest, then slipped the phone into his jeans pocket, so her call could be easily gotten to. He began walking toward Anastasie and Doug over in the Occupy the Arts area, but each stride seemed like stepping off some topmost stair into nothing but thin air. This wasn't the time for him to be near his French muse. And Mattie still was enthralled with her eco-protest project. So, Frazier stood there and began studying his sneakers along with the trampled grass right around them. The longer the opening licks of Iron Butterfly's "In-A-Gadda-Da-Vida" didn't sound from his phone, he became more and more convinced the thing to do was take Mattie and Doug home and have this conversation privately with Margaret after the kids went to bed. He didn't regret having phoned her from here. There was no way things would have transpired to give him the immediacy to confront the truth with Margaret had it not been for the crucible of this park and everything going on in it. One person's impetuousness being another's passionate convictions, how else would badly needed revolutions ever start, would love be winnowed out?

Absently his eyes lifted and scanned the park, until across the way he spotted Margaret walking directly toward him. She held an arm up, and in her hand was her cell phone. She sort of waved it at him, as if to say, "I got your call." She moved with bounce in her step, flashing him this almost beatific smile. Anytime an angel approaches that you recognize as such, it probably has been sent by a witch. What kind of punishment did she intend to put him through? Frazier gathered his wits as much as possible, which seemed barely at all, and began quickly making his way toward her. Maybe he'd get scoffed at for leaving the kids unwatched, but then, they were in good hands; besides, that was the least of his problems. This way, with a little luck, he could keep Margaret from seeing Anastasie and Doug together until having the chance to talk with Margaret, who had kept it no secret she knew what Anastasie looked like from her website. "A beautiful French slut" was how she'd first put it to Frazier several months ago.

As they stopped right in front of each other, before he could get a word out, she said, "Oh Frazier, this place has great energy, I can tell already. I wish I could've joined you sooner, but I've just had the most marvelous day with Grandpa Mandt." Pausing, she smiled knowingly. "Make that Oleg Mandelstam."

"So that's where you went to find your story," he said, suddenly even more confused. There was no denying it, Margaret seemed as happy to be here with him as his mom always had been with his dad when at the Lone Wolf diner most Wednesday evenings back in Monahans, Texas, each of them enjoying blue plate specials: chicken fried steaks with cream gravy poured all over the top and green beans on the side, a glass of heavily sugared iced tea for her, a beer in a frozen bowler for him. These weren't the only times Frazier had seen such effortless joy shown by a wife to her husband sans one iota of pretension, but certainly the earliest memory of the like, for this came to him now almost as a vision.

"Actually I found it on the page before I left for Grandpa Mandt's, and then with him I ended up delving back into the same story. Not by writing it out, at this place Nana started years ago. We almost literally dug it up."

"It doesn't surprise me you got into some good research there; I'm happy for you." It was exactly what Frazier didn't want to let happen, getting sidetracked. His silence on the matter at hand made him a damn cowardly husband, an anti-muse. He cleared his throat. "Margaret, what's this all about, really?"

She tilted her head. "It's all about me unearthing my lyricism, my poetic voice, with my pen as well as my hands, if you will."

He, too, tilted his head. "Didn't you listen to my voice message?"

"No. I got your call as I was getting off the subway, and I'm sorry, but I was lost in thoughts of piecing together my novel and let your call go. I knew I would be seeing you in just a little while, so I hope you don't mind too much. Why, is something wrong? Are the kids okay?"

"They're fine, over doing some stuff with the artists here." Margaret actually cared enough about writing her own story—not some HarperCollins assignment or a collaborative journalistic foray, but an entire book of solo fiction—to put him on the back burner, Frazier realized. There had been so many other excuses for her to all but forget him over the last several years, though none of them the right one, instead invariably directed at his inadequacies. Normally it would have been something for them to celebrate, her blossoming into this messy author hungry for the page, the way she'd always wanted to be but for suffering from creative blocks, an almost occult mantra he himself had lived by while falling into ambivalence over not getting published, then into slumbering. That is, until rising up from these doldrums so recently it felt like just now, obviously for both of them…and Frazier was about to toss out the biggest buzzkill between them ever. Yes, he was. There seemed to be no other way. "Margaret, Anastasie is here at Occupy Wall Street."

Margaret's forehead rutted miserably and she closed her eyes, as if inwardly looking directly at flames of fear Frazier and his French muse would eventually end up together, something she'd undoubtedly consigned to darkness each time this fire ignited in some chamber of denial but could no longer force the flames back down there. On finally opening her eyes, she said, "Did you two plan this? Is that why you weren't at home last night?"

"No, it just happened this way."

"What happened?" She placed a hand firmly against his chest. "On second thought, let's don't get into that just yet. I don't think I'm ready for it." *May never be,* she thought. The furrows in her brow smoothed some, as Margaret touching him somehow brought with it another way of calming herself, as though fanning a gust of wind that blew from the pile of glowing embers these ashes which instigated, if not peace, quite possibly a heartfelt truce.

Her touch had never before emanated to such places inside Frazier, so undeserved, a gift, the start of something new? He didn't move, not pressing into her hand, receiving it.

"What is it she gives you I haven't? And don't bullshit me, Frazier."

"Anastasie must find her story to survive, and she knows this. It seems until recently you and I merely sought to live creative lives in some overly romanticized or intellectual way, of course, me the former, you the latter." His words came immediately as though Hephaestus, the Greek god of fire himself, or the Christians' Pentecost spirit, or perhaps both working in some sort of divine conspiracy, singed him with them.

"So it's an act of desperation."

"Yes, I'm afraid so." Frazier smiled sadly.

She returned it. "Do you have your next story, Frazier? The one that truly awakens your own inner muse."

"I do."

"So do I."

A long moment, then she took her hand from his chest.

Somehow with this separateness—more than between their bodies, in their individual stories not needing anything from each other technically or with literary ideas or collaborative writing—mostly the need for Frazier and Margaret to be each other's muses rushed in on him and, from the way things were going, he believed for Margaret too. They had stepped right up to the abyss without holding hands, where you say yes to life or you jump in, companions indeed, no room for infighting or sappiness; it was simply too dangerous out here on the edge.

"What's your story about?" Frazier said at last.

"Dissident poets of the Arab Spring, but written in an entirely new way for me."

"Wonderful, Margaret, really."

"Thanks, really."

He nodded his you're welcome. "You should probably know that Mutt and Jeff are here as agent provocateurs. Perhaps you'll get a few chapters out of them even now."

She raised an eyebrow. "I just might at that. There's something you should know. When I called the office earlier today, I was told because of our article exposing Gary the mole's, shall we say, propagandistic tendencies, Harpers is shelving that rag of a book I had a hand in editing for him."

"Are you telling me you'll be the only person putting out the real story?"

She nodded sharply. "And with freedom to get at the essence of things by way of fiction."

"It should be a tremendous success."

The ruts in her forehead came back slightly. "After reading *My Long Journey Home*, I'm trying to define 'success' differently."

"Yes, me too." He meant this, felt good about it, though Margaret being published instead of him swarmed his joy for her like a hornet with its stinger extended.

"Would you like to tell me about your story, Frazier?"

He shooed the hornet away. Then, shared his plans to write of Felicia and Derek's foreclosure, which in one way or another was happening to millions, him already having great notes from people at Occupy who were part of these millions, how he wanted to get with them and ask for in-depth interviews. "I'll find so much more of the poetry in my story from these folks" was how he put it. When he finished telling her about this, she let him know she could hardly wait to read a draft of it should he be open to letting her have a copy of the completed manuscript. He readily agreed to do so. With that they stood there quietly, having exhausted their literary high.

Over the next several seconds, the curiosity sparking in Margaret's eyes was replaced by the anguished intensity he'd seen earlier.

"Did you fuck her? Yes or no," she said.

"No."

"Correct answer."

Frazier understood the better part of valor would be keeping his mouth shut. He stood there looking into her eyes for spiking glimmers that may well indicate she was of two minds with his response. Of course, there were some.

✐

Margaret learned in her dating days during university the best way to neutralize the competition was to befriend them. If Frazier and the French artist hadn't actually gotten it on all the way, then this could work, maybe, depending on how ruthless Anastasie Moreau happened to be. Then again, Margaret had no clue what you could attempt for turning a muse away, didn't know whether she wanted to even if this were possible. It sure as hell hadn't worked out very well for anyone being without their muses in Nana's life, in *My Long Journey Home*. Before reading that book Margaret had honestly considered the idea of muses almost quaint, some sort of dreamy non sequitur. Now she couldn't do without them inside herself as well as in the flesh, Alice's spirit, Grandpa Mandt...and yes, well, Frazier. And while she was at it, where was her handsome French artist muse or, better yet, some rugged Italian version thereof? In a way she felt cheated. "Where is Anastasie?" Margaret finally went on. "I'd like to meet her, and don't worry, I won't have my claws out too far."

Frazier envisioned a panther about to strike. "Doug is with her, over there." With an outstretched arm he indicated the Occupy the Arts area.

As Margaret spotted their son with Anastasie Moreau, it stole her breath. "Damn, Frazier, you're making this hard on me." Without another word she headed for the wavy-haired blonde, who looked every bit as striking as in her photos on the web. What's more, she and Doug seemed perfectly comfortable with each other. The muse Margaret shared Frazier with wasn't making this any easier either.

✐

Intently watching Margaret approach Anastasie and Doug, Frazier felt as if the orbit of his past was intersecting with the orbit of his future, and no telling what that would do to their gravitational pulls, three planetary trajectories about to be irrevocably altered, five counting Mattie's and Doug's. His thoughts drifted to Boris Pasternak as well as Osip and Oleg Mandelstam together with the women, Katya, Zinaida, Olga, Vika... When Margaret and Anastasie faced each other across the way, Margaret obviously having just introduced herself, Frazier began considering his womanizing friend, Buckminster Ross, a good comparison for sure, as those he was thinking of from the pages of *My Long Journey Home* shared the need to make themselves more whole by way of their complicated relationships, but the scars on Bucky's heart had to be so covered over by his one-dimensional cocksmanship they would never heal. Whatever came out of the two women meeting, whom Frazier cared the world for along with all the planets and stars, the three of their futures would be better than any of those with Bucky's stripes—which seemed to be multitudes. Yes, Frazier and Margaret and Anastasie happened to be that rare breed of poet who must always stay in the tension of harmonizing the masculine and feminine inside themselves by experiencing it in each other, moons needing suns just as well as suns needing moons.

Frazier walked over next to Mattie again, and then asked whether she thought it would be fun if he helped with the eco-house project too. His little girl was all over that idea. As he worked at the table cutting out more poster board flames, every now and then he'd glance over at Margaret and Anastasie, who had gone just outside the arts area, their conversation beyond the reach of Doug's ears. It unnerved Frazier so much they seemed to be getting along swimmingly, he came close to slashing the tip of a finger off with the scissors.

∅

When Margaret said coolly, "Hello, Miss Moreau, I'm Margaret Pickett, Frazier's wife, Doug's mother," the first thing she noticed was the soulfulness in the French artist's almost plum-colored eyes, this unflappable, what was it? availableness in her expression.

"Nice finally meet you," Anastasie said. "You have wonderful husband and childs. You must be good well as."

"Thanks, you're very kind," Margaret said, her tone softening more than she cared for. Something about Anastasie Moreau's accent and jumbled English was infectious. Perhaps either the French artist had few scruples when it came to marriage, or her honesty about its fragility presented little problem with meeting the wife, Margaret reasoned. No small part of her task would undoubtedly be to determine whether she was looking on this woman's mask or the real article. Margaret complimented Doug on his artwork, an honest critique, as her son's canvas actually brought her up short for a moment over the raw emotion in his bloody heart and the figures mocking it inside some very institutionalized-looking schoolroom. She viscerally felt the system of conformity closing in on that heart and, more than a little, on hers as well. She would rather become an ex-wife than one of those stick figures wagging their self-righteous fingers at the uncontrollable matters of love.

It impressed Margaret further that without any encouragement, Anastasie stepped away from her canvas and the two of them walked twenty or so feet from Doug so they could talk freely. There was so much Margaret had inwardly rehearsed to say to Anastasie Moreau should they ever meet. Had she really signaled Frazier with that artwork on her website? Did she make a habit out of vamping married men? What did she do to Frazier in bed that turned him on more than her? No time for false modesty, Margaret knew she herself was all but an acrobat in the sack. Had Anastasie Moreau gone so far as to actually bed down her husband? But right now all this together with more sort of funneled down to one thing and one thing only. "Are you going to steal Frazier away?" Margaret said flatly.

Anastasie Moreau's expression fell, lines from just outside the corners of her eyes all the way to her beautifully curved jaw forming an upside-down U. "You can take husband but can't take what happen free. I don't take husband."

"I see, indeed." Certainly a tenuous sort of assurance, more philosophical than actual hands-off-in-the-flesh with Frazier, it seemed to Margaret. Still, there was no denying—all of her Jewish and secular humanist moralizing aside—she agreed with Anastasie Moreau. Margaret wanted Frazier to herself more than ever before and sensed if whatever she said next came across in the least bit controlling, it would have just the opposite effect. Somehow she had to transform the lure of a not-so-clandestine extramarital affair into a less certain rebellion. An urge to slap the shit out of Anastasie Moreau flared in her almost as much as the desire to make Anastasie a muse of her own, like Olga and Katya had been, rather than lowering herself to the tough, clinging behavior reminiscent of Miss Zinaida. Margaret had done enough of that over the years. It was time for the skipped-over generation in the Mandelstam's bloodline to join the unfrozen part of the family. After all, Olga and Katya both had loved Pasternak, and it was as certain as the golden-orange setting sun beyond Manhattan she as well as Anastasie loved Frazier. Deft logic or some loosening hinge in her mind, Margaret was far from sure, but somehow, either way, that wasn't important at all. Something beyond reason inside her chest moved her now.

"I know this may seem as if coming out of nowhere, but do you like to read?" Margaret said. *Or is it you simply painted the cover of Steinbeck's* The Grapes of Wrath *to worm your way into Frazier's heart?*

Anastasie nodded. "I like read more than paint. I am hope write novel. Frazier make me think I really can."

The iciness of Frazier inspiring Anastasie Moreau, the budding novelist, suddenly succumbed Margaret's inclination to give her a copy of *My Long Journey Home*, get her reaction after reading it, see just how moved this woman would become over the book's message about the earth and the pen, love and muses. A test of sorts, though one that would be called off for the time being anyway. It was just too precocious the French artist found Frazier her *writing* muse, way close to home for Margaret to share her most prized personal and literary secrets with Anastasie Moreau. "He does have this…effect," Margaret could've kicked herself for saying, but the words seemed to come from that same place in her chest.

"Frazier your muse well as?"

Margaret nodded.

"Do you write book now?"

She nodded again.

"How's going?"

"Wonderful…lately."

"Good. I still look for story. Maybe have something, maybe not." Anastasie chuckled heartily. "Probably have return Marseille to develop it."

Despite everything Margaret was beginning to like Anastasie Moreau, whose eyes lighting up were those of a writer, not some faker, more like the cat that had swallowed the rat. Besides, she may be leaving the country to write her book! Certainly Frazier wouldn't abandon her and Mattie and Doug to be with Anastasie that far away, Margaret tried convincing herself, though with only moderate success. Anastasie seemed too unbound for any man to let go of easily. "Hang in there. I just found my story, and I've been on the search for it quite some time."

"I will."

"Good."

Anastasie glanced down around her feet, made a swoosh across the ground with her ballet slipper, as if indicating she was uncomfortable without anything else to add.

This conversation was done for Margaret too, so she looked over where Frazier had been and he wasn't there. On scanning the park, she spotted him with Mattie on one side and Doug the other, down on their knees in a large plot of vegetables. Peace Garden, she read the sign stuck in the ground over there. "Poetry minus the words," she said out loud, hardly realizing it.

"What you mean?" Anastasie said.

Oh, nothing really, Margaret almost replied. Actually it felt sort of magical just a few hours ago she, too, had been down on her knees among the potatoes with Grandpa Mandt at Sacred Cow Farm. Strangely it was as if Nana's spirit—her ashes mixed into the dirt, in some inexplicable way commingled with any soil put to good use—called them together, all of them, Frazier, Mattie, Doug, Margaret, *and* Anastasie. This notion came from Margaret's chest again, and there was no use trying to minimize it. Nothing had ever been clearer. She needed to find out what Anastasie and Frazier were like together, how Margaret herself would react with the two of them that close to Mattie and Doug, her family. And if Anastasie refused to come along, then, well, it would reveal her more as Frazier's mistress than his muse. A superb way to tease out some honesty on this as well as other things which, without such synchronicity, wouldn't amount to anything more than a fool's errand. *Thank you, Nana,* Margaret said inwardly.

⌀

Frazier had increasingly become a bundle of nerves with Margaret and Anastasie over there engaged in conversation; somehow it instinctively made him want to gather up his children. The closer his family came to falling apart, the nearer he wanted to be with them. Mattie and the others with the eco-house crew had put all the flames needed on it, so she had been up for another activity, readily agreeing to go with Frazier in search of it. He had been discreet on taking Doug away from the boy's artwork, not wanting to have Margaret or Anastasie spot him and possibly turn their tête-à-tête toward him any more than it already would be, or worse, get himself directly roped in with them. It had been his idea to head over to the Peace Garden with the kids. This was about the only thing he and the kids could do together other than join a march on the New York Stock Exchange that was forming, but he didn't want the three of them to leave the park without Margaret knowing. Besides, now that they were at it, digging his hands into the dark soil, churning loam, planting seeds, made Frazier feel as if he could sing in the desert or something, and from the intent expressions of Mattie and Doug while they helped him, the kids could have also. No contest, this was better than falling back into slumber. Yes, indolently enough, just before arriving at the idea of working in the garden, he had gone so far as reaching for the eyeglass case with the fake reading glasses in it down inside his backpack, though, managed to pull his hand back, stopping short of actually changing out his new John Lennon specs.

"Hello, everybody."

It was Margaret's voice, and Frazier along with Mattie and Doug looked up from their work. Anastasie stood beside Margaret. Frazier did his best to keep an even expression.

"Hi, Frazier, hi, Doug, and you are Mattie, yes." Anastasie's French accent floated over the top of Frazier, Mattie, and Doug's heads.

"Nice to meet you," Mattie said, then, "So you have a new friend, Mom, that's good."

"I think so too." Margaret then looked Frazier directly in the eyes. "Mind if we girls join you?"

"The more the merrier, I always say."

"It seems so."

Margaret got down on her knees beside Mattie while Anastasie did the same at the far end next to Doug.

Frazier's heart raced. What was Margaret trying to accomplish by bringing Anastasie with her?

The two women worked with a couple of chuckles and an "Oh, I see, that's how you do it," traded with the kids, while Frazier—caught in the middle—planted seeds with his head down. Sweat beaded on his brow, but it was too cool of a day for that to happen without duress. He dare not wipe it away.

✄

At first Margaret tilled with a fury as if that would wear out her inner turmoil, and then she began picturing, one after the other, every scene in *My Long Journey Home* where Katya worked the fields of Mashinska and Peredelkino…until finally she saw Katya as Alice not just working off anger at Grandpa Mandt for having those affairs, but also composing poems by immersing her hands in the ground. It took awhile but eventually the images of her mind's eye faded, and Margaret found herself foraging in this plot for herself, the gardening of her soul. She looked over at Anastasie, who seemed just as relaxed with her hands in the soil as herself. Frazier, though, was obviously tying himself in knots, sweat dropping from the end of his chin, his expression an overly stoic mess.

"It's okay, Frazier, truly it is," Margaret said.

✄

He met her eyes once more, and they were like gray pearls, creamy, soft moonbeams of understanding he could get lost in. "You mean it, don't you?"

"Yes."

He wiped the sweat from his forehead and face with his shirtsleeve.

"Just think about what you're doing now, Frazier," Margaret went on. "Not what you may or may not do in the future. Let life speak to you from the soil like it does in Nana's novel."

"Okay, I'll try." With that he went back to work. Initially he dug his hands into the soil as if burrowing a tunnel underneath a jail cell to freedom, but eventually he realized that's exactly what Margaret had gifted him—no need to dig singularly to be *libre* as the French say. Nothing had ever been more of a turn-on, as earthy and soulful as Pablo Neruda's love ballads. He slowed down, began gently patting the dirt over the top of his furrow scattered with seeds. Whatever was going on inside Frazier had the effect of making him want to have Anastasie as a muse and not a lover. For there to be more than a prayer around pulling that off, he'd have to stay head down in gardens much more of the time…and writing on his novel, he told himself. Then put his hands in the dirt and quieted his mind again.

∅

Margaret stole a few glances at Frazier so as not to get noticed and make him any more self-conscious. Pretty soon she realized he had seemed to lose most every bit of that malady. He was more and more staying in the moment, as though riding with Nana's spirit bareback on some white mare, and Margaret was right there with him. Whatever happened in the future, this was how they needed to be with each other as long as it lasted. Which of them would ever want that to come to an end? For the first time, Margaret felt completely sure she was Frazier's muse.

Her thoughts turned to Anastasie, who still seemed to be right with them in deed and spirit, except without her story Anastasie was a greater danger to their marriage, could easily apply too much feminine wile on Frazier to help her find it. What's more, there was a part of Margaret that now willingly wanted to assist Anastasie any way she could in finding her story. She trusted Anastasie as a writer, a kindred soul, a stealer of ideas, her husband's other muse, who she best make a partner in crime, honor among thieves being what it is and all. Margaret stopped working and sat up straight on her haunches. "Anastasie," she said, and the French muse removed her hands from the dirt, then looked over at her.

"*Oui.*"

"My grandmother wrote a book called *My Long Journey Home*. It helped me find my story in a very big way. Maybe it could help you find yours. If you'd like to read it, I could give you a copy."

"*Oui*, sure. *Merci.*" Anastasie smiled warmly, then returned to her gardening.

∅

Frazier could hardly believe his ears. What a generous thing Margaret just did and utterly disarming. He met her eyes again, and then, unable to help himself, even though knowing this could hurt Anastasie's feelings, he moved his face toward Margaret's.

But before he could kiss her, she almost imperceptibly shook her head, gave him a wink with devils dancing in her eyes.

Holy John Keats, she was being cool, cooler than Frazier himself, and right now he loved her all the more for this.

Doug got up and walked over to the far side of the garden to get a shovel that had a spade as big as his upper body. Frazier watched him as he made his way back with it, wobbling on his feet a little here and there. The thing was so heavy and long, it kept throwing him out of balance. "Hey, Dad," he said, "I'm gonna get more done than you with this." He proudly held it out toward Frazier using one hand, and he got so off-kilter that the little guy sort of threw the shovel to the ground. It clanked hard against something in Frazier's backpack, which he'd set down on the walkway next to the garden.

Along with the thud you could hear the sound of glass crunching.

"I'm sorry, Dad," Doug said.

"It's okay, pal. There's nothing in there worth worrying over."

Doug smiled hesitantly, then as if out of embarrassment went to work again in the garden using only his hands.

Frazier stood up and went over to his backpack. He removed the shovel, leaning it against a tree. He then opened the backpack and brought the smashed eyeglass case from it. While Mattie and Doug along with his two muses continued working in the garden, not as much as glancing his way, he took the fake reading glasses out of the case. The lenses were shattered. Without another word, he walked over to the nearest trashcan and threw them away.

ACKNOWLEDGMENTS

Those who have helped me change out my lenses, to want to see myself and humankind, in fact, all of creation more clearly—the anti-slumberers—are the ones to whom I give over my deepest gratitude. My father, Karl, and mother, Clarice, who carried around their tin drums, beating them relentlessly to their own songs and, by doing this, gave me my drum along with the sticks. My sis, Teensie, stalwart champion of my abilities, typing papers for me through the nights to get me through college, reader and consultant on my later manuscripts. My big brother, Karl, who by living through the very marrow of the Sixties and carrying on thereafter, gifted me with critical thinking. My other sis, Sissy, the poet of life and art by living so gracefully and strongly, that I, too, became a poet. My son, King Jr.—we change our lenses together by eagerly sharing what is going on in our daily lives and work, always heading toward passion. His future-ness infused with our bloodline inspires my words and actions like nothing else. And so much special gratitude to my wife, Lisa, the supporter of my dreams, a great and honest first reader, the love of my life.

Bob Whisnant, my Humanities professor in college, by holding me after class to say my writing was special, spoke the author into my heart. From that moment on, I knew my calling. Jack Dulworth once told me that he had learned from poetry so much more than he ever learned from his parents, and I have found this to be true. Then there was the actual Alice, in her late eighties when I met her, with those sapphire eyes glimmering youthfulness and vigor too rarely found in the chronologically young. Having penned eight novels and working on her ninth, she told me to start journaling and my story would find me. It has so many times over the years, and it certainly did again with *Letters to Alice*— which I must admit, in a big way is my love letter to the real Alice.

The manuscript was beautifully and carefully line-edited and its content improved by the folks at Writers Relief. This book would not be published without the expertise and excellent work of the entire WR team: Jill, Carol, David, Dave O, Matthew, Nicole, Joe, Kriste, Meg, Ronnie—well, all of you wonderful fellow bookies.

I couldn't be in better hands for the thoughtful and smart work of gaining flesh-and-blood readers by way of all those at Self-Publishing Relief and Randee Feldman at Get Noticed PR.

Written-down stories are surely inferior to the well-spoken word, for all that ink and so-called literacy so often serves to create hierarchy that separates us. Nevertheless, my life has been enriched by books: perhaps it has even been saved. Thank you, storytellers of today and those throughout the ages.